WELCOME TO
THE DUNGEON

It is a fog where time twists minds,
and voices call out from a swallowing darkness.

It is a jungle in which finned creatures dwell and
torment all that pass through its vines.

It is a maze whose tunnels trap the daring,
and whose creatures challenge the brave.

It is a chamber in which proportions are lost, and
fortitude is one's only weapon.

From the veldt of the dinosaurs to the gates of Tawn,
this is the quest of Clive Folliot, explorer and hero.

ABOUT THE AUTHORS

CHARLES de LINT's fiction has been described as "fantasy for people who don't normally read fantasy." On the official and definitive Charles de Lint website (at http://www.cyberus.ca/~cdl) the author continues: "I've taken to calling my writing 'mythic fiction,' because it's basically mainstream writing that incorporates elements of myth and folktale, rather than secondary world fantasy." A full-time writer, de Lint has published over forty books—including *Moonheart*, *Yarrow*, and *The Onion Girl*—and has others on the way.

Nebula and Hugo Award-nominated author RICHARD A. LUPOFF was born in 1935. He has worked in print journalism, in information technology, as a radio show host and in book publishing. His novels include *One Million Centuries*, *Sandworld*, *Space War Blues*, *Circumpolar!*, *Countersolar!*, *Lovecraft's Book*, *The Forever City*, as well as a number of mystery novels and a collection of his short fiction, *Before . . . 12:01 . . . and After*. Other recent publications include *Claremont Tales*, *Claremont Tales II*, and *The Great American Paperback*.

ABOUT THE ARTIST

ROBERT GOULD made his name in the 1980s with a series of groundbreaking covers for Michael Moorcock's fiction, among others, culminating in a World Fantasy Award in 1989. He founded Cygnus Press, publishing high quality prints and portfolios by such artists as Alan Lee and Barry Windsor-Smith. In the late 1980s, he started Imaginosis, devoted to "bringing magical worlds to life" through books, media and merchandising. He is also Vice President of Education First, an innovative children's charity based in Los Angeles.

PHILIP JOSÉ FARMER'S
THE DUNGEON

VOLUME THREE

THE HIDDEN CITY
CHARLES de LINT

THE FINAL BATTLE
RICHARD A. LUPOFF

Artwork by
ROBERT GOULD

ibooks
new york
www.ibooks.net

DISTRIBUTED BY SIMON & SCHUSTER, INC.

A Publication of ibooks, inc.

An ibooks, inc. Book

1230 Avenue of the Americas, New York, NY 10020

ibooks, inc.
24 West 25th Street
New York, NY 10010

The ibooks World Wide Web Site Address is:
http://www.ibooks.net

ISBN 0-7434-7447-3
First ibooks, inc. printing July 2003
10 9 8 7 6 5 4 3 2 1

*Special thanks to Lou Aronica, Betsy Mitchell,
Richard Curtis, David M. Harris, and Mary Higgins*

Cover art by Ciruelo
Cover design by Joe Bailey

Printed in the U.S.A.

PHILIP JOSÉ FARMER'S
THE DUNGEON

BOOK FIVE

THE HIDDEN CITY

CHARLES de LINT

for
Bruce
(we've got to stop meeting
in these kinds of places)

with special thanks to David
(not just for the candy,
but for holding the
whole thing together)

▪ FOREWORD ▪

"Heaven reveals nothing.//"Earth keeps its secrets to itself."

So wrote Li Ho, ancient Chinese poet (A.D. 791–817).

The final line of his poem goes somewhat like this: "See the man who raved while writing on the wall his questions to heaven."

Li Ho refers here to Ch'u Yüan, who lived during the third century B.C. Ch'u, while wandering through the ruins of the palaces and tombs of long-dead kings, went mad, and he wrote his questions beneath some murals. We do not know what the questions were. They must have been the same sort that drives the thinking person nowadays to despair or near frenzy. I say ."nowadays" though these questions have always been asked.

Why are we here? Why do we have to suffer? Why is there such injustice? Where do we go from here? Who is pushing us around?

The ancient Greeks believed that the Olympic gods interfered in human affairs, but that this interference was sporadic and usually for the personal benefit of a god or goddess. Never mind what happened to the unlucky man or woman or child who got in the way. The Greeks did not believe, however, that the deities conspired to wreak havoc, misery, and death among humankind, but that, generally, Chance or Fate determined the lot of the members of Homo sapiens. That this seldom resulted in good for Homo sapiens was just the way things were. Though the gods occasionally took a hand in man's destiny, the universe was a machine that cared nothing for what happened to the living. Or for that matter, the nonliving: the destruction of a mountain was as significant, or as insignificant, an event as the death of a mouse.

Other ancient cultures seemed to have much the same attitude, although the Egyptians and the Hebrews were exceptions. They seemed to believe that the gods monitored closely the lives and attitudes of their worshipers. In other words, they cared about humans. The Hebrews may have gotten this concept from the Egyptians while in servitude to them. But their idea of one God eventually evolved from the idea of many gods, though this may also have been the influence of Ikhnaton, the pharaoh who conceived monotheism.

The concept of a vast plot against humanity seems to have originated with the early Christians. This was probably influenced by various then-contemporary religions, most notably that of the Persians, from whom the modern Iranians are descended. The Buddhists did not blame other people or higher beings for the good or bad lot of individuals, and believed in no cosmic conspiracy against them. Every individual was responsible for his or her own fate.

The seeds of the conspiracy concept lay in the ancient Hebrew religion. The early Christians nourished this idea with Persian ideas, and the concept eventually grew into that of the great evil being, the superhumanly powerful anti–human being, the fallen angel called Lucifer, Satan, the Devil, and Old Nick.

In reality there is no abstract evil, no malignant, pervasive, ectoplasmic cloud floating around causing bad things to happen to us powerless humans. Evil is not a Platonic idea. The old folk saying, "Evil is as evil does," describes the nature of evil. Evil is what happens and what is caused to happen. What happens is the result of accident or chance or the deliberate action of human beings. The only conspiracy in this universe is that among sentients. It is not necessary to invent the devil to account for bad things. The philosophical and logical tool, Occam's Razor, cuts the devil out of the scheme of this world. The Englishman William of Occam, born A.D. 1285, gave his name to this principle, though others before him had stated it in various forms: "Entities are not to be multiplied beyond necessity."

That is, cut out the crap. Use the simplest explanation. Thus Satan is a fantasy, a totally unneeded accretion to the explanation of evil actions and reactions.

Even in this modern age, many people still believe in the existence of Satan as a living entity who personally begets all the evil thinking and behavior on Earth. "The Devil made me do it!" In 1990 there are many who think just as their Old Stone Age forebears did. They sincerely believe that "evil" is the afflatus spawned by the great conspiracy against "good" by Satan and his legion of devils, the lesser fallen angels.

But sincerity, as we know, is not confined just to "good" people. Nor is sincerity the test of validity. Hitler and Stalin and Jack the Ripper and the Inquisitor, Torquemada, were sincere. Nevertheless, the history of conspiracies generated by human beings is long and authentic. Extrapolating, we may safely assume that other sentients, those on non-Terrestrial planets and in other dimensions, must also have their history of conspirators.

The Dungeon series is based on, among other things, a Big Conspiracy. Richard Lupoff's Volume One contained the first hints of it, and Volume Five, by Charles de Lint, develops the idea tenfold. Though there are demons and references to Hell's Sire in this series, they obviously are not the Bible's, Milton's, or Dante's demons. Their origins and motives are based on reality, albeit reality in fictional form. They are flesh and blood, these demons and mysterious powers, and are not immortal. The Great Satan behind this conspiracy (or collection of conspiracies) is not the metaphysical creature invented by ancient theologians.

On the other hand, while previous books in the series did hint at or imply metaphysical situations, Volume Five dives headlong into metaphysical waters. I cannot elaborate without spoiling your sense of anticipation and surprise. You will recognize these excursions into the lands beyond physics when you encounter them. De Lint, I am sure, is not asking the reader to accept the ancient theology on which these episodes seem to be based. He connects the latest thinking of physicists to these theological/mythological ideas. He implies that such concepts as *heaven, hell,* and *limbo,* though presently religious in nature, may become physical in nature.

At one time physicists considered parallel universes and "other dimensions" to be the fantasies of romantic writers. Most physicists in the early twentieth century also regarded travel to the moon and the planets as impossible, as fiction writers' wild and irresponsible imaginings. Nowadays the more progressive physicists are not backwards about recognizing the possibility of such things as parallel universes, other dimensions, and interdimensional travel.

De Lint is saying that the concepts of *heaven, hell,* and *limbo* were derived from real worlds, the nature of which were unknown. The theologians embroidered on these concepts for their own uses. These other-worlds may become, however, much better known. They may someday be classed with the phenomena of black holes, wormholes, cosmic strings, chronons (wave particles of time), and the like. Their true nature will eventually be revealed as quite different from that portrayed by the theologians and metaphysicists.

De Lint includes several original concepts in this novel. If you do not agree with me on their originality, you will at least agree that his use of these concepts is novel. One scene herein raised the hairs on the back of my neck and chilled my skin. This does not often happen to me when I read a story. I hope that you will react as I did.

Another phenomenon accepted as possible in this series is telepathy. My personal attitude toward this, after reading much of the pro and con literature of psionics, is that the existence of telepathy has not been proved. Until it is, I remain a skeptic. If telepathy does exist, I believe it is quite rare, perhaps because very few of us have descramblers for telepathic messages in the receiving part of our brains. Only a tiny minority may have the power to receive, and that talent is probably intermittent and undependable.

Our band of adventurers develop both transmission and reception, the inference being that all sentients have, or have had, this power. Or perhaps, that one of their number is giving them this talent for his or her own (possibly sinister) purpose. There is no doubt, however, that this series is based on the premise that all sentient beings, human or otherwise, share a common substratum of icons and emotions. It also implies that all sentients have a basic need for companionship, affection, and approval. That seems valid to me. Certainly the "higher" animals on Earth share this need with Homo sapiens. It seems likely that not only mankind and the animals, but all sentients and the "higher" animals on their worlds, are born with this need. It is something that evolution or God, whichever you prefer (and you may like both), has endowed life with. Everywhere.

Meanwhile the band struggles against such harsh and cruel perils, both physical and metaphysical, that it is a wonder it has not broken down completely. Its trials far exceed those of rats in a maze or rats presented with seemingly insoluble problems in a laboratory. Alone, its members might go crazy. But they are together, and they share by this time a genuine companionship, affection, and approval. It was not so in the beginnings of their acquaintanceship.

Unlike the man about whom Li Ho wrote, our heroes have not gone mad. Made of stout stuff, reinforced by one another, they keep their sanity. And unlike Ch'u Yüan, they expect answers to their questions. This is in the spirit of my writings, especially those about Sir Richard Francis Burton of my *Riverworld* series. He plunged into the unknown after his involuntary journey into an alien world. He went into the deeper unknown because it was the unknown, and he wished to make it the known. And he not only expected answers to his questions. He demanded them.

We shall see what the answers are in the next and final book of *The Dungeon*.

—Philip José Farmer

▪ CHAPTER ONE ▪

The Dungeon was playing havoc on Annabelle's acrophobia.

Her fear of heights wasn't so much a fear of falling as a reaction against the desperate need that grew, whenever she was perched on some precarious elevation, to throw herself out into space. To simply let herself go tumbling over the edge and then let gravity take control.

And then you hit the ground.

And then you died.

But no matter how surely she knew that to be the logical conclusion, it didn't stop the terror.

In her own world only the small voice of logic, crying out under the unreasoning panic, could stop her from the simple process of shutting down all of her body's motor functions. The trouble with the Dungeon was that, time and again, as they went through the gates separating the various levels, the authority of that small voice of reason eroded as she fell incredible distances— at least through what felt like incredible distances— without physical harm.

Do you see? the heights appeared to ask her. *There was never any harm in just . . . letting go. . . .*

The voice of reason, presented with the irrefutable proof of her constant survival, was rapidly deteriorating.

Perhaps I was wrong . . . , it told her.

And that was more frightening than anything the Dungeon had thrown at her to date, because all that kept her sane when she was caught in the grip of her acrophobia was the knowledge—deeply hidden at times, it's true, but present all the same—that the base instinct of her sense of self-preservation would keep her safe, no matter how ardently the depths beyond her perch called out to her.

Because it *wasn't* safe.

Not for a minute.

It was true that the chance of being hurt was minimal, floating down through a gate as she was now—from the literal hell of the seventh level to who knew what awaited them on the eighth, Finnbogg's pawlike hand gripped in one of her own, Horace's in her other —but what if the next time their adventures took them to some precarious perch? A time when the curious cushioning that existed in many of the gates was absent and gravity merely hungered to draw her down to her death? If her self-preservation didn't cut in, if there was no one to help her . . .

Her boots came into contact with something hard at that moment, cutting off her train of thought with more pressing concerns.

"Heads up," she called softly to her companions. "Here we go again—"

She braced herself, but there was no real need. The surface underfoot was hard as pavement, but they landed as gently as feathers. Then one foot slipped on something greasy. She would have fallen, but Finnbogg and Horace kept her on her feet. The gray gauze of the gate that had blinded their vision as they fell drew away, and slowly their surroundings came into focus. A noxious odor clogged their nostrils before they could really register exactly where this gate had dumped them.

"Smells bad, very bad," Finnbogg said, his bulldog-like features wrinkling.

Annabelle nodded. And if it smelled this foul to her, she couldn't imagine how bad it would be to the dwarf's sharper olfactory senses. She looked down at what she'd slipped on and grimaced at the puddle of vomit that lay there on the pavement.

Pavement? She thought, then looked around.

They stood in an alleyway, brick walls rising on either side of them. There were garbage cans and litter strewn up and down its length. Through the mouth of the alley she could make out a vista of broken-down and burned-out buildings under a sullen sky that reminded her of nothing so much as the South Bronx.

Had they made it home? To the homeworld that she and Horace shared, at any rate?

She moved away from the disgusting puddle underfoot and cleaned her boots as best she could in the refuse spilling out of a garbage can. Her stomach fluttered and an unpleasant taste rose in her throat.

Get ahold of yourself, Annie B., she told herself. You've seen worse.

Good advice, but it didn't make their present surroundings any more appealing. Still, they *were* alive. And at least there didn't appear to be any immediate threat.

She looked at her companions. As she took in Horace, standing there with a shirt wrapped around his waist, a cloak overtop and nothing else, his head shaved bald under the black top hat he was wearing, his mustache and beard gone with his hair, she had trouble suppressing a grin. Quartermaster Sergeant Horace Hamilton Smythe, the queen's own man and at one time, before he was promoted, her many times great-grandfather's loyal batman. Right now he looked like a leftover extra from one of those old Monty Python flicks.

"Christ," she said. "Don't you look a sight."

Smythe wouldn't turn his gaze her way, which prompted Annabelle to realize that she didn't look much better herself. Having lost her shirt, all she was wearing were her boots and black jeans, with her leather-jacket overtop. Unzipped. Which was what was bothering Horace. She zipped the jacket up.

"Okay, Horace—I'm all decent now."

"I wish I could say the same," Smythe muttered, drawing his cloak tighter around himself.

He hadn't landed in the same puddle of vomit as she

had, but he was barefoot. Annabelle didn't envy him that—not here.

"Finnbogg hates this place," their other companion complained. "Hates it bad—not okay."

"Gotcha," Annabelle said. "We'll get moving as soon as the others arrive."

Which should have been only moments after their own arrival. What was keeping them? If Clive and the others had come through the mirror immediately after they had, they should have been here by now.

"I'm starting to get a bad feeling about this," she said.

Her companions nodded glumly.

"Only some new danger would have kept Clive from joining us," Smythe said.

"Or some caprice of the gate," Annabelle added grimly.

As soon as she'd spoken, she wished she hadn't. Finnbogg's long look grew longer, the worry in Horace's eyes deepened, while Annabelle had the unhappy thought that simply by voicing her concern aloud, she'd made it real.

"They'll be along real soon," she said.

"Real soon," Finnbogg repeated mournfully.

"Any minute now," Horace agreed.

But not one of them believed it for a moment. Not as time dragged on and there was still no sign of the rest of their party.

"Shit," Annabelle said. "Just when it seemed like we were really starting to get somewhere. . . ."

Now they were back to square one again.

A similar concern for their own missing companions troubled Sidi Bombay.

He and Tomàs had also arrived in a ruined cityscape, also alone. But while the other three had arrived in an alleyway, the Indian and his companion had landed on the roof of a building that towered a good hundred stories into a sky dirty with gray clouds.

On all sides of them spread a panoramic view of the desolate city to which the gate had brought them. They looked out over miles upon miles of blocks littered with ruined buildings, streets overgrown with dense vegetation and choked with the rubble of tumbled-down structures and abandoned vehicles. From their bird's-eye view it all appeared more like a map than an actual center of habitation.

"Madre de Dios," Tomàs said softly, looking over the edge of the roof and down, down, down to the street below. "This is not a place for Annabelle, *sim?*"

Sidi nodded. "Although the real question that comes to me just now is *where* is Annabelle? Where are the others? Why have we arrived here alone?"

"Could they have abandoned us?" Tomàs asked.

"Not through any choice of their own."

"That does not comfort me."

"Nor does it comfort me," Sidi said.

He glanced at his companion to see Tomàs checking his pockets.

"What have you lost?" he asked.

"The pistol I had. That . . ."

"Laser," Sidi said, supplying the word as he remembered the deadly weapon.

"Sim," Tomàs said. "From the Palace of the Morning Star. It is gone."

"You must have dropped it."

"Or it was stolen from me—as the Dungeonmasters stole the white suits from us."

Sidi nodded. "Or it was stolen," he agreed.

He remained by the Portuguese's side for a few moments longer, looking out over the city, then turned away.

"Where are you going?" Tomàs asked.

"To find a way down from this mountain of a building."

Tomàs looked down at the street far below once more, eyes narrowing as he tried to close the distance.

"What if when they arrived . . . ," he began.

"Yes?" Sidi prompted the Portuguese when he hesitated.

Tomàs turned once more from the view and leaned

against the balustrade. "What if there was not a rooftop awaiting them? What if they appeared in the air"— Tomàs waved in the general direction beyond the safety of the roof—"and fell to the streets below?"

"That is a terrible thought, Tomàs."

"Christo! Do you think it appeals to me? But we are alone here, we two—*sim*? If the others could come, they would be here with us—*sim*?"

Sidi knew that the anguish in his companion's features mirrored his own. He looked across the cityscape once more, then turned away again. The gravel footing of the roof rattled under his shoes as he made his way across to where a small structure stood.

"If we are lucky," Tomàs said as he caught up to the Indian, "there will be one of those 'elevator' devices such as they had in Dramaran. I do not look forward to walking down so many flights of stairs."

Neither did Sidi. The door in the small structure opened easily at his touch, but inside—whether there had been stairs or an elevator once—there was only a dark well now that descended for as far as they could see. The Indian kicked a piece of gravel down. It bounced against the walls as it fell, but though they listened for a long time, they never heard it land.

"We are trapped," Tomàs said. He looked about the rooftop. "Without food or water or shelter from the elements."

Sidi nodded. "Unless we find our own way down."

"But you can see for yourself—there are neither stairs nor device."

"I said our own way—by which I mean another way."

Tomàs regarded him for a long moment, then slowly shook his head. "Oh, no. You won't catch me trying to climb down the wall like a bug."

"Do you have a better suggestion?"

"Sim. We wait to be rescued."

"You said it yourself. We have no food, no water, no shelter. What if we must wait days? Weeks? Can you fast that long, Tomàs? And what if we are never rescued? What then?"

"*Asno,*" Tomàs muttered. "I didn't say you were wrong—only that it is *muy peligroso.* Very dangerous."

"I have climbed mountains in the Himalayas, while moving through a ship's rigging is almost second nature to you. I think we are better equipped for the adventure than you believe, Tomàs."

Returning to the balustrade, they both looked down. The building's face was not as sheer as it appeared on an initial glance. There was a webwork of cracks—due to weathering, no doubt. Faint in places, but present all the same for as far as they could see.

"You see? There are handholds," Sidi said.

"For a bug, perhaps."

"We need only go down to the next level. Perhaps we can find a stairwell there that hasn't collapsed."

"And if we don't?"

"We go on until we do."

Tomàs shook his head unhappily.

"I will go first to show you the way," Sidi said.

He removed his shoes and thrust one into each pocket of his jacket, then swung himself over the balustrade, toes reaching for the first series of cracks in the stone that he'd spied when he'd looked down.

"*Buena suerte,*" Tomàs said. "You are very brave, Sidi. I will say a prayer to the Virgin that she look after you."

The Indian nodded, knowing that Tomàs meant well. But among his own people a virgin deity was but an aspect of Shiva, and she preferred to see a man make his own way in the world.

"Don't keep me waiting too long," was all he said by way of reply.

Tomàs watched as Sidi inched his way from crack to crack, slowly making his progress away from the roof. In fifteen minutes he had gone no farther than a half-dozen feet. Tomàs imagined the cramps that the Indian would be feeling in his fingers and toes; all the weight of his body—no matter how slight—rested on those frail appendages.

Finally he stood back. He made the sign of the cross on his chest, promised a thousand candles to the Virgin if she would see him through this latest trial, then swung over the balustrade himself.

This was not encouraging, thought the eldest son of Baron Tewkesbury as he studied what there was to be seen of the Dungeon's eighth level.

He and Shriek had also arrived in a ruined city, but while the others had at least come to a place scaled to their own size, Neville Folliot and his companion had landed in a metropolis that must once have housed giants, for the pair were dwarfed by the immensity of their surroundings.

The buildings around them were made of brick. The windows, where they weren't broken, were glass. Vegetation had cracked through the pavement on the streets and sidewalks. Abandoned metal vehicles were scattered the length of the street. But whatever they laid their gaze upon was of such a gigantic scale that the pair had only a mouse's-eye view of it all.

They were no taller than the bricks that made up the walls of the nearest building. The clumps of weeds were small forests. The abandoned vehicles must once have been conveyances for creatures so large that just imagining the size of the city's previous occupants left their heads spinning.

Neville began to get an inkling as to how Jonathan Swift's hero must have felt when he first reached Brobdingnag.

"In a place such as this," he said to his companion, "we'd be considered no more than vermin, scurrying about in the shadows of those who created the place—an unpleasant concept for a peer of the realm."

Shriek regarded him with what passed for amusement on her alien features. *In the eyes of the Dungeonmasters, indubitably we* are *no more than vermin, Being Neville.*

"That, my dear spider woman, is an equally unpleasant concept, made more so by its obvious veracity."

Of more concern to this being is the whereabouts of our companions.

Neville nodded. "We appear to have been deserted."

The Clive Being would not do so willingly.

"That is only your opinion, madam. Myself, I would not be surprised."

Then you show only how little you know your brother.

Neville considered that for a moment, then shrugged. "I stand corrected. And since we are bowing to your wisdom, Mistress Shriek, perhaps you would care to offer a plan of action as to what we should attempt next? Press on? Or wait here for my ever-faithful sibling? I leave the choice up to you and will gracefully follow your decision. However, if I might make a suggestion, it would be to retreat to a more easily defended position for the nonce."

Little about their new environment put him at ease. They were too small, too easily prey to what in their own world would be considered no more than a nuisance. Here even an insect, in the scale of this immense city, could present a danger impossible for them to deal with—Shriek's hair spikes and his own sword notwithstanding.

Imagine a hunting beetle the size of a cart, armorplated. A bee with a stinger the length of a spear—or worse, a swarm of hornets, each the size of a large dog. . . .

It didn't make for pleasant conjecture, Neville decided.

"Well, madam?" he asked.

Shriek merely regarded him. *I see yet again why Being Clive is of two minds with you.*

"And why would that be?"

But the alien merely shook her head. *I agree with your counsel, Being Neville. We will seek a more advantageous vantage point and make further plans once we have—*

Her mental voice broke off as suddenly as if a switch had been thrown, cutting her off. The sudden silence jolted Neville. He had been studying the height of the lowest step leading up to the monstrous portal of the nearest building. Now he turned to see Shriek standing with her head cocked to one side, listening. One hand of four reached toward the hair spikes that covered her torso.

"What is it—" he began, but he got no further.

Hist, Being Neville. There is danger near. Mindspeak if you wish to communicate. Or else be still.

He couldn't mindspeak, Neville wanted to tell her, but he kept his own counsel this time. His time in the Dungeon had taught him this much: there was danger at every turn. If the alien perceived what he could not, he was more than willing to bow to her superior senses —with all honesty, rather than with the exaggerated civility he had offered her so far that owed a great deal more to sarcasm than to courtesy.

He waited patiently while she scanned their surroundings, his own head cocked. He heard nothing but remained quiet. It was only when the alien turned on him suddenly, upper arms pulling him close to her chest, that he could no longer refrain from speaking.

"Now you go too far, madam!" he protested.

Will you be still?

Her voice rang like thunder in Neville's head. With her lower arms she drew a thick silk thread from her spinnerets and tossed it to the top of the enormous step. No sooner had it attached than she drew herself up along its length, bearing Neville as easily as she might have a child.

Watch, she said when they were safely on the step, drawn back far enough from its lip to still see below.

Her voice was its usual volume now—no louder than spoken words, though for Neville still as disconcerting as having another's voice speak to one in one's own mind would always be. She loosed her grip on him, steadying him when he would have stumbled.

Take care, Being Neville. They are very close now.

Neville nodded. Close enough for him to hear, as well, what had first alarmed his companion. He peered over the edge of the step and looked toward the thicket of weeds from which issued the unmistakable sound of conversation and harnesses jingling. His sword hand drifted to the hilt of his saber, then fell numbly away as the party rode forth.

It was all Neville could do to stifle a cry of amazement.

Fairies, was all he could think to call them.

For they rode on rats—not the scurvy creatures to be found in any dockyard from London to the ports of Africa, but sleek, groomed creatures, their fur a pure white, their harnesses silver and gold, noses and tails the pink of a newborn baby's skin. And the beings themselves—how could he not call them fairies? They were slender, graceful creatures, men and women both in the small company of ten that rode forth; cheekbones high, ears topping to fine points, hair like a waterfall of fine golden fillets held back with jeweled tiaras, eyes dark like deep forest pools; the men in jackets, trousers, and boots all of green, weaponed with delicate épées and bows; the women in gowns like shimmering gauze that clung to their every charm. . . .

What else could they be but fairies?

Except . . . except . . .

They weren't the diminutive creatures of folklore and tale. No matter their appearance, nor their choice of steeds, the company was composed of beings the same size as he himself. Yet if one took in the scale of this city, they *were* diminutive.

As was he.

It all became a little too confusing at times. But this *was* the Dungeon, he reminded himself. Not England. Here the impossible was possible. If he could travel with an intelligent spider, then why could there *not* be fairies here as well, diminutive or not?

You know these beings? Shriek asked.

He turned to his companion and shook his head.

There was a look in your features . . . , Shriek began, then gave a mental shrug. *I still find it difficult to read the faces of your kind.*

Neville opened his mouth to explain the simple *wonder* of what he saw, but the alien laid one of her oddly shaped fingers against his lips.

Mindspeak only, she warned him yet again, but then she remembered that he had yet to be drawn into the neural web of communication that she shared with the lost members of their company. He *couldn't* mindspeak.

Before Neville knew what she was about, she had entwined her fingers with his, and their minds were in contact. More quickly than Shriek would have thought possible, more quickly than any untrained nontelepath with whom she had ever come into such intimacy with, Neville erected barriers between their minds. But the line of communication remained open—a gossamer thread running between them along which Neville sent his thoughts.

Ah, he said in her mind. *Now I see the trick of it.*

You cannot tell me that you are unfamiliar with this process, Being Neville.

I am merely a swift learner, Neville replied.

But to erect such barriers, so quickly . . .

I also value my privacy, madam.

They studied each other for a long moment, each trying to read the other's alien features, neither succeeding in breaching the other's barriers. Finally Shriek gave a mental shrug.

You recognized these beings . . . , she began again.

But then they both realized that during their time on the neural web that now linked their minds, they had been discovered. Two archers stood on the step above them, bows drawn taut, shafts aimed at their hearts. Below, the remainder of the party sat quietly on their mounts, looking upward. One stepped her rat a pace or two from her companions.

She spoke a few words in a completely foreign

tongue that utterly charmed Neville with its sweet, bell-like sound.

"I'm afraid I don't understand you," he replied in the common patois of the Dungeon.

"I asked," the woman replied in kind, "are you aligned with the Ren or the Chaffri?"

Neville and Shriek exchanged worried glances.

We must tell her the truth, Shriek said. *That we belong to neither.*

And what if she does?

What do you mean? Shriek asked.

Does the expression 'our goose will be cooked' mean anything on your homeworld?

I wish Being Clive were here, was all that Shriek could say then.

Looking at the fierce faces of the fairy woman's guard, Neville surprised himself by realizing that he too wished his twin were present. Weighing both their experiences in the Dungeon thus far, he was loathe to admit it even to himself, but for those keeping score—like those damnable Dungeonmasters—so far Clive had met with far more success than ever he had.

Clive had kept his party intact, while Neville had never managed to gather steady companions about himself.

Clive had that damned undefeatable optimism of his that kept him always pushing ahead, no matter what the odds—and what made it worse, his concern in doing so was never so much for himself, but for others. Coming in search of his twin, risking his life time and again for the motley crew of aliens and time travelers he'd assembled about himself . . .

Clive hadn't been reduced to being merely dinner for the Lords of Thunder.

But Clive was nowhere near to help them at this moment.

They had only themselves.

"Has anyone ever told you how radiant you look in that gown?" he asked the woman awaiting their reply below.

She regarded him for a long, cool moment, then made a quick motion with one delicate hand.

"Take them captive!" she told her guards. "But gently. I would question them while they are still in one piece."

What now, Being Neville? Shriek asked.

I believe that in a case such as this, he replied, his gaze never leaving that of the woman below, *discretion would prove to be the better part of valor—don't you think?*

Shriek sent only a wordless grumble into his mind.

Don't care for the Bard, do you, madam?

Don't care for you, Shriek replied.

Only the fact that his hand was clasped around that of his companion told Baron Tewkesbury's youngest son that he wasn't alone in this gray void between the Dungeon levels.

But Clive Folliot was less concerned with his immediate situation than perhaps he should have been. It was true that there was nothing to see—and as little to hear, or taste, or touch, save Chang Guafe's metallic grip in his own—yet he should have been concerned with their destination. The Dungeon was not a place where a man could let down his guard for an instant—not and survive as well. Yet Clive's mind churned with other worries.

As they fell through the gray, flickers of a brilliant blue flashed in his mind—reminding him of that earlier gate they had taken, after which their company split in two. The blue flashes brought him a nagging feeling that he was forgetting something of importance, but they did no more than that. They revealed nothing. They opened no doors in his memory. But they would give him no rest either, teasing and flickering behind his eyelids like torch shadows in the wind, and they quickly brought on the dull beginnings of a headache—an all-too-familiar sensation in the Dungeon.

But when he worked to put that nagging feeling from his mind, he saw instead the chess set placed on the board in the chamber they had so recently quit by stepping through a looking glass. The white pieces had included models of himself and the others of his party, but that was not what had so upset him.

It was the red pieces.

The half of the set that obviously represented their opponents.

It was the fact that among them stood miniature replicas of Sidi Bombay and Clive's current companion, the cyborg Chang Guafe.

Did their presence on the opposing team mean that all along the two waited only the proper moment to betray him? Were they working with the enemy—whoever that mysterious enemy might be?

Clive refused to believe it. It had to be yet another trick of the Dungeonmasters. But still . . . what did he know of either? Guafe was an alien—more so even than Shriek or Finnbogg, to Clive's thinking, for his thought processes were based on cold logic, nothing more. As for the Indian . . . Sidi Bombay remained the same enigma he had been from the moment he had come out of the darkness on that African night so long ago to join his party.

Clive's heart told him that neither would betray him. After all they had been through together, they were his friends now. He would trust them with his life.

Wouldn't he?

Damn these Dungeonmasters for the games they played with his mind. They made a mockery of everything he believed in. They gave lie to so much that it was next to impossible to trust one's own senses.

The pretenders to his twin's name and face that he had met throughout the upper levels of the Dungeon . . .

The vision of his fiancée in the molten pool . . .

The time he had spent reconciling with his father . . .

Lies.

All damned lies.

And now these chess pieces, so casually set out for him to spy.

More lies.

It had to be another lie. For if it wasn't, then who was to say that any one of his companions could be trusted? God help him, could he even trust himself? When he thought of what the Dungeonmasters had already done to Smythe . . . placing the implants in his mind to make him bow to their damnable will, an enslavement that only Horace's constant vigilance could keep at bay . . .

Who was to say they hadn't planted similar devices in each and every one of them? Would he turn on his companions at some moment of crisis? Would Annabelle?

God, he hated the creators of the Dungeon for what they did. To them it was all part and parcel of some complex game. An amusement, nothing more. But for him and his companions it undermined the very basis of their beings. Eroded loyalties. Made a mockery of truth. Challenged every perception.

In a place such as this how was a man ever to know what was true and what was not when he could not trust even himself?

His companion's metallic fingers tightened on his own just then, drawing him back to their present situation. A moment later, as he felt a solid surface under his boots, he realized that Guafe was merely warning him that they had arrived.

They landed in what appeared to be a central square of a large metropolis. Ruined buildings lay all about them, along with the metal shells of abandoned vehicles. Vegetation ran rampant, a jungle of growths that cracked their way through the stonework. Overhead was a dismal gray sky.

Clive blinked as he studied his surroundings. There was something wrong about what he viewed. Not just the desolation of the city—more as though his senses had gone subtly askew.

"It appears," his companion remarked then, "that

the original inhabitants of this place were only half our size."

That was what was wrong, Clive realized. When he looked at the nearest building, its doorway was sized down to a being that had only half his own height. It gave him an odd feeling, standing here as he was, too tall for his surroundings.

"And," Guafe added, "we are also alone."

And so they were. There was not a sign of any of the others who had gone through the looking glass before them.

Clive shot the cyborg a considering glance—Was this the beginning of the betrayal? he couldn't stop from asking himself—then firmly shut that disloyal thought away. He was damned if he'd play the Dungeonmasters' game.

"What could have happened to them?" he asked as he slowly looked about, scanning the deserted streets that led away from the square where they stood.

"Considering the spatial and temporal paradoxes we have encountered thus far in the Dungeon," Guafe replied, "they could be anywhere . . . or anywhen."

Clive's shoulders sagged as the reality of the cyborg's observation struck home. But when Guafe turned to look at him, he quickly straightened himself and gave a brusque nod.

"So be it," he said. "Then our first order of the day will be to discover the whereabouts of the others."

The red facets of the cyborg's eyes glittered as he continued to regard Clive, but he said nothing.

"Do you disagree?" Clive asked him, doubts arising once more no matter how he tried to keep them at bay.

Guafe shook his head. "On the contrary, I can but admire your loyalty to our companions."

"They have earned my loyalty—each one of them."

"Even your brother?"

When Clive thought of his twin, it was difficult to sort through the bewildering battery of conflicting emotions that helter-skeltered their way through his mind. Their differences were many. Neville had treated him poorly—to put it mildly—but he was still Clive's brother, and the more time Clive spent with him of late, the better he was beginning to understand some of what had driven Neville to do all that he had done.

Neville was haunted by his own private demons; the baron had compelled him as much as Clive had driven himself to compete against his brother.

He met the cyborg's steady gaze and finally nodded. "Even my brother," he said.

"I believe I am finally beginning to understand the Dungeonmasters' fascination with your family," Guafe said mildly, "particularly as it is embodied in you."

"I am no one special," Clive said.

"On the contrary, Clive Folliot, from my observations of your race to date, I would consider you very special indeed."

Clive couldn't control the sudden heat that rose up his neck and reddened his cheek.

"Yes, well," he said, "that's all well and fine, but it brings us no closer to finding the others. What can your sensors tell us of this place?"

Guafe remained quiet for a long moment before speaking.

"Simple observation on primary data-infeed levels indicates that this city fell victim to a localized disaster of major proportions—the detonation of a nuclear device, I believe, as I can still detect a faint radiation level—which is no longer harmful, I should add. The site of the blast must have been a few kilometers distant, hence the relative stability of the structures still standing about us. I would place the time frame for the disaster at approximately one hundred and thirty years as you count them. There are no life-forms in the immediate vicinity."

"What of the buildings themselves?" Clive asked. "Do you sense the same—circuitry I believe you named it—as there was in my father's . . . in the building on the previous level?"

"Negative. These structures are devoid of such apparatus. Below, however . . ."

Clive had a sinking feeling. Their worst moments in the Dungeon had inevitably occurred in its subterranean levels.

"Below?" he prompted.

"My sensors indicate considerable activity—electronic as well as mechanical."

"Which means?"

The cyborg shrugged. "Unfortunately there is insufficient data to elaborate further at this moment."

Clive took a last look around at their surroundings—all scaled to half their size. What manner of beings had dwelt here? Humans, such as himself? He wouldn't be willing to wager on it—not with all the varied races they had encountered thus far in the Dungeon. But that wasn't material at the moment. Finding their companions was the first priority. Once they were all together again, they could see about confronting the monsters who had created this hellish place for their own singular amusement.

There were debts to be paid; let the Dungeonmasters take note.

Enormous debts.

And Major Clive Folliot, presently on leave from Her Majesty's Fifth Imperial Horse Guards Regiment, was a man who always paid his debts.

"Below, is it?" Clive finally said. "Then I suppose that we must find a way that will take us underground."

▪ CHAPTER TWO ▪

"Okay," Annabelle said. "It looks like we're on our own."

Though neither of her companions relished the thought any more than she did, there was nothing either of them could offer to put the lie to her plain statement.

"So what we've got to do now," she went on, "is figure out where we are and what the score is."

"How can there be score," Finnbogg asked, "when is no game?"

"Oh, there's a game all right. We've got the Ren and the Chaffri and Christ knows who else messing about with us. We're working on simple survival, but to them it's all just a game."

"I wouldn't mind some new gear, ma'am," Smythe said.

That brought a trace of a smile to Annabelle's lips. Throughout their adventures the sergeant had always put forth that famous stiff upper lip of the British. But strip him down to not much more than his skivvies, and all he could do was squirm.

"New duds," she said. "Coming right up. Anybody know the way to Macy's from here?" At the blank looks she received from both her companions, she gave a shrug. "Never mind. Let's see if we can't scope out the scene."

Squatting on her heels, she zipped down her jacket far enough to reach the controls of the Baalbec A-9 device that were under the skin in the center of her chest. The computerized implants on her wrist began to hum as she lowered her hand, fingers widespread. On the dirty pavement in front of her, a gridlike map constructed of faintly glowing blue lines appeared.

"City blocks, for as far as the Baalbec can input," she muttered.

Finnbogg watched her with a worshipful gaze but kept his distance. Smythe crouched down beside her. He pointed to a small pulsing spot of light.

"Is that our position?" he asked.

"You got it, Horace. Looks grim, doesn't it?"

"I'm not sure I follow you, ma'am."

"Well, think about it for a moment. Each one of those squares represents a city block—that's, like, maybe a third of a klick, give or take a few meters."

"Klick?"

"Kilometer."

Smythe returned his attention to the map. "I see."

"Right. I've got the Baalbec turned up to max, so we're getting a long-range view of maybe thirty klicks. And this city's just truckin' on off my input range."

"Finnbogg doesn't understand," their bulldoglike companion muttered.

"It's simple, Finn," Annabelle told him. "It means we're smack-dab in the middle of one hell of a big city. For all we know, it could be like this for a hundred klicks in every direction. And if it's all like what we're looking at now—then we could be in deep shit."

"No food, no water," Smythe said.

"No new clothes," Annabelle added with a teasing grin.

Smythe frowned. "This is serious, Annabelle. How can we even begin to find the others in a place this immense?"

Annabelle's smile wilted. "You got me there, Horace."

Finnbogg suddenly lifted his head, nostrils quivering. "Someone comes. . . ."

"Bloody hell," Smythe muttered.

He stood up, trying to keep himself covered while

still maintaining a defensive position. He succeeded only in entangling his cloak around himself.

Annabelle rose to her feet as well. She faced the mouth of the alleyway where Finnbogg was looking, hackles rising at the nape of his neck. Her gaze darted to her immediate left and right, trying to spot something that she could use as a makeshift weapon, but there was nothing. Before she could look further, a shadow moved at the end of the alley and a man was standing there, peering in at them.

Finnbogg growled, deep in his chest.

"Easy," Annabelle said, as she took in the stranger.

He looked like nothing so much as a burned-out wino from her own world, the kind of grizzled, half-starved street bum you could stumble across in any of the major cities. He had a pronounced stoop, unkempt hair, a few days' growth of beard, raggedy clothes that just made his frail frame seem all that much thinner.

"Whoa," the stranger said, carefully holding his hands out in front of him. They were grimed with dirt and webbed with blue veins. "Jake don't want no trouble."

"It's okay, old-timer," Annabelle said as the bum began to back away. "We're all pals here."

The bum froze when she spoke, gaze darting from her to Finnbogg.

"That's some mean-looking dog you got yourself, lady."

Annabelle didn't bother explaining just what Finnbogg was. If they were back on her homeworld, it still made sense to keep a low profile. Let the authorities get their hands on someone like Finnbogg, and Christ knew what they'd do to him. She hadn't grown up on Spielberg films without learning something. The weird and the wonderful always got the raw end of the deal.

"What do you call this place?" she asked.

"You lost, lady?"

"Not a chance. We just came off a binge, is all, Jake,

and we're kinda muddy on exactly where we ended up."

"Well, you're in the Dives, lady. Not a good place for Downsiders, but I guess you already know that. Looks like you already run into some trouble."

"Downside?" Horace asked.

Jake tapped his foot on the pavement. "Under the streets—way down below the tunnels and sewers—where the spiffy folk live."

This didn't sound much like New York or any place in her homeworld, Annabelle realized. Wonderful.

"Does the city have a name?"

Jake shrugged. "Had one, I suppose, but I don't know anybody as recollects it. You folks have any liquid refreshment left, or did you finish it all?"

"Sorry, Jake," Annabelle said. "We're all out."

"Figures. Story of my life."

"Do you know anything about a gate to the next level?" Horace asked.

Jake blinked. "Say what?"

"The next level of the Dungeon—there must be a gate somewhere on this level."

"Shit, I just live here. I don't know diddly about no dungeons or gates or levels. This here's the Dives, mister, plain and simple. Nothing pretty about it, but it's all we got. Easy to get to—just get your ass kicked up from Downside—but once you're here, you're here for keeps. 'Less you got yourself a pass to get back in. . . ."

His eyes took on a considering look as he spoke.

"No passes here," Annabelle told him, "so you can forget trying to roll us."

Jake's gaze drifted back to Finnbogg. "Hell, lady. I didn't mean no harm. We're just talking, right?"

"Just talking," Annabelle agreed. "Is there any place around here we can get some provisions—you know, clothes, food, that kinda thing?"

"Just where the hell are you folks from?"

"Not from the Dives, and not from Downside either," Annabelle said.

"So what else is there?"

"It's a long, boring story. What do you say, Jake? Can you help us out? Steer us on our way?"

"What's in it for me?"

"Our thanks," Horace said.

Jake snorted. "That ain't going to take me far, mister."

"How about we don't let Finnbogg here chew off your leg?" Annabelle asked sweetly.

Finnbogg grinned. "Chew him now—can I, can I?"

Jake did a double take that would have been amusing under any other circumstances, but right now Annabelle didn't want to lose their connection to the only native they'd run into thus far, so she didn't crack a smile. Jake had already mentioned something along the lines of the Dives being a dangerous place. They might be able to avoid trouble if he'd come through for them.

That was if he didn't just take off first.

"Betcha Finnbogg runs faster than you can," she added.

"I . . . I wasn't going nowhere, lady."

"Never thought you were. So what do you say, Jake? Will you give us a hand?"

"Sure, sure. Old Jake's just smack full of charity, you bet. I'll take you round to Casey's."

"Which is?"

He shook his head as though he thought he was talking to a moron. "Casey's, for Christ's sake. What do you think it'd—oh, yeah. I forgot. You're not from around here. It's a club, lady. Won't be much going on there this time of day, but Casey'll be there. You talk to him, and maybe, if he's in a good mood—which ain't necessarily guaranteed, you understand—maybe he'll fix you up."

"Great. Let's go."

"But the thing is, lady, it's still gonna cost you."

Finnbogg growled and took a step forward. The bum went pale, knees visibly quivering.

"Hey, I'm not talking about Jake now. Like I said,

charity's my middle name. It's Casey. He don't do nothing for nothing."

Annabelle and Horace exchanged glances. They had no money—they didn't even know what passed for currency on this level of the Dungeon—and nothing to barter.

"What kind of a club does he run?" Annabelle asked.

"You know—drinks, a little fast food, got some music in the evenings. . . ."

"Well, you can just tell him I'm auditioning for a gig," Annabelle said.

Jake gave her a once-over. "Well, I don't know nothing about music, lady, or how good you'd be at it, but you look like you got the build of a dancer."

Dancer, Annabelle thought. Right. Read stripper. Read Casey was probably a pimp, pushing his "ladies" to make a little extra on the side. Some things didn't change no matter where you went.

"Don't even think about it," she told Jake.

"I never think about things," Jake assured her quickly. "Two things I'm good at—drinking and then drinking some more. I don't want no trouble with anybody, lady—not you or Casey."

"Suits me fine, Jake. Now be a pal and let's get this show on the road. Finnbogg here's getting awfully hungry."

"We're going, we're going. Just follow old Jake and keep that—is that a dog?"

"Close enough. He's a Finnbogg."

"Thought that was his name."

"It is."

Jake looked as though he wanted to work that out, then simply shrugged and set off, Annabelle walking at his side, Horace and Finnbogg bringing up the rear. Jake kept glancing nervously over his shoulder at the latter.

"Relax," Annabelle told him.

Jake nodded. "Sure," he muttered to himself. "Relax. Right. With the teeth on that sucker I'm supposed to relax? All the hell I was looking for was a drink. Plain and simple—no frills, thank you kindly. Instead, look what I got."

"A bunch of new friends," Annabelle said with a sweet smile.

Jake just shook his head. "Christ, I could use a drink. . . ."

The descent was simple.

One merely found purchase for fingers and toes in the narrow cracks that riddled the stone face of the building—clinging to them a thousand feet above the ground—tested each before putting one's weight on it, then reached for another. Yes, Sidi thought, but when one has also been placing the whole of one's weight on such frail digits, and the descent had tortoised as long as it had, difficulty was not the problem.

Stamina was.

Occasionally a wind would rise up, buffeting them where they held to their precarious perches. All they could do then was cling to the cracks and wait it out. Only when the wind died down once more could they continue their descent again.

Above him, Tomàs kept up a steady grumble that alternated between whispered promises to the Virgin and a stream of curses in his native tongue. Sidi might have joined him in either, but he believed that cursing was merely a waste of one's breath, and he was not a religious man—at least not by Western standards. The Indian followed a belief system that was a way of life, not merely a crutch one used in times of duress. Nor did he thank a deity for what he himself had accomplished.

He had been born a Hindu; now he was something else again.

To Westerners any definition of Hinduism remained inadequate, contradictory, and incomplete. But the Hindu Way, while it appeared overtly secular, was still a religion. It comprised a complex combination of religious belief, rites, customs, and daily practices and had given birth to a bewildering number of Eastern faiths that included Buddhism, Jainism, Sikhism, and various schools of tantra and bhakti. To an outsider—particularly a Western outsider—they were all part and parcel of one great heathen belief system; to the practitioner they were the very basis of life.

Sidi was not a good Hindu.

But once he had been. It was due to his wide travels and the contact he had made with the practitioners of other faiths that he had begun to question his blind acceptance of the caste system and other long-cherished institutions of the faith in which he was brought up. He began to realize that his very questioning of that faith reflected a weakness—not in Hinduism so much as in his own ability to adhere to its tenets. Consequently, as the years had progressed, he had drifted more toward a Taoist outlook upon life.

Lao Tzu had said, "The further one goes away from himself the less he knows." ·

This was more to Sidi's particular understanding of the world than to the faith of his parents. Though he could recall all the teachings by which he had been raised, it seemed to him that a man must work in harmony with the world in which he found himself. Every action had a reaction—some less obvious than others, but no less profound to one who took the time to contemplate them.

Man himself was a microcosm of the larger world about him. As he did, so was it reflected in the world, the depth of his deeds' ramifications dictated by his station in the world. But the leader of a country was no more important than the lowest field-worker; it was merely that the spread of his influence was more readily felt. Neither, Sidi believed, was more important than the other.

So it was that, as he made his descent, he contemplated inner mysteries rather than conducting a conversation of complaints and pleading with a deity. An inner peace stretched within him, allowing him full control of every sense required in the descent, but wrapping him in a state of timelessness so that he came

down the building's side without the same strength-
eroding anxiety that ate away at his companion.

Which wasn't to say that when he finally reached the
window of the story directly below the roof, he wasn't
relieved.

Sidi was a human first, subject to all a human's
strengths and frailties, and a Taoist second. His belief
system merely allowed him to deal more calmly with
the problems set before him. It didn't remove them.

As he clambered in the window, he stood for a long
moment on the floor inside, apparently motionless as
he eased the cramps in fingers and toes, in calf muscles
and back, in every muscle. Only then, still stiff but far
more comfortable, did he return to the window to help
his companion inside.

"Madre de Dios," Tomàs cried as he collapsed beside
the window. "Never again will I do such a thing. We are
madmen both—do you hear me, Sidi? *Muy loco."*

The Indian nodded. While Tomàs sat there massag-
ing his burning muscles, Sidi went exploring this floor
of the building. Tomàs looked up hopefully at his return.

"You have found stairs, *sim*?"

Sidi shook his head.

"Then here I will die," the Portuguese announced.

"I have found some discarded cable that we might
use as ropes to lower ourselves to the next floor."

"Cable?"

The Indian nodded. "It's a curious material—composed of many multicolored small fibers encased in a
hard rubbery substance—but it seems strong enough
to bear a man's weight."

Tomàs lifted his gaze and blew a kiss heavenward.
"Truly God is merciful," he said. Then he stood up,
groaning at the pain in his limbs. "Show me these
cables, *amigo."*

Neville and Shriek descended from that enormous
step employing the same process that they had used to
reach its upper lip, only this time Neville lowered him-

self down Shriek's silken strand rather than allowing himself to be carried a second time. When he reached ground level, where the main body of their captors waited for them, he studied the beings with frank regard.

The damned rats truly *were* the size of a horse. As he approached the one ridden by the apparent leader of the small company, he couldn't suppress a shudder at the presence of a rodent that large—tamed or not. The white groomed fur and tinkling harnesses couldn't disguise the disconcerting fact that they were still rats. He ignored the unpleasant feeling by fixing his attention on the creature's rider. Up close the woman was even more beautiful than she had appeared from his earlier vantage point.

"Do you have a name?" she asked.

"Indeed I do, madam. I am Major Neville Folliot, currently on leave from the Royal Somerset Grenadier Guards for the purposes of exploring East Africa. My companion's name is Shriek."

"You have a most military ring to your title."

Neville shrugged. "Then let me set your mind at ease by assuring you that we are merely lost and are trespassing on your company solely by accident."

"It seemed to me that you were preparing an ambush."

"Appearances can be deceiving," Neville said, laying a hand against his heart. "Trust me when I say, we meant neither you, nor any individual of your party, the slightest harm. Hearing your approach, we merely retreated to a more advantageous position. Strangers as we are to this land, we had no way of knowing if it was friend or foe who rode toward us." He glanced about at the archers who still had their weapons trained upon Shriek and himself. "To be blunt, might I add that we are still unaware?"

The woman made a quick cutting motion with her hand, and the archers lowered their weapons. Neville noticed, however, that not one of them relaxed vigilance.

"Your story has the ring of truth to it," she said, "but let me ask you again, are you aligned with the Ren or the Chaffri?"

Shriek replied before Neville could frame a response. *We are aligned with neither, Being.*

The woman's eyebrows rose slightly as she realized that the arachnid was sentient.

"Yet their names are familiar to you—are they not?"

Shriek nodded. *We have only heard of them—from other beings on previous levels of the Dungeon. As Being Neville has already told you, we are lost. We wish only to be reunited with our companions and to journey on to the gate that will lead us down to the next level.*

That's playing one's cards close to one's vest, Neville thought, shooting his companion a sour look.

The woman said nothing for a long moment, merely regarded them both until Neville could feel himself begin to fidget.

"You," she said finally, pointing to Neville, "are obviously of a devious nature."

Neville tensed. Now we're for it, he thought. He wished desperately to see what the woman's guard was doing, but he forced himself to keep a mild look on his features and to meet her gaze directly.

"I like that in a man," the woman said.

Neville relaxed and gave her one of his winning smiles, but she had already turned her attention to his companion.

"Yet," she added, "in our present circumstances I appreciate your honesty more, Mistress . . . ah . . . Shriek, was it?"

The alien nodded. *Shriek is the name this being presently utilizes, yes.*

"We are Tuan," the woman said. "I am the Song of the Wind; my speaking name is Alyssa."

Neither the name she gave her race nor her title meant anything to either Neville or Shriek. But she could easily be a song of his heart, Neville thought.

"A name as lovely as your charms," he said.

Alyssa glanced at him. "Yes, I'm sure," she said. The trace of a wry smile touched her lips. "But be that as it may, I would prefer to address other concerns at this moment. You are the first beings we have come across in this strange land—other than vermin and the like— that are of a similar stature to us. The greater number of the rest have been giants. Our diminutive height has helped us in evading many dangers thus far, but it also hinders our attempts to converse with the other beings we have met."

There was a certain stiffness in the woman's speech patterns as she spoke the Dungeon patois that had Neville wishing he could understand her native language. The bell-like tonality when she spoke in her own tongue had been like music—and utterly suited to her beauty.

We have seen a few giants, Shriek said, remembering the monstrosity on the bridge between the first and second levels and the living-dead Lords of the Thunder in Tawn, *but most have been beings of our own size—as you are. Helpful most of them have not been, no matter what their size.*

"We were snatched from our homeland and brought to this place against our will—can I assume you are in a similar situation?"

"That's exactly our predicament," Neville said. "Torn from our loved ones and left to fend for ourselves in this hellish place."

Alyssa nodded. "Yet for what purpose? All we have been able to discover thus far is that there are two warring factions who use the Dungeon as their gaming ground—the Ren and the Chaffri—but we have been able to learn no more of them except that they exist. They might be humanoid, or they might be"—she glanced at Shriek—"of a more alien appearance, as many of the beings we have encountered here have been; but one thing is certain: we mean no more to them than the pieces on a gaming board mean to us in our homeland."

She paused as though to give either of them a chance

to comment, but Neville was still more interested in the woman's charms at that moment than he was in her dialogue, while Shriek kept her own counsel.

"Are you aware that there may well be a third set of players in this game?" Alyssa finally asked them.

Neville focused on what she'd been saying. "A third set? We don't even know who belongs to which side of the other two. And if you say there are three, then why not four? A half dozen? Or every man for himself?"

The Tuan leader slowly shook her head. "I find it difficult to decide whether you simply *are* the rake you pretend to be, or whether you have some ulterior motive to carry on in such a superficial manner."

Being Neville can be impossible when he wishes, Shriek said, *but I believe, in his heart, he means well. He appears to be one who, when confronted with a situation over which he has no control, either ignores it or makes light of it.*

"Do you trust him?" Alyssa asked.

Neville wished they wouldn't speak of him as though he weren't present, but he said nothing. He too was interested in the arachnid's response.

Shriek turned to look at him, then back at the Tuan leader. *I trust his brother more,* she said. *Being Clive has no secrets.*

"And what secrets do you think I carry?" Neville demanded.

Shriek gave a mental shrug. *Only you would know, Being Neville.*

"I protest," Neville began, but broke off as that wry smile reappeared on Alyssa's lips.

"I too sense a mystery about you, Neville Folliot," she said, "but no danger."

Lovely, Neville thought. She saw him as a harmless crank.

"Shall we join forces?" Alyssa asked.

Our first concern is to find our missing comrades, Shriek said.

"I appreciate loyalty," the Tuan leader said. "Let us compare notes. Perhaps we will be able to help each other. To find missing comrades *and* bring this struggle directly to those responsible for all our troubles."

Being Neville? Shriek asked.

What do you want? he replied so that only she could hear him. *Me to make the decision or merely to agree to yours?*

I thought that since we are companions, of equal stature—the irony in her mindspeaking was heavy—*that the decision should belong to both of us. I believe that we should see if the Tuan can help us.*

Neville regarded Alyssa again and sighed.

"I'd be delighted to join forces with so charming a company," he said, a nonchalant wave of his hand taking in all of the Tuan party, but his gaze resting meaningfully on their leader.

"You are indeed a rake," Alyssa said. "I think I will enjoy the fruit born of this meeting."

Neville lifted his eyebrows quizzically. "How so?"

"I miss companionable banter. My own people are not so comfortable treating me as a woman rather than as their priestess."

Neville and Shriek exchanged glances. Wonderful, Neville thought. To date they'd not done terribly well in their dealings with the various religious groups within the Dungeon. But it was too late to back out of the situation now. Especially considering that the Tuan had the superior numbers.

If only Alyssa wasn't so damned attractive. The way her gauzy dress clung to her . . .

He looked away and indicated the immense structures that surrounded them, each towering monstrously high.

"Is everything so large on this level?" he asked, to change the subject.

Alyssa never looked at the buildings surrounding them. Instead she winked—not coquettishly, but there was a promise in her look all the same.

"That is something," she said, "that I'm sure we will discover, given time."

This was what he wanted, wasn't it? Neville thought. To sample her charms?

Then why did he feel so nervous?

There were benefits to their larger size, Clive realized—a larger size, at least, in relation to their surroundings.

They had followed the length of one long, deserted avenue after another, making a winding course around the abandoned vehicles and rubble, until Chang Guafe brought them to a halt before a wide set of stairs that led underground.

"Ah," the cyborg said. "This will do."

"What is it?" Clive asked.

"The entranceway to an underground transportation system—a railway system, I believe, by the signage."

A railway running under the streets? Clive thought. Well, why not? With all else they had come across thus far in their travels, why should he be surprised at anything the Dungeonmasters had created?

"Of course," he said.

Guafe glanced at him. On his metallic features passed what Clive could only consider a look of amusement—if such a thing were possible—but the cyborg made no vocal comment. Clive turned back to the railway's entrance.

"Underground railways," he added. "Common as dirt, really, in any truly civilized city. Only we do have one small problem. . . ."

Together they regarded the wreckage of the two vehicles that blocked the stairwell halfway down. They appeared to be wedged tightly enough to block any egress the pair might have attempted to what lay below.

"But we have the size now to overcome such a minor difficulty," Guafe said.

"Of course," Clive said, beginning to feel like a windup mechanical toy capable of only a few phrases and actions, which it repeated over and over again.

He glanced back at Guafe, who appeared to be waiting for him to make a decision.

Take command of the situation, Clive told himself.

But he was tired of commanding. One had only to look back a few hours to see how capable he had proved himself thus far—one scrape after another, and now their party scattered God knew where and, yes, perhaps even when.

All thanks to *his* command.

But he was an officer—on leave, it was true, but an officer all the same—and he had never been one to shirk his responsibilities.

"Very well," he said, stifling a sigh. "Let's see what we can do to clear a way through."

It was hard, backbreaking labor, and even with their increased size in relation to the vehicles, it might still have proved impossible without the cyborg's superior strength. It took them the better part of an hour simply to move one of the vehicles far enough away from the other so that Guafe could peer ahead through the gap, using the faint beams thrown by his red-faceted eyes to see in the darkness.

"This appears to be the only obstruction that I can see from this vantage point," he said.

Now they realized the negative aspects of their size. Had their surroundings been of a proper scale, the pair could have made their way through the gap right then. Instead it was another hour's hard work clearing an opening large enough for them both to squeeze through.

The odd red light thrown by Guafe's eyes dimly lit the stairs that continued on past the pair of wrecked vehicles, but Clive shook his head when Guafe was ready to go on.

"I need better light than that," he said.

Back on the street he braided thick grasses together until he had made a number of makeshift torches. Three he thrust into his belt. The fourth Guafe lit for him, creating sparks by hitting his metal forearm against a stone until the dried grass caught. With torch in hand Clive led the way down once more.

The ceiling was close, but they could just walk without bending their heads. The air, the farther they descended, took on a stale quality. Clive's torch sputtered, throwing odd shadows and giving off a thick black smoke. The stairs made two turns before they opened onto a wide platform that appeared to Clive no different from any railway station in his homeland.

Except it was underground.

In a desolate city.

He walked to the edge of the platform and looked down, holding his torch above him. Sure enough, there were two paired sets of tracks, both leading off into the tunnels to his left and right.

Which direction to take?

He turned to his companion, but before he could frame the question, Guafe spoke.

"Quick! Douse your torch."

"What?"

"Can't you hear it?"

"Hear what—?" Clive began, but then he realized what it was that had Guafe worried, as he too felt the vibrations underfoot.

God help them, there was a train coming. Here, under a dead city, a train was running.

They heard its whistle then—not a steam whistle, that friendly, if somewhat lonesome, sound that Clive knew from traveling by train in the English countryside. No, it was more like a quick, short blast of a siren.

Clive ground his torch underheel and withdrew with Guafe just as the engine's headbeams appeared in the distance of the tunnel on their left.

• CHAPTER THREE •

Jake led them by a circuitous route through the dead city, keeping to back lanes and alleys rather than the main thoroughfares. When they did have to go out on a street, he appeared nervous—shoulders drawn in tight, head hunched toward his chest as though he were trying to draw his head into his shell like a turtle. Annabelle, taking stock of the general sense of decay that lay about them, couldn't see what he was worried about.

Sure, there was a lot of rubble on the streets, and more than one abandoned car, not to mention trucks and buses, but there was plenty of rubble along the route they were taking as well.

"What gives?" she asked finally.

That got her another of Jake's anxious looks.

"C'mon," she said. "I'm not going to bite you—and neither's Finnbogg unless you screw us around—so tell me straight. What're we skulking through the alleys for?"

"Don't want to run into any of the gangs," Jake replied. "Most of them're sleeping off whatever the hell they was up to last night, but you get stragglers, or maybe some of the Baptists—John J.'s boys, you know —and ain't nobody with half an ounce of sense wants to run into any of them."

"Street gangs?" Annabelle asked.

Jake nodded.

"Making sure no one steps it out on their turf?"

"You got it, lady."

"These Baptists—are they a religious bunch?"

She was thinking of the Baptists back home—they

weren't her style, that was for sure, but they weren't connected to any street gang either.

"John J.'s like the new prophet," Jake explained. "Least he is if you listen to him. They're getting ready for the Third Coming."

"Third coming? Of Christ?"

"Yep."

"What happened to the second?"

Jake waved negligently around them. "Where the hell do you think this mess came from?"

Great, Annabelle thought. That was all they needed —another militant church. But that had always been the problem with people, didn't matter where you found them. Get a few of them together and soon enough they had themselves a religion or were worshiping something. Back home it was pop singers, movie stars, and TV evangelists—at least they ruled the heavens in Western society.

"You belong to a gang, Jake?" she asked.

"Huh! Who'd have an old fart like me? All the gangs want is the strong and the pretty." He shook his head. "What kind of a place are you from, anyway, you don't know that?"

The strong and the pretty? Annabelle thought.

"A place that's maybe not so different after all," she said. "Don't people ever get tired of this 'law of the jungle' bullshit?"

"Not so's I've ever noticed," Jake said.

"Burns my ass," Annabelle muttered.

Jake nodded. "The trick to getting by is you don't get yourself noticed. Mostly the gangs leave us street people alone, but ever so once in a while some guy like John J. gets a hard-on to convert the whole frigging world, and then you've really got to lie low."

It seemed as though he had more to say, but he went no further.

"Or what?" Smythe asked.

He'd been walking close enough to hear them and had been following their conversation.

"Or you really get to know the meaning of hard times," Jake said.

"What do you live on—you and the other street people?" Annabelle asked. "Or even the gangs, for that matter. I don't see anything—not a store, not a market stall, nothing. What do you eat? Where do you sleep? Where do you get your booze?"

"Oh we get by. Downsiders got a dump not far from here, and there's always good pickings there. They'll throw out food ain't hardly been touched. Booze we get out the back doors of the clubs—do the boss a favor and he helps you out. Me, I sweep the floors at Casey's every second night, so I get by. We sleep in any old building that ain't claimed by one of the gangs, and there's plenty of those. Plenty to go around. Ain't that many of us, you know."

"Why's that?"

"We get old, we die. Young kids that get kicked topside join the gangs—some 'cause they think it makes them special like they weren't Downside, others 'cause they figure it's their best chance to survive. But it don't matter much why they choose what they do. Being in a gang means that not many of them survive to my age. Not no more. So you get fewer and fewer street people every year." He shrugged. "That's just the way things go—nothing special about it. It's just life."

"Have you been here a long time?" Smythe asked.

"All my life. Got kicked topside when I was, oh I guess maybe nine or so, and I guess I'm about fifty-three now, so you figure it out. Didn't join no gang—that's what got me into shit Downside in the first place. I just made do. Made do, still do." He shot Annabelle a lopsided grin. "Real hard-luck story, huh?"

Annabelle glanced at him and caught the grin. "I've heard worse."

That sobered him up. "Yeah," Jake said. "Me, too. Heads up—here we go."

He paused in the mouth of the latest alley to point across the street. Astonishingly a red neon sign reading CASEY'S flickered above the door of a nondescript brownstone building that stood there. The door was open and standing just inside, surveying the street, was a tall black man with a physique right out of one of the muscle magazines Annabelle had laughed over in just about every 7-Eleven back home. He was wearing jeans, a T-shirt with the arms torn off and drawn tight across that broad chest, black boots, and shades.

"Maybe this wasn't such a good idea," she said.

If there were more like him inside—just as big and capable looking—and they happened to take a dislike to the three of them, as just about 90 percent of the Dungeon's other denizens had, they could be in big trouble.

"Too late for second thoughts," Jake said.

"That's Casey?" Annabelle asked looking over to where the black man was now waving them over.

"In the flesh."

"Well, boys," Annabelle said to her companions, "let's go check out Mr. Jones."

"Thought you said you didn't know Casey."

"I don't. It was a joke. Casey Jones was a railway man, back where I come from."

"Well round here," Jake said, "Casey Jones is something else again."

The old wino seemed to have lost all fear of Finnbogg and any of them now, Annabelle realized, and that made her bad feeling get worse.

"You coming?" Jake asked as he started out across the street.

Tomàs took charge of preparing the cable for their descent to the next story.

"*Son primo,*" he said when Sidi showed it to him. "It's made of what Annabelle calls 'plastic'—*sim*?"

"I believe so," Sidi replied.

It was a thick braid of hundreds of tiny copper wires, each wrapped in multicolored plastic, the whole encased in another layer made up of a thick black rubberized sheath. The cable was coiled around a large wooden spool, and it took the pair the better part of a half hour to wrestle it to the window. There Tomàs tied the loose end to a support beam that stood firm in the rubble of a nearby wall, using sailor's knots to make sure it remained firm.

To hoist the giant spool onto the low windowsill, they took a pair of long lengths of wood that had once been parts of the building's furnishings and used them as levers. Sweat dripping into his eyes Tomàs gave his companion a nod once they had the spool in place.

"Is there anything below?" he asked.

Sidi leaned over the casement to look down. "Nothing I can see from this height."

"Ahora bien," Tomàs said with a slight shrug that almost cost him his hold where he was bracing the spool, balanced precariously as it was on the sill.

The two of them gave it a mighty shove and stepped hastily back as it went over the casement, out the window, and down. The spool crashed against the side of the building as it dropped, the cable sending up a high-pitched whine as it unwound. Not until it was still and the cable lay taut against the casement did they look out through the window once more to study their handiwork.

The cable swung slightly back and forth below them. They could just make out its far end, some fifteen stories distant. The spool was impossible to spy from their height.

"Now this is more to my liking," Tomàs said.

Sidi nodded. "Like a ship's rigging."

"Un poco," Tomàs replied. "But enough to make our way much easier, *sim*? This time I will go first."

Sidi gave him a slight bow and waved forward. Grinning, the Portuguese hopped onto the sill where he clasped the cable between his hands.

"Do not go too fast, *amigo,"* Tomàs warned his companion.

Sidi nodded. One didn't need time in a ship's rigging to learn about rope burns.

"I will see you below," Tomàs said.

Still grinning, he began to slide down the cable,

slowly at first, but soon quickly enough for Sidi to grow nervous.

The man knew what he was doing, he told himself as Tomàs gave a happy shout from below. He swung over himself and began to swarm down, not so quickly as the Portuguese, but quickly enough so that Tomàs wouldn't be kept waiting when he reached the end of the cable.

This was, Sidi realized, the first time he'd seen Tomàs truly happy—despite the gravity of their situation. Undoubtedly because he was finally in a position where his own expertise could be brought into play.

Was that not a most human of human traits? All men and women wished to be considered of some worth—to see themselves respected in the eyes of their peers. It was a basic need that perhaps only monks could set aside.

'Let him be happy then, Sidi decided. Let Tomàs take the lead for a while. And who knew? If he truly had Folliot blood in him, it might well make the difference between success and failure for them all.

Alyssa proved to be as charming a host as any London gentlewoman, albeit her drawing room was but a small glade in a thicket of weeds—weeds that rose like trees around the small company.

Neville didn't much care for the sheer *oddness* of the immense buildings and gargantuan growths of even the commonest plant on this level of the Dungeon. The disparity between his size and that of his locale threw off his sense of perspective. Had he not had Alyssa's pleasant company, he would undoubtedly have been far more irritated than he was by the sense of insignificance with which his enormous surroundings left him.

But he did have Alyssa's company, and while she seemed overly flirtatious for a priestess, who was he to complain? Dungeon or no Dungeon, one did not look a gift horse in the mouth—especially when it arrived in such an attractive package as the leader of the Tuan.

Alyssa. Song of the Wind.

What exactly did her title mean?

As she introduced Neville and Shriek around, the litany of names—Maraja, Tuis, Fenil, Tama, Whies, and the like—all blurred in Neville's mind. The women—of which there were three all told, not including Alyssa—greeted the pair of them warmly, but the men—especially Yoors, the tall, cloudy-browed captain of Alyssa's guard—continued to regard them both with suspicion.

While the guards saw to their mounts, the ladies set out a meal that wasn't quite the fairy repast of elfin cakes and mead served in acorn cups that Neville had been half expecting, but was still welcomed by his growling stomach. Shriek politely tasted the various dishes that were set out, but she ate little.

"You have no appetite?" Alyssa asked.

I have a . . . shall we say different metabolism from your kind, Shriek replied.

"She eats flies," Neville said with a grin.

The Tuan women grimaced and hid smiles, but Neville didn't miss the flicker of—what? Disappointment, perhaps, that he saw in Alyssa's eyes.

It was a fair call, he realized. Mocking one's companions was scarcely a gentleman's behavior, whether it be at home in London or in this damned Dungeon.

"That was a bad joke and in poor taste," he said.

I'm sorry, he added privately to Shriek. *I wasn't thinking.*

You rarely do, the arachnid replied somewhat bitterly.

Neville nodded. *I deserved that.*

But if Shriek wasn't so quick to forgive, he was still rewarded by a smile from Alyssa.

"So," he said, deciding to lead the conversation onto safer ground. "Do you lead a nomadic life? I couldn't help but notice the packs your . . . ah, mounts are carrying. You seem well equipped for a mere afternoon outing."

"We call them silvers," the Tuan leader said.

"Pardon?"

"Our mounts. We call them silvers. And no, they bear no relation to the vermin that invest this city."

"I wouldn't think so," Neville said. "But to return to my question . . ."

He thought of what folktale collectors called the Trooping Fairies, for he still couldn't divorce his hosts from the magical beings that had peopled the stories of his childhood. But then what did that make Shriek and himself, when they and the Tuan were all of a size?

Perhaps, he thought with a half smile, Shriek and he had stumbled into Fairyland. Perhaps that was what the Dungeon was, and the men who disappeared for a lifetime in what was only a day in the real world had merely been trapped in the Dungeonmasters' games.

Reminded of their captors, he turned his attention back to Alyssa, who was far more pleasant to consider.

"Do you lead a wandering life?" he went on.

"Oh, no," Alyssa began. "We—"

Yoors, the captain of her guard, cut her off—politely, but firmly. "My lady, please. They are strangers. We know nothing of them."

Neville had been watching the man throughout the meal, growing progressively more annoyed with the man's all-too-obvious suspicion.

"Must we go through this again?" Neville demanded.

He stood up from where he sat with the ladies and faced the captain. Yoors's clouded brow darkened, and he put a hand to the hilt of his weapon as he rose to his feet as well.

Neville caught the movement. "Are you threatening me, sir?" he asked, his voice suddenly mild.

Neville, don't! Shriek sent to him.

You keep out of this, he told her. *This is between the good captain and myself and doesn't concern you.*

He returned his attention to the Tuan captain.

"I am warning you," Yoors said. "You are strangers, and until you prove yourselves, you will remain un-der—"

"I don't think I care for you," Neville said.

A thin, humorless smile settled on Yoors's lips. "Nor I you."

Neither of them saw Alyssa rise to her feet, and they only half heard her when she spoke. "I think this has gone quite far enough—the two of you, strutting like a pair of cockerels—"

"On the contrary, madam," Neville murmured. "We have only begun this discussion."

His sword hand came smoothly up to rest on the hilt of his saber, but before he could draw the blade, Shriek's voice resounded so loudly inside his head that he had to clasp his hands to his ears.

This is not the time!

He turned toward her. "Will you keep out of this!" he shouted.

There is danger—approaching rapidly.

That sobered Neville instantly. *Where? What?*

Before Shriek could reply, Neville felt a hand grip his arm. He was spun around and found himself face-to-face with Yoors—the Tuan's face inches from his own.

"No one turns his back on me until I—"

Neville slapped the hand from his arm. As Yoors reached for him again, Neville delivered a roundhouse blow to the man's chin that felled him on the spot.

Around him Yoors's men armed themselves. Arrows were suddenly notched to bowstrings. The ladies stepped back from the central part of the glade where they had been sitting with Neville, except for Alyssa who stood her ground and regarded him with studied worry. Neville lifted his hands—palms out.

"That was between the captain and myself," he said. "Before you act rashly, my companion"—he nodded to Shriek—"warns me that we have more pressing concerns."

This had better be good, he told her.

Some kind of dog approaches, Shriek said, broadcasting widely enough so that they all could hear.

"Are you sure?" Alyssa asked.

Reasonably. Is this bad news, Being Alyssa?

"Among the worst." She turned to her people. "Swiftly—mount up!"

Neville wondered a moment at the panic that ran through the Tuan, then he realized its source. If the approaching dog was of a similar scale to the city, then they had a very serious problem indeed.

He reached down to offer Yoors a hand up. The captain gave him a baleful glare, then took his hand. Neville pulled him quickly to his feet. In moments the Tuan were all mounted.

"Neville!" Alyssa cried, waving him over to where she bestrode her silver.

No one offered Shriek a ride, he noted, but the arachnid had already scuttled in amongst the treelike weeds. She stood hidden there, a hair spike in each hand.

Neville ran toward Alyssa. There was a crashing in the air—the sound of some huge thing pushing its way through the weeds—and a faint rumble underfoot. Neville saw Alyssa's eyes go wide and knew he was too late to escape with her.

"Go on!" he cried to her. "Ride on!"

Then he turned, saber filling his fist, to face the monstrosity that burst forth into the glade.

In the scale of the city it was no more than a small mongrel dog—part terrier, at least, though who knew what made up the rest of it. Half-starved. A feral glint in its eye. A dirty, mostly harmless thing that a man would kick away from his heels without much of a second thought.

To Neville the damned thing was at least the size of two elephants, and he knew he hadn't a chance in hell standing up against the thing armed with only his saber. It was like a mouse attacking a cat with a sewing needle for a sword.

No point in running. The monster would have him before he took two strides.

So. It was stand and fight.

The creature paused at the edge of the glade, snarling at him. It was probably puzzled, Neville realized, as to what something as small as he was doing, standing up to it.

"Come on, then!" he cried.

Oddly, Neville found himself thinking of his brother as he prepared to defend himself. I hope fate's treating you kinder than it is me, little brother, he thought.

Then the dog attacked.

Clive had his own troubles.

Hidden in the shadows that pooled deeply at the edges of the station's platform was another tunnel, much like that leading from the stairwell that they had descended, only this one maintained an even level. By the dim red light thrown by Guafe's eyes they could just see a half-dozen yards down the tunnel until it turned a corner. They had to bend their heads slightly to get inside, but there was room enough, and Clive felt that they could easily escape discovery.

Unless, of course, the riders of this underground train had this particular tunnel as their destination.

He turned to voice that concern to his companion, but then the train roared into the station. The noise of its entrance killed all hope of conversation.

Clive stared openmouthed at the machine.

It was nothing like the railways back home in England. In design it was sleek and streamlined. The engine appeared to be fueled by something other than wood or coal—in fact Clive doubted that it was a steam locomotive at all.

It pulled three passenger coaches. As soon as the train stopped, spotlights lit up on the roof of each car, flooding the station with a light so bright that Clive had to withdraw from his vantage point, rubbing at his eyes.

But he'd had time, before pulling back into the tunnel, to see the coaches unload their cargo. Men in baggy white suits with some form of glass containers enclosing their heads—How did they breathe? he wondered—and large backpacks.

"Spread out, men!" an authoritative male voice called out. "They can't be far."

He spoke in the patois of the Dungeon—strangely accented, it was true, but similar enough so that Clive and Guafe could understand what he said. The tonality of the voice had a hollow sound to it—as though it were speaking through an intercom such as Clive remembered from the lost city of Dramaran.

"That," Clive said, "is our cue to see where this tunnel leads us."

"Too late for that," the cyborg replied.

Clive gave him an odd look, but then realized that the mouth of the tunnel was filled with a number of the white-suited men. Some of them held what were obviously weapons. One pointed a device at them that was connected to a small metallic box attached to his belt. The box emitted a high-pitched clicking sound.

"Look at the size of them," one of the men said. His voice also had a hollow sound.

Size? Clive thought. But the man was right. Guafe and he were twice the size of these men.

Guafe linked his fingers with Clive, reestablishing the telepathic bond that Shriek had awoken in them all. *Do we stand and fight?* he asked.

Do you recognize the weapons they are carrying? Clive replied.

They appear to be sophisticated hand-held lasers. I would need a closer inspection of their actual specifications before committing myself to more at this point.

Deadly?

Yes—I believe we can assume so.

Perfect, Clive thought. First they had become separated from the others of their party, now they were being menaced by a band of midgets. Or perhaps—since they were underground—he should call them kobolds.

Clive held his hands out in front of him, meaning it as a peaceful gesture. The little men all scrambled back a few paces.

"We mean you no harm," Clive told them.

At that moment another of the little men arrived—one to whom the others all deferred. Obviously their leader, Clive decided. He cleared his throat to speak again, but the man ignored him, turning instead to the one with the clicking box attached to his belt.

"Readings?" he asked.

"Well into the red, sir."

The leader finally turned to look at Clive and Guafe. "You'll have to come with us," he said.

"Who are you?" Clive demanded. "What do you want with us?"

"I'll answer whatever question I see fit to," the leader said, "but only after you've been through the decam process."

"With what are we supposed to be affected?" Guafe asked.

"Radiation."

The cyborg shook his head. "Impossible. My own readings put us well within the strictest safety zone."

"Then your calibrations are off, 'borg." He looked from Guafe to Clive. "Will you come peacefully, or will you have to be sedated?"

Clive reached for his companion's hand again so that he could speak privately to Guafe through the neural web.

Sedated? he asked.

They want to put us to sleep.

Clive frowned. "We'll come peacefully," he said to the leader of the little men. *At least this way we'll have a chance to attempt a later escape,* he added to the cyborg.

Guafe gave a mental nod. *And they might have word of the others.*

I hadn't thought of that, Clive said.

"Glad you made the sensible choice," the leader of the little men told them. "Now if you two pussies would like to just stop holding hands and come out of that tunnel—nice and slowly now—we can get on with the business at hand."

Pussies? Clive asked.

Apparently some form of derogatory remark. The impression that I can gather is that he believes we are lovers.

Clive let go of his companion's hand as though he'd been gripping a hot coal.

"I'll thank you to keep your insults to yourself," he told the leader of their captors. "I'm an Englishman and a gentleman and a member of Her Majesty's Fifth Imperial Horse. I do not appreciate any insinuations as to my sexual inclinations."

"You'll thank me?" the leader asked. "How about I thank you to just shut up and do what you're told—think you can handle that?"

"We are your prisoners," Clive said stiffly. "Do we have a choice?"

The man shrugged. "First you get decammed, then we'll figure out your status, pal. Now let's go."

∎ CHAPTER FOUR ∎

"Well, now," Casey said as Annabelle and her companions crossed the street to where he was standing. "What've we got here?"

He lounged against the doorjamb of his club's entrance and gave them a sleepy look over the tops of his shades. Real casual attitude, Annabelle thought, but she wasn't fooled for a moment. Behind that lethargic gaze the club owner was giving them a hard once-over, no ifs, ands, or buts about it.

"New blood?" he added.

Annabelle nodded. "I guess you could say so."

She started to add to that—just to get things onto a footing where they all knew exactly where they stood —but then the music spilling out through the open door behind Casey stole away her attention. It was very familiar music—at least it was to anyone like Annabelle, who was up on that San Francisco sound from the late sixties that had a revival every decade or so. Guitar, bass, keyboards, and drums, playing a clean, old-fashioned kind of pop with that touch of psychedelia that the old players had told her was impossible to duplicate unless you'd been there in those days of flower power and free love and all that hippie shit. A woman singing overtop about a pill that could make you big, a pill that could make you small . . .

"Who you got playing in there?" she asked.

Casey shrugged. "New band—just up from Downside."

"They sound just like the Airplane—way back before they became the Starship."

∎ 57 ∎

"Don't know about no Starship," Casey said, "but we got the Airplane here tonight—no question about it."

Of course they couldn't be the real thing, Annabelle thought. No way. But it was weird how well they mimicked the real Jefferson Airplane from her own homeworld. She could swear that was Grace Slick singing, Marty Balin backing her up on the choruses, Paul Kantner and the rest of the band. . . . She had a DAT tape of a live gig of theirs, circa 1968, and damned if this didn't sound like a tune pulled right off that tape.

Course, this was the Dungeon, wasn't it? Anything could happen, right?

But the Jefferson Airplane playing in some hellhole of a club that looked as if it was set in the South Bronx?

Well, why not, Annie B.? She thought of Wrecked Fred. If only he were here. Wouldn't he get a kick out of *this.*

Then she thought about what she was saying. If only Fred were here? Christ, the guy was back home, where they all should be. Where she *could* have been if it hadn't been for Finnbogg.

She shot the dwarf a dirty look before turning her attention back to the club owner.

Casey gave her a toothy grin. "You're here kinda early for the show. Why don't you come back when it gets dark?"

At the same time that he spoke, the band hit the line about Alice being real small, and Annabelle realized just what song it was that they were playing. "White Rabbit." Right. Alice's adventures in psychedelia. Hard on the heels of their just stepping through a looking glass to get to this level of the Dungeon.

This was just too much of a coincidence.

"They're not here to catch the show," Jake said. "Lady wants to audition for you. She and her pals are looking for some food and gear and want to pay with an act."

Casey gave the three of them another long look. His gaze lingered on Smythe holding his cloak together with a dirty fist, his bare legs coming down from under it, bare feet on the pavement; Finnbogg almost as wide as he was tall with his mouthful of big teeth, set off by a pair of enormous lower incisors; Annabelle herself, decked out in her leathers.

"We're strictly a music establishment," he said. "Maybe you should check out some of the other clubs in the Dives."

"What the hell's that supposed to mean?" Annabelle demanded.

"Just what I said. I don't see no instruments, lady, and we don't offer any other kind of gigs here. Our clientele's into music, plain and simple. Do I got to spell it out any clearer for you?"

Annabelle had to laugh. When she thought of her initial fears about running into some pimp trying to get her on his string, it all had a certain feel of justice about it. Karma. She was putting the guy down before she'd ever met him, and here he was laying a trip on her because he thought the three of them had some kind of kinky sex act going.

"You mind sharing the joke?"

Annabelle shook her head. "You had to be there," she said. In my head.

"Yeah, well I got things to do."

He started to turn, but Annabelle caught his arm.

"Look," she said. "Everything's gotten off on the wrong foot. We've hit some hard times, and we could use a little help. My friend here needs some new gear, and we could all use a meal—not to mention some directions outta this place. I'm a singer, and a damned good one—at least that's what they tell me back where I come from. Can you use an opening act?"

Casey shook his head. "Getting outta Downside's real easy. Going back down's a whole other thing."

"We're from a little farther away than this city— Downside, Topside, the Dives, whatever part of it you want to name."

"Just where is it that you're from?"

"Can we talk inside? I'd sure love to get a peek at this band. They're like history where I come from."

Casey lowered his shades. His eyes narrowed as he studied her again. "Are you talking about the US of A?"

Annabelle nodded.

That got her another toothy grin. "Well, shit—why didn't you say so in the first place?" He stood aside to make room for them in the doorway. "C'mon in."

That easy? Annabelle wondered. But she took him at his word and went on inside. Smythe and Finnbogg hesitated a heartbeat longer, then followed.

"Ain't that something," Casey said, taking up the rear with Jake. "Finally we got ourselves another American."

The cable ended halfway between levels. Tomàs climbed back up it to the windows of the previous level and sat dangling his feet over the window ledge while he waited for Sidi to reach him. The Indian arrived in short order and took a seat beside his waiting companion. Gazing down, he saw that the street was still some forty stories below them.

"Have you looked for a stairwell?" he asked.

Tomàs shook his head. "I got here just before you, *amigo.*"

They sat in silence for a few moments, studying the city—a great deal of which was still spread out below them from their perch. The taller towers were more to their rear. In front of them was an area of the city that appeared to have suffered some catastrophe, as many of the structures had fallen in on themselves to make a rolling cityscape of stunted buildings and rubble. If they looked from left to right, they could see that their building was on the edge of that area of desolation.

"They're like mountains, these buildings," Sidi said.

Tomàs nodded. *"Sim."* He pointed in front of them. "And there are their foothills."

Sidi stood. He stretched a kink out of his neck and looked into the building. He made no move to enter.

"Where to now?" he asked.

When Tomàs looked up in surprise, Sidi kept his features bland. To let the Portuguese know why he was pushing him to take command would defeat the whole purpose of the exercise.

"Where to?" Tomàs replied.

Sidi nodded. He watched as Tomàs stood beside him, his carriage straighter, a more assured look in his eye than he'd had at any other point during their journeyings through the Dungeon.

"We look for a stairwell," Tomàs said. "Or more cable —*sim*?"

Sidi smiled. "*Sim,*" he said.

It was darker inside this level of the building than it had been above. Although the sun remained invisible behind the gray sludge of clouds outside, the day was lengthening. Light leaked steadily from the sky, deepening the shadows inside.

"We could use a torch," Tomàs said.

Sidi nodded. "Or Chang Guafe's eyes."

They moved away from the window, deeper into the building, then both men froze. Something was moving in the darkness ahead of them.

In a situation such as this discretion was the greater part of valor. Neville firmly believed that. It was only plain common sense that a man retreat from certain failure if he could. On the other hand, the elder Folliot was no coward. With his back up against a wall and no place to run, he could be as fierce as any lioness defending her litter.

So as the feral dog charged him—surely the monster weighed in at three tons—he held his ground until the last possible moment. Not until the monstrous jaws were almost upon him did he dart to one side, slashing with his saber.

The creature's teeth snapped on air. A shrill, ear-piercing yelp arose as the saber cut across its nose. The dog cut away, shaking its head. Blood sprayed.

Neville gave a quick glance to where the mounted Tuan watched from just within the shelter of the tree-like weeds surrounding the glade.

Too far for him to make the attempt to reach them.

The dog's hackles rose, and a rumbling growl came from deep in its chest—loud enough to be mistaken for thunder. Neville circled slowly, feeling like a mouse-sized matador in a normal-sized bullring, all advantage lying with his gargantuan enemy.

It wants but one thing, Neville thought with black humor. For dinner this evening, not beef Wellington, but Folliot Wellington. Served fresh. Utilizing only the finest ingredients, of course.

The dog paced his every movement, drawing closer with each step. Blood still dripped from the wound on its nose, but it paid no more attention to the injury. All its awareness was focused on the insect-sized creature that had stung him.

"I don't suppose you could do me the favour of bleeding to death?" Neville asked the creature in a mild voice.

The dog charged by way of reply.

Uncertain as to its intelligence Neville wasn't about to experiment at this moment by repeating his earlier trick. This time he charged as well, a bellow rising up from deep in his own chest, saber swinging. Paltry though the noise was, and for all the small target he made, the dog was thrown off by his attack.

It changed its mind halfway through its charge and tried to duck away.

Well, wasn't it said that mice frightened elephants? Neville thought.

Instead of backing off himself, he continued his own attack, getting close enough to cut one hind leg as the monstrous dog scurried aside. It yelped again—and then again.

The second cry surprised Neville until he saw that Shriek had come to his aid. Three of her hair spikes sprouted from the creature's muzzle. Given Shriek's command of biochemistry, Neville didn't doubt that she had adjusted the spikes to carry their maximum poisonous effect—but with the animal's great size, they did no harm. Yet they were enough to disconcert the dog some more. Then the Tuan guard came riding up at Alyssa's command, circling the creature on their silvers like some bizarre absurdist's portrayal of elfin bedouin.

They fired arrows from the saddle until the creature's head literally bristled with shafts. It yelped at the prick of each tiny shaft, shaking its head to and fro, snapping at the elfin riders. But now one shot took the creature in the eye—it would have to be from Yoors's bow, Neville noted sourly—blinding it on that side.

Howling, the enormous terrier fled off through the weeds.

"That's done it!" Neville cried, brandishing his saber above his head. "We've got it on the run now."

Alyssa pranced her silver near him.

"Quickly!" she cried. "To mount."

"But we've chased it off," Neville said. "What's the sudden hurry?"

Before the priestess could reply, a series of howls rose up from every side.

"Because," Alyssa added to the sound of the pack, "these dogs never hunt alone."

Of course not, Neville thought. Of course bloody not.

He sheathed his saber. Taking a running jump toward her mount, he leapfrogged onto its back. A moment later he had his arms around the priestess, the firm pressure of her back against his chest. This close to her his nostrils filled with the scent of apple blossoms and roses that hung about her. Strands of silvery hair tickled his cheek.

If only, Neville thought, he could relish her proximity without the nag of more pressing worries, such as simple survival. If they did survive, he'd allow himself that luxury. Until then . . .

Mistress Shriek, he called out on the neural mindweb he shared with the arachnid. *Can you keep up under your own locomotion?*

Have no fears for me, Being Neville, she replied. There was a moment's pause before the alien added, *But I thank you for your concern.*

The howls grew louder. No—they were simply closer.

Alyssa kicked her heels against her silver's flanks, and the whole company was off, darting through the gigantic forest of weeds like so many shifting shadows.

Inside the train coach there was no sense of motion. Nor could Clive hear a sound except for those that he or his captors made as they shifted in their seats. The interior of the coach had only two long benches along either wall by way of furnishings. Clive and Guafe sat against one wall, their captors across from them. Illumination was provided by overhead lights encased in long glass banks. The windows had been opaqued so that nothing outside the coach could be seen.

The little men kept their distance. Their unfamiliar weapons remained trained on both Clive and his companion, but they refused to converse, for all Clive's attempts to draw them out. When he looked at Guafe, the cyborg appeared to have shut down his systems, leaving Clive with only his own thoughts for company on the journey.

It was pointless to speculate on their captors' motives, he soon realized. The principal difficulty in attempting to second-guess any being he met in the Dungeon, no matter what level, had been brought home to him long ago. Each group of beings had such alien mental processes—no matter how close their resemblance to people of his own world—that any conjecture was futile. All that tied each diverse element of them together was the Dungeon itself . . . and the underlying thread of a plot that appeared to exist solely to confound his family.

It was at that moment that he realized that each group of their original party to have gone through the looking glass had in its number one member of the Folliot family—that was, if Annabelle's suspicions of Tomàs's origins were indeed correct.

But surely they had chosen who would go with whom on their own?

It had seemed so, but now Clive felt that it was not merely an unhappy coincidence. Coincidence, as such, did not appear to exist in the Dungeon. Once again he perceived the hand of the Dungeonmasters at work. How they had manipulated the choices, he couldn't begin to guess, but work it they must have.

How did the others fare? Had they arrived together in one place, or were they now scattered in four separate parties, in God alone knew what difficulties of their own?

Considering their ill-fated trials to date, it was no doubt the latter.

He wished that the neural web in which Shriek had initiated them could operate without the need for physical contact. He didn't need such contact to communicate mentally with Shriek. He had tried to reach her numerous times since arriving through the looking glass to this world—as he had been able to do on the previous level—but there was simply no reply. It was as though the bond between him and the arachnid had never existed.

Or worse—as though something had happened to the others. Something worse than the fix he and Guafe were in at the moment. If he could just reach out to touch the arachnid's mind, or Annabelle's—if he could at least know that they were safe—it would make his own captivity that much easier to bear. But as it was, he had to consider not only how to extract Guafe and himself from their present predicament, but also how to gather the rest of them together once more.

The task—from his present perspective—appeared hopeless. No doubt whenever they arrived at their destination, they would be confronting yet another replica of his brother Neville. Or of his father. Clive ground his teeth together. If only it could be the Dungeonmasters themselves. If he could be allowed but a few moments alone with them, a good sword in hand, he'd have the damned truth out or he'd cut out their—

The leader of what Clive had named—in his own

mind—kobolds entered the coach at that moment, breaking off what had begun of a very pleasant fantasy.

"Well, sweethearts," the leader said. "End of the line."

Beside Clive, Guafe became functional once more. He stood up, the red facets of his eyes glittering. Clive rose to stand beside him.

"Who are you people?" he asked the leader. "What do you want with us?"

"We're real people—not freaks."

Clive glared at him. "We are not—"

"Just shut up and do what you're told, and we'll all get along fine—okay?"

Clive took a step toward him but immediately stayed his advance when the kobolds brought their weapons up. The shift from casual guarding positions to those of a more threatening nature was swift as thought. Clive stood stiff and straight, hands clenched at his side.

"Attaboy," the leader said. "Just come along nice and easy."

They were led from the coach onto another platform, but this one bore no resemblance to the deserted station where they'd first boarded the underground train. The area was lit with blindingly bright lights set in the ceilings. The surface of the platform was so polished it gleamed. More of the little men were waiting for them—all in the white suits with the glass bubbles on their heads.

From the platform they were taken down a long corridor that eventually brought them into a small square chamber.

"Strip," the leader told them.

"I protest," Clive began, but a weapon aimed at his face quickly stilled him.

"Just strip."

Clive turned to his companion, but Guafe was already removing his clothes. Face hot under the kobolds' stares—especially that of the leader who stood watching with a smirk on his lips—Clive followed suit. When they were both stripped down, the kobolds collected their clothing and retreated back into the corridor. A door slid out of the wall, locking Clive and Guafe in the chamber.

"God in heaven," Clive muttered. "What kind of men are these?"

Guafe merely shrugged. He took a seat on the floor, back against the wall, and shut down his systems again.

"Thank you for your companionship," Clive told him.

The cyborg gave no response.

Clive prowled the confines of the small chamber, starting back in alarm when a cloud of gas began to issue from the ceiling. In moments he grew drowsy and had to sit down himself. His head began to spin once he was seated. He put it between his legs and tried to breathe as shallowly as possible, but the gas was already in his lungs, coursing through his blood system.

What an ignoble fate, he thought. He hoped the others had managed to escape the kobolds' clutches—though knowing the Dungeon even as little as he did, they could well be in worse straits.

He tried again to stretch the neural web that he shared with Shriek and the others, calling out to them. As his consciousness began to slip away, he thought he could hear someone returning his mental cry.

Clive. Clive . . . ? Can you hear me, Clive . . . ?

Just as the darkness took him, he realized that the voice was very much like that of his old friend, George du Maurier.

▪ CHAPTER FIVE ▪

The band looked just like the old vids that Annabelle had seen of them—except they were onstage, front and center and big as life, not squeezed down onto a vid screen, the image flickering with imperfections. Slick and company had begun another song—one Annabelle didn't recognize—but that psychedelic sound remained, augmented with visuals now because there was a screen in back of the band on which colored patterns kaleidoscoped liquidly in time to the music. And the band, just cooking with that old-time music . . .

"Jesus," Annabelle said softly. "Talk about a time warp."

Smythe nodded beside her. "Warped, indeed. It's ghastly."

"You're jiving me—right, Horace?"

Her however-many-times great-grandfather's companion just blinked at her.

"You *like* this . . . noise?" he asked finally.

Annabelle shook her head, dismissing him. Instead she drank in the sounds that came from the stage. Her fingers twitched, looking for the neck of her Les Paul, as she watched the band play. It was long moments before she could pull her attention away to take in the rest of the club.

It wasn't much different from a hundred others she'd played in New York, LA, London, or any place in between. It was dark, the walls covered with old band posters. Small round tables, three or four chairs to each, were scattered across the floor. There was a dance floor in front of the stage. A bar along one wall with a door leading back into the kitchen. Familiar territory for Annabelle. She didn't realize just how much she'd missed it until she was standing here, letting it all wash over her again, firing up her blood.

But then her gaze fell on a woman sitting near the stage—a pretty white woman, blond and slender in a simple flower-print dress, nursing a mulatto child at her breast.

"That's my old lady Linda," Casey said, coming up beside her. "And our daughter Cassandra."

Annabelle hardly heard him. The pride in his voice never registered. All she could do, looking at the mother and child, was think of what she'd lost.

Amanda, her own daughter.

Who'd be thinking that her mom was never coming back by now.

Amanda.

Whom the Dungeonmasters had cloned into a kind of vampiric creature and set upon her.

Amanda.

Who was going to grow up without a mother or a father now.

Amanda.

Her vision filmed over with tears. Forgotten was the band and its marvelously archaic music. Forgotten was the club, Finnbogg, and Smythe standing near her, Casey still talking to her. All she could think about was this frigging Dungeon and what it was doing to her. Because of the band onstage, no doubt, the lyrics of another old song came to her. Something about the games people played.

Why was it all happening to her? What did the Dungeonmasters want with her or any of her family? What was so goddamned important about the Folliots anyway?

"You okay?"

She blinked, turned slowly to see—through a film of tears—Casey regarding her with an odd look on his features. She shook her head.

"No, I'm not okay. I'm being fucked over no matter which way I turn—think that'd make you feel okay?"

Casey took a step back from her, hands held out in front of him. "Take it easy, lady. You're the one that's come to me looking for—"

Annabelle reached out to one of his hands with a feather-soft touch, fingers fluttering for a moment on the dark skin, before she dropped her hand to her side. She sniffed and wiped her eyes on the shoulder of her jacket with a quick motion of her head.

"I'm sorry," she said. "I'm just . . . seeing your wife there with her kid . . . it reminded me of everything I've lost. . . ."

The band had stopped playing. One by one they shut off their amps and the PA system and drifted off the stage. Most went out the door that led to the kitchen. The one that looked like Kantner took a seat at the bar.

"C'mon," Casey said. "Have a seat. I'll get you something to drink."

Annabelle let herself be led to a table and sat down. Finnbogg and Smythe joined her while Casey went to the bar. There he served Kantner a beer, before returning to the table with a tray laden with four frosty brown-bottled beers, moisture beading on their sides. He handed one to each of them, hesitating over Finnbogg until the dwarf reached out and took the proffered bottle. His wife—now that the baby had finished suckling—lowered her blouse over the one bared breast and joined them, jiggling the baby against her shoulder.

"You want to tell me about it?" Casey asked.

Annabelle looked at him. He looked different up close, with his shades off. His features were warm with the obvious affection he had for his own little girl as he took Cassandra from her mother to hold her for a while. Not so much like some tough punk as just a hard guy with a lot of heart. She'd known a lot of men just like him—back in her other life. Roadies. Bodyguards they'd used from time to time. Or just the plain everyday joes that she used to meet back when her band still played the club and college circuit.

So while she didn't know Casey from Adam, she did know a lot of guys who wore a one-dimensional image like a flag, like a biker did his colors, though unlike most bikers the ones she'd liked seemed to carry something softer in their hearts—hidden away where it couldn't get so easily tromped on. She could easily see herself spilling out all her hurts to him. Sitting here in a club so like the kinds of places where she used to hang out that she felt homesick, with a real genuine woman at the table—not some exotic alien, just plain folks.

But could she trust these feelings? The frigging Dungeonmasters seemed to know just what strings to pull to get the reaction they wanted. Was she just letting herself in for more hurts? She couldn't forget the too-obvious coincidence of the Airplane playing that big hit of theirs, about Alice and all that Wonderland shit, just as they got here through a mirror of their own.

She looked at her companions, first Smythe, then Finnbogg. The three of them needed some help—no question about it. She sighed, then cleared her throat.

"Like I said," she began, "we're not from around here. . . ."

Casey nodded. "You heading on, or do you plan to go native?" he asked, looking at her from around the nodding head of his infant daughter.

His wife put a hand on his arm. "Let her tell it in her own way, Case."

After another brief hesitation Annabelle did just that.

Sidi and Tomàs backed slowly to the window until it was directly behind them and they could go no farther. From the darkness in front of them the sound of movement continued as whatever hid in the shadows drew nearer. Sidi looked about the floor at their feet, but there was nothing lying about that they could use as a weapon.

"*Madre de Dios*," Tomàs murmured.

Sidi looked up to see that a tall skeletal creature had stepped forward from the darkness. It was at least two feet taller than either of them, a humanoid shape that appeared to be literally just skin covering bones. It had an extra joint in each of its four limbs, which made it appear to be standing slightly askew when it stopped its forward motion. Its vestigial nose and ears gave its oval head a pronounced almondlike shape. Its eyes were tiny and black, reflecting back the light from the window with a bright glitter that reminded Sidi of Shriek's multifaceted eyes.

Tomàs leaned closer to him. "What is it?" he asked softly.

Sidi shrugged. It appeared nonthreatening, but this was the Dungeon, so that meant little.

"Can you speak?" he asked the creature in the patois of the Dungeon.

It lifted one hand to chest level, and Sidi saw that while it had only three fingers, they too each had an extra joint. Its opposable thumb had only two joints. One long finger tapped its skeletal chest.

"Brezhoo," it said.

Sidi cocked an eyebrow. "Yes?"

Was it the creature's name, or a description of what it was? Perhaps, as with Finnbogg, it was both.

"Brezhoo," it repeated.

Sidi and Tomàs exchanged glances, then the Portuguese touched his own chest.

"We are men," he said. "I am Tomàs. My *amigo*'s name is Sidi." He offered it a quick smile.

"Mehn," the creature repeated bobbing its head. When it copied Tomàs's smile, its lips drew back to reveal rows of sharp teeth with two long, pronounced fangs in the front.

Tomàs swallowed thickly. "Yes," he said. "Men."

"Tayste ghood—mehn?"

Before either of them could react, that strangely jointed arm whipped out. Its fingers caught the Portuguese by the front of his shirt and hauled him in close. Sidi immediately launched himself at the creature, but the other arm lashed out with blinding speed and sent him stumbling into the shadows until he tripped on some obstruction hidden by the darkness.

He fell to the ground but recovered quickly. When he turned, it was to see his companion still struggling in the creature's grip. But no matter how desperately Tomàs battered at the creature with his fists, the long fangs were lowering steadily toward his throat.

With a wordless cry Sidi launched himself at the creature again. Sensing his attack, it sidestepped lightly, this time striking the Indian with enough force to knock him out the window.

The Tuan's silvers ran with a far smoother gait than Neville was accustomed to in a mount—due no doubt, he realized, to their relation to the rodents of his own world. They didn't gallop so much as scurry through the forest of tree-high weeds, but at a speed that would have left a good English horse winded in no time at all. Unfortunately the pursuing pack of gigantic hounds was making better progress still.

With his arms firmly wrapped about Alyssa's slender waist, he leaned over her shoulder to speak.

"I don't suppose you have any fairy spells at your command?" he asked. "Some wand or similarly useful device that you could wave about and make the damned beasts disappear?"

"We're not witches," she replied.

"No. No. Of course not."

But they still appeared—to him, at least—for all the world like the fairies from the old folktales that nannies delighted in telling to their charges back home in England. How could he not see them so? They were delicate-boned and silver-haired, the women beautiful beyond compare, the men handsome, their mounts enchanted. Surely Oberon and his court would have appeared so? There was really no difference that he could perceive. Except, of course, for their size.

They weren't the diminutive creatures of those tales

—at least not in relation to his own size. When one considered this oversized world, however . . .

A new thought occurred to Neville that brought a sinking feeling to his stomach.

What if this world *was* normal-sized and it was just they who had been reduced? The Tuan, Shriek, and himself. He had yet to discover how the Tuan had arrived in the Dungeon; but stepping through a looking glass, as he and Shriek had, in a manner that only Reverend Dodgson could have invented for his heroine . . .

Hadn't she, at some point in Dodgson's narrative, been reduced in size as well?

When one considered the resemblances between the two worlds . . . the underground Wonderland as Dodgson had described it was a place almost as absurd as the Dungeon—if not quite so perilous. Still, it had talking rabbits with pocket watches, packs of cards that came to life, and all manner of preposterous creatures and situations. It would be so like the Dungeonmasters to place his party in such a situation.

Could he—Lord help him—now look forward to encounters with hookah-smoking caterpillars, disembodied cat's grins, and the like?

And what of the others—Clive, Smythe, and all? Were they wandering about this ruined city as well, mouse-sized and in similar dire straits?

Better not to think on it, he told himself. Better to concentrate on the situation at hand, for the monstrous dogs were steadily gaining on them, and if something wasn't done about them, and done quickly, it wouldn't matter how absurd the Dungeon became, for he wouldn't be here to see any of it.

He chanced another glance back to see that the foremost of the dogs was advancing far too rapidly. What small lead they had gained on the pack was quickly being swallowed by the extended gait of the huge animals' broader step. The agility of the silvers as they bore their riders through this forest of vastly oversized vegetation gave them little advantage when the dogs could simply plow through it. To the pack this was simply a field of weeds—not the forest it was to Neville's company.

"Duck your head!" Alyssa cried suddenly.

Neville looked forward and bent quickly, his chest pressed against her back. They were approaching a curb where the buckling pavement of the street met the sidewalk. There was a small rectangular crack in the lip of the curb, set in the gutter near a sewer grate. The riders ahead of them entered it, two at a time. The silver bearing Alyssa and himself darted in after them, taking them into the safety of its darkness. Shriek followed, hard on their heels.

Once inside Alyssa brought her mount to a halt, and the whole company turned to face the narrow entranceway. Moments later the light was blocked as the first enormous dog's head pressed close, snarling at them, but the entrance was too small to permit it to come in after them. It dug at the pavement all the same, scrabbling to get near them.

In the close confines of their hiding place, the sounds of its growling boomed uncomfortably loud. Shriek tossed a hair spike directly at the monstrous beast's nose, which caused it to retreat, but another dog immediately took its place.

Alyssa turned away to look at her guards.

"Is there an exit?" she asked Yoors.

The captain shook his head. One of his men had already gone as far into the darkness as he could, but the way was blocked with rubble and ancient refuse. There was no telling how deep the blockage went.

Alyssa sighed. "Then we wait."

Neville dismounted and lifted her down. "Wait?" he asked. He thought of the dogs from his own world and how difficult it was, unless they were very well trained, to heel them once they had a scent. "But hounds such as these—"

"Will be tenacious," she said with a nod. "I know."

Neville surveyed what there was to see of their refuge, little that there was of it. There was a dankness in the air. The ceilings were low. But at least it was large enough so that their quarters would not be too crowded.

The dogs had given up their attempts to enter. Stepping close to the opening, Neville saw that they lay outside in a half circle, gazes locked on the narrow entryway. Growls greeted his appearance. When one enormous beast rose to its feet, Neville ducked quickly back inside.

"It could be a long wait," he said.

When Clive became aware of his surroundings once more, he realized that they'd been transported from what the kobolds' leader had called the decam chamber to yet another unfamiliar room. Both he and Guafe were no longer nude. They wore white gowns that came down to their knees—garments that appeared to have been hastily stitched together to fit their larger size. The room's walls were paler than the bright glare of the decam room—easier on the eyes. Pallets had been made for them on the floor by the simple expedient of dragging together a number of smaller mattresses, large pieces of some man-made material serving as sheets.

There were no other furnishings in the room. No windows, no sign of a door, although one side of the room was completely taken up by a mirror. Of their captors there was not a sign.

Chang Guafe lay motionless on his pallet, all systems shut down once more. Clive reached over and put his hand on the cyborg's shoulder.

Chang? he asked.

The red-faceted eyes flickered open immediately.

Are you well? Clive added.

The cyborg sat up. For a long moment he was motionless, attention apparently turned inward as he took stock of his body's present condition.

Nothing appears to have been tampered with, he said finally. *And you?*

Well enough. Confused, but well.

Guafe looked toward the mirrored wall, then faced his companion again. *We are being observed.*

As Clive started to look, the cyborg sent a quick warning into the Englishman's mind.

No, he said, continuing to use the neural web that connected their minds when they were in physical contact. *Do not look. They are behind the mirror, watching us.*

Behind the mirror? Clive thought. How was that possible? But then he remembered how they'd arrived on this level of the Dungeon.

Is it another gateway? he asked.

Something far simpler, Guafe replied. *A two-way mirror. It allows them to observe us, while remaining unseen themselves.*

But to what purpose?

Guafe gave a mental shrug. *I expect it is because we are something unexpected—beings that do not fit into their normal scheme of what should and should not be. I assume they are observing us to see what action we will take, if any. If we remain docile, they will have to come to us.*

I find the waiting hard—not knowing what to expect.

Exactly, Guafe replied.

Clive waited for his companion to continue, then realized that there was nothing to add. Their captors wished to keep them on an uneven keel—it was as simple as that.

I had a strange experience, Clive said after a few moments, *just as I lost consciousness earlier.*

What was that?

I tried to reach Shriek or one of the others through the neural web.

You had some success?

Not exactly. It wasn't until I began to lose consciousness that I received a response. But that response was from none of our companions. I—this will seem far-fetched, Chang—but I heard the voice of a man from my homeworld calling to me. That of my friend, George du Maurier.

What did he say to you?

Clive shook his head. *He was merely calling out to me. I lost consciousness before I could respond.*

Interesting, the cyborg said.

But how was it possible? I must have imagined it, for other than mindspeaking with Shriek, we've never been able to speak to each other *without physical contact, let alone reach out beyond the Dungeon. Only Shriek had that ability, and even she has never been able to communicate beyond the Dungeon's borders.*

I believe it has to do with the decontamination process we underwent, Guafe explained. *They ran some very complex tests on our neural cortexes. Something in the process must have allowed you to project your thoughts to your friend and then receive his.*

What does it mean? Clive asked. *This confuses me. Those of us taken from my world have arrived here from many different times. Are they all one single time line, or are there many different ones—some where I return to England, others where I have never left in the first place? And if that's true, then is the time line that I know the real one?*

And where did that leave Annabelle? he wondered. As a figment of a possible future? Perhaps as another construct of the damned Dungeonmasters?

God, he hated how they had brought him to a state where he must question every loyalty, every truth.

Not necessarily, Guafe said. *If the Dungeonmasters can pluck us from any number of worlds and times, it stands to reason then that communication between all those various places and times would continue to exist.*

Clive gave a mental nod in agreement. No matter how preposterous such things would be considering the physics of his own world, it sounded logical enough for the Dungeon. He thought again of that voice he'd heard—he was as sure it had been du Maurier's as he could be of anything—and then another concern arose in him, for he remembered something else that he'd sensed, just as that unconsciousness had swept over him.

He'd had the feeling that a hidden memory was trying to surface in his mind—something important, something forgotten, something disturbingly lost. Reaching for it was like knowing a word but being unable to grasp it while in the middle of a conversation. The more he tried to recall that memory now, the further it slipped away from him.

I'd give a great deal for some answers, he said.

As though on cue a door slid open in one of the walls closest to the mirror. The leader of the kobolds stood there with two men. None of them wore their bulky suits or the glass bubbles over their heads any longer, but the two men accompanying the leader still carried their weapons, both of which were trained on Clive and Guafe.

"The Speakers are ready to question you now," the leader said. Before Clive could frame a word, the leader held up his hand. "Yup, and they just might answer some questions too, if you're real lucky. So up and at 'em, now. Look sharp. Nobody's going to hurt you unless you start making trouble first."

A sharp anger rose in Clive at the amusement he saw in the leader's eyes, but he kept his own counsel. Letting go Guafe's shoulder and so breaking their neural contact, he rose stiffly to his feet.

You and I, he thought, looking at the leader. *We will have our day yet—don't ever doubt it.*

But for now he let himself be led, docile, down yet another long white corridor.

■ CHAPTER SIX ■

There was a long silence as, another round of beers later, Annabelle finished up her story. That silence stretched around the table until Casey finally nodded his head.

"We've been there," he said. "Linda and me—we met up a couple of levels back and made it this far before we realized she was carrying Cassandra. Figured it was time to stop then. Got settled in here and" —he shrugged—"just never went any farther. Kinda hard to keep on going when you've got a kid in tow. I mean, the Dives ain't no great shakes, but the weirdness you know—especially in this place—sure beats the weirdness you might be heading into."

"But why?" Smythe asked. "What can they possibly want with so many different kinds of peoples?"

Linda pushed her hair back from her face and took Cassandra from her father. She lifted her blouse to nurse the baby again, and Smythe averted his gaze. Annabelle and Linda exchanged smiles.

"I got kicked out of a mall back home," Annabelle said, "for nursing Amanda in a public place. It gets so bizarre. The theaters've got posters up with guys ripping each other's hearts out, every 7-Eleven's got skin mags sitting right beside the candy bars, but something natural—something positive—like nursing your kid . . . well, that's just obscene."

Linda nodded. "I've been thinking about what you found out in the baron's library on the last level," she said, bringing the conversation back to the matter at hand.

■ 80 ■

"You mean Tomàs being related to the Folliots?"

"Yes. Did you ever read much Jung—you know, racial subconsciousness and all that?"

Smythe and Finnbogg just looked blank, but Annabelle nodded.

"I know the basic theory," she said.

"Well, for us all to share a racial subconsciousness," Linda went on, "there's got to be some connection between us all—right?"

"I suppose."

"No, think about it for a moment. If you compare the world's population in the late sixties—Casey's and my time," she added before Annabelle could correct her. "Compare it to the world's population a thousand years before that—we're growing by leaps and bounds. You take interracial couplings—and they've been going on for as long as there've been people. I mean it can be as simple as an Arab marrying a Greek, okay? Well, the gene pool has got to include a bit from just about everybody that ever existed. We have to ignore some cultures—certain Australian aborigines, for example, who have never married outside of their cultures. Or Inuit —those kinds of peoples. But other than that, maybe we really *are* all brothers and sisters under the skin."

Annabelle nodded. "By the nineties—in our world— genetic archaeology's pretty well traced all of humanity back to a common ancestress who lived somewhere in ancient central Africa."

"Which proves my point."

"The Age of Aquarius," Annabelle said with a smile.

"Could be it's not so farfetched," Linda said.

"Then what about the aliens?" Smythe asked. "Beings like Shriek, or our friend Finnbogg here?"

Linda turned her gaze to the dwarf.

"And this," Casey said, "is where our theory gets its first hole."

"Maybe," Annabelle said, "and maybe not. Depends on whether you believe the tabloids or not."

"Tabloids?" Smythe asked.

"After your time," Annabelle told him. "They're like

newspapers, except they carry just the juciest and most farfetched stories. 'Biker Nuns Kidnap Pope' or 'Man Gives Birth to Collie Pups'—that kinda thing."

"Just a load of crap," Casey said.

Annabelle grinned at the expression on Smythe's face.

"But that kind of thing is impossible," the Englishman said.

"Sure it is. Just like all the reports of UFOs and aliens taking people away to study them are. But what if they're not? What if cataloged with all the crap are some truths, but we just don't have any way of telling one from the other? I can't tell you how many times I've seen articles about people who were supposed to have been taken away by flying saucers, studied like lab animals, and then returned. There's guys that've made a living writing books about this kind of thing.

"So what if some of that was real? UFO reports go back for as far as there is written history—maybe further back if you take the oral stories about fairies and stuff like that as just the only way those people back then could talk about extraterrestrials."

"So you're saying the gene pool could cover the whole universe?" Linda asked.

Annabelle shrugged. "I don't know. I always thought all this 'the aliens have landed' stuff was crap, myself. But maybe it isn't. If there *is* something special about the Folliots that gets them dumped into this Dungeon, then maybe that's why we've got Finn and the rest of them in here with us."

For a long moment no one spoke. Then Smythe said, "Because they're related?"

"You got it, Horace."

"But then why am I in here?"

"You were with Clive when he got snatched."

"And what about us?" Linda asked.

Annabelle shrugged. "If Finnbogg can be related to the Folliots, then there's nothing stopping you from being related as well."

"Interesting theory," Casey said.

"But you're not buying it?"

"Didn't say that. Just said it was interesting. Course, you gotta remember that there's going to be a certain reproductive incompatibility between species. Seems to me if the Ren and the Chaffri are into filling the place up, then there just aren't going to be enough Folliots around to do it. Not enough pure ones—because it seems, with all the trouble they're going through with your great-grandfather and great-uncle, that they want the pure ones."

"I'm holding onto my theory," Annabelle said. "At least until a better one comes along."

Casey shrugged. "The way I see it, it doesn't make much difference anyway. We're still stuck here."

"Then you'd better think about it some," Annabelle said. "Because if it *is* on the level, then that means holing up here in the Dives isn't going to make a whole lot of difference in the long run. The Dungeonmasters'll be after you sooner or later to bring you back into the game."

"Unless this is our part in the game," Casey said.

"What do you mean?"

"Sitting here with you. Giving you a moment to catch your breath before you go on. Providing some new gear and provisions—and directions?" he added. "I mean, you are going on?"

Annabelle gave him a long, hard look and wished he hadn't said that. She was just starting to relax a little bit, but now he had to go screw it all up. She looked away, around the club. Kantner had left the bar now, joining the rest of the band backstage, probably. Jake, the old wino who'd brought them here, was sleeping with his head on a table just a few yards away. Otherwise they had the place to themselves.

Nice place for an ambush, Annabelle thought, but then realized that with the way things were going, if this was an ambush, it was a mental one. Of course, that wouldn't make it any less dangerous.

Not here.

Not in the Dungeon.

"We don't have any other choice," Annabelle said.

Linda shook her head. "There's always choice."

Annabelle grinned. "Can't see a world without free will, can you?"

Linda shook her head.

"Well, welcome to the Dungeon," Annabelle told her. "Because the only free will you'll find here is what the Dungeonmasters'll give you."

It was pure instinct that saved Sidi as he went hurtling out the window. Without stopping to think, his hands reached out for the cable that his subconscious mind, at least, knew was there. By the time his conscious mind remembered the cable, he was already holding onto it, the force of his body's impetus swinging him away from the building.

Tao, he thought. Every action has a reaction.

Then the cable was swinging back toward the building. The window loomed up in front of him. He tucked in his legs, rode the cable to the end of its short arc, and launched himself at the creature again.

This time he succeeded in dislodging its grip on Tomàs. The Portuguese fell in a bundle of limp limbs as the creature was knocked back into the shadows from which it had first issued.

Sidi rode the creature, making sure it took the brunt of their fall when they landed. Something cracked under him as they hit the floor. The sound was like the snapping of a dry bone. Sidi didn't take time to investigate the damage he'd inflicted on the creature. He scrambled back into the lighted area by the window, rising in a defensive posture over his fallen companion.

When the creature came stalking forth from the shadows once more, one forelimb hanging limply at its side, Sidi took a step forward, putting himself between it and Tomàs. Behind him the Portuguese coughed, trying to catch his breath. The dry hacking sound was loud in the stillness. In front of him the creature's eye gleamed with pain and anger.

"Hurtz," it said.

It took another step forward, but before Sidi could mount an offensive against it, a small shaft sprouted in the creature's forehead. It gave an odd squawking sound, its eyes widening with surprise, then fell stiffly to the ground.

Sidi turned slowly. Behind Tomàs, who was now sitting up, Sidi saw perched on the windowsill a small being that he could only describe as a feral child.

The newcomer was no more than four feet tall and dressed in worn leather trousers and a tunic of sewn-together rodent pelts. His feet were bare. His features were worn to the bone, hair a rat's nest of brown curls, eyes like a mongoose's, flashing and alert. In his hands was a small bow, notched with a second shaft, the point of the arrow aimed directly at Sidi.

The Indian stood perfectly still. "We owe you our lives," he said.

The newcomer grinned, showing a mouthful of human teeth that were stained yellow and brown.

"Got that g'ant good," he said.

He didn't lower the bow.

Sidi nodded. "Is that what it was?" he asked. "A g'ant? The creature called itself a brezhoo."

"That's what they call 'emselves. We call 'em g'ants 'cos that's what they're looking like—all g'ant and spid'ry."

Tomàs had recovered enough to take in the newcomer as well. *"Christo,"* he muttered. "Now what?"

"This . . . ah, being . . . has just rescued us," Sidi said. He didn't take his gaze from the feral child.

"I'm Poot," the newcomer said. "Frenchy calls us EPs, but we all got names just like real people do."

"EPs?" Sidi asked.

"Les enfants perdus," Poot said.

"The lost children," Sidi repeated, translating the newcomer's terrible French to the Dungeon's patois. It suited the child.

"Are there many of you?" Sidi asked.

"Thousands," Poot assured him.

"And can we be friends?"

The child shrugged. "What for? Don't trust nobody over ten—that's what Frenchy says. 'Cept for him. You gotta trust him, or he'll sew your ears to your shoulders. Said he would, for sure, and Gren says she maybe saw him do it once."

"We've only been in the Dungeon for a few months," Sidi said. "How old does that make us?"

Poot appeared to consider this for a long moment, then he slowly lowered his bow. "Not even a year, I guess. I dunno. Frenchy'd know. Let's go ask him."

As he turned to look out the window, Sidi and Tomàs exchanged glances.

"What is going on here, *amigo*?" Tomàs asked.

"You coming?" Poot asked before Sidi could reply.

"Coming where?" Sidi asked.

Poot pointed out the window to where a rope ladder hung beside the cable they had used to descend from the roof of the building. The two men joined the boy at the window and looked up.

"*Asno,*" Tomàs said. "What is it?"

"A balloon," Sidi replied. "A hot-air balloon."

Looking down at them from over the rim of its basket were the faces of three more feral children, not one of them older than Poot. Their faces seemed very white in the fading light—like the heads of three small ghosts, peering down at them.

"If God had meant us to fly . . ." Tomàs began, but he broke off as Poot gave him a suspicious look.

"You're not coming?"

"*Ahora bien,*" Tomàs told him. "Of course we will come. We only need our heads examined, eh?" he added to Sidi as he climbed back onto the windowsill. He began to ascend the ladder then, mutterings of "*Muy loco*" drifting down as he went.

"Your friend talks funny," Poot said to Sidi as the Indian joined him on the windowsill.

Sidi shrugged. He was more worried about what would happen when they met this Frenchy that the boy had spoken of. They might be able to trick Poot into thinking they were under ten, but a grown man would be another thing altogether. Especially one who could command an air vehicle such as this for his charges to ride about in.

Then he was on the swaying ladder himself, climbing up. As soon as Poot stepped onto it as well, one of the children in the basket threw off their moorings, and the balloon began to drift away from the building, Sidi and the boy swinging on the ladder below it.

Neville had never been one to wait patiently for anything or anyone. In a world of doers and those done to, he preferred to count himself amongst the former, for all the Dungeonmasters' attempts to fit him squarely in amongst the latter.

It was true that the company was pleasant—if one discounted the scowling Captain Yoors and his fellow guards—but the situation itself irked the elder Folliot to no end. Bad enough to be trapped by a pack of common dogs, but in such a place? The dampness had gotten into his clothes, making them stick uncomfortably to his skin. The air was foul, as though something had died and then rotted in here.

He found himself pacing back and forth in front of the entranceway, until Alyssa finally asked him to please sit still for at least two minutes running as he was driving her mad. That was all Neville needed.

Grunting some unintelligible reply, he made his way to the back of their hiding place to investigate the blockage.

"I've smelled composts that had a better odor," one of the Tuan guards said, joining him there.

Neville studied him for a moment, his mind replaying the moment of introduction, until he had a name.

"You're Fenil?" he asked.

The guard nodded.

"You don't mind talking to the enemy?"

A slight frown touched Fenil's features. "What do you mean?"

"Your captain doesn't think much of me."

Fenil smiled then. "Yoors doesn't think much of anyone unless he can trace his bloodlines back to the High Forest. It's our lady who commands this company, and as she has accepted you, then I will do the same."

Unless I betray that trust, Neville thought, completing the guard's unspoken thought.

What are you playing at now, Being Neville? Shriek asked.

Neville glanced at where the arachnid was resting near the doorway so that she could keep watch on the pack outside.

Nothing untoward, Neville replied. *That I promise you, madam watchdog.*

A mental sigh carried from Shriek to him, but she spoke no more.

Neville turned back to study what he could of the blockage. It was composed of tightly packed refuse—rags, rotting material, and Lord alone knew what. He gave a piece of tightly wadded cloth an experimental pull. It came away easily, but a noxious odor quickly arose as the material was moved through the still, dank air. Behind him the silvers shifted nervously in their harnesses.

"There's no telling how deeply it's blocked," Fenil said.

Neville nodded. "So one of your fellows mentioned earlier. But there's a simple, if not pleasing, way to find out—don't you think?"

Fenil wrinkled his nose but nodded. "I can't abide waiting either," he said.

They set to it then. At first they were careful to touch the unpleasant material only with their hands, but soon they became inured to the stench and fell to it without consideration as to how much of the foul slop they got on themselves.

Their companions kept well away from them as the stink pervaded the whole of their hiding place. They kept as close to the cleaner air that came from the entranceway as they could without arousing the dogs. But Shriek came to join them, and then another of the guards, one named Thulen, and soon they began to make better progress still.

It was when Alyssa herself came to join the workers that Yoors finally arose.

"My lady," he said. "Now you go too far."

"Propriety means nothing in a situation such as this," she replied. "Would you have them labor on our behalf and do nothing to help?"

Gladly, his eyes said, but he shook his head and called to the remainder of the guards to join him. But Neville and the others had already worked their way seven or eight feet in, and a part of the blockage gave way to fall on the opposite side of where they were working just as the guards approached.

"Too late, old chum," Neville told Yoors. "We're through."

"Torches," Alyssa said.

Guards brought them out from their saddlebags as Neville and his companions continued to widen the hole. By the time the torches were lit and brought forth, the opening was large enough for a man to step through.

Covered with slime and stinking like a pair of sewer rats, Neville and Fenil grinned at each other.

"Do the honors," Fenil said, handing Neville a torch.

The Englishman winked at Alyssa as he took the light.

"Gladly," he said.

Thrusting it through the hole ahead of himself, he stepped through to the other side.

The Speakers were a pair of small dapper men and an overweight woman, all three dressed in loose-fitting robes the color of a robin's egg. Their hair—even the woman's—was cropped close to their scalps. Their features held little expression and seemed all of a kind, even taking into account the woman's broader face. One of the men wore a pair of spectacles.

They sat behind a long steel-framed desk with a glass

top and looked up as Clive and Guafe were brought in. They made no greeting.

The man with the spectacles returned his attention to a small stack of paper on the glass surface of the desk in front of him. The other two merely regarded the prisoners with what Clive could only describe as boredom.

The two guards and their leader directed Clive and Guafe to a pair of makeshift chairs—roughly sized to their larger stature—that had been placed directly across from the desk. Beside them stood another man and woman and a small trolley on which sat an array of technical equipment. Clive regarded the gear with suspicion before turning his attention to the Speakers.

"I think we've been patient for quite long enou—" he began, but the guard leader tapped him on the shoulder with the butt of his weapon before he could finish.

"Be good," he said, "and maybe you'll get a chance to say your piece."

Clive clenched his fists but kept silent. Beside him the female technician was studying Guafe.

"I'm afraid the evaluators can't be trusted in regard to this one," she said to the Speakers. "We'd have to take him apart to find out just where the flesh leaves off and the cybernetics begin. And then we'd still have to recalibrate the evaluators."

The man without the spectacles nodded. "We'd like them in one piece for the present," he said. "Hook up the other."

"We can judge some of the validity of what the cyborg has to say from this one's reactions," the male technician said as he approached Clive. "But we won't guarantee any of it a hundred percent."

He pulled a wire with a suction cup attached to its end from the belly of the largest machine and lifted it toward Clive's brow. Clive shrunk back until he felt the muzzle of one of the guards' weapons touch his back. Then he froze.

"It's merely an advanced form of a truth detector,"

Guafe said. "I believe it works on a neural level—isn't that correct?"

The technician appeared surprised at the cyborg's knowledge, but he nodded. "It's completely harmless."

Harmless or not, Clive wasn't happy as the electrodes were attached to each temple, his wrists, and his ankles, with three more placed on his chest.

"Can we get on with this?" the woman Speaker asked.

The man with the spectacles nodded. "Let's just give the evaluator a quick test." He looked directly at Clive. "How many of us are sitting at this table?"

"This is nonsense," Clive said.

The muzzle of the guard's weapon jabbed his kidney.

"Three," he said then.

The machine hummed on the trolley beside him, and Clive suddenly felt an odd buzzing sensation run up and down his spine. It spread out to touch his every nerve end, but one part of it remained centered at the base of his spine. A warmth sat there; not unpleasant, but not natural either.

It was the machine that was causing this, Clive thought. This evaluator. But while that might be the origin of what he felt, he couldn't shake the apprehension that the device was waking something more than merely an evaluation of how truly he replied.

"What is the color of our robes?" the Speaker went on.

"Blue."

"Are you a native of this world—please answer in the affirmative."

"I am not a—"

"A simple yes, if you please."

Again the jab in his kidney.

"Yes," Clive said.

"Thank you," the Speaker said. "Do you have enough data, Chary?" he added to the female technician.

She nodded. "There appears a slight anomaly—a ghosting in his neural pattern that the program can't explain—but with that taken into account, we shouldn't have any difficulty in obtaining a reading."

Before anyone else could speak, Clive leaned forward. "Could someone please explain"—he ignored the sudden jab in his kidney as the guard tried to stop him from speaking—"just exactly what it is that you want from us?"

"We are *not* here to satisfy your curiosity," the Speaker without the spectacles replied.

"Oh, give the man a break, Hoyd," the female Speaker interrupted.

Speaker Hoyd frowned, but the third Speaker nodded. "Go ahead, Lena," he said.

"It's really quite simple," Speaker Lena said. "We are trying to find out if you really are Clive Folliot, or merely a clone grown from one of his cells."

"A clone!" Clive cried.

The machine hummed at his side as he spoke. The curious buzz followed the traceries of his neural system.

Speaker Lena ignored his outburst and went on. "The Dungeon's been up to its ears in Folliots of every size, shape, and description lately—some with true blood, most not even vaguely related but who take the name for their own, all the same."

"I *am* Clive Folliot, madam," Clive said. "Make no mistake about that."

Again the machine's hum. Again the accompanying sensation in his nervous system.

"He's telling the truth," the male technician said.

"Check your data infeeds," Speaker Hoyd said, "because whoever he is, he can't be Clive Folliot. What we need to ascertain is what he hopes to accomplish by this charade and most importantly *how* he has acquired a body that contains all the necessary traces for him to have grown up in the England of the true Folliot's time. He even has the real Folliot's scars—all correctly aged!"

"That's because I *am* Clive Folliot!" Clive shouted.

The machine hummed beside him. The accompanying buzz was accentuated—it was sharp this time, awaking a slight pain between his temples and behind his eyes.

"The evaluator is not malfunctioning," the technician stated firmly.

"How's it possible?" the Speaker with the spectacles asked.

"The Chaffri will stop at nothing to best us, Kian," Speaker Hoyd said.

"But his size . . ."

"My size?" Clive asked. "There's nothing wrong with my size—it's you who are diminutive."

The evaluator made a crackling noise, and Clive began to shake.

"Oh no," Speaker Kian said. "I can assure you of this much, whoever you are—the real Clive Folliot and we are all of one size. Not giants such as you and your companion."

"Freaks," the guard leader muttered softly behind him.

The mirror, Clive thought. It was something to do with the mirror. Just as Dodgson's Alice had shifted in size in her Wonderland . . .

He couldn't continue the thought. The machine beside him shorted out, and his back arched as blue fire ran through his nerve ends. He would have fallen forward, but the female technician caught the bulk of his weight and, with the help of a guard, pushed him back into his chair. His eyes rolled backward, and he lost all awareness of the questioning room.

He saw instead a uniform grayness. A strobing blue light flickered behind his eyes—reminding him of that lost memory that he could not quite grasp. It burned in a lost, dark place in his mind, almost present, but frustratingly just out of reach. Then his attention was snared by other matters as, slowly, a portion of the grayness in front of him cleared—a section in the shape of an oval mirror. And then it seemed he was looking into a Victorian sitting room—directly into the astonished features of his friend, George du Maurier.

"Clive?" he heard du Maurier say. "Good Lord, man. What are you doing in my mirror?"

"Mirror?" Clive replied. "What are you doing in my dream?"

Before du Maurier could reply, the grayness took Clive away again.

▪ CHAPTER SEVEN ▪

Twilight had come and gone while they talked. Darkness held the streets now. With the coming of night the bar began to fill up with the oddest collection of people Annabelle had run across since her time in the khalif's prison, way back on the Dungeon's first level. Linda had left for the apartment she and Casey had in back, taking her daughter with her. She offered the place to Annabelle and the others to rest up, but Annabelle shook her head.

"I want to check out the scene," she said.

No, be honest, she told herself. What you really want is to hear some good ol' rock 'n' roll.

Casey took up his position behind the bar—but not before providing Smythe with some new gear. The trousers and shirt were old and patched, the shoes a little tight—but the canvas would stretch, Casey assured him.

"And it sure beats walking around bare-assed under that cloak—don'tcha think?" Annabelle had added.

So now they sat near the stage, watching the club's regular patrons drift in. Almost all were human; fashion was what set them apart. There was everything from full-body tattoos and shaved pates to bewildering arrays of multicolored rags and the most amazing peacock hairstyles that would have put to shame the old punks from the eighties in Annabelle's homeworld.

It was only on closer—if circumspect, after staring got her some fierce scowls—inspection that Annabelle began to notice physical differences. Noseless beings with odd, flat faces. A beard that proved to be hundreds of thread-thin tentacles. A woman with three breasts, running in a row down the center of her chest. What looked like a beer-bellied tattooed biker who proved to have instead a marsupial pouch from which a small head poked as soon as he was served.

There were two waitresses who were kept on their feet in a constant rush from bar to tables for the first hour as the club filled up. Then things finally settled down, and the moment Annabelle had been waiting for came as the Airplane took the stage again.

For a good half hour Annabelle was taken away from all her troubles. She didn't think about the Dungeon, about their missing companions, about anything but the music. Smythe left to take up Linda's offer as soon as the first song ended, but Finnbogg stayed with her, singing along on every chorus whether he could pick out the words or not. It wasn't until the band ended their first set with "White Rabbit" that Annabelle came down from her high.

The three men who suddenly sat down at her table didn't help.

All three wore leather vests to show off their muscular chests and arms. Greasy black hair was tied back in ponytails. One—the obvious leader—went so far as to be wearing a pair of shades. He grinned at Annabelle, showing a gold-capped front tooth.

The band had left the stage as soon as the song ended, and the club filled now with crowd noise as its patrons stretched their legs and began to talk with each other.

"You're new," Gold-tooth said to her.

"Don't think so," Annabelle said tiredly. "I feel all grown up."

That gave Gold-tooth and his friends a chance to give her a long once-over, smirking the whole time. A quiet growl rumbled deep in Finnbogg's chest.

"I meant, new around here," Gold-tooth said. "I like to check out the new blood, y'understand. See what they're made of. Whatcha got there?"

He pointed to where the Baalbec A-9 merged with the flesh of her forearm.

There was no way this could end pretty, Annabelle thought. Here and there throughout the crowd she could spot other men wearing the same black vests, their chests bare. Some kind of gang—no question about it—which was not going to make things easy, even with Finnbogg at her side.

She was just trying to figure how far she should let this go when Casey suddenly appeared beside their table to glower down at Gold-tooth.

"Don't push it, John J.," he said.

Great, Annabelle thought, remembering what Jake had told her about the Baptists and their leader. It had to be the Prophet himself. This she really needed.

"Easy," John J. replied. "You look after secular matters, brother, and leave the people's spiritual welfare to me."

Casey shook his head. "I told you—you and your boys are welcome here any time you want—but no preaching. Save it for the streets."

"It's cold out there on the streets," John J. replied. "Real cold. A hard, tough world. Shame if you had to relocate on a street corner, what with being a new daddy and all."

"That does it," Casey said.

He started to reach for John J., but the Prophet put his hands up placatingly. "Hey, hey, Casey—be cool. You got a lot of friends in this here club right now, but we've got some numbers here too. You want this place coming down around your ears?"

Annabelle was completely bored with all the macho posturing going on—both from John J. and her own rescuer. All she'd wanted was to listen to some good music for a couple of hours before she had to hit the battle lines again. Was that really too much to ask?

"Listen up," she said.

They both turned to look at her.

"I appreciate the concern, Casey, but I don't want to bring trouble down on this place."

"See?" John J. said. "Lady likes my company."

"As for you," she told him, "whatever you're selling —I don't want it, so why don't you go bother somebody else?"

"I'm here to look out for your soul, lady."

Annabelle shook her head. "My soul's in great shape, so take your business somewhere else. This table's reserved."

She could see him flexing his muscles, wiring himself up for a challenge.

"Oh yeah? Or else what?"

She saw Casey shaking his head. Right. Don't antagonize him. I'd love to take this outside, Annabelle thought, but you can only play 'em as they come.

"I'm trying to be real nice about this," Annabelle said. "Why don't you do us both a favor and find somebody else to hit on?"

He moved so fast that she never saw it coming, never had a chance to activate her Baalbec. He just reached out across the table and half pulled her back across it, using a handful of her jacket's lapels to hold her by. Drinks fell off the table. Casey started to move in to help her, but two other Baptists rose to block his way.

John J. was just grinning in her face—that gold tooth flashing—when Finnbogg lunged across the table, breaking John J.'s grip on Annabelle. Off balance, she fell to the floor. By the time she got up, it was to see Finnbogg pinned to the floor by a couple of Baptists, John J. holding the edge of a long, wicked blade against the dwarf's throat.

Where the hell was he hiding that? Annabelle wondered.

"The Lord's talking to me!" John J. cried, raising his voice so that it carried throughout the club. "Hell, yes. He's talking and I'm listening. And you know what he's telling me, brothers and sisters? He's telling me it's time for this little dog-boy lying here at my feet to meet his maker."

Oh shit, Annabelle thought.

John J. chose that moment to look right at her. "Can I get a big amen from you all on that?"

The balloon drifted slowly over the ruined city. The tall buildings reared darkly about them as though the balloon were nothing more than a seed pod floating in some immense forest. But when was there ever a forest this large? Sidi wondered. When was there ever a city this large?

Only in the Dungeon . . .

With the fall of night they could see pinpricks of light below them. Some were from open fires—but others appeared to be of an electric origin, which puzzled Sidi. He'd already seen on previous levels what sort of complicated equipment was needed to furnish even the simplest current. If such devices existed below, then it would seem the city was not nearly so deserted as it had first appeared.

That brought a smile to his lips as he took in their youthful companions. No, it wasn't so deserted at all— was it?

"Watcha smiling for?" Poot wanted to know.

"I'm just happy that we've escaped danger and are with friends," Sidi replied.

"EPs make real good friends," Poot assured them.

"They look kinda old," the female of the remaining EPs noted dubiously.

She'd been introduced to them as Nacky. The other two were Agog and Merrybe.

"Not even a year old—either of 'em," Poot told her.

Nacky scratched at the tangle mat of her hair and shrugged. "Dunno. . . ."

"Frenchy'll know, you betcha," Merrybe said.

"Maybe," Nacky said. "Maybe Frenchy'll box us good, bringing home just a couple of Topsiders and no good loot."

Simple they might be, Sidi thought, but that didn't make them simpletons.

"You got any good loot?" Agog wanted to know.

Poot nodded happily. "Yeah, give Frenchy some loot, and he'll be happy. Maybe make you EPs, too."

"Loot?" Sidi asked.

"Treasure," Tomàs explained.

He had been standing at the rim of the basket, looking down at the dark streets passing below. He turned now and leaned with his back against the rim to look at the feral children.

"Eh, *mi niños*? Is it treasure that your Frenchy collects? Gold and silver and sparkling gems?"

Nacky shook her head. "What good's that?"

"It can buy you whatever you wish."

"Buy?"

The faces of the children creased as they pondered the word.

"What do you call loot?" Sidi asked them.

"Toys," Poot said promptly.

Agog nodded. "With working parts—Frenchy likes them best."

"Like this," Nacky said, and she pulled a small pistol from the pocket of her jacket and waved it in front of them.

"Be careful where you point that thing," Tomàs said.

Nacky just laughed. She aimed the muzzle straight at him and pulled the trigger.

"Bang!" all the children shouted together.

They laughed uproariously at how Tomàs jumped. The Portuguese gave Sidi a pained look.

"Madre de Dios," he said. "They are *loco*."

"They are children," Sidi said. "As we are," he added quickly when Nacky frowned at him. "We are all children, and children like games." He stuck his hand in his pocket. "What have I got in my pocket?"

"Your hand!" Merrybe cried.

"Grub!"

"Loot!"

"A dead mouse," Poot said.

While the children continued to guess, Sidi shook his head each time they were wrong. Caught up in the game, no one paid any attention to where the balloon was drifting until it bumped into the side of a building. Tomàs, still leaning on the rim, grabbed at the rigging to keep himself from falling over.

"We're home!" Poot cried.

"Home, home, home!"

Agog leaped up onto the rim where he balanced precariously for a long moment before jumping from the basket to the ledge of the nearest window. Merrybe threw him a rope, and in moments the balloon was firmly moored to the building. He and Poot joined Agog on the ledge, quickly followed by Tomàs.

"What *did* you have in your pocket?" Nacky wanted to know before they joined the others.

Sidi took from his pocket a small round pebble pocked with bits of quartz. "A lucky stone," he said. "Here. You can keep it."

Nacky's eyes widened. "For true?"

When Sidi nodded, she grinned and stowed it carefully away in an inner pocket of her jacket.

"I never saw a stone that good before," she said.

"C'mon, c'mon!" Poot cried from the window ledge.

"Hang onto your shirt!" Nacky shouted back. She gave Sidi another big grin, obviously having decided that he could be a friend. "Let's go see Frenchy."

Ah, yes, Sidi thought as he followed her across to the ledge. Frenchy.

He doubted the EPs' leader would be won over by anything so simple as a kind word or a lucky stone.

"I hope you have something in mind, *amigo*," Tomàs said as the EPs led them deeper into the building.

Sidi only wished he did.

Tomàs nodded at the look on the Indian's face. "I didn't think so," he said.

Already his shoulders were sagging, the momentary sense of self-worth that had awoken while descending the tower was quickly wearing away.

"Don't worry," Nacky told them. "Frenchy likes all us EPs. You'll see."

We will see, Sidi thought. True enough. But will we like what we see? Or more to the point—will Frenchy?

Then they were led down a last corridor into a broad room and the time for wondering was gone.

The room was enormous. Torches thrust into brackets in the walls cast a flickering light over a scene out of a madhouse. There were children everywhere—all of them dressed in rags and tatters. Their hair was long and matted, or cut short into uneven tufts. Their faces were all thin, their eyes both childlike and feral. But strangest of all was the figure propped up on cushions at the far side of the room who could only be Frenchy.

He was not a man—that much was plain. He reminded Sidi more of some gigantic caterpillar or slug, given somewhat human features and two slender forearms. On his bald pate was a red fez. His only other garment was a yellow-and-green vest, pulled tight over his bulbous chest. In one of those impossibly slender hands was the mouthpiece of a hookah pipe. As he drew in the smoke, the water in the pipe bubbled. He let a slow stream of smoke out through the broad nostrils set dead center in his face. There was no nose to go with them.

His eyes were tiny, almost lost in the folds of fat that blurred his features. His mouth was a wide slit that ran literally from ear to ear. The head was as big as a normal man's torso; his body's bulk many times that again. All over the cushions, and scattered on the floor around them, were heaps and piles of small mechanical devices in various stages of repair.

His loot, Sidi realized.

"Brought you some new EPs, Frenchy," Poot said proudly.

The creature's tiny eyes studied Sidi and Tomàs while he inhaled another lungful of smoke from the hookah.

"Did you now, *mon petit* Poot," he said finally.

His voice was surprisingly thin and high-pitched, coming as it did from such an immense body. How did he move? Sidi couldn't help wondering.

"Found 'em, we did—up in an old tower," Poot said, grinning happily.

"But these are too old to be EPs," Frenchy said.

Poot's grin faded. He took a couple of steps away from Sidi and Tomàs, as did Agog and Merrybe. Nacky hesitated at Sidi's side, before sidling away as well.

"Didn't know," Poot said. "They said they were only a year old."

"Actually," Sidi spoke up, "what I said was that we had only been in the Dungeon for a few months. I'm afraid the boy misunderstood me."

Frenchy nodded slowly. "You're not Topsiders either," he said.

Sidi noted that Nacky and the others visibly relaxed at that.

"No," he said. "We're from another world entirely."

The sluglike face remained impassive. More smoke was inhaled, then exhaled in a series of smoke rings that made a number of the EPs clap their hands with delight.

"Alors," Frenchy said finally. "Tell me about it."

Once Neville and his companions made their way past the blockage, they realized that they had found an entranceway to the city's storm-sewer systems. For a company that was proportional to the size of the city, it would have been cramped quarters at best—and impossible to traverse with mounts. But to their diminutive company the rounded passages were enormous and presented no problems whatsoever.

There were other hazards to their small size, however.

The flickering lights of their torches sent odd shadows scurrying in all directions. The tunnel walls were slimy to the touch, the footing slippery—even for the clawed toes of the silvers. Lying on the bottom arc of the immense concrete pipes was an endless series of large pools that they had to take care to circumvent.

The still surface of the water gave off odors more noxious than that of the blockage they'd had to remove to enter the tunnels in the first place, while the basins were deep enough in places to easily drown a man and his mount. The cesspools had been left behind since the last storm waters entered the tunnel, which left them all with a sobering thought.

"Pray it doesn't rain," Neville said to Alyssa as they rode along at the fore of the company.

She nodded. "And that we don't meet up with the feral cousins of our mounts that haunt these tunnels."

"So you know your way about in here?"

"No. Do you?"

"Not likely," Neville said. "We arrived on this level of the Dungeon only moments before meeting you."

They rode on in silence for a while after that until they came to a pool that spread so wide across the tunnel that they couldn't circle it without falling in.

"Now what?" Yoors asked, riding up.

Shriek? Neville called to the arachnid. *Can you lay webbing along one side of the wall that we can use as handholds?*

I believe so, Being Neville.

Can I help?

A mental chuckle was her only reply as she moved to where the edge of the pool met the steeper wall.

"My companion will lay down a web that we can crawl along," Neville said to Alyssa.

"What of the silvers?" Yoors asked.

"They'll have to swim."

"In that foul muck?"

Neville shrugged. "It's that or you carry them."

In the end the silvers swam through the pool while the company slowly edged their way along the steep wall, using the web spun from Shriek's spinnerets to cling to. They reached the far side without mishap, though the silvers were befouled and gave off a smell strong enough to make them all choke. The unpleasantness was compounded when the beasts shook themselves dry.

"How far do you think we've come?" Fenil asked as he worked on the coat of his mount, trying to clean away the worst of the muck.

"By our reckoning," Neville said, "in consideration of our size, I mean—perhaps half a league."

Not far, Shriek said.

"No Tuan has ever been very far into the labyrinth of tunnels that lies beneath the city," Alyssa said. "We've done a little exploration of them about our base camp, but we run into continual dead ends."

Neville nodded. That was his fear as well—that they'd come up against a blockage too tightly and too deeply packed to allow them through. He let her comment about a base camp pass for the nonce. It hadn't surprised him, as he'd already surmised that the Tuan had come to the Dungeon in a much larger company than the few of them he saw represented here.

"Dead ends, is it?" he said. "Then it's best we find a way out as quickly as possible."

"Or a way down."

"My lady," Yoors protested. "You speak too much."

Both Neville and Shriek ignored the captain to give Alyssa considering looks.

What do you mean by that, Being Alyssa? Shriek asked.

"The entrances to the next level—they're supposed to lie in an enormous living city that lies under this dead one."

Neville looked at the ground underfoot. "Another city?"

"Where the principal players in this Dungeon dwell: the Ren and the Chaffri. Half belongs to the one—half to the other."

Shriek nodded slowly. *You said earlier, Being Alyssa, about there being a third set of players . . . ?*

"So we've been led to believe."

"And are they in this city as well?" Neville asked.

"No. The way to them is through a gate to the next level of the Dungeon."

"And as the gates lie in the city . . ." Neville began.

Alyssa completed his sentence. "Then we should be looking for a way down, not up. Exactly."

* * *

When Clive regained consciousness, he found himself in yet another chamber. Unlike any of the rooms he had seen so far, this one was pleasantly furnished, albeit to a being half his size. Brocaded velvet drapes hung on either side of a large window that overlooked a brightly lit plaza where the people of this underground city went about their business under the simulated sunlight of man-made lighting. There was the oversize bed upon which he lay, ankles dangling over the end, a table and chair near the window, paintings of scenes from his own England on the walls, a dresser on the far side of the room with a mirror above it.

Remembering his hallucination in the questioning room when he'd thought he'd seen du Maurier speaking to him again, Clive studiously avoided looking into the mirror.

The diminutive size of the furnishings gave him an odd sense of misappropriation—as though he'd been left to sleep in a child's playhouse. That sensation was accentuated when the small door opened. Speaker Lena and a guard entered, both of them still only half his own height.

"How are you feeling?" Speaker Lena asked.

Clive sat up—moving gingerly when the bed creaked under the shifting of his weight.

"Where am I? Where is Chang?"

"You are in one of our guest rooms—one that a certain Speaker had been known to use for his private parties, which is why the bed is closer to what would be comfortable for your size than you might find in some of the other rooms. Your companion is waiting for us in the dining hall. Do you feel up to joining him?"

Clive had that uncomfortable feeling of having missed something important.

"Why are you suddenly being so friendly?" he asked suspiciously.

Speaker Lena shrugged. She turned to the guard. "You may go now," she told him. When the guard had closed the door behind him, she sat down on the end of the bed.

"You feel safe in my presence?" Clive asked.

"Oh, yes. I only had Guard Ourn come with me in case you woke in a state of disorientation and tried to attack me. There's no need for him to be here now."

"How do you know I won't attack you?"

"Because—with the evidence laid irrefutably before us—there can be no doubt that you are the true Clive Folliot. And the true Clive Folliot is a reasonable man, and a gentleman. I believe you'll hear us out first."

"And . . . and my size?" Clive asked.

"We realize now that the Chaffri must have been responsible for altering it. We have our own technicians working on a solution at this very moment."

"I am feeling confused, madam. Why should my being who I am alter your feelings toward me?"

"Because we want to be your friends, Clive Folliot. Because only you can help us in our struggle against the Chaffri."

"And why would I do that?"

"Because you will be helping yourself." Speaker Lena stood then. "We had a seamstress take your size while you slept. Using your decontaminated clothing as a model, she has sewn you a new wardrobe."

Clive glanced at where she pointed to see the clothing set out on a chest that lay at the end of the bed.

"We thought you would be more comfortable in your own familiar style than in the fashion of our city."

"Thank you," Clive said absently.

"You're very welcome. I'll wait for you outside. I'm afraid you'll have to bend a bit to get through the doorway, but the door's unlocked."

Clive nodded. When she left, he got carefully out of the bed. Sitting on his haunches in front of the dresser, he peered into the mirror.

"George?" he said softly. "Are you there?"

There was no reply.

Of course there would be no reply, Clive thought. Had he gone mad? Twice now he thought he'd received a communication from his old friend—and one of those times he had actually seen Du Maurier—but both events had occurred during moments of extreme stress. They were hallucinations, plain and simple. They were what he *wanted*, not what was.

He had confronted so much madness in this Dungeon that he longed with all his heart to touch something of his old life—just to feel that there was a real world beyond this house of Bedlam. Naturally he would imagine George to be the one he could reach— George being the only one of his friends fascinated with paranormal phenomena. Who else to reach for? But what he wanted and what he received, in this place, were never the same. If he wished to communicate with George again, he must first win free of the Dungeon.

It was that simple.

But if he could reach out to Du Maurier . . . pass a message on to his lover Annabella so that she would know he had not deserted her . . .

Clive frowned. That nagging sense of his missing something returned again. There was something about Annabella and du Maurier. . . .

But no sooner did he reach for the memory, than it was gone once more. Clive turned from the mirror to dress, irritated with himself for wanting the impossible to be real. It was time to deal with the present situation. Attempting to salvage some kind of sense from this latest morass of confusion that the Dungeonmasters had placed him in—that would require all of his concentration.

But it was a hard thing to do to put the past aside. Hallucination or not, seeing Du Maurier, hearing his voice again no matter that none of it had been real . . .

Enough, Clive told himself. Dressed in his new clothes, hair combed with his fingers, he bent low and stepped out the door into the hall where Speaker Lena was waiting for him.

▪ CHAPTER EIGHT ▪

Neither Annabelle nor Casey was in a position to do a thing to help Finnbogg. Annabelle was still off balance, just rising from where she'd fallen, one hand gripping the edge of the table that lay on its side beside her. Casey was held back from interfering by a pair of the Baptists. That left Finnbogg on his own. With the Prophet's knife at his throat.

"I didn't hear nobody tell me amen," John J. said. "Are y'all heathens?"

There were Baptists scattered throughout the crowd —enough so that if it came down to a fight, the sides were pretty evenly matched. A lot of people stood to get hurt, not to mention the fact that the club would get trashed.

"C'mon," Annabelle tried.

She straightened one of her legs, then drew it up under herself to give herself something to push off with. Big gang or not, there was no way she was going to let Finn die without giving it her best shot.

"He never did nothing to you," she said.

"I don't want your dog-boy's blood," the Prophet told her earnestly. "It's the Lord wants it. Guess He doesn't like to hear some smart-mouthed slit giving one of His people a hard time—you hear what I'm saying."

"Is that all?" Annabelle asked. She lifted her hand to her bodice as she spoke and activated her Baalbec A-9. "Hell, let's you and me go have some fun. Just leave my friend alone."

John J. shook his head. "Kinda late for that. It's not

▪ 109 ▪

just me that's pissed now, y'see. You got the Lord wanting His righteous cut."

"Whatever," Annabelle said.

Because as soon as that knife was away from Finn's throat, John J. was going to find out just how close the Baalbec would let him—never mind his Lord—get to her.

But the Prophet never did get to find out.

"Is there some kind of problem here?" a new voice asked.

· John J. looked up into the muzzle of a nickel-plated .44 automatic held in the steady hand of Jack Casady, the Airplane's bass player.

"Butt out, pal," the Prophet told him. "This isn't your business."

Casady shrugged, but the .44 never wavered in his hand. "Seems to me that when a guy's got a knife to the throat of someone in my audience, that makes it my business. Let the kid go."

"It's not a kid," John J. said. "It's not even human."

"More human than you, maybe," Casady replied.

"You're buying into more trouble than you can handle, pal."

Casady laughed. "You think this is trouble? Try calming down a club full of whacked-out Angels sometime."

"Angels?" John J. asked.

Annabelle knew what he was going to say even before Casady spoke. Angels, all right, though they were anything but.

"Hell's Angels," Casady said.

The Prophet's eyes narrowed as he looked up above his glasses at the bass player. "Siding with Satan," he said. "That's blasphemy."

Casady shook his head. "I didn't say I rode with 'em; I just said I've had to deal with them in my time. But you want to talk about taking the Lord's name in vain, you ever stopped and had a real hard look at what you're trying to put across as His word?"

By now others in the band had wandered over to see what was going on.

"Trouble?" Kantner asked.

"Nah," Casady told him. "Guy's just having a little fun. Now he's going to put the knife away and let the kid up—right, friend?"

Ever since the Airplane's bass player had drawn down on the Prophet, there'd been a shift of mood in the room. Annabelle didn't doubt it was a hard life in the Dives. A gig like this one tonight was one of the few chances they had to let go and forget those bad times— just as she'd been trying to. Right about now those who didn't wear the Baptists' colors were sick of screwing around.

"Let's have some more music!" somebody called out. "Yeah!"

"Everybody's waiting, friend," Casady told the Prophet.

For one long moment Annabelle was sure that John J. was going to cut Finn's throat anyway—just out of sheer perversity. But then he pushed Finn's head away and rose smoothly to his feet, the knife disappearing back into its sheath in his boot.

Casady's automatic tracked the whole movement. Finally freed, Finn turned, a deep growl coming up from his chest until Annabelle thumbed off her Baalbec and caught him by the shoulder.

"Never mind him, Finn."

Under her hand his muscles trembled.

"Why don't you take a little hike around the block," Casady told the Prophet, "just to cool off? And take your boys with you. We're here to have some fun tonight—nobody wants any trouble."

John J. stabbed the air in Casady's general direction. "You're dead meat. You, the girl, and the dog-boy there. The good Lord forgives, but I don't."

Casady laughed again. "Hey, I'm on contract," he said. "I don't live, so I can't die. When my time comes, I'll just fade away."

"Not before I get a piece of you," the Prophet muttered.

But having already been forced to back down once,

he knew it was too late to try to regain the upper hand. Before, when half the crowd was still undecided and nobody really wanted trouble, the Baptists would have had no problem—taking out half the hardasses before anyone really knew what was going down. But now, with everyone primed and ready to dance on Baptist heads, all the Prophet could do was retreat.

But there was going to be a later—and it was going to come real soon. That promise lay in the Prophet's eyes as he backed away through the crowd. Casady waited until John J. was out the door, then winked at Annabelle and headed for the stage, where the rest of the band was getting ready to start the next set.

"What did he mean by that?" Annabelle asked Casey.

"We've got to get you out of here," Casey said. "And fast. If John J. rounds up enough men and comes back looking for you, there'll be all hell to—"

"What did Casady mean about not being alive?" Annabelle demanded.

Casey blinked and looked over at the band. "I got 'em off a batch of GBCs that were boosted from Downside. Friend of mine who got them for me knew the kind of sounds I'm into—my own time in the good ol' US of A."

"And what does that mean?"

"What does what mean?"

"GBCs."

"Genetic blueprint cards—like these."

He pulled what looked like a pack of credit cards from his pocket and showed them to her. Familiar faces rolled by. Hendrix. The Stones. Moby Grape. Lothar and the Hand People. Joplin.

"What are you telling me?" Annabelle asked.

"Look, we've really got to get you out of here," Casey said.

She grabbed his arm as he started to turn away. The band struck up a new song, and she had to shout over the music to be heard.

"What the hell are those things?"

"I told you—they're GBCs. Each of them holds the genetic blueprint for the person pictured on them. That's what they use for entertainment Downside, except once the gig's over, they usually boot the kids back into their cards. Me, I figure if they're good enough to play for me, they can do what they want when the gig's done. Only problem is, it's like Casady says: if they don't get to plug into some sounds on a regular basis, they fade away. They get real hazy until you can almost see through them, then"—he snapped his fingers—"they're gone like they never existed."

"There's people in those cards? Real people?"

Casey shrugged. "I don't know how it works. They're just like real people, but they fade if you don't keep 'em busy."

"You've grown clones of all those musicians?" Annabelle asked, pointing at the GBCs that were still in Casey's hand.

"They're not clones—they're replicas. You'd see the difference straightaway if you saw the real McCoy standing side by side with one of them."

"How do you grow them?"

Casey shook his head. "I told you, they're not clones. You need a projection box. Then all you do is stick the card in, flick a switch, and you got yourself some entertainment."

"That's obscene."

"Maybe the way they use 'em Downside—where you're going—is obscene, but I treat 'em good. Treat 'em like people. Why the hell do you think they stepped in and helped out like they did?"

Annabelle looked up at the band onstage. Casady caught her gaze and nodded to her. She smiled weakly, then looked away.

"I feel sick," she said.

Finnbogg touched her arm, concern plain in his features. "Don't be sick, Annie."

"Yeah," Casey said. "Save it for Downside. This kinda shit's tame to what you're going to find when you get down there."

"Yeah, but—"

"Now are you coming? Or would you rather have another waltz with John J.?"

Annabelle took a last look at the band, then nodded. "I'm coming."

"Well, let's fetch Horace and get you the hell outta here."

Sidi regarded the flat features of the EPs' caterpillar-like leader and thought, tell him about how they had come to be here? Frenchy appeared to accept without question that they were from another world than the Dungeon, but how could anyone be expected to believe all that he and his companions had been through since they had first arrived? There were times he had difficulty believing it all himself.

And there was simply so much to relate.

"Where do I begin?" he said.

Frenchy blew another series of smoke rings to the delight of his entourage of *enfants perdus*. His tiny eyes glinted behind the smoke.

"How did you arrive in the Dungeon?" he asked. "Where did you come from? Tell me all. Time is one thing of which we have no lack, *mes amis*—not in this place."

Sidi glanced at Tomàs, who merely shrugged as though to say, you tell it. So the Indian did just that.

Not long into the story most of the children drifted away to amuse themselves rather than listen to Sidi's dry description of the events that had befallen him and his companions over the past months. But Poot and Nacky stayed, as did a few of the other children, and Frenchy himself proved to be an attentive listener.

"You were old and now you are young," he said when Sidi described his time spent in the Chamber of the Venerated Ones. *"C'est merveilleux."*

"Perhaps," Sidi replied. "But it wasn't an experience I'd care to repeat."

"I understand," Frenchy said. "Perhaps better than you might imagine. But please. Go on."

Sidi continued the story then. Frenchy made no more interruptions until Sidi described how Baron Samedi had destroyed the clone banks on the previous level.

"You are certain?" the EPs' leader asked sharply. He lifted himself slightly, rolls of flesh jiggling like gelatin with the movement, and leaned closer. "It was all destroyed?"

There was something in the tone of his voice that Sidi couldn't quite put his finger on—an intensity that belied the nonchalant attitude he had presented to the travelers since they'd first arrived. Sidi and Tomàs exchanged nervous glances.

"Answer me!" Frenchy cried.

All around the room the various EPs froze where they stood to turn nervous faces toward their leader. Beside Sidi, Nacky and Poot were visibly shivering.

"Yes," Sidi said. "So far as we could tell, it was all destroyed."

Frenchy pinned him with a long, considering glance, then slowly settled the vast bulk of his body back onto the pillows. The various EPs relaxed once more. Frenchy turned his gaze skyward.

"*Sacré mains,*" he said softly. "Perhaps God will answer prayers even in this *damné* place."

"You are familiar with that level of the Dungeon?" Sidi asked.

Frenchy touched his bulbous chest with one slender finger. "How do you think I came to be like this? I too was drawn into this Dungeon through no choice of my own. I made my way through the levels until I was taken on the previous level and . . . experimented upon."

"We were told that those were clones growing in those vats," Sidi said.

Frenchy nodded. "But it amused my captors to manipulate the source bodies as well. What I have seen in that place . . . it was *monstrueux.*"

"You were not always as you are now?" Sidi asked carefully.

"I was born in Paris, *mes amis,* in the year of the revolution—1789. My name was Georges Corbeil. I was still a boy when I was first captured, but I never had a chance to become a man. Instead I was made into this creature you see before you now. The boy I was still lives within this grotesque body, but I am the only one to remember him now."

"Christo," Tomàs breathed.

"And so you gather around you children," Sidi said, "who will not remind you of the monsters disguised as men and women who did this to you."

Frenchy nodded. *"Mes enfants perdus."*

"May we call you Georges?" Sidi asked.

"Georges Corbeil is dead," Frenchy said bitterly. "The only name I have now is the one my cellmates gave me before it was my turn to be taken to those *laboratoires damnés* where this was done to me. You have my eternal gratitude for helping to wreak my vengeance upon those monsters."

There was a long moment of silence during which it seemed no one even breathed. Sidi and Tomàs thought of that room with its hellish vats. Imagining a similar fate befalling themselves, they could only shudder.

"I am very sorry for you," Tomàs said sincerely.

Frenchy shrugged. "It was a long time ago. I do not let it trouble me now."

No, no, Sidi thought. You don't let it trouble you at all.

"Please," Frenchy went on. "Continue with your story. After you destroyed the vats, eh? What befell you then?"

The rest was simple to tell.

"From reports they have brought me," Frenchy said when Sidi was finally done, "I believe that my children have seen some of your companions. But tell me— were you not all of similar proportions?"

"What do you mean?" Sidi asked.

"The children have told me of two groups of new-comers to the Dives. One of these could well be your mechanical being and his companion, but the children tell me that these two are twice the height of a normal man."

"Do they exaggerate?" Sidi asked.

That got him an elbow in the ribs from Nacky, who was still sitting beside him.

"Not if they know what is good for them," Frenchy replied. "Perhaps the Dungeonmasters experimented on them?"

"That would not be possible," Tomàs said. "We all went through the mirror at almost the same time."

"Then these must be clones of your friends—clones grown twice their size. The children tell me that they went below."

Sidi nodded. "What of the other group the children saw?"

"That one had a woman leading them."

Annabelle! Sidi thought. She was still alive. His heart skipped a beat, as it did whenever he thought of her.

"And she had with her?" he asked.

"A broad dwarfish being with the features of a dog, and a hairless man wearing little more than a cloak."

That would be Finnbogg and Horace. Sidi turned to Tomàs, and they shared a grin. At least three of their companions were safe.

"Can your children take us to them?" Tomàs asked.

Frenchy nodded. "But I would not advise it, *mes amis.* They have gone to a dangerous area in the Dives. Tonight the voice of the streets tells me that the Baptists are angry and gather in strength in the very area where your friends were last seen. You would do better to wait until the excitement has died down."

Sidi didn't know who or what Frenchy meant by the Baptists, but he did know that if there was trouble brewing near to where their friends were, then the odds were better than good that Annabelle and the others would be in the middle of that misfortune. That was simply how it seemed to work in the Dungeon.

"We have to join them as soon as possible," Sidi said.

"*Alors,*" Frenchy said. "I am indebted to you, so I will help you as best I can. I will have one of my children take you near to where your friends were last seen, but I cannot risk more of them than that."

"I'll take them," Nacky said. "I'll take them right into Casey's. I ain't scared."

"And what, *ma petite,* if you do not find it so easy to return? If the Baptists catch you, they will not be kind. They will keep you from me and your brothers and sisters, and then you will grow old. Would you like to risk that?"

Nacky simply shrugged. "I ain't scared," she repeated. "I kicked a Baptist once—right in his knee— and took off fast. He never even tried to catch me."

"We don't want to risk your children," Sidi said, "but we will need a guide."

"Malheureusement," Frenchy said, "this body of mine, *c'est immobile.* It will have to be one of the children."

"I'm really not scared even a bit," Nacky assured them.

"Me neither," Poot added.

"I was never scared, ever," another of the EPs, whose name they didn't know, piped up.

Tomàs smiled. "One guide will be enough, I think."

"Perhaps it will be one too many," Frenchy said. "You don't know these Baptists, *mes amis.* They are very strong and tonight—I have been told—they are very unhappy. If they were to catch you or your friends . . ."

"But they are our friends," Tomàs said.

Sidi nodded. "If there is a chance that they are in danger, how could we not go to help them?"

Frenchy nodded wearily. *"C'est vrai.* In a place such as this we have only our friends. Go then—with my blessing. Nacky will guide you, since she seems so eager to go."

"I've got a lucky stone," Nacky said, "so everything'll just work out better 'n good."

Sidi and Tomàs rose to their feet. Nacky started to tug on Sidi's hand, but he held back long enough to give Frenchy a short bow.

"It's been an honor to meet you," he said.

"If you survive, bring your friends to speak with me," Frenchy replied. "I can show you a way below."

"Below?"

"Into Downside. If you wish to go on to the next level, you must go among the Chaffri and the Ren to do so."

There would be time to worry about that later.

"We will try to return to see you," Sidi said. Then he gave in to Nacky's insistent cries of "C'mon, c'mon," and her tugging on his arm.

"Adiós," Tomàs said. He tapped a forefinger against his temple in a quick salute before he hurried off to join Sidi.

Frenchy nodded to himself as they left. *"Oui. Adieu et bon chance, mes amis,* but I fear I won't be seeing you again."

Tomàs and Sidi heard that, but then a crowd of laughing children were clustered around them to see them off, and if Frenchy had anything more to say, they didn't get to hear it.

"What do you think these Baptists are?" Tomàs asked Sidi as Nacky led them into a stairwell.

"They're bad and ugly," Nacky called back over her shoulder.

Of course, Sidi thought. They were a danger of the Dungeon, so what else could they be? But he thought of the tragic figure they had just left behind them, of Shriek and Finnbogg and others he had met who didn't fit into a certain consideration of what was beautiful, and realized that he was doing Frenchy, and many another victim of the Dungeonmasters, or perhaps just victims of simple fate, an injustice.

It was those who wore ugliness in their hearts—of them one must take care.

Impossible as Neville might have thought it, he and his companions eventually grew used to the noxious stench that pervaded the sewer system. It was worse when their mounts had to disturb the still pools, but only nominally so, and they soon became inured to that as well.

More disturbing was the increasing appearance of heaps of rubble where parts of the ceiling had fallen in. Though each time the debris proved passable, they could not help but worry that the next time their route would be well and truly blocked, and they would need to turn back.

They kept track of the hours by the lifetimes of their torches. As a torch lasted approximately twenty minutes, Neville reckoned that they had been in the sewer system for almost two hours when they finally rested on a low platform that the silvers reached by means of a sudden, heart-stopping scrabble up a face of loose stone.

Of them all Shriek appeared the least discomfited by both their surroundings and the rough terrain.

My olfactory senses do not have the same reference points as do yours, Being Neville, she explained when Neville complained to her about it, *so I am not as troubled with the smell. And my physique is better suited to navigating our route than are either yours or the Tuan. Our positions were reversed on some of the other levels.*

And she had offered no complaint then, Neville thought. But of course Shriek, being who she was, left that unspoken.

I'm merely frustrated, he told her. *Rationally, I'm happy that it goes so easily for you.*

What Neville had come to recognize as a smile passed briefly over the arachnid's features. *But physically, it is not so easy to be logical,* she finished for him.

Exactly.

He leaned back against the side of Alyssa's mount, which lay stretched out on the platform, eyes closed, breathing even. Alyssa sat a few feet away from him.

"I think you and Shriek have brought us luck," she said, turning to look at him.

"How so?"

"We've never come this far before in any of the tunnels."

Neville laughed. "Thank the dogs then—not us."

Alyssa shook her head. "How do you keep your spirits so cheerful? My own people make no pretense of how little they're enjoying this place."

She nodded to her companions who, all except for Fenil, lounged against their own mounts, dour looks on their faces. Fenil leaned over the edge of the platform, torch held out above his head, trying to spy what he could of the road still to come.

Neville shrugged. "I could make a joke and say I've seen worse."

"But . . . ?"

"It's no joke, but I have seen worse. At least here no one's trying to loosen my head from my neck. These tunnels are as charming as swimming in a privy, but we are still free. We do what we do by our own inclination. And . . ." He laughed again, but this time there was a sardonic note to his humor.

"And?" Alyssa prompted him again.

"Each step we take brings us closer to the bastards who have put us into this situation in the first place."

Alyssa said nothing for a long moment, only staring off into the darkness, then she slowly nodded. "I too have words I wish to share with the Dungeonmasters." She turned to look at Neville. "How long has your party been trapped in here?"

When Neville shrugged, Shriek said, *It varies. I have been here for a few of what Neville terms years; for Neville it has been a year or so. One of our companions claims a residency of ten thousand years.*

Neville smiled, thinking of Finnbogg and his preposterous tales. But it was true that each one had some kernel of truth hidden in it.

"I believe it," Alyssa said. "In this place I will believe anything. In my homeland we have tales of the Weeping Desert—where souls go who have not served the Great Wind with all the heart, strength, and loyalty that they might have. They are sent to the Weeping

Desert—there to suffer until the Great Wind's Second Moon returns. This Dungeon has appeared too much like the Weeping Desert, at times, for my liking."

Neville began to describe the last level they had passed through, which had been so much like the hell of his own homeland's religion.

"We saw no such place," Alyssa said. "Neither the place of fires, nor the barony, nor the medicine tent with its evil twins."

"Not twins," Neville said. "One of our companions— the cyborg Guafe—explained it to us. The Dungeon-masters can grow exact replicas of us from the smallest particle of our body. He called them clones. But they are not like twins that have grown together in the same womb."

"How can you be so sure?" Alyssa asked.

"Because one of our missing companions is not only my brother, but my twin as well. And as Shriek will vouch for me, I'm sure, we bear little resemblance to each other, save for that physical family resemblance that any siblings might share."

"But these vats . . ."

Neville nodded. "I agree. It's an evil process."

But blame not the creatures themselves, Shriek added. *Rather, blame those who created them.*

"I'd sooner kiss the butt of the Night Troll," Yoors said, speaking for the first time, "than forgive such monsters."

Neville smiled to himself. He had been certain that the captain hadn't been dozing as he'd pretended but listening to the whole of their conversation.

"They killed his brother, Shian," Alyssa explained.

Yoors shook his head. "They didn't kill him—they butchered him. Butchered him like some animal while we were forced to flee without giving him his final rites."

If one looks deep enough, Shriek said in her mild voice, *we can see a reason for every being's temperament.*

When no one replied, Neville realized that she had narrowed her neural broadcast so that only he could hear what she said. He nodded, understanding what she meant.

I'll try to be easier on him, he told her.

He could feel her smile in his mind. *There is hope for you yet, Being Neville.*

Alyssa was unaware of the conversation that had gone on between the two. "It was in that damned desert," she was saying, "the one that finally led us to this level."

"You saw no looking glass? None of what I described?"

Alyssa shook her head. "Only what seemed to be an endless waste. And there were creatures in it—dry, scaly monsters that thrived in the desolation. Shian was killed by one just as we reached the entranceway to the gate. . . ."

"I'm sorry, Yoors," Neville said. "For everything."

The captain gave him a hard look before turning away.

Neville glanced at the arachnid. *I'm trying, Madam Shriek, but he's not helping. What does he want?*

Perhaps a chance to come to grips with his loss? she replied.

"What made it worse," Alyssa said, "was that we were so close to escaping. All we needed were another few moments and—"

Fenil hissed suddenly. He drew back from the edge of the platform. Yoors was immediately on his feet, quickly followed by the others.

"What is it?" the captain asked.

"Something is approaching," Fenil replied. "Something very large."

"Perhaps more than one something," Yoors said as he reached the edge of the platform and peered off into the darkness.

Lovely, Neville thought. Trust the Dungeonmasters to make certain that there was never a dull moment.

* * *

Like the room in which Clive had woken the hallway where Speaker Lena waited for him would not have been out of place in any good London gentleman's home. Its very familiarity reawakened Clive's homesickness once again.

East or West, Home is Best.

Clive had always thought of that little homily as a middle-class ideal, but now, after months in the Dungeon . . . What he wouldn't give to be home once more. His present surroundings merely accentuated that yearning.

The hallway was carpeted underfoot in a deep burgundy. The walls held sconces converted to electrical lighting and portraits of muttonchopped gentlemen and charming ladies in scenes that reminded Clive of his friend Du Maurier's work for *Once A Week* and *Punch.* Side tables with decorative urns and statuary could be found every ten feet or so, and the ceiling, while uncomfortably close because of Clive's current size, was delicately arched.

Clive felt like some lumbering beast as he followed Speaker Lena down the hall, their footfalls masked by the deep pile of the carpeting.

"This building is the Speakers' Hall," Speaker Lena explained as they walked. "It lies across the city from where you were first brought in. This particular wing is dedicated to English Victoriana—the patterns and expressions of your own particular era."

"Why?" Clive asked.

Speaker Lena paused to look at him. "I'm sorry?"

"Why is this wing dedicated to my era?"

She smiled. "Because there are many among us who have taken a great liking to your particular period." She began to walk on again. "Your time was one of glorious advances in the arts—a flowering of science and creative expression."

Clive thought of all the progress the world had come to know in the century after his own—of all that his great-granddaughter had described to him during their months together. From all he'd seen of this city so far, its inhabitants were easily as technologically advanced.

"I would think you would see us a primitive people," he said.

"In some ways—yes, of course. But the spirit of your time was so open to that which was new. . . ."

Clive blinked. Open to that which was new? He considered the society of his time, the Church of England, social mores, class structure. . . . When he compared their likes to how men and women could live together, as he'd come to understand through his relationship with the lost members of his company, he knew that there was a great deal that could be changed in English society—and all for the better.

It was still home, to be sure, and he longed for it, but if ever he could return, he would be a far different man than he had been before he had put England's shores behind him.

"I believe you have an idealized impression of my time," he said.

Speaker Lena shrugged. "Probably."

"And have you been there?" Clive asked.

He had been wondering for some time if the beings that inhabited the Dungeon ever crossed over to the worlds from which the Dungeonmasters kidnapped their unwilling game pieces. And then there was the consideration that anyone he met in this place might actually *be* one of the Dungeonmasters. So he meant to question and learn all he could; to be friendly but to keep his own counsel; and above all to look for the chance to escape so that he could get back to the true business at hand—reuniting with his companions and defeating the Dungeonmasters.

"Well?" he prompted the Speaker when she didn't answer him at once. "Have you?"

Speaker Lena smiled. "Of course—but I'll never actually live there, so what harm does idealizing do?"

There was harm in the spread of any lie, Clive thought, even when its basis merely lay in ignorance or thoughtlessness, but he was hard put to explain exactly why—even to himself. Until he could, he saw no point in contesting the point with his present companion.

"What of the Hall's other wings?" he asked instead.

"I was going to tell you to prepare yourself," Speaker Lena replied as they approached a door at the end of the hallway.

The door was enormous—solid wood panels with brass gilding and knobs. On either side of it stood tall vases, brimming over with bouquets of fresh roses. The blossoms seemed tiny to Clive. Unreal.

"Prepare myself for what?" he asked.

"Each wing has a different decorative theme. We are a people who delight in the acquisition of cultures, wholeheartedly embracing whichever appeals the most to us—at least until another, more attractive one comes along. The houses and apartments in the city might have a room dedicated to, say, the Sak of ancient Heline—a race of beings who would spend their formative years in a cocoon, before emerging as brilliantly tattooed insectoids—side by side with another given over to the Ming Dynasty of your own world's China, or the sand-faring Lem, the artifacts of whose entire culture are based solely on spheres."

"And beyond this door?" Clive asked.

"Lies the Hub of the Speakers' Hall, which corresponds roughly to Central Plaza—the inner core of the city, which is given-over to our own culture."

She opened the door as she spoke, and Clive found himself looking at whiteness. Walls, floor, ceiling, the clothing of the people—it was all blank. Ciphers. Everything was utilitarian. There were no statues, no paintings on the walls. Angles were precise with an utter lack of decorative appeal.

He turned to give his companion a puzzled look. "But . . ."

Speaker Lena nodded sadly. "We are a chameleon people," she said. "We have no culture of our own—only what we borrow from others."

"But I don't even see that."

"It's not considered good form to wear one's obsessions in public."

"I see," Clive said.

But he didn't. How could a race of people exist without a culture of their own? Surely it was impossible. At some point in their history they *had* to have had fashions and fads that they could call their own. Didn't they?

"Come," Speaker Lena said.

She led him out into the Hub, which proved to be an enormous room inside which could have easily fit a half dozen of the Great Exhibition's famous Glass Palace. Here their shoes clacked on the floor, and Clive was very much aware of the attention he drew. From the looks upon the faces of those he passed, he saw that they viewed him in much the same manner as had the leader of the guard who had first captured him and Guafe in the underground railway station.

He could almost hear the guard captain's voice hissing, "Freak," in his ear as he watched their gazes slide from his own. The rising grumble of their voices as they spoke of him followed unpleasantly in his wake. Their antagonism, coupled with his recent thoughts of du Maurier, brought an odd memory to mind—that of the time he'd met the tragic Mary Wollstonecraft Shelley not long before her death in fifty-one.

After meeting the poet's wife he had searched out and read her novel of the Modern Prometheus with great interest, even going on to take in the London stage production of the book.

There had been a pathos about the monster that had deeply moved Clive—more so in the novel than in its adaptation to the stage. He had found himself thinking, in the weeks that followed his first reading of the novel, of just how the monster had felt, trying to imagine himself in a similar position.

Now he knew.

He wasn't the same hideous monster—at least not to his own gaze, nor from the image he had seen looking back at him from the mirror earlier today—but to these people he was a freak of nature all the same. How else could they perceive him as he towered above them, twice as tall as the tallest in their number?

"Perhaps we should have taken another route," Speaker Lena said softly at his side.

Clive bent lower to hear her. "Why's that?"

"Because I have the uncomfortable feeling that things are about to become very ugly," Speaker Lena replied. "Quickly! Make for that far door."

But it was already too late. Though they still kept their distance, the crowd was thickening, and their epithets were no longer muttered under their breath but hurled at Clive in loud voices instead.

Things were becoming ugly indeed, Clive realized as one of the crowd threw the core of a piece of fruit at him.

▪ CHAPTER NINE ▪

Horace was waiting for them by the door that led back into Casey's apartment. He had a crowbar, the only weapon he could find on such short notice, in his hand. Linda stood beside him, a worried expression on her face.

"Thanks for the thought," Annabelle told Smythe, "but the crisis is over." She glanced at Casey. "Isn't it?"

He nodded. "If we get you out of here right away. Back on the floor John J. might've let his boys cut loose if Casady hadn't got the drop on him. We let him stew a while, and he could get up enough hardasses to make a run at the club. But if he knows you're gone, things'll cool down. No matter what John J. says, his Baptists like to have themselves a drink and some good music once in a while, and this club's the best there is in the Dives. They won't wreck it."

"What about you and Linda?"

"I'm telling you, Annabelle. We'll make do. You're the one that's got to get outta here. Pronto."

"And Casady?"

"He's a GBC replica. What's John J. going to do to him?"

Behind them in the club the Airplane were still cooking on the stage, a raunchy rock 'n' roll number with Slick's cool voice soaring overtop. Replicas, Annabelle thought. Jesus.

"I guess the thing that bothers me the most," she said, "is that they know what they are and it doesn't seem to bother them a bit. I mean, what kind of a life is that?"

Casey shrugged. "The only kind of life they'll ever know."

That woke an echo in Annabelle's mind. She chased it down until she came up with the song: "Tobacco Road," on *Takes Off.* Right. A little too apropos for her present mood.

"I know it doesn't seem right," Linda said. "We felt the same way you did until we got this latest batch of cards and talked to them. The originals are still out there in the real world, doing what they do best. The replicas really are happy just playing their tunes."

"Those originals aren't all out there anymore," Annabelle said.

Casey gave her a hard look. "What's that supposed to mean?"

"People die—musicians just the same as everybody else. Hendrix, Morrison, Joplin, Lennon . . . they're all gone now. All that's left is their music—at least that's all we ever thought was left. But I come here and find that the Dungeonmasters have managed to steal a piece of their souls, or whatever the hell it is that they do to get 'em into those cards, and you've got their ghosts up playing on a two-bit stage." She shook her head. "I always thought rock 'n' roll heaven was going to be different, you know?"

"Hendrix . . . Joplin . . . they're dead?"

Annabelle nodded. "You don't want to hear the whole roll call—believe me."

"Morrison too?" Linda asked. "And Lennon?"

"I always thought they'd get the band together and start playing again," Casey said.

Linda nodded. "Who else is gone?"

"Like I said: you don't want to get me going," Annabelle said. "You've gotta understand, I'm from the ass-end of the twentieth century—the big one-nine-nine-nine. I recognize the faces on those cards you've got 'cause my mom turned me onto all that old music. But I don't think any of those people are even players anymore. Kids don't want to get their rock 'n' roll from some grayhead, old enough to be their grandfather."

"Man," Casey said. "I'd never want 'em to stop playing."

Annabelle shrugged. "Well, you got a point. A lot of the old guard's still going strong. Course, what keeps those bands on stage and cutting CDs is that the fans who grew up listening to 'em are now investment bankers and brokers and the like, and they can afford the pricy concert tickets and shit." She shook her head. "I remember seeing a poster for Garcia and the Dead playing a concert in Wembley just before I got dumped into this place."

"You'd never want the Dead to stop playing."

Annabelle gave him a sad smile. "Guess that's what keeps them grateful, right? But it don't do much for those who are really gone. . . ."

Casey straightened up. "Okay. That's a bummer, but we don't have time for any of this. I'd love to sit down and talk about the Fillmore and all, but we've got to get you out of here, or you won't even get the chance to have a replica on one of these cards."

"What makes you think I'd want . . ."

Annabelle's voice trailed off as the thought struck home. What was she saying, she didn't want to have a part of herself in one of those cards? Knowing the Dungeonmasters, they already had pieces of her playing gigs all over the frigging Dungeon.

"I really think I'm going to be sick," she said.

"You don't have time for that kind of shit," Casey told her.

Linda pressed a small sack of provisions into Finnbogg's arms.

"Take care of yourselves," she said.

"Thank you, madam," Smythe said. "And you, Mr. Jones."

"Now listen up," Casey said as he led them to where the club's back door opened into an alleyway. He gave them quick, concise directions on how to find safe passage to Downside.

"Once you're heading down through the tunnels, just keep the paint splashes on your left—they're about shoulder level," he finished up. "You should do okay. Linda threw a couple of flashlights in your pack that've got enough juice in 'em to take you all the way down. Just don't go wandering, 'cause I don't know how long they'll last after that."

"How do you know about this passage?" Smythe asked.

Casey grinned. "It's a smuggler's route, and you, folks, are looking at one of the prime movers of Chaffri goods in the Dives. Don't worry. I'm not steering you wrong."

Smythe nodded. "Anything else we should know about the passage?"

"Just stick to my directions, and you'll do fine. You shouldn't run into any of the Chaffri's zeros, but you've still got to keep your eyes open. They've got more snares down there than you can shake a—"

"Zeros?" Annabelle asked.

"They're a kind of simulacrum—all fiber and plastic and metal, but they've got human brains housed inside, wired up to computerized motor units." He took in the looks on Annabelle and Smythe's faces. "I told you there was weirder shit than the GBCs down there."

"Can you give us any weapons?" Smythe asked. "Even just a saber?"

Casey shook his head. "That's prime goods up here, and something the smugglers don't run up to us real often. They're too hard to boost from the Chaffri. I mean you figure it—if you were the Chaffri, you might let toys and shit get into our hands, but weapons? That's just buying trouble."

They had reached the back door now.

"Hang loose a minute," Casey said.

He eased the door open and slipped outside, returning in a few moments.

"I don't know. It feels quiet—maybe too quiet for a night in the Dives."

"We can't stay," Annabelle said.

She gave Linda a kiss on her cheek and accepted a

hug from Casey before leading her small company out the door.

"Give 'em hell," Casey said before he closed the door.

"You bet, sailor," Annabelle told him.

The club door closed with a soft snick, then they heard the bolt being engaged as it was locked. Annabelle looked at her companions.

"Okay, kids," she said. "Time to boogie."

"Amen," a quiet voice from behind her added.

They turned to see the alleyway filling with Baptists, John J. in the fore. By the time they looked back the way they'd been heading, it too was blocked by gang members.

"Time to say bye-bye, sweet world," the Prophet told them, "because the Good Lord's best shepherd is looking to harvest your souls. And the real sad thing— least it's sad from your point of view—is that there ain't no GBCer here to save your asses now."

Nacky kept up a constant chatter as she led Sidi and Tomàs from the tower of *les enfants perdus* and out into the night-cloaked streets of the ruined city. When they finally reached the ground floor of that first building and stepped out onto the cracked and buckling pavement, Tomàs stamped a foot on the ground and grinned at his companion.

"Por ultimo," he said. "No more desperate climbs or swinging like monkeys from a rope, *sim?"*

Sidi smiled back at him. He too felt relieved to finally be on the ground once more.

"I would think," he said, "that as accustomed as you are to a ship's rigging, you would have been more comfortable in the heights."

"There is a *grande diferencia* between the two," Tomàs replied. "Trust me."

Sidi looked up the clifflike face of the building behind them. It seemed to rise as tall as the heights of the Himalayas in the darkness.

"A very big difference," he agreed.

"C'mon," Nacky said impatiently, tugging on Sidi's arm again. "Lots of way to go still."

"Then lead on," Sidi told her.

She kept steadily to a quicker pace than either of the men would have assumed a child could. Mostly they went by main boulevards, skirting the heaps of rubble, pushing through waist-high fields of weeds that grew right out of the pavement. But from time to time they would spy a fire ahead, and then Nacky would lead them by circuitous routes through alleyways and deserted buildings.

"Whose fires are those?" Sidi asked her as they bypassed yet another.

He could dimly make out figures gathered around the fire, warming their hands to the flames, lounging on the ground, sharing bottles of what he assumed was alcohol.

Nacky shrugged. "Rubbies or gangs. At this time of night it don't matter which. They're all trouble."

"Rubbies?" Tomàs asked.

"Bums," she explained. "They've got no home like Frenchy made for us, and they're too old to belong to a gang."

"Ah," Tomàs said. "Beggars. Yet who do they beg from?"

"They just make do, like we all do, 'cept they don't make do as well."

They skirted the fire, entering the ruin of a building that was merely support beams standing like dead tree limbs over the building's original foundation. A mountain of fallen stone showed where its walls had fallen— so long ago now that the sharp edges of the stones were rounded by vegetation.

Two more back alleys through increasingly better-weathered buildings brought them out onto a main thoroughfare once more. Ahead of them they could now see another fire, but there was something different about this one. A few blocks closer and they could see that it was an enormous burning cross.

"Oh, this is bad," Nacky said.

She hid behind a mound of fallen stones, pulling at her companions' sleeves until they crouched down with her.

"What is it?" Sidi asked.

Nacky pointed to the cross. "That's the Baptists," she said.

Sidi could count close to fifty men gathered around the fire. They wore only trousers and vests, their bare skin gleaming in the light cast from the burning arms of the cross. There was something at the base of the fire that had their attention. Because of his angle of sight, Sidi couldn't make out what it was that interested them so.

"Can we go around them?" Tomàs asked.

Nacky shook her head. "See that sign?"

Now that it was pointed out, both men could see the neon CASEY'S that hung on the wall of the building behind the gang.

"That's the club where your friends went," Nacky explained.

"Isn't there a rear entrance?"

"Oh, sure. But look."

Once more Sidi studied the open ground where the Baptists were gathered, and this time he saw what he'd missed before. There were gang members standing on guard the length and breadth of the area. He started to turn to Tomàs, but then the Portuguese's hand touched his arm, fingers tightening.

A shift in the crowd had made enough of an opening for Sidi to catch the familiar crest of Annabelle's short-cropped hair. A moment later he spied Finnbogg's bulk, then the crowd shifted again, and the two were lost from sight.

"We won't need to go to the club anymore," he told Nacky.

"You don't want to help your friends now?"

Sidi nodded toward the burning cross. "The Baptists have our friends."

"Better say bye-bye to them," Nacky said. "Better

say it from here and real quietly, 'cause you can't do nothing else now."

Sidi turned to look at Tomàs.

"*Asno,*" the Portuguese muttered unhappily. "What can we do now?"

Sidi's hands clenched into fists as he stared out at the Baptists once more. The flickering of the flames on the burning arms of the cross sent shadows skittering across the gathered men and out to where the darkness pooled deeper by the buildings. The constant motion of the Baptists and the red tinge of the light gave the scene a hellish quality all too reminiscent of the fire fields they had passed through on the previous level.

Barely passed through.

"I don't know," he said. "There are so many of them. . . ."

"We must do *something,*" Tomàs said.

Sidi nodded. Yes, of course. They would do something. Those were their friends out there. And Annabelle . . . They had to do something more than crouch here and watch.

Only what?

There was no need of their own torches to cast light on the two immense beings that were coming down the tunnel toward them, for they gave off a pale luminescence that appeared to originate from their own skin. Taking in their height, their enormous bulk, Neville realized that he had not in fact had even an inkling as to how Swift's hero had felt when he first reached Brobdingnag.

The buildings above, huge in scale to his own size, the feral dogs . . . neither could have prepared him for the helplessness he now felt regarding the two beings that presently approached them.

They were scaled to the size of the city, and, had Neville been in proportion himself, would have stood a head shorter than he. But what they lacked in height they more than made up for in bulk. They were balloonish creatures—round heads attached to round bodies without the benefit of visible necks. Their legs were squat, their arms insect thin.

And they were as alike as two peas in a pod.

Twins.

Enormous, grotesque twins.

"What have we . . ." one began.

". . . got here?" the other finished.

"Little . . ."

". . . people."

"Small as . . ."

". . . mice."

Their voices boomed in the confines of the tunnel. More disconcerting was the way the one finished the other's sentences, as though they shared one mind. Their enormous faces bent down to look at Neville's party, eyes like saucers, smiling like a pair of bedlam inmates, their grins stretching from ear to ear.

"But we've . . ."

". . . seen their like before."

"Haven't . . ."

". . . we just?"

"Dip them in . . ."

". . . chocolate, wrap them in . . ."

". . . pastry, and won't they taste . . ."

". . . just fine?"

The two fat faces turned to each other, happy as a pair of bedlamites. If it was possible, their grins had widened. Two large hands rose, fat fingers reaching toward Yoors and Fenil.

While the rest of their party could only gape at the pair, Shriek quickly tugged free a handful of her hair spikes. Quick as an adder's strike she threw them. By the time the first pair of spiked missiles struck—one in a left eye, the other in a right—there were four more spikes already in flight.

The monsters roared. Clasping at their eyes, the remaining spikes punctured their fat hands. They reared to their full height, bellowing with pain. The sound rumbled like thunder and was answered by alarming groans from the walls and ceiling of the tunnel.

Fly! Shriek cried to her companions.

In moments the Tuan were mounted—Neville sharing Alyssa's silver once more—and the quick beasts skittered down the face of loose stone that led up the platform where they had been resting. The well-trained animals responded to their riders' commands and darted between the legs of the giants, who lumbered about, shouting with pain.

"Kill them . . ."

". . . all!"

"Mash them, smash them . . ."

". . . flat as cow turds!"

The giants stamped about, trying to stop the fleeing Tuan. They roared and howled, batting at the air as though to ward off a cloud of stinging gnats. But these gnats were Shriek's hair spikes, which she continued to toss with great effect at the pair until the roof over the platform began to give way and she had to make her own escape.

She ran at the heels of the rearmost Tuan and was only a few feet behind them when a great foot came down and squashed both rider and mount flat. Blood and less easily defined matter sprayed over the arachnid and the floor of the tunnel all about her. She lost her footing and fell, gaze turned upward to see another foot coming down at her.

She rolled desperately aside, but she was so close to the descending foot that she felt a rush of air as it hit the ground. She cast off with a thread from her spinnerets, snagging the rough cloth of the monster's trousers. When he lifted his foot again, she rode up with him, casting out another thread as his foot came down once more.

This one snagged the tunnel wall so that, when she let the first loose, she swung out and away from under the feet of the two monsters. Each blind in one eye, they could still see enough to realize that all save one of their prey was escaping.

"Catch . . ."

". . . them!"

Shriek! Neville cried, looking back over his shoulder. Clouds of rock dust hid her from his sight.

Coming . . . Being . . . Neville . . . Shriek managed to reply as she swung herself to the floor.

As soon as she touched ground, she was off and running, the monsters hard on her heels. All around them the tunnels grumbled and groaned. Dirt and bits of stone cascaded down in blinding showers. The ground shook under the monsters' tread. The tremors threw off her sense of equilibrium, making it difficult for her to keep her balance.

Shriek! Neville cried again.

He looked back, trying to spot her amid the falling debris.

He saw only a fog of powdered stone.

Shriek! he cried again, desperately now.

For all his attraction to Alyssa, for all that the Tuan seemed more his kind than the alien, it was at that moment that Neville understood that a bond had grown up not only between Shriek and himself, but between all the members of their original party. He realized that he'd rather die with his companions than seek safety on his own or with comparative strangers.

The intensity of the bond surprised him, but he put further conjecture along those lines behind him. There was no time for it just now.

He loosened his grip from Alyssa's waist.

"Neville . . . ?" Alyssa began to ask.

But Neville's attention lay only on their backtrail.

Shriek! he tried one last time.

Still no reply.

He was about to leap off Alyssa's mount then, to go back and help the arachnid, when he saw her burst through a cloud of dirt, her body wreathed in gray dust. She seemed shaken, moving not so quickly as she was normally able.

But she was alive.

She raced to catch up. When the dust briefly cleared again, Neville saw one of the giants fast approaching as well. A moment later, and the other was in view as well.

Just when Clive was certain that the unpleasantness in the Hub was about to develop into a full-scale riot, the door that Speaker Lena was steering him toward opened, and a number of guards stepped through, led by the captain who had first captured him in the underground station.

The crowd shuffled uneasily at their appearance. When the guards brought their weapons up to firing positions, they immediately began to disperse. In moments Clive and the Speaker were alone with the guards in the center of the immense chamber. Around them the Ren went about their business as though nothing untoward had ever occurred.

"A fortunate arrival, Cavet," Speaker Lena said.

The guards' captain shrugged. "We've already been through the same thing with our other"—he paused significantly—"guest. Not that I can see why you'd bother."

"Cavet . . ." Speaker Lena warned.

"I know, I know. But look at the size of him. He's like something that grew on the underside of a Chaffri breeding tank, and the 'borg—you can't tell me he isn't a Chaffri construct."

"That will be quite enough. It's no fault of our guests that the Chaffri did this to them."

"Yeah. Right."

All I would need to do, Clive thought, would be to just bring my fist down on the top of his tiny head. Perhaps there were benefits to this size. Though, of course, with those guards and their weapons . . . He didn't doubt that it wouldn't take much for the weapons to be trained on him rather than to protect him as they were now.

"It seems I'm not well liked here," he remarked to the Speaker. "It makes me wonder, yet again, why I would want to help you."

He kept his tone mild, but the Speaker didn't miss the flash of anger in his eyes.

"An unfortunate accident," she began.

Clive shook his head. "I don't think so. What strikes me as particularly odd, however, is how a people so enamored with alien cultures can dislike aliens as much as they do."

"It's not that they perceive you as alien," Speaker Lena said. "It's that they see you as an ally of the Chaffri."

"At this moment," Clive replied, giving the captain Cavet a hard stare, "I am an ally of neither your enemies, nor you."

Now the anger was reflected in the Speaker's eyes, but it wasn't directed toward Clive.

"Guards," she said, "you will answer directly to me now."

"Speaker," Cavet began.

"You, Captain Cavet, are hereby relieved of duty and under house arrest. You will turn in your weapon and remain at your apartment until a board of inquiry has been convened to judge your actions—actions, I would like to add, that are in direct contravention of your orders. Clive Folliot and his companion are our honored guests." Her gaze raked the remainder of the guard. "You would all do well to remember that."

The men shifted uneasily, not one of them willing to meet her gaze.

"Cavet," she said. "Your weapon."

For one moment Clive was sure the man would refuse, perhaps even use the weapon on the Speaker or himself—guest or no guest—but then slowly he handed it to one of his men. Turning abruptly, he stalked off.

Speaker Lena pointed to one of the guard. "You will go with Cavet to see that he does indeed return to his apartment, and will remain on guard at his door until you are relieved. The rest of you will accompany us."

Respectfully guards held the doors open for them both, following once the Speaker and Clive had entered. This hallway had a completely machinelike appearance. If Annabelle had been with them, she would have described the decor as having the appearance of the innards of a computer. Circuitry and wiring rambled in a bewildering pattern across floors, walls, and ceiling. Banks of tiny red light flashed in confusing patterns. To Clive it was reminiscent of what he'd spied of Guafe's inner workings the times when the cyborg opened one of his bodily panels to make some adjustment or other.

He imagined a cyborg yet larger still than either he or Guafe, a simulacrum as large as a city, and they were walking about inside it. . . .

The idea brought a queasy feeling to his stomach. To allay it, he turned again to his companion.

"I don't think your people's animosity has anything to do with who I am or am not allied with," Clive said as they set off down the corridor.

"No, truly—"

"They see me as a monster," Clive interrupted. "I've seen the look before—it's not easily forgotten."

He didn't add that it had been on his own features when he was first confronted with Shriek or some of the other more alien beings he had previously encountered in the Dungeon. He was not proud of those reactions—not now, when he realized how true those same alien beings had proved to be, time and again.

He thought again of Mrs. Shelley's novel, and that monstrous creation of the doctor that wreaked such havoc in its pages. The monster hadn't been evil of itself—rather, it had been driven to its evil actions by the wrongs committed to it. Considering his own feelings when confronted by the crowd in the Hub, he saw how easily such a point of view could be acquired.

"A monster," he repeated.

He turned to look at the Speaker. When she wouldn't meet his gaze, he nodded to himself.

"My people are enamored with alien cultures," she said finally. "Unfortunately, they hate the aliens themselves for having those cultures where they have none."

"And you?" Clive asked. "Do you hate as well?"

Speaker Lena glanced briefly at him, then pointed to the walls. "This was patterned after a cyborg race—related, perhaps, to your companion Guafe—who created a culture of their own in a derelict space station near the planet of Elex. Elex itself was devastated by a nuclear holocaust two centuries ago, as you count time. . . ."

Clive shut her explanation off and thought instead of his missing companions. He prayed that they were in more fortunate circumstances than he and Chang had found themselves, though he doubted that would be the case.

They were all mad—Ren and Chaffri and whoever else was in charge of this Dungeon. He didn't want to help them. Not for a moment.

All he wanted was to bring them to their knees for what they had done to him, to his family and friends, and then be done with them all. For that he needed to be patient a while longer.

But patience was a virtue that he found harder and harder to embrace with each moment he spent in the Dungeon.

∎ CHAPTER TEN ∎

Annabelle didn't even have time to activate her Baal-bec before the Baptists were upon her. In moments she was knocked to the ground, her arms pinned. Coarse ropes were unwound from Baptists' waists to tie her hands together behind her back, then she was dragged to her feet.

Weaponless as he was, Smythe hadn't had a chance either. Only Finnbogg put up a decent struggle, taking out a half dozen of the bare-chested Baptists before he too was overwhelmed. When they finally tied him, it was with enough ropes to hold a half-dozen men, but still the dwarf bristled and snarled at them.

"Don't hear you mouthing off much now," John J. said. "All I see is a slit who's going to learn her place—like the Good Lord made her to. Don't matter how much you hate me, 'cause it ain't going to change a thing."

Annabelle glared at him. He'd removed his shades since leaving the club to reveal the eyes of a fanatic. The Bible-thumpers back home could be fanatics as well, but at least most of them were pretty conservative. You'd never catch a real Southern Baptist in the getups of the Prophet's followers, running in street gangs like LA homeboys, looking brain dead instead of religiously inspired.

These Baptists seemed more secular than born-again, for all the Prophet's rhetoric. They were just a bunch of bad-news crazies. Capable of just about anything.

Where did the Dungeonmasters dig these guys up?

Probably didn't, she realized. It was the Dungeon that did this to them.

So should she feel some empathy for John J. and his merry men?

Not bloody likely.

Because whatever John J. had planned for them, Annabelle didn't doubt that it'd be more along the lines of the Inquisition than a Bible meeting. It was hard to feel empathy for somebody who was about to go pogoing on your bones.

John J. peered more closely at her, laughter dancing in his eyes at her impotent fury.

"Heaven has no room for hatred," he told her.

"Do tell. Then how're you getting in?"

He laughed. "I've been there and back again, slit. I'm John the Baptist, born again."

"Yeah? So what's the *J* stand for? Jerk?"

Real bright, Annie B., she told herself as he cuffed her across the face. It was an openhanded blow, but it struck her hard enough to knock her to her knees and make her ears ring.

Finnbogg growled fiercely, deep in his chest, but the Prophet simply ignored the dwarf. He grabbed Annabelle by the lapels of her jacket and hauled her back to her feet.

"Look," he said.

He steered her toward the end of the alley. Other Baptists brought Smythe and a snarling Finnbogg along.

"Do you see where your mockery of the Lord brings you?" John J. asked.

Annabelle stared at the cross the gang had erected directly opposite the club's entranceway. There were dozens more Baptists gathered around it, many of them holding aloft torches that made shadows flicker on the cross. The smell of gasoline was strong in the air.

As they stepped from the alley, the Prophet gave a signal. A Baptist touched his torch to the cross, and the gas-soaked wood burst into flame; then the three captives were brought close enough to feel the heat blistering at their skin.

"Do you have any faith at all?" John J. asked her. He used an orator's voice now to speak above the crackle of the flames.

"Because if you do, you're about to become a martyr to it, slit. When the Baptists call you to prayer, y'see, you either pray, or you burn in hell. Now I know that sometimes the odd mistake gets made, so just to make sure that you don't get accidentally shuffled out of purgatory, I'd like to make sure you get a taste of the flames as you're heading on your way."

Annabelle couldn't believe this was happening to them. After all they'd come through on the previous levels of the Dungeon, to be burned at the stake by this bunch of losers seemed the most unfair fate of all.

She swallowed dryly. Well, she'd be damned if she'd give them any satisfaction.

"Real . . . thoughtful of you," she said.

The Prophet shook his head admiringly. "Unrepentant to the end—I like that in a martyr. Tell me—do you hear voices at all? Have you seen visions?"

"Screw you," Annabelle told him, and spat in his face.

That earned her another cuff.

"Okay," John J. said. "Fun's over. Throw 'em in, boys, starting with the slit."

Finnbogg howled and strained at his bonds. With so much attention suddenly trained upon the dwarf, Smythe chose that moment to act. He'd remained so passive that the Baptists had thought him thoroughly cowed. He had played the part of an utter coward, trembling and shaking, his entire carriage that of a smaller man, fearful of his own shadow, never mind the Baptists.

As Finnbogg struggled madly in his bonds, actually snapping a few of the ropes, Smythe moved suddenly, breaking the grips of the two men restraining him. Before they could recover, he threw himself at Annabelle, butting his head at her chest.

The blow broke her free of the hands that had been holding her captive and sent her stumbling toward the flames before any of the Baptists could carry out John J.'s order. With the heat of the fire right in her face, Annabelle backpedaled furiously. She ducked the grasping arms of the Prophet's followers, getting far enough away from the burning cross so that the Baptists' leader was between her and the flames.

Cursing, John J. grabbed at her himself.

"Sidi," Tomàs cried in a harsh whisper. "We can't let them die."

The Indian nodded. "We will work our way closer."

"But the guards . . ."

"Let me deal with the guards."

Sidi rose from their hiding place. Crouching low, he moved forward across the cracked pavement like a ghost. The nearest Baptist guard, attention on the action near the burning cross, never had a chance.

Not against what Sidi was.

When he first began to question the more orthodox Hindu beliefs in which he'd been raised, Sidi had briefly become involved with a sect of Phansigars and trained with them until he realized that life as one of Kali's Thugees was not what he was looking for either. But he had appreciated the skill of using one's body to its fullest—of the combination of meditation and physical training that made both mind and body, and hence one's spirit, strong.

So he looked to other belief systems that combined the two. When he finally embraced Taoism, he trained in one of their esoteric martial arts schools until he was adept, not only with the sacred weapons, but in *muto* as well—the art of fighting without weapons, where one used everything, and nothing, to bring about victory in combat.

When he was so close he could have reached out and touched the guard, Sidi rose suddenly to his feet. The heel of his hand struck the guard across the throat, breaking his windpipe. As the guard fell, the Indian grasped his hair, jerking the man's head back and snapping his neck. Slowly he lowered the corpse to the ground and checked the man for weapons, coming up with a knife that had a ten-inch blade, edge honed sharp as a razor. Thrusting the knife into his sash, he moved still closer to the burning cross, keeping to the shadows just beyond the light thrown by the flames.

A second and then a third guard fell to his silent attacks. He collected their weapons as well, passing one to Tomàs as the Portuguese and Nacky joined him. They were now close enough to the cross to see that the Baptists had captured three of their missing companions—Annabelle, Smythe, and Finnbogg.

"What now?" Tomàs breathed in Sidi's ear.

What now? Sidi weighed the odds, but no matter what plan of action he considered, there were simply too many of the Baptists for them to deal with. With only the knives he had taken from the men he'd killed, they might as well still be weaponless. Yet to leave their friends . . . that was unthinkable.

They needed to divide the Baptists' forces. If they could create a diversion . . .

He turned to Tomàs, a plan beginning to form in his mind. But just then Finnbogg went mad. Bound as he was, the dwarf fought his captors all the same. The ropes that bound him were snapping free, and the Baptists fell upon him with fist and toe. Sidi watched as Smythe used his own guards' momentary loss of attention to butt Annabelle in the chest with his head, knocking her toward the flames. Annabelle spun away from the fire, but then the leader of the Baptists reached for her.

There was no time to create a diversion, Sidi realized. There was time now only to act.

Without a word to his companions he drew his two stolen knives from his sash and charged into the melee, cutting at the Baptists with a blade in each hand.

If Neville and his party didn't have quite so many enemies to deal with, the two that they did have more than made up for their lack in numbers by the sheer bulk of their size.

Hurt as the giant twins were, all their mad humor had left them. They appeared now to be a pair of mobile mountains—two great heaps of flesh with but one objective, and that was to eliminate their tormentors. But while their humor had vanished, their madness had not, for they were singing as they pounded their way through the tunnels.

"Here we go . . ."

". . . round the . . ."

". . . mulberry bush . . ."

The children's song took on a hellish quality, for they sang in time to their monstrous tread, their voices high and shrieking, the volume making the tunnels rattle and Neville's ears ache. Whenever they came to the final line of the refrain, they shouted it in unison—

"ALL! FALL! DOWN!"

—stamping their feet in time.

And indeed, sections of the tunnels did fall down, in ever larger clouds of debris.

Shriek ran alongside the silver that bore Neville and Alyssa. She had caught hold of the hind bow of its saddle, but while the silver helped her keep up, what with two riders and the arachnid leaning on it more and more, the poor beast was falling well behind those of the other Tuan.

And the giants were rapidly catching up.

Shriek, Neville told her. *You must let go.*

The arachnid's weariness was apparent in the tone of her reply. *Yes, Being Neville. There is no reason that we should all three of us die.*

Neville gripped her hand before she could let go of the saddle. *I don't mean that!* he told her. *You have to get ahead of us, if you can. Far enough ahead of those monsters to stretch your web across the tunnel so that we can go under it, but it will trip them.*

A fine plan—but I have not the strength.

Then find it, Neville told her, his voice ringing harshly in her mind, *or lie down and die now.*

Shriek's head snapped up. For all her alien features Neville could read the rage in her eyes. He lifted his hand from where it had gripped hers.

Go on, he said. *After all you've been through—give it all up to the likes of them.*

He nodded to their rear where the giants followed, still singing their mad children's song.

". . . mulberry bush . . ."

". . . mulberry bush . . ."

"ALL! FALL! DOWN!"

The ground quivered underfoot as though shaken by an earthquake.

Shriek glanced back. *Damn . . . you . . . Being Neville. . . .*

She let go and darted ahead. Where she found the necessary strength, Neville couldn't even guess, unless it was fueled by her anger at him—and that was exactly why he'd spoken as he had. He just hoped that they would survive so that he could explain it to her.

But Shriek had already guessed it for herself. Her new strength came not from the anger that she'd initially felt, but from another source entirely. She had secreted a concentrated dose of what worked as adrenaline in her alien physiology into one of her hair spikes, then injected it into herself. It gave her the necessary stamina—but it was a highly dangerous action, for it could easily burn out her nervous system as well.

But for now she was running as she had never run before, gaining on the other Tuan, then passing them. When she was well ahead of even the foremost of the Tuan, with the sound of the giants' pursuit considerably lessened, she flung herself at a wall, spinnerets creating silk at many times their normal rate.

She attached the thread to that wall, leapt across the tunnel to the other, pulling the thread high and taut just before the first of the Tuan rode under it. Back she went again, then across once more. By the time she'd attached the third thread to the wall, she could no longer move.

All she could give, she had given.

She collapsed against the wall, her body's reserves of strength drained and used up. She wasn't sure if three threads would be enough, but it was all she could do. She let her mind go blank.

Clouds of stone dust covered her at the approach of the giants. Neville and Alyssa passed her, not needing to duck under the thread as she'd fastened them high enough to let them get easily by. Neither of them saw either the thread, or Shriek, where she lay with her limbs splayed out.

". . . mulberry bush . . ."

". . . mulberry bush . . ."

The giants came, with their shrieking voices and thundering tread. The foot of the first snagged on the thread. It pulled, stretched, far, and farther, almost to its breaking point. . . .

But it held.

And the first giant went sprawling out the length of the tunnel. His twin saw the danger, but he was moving too quickly to stop himself. The resulting impact when they both hit, first one, then the other, brought half the roof down on top of them.

Neville and Alyssa had pulled up as they saw the giant falling.

"All fall down," Neville said with a hard smile.

They braced themselves for the crash, but nothing could have prepared them for its violence. They were both thrown from the back of their silver, Neville cushioning the Tuan as best he could.

The ground shook with long, tumultuous tremors. Parts of the tunnel collapsed all around them. The air filled with dust, so thick they choked and were blinded. When the dust finally began to clear, they could see the two giants, one on top of the other. The bottom one had cracked open his head when he fell. The one on top had a length of sharp rock embedded in the back of his skull.

Dead, the pair of them. And half-buried in a makeshift cairn that was more than either of them deserved, Neville thought.

He rose shakily to his feet and helped Alyssa to stand. The other Tuan returned, Fenil catching Alyssa's frightened silver and calming it as they all regarded the dead monsters.

"We've Shriek to thank for our rescue," Neville said, "both when the giants first attacked, and now for their death."

Alyssa nodded. She turned to look for Shriek amongst her company but couldn't find her.

"Where is she?" the Tuan leader asked.

Fenil pointed toward the giants and the rubble that almost covered them. "The last I saw of her was back there—when she was setting the trip wire for the giants. . . ."

Neville gazed bleakly at the mess.

Shriek, he called. *Shriek!*

There was no reply.

Shriek!

He reached out with his mind but could not find that familiar neural web by which he knew the arachnid's mind.

"If she was caught under that," Alyssa began.

She didn't finish, but Neville knew what she left unspoken. If Shriek had been caught under that rubble, she was dead now. There was no possible way she could have survived.

But he refused to believe it.

By the light of their torches it was hard to see if the tunnel was completely blocked now or not. But it didn't matter. He'd dig through it, if he had to. He started back toward the bodies of the giants and began to climb the rubble.

After a moment Fenil, then Alyssa, climbed up behind him.

Guafe was easy to spy in the dining hall when Clive and Speaker Lena finally arrived. He was on the far side of the room, his metalplated head and eyes rising above the crowd. For though he sat on his haunches, he still reared taller than either of the two techs who shared the table with him.

To Clive the hall had the appearance of a large restaurant, but one entirely devoid of even the simplest decor. There were perhaps half a hundred tables, at which sat various of the Ren, each of them dressed alike, the food colorless and bland in appearance, their plates and cutlery all identical, giving the entire place an antiseptic air. It seemed more like the laboratories Clive had seen on previous levels than a place in which to have a meal.

All conversation halted as he and the Speaker stepped through the door, but here, unlike the Hub, the Ren merely returned to their meals after a long, curious gaze at the second giant in their midst. Their scrutiny brought a flush to Clive's cheek, and he forced himself not to fidget under their gazes, matching their curiosity with a calm disregard. He was only partially successful.

The Speaker led Clive to the table where the others were waiting for them.

"Are you hungry?" she asked Clive.

She indicated an area on the far side of the room where various Ren were filling trays with foodstuffs displayed under glass coverings. It all had the same unappetizing appearance.

Clive shook his head. "Only for answers."

The techs sitting with Guafe were the same pair that had seen to the equipment when the Speakers were initially questioning Clive and Guafe. The female was named Chary, Clive remembered. The male was now introduced to him as Howell. It was the male who addressed their immediate problem.

"We've isolated the discrepancy," he told the Speaker, "between our records of the subjects and their actual physical appearance."

"And?"

"It has to do with the mirror the Chaffri used to send them to this level."

"I see."

"Well, I don't," Clive said.

He felt irritable and awkward crouching by the table. It made him feel as though he were visiting children in their playhouse, all the furnishings scaled down to half his size. The surreptitious glances he was continually given by the Ren at the other tables only heightened his discomfort.

"It appears," Guafe explained, "that the device used to bring us here—the mirror we stepped through—was in fact a teleportation mechanism that utilizes a form of molecular disruption to transfer physical objects over great distances. It's because it hadn't been coded to our particular party that we ended up arriving in different places—and, in our case, a different size."

"The others have been found, then?" Clive asked eagerly.

Chary shook her head. "But we're working on it. What we can do now is put you through a properly coded teleporter and return you to your normal size."

"By sending us where?"

Chary laughed. "It won't be necessary to send you anywhere. The whole procedure can be done in one of our labs."

"There'll be no danger," Howell added.

Well, that would be half their problems solved, Clive thought. But he wondered—could they trust the Ren not to teleport them into some new, worse danger while supposedly "helping" them through this problem?

He wished he could take Guafe aside to discuss it with him, but there didn't appear to be much opportunity for privacy in the Ren city. More troubling was how comfortable the cyborg appeared with their captors. It was true that these two were mechanics, and so able to answer the questions thrown up by Guafe's insatiable curiosity; but all the same they appeared to be getting along too well for Clive's liking.

Because he remembered . . .

Try to put it from his mind though he did, he couldn't forget that chessboard he'd seen, before stepping through the mirror, and the two traitorous playing pieces.

Guafe and Sidi Bombay.

If they *were* working with the Dungeonmasters . . .

Clive shook his head. It had to have been just another trick of the Dungeonmasters—just something else to throw him off his stride—of that he was sure.

Wasn't he?

"If it'll make you feel any better," Chary told him, "I'll step through with you—just to prove that there's no danger."

Was his face that easy to read?

Clive sighed and nodded stiffly. "That would do much to set my mind at ease."

"Your other questions—" Speaker Lena began.

"Can wait, I think," Guafe broke in. "Don't you think, Clive? I for one would prefer to conduct any further conversation on a more equal footing."

To stop being a freak in the eyes of the Ren, to stop feeling that his smallest movement would create the same disaster as a bull let loose in a lady's sitting room? Much as Clive wanted answers to all the troubling questions, he could not agree more.

"First this teleportation device," he said, "but then" —he glanced meaningfully at the Speaker—"some answers."

Speaker Lena nodded. "We will help you in any way we can, Clive. Though you still don't trust us, I assure you—we share the same foes. The danger they represent is enormous. They must be stopped, but neither of us can do it on our own. We need your help, as you need ours. And time is running out for all of us."

■ CHAPTER ELEVEN ■

As the Prophet grabbed her, Annabelle realized just what it was that Horace had been up to. He'd activated the controls of the Baalbec A-9 in her bodice—the controls she couldn't reach herself because her hands were tied behind her back.

With the protective device operative, the leader of the Baptists was bounced away as soon as he laid a hand on her. He was flung backward, knocking over a can of gasoline as he was driven straight into the burning cross. The spilled gasoline ignited with a thundering whoosh.

Wide-eyed, Annabelle saw the Prophet go up in flames.

He howled—a raw, wailing cry that didn't seem human. Staggering from the fire, he was a flaming pyre in human form. He came straight for Annabelle, arms outspread.

She backed away. No matter how much she'd wished him dead, she hadn't wanted this. No one deserved to die like this.

Watching their leader burn, the Baptists were all frozen for a long moment—long enough for Finnbogg to snap the last of his bonds in a sudden frenzy of desperate strength. John J. lurched forward, two, three more steps, then collapsed, the howl of his pain fading to a whining shriek. Then dying completely.

They all stared at the black thing lying there in the light of the flames. It was difficult to believe that it had once been human. The raw smell of burnt meat filled the air. Then the full understanding of just what had happened to their leader settled among the Baptists.

The momentary tableau dissolved into an out-and-out melee.

The Baptists fell upon their captives, but their attack came a little late. Adrenaline pumping through her, Annabelle watched the world fall apart for the gang members.

Finnbogg was on them like a werewolf from one of the old Hammer flicks that Chrissie Nunn—the keyboard player from her lost band—used to watch over and over again. He was all tooth and fang—a literal killing machine that the disoriented Baptists found impossible to contain this time.

One of the gang members came at her, a long, wicked blade in his fist, but her Baalbec flung him back against his companions. Two more attacked Smythe. Annabelle ran toward him—Baptists flung away on either side of her as they tried to grab her—but knew she was going to be too late. The knives were slashing out. Horace was going to die. . . .

But then a familiar figure was there, a knife in either hand, cutting down the Baptists, taking time to slice through Smythe's bonds before he spun away to where the gang members were thickest.

Sidi!

Annabelle couldn't believe it. The frigging cavalry had arrived.

She saw Tomàs as well, in the crowd, holding his own against the Baptists as he fought his way to her side. He started to reach out toward her wrists to cut her free.

"Don't!" she cried. "The Baalbec!"

The Portuguese hesitated, then nodded, turning to help Smythe, who was waging an unequal battle with another pair of Baptists.

They were going to do it, Annabelle thought. Jesus, they were really going to take the bastards down.

She looked for the others of their party—Clive and Shriek and the rest—but saw only a small, feral-looking child. A Baptist came at her, and the girl kicked him in the groin. When he doubled over, she hit him on the back of the head with the length of pipe she was carrying, laughing delightedly as though this were only a game.

Where was everybody else? Annabelle wondered.

She'd have to worry about that later, she realized, as another Baptist threw himself at her only to be flung away by the Baalbec for his trouble. Annabelle grinned at the stunned look on the man's face, but the grin faltered when she realized that the Baptists were recovering from their initial disorientation. They had backed away to form a half circle that enclosed the six of them—Smythe and Tomàs; Sidi, Finnbogg, the feral child, and herself.

Behind them was the cross. Behind it the front of a building, its windows set too high in its walls for them to get through, the doorway blocked.

"Okay, mothers," the foremost of the Baptists shouted. "You had your fun. But you don't kill a Prophet and live to brag about it. No way. No *way!*"

By the light of the burning cross Annabelle realized that the man actually had tears in his eyes.

"You got to pay," he went on. "You got to *pay!*"

The Baptists roared in unison—a loud, wordless cry that held all their anger and despair. They lifted fists in the air, and the night air bristled with knives, clubs, and makeshift weapons.

"Oh, Jesus," Annabelle muttered.

She moved to the front of her small group.

"Don't, Annabelle," Sidi said.

She gave him a quick, small smile. "At least they can't touch me," she said. "I'm going to buy you some time—so get moving. Just take one of those alleys on either side of the building and get out of here!"

Her companions merely ranged themselves at her side.

"We'll chew them to pieces," Finnbogg growled.

"Yeah, right. With the odds still four to one we're really going to make a statement." She glanced at

Smythe. "Horace, you've got some sense—get everybody out of here."

Smythe merely shook his head. "We're in this together."

The Baptists were still working themselves up to attack. Any moment now, Annabelle thought, and it's going to be game over.

"Sidi?"

"I've just found you again and you expect me to leave?"

Annabelle sighed.

"This is your friend?" the feral child asked the Indian.

Sidi nodded.

"How come no one cuts her loose?"

Before Annabelle could explain about the Baalbec, the Baptists' cries rose to a sudden crescendo.

"Heads up," Annabelle said, "here they come."

And come they would have, if the big boom of a handgun hadn't cracked across the Baptists' cries. All gazes turned to the source of the sound.

"Hole-lee," Annabelle said.

It was a real cavalry.

Ranged in a long, ragged line in front of Casey's were the members of the Airplane and a half-dozen other bands. Casey himself stood in the center, with the old wino Jake on one side of him and Jack Casady on the other. It was Casady who'd fired the gun. Here and there Annabelle spotted other handguns in the hands of some of the musicians.

One of the Baptists took a step toward the club, and a long-haired man that Annabelle vaguely recognized as belonging to some late sixties, early seventies band, leveled his weapon and fired, dropping the Baptist in his tracks.

What did Casey do? Annabelle wondered. Call up the whole pack of GBCers he had? And where had they got the weapons? Better still, why hadn't they given her group any?

That was easy to answer, she realized. Her group was

going on and might be able to pick up gear wherever they went, but Casey and his people were stuck here and needed whatever they had just to survive.

"Okay," Casey cried. "It ends here."

Beside him Casady waved his .44 automatic, the silver weapon glinting in the firelight. "Anybody have a problem with that?" he asked.

The remaining Baptists muttered, but none of them seemed ready to take it any further.

"Now you boys are going to wait right out here with us," Casey went on, "while our friends head on their way. Where they're going, they won't be back, so this thing's over—everybody agree?"

Finally one of the Baptists spoke up. "Yeah? And what about the Prophet?"

Standing beside Jake, a bare-chested man in leather pants and long dark hair smiled grimly. "Well, that's what you get when you play with fire."

Annabelle blinked when she recognized the man. Jim Morrison. Her mother was forever playing his albums.

"It's got to end right here and now," Casey said. "One way or another."

The man who'd shot the Baptist a few moments ago patted his handgun meaningfully.

"Okay." The Baptist who'd been doing all the talking put his knife away in its boot sheath.

Casey and Jack Casady came across to where Annabelle and the others were standing, circling around the Baptists.

"You saved our asses," Annabelle said, looking at Casady. "Again."

Casady laughed. "Like I told the man inside, you got to take care of your people, and seeing how Casey tells me you're a player too, well, hell. We're supposed to let them get away with this kind of thing?"

"Well, thanks."

"You remember the way I told you to go?" Casey asked.

Annabelle nodded. "Just let me get these ropes off."

Sidi went to cut her free, but Tomàs caught him by the arm.

"Remember her device, *amigo,*" he said.

"Just give me a sec' here," Annabelle said.

She went over to where the remains of a street sign stood poking up out of a thicket of weeds. Leaning over, she pressed the Baalbec's control against the end of the sign, shutting the device off.

"Okay," she said. She turned around and offered up her hands. "Who's going to do the honors?"

When Sidi had cut her free, she took the time to give him a hug before rubbing at her chafed wrists.

"I hate to push," Casey said, "but you've got to get moving. We're holding them now, but just looking at you long enough's going to make them think, what the hell. The next thing you know, they'll have a go at us anyway."

"You'll be all right?" Smythe asked him.

"No problem—trust me. Just get going before the shit hits the fan again."

"I'll go with you a ways," Casady said.

Annabelle glanced at Casey's pocket where she knew he kept the GBCs that had called up the various musicians in the first place.

"I thought . . ." she began.

"That's right," Casady said. "If we don't play, we just fade away." He smiled. "But it's no big deal. We just end up back in the cards, so many digitized bits of data, until we get called up again."

"But . . ."

"It bothers people around us way more than it bothers a GBCer. Now, c'mon. Let's go before Casey pops a vein."

He led off. With a final wave to Casey and a nervous look at the Baptist, Annabelle and the others followed. Once they were out of sight of the gang members and the burning cross, she and Sidi filled each other in on what had happened since they'd each stepped through the mirror.

"You haven't seen anything of the rest of them?" she asked.

"Nothing of Clive?" Smythe asked almost at the same time.

Sidi shook his head.

Annabelle looked back the way they'd come. "Christ, I hope they landed in a safer place than we did."

There was enough room at the top of the heap of fallen stone that covered the giants for Neville and his two companions to squeeze through. By the light of their torches they searched for Shriek. When they finally found her, lying where she'd fallen, limbs splayed loosely about her and covered in stone dust, Neville feared the worst.

He scrambled up to where she lay, blinking away the sudden dampness that blurred his sight.

Shriek?

He searched for her mind, but there was still no reply. The neural web joining the two of them was gone as though it had never existed.

"Damn them," Neville said. His voice had a strangled sound to it. "Damn the Dungeonmasters, and damn their bloody games."

Alyssa stood beside him, looking down at Shriek's body, and laid her hand on his shoulder. "Is she dead?"

Neville nodded.

"Are you sure?" Fenil asked.

Dangerous lights flickered in Neville's eyes as he looked up at the Tuan. "What's *that* supposed to mean?"

Alyssa's fingers tightened on his shoulder. "We are all friends here, Neville."

Fenil nodded. "Her body—it's so different from ours. . . . I was wondering if perhaps, when her kind is hurt, they withdraw into themselves to make their healing easier."

Neville thought then of his travels in India and Africa, of the fakirs and shaman he had met and the things they could do with their bodies. Some could slow down their bodies' metabolisms to such an extent that they appeared dead—even to the closest scrutiny.

He looked back down at Shriek again.

Is that it? he asked. *Have you taken yourself away to heal?*

When he thought of the effort it must have taken for her to get as far ahead of their party as she had to set the trip wire, of the terrible toll it must have taken . . .

But she lay stiff and silent. Unresponsive.

Perhaps he wasn't focusing his mind properly. He recalled the exact order of events when Shriek had first opened the neural web between them—and remembered something of importance. It had begun with physical contact. Her chitinous skin touching his in a hand grasp.

He laid a hand on either side of her head and bent over her until his forehead rested against her own. Closing his eyes, he sought the web again.

Shriek . . . ?

There was still no response. But now, far off in the darkness behind his closed lids—a darkness that was a mental realm, rather than a physical one, he quickly realized—he thought he saw a glimmer of movement. A spark that flickered in the endless dark, teasing and distant.

He narrowed the focus of his searching thoughts and sent them deeper into the darkness, pursuing that flickering spark. It fled away from him, so that he never drew any closer to it, no matter how quickly he pursued it.

But he refused to give in. He kept at it, forcing his thoughts to follow the spark. He lost all sense of his body where it crouched in the tunnel above hers. When the last sense of contact with his physical form slipped away, he suddenly gained on the spark.

His thoughts, fueled by that success, increased their speed until he was upon the spark, hard on its heels, then close enough to touch. He grabbed at it, and the darkness melted away in a flare of blinding light that stunned him.

He had the abrupt sense of vertigo—as though he were falling for miles through the heart of a star. Try though he did to stop his plummeting descent, the fall had all the unyielding grip of gravity running its course. When it finally ended, it was through no effort of his own, but because he had come to the end of his passage.

The blinding light dimmed to normal lighting. He found himself occupying the semblance of a body—his own body—standing on an alien landscape. The sky was a deep orange all about him, the land a place of flat gray expanses, dotted with odd purple-and-blue growths. And in front of him, creating a massive silk web between two upright black stones that had all the look of the ancient stoneworks in Neville's own England, was Shriek.

For long moments Neville could make no sound. His throat was constricted and dry. The alien quality of the landscape left him with a sense of both estrangement and an odd reverence. It was as though to speak here would be as disrespectful as carousing would be in a cathedral.

But finally he spoke all the same.

". . . Shriek . . . ?"

At first he thought the arachnid hadn't heard him. She continued to weave her giant web, spinnerets producing the silk, her limbs drawing it forth and setting each strand in place with an assuredness that was both aesthetic and mechanical, all at once. It was only when he was about to call her name again that she finally halted her work and turned to regard him.

There was an odd look on her features—almost, Neville thought, as though she didn't recognize him. Then she smiled.

Being Neville. What are you doing in my death dream?

"Your what?"

My death dream. Before the spirits of my people

vacate their physical forms, they come to this holy place to make a pattern of their dying with the threads of their life and weave it as a remembrance of what was, but will be no more. This realm exists in our communal mind. Some of our Wise have seen it in visions, but most of us view it only at the time of our death dream.

It was an odd concept, but no odder than many they'd come across in the Dungeon, Neville thought. No odder than many of the conceits of the various peoples who lived on his homeworld. Heaven and hell. Reincarnation. Karma. There were as many theories of what lay beyond life as there were cultures.

But here, at this moment, Neville wasn't interested in hearing any of it. He didn't want to hear Shriek speak of her dying. He wanted her alive and walking beside him, searching out their comrades, bringing their final judgment on the Dungeonmasters when they eventually caught up with them—as catch up to them Neville was determined they would.

For that to occur—for any of it to occur—he had to bring Shriek back with him. However that might be done.

"But you're not dead," he said.

He felt her smile in his mind. There was a beatific quality about her presence on the neural web.

I must be, she said, *or why would I be in my death dream?*

Neville thought quickly. Perhaps she was, but he wouldn't let her stay here. Not when there was a chance to bring her back. Only where to begin? How to convince her? For he saw that it was a matter of her point of view that had brought her to this place. If he could only convince her that she still lived . . .

And then he had it.

"It's another trick of the Dungeonmasters," he said. "Another play in their damnable game."

I don't think so, Being Neville. I have been in danger before, but never have I been in this place before today. I must be dead.

"Then am I dead too?"

That brought a puzzled look to her features. *I* . . .

"And if I am dead, then why am I here—in your afterlife, rather than in my own?"

You . . . Her shock passed like an electrical spark from her mind to his own. *You are inside my mind . . . ?*

Neville nodded. "I came to bring you back."

You don't understand. If you are here when the Gatherer comes to take me, you will be taken with me.

"I can't leave. I don't know the way back by myself. Show me the road."

But the Gatherer has already been summoned. I can feel Her breath on the wind.

There *was* a noticeable cooling of the air, Neville realized. He looked to the east and saw a darkness spreading across the orange sky.

"Quickly!" he cried. "Come back with me."

Shriek sadly shook her head. *Too late, Being Neville. The Gatherer comes because I've summoned her. My life web is almost done. She will take me home now—to the Beyond Beyond. And She will take you with me. . . .*

Neville looked at the eastern sky again. The darkness was spreading. And now he saw, in that blackness, a sense of enormous eyes, a cavernous mouth.

"Shriek," he said. "We must leave now."

Too late, too late, Shriek sighed.

The darkness was almost upon them now. Neville searched for some tie to his body, but the thread that bound him to his physical form was gone. He'd hoped, as a final measure if he couldn't talk her into coming back with him, to simply grab Shriek and use that thread to take them back to where their bodies waited for them.

But now he couldn't even return himself.

The darkness swallowed the orange skies until everything went a flat black. Only Shriek's web and the arachnid herself glimmered with a soft luminescence like phosphorus shimmering on water. Neville lifted his own hand before his face and saw that he too was glowing.

And then the Gatherer was there.

The only difference between the laboratory to which the Ren brought Guafe and Clive and the restaurant they had quit was that it had a banked wall of electrical equipment and other devices, and a huge mirror that was set a few feet out from another wall. Otherwise, it had the same sterile environment—white walls, expressionless Ren lab techs in their colorless suits—with nothing of a personal or cultural nature to be seen, no matter where one looked.

What made the lab yet more sterile, to Clive's way of thinking, was the bewildering maze of corridors that had led them to it—a stunning mishmash of alien cultures that Speaker Lena explained was a duplicate of a marketing satellite that served as a trade center for a number of space-faring races in a solar system far from the one in which the Dungeon was situated.

Clive was merely relieved to step from the confusion of stolen cultural artifacts in the corridors into the relative sanity of the lab.

"This'll just take a moment," Chary said as she went to confer with the techs. "I have to input our neural and physical characteristics."

Clive studied the mirror while they waited for her, a calm expression fixed determinedly on his features.

"I can go through first," Guafe said. "I rather relish the novelty of the experience. Knowing what to expect, I can study the changes as they occur."

"I'll be fine," Clive said.

But he couldn't stop the small twitch of uncertainty that arose in him at the cyborg's words. Of course Chang wasn't worried—not if he was allied with the Ren as the chessboard on the last level had seemed to indicate.

It was an unfair assumption of distrust, Clive knew, but it wouldn't leave him. Because what did he really know about the cyborg? Lord help him, what did he know of any of his companions, truly?

Annabelle had some physical resemblance to his lover Annabella Leighton, but he had no real proof that they *were* in fact related.

Smythe had been acting most oddly from when he first contacted Clive on the ship from England, disguised as a mandarin.

Sidi Bombay had appeared out of the African night— as if from nowhere. Perhaps from the Dungeon itself?

Neville . . . Neville was his twin, it was true, but with all the replicas that the Dungeonmasters could create, how could he ever be sure that the man wearing his form was truly his brother?

And the others. Shriek, Finnbogg, Tomàs . . . all he knew of them was what they had told him of themselves and how they had conducted themselves since they'd begun to travel together.

God help him, they could all be his enemies.

But this was exactly what the Dungeonmasters wanted, wasn't it? For some unfathomable reason they delighted in breeding mistrust amongst allies. Clive had the feeling that if he could simply understand some small aspect of the riddle—why they felt the need to foment this distrust, what was the importance of the Folliots—that the entire mystery of the Dungeon would begin to unravel for him.

Speaker Lena claimed they should be allies, that they could help each other. Would whatever responses she gave to his questions help solve the greater puzzle? Or would they make matters worse?

"Clive?"

Clive blinked at the mention of his name to see that Chary had returned from her conference with the techs and was waiting for him. She offered him her hand.

"We should remain in physical contact," she said. "It's not absolutely necessary, but it does make for a smoother run-through."

Clive shook his head. "That won't be necessary." He

walked toward the mirror and studied it without really taking in his own reflection. "What do I do? Just . . . ah, step through?"

"It's as simple as that," the male tech Howell said.

"You'll feel a moment of disorientation," Chary added, "but it won't last long. You'll be back here in just a few seconds."

Clive nodded. Steeling himself, he stepped toward the reflective surface, shivering as he passed through.

A momentary sense of vertigo caught hold of him. Warned to expect it, Clive still felt panic come bubbling up inside him. He reached out with those mental muscles awakened in Shriek's neural web, and a sudden wrenching sensation shook him, immediately followed by an unnatural calmness.

He felt as though he were floating in a vast gray sea. He held his hand in front of him but could see nothing. Only the grayness. The unending sea that spread out from him in all directions. The grayness both in which he floated and of which he was a part.

If he had a hand, if he even had a body anymore, in this strange sea it was invisible to his sight.

The Ren had said nothing of this.

The sense of calm that the grayness had given him began to unravel.

What if the source of this place was something other than the Ren?

He called out, not with a physical voice, for all sense of body was gone, but with a voiceless cry that went winging off into the grayness on the neural web.

And he was answered.

Not by Shriek. Not by any of his other companions who had shared her neural web with him. Not even by du Maurier. But he knew who it was all the same.

The voice that rang inside his mind—that flexed the invisible muscles of the gossamer spider's web that was now his mind—was one he would never forget.

It was the bodiless voice of the maze. The voice that had come to him but twice in his life—

No, he realized. He had heard it more than twice. He had heard it when—

At that moment the annoying flicker of lost memories returned to Clive in a rush. He remembered, remembered it all. Lord help him, how could he have forgotten?

Falling through the azure blue.

Stolen by the Dungeonmasters to a dream of London.

A dream of Annabella and their life made perfect with his receiving a promotion and therefore being able to propose marriage to her.

A dream that had gone sour when he had seen through its lies.

And then the Dungeonmasters had taken him someplace and erased the memories so that he would not be aware of their machination. Returned him to the blue void of the gate and let him arrive with the others, never realizing what he had experienced.

God, but he hated them.

And that voice he heard now—it had been there as well. He had begun to consider it not so much as an entity in its own right, but rather as the voice of his own subconscious. It had rescued him then.

What did it want of him now?

It is time, that voice said.

Time? Time for what? Clive asked.

Time for you to finish the journey on your own. Your companions—whether they play you true or false—will only hold you back now.

Who are you? Clive demanded.

Silence replied.

Damn you! Stop playing games. If you are one of the Dungeonmasters, then come out and face me like a man.

I am neither Dungeonmaster nor man—not a man as you know the term.

I'm not so easily shocked anymore, Clive replied. *God knows I've seen my share of odd beings since first entering this damned place. So step forward and show yourself.*

Though he fought to hide it, it shook Clive to the very roots of his essence to think that the Dungeonmasters had set him up as one of their gaming pieces from as early a time as his tenth year. For all he knew, from before his birth.

I ask you again, he said. *Name yourself.*

The ensuing silence was long enough that Clive thought the disembodied entity was again refusing to reply. But then a long sigh echoed along the neural web.

Had I lived, had I been born, the voice said, *my name would have been Esmond. Esmond Folliot.*

What!?

When our father's sperm first seeded our mother's egg, we would have been born as triplets. Bearing twins killed her. Had she carried all three of us to term, none of us might have survived, so I, as the youngest, was taken away.

Taken? By whom?

I don't know. I am simply here, in this place. I have been able to watch you both, my two brothers, but rarely has the veil between the worlds been thin enough that I might communicate with either of you.

And what of now? Clive asked. *How did you come to me now?*

I did not come to you, the voice replied. *You came to me—to the place of unborn souls; souls that should have been born, but were not.*

This is madness.

Perhaps. If you had dwelled here all the years I have . . . Perhaps I am mad. But I am still a Folliot. I am still determined that the creators of this place shall not have the better of us.

You know them? Clive asked. *Who are they? What is their purpose for entrapping us and all the others that have come to be imprisoned in this damned place?*

I don't know, Clive. I know only that you must go on alone now. It is in you that the hope of every prisoner of the Dungeon lies. But what you do, you must do alone.

I can't do that. I can't forsake the others.

Your loyalty will be your downfall.

What use winning, Clive asked, *if your method of doing so leaves your life a lie? I am the man I am. You say the hope of the Dungeon's prisoners lies in me. If I go on alone, if I forsake the others, then I will become someone else. Will I still prevail?*

There came a long pause. Then the voice sighed again.

You offer a formidable logic, it said finally.

Are you truly my brother? Clive asked.

Had I been born . . . then, yes. We would have been brothers.

It had to be yet another damnable trick of the Dungeonmasters, Clive thought, for surely this wasn't possible. How could he and Neville have an unborn brother?

But because this was the Dungeon . . . because here the impossible was not only possible, but probable . . .

How can you prove this? he asked.

This is a thing that can be accepted only on faith, the voice replied.

But an unborn brother . . .

He tasted the name in his mind. Esmond. Esmond Folliot. Damned if it didn't ring true.

When the others are safe, the voice asked. *Will you then do as I counsel?*

You'll help me find them?

A sensation very like a mental shaking of a head moved in Clive's mind.

I know only the whereabouts of you and our brother, the voice replied.

Can you at least lead me to him?

I can show you a road on the neural web that can take your thoughts to him.

A glimmering thread appeared in the grayness,

originating in the place where Clive sensed himself to be and leading off into the distance.

You have but to grasp it with your thoughts, the voice told him.

And if Neville's mind was on the end of this thread— what would that prove? Clive asked himself. That the voice was indeed that of an unborn brother named Esmond, or that of a Dungeonmaster with yet another of their mad ploys to play?

Will we speak again? he asked the voice.

I don't know, it replied. *You will have to come to me. Through a mirror?*

There was no reply.

Wait! Clive cried. *Where have you gone?*

Still only silence.

And now the shimmering thread was beginning to fade.

Esmond! Clive tried one last time.

Still no reply, and now the thread was nothing more than a ghost, fading swiftly.

He caught it with his thoughts and let the thread pull him away, deeper and deeper into the gray.

• CHAPTER TWELVE •

Both Jack Casady and the feral child, who was introduced to them as Nacky, knew the way to a secret route leading to the underground city. Casady let the little *enfant perdu* lead the way while he walked with Annabelle and Sidi.

"I thought this was supposed to be some secret smugglers' route," Annabelle said.

"It is," Casady told her.

"Then how come everybody and his brother knows how to get there?"

Nacky turned and flashed her a toothy grin. "Frenchy likes to know everything that goes on in the Dives," she said. "You can't keep a secret from an EP—no way at all."

Frenchy, Annabelle thought. Right. Sidi and Tomàs had told her about him. A genetically altered Frenchman who now bore more resemblance to a giant caterpillar or slug than to the man he'd once been. Holding court over a gang of Peter Pan-like Borribles and smoking a hookah. More shades of Wonderland, with a little Barrie and de Larrabeiti thrown in for good measure. Were they going to run into Toad of Toad Hall next?

"And besides," Casady added. "There's nothing for a Diver down there anymore, anyway."

"What do you mean?"

"Getting out's easy; getting back in . . . well, even if you could, you couldn't hide out for long. Everyone's got an ID card—coded to their genetic makeup. You can't cheat with them. And if you try to sneak around, they've got all kinds of ugly little watchdogs running around there, just itching to round up a few strays."

"The zeros," Annabelle said.

Casady nodded. "Casey told you about them?"

"Oh yeah."

It was kind of hard to forget Casey's description of the simulacrum. Made up of fiber and plastic and metal, but with human brains housed in their synthetic bodies that were wired up to their computerized motor units.

"You ought to stay," Casady said.

"Can't."

"It's not so bad. We can fix you up with your own GBC so that, even if what you're wearing now does bite the bullet, you'll still be around. Or at least some of you will—the important parts. Casey told me you're a player. We've got a good scene happening in the Dives."

"You don't understand," Annabelle said. "We've got friends to track down still. And a score to settle."

"From everything I hear about the guys running this place, you'd have better luck being a black woman in the middle of a Klan meeting."

"It's still got to be done," Annabelle said.

"We don't really have a choice," Sidi added. "The Dungeonmasters appear to have a special interest in some of the members of our party. Even if we did try to find a refuge, they would come looking for us."

"Bummer."

Annabelle smiled at the word. "Right. A major bummer."

Nacky came dancing back through the rubble just then. "Found it!"

"Never thought you wouldn't," Annabelle said.

The EP led them down to the end of the alleyway and across the buckling pavement of a side street to where an old subway entrance stood. Its opening was choked with vegetation that proved to be easily pulled aside. Using one of the flashlights that Linda had given her, Annabelle pointed its light into the darkness.

The stairs leading down were in good shape. The air coming up to them was only slightly stale, with a hint of dampness in it.

"This is it," Annabelle said to Casady and Nacky. "End of the line for you guys. Thanks for the escort."

Nacky shook her head. "I'm coming."

"That's impossible," Tomàs told her.

"Can't stop me."

The Portuguese knelt down in front of her. "This is a very bad place we are going to, *muchacha*. There is no coming back from it."

"I wouldn't want to come back. Want to go with you and Sidi."

"And what of Frenchy?" Sidi asked. "Who would look after him?

"He's got lots of other EPs."

"Yes. But I think you are a favorite of his."

The little feral face looked earnestly from him to Tomàs. "You think so?"

"Verdad," Tomàs said. "I think so, *sim."*

"You won't forget me, will you? Frenchy says that that's the only way you can live a long time—is by what people remember about you."

Tomàs enfolded her in a quick embrace. "We won't forget you," he said.

When he let her go, Sidi embraced her as well. "How could we forget one so brave and true?" the Indian asked.

When Nacky stepped back, she was chewing on her bottom lip. She looked around at the others, hesitating for one more long moment, then she lifted her hand in a quick salute and sped off into the ruins, disappearing almost immediately.

"I hate to leave her here," Sidi said.

Tomàs looked at him. *"Sim.* But where we are going . . ."

"It will undoubtedly be worse," Sidi said with a slow nod.

"That leaves you, Jack," Annabelle said. "You take care of yourself and thank Casey for us again—okay?"

Casady smiled. "You won't get rid of me that easily. I've got a hankering to see what the Chaffri've been doing with their digs since the last time I was there."

"A 'hankering'?" Annabelle asked with upraised eyebrows.

"I like country music—so sue me."

"But . . ."

"Look—anything happens to me, I just fade away and old Casey can call me up again. No problem."

He took one of the flashlights from her and started down. Annabelle shivered. This whole GBC business just gave her the creeps.

"I don't understand," Smythe said, stepping up beside her to look down the stairs. "One's either alive, or dead."

Annabelle nodded. "Yeah. You'd think so. But this is—"

"The Dungeon," everyone chorused.

"Right. Where any frigging thing seems possible."

"You coming?" Casady called from down below.

"We're on our way," Annabelle called back. She looked at her companions. "Well, kids. Ready for the next mess of bad-news craziness?"

One by one they followed her down the stairs to where Casady's flashlight was beckoning to them.

The Gatherer's features filled the entire sky. A darkness spread from the immense being, a deeper darkness within it that appeared to be the Gatherer itself. Neville didn't understand how he could discern differences in that stygian shadow, but he saw distinctions all the same. Within the cloak of blackness the Gatherer's features were like Shriek's, reflecting the beatific serenity echoed in Shriek's own visage.

As Neville stared up at the being, a sensation of utter peace settled in him. He understood now why Shriek had been content to pass on into the afterlife of her people. He understood, as well, why none among the living should be given a view of it.

Once tasted, who would not embrace his death?

He too, like Shriek, yearned to reach out and be taken in by the Gatherer. Vestiges of creatures his ancestors had been, drawn from the evolutionary ladder his race had once climbed, had him casting his own web of memory between the stones where Shriek hung. That the memories remain there, while he could go on.

Into the peace.

To be at peace.

Only . . .

A part of him rebelled.

Remember, he told himself. Death, peaceful though it promised to be, was not for them. Not now. Not so soon. Not with their companions still lost. The Dungeonmasters still unpunished.

"Wuh . . . wuh . . ."

He tried to speak but could not frame even the first word.

We cannot come with you. He sent the thought up to the Gatherer. *There is too much undone.*

Her voice, when she replied, was a breath of soft wind that made his soul shiver. *Others remain to do; your time is done.*

It was true, one part of him argued, yearning for what the Gatherer promised them. Let the others take up the battle. He and Shriek . . . they had struggled long enough.

Come with me.

Yes. It was that simple. Just let go of his last memories of life and go with her. Let her gather them in her peaceful embrace and take them away. . . .

Slowly Neville shook his head.

We cannot, he told her. *God help us, though every fiber of my being bids me to let go and come with you, we cannot.*

Someone must come with me, she replied. *I am like the sword drawn that must taste blood before I return to my sheath. One of you must return with me.*

We cannot, Neville repeated, for all that it broke his heart not to simply let himself go with her.

This is not a matter for discussion, the Gatherer said. *One must come with me—that is the law.*

I will come, Great Mother, Shriek said.

No, Neville said. *I . . .*

He would what?

The unselfish thought that had risen in him—that was related to the same impulse that had sent him here looking for Shriek—surprised him as much as it would have surprised any that knew him. He realized again that here, in this Dungeon, he was part of a group. It was not Neville Folliot who was most important in this place—it was the group as a whole. And their ultimate goal. To foil the Dungeonmasters. To see to it that as many of the party escaped as could.

His brother had already proved to be a better leader than he in this place. And he had not as much to offer to the company as did Shriek. So it was best for him to make the sacrifice.

Yes, but was that such a hard choice? a part of him asked. *The Gatherer promises peace. Every part of your being yearns for what she offers. Is that such a sacrifice—to go with her?*

But it was. For he realized that, no matter how much he yearned to go, he wanted to live more. It was not that he thought the Gatherer's peace a lie; it was that the impulse to live was stronger. But if his death would save Shriek, if it would help the others . . .

I will come with you, he told the Gatherer.

There is no need for you to sacrifice yourself on my behalf, Being Neville, Shriek told him. *I called her; I will go with her. Understand, Being Neville, if the Great Mother does not take me now, the peace that lies as a promise at the end of my people's lives will never be mine.*

You'll also be dead, Neville said.

It is my time, she replied simply.

Neville shook his head. But before he could reply, a new voice spoke.

I will go, it said.

Neville turned slowly. He saw his brother standing nearby.

Clive . . . ?

Clive here? How was it possible?

But before he could even begin to unravel that riddle, he realized it wasn't Clive who had spoken. Behind his twin there was yet another presence—no more than a ghostly shimmer at his brother's shoulder, but a presence all the same.

Clive had little time to puzzle out his own surroundings, or what Shriek and Neville were doing in this place. With as much surprise as evinced by his brother, he turned himself to see the glow hovering near him. But unlike Neville he had a name to put to that presence.

Esmond?

Yes, the glow replied. *It is I. Let me go with the Gatherer—allow me to find a moment's worth in a life that never was.*

Who is this? Neville asked.

Clive turned to him. *Our unborn brother, Esmond.*

Neville shook his head slowly. *Now I'm certain that we've all gone mad.*

Had he lived, Clive explained, *he would have been our brother Esmond. We were meant to be triplets, not twins.*

Clive, do you hear what you're saying?

It is the truth, Esmond said.

But . . .

Go now, Esmond continued. *Your bodies await you. You have tasks yet to perform. Let me do this thing.*

No, Shriek said. *This is my covenant to fulfill.* Then she turned to Clive. *I welcome this chance to say farewell to you, Being Clive. It does my heart good to see you still alive.*

You can't die, Neville protested.

I am as good as dead, Being Neville, she replied. *To go with the Great Mother is merely the final step in my journey. Go back to your lives with my blessing.*

No, Esmond said.

In the glimmering shape that was Esmond's presence, vague features began to form—as surely a Folliot's features as either Clive or Neville had ever seen. Their father was in them—and their mother, whom they had known only from portraits.

Esmond turned to the Gatherer.

Will you take me? he asked.

For a long moment the dark presence in the sky was silent. Clive could feel the tug of his body. He saw two flickering threads grow out of the darkness. One touched Neville's lower spine, the other attached itself to the centermost position of Shriek's chest, equidistant from the joints of each of her four upper limbs.

Come, the Gatherer said softly.

No! Shriek cried, but she was too late.

Esmond's presence lifted to float toward the Gatherer. The shadows enveloped him and began to draw away once more, leaving a swath of orange sky behind that was so bright after the darkness that it hurt the eyes of the three who watched from below.

No, Shriek cried again, but more softly now, her voice heavy with regret and promises lost.

Good-bye, my brothers. . . .

Esmond's voice whispered in both Clive and Neville's minds. The twins regarded each other.

He . . . Neville began. *That presence. Surely he wasn't . . .*

I can't explain it myself, Clive replied. *But I believe he truly was who he said he was.*

But that's impossible.

Clive nodded. *So one would think. I doubted him myself—but now, with his sacrifice . . . I find it hard not to believe.*

To have never lived . . . Neville said softly. *What would it be like, to be aware, but never actually living?*

Hard, Clive said. *Desperately hard.* He looked about himself. *What is this place?*

Neville started to shape the explanation in his mind, but suddenly the tug of his body was too strong. He felt the brush of Shriek's mind as it touched his, the neural web enveloping them, and then they were gone.

For long moments Clive remained behind, standing there in that alien landscape; then his body made its own demands on his spirit and he too was drawn away. . . .

· CHAPTER THIRTEEN ·

"What's with Tomàs?" Annabelle asked Sidi.

The Portuguese was walking ahead with Casady; Smythe and Finnbogg brought up the rear. Sidi gave her a questioning look that was lost in the shadows.

"Wrong?" he asked.

"You know—he's acting almost human."

"I think Tomàs needed to acquire a sense of his own worth. You must remember that he comes from a time when a man such as he has no future and was considered to be of little value. One does not hear of the crews of those old sailing ships—only of the captains. And then only when they have accomplished some great deed of exploration or war.

"At first coming to the Dungeon did little to change that lack of self-worth in Tomàs. But now . . ."

Annabelle turned to look at Sidi, aiming the flashlight's beam up to his features. There was a thoughtful look in his eyes.

"And now?" she prompted.

The Indian shrugged. "I believe the more responsibility we give him, the more he will prove his value— not only to our company as a whole, but to himself as a human being."

Annabelle aimed the light back at the ground and nodded slowly. Made sense. And when she thought of how Tomàs had been saying good-bye to the little *enfant perdu* and how he'd been this past hour—helpful, easy to get along with—it seemed to be working too.

"Awfully modern psychology," she told Sidi, "for a nineteenth-century Indian."

"Your time isn't the only one concerned with the workings of a man's mind."

"I know. But with that caste system you guys've got . . ."

Sidi smiled. "I was born to the *varna*," he said. "In India I would still be perceived as belonging to what I was born to. But I left India a long time ago. I left *varna* behind with it."

Their conversation came to a halt as they reached Tomàs and Casady, who were waiting for them. The stairs they had originally taken at street level had brought them down into a network of tunnels; now the tunnels had deposited them in a large open area.

"What's this?" Smythe asked as he and Finnbogg arrived as well.

"A disused Chaffri loading area," Casady explained. "Back when there was still trading going on between them and the Ren, they used to move the goods through this sub-subway system. The only goods being moved through it now are by smugglers."

"How far are we from the city?" Annabelle asked.

"Ten minutes."

"And the gate?" Sidi added.

Casady shook his head. "Don't know about the gate. Stands to reason that it'd be smack in the middle of wherever the Chaffri are thickest—seeing how they're the only ones using it."

"What about the Ren? How do they get to use it?"

"They've got their own gate."

"Figures."

Annabelle shone her flashlight around the large chamber. The light wasn't strong enough to reach its far walls.

"This war between the Ren and the Chaffri," she said finally, looking back at Casady. "It's not just about the Dungeon, is it?"

"You're asking the wrong guy about details. I've been in both sides of the city—a GBCer doesn't get to pick where he gets called up—and all I know is they've been at each other's throats for about as long as the

Dungeon's been in operation. And that's a long time, by any standard."

"Thousands of years," Finnbogg said.

Casady nodded at the dwarf. "What he said. Thing is, both sides are getting antsy now because there's a bunch of new players in the game. I've heard that they're another race entirely that stumbled on the Dungeon and want to take it over, but I've also heard that they're the original creators of this place and they want it back. They've got their own agents moving through the levels, getting things ready for some final showdown."

"Agents?" Smythe asked.

Casady grinned. "That's what the word I've heard says. Got it in both sides of the city. One's the Madonna, another's the Cloak, a third's a mismatched bunch of outsiders that follow a couple of guys named Folliot. . . ."

"*Christo!*" Tomàs said. "That is us."

"And let me set you straight, Jack. There's no way we're aligned with any of the Dungeonmasters," Annabelle said.

"I'm only telling you what I hear—not what I believe."

"I've heard of this Madonna in Tawn," Smythe said, "but not of the one you call the Cloak."

"He's supposed to be a little guy who makes a real good business out of hiding in the shadows, manipulating the people around him, just generally causing trouble. Supposed to have a pair of small horns growing out of his brow, and also goes by the name of the Lightbringer."

"Lucifer," Annabelle said.

Tomàs crossed himself.

"Close enough, I suppose," Casady said. "They got the Mother of God and the Big D. both working together against the Ren and the Chaffri."

"I don't understand," Smythe said. "Why the religious motifs? Why religions from our world, for that matter?"

Annabelle nodded. "Yeah. Why's there so many weird twists on the religions of our world? Everywhere we turn there's some new variation on the theme. It doesn't make sense. If they've got the whole universe to draw on, why center so much of it on our world?"

"Got me," Casady said. "I'm just passing on gossip."

"I wish we could find someone who *did* know," Annabelle said.

Casady shrugged. "My bet's that not even the Dungeonmasters really know what's going on anymore. I figure this started out as a game, and somewhere along the line it took on a life of its own and went right out of control. All they've been trying to do since, when they're not fighting with each other, is bring it back to what it once was—their own personal, private playground where they could get a kick out of messing with people's heads.

"See the thing is, they've got all this technology, but nothing's working quite the way it's supposed to anymore. They've had their agents out on the other levels, supposedly getting things back in control, but in reality, they're just setting up their *own* little private playgrounds. Place is splintering into so many different groups that you need a scorecard just to—"

He broke off suddenly.

"Kill the lights!" he told Annabelle and Smythe as he switched off his own flashlight.

"What is it?" Annabelle whispered.

"Thought I heard someth—"

They all heard it now—the quiet scrape of metal against stone. They turned slowly, studying the darkness around them.

Annabelle felt someone press in close to her. Her hand reached for the controls of her Baalbec.

"Zeros," Casady breathed in her ear.

She saw the red glow of their eyes now—three pairs, low to the ground.

Zeros. Right. She should have figured that there was no way were going to get down to the next level without first having a run-in with these things.

"Too late for hiding," Casady said as he moved away from her.

He flicked on his flashlight. The beam stabbed the darkness, glinting on three forms made of metal and plastic. They were the size of German shepherds and stood on all fours, with torsos rising from where their necks should be. A head and a pair of arms were attached to each torso.

Little cybernetic centaurs, Annabelle thought looking at them.

Their heads were composed of a transparent plastic. Turning her own flashlight on them, Annabelle could see the human brains floating in some kind of thick liquid inside each head.

"Can they be reasoned with?" she asked Casady.

"Not a chance."

Annabelle nodded. "Okay, everybody back up slowly to the tunnel entrance."

They started to do so, all except for Annabelle and Casady.

"Annabelle," Sidi called.

She shook her head. "I can handle this."

"But . . ."

"No arguments, please, Sidi. I know what I'm doing." At least I hope I do, she thought.

Casady switched his flashlight from his right to his left hand and drew his handgun from his belt. "You heard the lady," he said without looking over his shoulder.

"Is that going to do any good?" Annabelle asked.

"Against their armor? Not likely. But don't forget, I don't die, I just—"

"Fade away. Right. Well, let's try my idea first, shall we?"

"You're the boss," Casady said.

"Neville?"

The voice seemed to come from a great distance. It echoed vaguely in the fog that choked Neville's mind but seemed too obscure a sound to make any sense.

"Neville."

The insistent repetition of the word finally spoke through the fog. It was a name. Of course. *His* name.

"Neville."

It took an immense effort for Neville to open his eyes and focus on the concerned features of Alyssa and Fenil.

"Thank the Great Wind," Alyssa murmured. "He lives."

Neville sat up slowly, head spinning. "Sh-shriek . . . ?" he asked, then realized that he'd been sprawled across her chest.

He turned so that he was facing her and watched her many-faceted eyes flicker open to regard him. The beatific expression she had worn in her death dream had been replaced by a look of such utter loss that Neville realized a deep pang of regret himself.

She had been on the doorstep of heaven, and he had drawn her back. For what? Merely to continue this damnable struggle in the Dungeon.

I'm sorry, he said. *It seemed the right thing to do at the time.*

I understand, Being Neville, she replied. *But it is hard . . . to be back in this world of flesh and blood when that peace was almost mine.*

It will still be waiting for you.

For a long moment the archanid said nothing. Finally she sighed.

Perhaps, she told him.

What do you mean?

Can one touch that moment of utter peace more than once in one lifetime, Being Neville?

Gods! I . . . I never thought . . .

Shriek slowly shook her head. *Do not berate yourself, Being Neville. You meant to perform a brave and selfless deed.*

But if you've lost your chance at heaven . . .

Only the Gatherer knows if your brother has taken my place in the Beyond Beyond, or if there is still a place there, waiting for me. She paused, then added, *At least we now know that Being Clive is well.*

Yes, Neville said. *But—*

What's done is done, Being Neville.

As she began to sit up, Neville moved back from her.

"What happened?" Fenil asked. "Where did you go?"

"Go?" Neville asked.

He was only half-returned to the real world. The remainder of his being was still caught up in Shriek's death dream.

"He went inside," Alyssa said. "Into her mind."

"Inside?" Fenil regarded both Neville and Shriek with an odd expression. "What was it like?"

"It . . ."

Neville's brow creased as he remembered. Shriek's web of memories that she wove between those tall black stones. The Gatherer, filling the sky with her benevolent presence. The arrival of his brother Clive. And that other presence. The one who made the sacrifice. Supposedly his unborn brother.

Could such a thing even be possible?

Neville briefly described their experience.

"I have heard of such beings," Alyssa said. "Those spirits who lose their chance at birth are considered blessed in the eyes of the Great Wind."

"It seems so . . . so preposterous," Neville said.

Alyssa smiled and gave him an understanding look. "Many are the Mysteries of the world—but few exist who can unriddle them. If the Mysteries were so easily understood, they would scarcely be Mysteries, now would they?"

That wasn't what Neville wanted to hear at the moment, but he realized it would be all that he'd get. He had wanted Alyssa to tell him that it was impossible, that he could have no second, unborn, brother who would have been named Esmond. Who would sacrifice himself, as this entity had done.

Allow him the strength of his offering, Shriek said.

"Can you read minds as well as the thoughts projected from them?"

Hardly. But I've learned how to read the features of your people, Being Neville. Yours were what you would call an open book.

Neville nodded. He stood up and brushed from his clothes what he could of the dirt that had been ground into them, then helped Shriek to her feet.

"Remind me not to play cards with you," he said.

The arachnid was unsteady at first but slowly regained her sense of balance. She looked at the two dead giants, half-covered with rubble.

We dealt with them well, she said.

"Most permanently, madam," Neville said.

She turned to look at him to see, not that familiar mocking look that she expected, but a genuine smile on the Englishman's features.

"I'd offer you my arm," he added, "but I don't know the proper protocol among your people."

We spin a web, Shriek said, *to bind us close.*

"I believe I'll pass."

With Fenil and Alyssa's help the pair rejoined the rest of the party. The Tuan was waiting for them on the far side of the mountain created by the fall of the twin giants.

"Do we go on, my lady?" Captain Yoors asked.

"Indeed," Alyssa replied.

Yoors nodded. "I thought as much. I sent Thulen to scout ahead, and he came back with word that he's found a way into some new sort of tunnel—obviously man-made and more in scale to our size."

"Is it far?"

"A half hour—no more."

Alyssa regarded Neville and Shriek. "Do you need to rest, or can we press on?"

"Press on," Neville said. "Only God and the Dungeonmasters know what else is lurking down here in this sewer system. The sooner we get out of it, the happier I'll feel."

He glanced at Shriek.

I am weary, but I—she gave what passed for a smile on her alien features— *I vote that we go on as well.*

Neville was familiar with the concept of voting—the House of Lords ran by voting, while the Commons was elected by a limited, popular vote. Electoral reform was one of the great issues of his day. Neville wasn't decided yet on the finer points of the system, but while he generally considered it fitting enough for Parliament, he wasn't so sure that it was the best method of decision making for a military-styled unit such as they had at the moment.

It was Annabelle's influence, Neville decided, all this business with voting and the whole of a group having a say in what they did rather than following one leader. He admitted to the system's basic fairness but still believed that the most expedient procedure—in practical terms—was to have one man make the decisions. Otherwise the group could spend the better part of its time arguing among themselves rather than forging forward under their common goal.

On the other hand, the Dungeonmasters were a perfect example of the other extreme, so perhaps there was something to be said about democratic action even in a group this small.

Mounted once more, they set off with Thulen in the lead to show the way. The company kept their silvers to a slow pace to accommodate Shriek's slower gait, so it was closer to forty-five minutes before they reached the new tunnel that Thulen had discovered.

"It's a ventilation shaft!" Neville cried when he saw it.

Portions of the tunnel had worn away to show a join between two metal plates of what indeed had to be a ventilation shaft. Some beast had worried away at the join, pulling it apart enough to allow egress for beings of their diminutive size.

"The city below," Alyssa said as understanding dawned on her.

Neville nodded. "It would have to have ventilation. This will lead us directly to it."

There was no need to discuss what was to be done next. One by one they squeezed into the ventilation shaft's narrower confines. The floor of the shaft lay on a gentle gradient. Because the city they sought lay below, they took the downward slope.

Clive stepped from the mirror, feeling as disoriented as Shriek and Neville had coming from the arachnid's death dream. He would have stumbled had Chary not caught his arm and steadied him. He regarded her for a long moment. There was something wrong with her, some discrepancy that he couldn't quite focus on.

"Are you ill?" she asked.

Clive started to shake his head, but then he had it. "You've grown," he said. "You're the same size I am."

The tech smiled back at him. "It's more like you've come down to our size."

Clive looked about the room. It was true. Suddenly everything was in proportion once again. It was a dizzying sensation to look at it all—especially coming hard on the heels of his recent experiences as it did.

"It's so odd," he said. "I've been gone so long, but time seems to have stood still here."

No one appeared to have moved from the positions they had been in when he had left.

"So long?" Chary asked. "The procedure only took" —she looked at a nearby dial—"five point three six eight seconds."

"Only . . . ?"

Clive's sense of disorientation grew stronger.

"What is the matter?" Speaker Lena asked, concern plain on her features.

"Nothing. I just . . ."

He let his voice trail off. Time had passed at different speeds for him, while he stepped through the mirror, and for those who'd remained here. His mind was filled with the bewildering flurry of what he'd recently experienced—meeting his unborn brother, the rescue of Shriek and Neville, discovering the truth about his lost memories. . . .

It took a great effort to put aside the rage that came over him as he remembered what the Dungeonmasters had done to him. Going into his mind to rearrange his memories . . . that seemed the worst a man could do to another. For what was a man, if not the sum total of all he had been? Take some of that from him, and he is that much less the person that he could be.

Around him the Ren and Chang were still regarding him with varying expressions of worry and curiosity. Tell them nothing, he thought. For the moment, at least, he should keep what had occurred to himself. Knowledge was power—even when the owner of such knowledge did not yet know the best method to use it.

He let Chary lead him to a seat into which he gratefully sank. He watched Guafe step into the mirror and reappear moments later, returned to his proper size as well. The cyborg appeared to suffer no ill effects whatsoever.

"How did you find the experience?" Clive asked him.

Guafe shrugged. "It was over so quickly, it scarcely had time to register."

I am going mad, Clive thought. In my mind, I was gone at least an hour.

He recalled speaking to a man who had fainted from the heat once, who had told him that the experience seemed long enough for him to have been caught up in some long dream. His comrades, however, who had brought him around, assured him that he had been unconscious for only moments.

Perhaps this was similar.

All a dream.

When he thought of his experience with the voice from the maze—who claimed to be his unborn brother Esmond—that seemed the logical explanation.

But then he considered the realization that had come to him of how the Dungeonmasters had toyed with his mind, then manipulated his memories to forget the incident. . . .

Perhaps his mind had been manipulated again. The

Dungeonmasters appeared to be divided among themselves. Could one group now be playing him against the other with a new set of false or lost memories?

Madness or dreams? Both seemed too possible. Except what he had experienced had seemed so real. And Shriek and Neville . . .

When he finally found them again, he would ask them if they had ever been in that place he had seen with its orange skies and the huge dark face in its midst. Until then he *would* keep it to himself.

"Well, Clive," Speaker Lena said. "We've kept our side of the bargain and helped you. Will you return the favor?"

Clive shook his head. "Not so quickly. There's still the rest of our party to track down."

"That could take a very long time. Believe me, if they are in danger, then that danger comes from the Chaffri. Every moment you waste could be placing them in more danger. Help us, and we can help you."

Clive remained firm.

Speaker Lena argued further, but when she saw that Clive wouldn't budge from his position, she finally sighed.

"Very well," she said. Looking at Chary, she added, "Do what you can to find his companions—we'll be in the DSL."

"Which is?" Clive asked.

"The Data Storage Library. I want to show you some history."

She led the way out of the laboratory. Once they were in the hall, Guafe surreptitiously laid a hand on Clive's shoulder.

You do well to remain suspicious of them, the cyborg told him through the neural web they shared. *I don't believe they are telling us the entire truth.*

I thought you were on their side, Clive replied.

Hardly. It's simply easier to gain access to the information one requires by ingratiating one's self with one's hosts.

What have you learned, then?

*That there is a war between our hosts and the Chaf-
fri, and there is a third group in the Dungeon, but I
believe that our hosts' motives to gain your help are not
quite so altruistic as they would like us to believe. To
use an analogy you will find simple to understand, we
are all chess pieces in this Dungeon, but while most of
us are pawns, there are some, such as yourself, who
have a more important value.*

Oh. I'm a king now, am I?

Guafe gave a mental headshake. *Not a king, but at
least a knight or a bishop.*

And what do you suggest we do?

*Wait. Watch and learn what we can. But take the first
opportunity that arises to make our own way once
more.* The pressure of the cyborg's fingers increased
slightly on Clive's shoulder. *Mark this well, Clive Folliot. The first opportunity either of us gets to escape—
we should take it. I know I will.*

And what of the other?

*We must hope to escape together, but if the occasion
arises where I can escape only on my own, believe me, I
will do so.*

Before Clive could respond to that, Guafe removed
his hand from the Englishman's shoulder. Speaker
Lena turned to look at them.

"You're awfully quiet," she said.

"We have much to think upon," Guafe replied.

Much indeed, Clive thought. Such as Guafe's chess
analogy. He thought again of that chessboard he had
seen on the previous level—of the two pieces that wore
a different color from that of the remainder of their
party.

The cyborg and Sidi Bombay.

Whose side were they truly on? And if Guafe *was*
opposed to him and the rest of their party, then what
purpose did this last conversation prove? A moment of
weakness for the enemy? Or was it simply an honest
warning as to Guafe's own purposes?

Gods, but this place played havoc on one's sense of
trust.

CHAPTER FOURTEEN

As soon as Annabelle began to approach the zeros, a low electronic growl rose from the voice boxes attached to their chins.

"You get the idea they're trying to tell me something?" Annabelle asked Casady.

Lips dry, heart thumping in her chest, Annabelle flicked on her Baalbec and continued her approach. As she took a couple more steps forward, the first of the creatures made a sudden rush at her.

Annabelle didn't hesitate.

Annie B., you're not operating on a full load, she told herself as she met the creature's attack.

The force of the zero's forward momentum knocked her off her feet, but before the Baalbec could kick in and fling the creature away from her, Annabelle wrapped her arms around it. The Baalbec's electrical force field, surrounding the creature as it was, exerted its terrible pressure. For one long moment the tableau held, electric charges ionizing the air about them, blue-white currents flickering up and down the creature's metallic body. Then the zero imploded.

Protected by the Baalbec, Annabelle wasn't hurt by the exploding metal and plastic. She was thrown back by the violence of the discharge, ears ringing, but stumbled quickly to her feet.

The remaining pair of zeros had begun their own approach. They halted now as Annabelle stepped toward them. The fluid surrounding their floating brains was agitated, bubbling into a froth inside its protective bubble. Their electronic eyes flickered like hazard lights. But they backed up as she continued to move toward them.

A moment later they turned tail and were gone.

"If I hadn't seen it myself," Casady said slowly, "I wouldn't have believed it."

Annabelle turned off the Baalbec and merely shrugged. But her pulse was drumming a rapid tattoo. Her heart felt as though it were rattling against her rib cage.

"You okay?" Casady added.

"Yeah. I . . ."

She wasn't about to tell anyone that she hadn't been sure her plan would even work in the first place. Giving Casady a quick grin, she looked at her handiwork. The creature lay in pieces all over the floor, and the adrenaline charge running through her changed into a flip-flopping nausea that settled in the pit of her stomach.

It was hard not to think of the human brain encased in the intricate cybernetic mesh of plastic and metal that had made up the zero's body. If she closed her eyes, she could see it imploding again. . . .

"I just feel a little . . . sick, that's all."

"Well, let's get a move on," Casady said as the rest of the party emerged from the tunnel behind them. "We hang around here any longer, and we'll have Chaffri all over our asses."

Annabelle nodded.

"That was a nice trick with the zero," Casady added, "but don't go getting cocky. The thing you just killed is only the smallest model they've got running around down here."

He looked around at the others, then led them quickly across the cavern to where another tunnel ran off toward the Chaffri side of the underground city. This one was wider than the one they'd just quit. The floor and walls, where their lights cut across them, appeared to be in better repair.

The city was ten minutes away, Annabelle thought as they hurried down this new passage. But she already felt as though it'd been an hour since they'd left the cavern behind.

"How much farther?" she asked Casady.

"Almost there."

Looking ahead, Annabelle could see a square of light ahead of them.

"Quiet now," Casady added. "This lets us out on a back street in a part of town that isn't being used anymore."

"Why's that?"

"Both the Chaffri and Ren are suffering from lower birthrates. Every year they end up abandoning more and more of their living and working space."

"But—"

"Later," Casady said.

He slowed their approach as they neared the square of light. They could see outside the tunnel now—a small plaza surrounded by buildings that had once been white but were now a dirty gray. Casady paused at the entrance and looked carefully out. The others waited impatiently.

"Okay," he said finally. "Looks clear. See that alley across the plaza to the right?"

Annabelle nodded.

"Head for it and take the second door you come to—on your right. We'll figure out the rest of your route once we get there. Out here we're sitting ducks for the first passing zero patrol."

Without waiting for them to agree or disagree, Casady left the entrance at a quick run. The others hesitated for only a moment, then followed. They got about halfway across the plaza when zeros stepped out of the side streets on every compass point.

Oh, shit, Annabelle thought.

Casady's warning had been well-taken. These zeros were five times the size of the ones they'd encountered back in the cavern. The brains floating in their plastic head casings were the same size, but everything else was multiplied. The new creatures bristled with projections that were all too obviously armaments of one kind or another.

There was no way her trick would work on these, Annabelle realized.

Casady had come to an abrupt halt. As the rest of the party joined him, they made a circle, backs to each other, facing outward. The zeros moved in closer, effectively cutting off their escape from any direction.

"I think we blew it," Casady said softly.

"No kidding." Annabelle said. "Try end of the road."

Oddly enough she felt utterly calm. Maybe it was because she'd never really thought that they'd ever get out of this place, that they'd ever have a chance to confront the Dungeonmasters—to beard them in their own den, as it were.

She flicked on her Baalbec.

"Well, screw 'em all," she said. "I'm going down fighting."

The ventilation shaft led Neville and his party along a gentle downward slope for long miles—or at least what felt like miles.

It was another benefit of their stature, Neville thought as he rode behind Alyssa. If their party had been of the same scale as those that this shaft serviced, they would have had to leave their mounts behind and crawl the length of the shaft.

They made a number of halts, during which one or another of the Tuan would scout ahead while the remainder rested. Shriek took full advantage of each of these interludes, snatching every moment of respite that she could before it was time for them to press on once more.

Neville dismounted from Alyssa's silver at each stop and sat beside the arachnid, lending her the comfort of his moral support. At their latest halt he joined her once more, squatting in front of her.

"How goes it?" he asked.

A sense of mild amusement sparked from her mind to his, tickling his thoughts.

I am not an egg, Being Neville, she said, *for all that you insist on treating me as one.*

"I'm concerned."

I know. I am doing better. I am not so much there anymore.

Neville knew exactly what she meant. Though the experience hadn't had the same intensity for him as it had for her—it was, after all, part and parcel of her racial background, not his—he could still empathize with her. Like the protagonist in Milton's famous poem he knew now what it was like to lose Paradise.

The memory sat in the back of his mind, rising up in the middle of the most mundane thought to remind him of what was now gone. Calm unclaimed. Peace lost. Solace thrown away. And for what? To struggle on in this hellish Dungeon.

It made one reconsider one's own sanity, Neville couldn't help but think at times.

What I fear the most, Shriek said, *is that we will have gone through all we have but never learn the why of it. Never to understand why it was we that were chosen . . . what the Dungeonmasters want with us . . . what any of this madness* means. . . .

She looked at Neville, and Alyssa sitting beside him. *Do you understand that fear?* she asked.

Neville nodded. "All too well."

Shriek continued to study him for a long moment. *You have changed, Being Neville,* she said finally. *And that change is not simply due to your meeting the Gatherer.*

"All men change," Neville said with a shrug.

He could feel her smile in his mind.

Yes. But not all change for the better.

They sat quietly for a few moments. The only sound was the quiet murmur of the Tuans as they spoke to each other, the fairy jingle of the silvers' harnesses when the animals shifted their positions. The light of their torches flickered, throwing shadows. The air within the shaft was basically fresh—far more so than it had been in the storm sewers—though it did have a very slight chemical scent to it.

"Among my people," Alyssa said, "it is the journey that is important, not the destination itself. When one seeks knowledge, the quest is the thing, not the final solution for which we aim. All too often that solution proves to be of far less import than what we learned on our route to reach it."

"Small comfort in our present situation," Neville said.

But Shriek was nodding her head. *I understand what you mean, Being Alyssa,* she said. *We have a similar philosophy on my homeworld.*

"I think it's a concept put forth by the philosophers of every culture," Neville said. "It's simply not what I want from this adventure. I want answers. I want satisfaction from those who have treated us as though we were nothing more than gaming pieces for them to move about on their game board. And one way or another I will have it."

"Brave words."

Neville looked up to find that Captain Yoors was standing near them.

"I mean what I say," he told Yoors.

"I don't doubt that you do."

Neville studied the Tuan's serious face. Yoors met his gaze. There was no give in him—not an inch.

"So you've finally decided to accept us?" Neville asked.

Yoors shrugged. "I'm not ready to count you among my friends—for all that, I know now that you are not ranked with my enemies."

A hard man, Neville thought. But they all needed to be hard if they were to survive in this place—men and women both.

"But when we do find these Dungeonmasters," Yoors added, "you will have to wait to have your turn with them, for they and I have the matter of an old debt to clear up first."

"They owe many debts," Neville said.

Yoors merely nodded, then returned to his mount and began to adjust its harness.

"We should ride on soon," Alyssa said.

Shriek rose wearily to her feet. *My body yearns for its nest, but I still have the strength to press on.*

Neville stood up beside her. Trouble made for odd fellowships, he thought. Here he felt closer to a creature that in England he'd be more likely to step on than attempt to speak with. Instead he counted her as his friend and gave little consideration to her bizarre appearance.

As for Alyssa—whose appearance left nothing to be desired—ever since the attack of the giant dogs she had exchanged her earlier flirtatious behavior for the responsibility of being the leader of her company. Surprisingly Neville found himself more attracted to her because of that. He had never considered it before, but it stood to reason that a man could do little better than to have a woman who stood beside him, rather than one who deferred to his wishes.

You have changed, Shriek had told him earlier.

Neville nodded to himself. He had, indeed. Far more than even she might realize.

"You look thoughtful, Neville," Alyssa said to him as he approached her silver. "Is something troubling you?"

"No more than troubles us all," he said.

He gave her a leg up. The Tuan who had been scouting ahead returned with no news except that the shaft continued with its gentle descent for as far as he could see.

"How deep does the city lie?" Neville asked.

There was no response from the Tuan until Fenil spoke.

"No one knows," he said.

Neville nodded. "Then we'll simply have to find out for ourselves, won't we?"

Fenil flashed him a quick grin.

When Neville was mounted behind her, Alyssa gave the signal to ride, and the company set off once more.

They rode quietly. Alyssa and Neville rode at the fore, with Shriek at their side. The rest rode single file. The only sound that accompanied them was that of the jingling harnesses and the soft click of the silvers' claws on the metal floor of the shaft. Their torches sent shadows scudding ahead of them.

Neville didn't mind the slowness of their pace. At this point it didn't matter to him how long it took them to reach the Dungeonmasters—just so long as they reached them.

He touched the hilt of his sword.

You'll have to be quick, Yoors, he thought, if you mean to collect your debt before I collect mine.

The Data Storage Library was like no library that Clive was familiar with in his own world. There were no club chairs and lights, no carpeting underfoot, no paintings, no sculptures. For God's sake, there were no bookcases—no books!

It was a long, rectangular room, garishly lit by overhead banks of lights, flanked on either wall by rows of cabinets. Desks ran down the central length of the room, dotted with computer stations that Clive recognized from their stay in Dramaran.

But where were the books?

"The data is digitally stored in CCs—compact cubes," Speaker Lena explained when Clive asked.

She went to the nearest cabinet and opened the drawer to show row upon row of small translucent cubes.

"One of these," she said, picking a cube at random, "holds as much data as a hundred books."

Clive let none of the surprise he felt show on his features. A hundred books on each cube? He began a quick calculation—the cubes in this drawer, times the number of drawers in each cabinet, times the cabinets —and gave up before he'd reckoned the amount of books that one drawer could hold.

"You said something about histories?" he said.

Speaker Lena replaced the cube and moved down

the room to another drawer. Taking a new cube from it, she sat down at one of the computer stations and beckoned the pair of them closer.

"History," she said as she inserted the cube.

She indicated that they should pull up chairs on either side of her. Once they were seated, she attached a cable running from the computer's main housing to a small socket on a plain metal bracelet that she wore on her wrist. Laying her hand flat on the table in front of the monitor, she moved her fingers in a quick, complex pattern on the tabletop. The screen came to life.

"This is the Dungeon," she said.

Clive gazed uncomprehendingly at the image on the monitor. It showed the vastness of space, constellations dotting the darkness in unfamiliar patterns—except for one that was too familiar, and that was the star pattern Clive remembered from when he had first entered the Dungeon. Close up was a large rock, floating in the center of the screen.

"What is this?" he asked. "What are you trying to tell us?"

Guafe explained what the image meant, then turned to the Speaker.

"Are you telling us that the Dungeon is an asteroid circling some unknown planet?" he asked.

"Not unknown." She manipulated her fingers on the desk once more and the view changed, from the asteroid to the planet beyond it. "This was Aralt—the homeworld of my people and the Chaffri. We discovered the Dungeon on our first manned flights beyond Aralt's atmosphere. All our subsequent technical advances sprang from what we found within it."

"You said 'was,'" the cyborg said, making a question of the statement.

Speaker Lena nodded. "Aralt was destroyed in one of our wars with the Chaffri. We have fought across the galaxies, leaving similar destruction in our wake wherever our forces have met."

There was no real regret in her voice, just a simple stating of the facts.

Guafe nodded slowly. "And then why does the Dungeon still stand unharmed?"

"Happily some part of the Dungeon itself has always intervened. But now . . ." She turned from the screen to look at Clive. "Our spies have learned that the Chaffri have cracked the coded seals on a Gannine weapons store. Once they have the weapons operational, they will move against us, then on through the gates to conquer other times and worlds."

"Gannine?" Clive asked.

"The original race who created the Dungeon."

"And just what *is* the Dungeon?" Guafe asked.

"The closest we can guess is that it is some form of space station—a giant laboratory that the Gannine used to study the various races they came across on their journeys through the vastness of space."

"And the Gannine?" Clive asked. "What happened to them?"

Speaker Lena shook her head. "No one knows. They were absent when our ancestors first commandeered the Dungeon, but lately it appears that they could be returning to reclaim their own."

"It seems curious that they should ever cast aside their work in the first place," Guafe said.

"We have always felt that they simply moved on to other endeavors," Speaker Lena replied. "The Chaffri held to the theory that they were sleeping—hidden somewhere in the vastness of the Dungeon—and that they would wake again. It appears that the Chaffri were correct."

Again she turned to Clive. "So you see our problem. If the Chaffri have gained the use of the Gannine weapons technology, we are all in equal danger. And if it is the Gannine returning—our danger is multiplied a hundred times."

"I still don't see what it has to do with me," Clive said. "I don't even understand the half of what goes on in this place, so how could I be of any importance?"

"You . . ." the Ren Speaker hesitated. "You are a

born leader. You can consolidate our forces, plan our attack. . . ."

Guafe leaned forward as though to study the screen more closely. He used the motion to disguise the movement of his hand that reached behind the Speaker's back to touch Clive's shoulder.

She's lying, he said on the neural web.

About what? It all seems preposterous.

Probably about everything except the fact that the Chaffri are a threat, that there is a third party out for both Chaffri and Ren blood, and that she needs you. The question is—what does she need you for?

Remember Annabelle's theory? Clive guessed. *It must have something to do with my Folliot blood.*

Yes. But what?

Guafe let his hand drop. Aloud he asked the Speaker, "Have you never searched for the Gannine before?"

"Oh, yes. That has always been an ongoing part of our research—both ours and the Chaffri's. Over the years we have had to conclude that, for whatever reasons they had, they simply abandoned the Dungeon to move on to other concerns. Left to its own devices, the Dungeon evolved on its own, factions forming and changing as the years went by. When we arrived, we took control of what we could—roughly an even division between the Chaffri and ourselves."

"And," Guafe said, "can we assume, by our own presence here, that both you and the Chaffri have continued the Gannine's work?"

"What do you mean?"

"Are we not here to be studied as well?"

"Oh, no. We each bring in new beings to foil the plans of the others. We have to. The Dungeon will not allow us to work directly against each other, so we must use intermediaries."

It *was* nothing but a game, Clive realized.

His fist clenched at his sides, but he kept his own counsel. Taking a deep breath to steady his anger, he reached behind the Speaker's chair to touch Guafe's shoulder.

We have to play along with her, he said.

I am not so certain that that is a wise course anymore, Guafe replied. *Better we put our minds to escape—and quickly.*

Agreed. But until that opportunity arises, we have to keep up a helpful pretense.

He dropped his hand from the cyborg's shoulder as Speaker Lena turned to him.

"I see now your problem," he told her, "and it *is* our problem as well. I will do everything I can to help you."

The Speaker's features beamed. "I knew you would help. I told the others you could do nothing else but help us, once you knew the truth."

I've yet to know the truth, Clive thought, but he doubted he would find it anywhere in the Ren's part of the city.

"Can you call up a map of this level?" Guafe asked. "I am feeling somewhat disoriented as to exactly where we are in the Dungeon."

Speaker Lena nodded. Manipulating her fingers on the desktop, she called up a series of maps. Clive and Guafe watched the levels go by—all those miles they had struggled through on foot, all those places of danger, flitted by in moments where it had taken them months to travel. Finally the screen stopped with a map of the eighth level.

"This is where we found you," the Speaker said, indicating a spot on the map displayed on the screen. Her fingers made another quick movement on the desktop. "And this is the city we share with the Chaffri. The demarcation line between our halves of the city is here."

Both Clive and Guafe leaned forward. They noted the position of the Data Storage Library and its proximity to the gate leading to the ninth level. The greater bulk of the Ren's part of the city lay between the two spots.

"Why do you use a gate such as this," Guafe asked, "when you have the teleportation device in your laboratory?"

"The device is something we made for ourselves—
the Dungeon has its own gates, one of which is what
you see here. We can't open or close them—they simply are."

"Do the Ren have similar teleportation devices?"

"Unfortunately, yes. Why do you ask?"

Both Clive and Guafe caught the sudden suspicion in
her voice. Clive glanced at his companion.

Well? he thought. Come up with something quickly.

"If you were the only ones to have such devices, it
would put you at a great advantage. It's advantages
that we must be looking for, is that not true?"

Speaker Lena relaxed. "Exactly. And with Clive's
help we'll be able to do just that."

"What exactly is it that you want me to do?" Clive
asked again.

"I'll tell you that when we've rejoined the other
Speakers. Have you seen enough in here?"

More than enough, Clive thought.

"For now," Guafe said. "We will most likely have to
return for more data, once we have spoken with the
other members of your council." He stood up from the
chair. "Shall we go?"

While Speaker Lena disengaged the computer cable
from her wrist and was returning the cube to its
drawer, Guafe moved closer to Clive so that their
shoulders brushed.

Keep her occupied, if you can, he said.

Do you have a plan?

Yes. I—

He broke off when the Speaker turned and moved
away from Clive. Letting the two of them take the
lead, he followed along behind.

"What luck do you think your scientists will have in
tracking down the rest of our party?" Clive asked the
Speaker. He spoke as much out of concern for Annabelle, Smythe, and the others, as he did to keep the Ren
busy.

"We can ask after their progress as soon as we're
finished with the council," she replied.

Clive immediately asked another question, wondering all the while what it was that Guafe had planned. When they reached a door that led back out into the Hub, both he and the Speaker found out at the same time.

Looking behind them, they realized that the cyborg was no longer with them.

The maps, Clive realized. Guafe had memorized the maps, learned what he needed of how the city was laid out, and was making his escape.

Wonderful. He was left here on his own amongst their enemies while Guafe went free.

An image of a chessboard arose in his mind—the pieces resembling Sidi Bombay and Guafe on the opposing sides of the board.

It had been a warning.

And now . . . Chang was gone, and the Ren would think he had played a part in the cyborg's escape unless he covered up his own part in the plan.

"Where on earth . . . ?" he began.

Speaker Lena regarded him coldly. "Where indeed?" she said.

Lifting her wrist, she pushed a small indentation on her bracelet and spoke rapidly into it. Clive couldn't understand a word of what she was saying, but he would have had to be both blind and deaf not to see the anger in her eyes or to hear the tightness in her voice.

Somehow he didn't think she was about to believe in his innocence.

▪ CHAPTER FIFTEEN ▪

Annabelle got ready to charge the zeros.

Maybe they were five times bigger than the little sucker she'd taken out back in the cavern, and maybe her ass'd be grass if she tried the same trick on these guys, but she was damned if she was going to just be docilely taken away again.

She was done with prisons.

Done with being played for a patsy.

Done with fighting for her life every second step of the way.

She'd had it up right to here, thank you very much, with this frigging Dungeon.

"Don't do it," Casady said as she took her first step.

"Screw you too," she said.

But then Casady grabbed her, and Annabelle's world just did another skidding flip-flop. She had the Baalbec turned on. There was no way—no *way*—he could grab her. But she could feel his fingers on her arm, his hand reaching through the Baalbec's field as if it weren't even there.

"You can't . . . that's impossible. . . ."

The Baalbec had to be malfunctioning.

Casady shook his head. "You keep forgetting—I'm not really here."

"But I can feel you. . . ."

He shook his head again. "It's a play on your senses. I'm just a collection of juiced-up molecules, made up to play Jack Casady. I feel real to you because your head tells me I'm here. I feel real to me because that's the way I've been programmed. But I'm just a glorified piece of playback, Annabelle, fired up with a high-tech AI program. Your Baalbec knows I'm not here."

"But your gun . . ."

"It's a real gun—fires real bullets."

"How can you hold it?"

"Because the molecules I borrow to make me exist can be as solid or permeable as I want 'em to be. I keep going just so long as the program's juiced up."

"And when the music fades . . ."

"I fade."

"Annabelle?"

So intent had she been on what the GBCer was telling her that she'd entirely forgotten the danger they were in. At Smythe's quiet call she looked up to find that the large zeros had closed in on them, leaving them no room to maneuver.

The cybernetic creatures made no move; they just boxed the group in, not allowing them any egress from the square. With their shining metal and plastic hides they looked like something an engineer might've designed on an acid trip in a hardware store.

Annabelle took a step forward, and a bright red laser cut the pavement before her feet, slagging the concrete. She quickly stepped back, not wanting to test her Baalbec's capabilities. Not when the GBCer could put his hand through its field. Didn't matter how reasonable an explanation Casady had to give, the experience had spooked her.

"Now what?" Annabelle said, staring one of the ugly suckers straight in the face. "So you got us. What're you going to do with us?"

A voice, its tone metallically nonhuman, spoke from the voice box under the chin of the zero directly in front of her.

"You will remain passive until an agent of authority arrives. Please be warned, any untoward movement will require the mobile tactical units to fire."

"At least they don't mean to kill us," Tomàs said.

Annabelle nodded without any enthusiasm. "Yeah, they want to save that pleasure for themselves. What'll it be this time, guys? A takeoff on an Inca sacrifice? Or maybe we'll get to play Christ on a cross."

"We've escaped from worse situations," Sidi said.

Annabelle regarded him for a long moment, knowing he meant well, but she was just too depressed to be able to find anything optimistic about their situation.

"Hooray," she said as she turned off her Baalbec and sat down on the pavement.

The lasers mounted on the bodies of the nearest zeros tracked her every movement. She turned her back on them.

One by one the others followed her example. Her foul mood was affecting them all. Finnbogg sat mumbling to himself. Tomàs looked more as she remembered him from before, sullen and with secrets brooding in his dark eyes. Sidi sat unsmiling with Smythe beside him; the Englishman was stoic as always, but grimly so now. Only Casady seemed unaffected.

Of course, she thought, he wasn't real.

He sat down close to Annabelle.

"You're doing this to them," he said softly.

"Doing what?"

But she knew. They were all picking up on her bad vibes, and the whole thing was just feeding on itself now.

"You're the leader," Casady said. "No matter what expertise the others might have that you do not, you have that one special quality to set you apart. They will follow you."

"Great. Look where it's gotten us."

Casady ignored her sarcasm. "Yes, look," he said. "All the way down to the eighth level of the Dungeon, whereas most prisoners don't even make it past the first few."

Annabelle shook her head. "You don't understand. We can't win this one on points. We either get to the end and win, or we end up like we are now—royally screwed."

"As your friend said—you've made it through worse."

"Yeah, but every time it takes a little more out of you until it gets to the point where you've got nothing left and it doesn't matter diddly anymore." She looked over at the zeros, then back at him. "I don't think you *can* understand. I mean, the worst that can happen to you is you run out of the juice that the music gives you, and you end up back on your card until somebody else comes along and calls you up—am I right?"

"Yes, but—"

"You've got this sixties mentality that you never grew out of—a weird combination of peace, love, and karma, and some kick-ass that you never left behind from before you got enlightened."

"So?"

All Annabelle could do was look at him.

So? Right. Maybe more to the point, so what?

It was like Philosophy 100 and "Why?/Why not?" Or that quote she'd heard about some traditional Irish musician who, when asked why he played so fast, simply said, "Because I can."

It was all in your attitude. That was what Casady was trying to say. Didn't matter if he was just a GBCer playing at being real, or a flesh-and-blood holdover from the sixties, marooned here in the Dungeon with them. What he said was true. It still came down to your attitude.

Think like a winner, and you win.

Why climb that mountain? Because it's there.

Like all that pop psychology bullshit that started up in the seventies and kept right on trucking, all the way into her own decade.

You can do it if you want to.

Think frigging positive.

But it was all a front. Most of the time, while you were playing smart and brave and on top of things, you were just scared shitless inside and feeling like a dummy. And it got harder each time, not easier.

She looked at her companions, at the circle of glum faces, most of which didn't even bother to look back at her. And sighed.

"I guess you remember sit-ins and be-ins—right?" she said to Casady.

He nodded. "Why do you ask?"

"My mom used to talk to me about them, about how people would just get together and not budge until something got done. About how maybe you couldn't change the whole world, but if you at least changed yourself, you were doing *something*. That kinda bullshit."

Casady smiled. "I can see why you'd think that way. Sometimes we got our asses kicked, but sometimes . . . sometimes it worked."

"Yeah. I know. I got the point already. What I'm trying to say is thanks."

Before he could reply, she stood up and hauled Tomàs to his feet beside her.

"Christo!" he muttered. "Now what—"

She shut him up by starting to sing "We Shall Overcome."

Tacky, she thought, but hell. It had easy words and a nice, simple melody line.

Casady rose to his feet, pulling Finnbogg up beside him. Sidi and Smythe joined them. Arms linked, they all sang as loud as they could, cleaning the fear out of their hearts, just letting the music ring there, hard and sure.

If I saw this on the nightly news, Annabelle thought, I'd think we were all whacked out.

But it was a different world here. They were all feeling down. And damned if sometimes the old bullshit didn't cut straight through the new.

They were still singing when the Chaffri arrived.

When the torches finally gave out, Neville's party lost not only their source of light, but their means of measuring time as well. Knowing that each torch had lasted for twenty minutes made it easy to reckon how long they had been traveling and to schedule rest stops. With the last torch gone they were reduced to feeling their way along the shaft, slowed down to a snail's crawl, and time lost its meaning.

In the darkness a minute and an hour took on too similar a denotation.

They made slow progress—even if, with the endless similarity of the ventilation shaft, it seemed as though they made no progress at all—and they all began to suffer from a mild sense of claustrophobia. It was not until their third rest stop after the torches ran out that they began to perceive a difference: that chemical scent in the air, faintly detected when they first entered, seemed somewhat stronger now.

And then a scout brought back the welcome news that he'd spied light ahead.

Though they had been resting only a few moments, they were all so heartily sick of the shaft, of the darkness, of their interminable journey through both, that they immediately mounted once more and set off to find that source of light.

It proved to be a grating that looked out on an immense city.

Neville marveled to look out on it—such an expanse of streets and buildings, all nestled here underground, lit by long banks of lights on the cavern roof above that were too bright to look at for long. It seemed a great waste to him that, with so much knowledge and ability in their hands, the Dungeonmasters used it for no more than vexing the prisoners that they kidnapped and placed in the game-board maze that the Dungeon was.

What a man could do with what they had!

"Thank the Great Wind," Alyssa said. "We've done it."

The grating was so small that only three of them could stand shoulder to shoulder and look out at one time. They each took their turns, studying the streets below them. Like the city above this place appeared to be deserted as well. But here there was no rubble, no sense of decay or destruction. Simply an emptiness.

"How to get down from this shaft," Neville said. "That's our problem now."

I could spin a line, Shriek said.

Neville nodded, remembering what he'd heard of an earlier descent that she and the others of her party had made from one level to another.

"Perhaps," he said. "Though first we'd have to get through this grating. . . ."

But the spacing between its bars was too small to allow them egress. And the immense screws locking the grate to the walls of the shaft were too large and too firmly in place to budge, even when they tried two at a time on one screw.

"So we travel on," Fenil said.

"And a good thing too," Neville said quietly as he looked through the grating once more.

"Wha—" Alyssa began, but Neville laid a finger across her lips.

"Look," he said softly.

On the street below them a pair of monstrously large creatures had appeared, pacing slowly down the smooth pavement. They were like the cyborg, Chang Guafe, Neville thought. Some combination of metal workings, fused with a living creature. Mechanical centaurs—if one exchanged the horse and man for a dog and dwarf.

Of course their large size was a matter of scale, Neville realized. To his party they were giants—as every other creature had been on this level except for the Tuan—but in relation to the buildings and streets below, they were the size of large terriers.

"What are they?" Alyssa asked.

"I don't know. But we had a member of our party—human in shape—that reminds me of them."

Guafe, Shriek said.

Neville nodded. "Still, I wouldn't be so likely to trust these creatures as I would our erstwhile companion."

They waited until the creatures had traveled the length of the street and disappeared from view before moving on themselves. Their own route was easier now, for the gratings were spaced regularly enough so that the darkest it became was at those places equidistant between two apertures, and there it was no more than the deep twilight just before night that Neville remembered from his homeworld.

Making good time, they reached a branching in the shaft about an hour later. Part of the shaft continued on at the same level; the new branch led downward at a sudden steep angle. After some discussion they chose the route that would take them down.

The claws of the silvers scraped and slid on the metal floor of the shaft as they made their steep descent. Eventually it grew so difficult that Shriek had to release a line from her spinnerets. She attached one end to the wall of the shaft where they were, then took the lead on the way down, playing out the sticky thread behind her. The silvers, once the Tuan showed them how to walk on the thread, soon picked up the knack of using it for a brake for the remainder of the descent.

At the bottom of the shaft they had a choice of dozens of new routes. Through the gratings here they could see inside the buildings. The shaft they chose eventually led them into one of the buildings. Here they found shafts that led them straight into the casings of a number of large machines that reminded both Neville and Shriek of the computer banks they had seen on previous levels.

"We can get down to the ground now," Fenil remarked the next time they paused to take stock of their surroundings.

He indicated a spiraling descent created by loops of cables inside the machine where they were resting. At the floor level they could see that there was enough space between the sides of the machine and the floor to allow them to creep through.

"True enough," Neville said. "But this part of the city appears to be deserted. We might as well continue through the shafts until we reach a peopled area."

"If there is one," Yoors said.

"Oh, there will be one," Alyssa said. "I can *feel* other presences."

She closed her eyes, then with a loose wave of her

arm indicated the direction in which they were already traveling.

"That way."

Neville gave her an odd look. Was she going to prove to be a psychic now? But then he remembered that she was the priestess of these Tuan, as well as their secular leader. Who knew what a Tuan priestess was capable of? In this Dungeon he had seen too much that was strange simply to dismiss such a thing.

Being Neville has the right of it, I believe, Shriek said. *Once we reach a peopled area, we will have a safe vantage point from which to spy on them in these shafts.*

"And we can take further counsel at that point," Alyssa said.

The only drawback that Neville saw to this, even if it had been his idea in the first place, was that he was soundly tired of feeling like a mouse or a rat, scrambling about inside these walls.

"And if we can't descend from the shaft in those peopled areas?" Yoors asked.

"It's a trade-off," Neville replied. "No question about it."

"But a chance we will take," Alyssa decided.

There was no argument from the Tuan once she had made her decision.

Counsel taken and their course determined, they set off again.

For the second time in as many days Clive found himself connected to the Ren's truth detector, the electrodes attached to each of his temples, his wrists, his ankles, and his chest. Once again three Speakers sat at the desk before him. Speaker Lena was not amongst them. She sat to one side of the desk, glaring at him. There were three guards present—standing watch behind Clive—and two techs to run the machines.

"I don't believe you had anything to do with your friend's escape," Chary told him in a soft voice as she and Howell were connecting him to the machine.

Clive gave her a weak smile. That was small comfort when the truth detector would proclaim his lies.

Damn Guafe for putting him in this position in the first place.

He was in for it—no question about it—unless . . . Clive nodded to himself. Unless he told the truth. Not enough to incriminate himself—just enough to keep the evaluator from setting off its alarm, or whatever it was that it did to tell the Ren that its subject was playing them false.

Chary turned on the machine, and it began to hum on its trolley beside Clive. That odd buzzing sensation that he remembered from his previous experience with the evaluator returned. It traveled the length of his spine, spreading out to every nerve end while an unnatural sensation of warmth settled in the base of his spine.

"How many of us are sitting at this table?" the centermost Speaker asked him.

He was the same one who had been present the last time. His name was Kian, Clive remembered. The other two Speakers had been introduced as Ovard—he was on the left, yet another short, dapper man—and Berna, a red-haired woman with cold gray eyes. Speaker Lena appeared to be merely observing the proceedings this time.

Speaker Kian frowned. "I asked you—"

Lord, this infantile test again, Clive thought, but he replied before one of the guards behind him jabbed him with the muzzle of his weapon.

"Three. Four if you count Speaker Lena."

"What is the color of our robes?"

"Blue."

"Are you a native of this world? Please answer in the affirmative."

"I am."

With each reply Clive made the evaluator hummed at his side, sending that curious buzz to follow the traceries of his nervous system. He felt a sense of disorientation creep over him. His surroundings took on a surreal quality, while his mind seemed to sharpen. It was almost as though he could see *within* the objects about him.

The stark furniture blurred as though it were slightly vibrating. The Ren were still human shapes, but their features and bodies had clouded into smears of swirling color.

Clive blinked away the sudden sheen of perspiration that dripped into his eyes.

Speaker Kian glanced at the techs.

"Can we continue?" he asked.

"Adjustments have been made," Howell said. "You can question him now."

Speaker Ovard steepled his fingers and gave Clive a long, serious look. "What is your purpose in this Dungeon?" he asked.

Clive made an effort to concentrate on his reply. But it was difficult. The Speaker's words appeared to issue from his mouth as both sound and swirls of color.

"To find my companions and to escape," Clive said.

The buzz whined through his nerves.

"And?" Speaker Berna asked.

"Have our satisfaction from the Dungeonmasters for how they have treated us."

Again the machine's hum. Again the quiver running the length of his neural system.

"Are we your enemy?" Speaker Kian asked.

Clive blinked as more sweat pooled in his eyes. The entire room seemed to be shimmering.

"I . . . I don't know."

That appeared to perplex them, for the three Speakers at the table bent their heads close together and whispered amongst each other for a few moments.

"Where has your companion gone?"

"I don't know."

"Why did he abandon you? What is his purpose?"

"I presume the same as all of us—to escape."

Each reply Clive made intensified the evaluator's response on his nervous system. He felt as though his

entire body were humming along in concert with it—
each cell vibrating. Faster and faster.

Lord, he thought. What is happening to me?

"I ask you again," Speaker Kian said finally. "Do you
perceive us as your enemy?"

It took a long moment for Clive to gather his
thoughts. It was increasingly difficult for him to concentrate on any one thing for longer than a moment.
As soon as he focused on an object or a thought, his
entire being appeared to spin about it.

"I don't know what you want with me," he managed
finally. "If you are asking me, do I trust you"—he
paused to let the swirling room slow down enough for
him to complete his sentence—"then the answer is
no."

"He is speaking the truth," Howell said. His voice
was so clinical that it cut through the blur affecting
Clive, giving Clive a momentary respite.

Speaker Ovard pursed his lips. "And your companion? Why did you help him escape?"

"I . . ."

Then it happened again. There was a hissing and
popping sound from the evaluator beside Clive as it
shorted out. The room became a plummeting mael-
strom in which he bobbed helplessly like a piece of
flotsam, tugged free from some safe harbor. Dimly he
could hear voices crying out in alarm.

"The evaluator—it's feeding back again!"

"Cut the power!"

Blue fire ran through Clive's nerves. He could feel
Chary plucking the electrodes from his skin. They
popped free with sounds that echoed in Clive's mind.

"I told you we shouldn't have used this on him
again," she was saying. "Something in his neural system sets up a feedback and shorts everything out."

Clive lolled in the chair, head on his chest, eyes
rolled backward. Once again he lost all awareness of his
surroundings and went traveling through a gray mist.

Esmond, he called into the fog, but there was no
reply.

Of course there wouldn't be. Esmond, if he had ever existed, had sacrificed himself and been taken away by the Gatherer of Shriek's afterworld.

Free-falling in the mist, his thoughts coalesced into a more orderly form. With only the grayness about him his mind was no longer confused by the bewildering input of surreal data with which it had been forced to contend.

That machine of the Ren. Lord help him, what did it *do* to him?

An oval clearing appeared in the grayness. Drifting directly before it, Clive found himself looking into a Victorian sitting room—just as he had the previous time that the evaluator had sent him into this place— only this time the room was empty.

He leaned as close to the oval as he could propel himself.

"George?" he called softly.

From his vantage point he could see what he supposed was du Maurier's desk. The green blotter held a scatter of manuscript pages and half-completed pen-and-ink drawings. Clive's shocked gaze centered on one almost-complete drawing.

It was that of a woman, obviously attending a fancy dress ball. Her costume was that of Little Bo-Peep, illustrating, Clive realized, a poem of the same name that lay on the desk beside the drawing. But it was neither costume nor poem that drew and held Clive's gaze.

It was the woman's face.

Those familiar features.

God help him. A pen-and-ink Annabella Leighton looked back at him from that drawing. Du Maurier had used her as the model for that piece.

Clive knew such a pang of loss that all he felt was a bleak emptiness inside. He already knew, from what Annabella's own descendant Annabelle had told him, that he had never returned to England. Never returned to Annabella, pregnant with their child.

But he had once—in that damnable dream that the

Dungeonmasters had forced upon him. Perhaps, he thought, despair lying thick on him, he should have closed his mind to the lie of it. Perhaps he should simply have remained in that dream because, for the first time since coming to the Dungeon, the fact hit home that he would never actually escape this damnable place.

All that he had been, all that he might have been, had been stolen away by the machinations of the Dungeonmasters—God curse their souls!

He tried to turn his gaze from the drawing but could not. He reached for it, through the oval opening, but it was as though he were outside a window, looking in. His fingers were stopped by invisible glass.

The door of the room opened then, and Clive finally dragged his gaze from the drawing to see du Maurier enter the room.

"G-george . . ."

Du Maurier stopped dead in his tracks and stared at him. The shock of familiarity ran across his features as he recognized Clive.

"Don't leave so quickly this time!" he cried as he hurried toward the oval opening.

But already Clive could feel the Dungeon pulling him back—away from the oval that allowed him to look upon, but not touch, the England he had lost. Away from his old comrade.

If he could just pass a message to Annabella through him . . .

"Tell her," he began.

The pull of the Dungeon grew too strong, dragging him back into the gray mists.

"Clive!" du Maurier cried. "For God's sake, man! Don't go."

"Tell her . . ."

But the gray mists washed over the oval, shutting it from view like draperies being drawn across a window, and the hole that let him look into his old life was lost again.

The fog settled in his head, clouding his mind.

"Tell her that I love her still," he said. "That I always will."

But there was no one there in the mist to hear what he said.

When he finally regained consciousness, it was to find himself back in that chamber modeled on the Victorian world he had lost, the same chamber he had awoken in when the machines had malfunctioned the first time and sent his mind spiraling away into the grayness. Chary and Speaker Lena were both sitting there, watching him.

He sat up slowly.

"I apologize," Speaker Lena said. "The evaluator shows you spoke the truth. You knew nothing of your companion's plans."

"I told you things would work out," Chary said.

Clive realized that the female tech was interested in him—as a man, rather than simply as a subject for her labs. But with that pen-and-ink drawing of Annabella still fresh in his mind, he knew he would not reciprocate her feelings.

He swung his feet to the floor.

"Tell me what it is you want me to do," he said to Speaker Lena.

"I'm so sorry about the accident with the evaluator," the Speaker said. "But you must understand. We are surrounded on all sides by enemies. Without assurances—"

Clive was rapidly losing all semblance of patience.

"Didn't you hear me?" he said. "Tell me what you want done, and I will do it. Not tomorrow. Not when your Speakers can bring themselves together long enough to convene some new council. But now."

Speaker Lena regarded him for a long moment, then quickly nodded her head. She rose to her feet.

"Come with me," she said.

· CHAPTER SIXTEEN ·

Annabelle's first impression of the Chaffri was that they looked like a bunch of Mardi Gras Indians, all decked out in colors so bright it hurt her eyes. She'd been leading her companions through a version of the Wailing Men's "Anger's Not Enough"—a moldy-gold hit from 1991—and their voices all trailed off at the newcomers' approach.

There were a half dozen of them, two women, the rest men, all of them white-skinned, but everything else screamed color. Serapes, trousers, and baggy shirts painted day-glo bright, headdresses and vests of multihued feathers, faces daubed with garish makeup thick as war paint—exactly the kind of whacked-out madcap inventors who would put together cybernetic machines like the zeros with their metallic bodies festooned with what looked more like decorative additions than anything serviceable.

But, she reminded herself, those decorations on the zeros hid laser mountings—lasers powerful enough to slag the concrete at their feet. Who knew what the hell the Chaffri had going for them under their feathers and gear?

She started to flick on her Baalbec, but then thought twice about it.

Right. Real compassionate of you, Annie B. Stand here cocooned in the Baalbec's force field, all nice and protected, while her friends had to face their captors with nothing but their clothing and skin to protect them. Because ever since their escape from the prison in Q'oorna, the Baalbec was no longer operating at its full potential. Time was she could have held them all in its force field. Since then it just barely worked on herself and—considering what had happened with Casady—she couldn't even be sure of that anymore.

She let her hand fall back from her bodice.

"Which of you is the Folliot?" the foremost of the Chaffri asked, speaking the patois of the Dungeon with a stiff accent.

"Depends," Annabelle said after a pause that was a heartbeat long, "on how true-blue you want the blood."

The Chaffri's gaze shifted to her, eyes narrowing. "You are a descendant?"

Annabelle shrugged. "Got the blood—that's all I know. Can't show you a pedigree, but of course you folks already know that."

"What is that supposed to mean?"

"Well, it's because of you that Clive never got back to England to make an honest woman out of my ancestor—not that any Leigh ever really gave a shit about that kind of a thing."

The Chaffri continued to study her. Finally he nodded.

"My name is K'cholik," he said. "We will require your assistance in a matter of great urgency."

He started to turn away.

"Say what?" Annabelle said.

K'cholik turned back to look at her.

"Is your hearing impaired?" he asked.

"Not as much as your brain is, pal. Who the hell do you think you are, ordering me about? And what makes you think I'm going to help you anyway?"

"It is not a matter of whether you are willing to or not," another of the Chaffri replied—one of the women this time. "It is something that must simply be done, or you will suffer the consequences."

Annabelle shook her head. "I don't believe you guys. What is it? Something in the air down here that makes you crazy? I'm not doing diddly until you straighten out a few items—starting with sending away your watchdogs here."

"Impossible," the woman said.

K'cholik turned to her. "There is no need to argue with them, Unaa. The zeros will bring them along for us."

Annabelle glared at him and took a step forward, fists clenched at her sides. A laser immediately burned the concrete at her feet once more, filling the air with the reek of burnt ozone.

She stepped hastily back.

"We brought you here," Unaa told her. "You are ours to do with as we will."

"Uh-uh," Annabelle told her. "Nobody owns us."

A third Chaffri joined the conversation then—a slender man with soft dark eyes and lips so thin they were almost nonexistent. He wore his feathered headdress like some archaic punk's Mohawk.

"It won't hurt to explain," he said.

"Don't begin that old argument, Peotor," K'cholik told him.

Peotor ignored his companions. "We require your help against the Ren and Gannine," he told Annabelle. "They have joined forces recently and are moving against us."

"The Gannine?" Sidi asked.

The Chaffri's gaze shifted to him. "The Ren woke them when they finally broke the codes on one of their arsenals."

"Fascinating, I'm sure," Annabelle said. "Only who or what are the Gannine?"

"They created this gaming board—the Dungeon."

"*You're* not the Dungeonmasters—you and the Ren?"

"We were—until the Gannine woke. Now that they *are* awake, it's anyone's guess as to who will come out ahead. If they have joined with the Ren, as our spies tell us . . . we have no hope of standing against the Gannine weapons without your help."

"And just what kind of help is that, guv'nor?" Smythe asked.

Peotor blinked in surprise. "Why, blood, of course. We need the Folliot blood to power our ghosters."

"You want to drain my blood?" Annabelle said slowly.

"You won't feel any pain," Peotor assured her. "And we'll store your mind pattern and a cell sample so that we can regrow you after the final battle is done."

All Annabelle could do was stare at him. "Ghosters?" she said finally.

"Both we and the Ren have been developing them for years—it's all we have that will stand against the Gannine's superior technology. At least we hope it will. Unfortunately they require a certain rare blood type that we have, after searching hundreds of worlds, found in only one family—the Folliots."

"You're kidding—right? This is some kind of weird joke?"

"Probably not," Casady said from beside her. "Neither the Chaffri nor the Ren have any morals—and they're both experts in cybernetic construction."

The Chaffri woman named Unaa took a small tube from her pocket and pointed it at Casady. "That will be enough," she said.

Casady shrugged. "Hey, I'm only trying to tell it like it—"

When the woman pressed on the tube, there was the sound of a small whuft of displaced air. A tiny projectile struck Casady. His entire form shimmered and crackled, like the picture on a TV screen going haywire, then he literally disappeared. All that remained was the gun he'd been holding, which fell to the pavement with a loud clank.

Annabelle bent quickly to pick it up, but a zero's laser slagged the weapon before she could touch it.

"Damn GBCers," Unaa muttered.

Annabelle just stared at the place where Casady had been standing, her face registering the shock that had frozen her thoughts.

She'd known that he hadn't been real—that he was some kind of projected image, an AI program that fed on sound—but knowing and actually accepting it were two different things. Intellectually she'd known. But emotionally she'd seen him as a flesh-and-blood human being. A real person that the Chaffri had snuffed out of existence the way someone in her own world would change a channel.

"You bastards," she said as she slowly rose to her feet. "It'll be a cold day in hell before I help you."

Peotor shrugged. "Whether you want to help us or not is immaterial. We'll use your blood, with or without your consent."

"Take them away," K'cholik ordered the zeros. "Keep them in storage while we prepare the ghosters for an infusion of her blood."

"It has to be fresh, you see," Peotor told her, his voice sweet, his thin lips shaping an unpleasant smile.

"We will fight them," Tomàs said softly from behind her.

"Just say the word," Smythe added.

Fight them? Annabelle thought. Yeah, right. Like they had a hope in hell of taking more than one step forward before the zeros cut them down.

"No fighting," she said. "We don't have a chance."

She turned to look at her companions, her eyes adding, Not here. Not now. Let's wait for better odds.

And if they never got better odds?

Annabelle refused to let herself think about that.

You're the leader, Casady had told her. They will follow you.

If she held up, if she put forth a strong faith, kept hope alive, then it would at least stop her companions from despairing.

"How pleasant to see you coming to your senses," Peotor said. "This whole experience could be quite invigorating, you know. Imagine the new body you'll have. If you like, you can design adjustments, which we'll see are implemented before it comes to term. Would you like smaller breasts? Gills? A penis? It can all be arranged. And naturally your memories will all remain intact."

Annabelle looked down at the slagged handgun—all that was left of Casady—then slowly raised her gaze to meet Peotor's.

Hope, she reminded herself. Keep the faith that we'll pull through again.

She smiled at Peotor. "Before this is all over," she said, "I'm gonna have a piece of you, sweetheart."

Her companions ranged closer to her. Finnbogg started to hum under his breath "We Shall Overcome."

Annabelle glanced at him and ruffled the hair on his head. Hard to remember how pissed off she'd been with him once.

"You've got it, Finn," she said.

She turned back to face the Chaffri and held out her hands offering up her wrist. "So, are you going to chain us up or what?"

"That won't be necessary," K'cholik said. "We have a holding cell prepared for you."

Annabelle's eyes narrowed at that comment. They had a cell prepared already? So who the hell had told the Chaffri that they were coming?

"Take them away," K'cholik said.

No one in Neville's party was entirely certain as to what exactly they were looking for. They were all agreed on a confrontation with the Dungeonmasters and discovering a means of escaping the Dungeon itself. Shriek was determined to seek out the missing members of their previous company. Yoors wanted simple revenge—he no longer cared about escape himself. Alyssa was determined to understand the whys and wherefores of the Dungeon and to learn what part the Tuan had to play in it.

Neville was in basic agreement with them all. He wanted to find Clive and the others. He wanted satisfaction from their captors. And he wanted to understand.

Only where to begin with any of those courses? It was over that, that they were constantly arguing.

"We've been wandering aimlessly for hours now," Yoors said as they rested once more.

"And found nothing," another of the Tuan guards chimed in.

Fenil nodded. "No inhabitants to this place—only those machines."

"I know," Alyssa said, "but what else can we do?"

"Capture one of the machines," Yoors said promptly.

Alyssa frowned.

And do what with it, Being Yoors? Shriek asked. *They might not even be sentient. What if we put the entire party at risk to capture one of them, only to find that it* is *no more than a machine and can tell us nothing?*

"Machines don't move in random patterns as these things do," Yoors said.

"I disagree," Neville said. That earned him a glare from Yoors. "The Dungeonmasters are perfectly capable of creating machines that are sentient. Lord, Shriek. Think of Guafe. He wasn't created by the Dungeonmasters, but I'd call him more machine than man."

Shriek nodded. *It's true. He is a hybrid. And those creatures we've spied do appear to have some form of organic matter housed in their head casings.*

"So," Neville said, "while we have our differences"—he glanced at Yoors—"I also agree that if we don't come upon some human inhabitants soon, we should attempt to capture and question one of the creatures."

That earned Neville a glare from Alyssa.

"And how do you propose to do that without putting us all terribly at risk?" she asked.

Neville sighed. "Every moment we are in this Dungeon we are at risk."

"Yes—so why call it down upon ourselves, when it comes unasked for all too often?"

She looked from Neville to Yoors. The Tuan captain remained silent—no doubt, Neville thought, because

Yoors knew that Neville would argue the case, saving Yoors from yet another argument with his leader.

"Sometimes the risk is necessary," Neville said. "We need information, and I see no other method of gaining it."

Alyssa said nothing for a long moment. She looked out the nearby grating, gaze fixed on the interior of the warehouse through which their shaft was presently traveling, but Neville doubted that she saw anything. She was looking within.

"How?" she said finally, turning back to look at them. "How will we bring it down? We know nothing of its defenses. For all we know it could be linked to some central agency—by its mind, by radio, by who knows what. In some small building in the center of the city's defenses, there might well be men and women using their advanced equipment to look through the eyes of those creatures to see everything that they see."

To relatively primitive technological societies such as Neville's own, or ones that had no technology to speak of such as the Tuan's, the mechanical marvels of the Dungeon were still unfamiliar enough for them not to take every aspect of them into consideration. It was too easy to forget just what the Dungeonmasters' creations were capable of, but they had all seen enough on the previous levels for Alyssa's warning to strike home.

Such things are possible, Shriek said.

Neville nodded glumly. "All too possible."

Though he was reluctant to do so, Yoors had to agree as well. "But that still doesn't solve our problem."

"No," Alyssa said. "My suggestion is that we follow the next of these creatures we spy."

"But they move too quickly," Fenil said. "We're no more than bugs to them. How could we keep up?"

I could keep up with them, Shriek said.

Neville shook his head. "It's too soon since your ordeal."

I am much recovered now, Being Neville, though I thank you for your concern.

"Would we wait for you here?" Alyssa asked.

No. Travel on. I will find you when I have need to.
Through the neural web they shared, Neville realized.

He caught Yoors regarding Shriek and himself with new suspicion, but he said nothing to allay the Tuan's worries. The wise man didn't show all his cards.

They traveled on then, through length upon length of the ventilation shafts, following the bewildering network until they found one that brought them out of the building they were in, to a place from which they had a view of the streets once more.

"There!" one of the Tuan called softly.

Below, a pair of the curious mechanical creatures were moving down the street. They walked one to a side, staying close to the buildings that reared up tall beside them.

Shriek immediately sped back the way they had come, heading for the descent to ground level that they had passed inside the building. Neville and the Tuan remained at the grating, taking turns watching the mechanical creatures fare the length of the street.

"She's too late," Fenil said.

"Don't speak too soon," Alyssa said.

She pointed to where the tiny figure of the arachnid had just reached the street. Shriek hurried down the pavement, pausing at the corner to peer cautiously around it. They saw her look back in their direction for a brief moment; then she turned the corner and, like the creatures she followed, was lost from sight as well.

"And now?" Yoors said.

Alyssa glanced at him. "Now we go on."

"I would still like to know how she will find us again," the Tuan captain said. "It seems odd to me that she would be able to do so with any ease—unless, of course, she knows this city well."

He turned to look at Neville, who merely smiled back.

How are you doing, Shriek? he asked the arachnid, broadcasting his thoughts to her on a narrow beam so that only she could hear him.

Well enough, came her reply. *They do not appear to move too swiftly. I should have no trouble keeping up with them.*

Be careful.

I will.

Call in your position at the first sign of trouble, and for God's sake, keep out of their way.

You worry too much, Being Neville.

"I was speaking to you," Yoors said.

Neville blinked at him. "I hadn't realized it was a question."

"I want to know how your companion can find her way so easily about this city."

Neville sighed. "I can sympathize with your loss of your brother, Yoors," he said, "and I understand that you're far from home and frustrated that you can't do anything to strike back at those who have put us in this position. But I grow increasingly weary of your glares and bad humor."

Yoors growled something unintelligible and reached for his sword, but Alyssa's hand was quicker. She caught his wrist. But before she could speak, Neville leaned closer.

"You can go on by yourself," he said. "Pick any direction that suits you, and I'll go the opposite way."

"No," Alyssa said. "We will continue on together."

Neville ignored her, all his attention fixed on the Tuan captain.

"I too have lost companions who might well be dead, for all I know. I too want satisfaction from the dogs that brought us here. But while there's little I can do about either of those except for pressing on, I'll be damned if I'll put up with any more from you."

For a long moment no one spoke. Then Yoors surprised them all. He nodded slowly and reached out a hand to Neville.

"I . . . I'm sorry," he said.

Neville looked down at the proffered hand, then lifted his gaze to meet the captain's own guileless eyes.

Well, I'll be damned, Neville thought. Unless Yoors

was a better poker player than himself, it seemed the Tuan was genuinely sorry.

Neville took Yoors's hand in a firm clasp.

Perhaps he was being a fool in doing so, but Neville believed at that moment that one trust deserved another.

"We speak," he told the Tuan, "my companion and I —we speak mind to mind."

"Our agents acquired the design from the Chaffri," Speaker Lena explained.

Clive stared at the thing. It stood as tall as he did himself, but on four legs, and appeared to be made entirely of clear crystal. It had a head like a dog's— streamlined, powerful jaws, clear eyes set to either side of its face above the muzzle. Its body was a combination of an ape and a large hunting cat—a tiger or a lion. The limbs were flexible, talons on the end of each articulated finger, opposable thumbs on front and hind paws. The torso, the powerful chest and shoulders, were that of a lion.

"Acquired?" Clive said with a trace of mockery in his voice.

As Speaker Lena began a complicated explanation of just how the blueprints had fallen into the Ren's possession, Clive stepped closer to the construct and ran his fingers along its smooth skin. It was housed in yet another of the Ren's labs, deep inside their innermost complex. Most of the chamber was taken up with what Clive assumed was the apparatus with which they had created the thing that stood before him; but one wall showed the flat surface of what first appeared to be a mirror, except that it gave back no reflection.

Mostly it showed a grayness as unrelenting as that in which Clive had found himself when the evaluator malfunctioned again. But from time to time places appeared—unfamiliar views that seemed so realistic that the glass surface could only be a window looking onto each separate scene that was shown. A jungle, a city street, a frozen arctic waste, the surface of an asteroid such as the one the Dungeon was purported to be, a coniferous forest, the interior of some form of ship that moved through the dark void between planets—Clive believed that either Chang or Annabelle had once identified such ships to him as spacecraft.

The images remained for only a few moments before the grayness swallowed each in turn.

It was a gate, Clive realized. Either some new mirrored gateway that the Ren controlled, or that Gannine gate that led from the eighth level down to the ninth.

He made sure that he gave the glass no more than a curious glance before turning to study the construct that Speaker Lena had brought him here to view. But he continued to steal surreptitious glances at it as each new scene appeared. The number of different views appeared to be finite, for Clive soon recognized repetitions. The scenes passed by in the same order each time.

"What is this thing made of?" Clive asked when Speaker Lena fell silent once more.

He tapped the construct with a fingernail.

"Ordolite," Chary explained. "It's a form of plastic that's strong enough to withstand anything up to and including a direct laser hit, but flexible enough to allow complete mobility. The Gannine created it."

"The construct?"

"No. The ordolite. The Chaffri created the construct."

"They call it a ghoster," Speaker Lena added.

"I see. And what does it have to do with me?"

"All the construct needs now is to be fueled," Chary went on. "Through advanced biotechnology the fuel will replicate itself infinitely. As everything about the ghoster was constructed of ordolite, once it is operational, it will never need to be serviced again."

"And what will you use to fuel it?" Clive asked.

Chary hesitated and glanced at Speaker Lena.

"It will require your death," the Speaker said.

Somehow Clive was not surprised. All that did surprise him was how calm he felt.

"I see," he said. "And that answers my earlier question as well."

"It's not what you think," Speaker Lena hurried to assure him. "It's true this body you are wearing will die, but we will save your brain pattern and reinstate it in a new body once we have grown you one. Your new body can be exactly the same as the one you now wear, or modified to your own specifications."

"You mean to clone me, then," Clive said, the unfamiliar word coming easily to his lips.

Chary shook her head. "Not exactly. It's true that your new body will be cloned from cell samples that we will take from your old one for that purpose, but your brain pattern and personality—everything that makes you *you*—will be the original. When we bring you back, you will feel as though you're just waking from a long sleep. There will be no discomfort."

"This thing needs my death to fuel it?" Clive said.

"Your blood—yes. Folliot blood."

"Why Folliot blood?"

Both Chary and Speaker Lena shook their heads.

"That is how the Chaffri designed it," Chary said. "But as they probably stole the blueprints from the Gannine, who knows why it will work only in this fashion. We have tried other blood—but without success."

"So it will work only with my blood, or my twin's?"

"With anyone who has your blood—such as your descendant, Annabelle Leigh."

"Why didn't you merely bleed one of us when you captured us on the various other levels? Or does it require a willing sacrifice?"

"Oddly enough," Chary said, "that's exactly it. According to the data we've acquired, if the donor is not a willing participant, it will set off an imbalance in the blood, and the ghoster will not function."

"Why haven't you used any of the clones you've made of us?"

"Again," Chary said, "for all that a clone is an exact replica of its subject, only the original will work."

"Or so say the design plans we acquired," Speaker

Lena said. "We have experimented with everything except an original Folliot—all without success."

"That does not sound promising," Clive said.

"There's no need to be afraid," Speaker Lena assured him. "Even if the experiment proves to be another failure, we can still reinstate you in a new body with everything about you intact. You risk nothing."

Clive frowned, thinking. "If the ghoster's fuel can replicate itself infinitely, why must you kill me to fuel it? Why not take just a few pints?"

"Because," Chary explained, "the initial fueling requires ten pints—which is about as much as you have in your body at any given time."

"I tell you again," Speaker Lena assured him. "You risk nothing."

Nothing? Clive thought.

He looked at the ghoster construct again.

What of his soul?

For that appeared to be the flaw in their reasoning. How could their machines transfer a man's soul from one body to another? Thoughts and memories . . . After all he had seen in the Dungeon since he first arrived, with the way the Dungeonmasters had so easily manipulated his memories, he could see how thoughts and memories might be successfully transferred. But not a soul.

And that was the key to this ghoster construct, he believed.

It didn't simply require his original Folliot blood to function—it required his soul. And that was too dear a price to pay.

Not that he had ever had any intention of helping either the Ren or the Chaffri in the first place. He meant to bring them low, plain and simple, and to take down the Gannine while he was about it. They were monstrosities—all three races.

He laid his hand on the construct's smooth synthetic skin once more, then slowly turned to his companions.

"When do we begin?" he asked.

Speaker Lena appeared taken aback for a moment, but she quickly recovered.

"Why, immediately," she said. "It will take us a few moments to set up the proper procedures. . . ." She glanced at Chary.

"We can be ready to go in fifteen minutes," the tech said.

"That quickly?" Clive said.

Speaker Lena turned back to him. "You are absolutely certain you wish to go through with this?" she asked.

"Oh, yes."

"Then I'll take you to a more comfortable place where we can wait while the techs ready their equipment."

"I'd prefer to wait here," Clive said, laying his hand on the ghoster's shoulder once more. "To meditate with my . . . I suppose we could call it my descendant, couldn't we?"

"I suppose you could," Speaker Lena said with a slow nod. "Chary, will you see to the preparations?"

"Right away."

Clive waited until the tech had left the room. Once he and Speaker Lena were alone, he turned from the ghoster to look at her.

"You must think very badly of us," she said.

Clive found a smile. "Not at all." He stepped away from the construct, closer to her. "You are fighting for survival—it's a very understandable reaction."

"I knew you would understand."

"As I hope you'll understand this," Clive said.

Before the Speaker could move to escape him or sound an alarm, he struck her with a roundhouse blow in her solar plexus. Speaker Lena dropped like a felled ox. Clive darted for the mirrored wall.

"N-no!" Speaker Lena cried from where she lay.

Clive turned to see her struggling unsuccessfully to regain her feet.

"I'm fighting for survival too," he said.

He glanced at the gateway. Damn, he needed more

time. The view of the city street was just disappearing. That meant the next one would be the arctic tundra, followed by the asteroid—at least two views before there was another suitable one, which would be the forest.

He could hear someone at the door.

"Those are . . . are Randoms pictured there," Speaker Lena said, obviously fighting nausea. Her eyes implored him not to step through.

The gate showed only grayness.

Clive heard a sound at the door.

Damn them all, they were coming back too soon.

"Randoms are . . . they are . . ." Her throat convulsed as though she were holding back bile.

The door opened with a crash, armed guards appearing in its threshold.

The grayness of the gate changed to the arctic scene.

"They are only . . . Gannine fictions. . . ." Speaker Lena managed.

Clive didn't know what she meant by either Randoms, or fictions. All he knew was that he had this one chance to escape. He would get no other.

"D-don't!" Speaker Lena cried.

But Clive was already stepping through.

CHAPTER SEVENTEEN

The Chaffri's holding cell turned out to be an area of general confinement where they locked up both their own criminals, and trespassers into their half of Downside. Of the two dozen or so others who were their fellow prisoners, most were humanoids, Annabelle noted as she was pushed inside with the rest of her party. But there were a few of the truly alien beings that she'd run into more than once in the Dungeon.

She spotted one, with a chitinous skin and six limbs, that reminded her of Shriek, though the arachnid had two more limbs; in another corner a ball of fur unrolled enough so that a pair of eyes could examine them, before whatever creature it was rolled itself up again.

She turned back to look at the Chaffri as the cell door closed behind her.

"We will be coming for you soon," Peotor told her as he locked the door. "You'd do best to compose yourself —the ghoster requires your willing participation."

In their feathered finery and day-glo clothing, with the gaudy face paint on their white skin, the Chaffri reminded Annabelle of nothing so much as clowns.

Right. Clowns, she thought. Make that death clowns.

"You'll rot in hell before I help you," she told him.

Peotor smiled. "I know you mean that, but you'll come willingly all the same. It's that, or we'll take your friends apart in front of you—one piece at a time."

"You—"

"Really, you have no reason to be so upset. Help us, and your friends live, and you will come out of this with a new body."

Before Annabelle could reply to that, he turned and joined the remainder of the Chaffri who were leaving the holding cells.

"I'll have your balls, you lowlife!" Annabelle shouted after them, but the metal door locking the holding cells from the remainder of the Chaffri's security complex had already closed with a large clank.

She sighed and turned to look at her cellmates again. When three familiar figures rose from among the strangers, she blinked with surprise, her anger momentarily forgotten.

"Jesus—how'd you guys get here?"

Facing her were two of the Japanese from New Kwajalein, back on the Dungeon's first level—Sergeant Nomura, who had been in charge of the Japanese fighter plane, the Nakajima 97, and Chuichi Fushida, the sergeant who had been in command of the raiding party that captured Annabelle. But the one who took up her immediate attention was the cyborg, Chang Guafe.

"Where's Clive?" she asked. "And the others?"

"You are the first of our party that I have seen since Clive and I were separated in the Ren half of this city," Guafe replied. "I was making my way to the Chaffri gate when I was captured."

Smythe pushed closer. "What about Clive?" he demanded. "How is he? Damn it, man, *where* is he?"

"Still with the Ren. He has . . ."

The cyborg hesitated—an unusual action for him, Annabelle realized with a sinking feeling. Whatever he was going to say, it was going to be very bad.

"He's what?" she asked, not sure she even wanted to hear it.

"He has joined forces with the Ren."

"But they are our enemies," Tomàs said. *"Christo!* Surely he is just pretending to help them?"

"I hope so."

"You don't sound so sure about that," Annabelle said.

Guafe shrugged—another unfamiliar gesture. "He did not confide his plans to me."

So just how did they get separated? Annabelle wondered, but she decided that now wasn't the time to get into it. If Guafe had wanted to talk about it, he'd have told them.

She turned to the Japanese. "It is good to see you both again," she said, giving them each a quick short nod of her head. "Fushida-san, Nomura-san."

The Japanese seemed very happy to see a familiar face. "We are pleased to meet with you again, Sacred One."

Annabelle sighed. Christ, not this again. But she didn't have the energy to argue it with them.

"How did you get here?" she asked.

"These people—the Chaffri," Fushida said. "After we recovered the Nakajima from where you abandoned it—"

"Oh, yeah. Sorry about that."

"—the Chaffri raided New Kwajalein to steal it from us."

"What do they want with that old plane?" Annabelle wondered aloud.

Nomura shrugged. "They have not confided in us, *neh?*"

"We were working on a new fuel system," Fushida went on, "when the Chaffri attacked. They had a machine that swallowed the Nakajima whole—with us in it. The next thing we knew we were in this city. When the Chaffri discovered us, they locked us up in these cells, and we have been here ever since."

"They will tell us nothing," Nomura said.

Fushida spat on the cell floor. "They have no sense of honor."

"They don't have much of anything worthwhile," Annabelle said. She was about to question them further when they were approached by one of the other prisoners.

He was tall and lean, skin a dark mulatto that told Annabelle that he wasn't a renegade Chaffri—not unless there was more to them than the bunch who'd captured her. This man had the look of the street about him—quick eyes that took everything in, a stance that left him ready to move in any direction. A careful man. But when he spoke, Annabelle couldn't help but put him down for yet another lunatic.

"He called you the Sacred One," the man began.

"Yeah, but he—"

"You must call them down to help us. The Chaffri aren't just sending us up to the Dives anymore. They're building zeros like crazy, and it's our brains that are going to be sitting in those frigging ordolite heads."

"Call who?" Annabelle asked.

"The Gannine. You *are* the Madonna, aren't you?"

Annabelle had to laugh. "Me? I don't think so, pal. I never could hold with that virgin birth crap."

"No, no," the stranger said. "I'm not talking about mythology. I mean, the Madonna of the Gannine—their agent."

Another man approached then—shorter, hair curly as a corkscrew, slight of frame.

"She might not know, Kan," he said.

The first man turned to look at the newcomer. "What do you mean?"

"Remember what the Cloak told us?"

The man named Kan nodded slowly. "I see."

"Yeah, well I don't," Annabelle said. "Would someone tell me what the hell's going on here?"

"Well, you see—" the second man began.

"Hold on—what's your name? And what are you guys doing in here?"

"I'm Sordiam and my friend here is Kan. We're Divers. We got picked up on a smuggling run."

"Okay." Annabelle made the introductions around her own party. "So this Cloak you were talking about—he's an agent of the Gannine?"

She remembered Casady talking about the Cloak, something about how he was also called the Lightbringer—Lucifer.

Sordiam nodded. "Only he didn't know it until very recently—when he was contacted by the Gannine and taken down to the ninth level."

"If he was taken down, how did he come to speak to you about it?"

"We were there when they took him," Kan said.

"What did he look like?" Annabelle asked.

Now she was afraid that if they thought she was the Madonna, someone might decide that Clive or Neville was this Cloak. If either of them had been taken down to the ninth level by the Gannine, she might never see them again.

"Better yet," she added before either man could reply, "what do the Gannine look like?"

"We don't know," Sordiam replied. "It happened in a back alley, Topside, where it was dark as shit and all we could hear were the voices."

"And the Cloak?"

"He's a black man."

Sordiam went on to describe a figure that seemed very familiar to Annabelle.

"That sounds like Baron Samedi."

Kan nodded. "That was the name we knew him by."

"But he's dead. We saw him die on the seventh level."

"Several times," Sidi added.

"Those were his clones that died."

"Oh, Jesus," Annabelle said, rubbing her temples. "When are things going to start making sense?"

She looked at her companions and saw the same mix of bafflement and exasperation on their faces.

"We heard what the Chaffri pig said to you," Sordiam went on. "He wants to bleed you to fuel their ghosters —right?"

Annabelle nodded. "He said they'll run only on Folliot blood."

"I've heard that name before," Kan said.

"Where?" Smythe asked eagerly.

"From the Gannine, when they were talking to the Cloak—Baron Samedi. They made it sound like Folliots and the Gannine were one and the same thing."

"Makes sense when you think about it," Sordiam added. "The Chaffri stole the design of the ghosters from the Gannine. Why wouldn't it take Gannine blood to make them run?"

"Now wait a minute," Annabelle said. "There's no way I'm related to the people running this place. I'm not their Madonna, Folliots are Englishmen, not Dungeonmasters, and—"

The door to the holding cells clanged open and Peotor was there with a pair of zeros, each the height of a human. Further conversation died on their lips as they nervously regarded the Chaffri.

"Such a fascinating discussion," he said.

"Listen, you—" Annabelle began, finding her voice, but Peotor cut her off.

"Have you made your decision? Do you come willingly, or must we take apart a few of your friends first?"

"I . . ."

Sidi stepped close to her side. "Don't worry about us, Annabelle."

"Sim," Tomàs said, flanking her on the other side from Sidi. "We will stand or fall together."

Smythe and Finnbogg ranked themselves beside her, as did, much to her surprise, Guafe and the two Japanese. Sordiam and Kan each took a step away from her and watched the proceedings with interest.

"Sorry, guys," Annabelle told her companions. "But I've gotta go."

Because she couldn't stand by and watch anyone die for her. No way. It would serve no purpose.

Was this the position that Clive had found himself in? she wondered. Forced to join their enemies—or at least pretend to join them—until the chance arose for his own escape?

"No," Sidi said. "You can't—"

But Annabelle just shook her head. "I've got to," she said. "I . . . I'll see you around sometime. Say hello to Clive and the others if you run into them."

"Do not trust them," Tomàs said. "They will kill us anyway—turn us into"—he glanced at Sordiam and Kan—"into those zeros, as these men have told us."

Annabelle just shook her head. Turning from Peotor's view, she gave them all a wink and lifted her hand to her bodice, reminding them of all it would take to activate her Baalbec.

"I'm taking the chance that they'll keep their word," she said.

"Of course we will keep our word," Peotor said.

While his zeros kept their lasers trained on the prisoners, the Chaffri unlocked the cell door and ushered Annabelle out.

"If you will follow me," he said, once he had relocked the cell.

Annabelle lifted a hand to her friends, then the door shut behind her, and she was in a long hall with Peotor and the zeros, the holding cells lost from view. The sound of their passage echoed hollowly down the corridor.

Neville was attempting to describe a London theater to Alyssa when he finally heard Shriek's voice in his mind once more. He and the Tuan had traveled through miles of ventilation shaft—miles by the reckoning of their size, at any rate—since taking their leave of the arachnid. Through all that time there had been no word from Shriek, and Neville had hesitated in contacting her himself for fear of interrupting her at some crucial moment when she might need all of her concentration.

As the hours had passed, he couldn't help but worry.

Being Neville?

I hear you, Shriek, he replied, the relief obvious in his voice. *Have you run into trouble?*

Not yet. But I have found others who need our help.

Others?

Neville could feel her smile in his mind.

The missing members of our company, she told him.

You have? How are they? Where are they? Have you spoken to Clive?

Shriek hesitated for a long heartbeat before replying. *Your brother is not among them,* she said.

Where is he? What happened to him?

I do not know. I do not see the Guafe being either.

An image suddenly filled Neville's mind, and he realized he was seeing through Shriek's eyes. It was a fly's view of a hallway down which marched the various members of their erstwhile company. Annabelle and Smythe, Sidi and Tomàs, loyal Finnbogg. They were obviously the prisoners of the cybernetic creatures and gaudily clad humans who walked with them.

The latter, Neville realized, must be the elusive inhabitants of this city.

Where are you? he asked.

From the strength of your voice I believe we are fairly close to each other, Shriek replied. *I will keep our mind link open so that you can use it to home in on my position.*

We'll be with you as soon as we can, Neville said.

He opened his eyes and looked at Alyssa.

"Shriek has found my companions," he said.

"Where are they?"

"Not far. The Dungeonmasters have them prisoner." He rose to his feet. "Will you come with me?"

Alyssa nodded and stood as well. "Of course," she said, adding to her people, "To mount!"

In moments the Tuan were mounted and riding their silvers at a swift pace through the ventilation shafts, following Neville's lead. Twice they ran into dead ends and had to backtrack, but they were quickly gaining on Shriek, for her mental voice continued to grow stronger in Neville's mind.

A word of caution, Being Neville, she warned him at one point.

And that is?

There is an enormous size discrepancy between ourselves and the others of our party.

What do you mean?

But even as he asked, Neville already knew what she would say. He'd guessed it himself. Somehow that mirror they had traveled through to reach this level of the Dungeon had altered their size.

We would fit into the palms of their hands, Shriek replied.

Wonderful, Neville thought. Tiny as they were, how could they even hope to effect a rescue of the others?

The ventilation shafts continued to unwind beneath the quick pace of the Tuan's silvers.

They've stopped now, Shriek called back to Neville. Again his mind filled with images of what she saw.

A prison cell, Neville said.

Shriek gave a mental nod. *And I see the Guafe being. But not my brother.*

I will wait until their captors leave before approaching them.

No, Neville sent back. *Wait for our arrival instead. If one of the other prisoners mistakes you for a—pardon me, Shriek—a bug . . .*

I will contact them through mindspeaking.

I still say wait for us. Who knows? Perhaps their captors can communicate mentally as well. If you mindspeak while they're present, we could all end up prisoners.

Then come quickly, was all Shriek said in response.

Alyssa picked up the company's speed when Neville had conveyed the latest conversation to her, but it still took them the better part of a half hour before they reached the holding cells that Shriek had shown Neville. He and Alyssa peered down through the nearest grating to look at the prisoners. Shriek clung to the other side of the grate.

"I don't see Annabelle," Neville said.

They've taken her away. She hesitated, then added, *They mean to kill her.*

"Do you know where they've taken her?"

Shriek shook her head. *No, but I can follow the trail of her thoughts.*

"Contact the others," Neville said. "See if they can get us out of this damned shaft."

The confusion that Shriek's sudden appearance evoked in their companions would have been comical to behold if the situation hadn't been so serious. Guafe was the first to recover.

"Clive and I came through as giants," the cyborg said.

"Nothing strikes me as impossible anymore," Smythe added.

With a boost from Guafe, and using the buckle from his belt, Smythe pried loose the screws that held the grating in place. One by one he carefully passed Neville, the Tuan, and their silvers down to the waiting hands of the others.

"*Madre de Dios,*" Tomàs muttered. "What will they do to us next?"

Sidi quickly filled Neville in on what had befallen Annabelle and Clive.

"He's in the other half of the city?" Neville asked.

"He was when I last saw him," Guafe replied.

"Annabelle is the more immediate concern," Sidi said.

Neville nodded slowly. "But what of Clive?" he asked. "If these Ren mean to use him in a similar fashion . . ."

"I know, sah," Smythe said, obviously troubled himself. "But Annabelle is closer."

"I'll grant you that," Neville said. He glanced from his perch in Smythe's hand to the prison's bars, then to the cyborg. "Can you get us out of here, Guafe?"

"I can try."

The cyborg crossed the cell to the bars. Bracing himself, he took ahold of a bar in each metallic hand and began to exert pressure on them. For the longest time nothing appeared to happen. Unlike the features of a man Guafe's face showed no sign of the strain he was undergoing. His metallic brow remained dry, his features showed concentration, but little else.

Placing Neville down on the floor, Smythe went to give a hand. A moment later Sidi and Tomàs joined him, soon followed by the two Japanese and the pair of smugglers, Sordiam and Kan. With that many backs put to the task, there was no question as to their success.

Slowly the bars began to give.

When the space was large enough to allow a man egress, they fell back from the bars and gave a short cheer. Neville went into Smythe's breast pocket, Shriek perched on his shoulder, Alyssa and her mount in one side pocket, another Tuan and silver in the other. The rest of the Tuan were quickly tucked into the pockets of the others. Then they made their way through the bars to the hallway beyond.

"Now this door," Tomàs said.

Unlike the cells this door was solid metal, top to bottom, except for a small window set just at eye level. Guafe peered through the window.

"The hallway is clear," he said.

Before anyone could ask how he meant to get through this door, he placed one hand on the top doorjamb and hoisted himself into the air. When he was high enough, he broke the window with the heel of his free hand, then thrust his arm through. A moment later they all heard the door's lock snick open.

Guafe lowered himself back down to the floor. When he gave the door a push, it opened silently onto the hallway. Guafe stepped out, glass crunching underfoot.

"Why didn't you break out sooner?" Smythe wanted to know.

The cyborg shrugged. "I arrived no more than a half hour before you did," he said. "I was merely waiting for an opportune moment."

He glanced at the tiny Shriek who clung to Smythe's shoulder.

"Which way now?" he asked.

The arachnid closed her eyes for a moment, then pointed to their left with one chitinous forelimb.

That way.

· CHAPTER EIGHTEEN ·

The place Peotor took her to was an enormous chamber—easily a quarter the size of a football stadium. Annabella stopped in the doorway and stared across its immense distance, the two zeros flanking her on either side, eyes tracking her every movement. Slowly she took in the amazing view.

One full wall was taken up with what she assumed was some kind of video screen. Mostly it showed a pattern of unrelieved gray, but images appeared on it in a regular rotation, separated from each other by those times when the entire screen went gray again. She saw the bleak surface of an asteroid, fade to gray, a coniferous forest, deep and thick as those in upper New York State, fade to gray, the interior of a spacecraft. . . .

Lining another wall, their crystalline ordolite surfaces highlit by the flickering video images, was a long line of the ghosters that her blood was going to awake. Annabelle didn't look at them long. They obviously existed solely for the purpose of war, and the fact that something in her was going to make them operative just left her with a sick, empty feeling inside.

But what could she do?

The Chaffri were going to kill her friends if she didn't go along with them—*willingly* go along so that the chemical balance of her blood would be just right to make the ghosters function. Yet what kinds of destruction would these machines cause? Would the Chaffri settle with just taking over the Dungeon? Once it was in their power, wouldn't they just move on to all those worlds from which they stole their prisoners—all those poor souls who were no more than gaming pieces in the Chaffri's senseless struggle with the Ren and Gannine?

She imagined these ghosters coming to her own world—wreaking destruction there. . . .

She thought of her daughter, Amanda. Of the members of her band. Of her friends and family. Of all the people that made up the crazy confusion that was her planet. Of all those hundreds of millions of beings on all those various worlds and times from which the Dungeonmasters had gathered their cannon fodder.

How could she be responsible for all their deaths?

Because it would be her blood fueling those damned machines.

She would be a part of the ghosters.

She *would* be responsible. . . .

She had always had a certain streetwise toughness, something that the Dungeon had brought to the fore, more and more, the longer she was trapped in it; but she'd never been a hawk. Never rooted for war. Though she was willing to fight for what she believed in, she took no delight in instruments of pain. Things that existed only to cause destruction.

And those ghosters . . .

On the large screen a jungle scene appeared, faded to gray.

Her gaze drifted across the wide expanse of the floor to the opposite side of the room from the ghosters. Her eyes lit up as she saw the Japanese Nakajima 97 standing there with a deflated hot-air balloon, a curious machine that looked like the proverbial saucer-shaped spacecraft, and some other winged machines that she didn't recognize but assumed were planes of one sort or another.

"What are those doing here?" she asked Peotor.

The Chaffri shrugged. "Sometimes when we bring people through, they've come in vehicles. We let them keep them, so long as they're not operative, but if they can get them to work, we have to take them away."

Annabelle remembered something that Clive had told her about his time in Dramaran. "What about those air scooters that the Dramaranians have?"

"We confiscate only those vehicles that can reach a certain altitude. The atmosphere in the Dungeon isn't the same as it would be on a world such as your own. It thickens the higher you get. We're afraid that a craft such as the Nakajima might irreparably rupture the sky."

The gray video screen cleared to show a crowded city street, alien creatures bustling along its length, strange vehicles moving slowly where the sidewalk would be in Annabelle's world, the pedestrians walking down the middle of the street.

The image faded to gray.

Annabelle looked at the Nakajima, remembering her flight in it. The green paint on its fuselage and wings was chipped and fading; the red circles on the wingtips and near the tail assembly were in as bad a condition, but the craft still looked splendid to her. Here was something made for war but that need not necessarily be used for war.

On the video screen a view of an arctic waste appeared. Annabelle just caught a glimpse of some figure on the ice, but then the image was gone, fading to gray.

"What are those images?" she asked, pointing to the screen. "Some kind of—what?—video meditation or something? They keep running through the same pattern, the same views repeating. . . ."

"That is the gate to the ninth level, where the Gannine have wakened," Peotor told her. "We'll be sending the ghosters through it once they've been activated."

"All those different places are on the ninth level?"

Peotor shook his head. "Not exactly. Those images you see are Randoms—a multiple of pocket worlds that the Gannine have created on the ninth level to confuse our calibrating machines when we make the jump between the levels. The images have been increasing day by day—soon there won't be any gray left at all, and then the ninth level will be closed to us through this gate."

"When the screen's gray, then the gates are opened to the ninth level?"

"That's correct."

The asteroid surface was back, fading to gray.

"So these places they show aren't real?" Annabelle asked.

"Oh, they're real all right—we just don't know *where* they are."

"But surely with your tech you've got your own gates in operation by now?"

Peotor nodded. "Yes, but something about the ordolite that we use to make the ghosters and our zeros won't allow them to jump through anything but the gates created by the Gannine."

On the screen the grayness became the coniferous forest, faded to gray again.

A tech approached them from the side of the room closest to the door they'd come through. Banks of electronic gear and other apparatus stood there, with gaudily clad Chaffri bustling about, busy as ants.

"We're ready for her now," the tech said.

Peotor took her arm. "Remember," he said as he led her over. "You must do this willingly."

Annabelle just looked at him. "Willingly. Right. Give up my life so you can use my blood to fuel all those monsters, just so's you guys can kill more efficiently."

"Not all of them," Peotor explained. "Just one. Each takes ten pints of Folliot blood to fuel initially."

"So you're going to need other Folliots to fuel the others?"

Peotor nodded. "We're already working on that."

Oh, Christ, Annabelle thought. What if they go after Amanda?

"But," Peotor said, "one is all we need functional for the moment."

Annabelle glanced at the ghosters and fought back a shiver. The arctic waste image caught her eye on the video screen. Just before it faded to gray again, she realized that there was a man out there on the ice. And not only could she see him, she could recognize him.

It was Clive.

The screen faded to gray.

Annabelle turned to the Chaffri holding her arm. "Out there on the ice," she began.

"I know," he said. "It's your ancestor. A pity we couldn't have gotten to him before he was swallowed by a Random, but we're not about to risk ourselves going after him. To cross over is easy—getting back is something else again."

"But—"

"At least the Ren don't have him. I just wish we could say the same for his brother. . . ."

All the while he spoke, he was leading Annabelle to where the techs were getting ready to transfer her brain pattern into their computers and then harvest her blood to fuel the ghosters.

"You're a real bunch of sons of bitches, aren't you?"

Peotor made a tut-tutting sound. "Willingly, now," he said. "Don't forget. Or your friends will suffer."

Willingly.

That was a laugh. And who was to say they'd let the others go anyway?

As she was surrounded by smiling techs, all ready to wire her up to their machines, she realized that this was really the end of the road.

Annie B., you are in deep shit, she told herself.

What a brilliant realization. She thought about Jack Casady, about positive thinking, about all the pop psychology that said, yes, you too can be a winner, if you just *believe*.

Somehow she didn't think singing a song was going to do that much good right about now.

The first zero they came upon was more surprised to see them than they were it.

Guafe was in the lead when they came around a corner to confront the dog-sized creature. Before it had a chance to train its lasers on the party, Guafe closed the distance between himself and the creature. He brought a metal fist down upon the protective covering that housed the zero's brain.

His first blow cracked the transparent covering; the second broke it. Fluid spilled out over the creature's body, sizzling and sparking on its electrical components. The brain collapsed in its housing. One unaimed laser sprayed a wall, nearly reaching Smythe and cutting him in two, before the zero's systems shut down and the creature collapsed.

"Right," Kan said. "I'm out of here."

The other smuggler, Sordiam, nodded in agreement. "Another few minutes and this place will be crawling with zeros—big suckers, not like this."

We are very close to where they have the Annabelle being, Shriek said.

"That's okay," another of the prisoners said. "Chase after her if you want, but I'm with Kan. No way I want to head down to the ninth level."

Kan nodded. "If you folks are smart, you'll come back up into the Dives with us."

"Staying here will be suicide," Sordiam added.

But Smythe merely shook his head. "I'm going on."

"As am I," Sidi agreed. He looked around at the other prisoners. "You are free now—make your own choices."

When they finally moved on, their company was composed of only Guafe, Smythe, Tomàs, Sidi, and the two Japanese. In their pockets, and on Smythe's shoulders, rode Neville, Shriek, and the Tuan with their mounts. Guafe remained in the lead, carrying one of the downed zero's laser mountings, complete with its power pack. It made for a bulky burden, but they all felt safer for having it with them.

"Lord, what a ragtag band of ruffians we make," Smythe said.

We must hurry, Shriek urged them. *I can sense the Annabelle being growing more agitated.*

"Ahora bien," Tomàs said. "Tell her we are coming."

Is anyone aware of the Chaffri having telepathic

abilities? Shriek asked, worried as to whether her contacting Annabelle would give their enemy warning of their approach.

The wail of a distant siren ended the need for any caution. It was obviously an alarm, and that meant that the Chaffri were already warned.

"Run!" Guafe cried, and he broke into a quick trot, Smythe running at his side.

As they approached a sudden widening in the corridor, Shriek called out:

This is it. The Annabelle being is beyond those doors.

Zeros appeared at the far side of the corridor—human-sized, their lasers swiveling in their housings to train on their party—but Guafe cut them down before any of them had a chance to fire. Then he aimed the weapon on the door in front of them and fired again.

Shriek's warning came just as the techs were attaching the first electrode to Annabelle's temple.

Being Annabelle! Do not let them hurt you. We are on our way.

They were on their way?

For one long moment Annabelle went blank. That was Shriek's voice in her head. Shriek, who, along with Neville and Clive, was still unaccounted for. What was she doing here?

Then her sense of self-preservation kicked in.

"Got an itch," she said.

She reached up as though to scratch and activated the Baalbec. The tech attaching the electrode was thrown back as the Baalbec's force field cut in. The tech hit the banks of equipment hard enough to shatter the glass on VU meters.

"What the—" Peotor began.

He grabbed at her, and he too was thrown away from her. He collided with one of the zeros, and the two fell in a tangle to the floor. The other zero immediately opened fire.

"No!" Peotor shouted.

Too late. The laser's beam skidded off the force field

and struck the banks of equipment. Plastic and metal were slagged. Sparks erupted and smoke billowed from the machines.

The other techs took long moments to recover. As a warning siren cut in, they ran for weapons. The zero fired again at Annabelle. This time the deflected laser cut down two of the techs, and the air was suddenly filled with the too-sweet stench of cooked meat.

The other zero had recovered, and it too opened fire, but as had happened with its mate's shots the deflected laser beams did more damage to Chaffri equipment than to their prisoner.

Then the door to the enormous chamber burst open, and Annabelle's companions were there.

"Go through the screen!" Annabelle cried to them. "When it's gray, it'll take you down to the ninth level."

The zeros turned to meet the new attack, but Guafe's laser cut them both down. Peotor was caught in the swath that the laser beam fanned across the room. He was cut almost in two, blood fountaining from his torso as he fell.

And what about you? Shriek asked.

"I'll follow," Annabelle told her.

She ran toward the Nakajima.

Guafe cut down the remaining techs and their whole party headed for the screen. The jungle scene appeared, its sun-bright glare sending strange shadows scurrying across the room, before it faded to gray.

Being Annabelle? Shriek called to her.

Annabelle had reached the wing of the Japanese plane and was climbing up to the cockpit. Once she'd slid open the glass canopy, she looked over to where her friends were all gathered near the screen that was in reality a gate.

Where the hell was Shriek? she thought.

What are you doing? the arachnid asked.

"I'm bringing the plane!" she called back. "Get going —I'll meet you on the next level."

Peotor had told her that it might be impossible to get out of one of the Randoms once you were in. No way everyone should risk their ass in there, but no way she was leaving Clive on his own either.

But . . .

"Just do it!"

She was inside the cockpit now. As she slammed the canopy closed, she could see the screen go to gray. Her friends hesitated for a long moment. Annabelle started up the Nakajima. Its engine whined, broke into a cough, before it snarled like some living animal and steadied into a throbbing hum.

She started the Nakajima rolling toward the screen.

More zeros appeared in the doorway Guafe had burst through—the big ones this time, Annabelle saw.

Get going, she willed her friends.

As though they'd finally heard her, they went through, all in a group, the grayness swallowing them.

Now there was just Annabelle and the zeros.

She knew the Nakajima was made for combat, but somehow she didn't think it would take too many direct hits from those lasers.

She turned the plane to get the best run she could get in the huge room. When she faced the screen again, she forced the engine to give her all it had to give. The Nakajima taxied toward the screen, picking up speed. She just got the nose up as the scene of the frozen waste appeared, the small figure of Clive standing out in the tundra.

It's got to be now, she thought.

The zeros' laser blasts exploded all around her. A number hit the plane but didn't cause enough damage to stop it from lifting off the ground.

And then she was through.

Airborne over the frozen tundra, no sign of the gateway behind her. On the ice fields ahead of her the figure turned at the sound of her engine. High above him, rotating slowly in the bright twilight sky of the tundra, was a spiral of stars that Annabelle recognized. It was the same as the symbol tattooed on the back of Horace's hand. The same as the stellar formation that

Clive had described to her, the one that had heralded his arrival into the Dungeon.

What the hell . . . ? she thought.

No time to think of it now, she realized as she banked the plane and came swooping back. The spiraling stars now at her back she checked the sky ahead of her. Wherever the gateway she'd come through was, it wasn't visible from this side.

Don't worry about that either.

She turned her attention back to the figure on the ice below.

Here I come, Clive. Let's just hope the hell I can get us out of here again.

The following drawings are from Major Clive Folliot's private sketchbook, which was mysteriously left on the doorstep of *The London Illustrated Recorder and Dispatch*, the newspaper that provided financing for his expedition. There was no explanation accompanying the parcel, save for an enigmatic inscription in the hand of Major Folliot himself.

Much to our great despair, we arrived on this level of this blasted Dungeon with our party fragmented. Into four groups we were split, and some of us with our proportions drastically changed! And what a wretched place we find ourselves in.

It is owed to some small good fortune that we were reunited. Thus, we forge on, strengthened by our numbers, in our search for an escape from this peculiar and frightening place. *If* and *when* we return, will we ever be the same?

SELECTIONS
FROM THE SKETCHBOOK
OF MAJOR CLIVE FOLLIOT

ALYSSA, THE SONG OF THE WIND, AND HER PARTY RIDING THEIR SILVERS.

MR. JAKE, WHO GUIDED ANNABELLE, FINNBOGG, AND SMYTHE IN THE DIVES.

CASEY'S PLACE
A TYPE OF TAVERN
WITH MUSIC.
FROM
ANNABELLE'S
DISCRIPTION,
IT IS A LESS
THAN RESPECTABLE
ESTABLISHMENT.

SIDI AND TOMÀS
ALMOST FELL PREY
TO THIS MULTI-
JOINTED CREATURE,
BREZHOO.

POOT, ONE OF LES ENFANTS PERDUS, WHO SAVED SIDI'S AND TOMAS'S LIVES WITH HIS EXCELLENT SHOT.

THEY MADE THEIR NARROW ESCAPE IN THE BALLOON.

I WAS INTERROGATED BY THESE THREE "SPEAKERS." THEY WISHED TO DETERMINE WHETHER I WAS THE TRUE CLIVE FOLLIOT!

FRENCHY - MENTOR OF
LES ENFANTS PERDUS.

THE PROPHET
SUFFERS A
TERRIBLE FATE.

NEVILLE AND SHRIEK HAD THE UNFORTUNATE
EXPERIENCE OF MEETING THESE TWO GIANTS,
TRAVESTIES OF NEVILLE AND MYSELF, OR
OF REVEREND DODGSON'S TWEEDLEDEE
AND TWEEDLEDUM?

SHRIEK, AS
(NEVILLE FOUND HER IN THE
DEATH DREAM; AWAITING THE
GATHERER TO BRING HER TO
HER DESTINY.

THESE CREATURES
WITH HUMAN BRAINS
AND GLOWING EYES
WERE THE
WATCHDOGS
OF THE
UNDERGROUND.

ARALT, THE HOME PLANET OF THE REN, AND AN ASTEROID BELIEVED TO BE THE DUNGEON.

THE CHAFFRI, ONE OF THE THREE RACES WHO COMPETE FOR CONTROL OF THE DUNGEON

BOTH REN AND CHAFFRI SOUGHT THE BLOOD OF THE FOLLIOTS TO FUEL THIS HORRIFYING MACHINE OF WAR, THE GHOSTER.

THE POWERS OF THE DUNGEON
HAVE REDUCED SHRIEK AND NEVILLE
TO MINIATURE.

ESCAPED TO THE
EXT LEVEL THROUGH THIS SCREEN.
NNABELLE ATTEMPTED TO FOLLOW ME IN THE NAKAJIMA!

PHILIP JOSÉ FARMER'S
THE DUNGEON

BOOK SIX

THE FINAL BATTLE

RICHARD A. LUPOFF

Foreword

PHILIP JOSÉ FARMER

FOREWORD

Here at hand is a book which resembles, in many respects, the final book of the Bible, *The Revelation of Saint John the Divine*.

All things are explained; all loose threads are tied together. The mysteries and The Mystery are revealed. The trumpets of the angels announce the falling away of the veils, and we see who are the angels, who are the devils, who are the villains, and who are the heroes and heroines.

I won't disclose who wins this mighty battle. Read for yourself.

This is Volume VI: *The Final Battle* of *The Dungeon* series. It is the last of the epic that began with Volume I: *The Black Tower*. Both were written by Richard Lupoff. Volumes II-V were created by different writers. These were derived from the "spirit" of my own works, not as spinoffs from any one of my series or stands-by-itself stories.

I have been worrying—somewhat—about the immense task Richard Lupoff would have when he wrote this concluding volume. He gave it a magnificent start, started the ball rolling. No, that's not accurate. What he did was to start an avalanche. His first book was the explosion that caused the avalanche. Each succeeding book added to the mass sliding and rumbling down the mountain. And Lupoff had no idea how each writer would develop the plot and introduce new themes, twists, and characters which he did not have to explain.

It was like five weavers working on one tapestry, and four of them given only general directions about the pattern to be woven. When these had done their work, the first weaver became the last one. It was his goal to finish the pattern and to make sense of the work of the other four. He had to make a pattern which would, in a sense, magically reshape the other patterns so that the result was one self-consistent work.

On the whole, this goal was achieved.

Only a writer would know how much Lupoff had to sweat and strain and reach way down into his pocket of imagination and ingenuity to find explanations for things which he had not dreamed of when he wrote the initial volume.

He had to dive deep to bring up the pearl of great price.

You not only have this pearl at hand. You have a book (considering this volume as part of one six-volumed book) which is a sort of encyclopaedia—or compendium—of most of the traditional themes of science fiction and fantasy. In addition, there are new themes. But the traditional ones are recut to make novel facets.

Old or traditional themes, such as time travel, parallel worlds, alternate universes, shape-changing, and so on have never died out or become obsolete. They are being reworked and will always be reworked. Human ingenuity finds new uses or applications and new explanations for the traditional themes.

This set of six volumes (a sexology?) has all of them or almost all of them. In fact, if I had written the final volume, I might have slyly inserted a Magical Kitchen Sink. Or a Chirality or Superstring Kitchen Sink in order to make it scientific-sounding.

Doing this is one of my weaknesses. I can't help it if I am sometimes facetious.

One of the inventions I admire in this series is Esmond the Unborn. There may be a literary precedent for Esmond, but I don't know of it; although there is a reference to an Uni the Unborn in a genealogy in the Icelandic saga, *The Story of Burnt Njal*. But this is just a name with no explanation about the epithet. (How would you like to go through life with this name?) I doubt if this was the source for the character of Esmond.

You have here a work the range of which exceeds that of the poet John Milton (1608–1674). His great epic works were about Heaven and Hell and the conflict between good and evil. These were *Paradise Lost* and *Paradise Regained*. This series, *The Dungeon*, not only covers the above subjects and locales, it goes beyond them into other dimensions.

The language, of course, is not Miltonic. If it were, you probably wouldn't be reading this series. (My apologies to those who would read both.) But its scope certainly is Miltonic, and it, too, is about the battle between good and evil. The good guys, however, reflect reality. They have certain touches of evil; they're not perfect. But the hero, for instance, while battling Nature and hostile beings and forces, is also battling inside himself to overcome his prejudices and irrational attitudes.

In this respect, Clive Folliot is human, unlike Milton's Satan. Being a fallen angel, Satan has no self-doubts or any consciousness of being wrong. His only doubts are whether or not he is going to win the battle against Heaven. Our hero, Folliot, has his doubts about winning over the forces of evil, of, in a real sense, the hosts of Hell. But, since this is a science fiction story, Hell is something different in origin and nature from Milton's Hell. And it does not spawn beings of the same origin, though their nature is the same.

In fact, without a program, you can't distinguish the angels from the devils. You have to wait for the final act.

But isn't this true of our own world, of the Earth we know? Haven't we mistaken angels for devils and vice versa? And, though people can't change their shapes in this real world, don't they do the equivalent? Put on different masks, play different roles, depending upon their environment and the people they deal with?

We're all shape-changers, if you define "shape" as "role" or as "behavior adaptation."

Another unexpected concept is the introduction of a character whom we thought existed only in fiction but who is portrayed here as existing in reality. I was surprised by this, though I suppose I should not have been. After all, I've done something like this in a similar fashion. And Lupoff, mindful that this series is in my "spirit," out-Farmered Farmer.

I won't reveal just who this character is, but it'll be familiar. Even those who haven't read about it will know it from the movies. I was delighted with its sudden entrance.

We have here a work which exemplifies the classical Quest story. It resonates with *The Odyssey*, the tale of Jason and the Golden Fleece, the search for the Holy Grail, the fairy tale of the little tailor, the saga of Sigurd, the slayer of the dragon Fafnir, of the great seductresses Lilith and Ayesha, of Castor and Pollux, of the journey underground by the hero, and, indeed, of the hero-cycle which Joseph Campbell and Robert Graves have depicted.

That is all to the good because it plucks at the strings of our unconscious mind, that part of the collective unconscious which contains these primal stories. But the music brought forth from the plucking has notes which would be strange to the ears of the ancients. They knew nothing of time travel, of voyages to the distant stars, of the fearfully destructive weapons in this story, of other dimensions, of computers, of superstrings.

They did know about shape-changing. This concept must have been popular among the Old Stone Age people long before literature was invented. In fact, it was universal among the preliterates encountered in modern times. Such stories must have existed since humans began to speak.

I also suppose you could say that the concept of other dimensions was foreshadowed in the ideas of Heaven and Hell, of the underground afterlives of the ancient Egyptian and Greek religions, of the Tir na nOg, the other world of Irish myth. But these did not have a scientific or pseudo-scientific rationale. They belonged strictly to the supernatural.

The hero, Clive Folliot, is a man of whom I approve as a Ulysses or Parzival. He starts off with a quest for his lost brother and ends up being something he had not dreamed of when he began his long painful search. In fact, he could not have imagined such a quest because he did not know, could not have known, that such things could exist. Nor had he ever read about them in the wildest novel that had ever come his way.

Wildness of imagination is, I believe, one of my traits. The book at hand, the entire series, certainly reflects that aspect of my character and so displays the "spirit" of my writings.

Herein is a wild book in the best sense of the word. Like all wild things, its actions cannot be predicted. It is full of wonders and surprises.

Philip José Farmer

· CHAPTER 1 ·
The Ninth Level

For a moment he was too dazzled by whiteness to notice anything else. Not the cold, not the wind, not the clouds that swirled and dived overhead like living things. All of these he would notice—but not yet.

Clive Folliot clasped his hands to his eyes.

It was as if he had been struck by a solid mass of light, a pure essence of undifferentiated color so overwhelming that it forced its way past the irises of his eyes and filled his whole skull. His brain reeled before the dazzling onslaught. He grew dizzy, felt himself stagger, folded onto his knees.

Instinctively, he dropped one hand, resting his knuckles on the hard surface to give himself a sense of balance, to assure himself that he would not fall prone. If he permitted himself to do that, he feared, he might slide, tumble, roll into nothingness.

His sense of direction had been snatched away from him.

He had no inkling of east or west, of up or down. He felt as if he might plunge into the earth itself, or into the sky.

He forced the fingers of his other hand apart. Between them the whiteness still smote at him, but he was able now to control it somewhat. And his eyes were adjusting. Recovered from the initial shock of unbearable lightness, they were beginning to provide him with a fuzzy image of the world into which he had fallen.

Whiteness in all directions. Whiteness above and below.

And now he began to notice other things. Now he

noticed the cold, and now he noticed the wind that stung his cheeks and hands, and now he threw back his head and squinted at the sky above him. Shards and fragments of cloud still swirled overhead, chasing one another like ferocious beasts in cannibalistic pursuit.

Was this the ninth level of the Dungeon? A wilderness of windswept, frigid whiteness? His mind returned to his first entry into the Dungeon, that strange world (or series of worlds—he could never be certain even of that) where he had wandered for he knew not how long.

His first entry into the Dungeon had occurred in the Sudd, that mystery-laden swamp north of the Equatorian lake country where he had sought the answer to his brother Neville's disappearance. Neville, who had set out to find the headwater of the White Nile and vanished from the continent of Africa and the face of the Earth.

Traveling with Quartermaster Sergeant Horace Hamilton Smythe and the ancient and wizened Sidi Bombay, Clive had found himself tumbling through a rock like a great shining diamond with a heart of pulsing ruby, into a world of blackness and mystery. The Sudd had been a place of prostrating heat, and the Dungeon . . .

The first level of the Dungeon, the World of Q'oorna, had been a world of blackness. Black earth, black vegetation, black landscapes through which black rivers wound beneath eternally black skies. Overhead the enigmatic spiral of brilliant stars.

Clive had made his way through eight levels of the Dungeon, and now he found himself in what seemed to be the ninth. The ninth: this world of blinding whiteness and numbing cold.

The wind keened in his ears, but somehow through that keening he heard another sound, a sound like the buzzing of an engine. He was able to scan the sky, by this time, without recoiling in pain from the sheer burning brilliance of its whiteness. He turned slowly on his heel, scanning the sky until he caught a glint.

It came again.

He was able to identify it with the source of the buzzing.

And now he was able to see it as a black speck against the grayish whiteness. A speck that grew and took shape.

It resembled a cross, and for a moment he feared that he was going mad, was experiencing a religious hallucination, but then as it grew larger he was able to make out a tail structure, and a whirring disk at its front end that he knew was an aerial screw. A propeller, his great-great-granddaughter Annabelle had called it.

It was an aeroplane, its configuration and painted markings identifying it as the same Nakajima 97 in which Annie had escaped the Japanese encampment at New Kwajalein Atoll back on level— He couldn't even remember which level of the Dungeon they had been on when they had encountered the Imperial Japanese marine detachment.

The Nakajima waggled its wings.

Clive waved his hand in response.

The aeroplane dipped lower. He could see Annie in its cockpit, her hands on the Nakajima's controls. He waved both arms frantically. Annie raised one hand and returned the greeting. Clive could actually make out her features, see her smiling at him.

And then the Nakajima disappeared.

There was little or no sound—possibly the faintest of *pops* that was drowned out by the keening polar wind. There was a wink of colored light, a lurid purple that faded to lavender and then disappeared.

And the Nakajima was gone. There remained a small, glowing spot in the sky, as if a seaman's distress flare had burned and died. Then that was gone, and there was a tiny fluff of cloud that accelerated, and faded, and then was totally gone with the wind.

Clive blinked and rubbed his eyes. Had the aeroplane been there? He had thought at first that he was experiencing a religious hallucination. Clearly, that was not the case. But had this been a hallucination of another sort? Had his tortured mind and half-blinded eyes conjured up the illusion of the aeroplane?

Or had the Dungeon added still another puzzle—and potentially, still another horror—to its long roll-call of mysteries?

Through the whirling wind a softer sound seemed to whisper, then to grow louder. It was a metallic clicking, a mechanical, almost metronomic clattering.

Clive spun and saw something that looked like a child's spring-driven toy moving across the ice toward him. At first glance it appeared tiny, but as it approached him more closely he realized that it was neither tiny nor toy-like, but was in fact larger than he. The clicking sounds had come from the contact of its metallic feet with the surface of the ice.

"Clive Folliot! Being Clive Folliot!"

The voice was mechanical and uninflected, but Clive recognized it at once and felt his heart leap with joy. "Chang Guafe!"

"It pleases me to see you still functioning, Being Clive!"

"And it pleases me to see you as well, old friend. I feared that I was alone, stranded here on the ninth level of the Dungeon. Chang Guafe, did you see the aeroplane with Annie in it?"

"Is that where we are—the ninth level? No, Being Clive, I saw no aeroplane."

Clive turned slowly, surveying the unbroken vista of whiteness. If only Chang Guafe had arrived minutes earlier, even seconds earlier, he could have verified Clive's sighting of the Nakajima. He might have been unable to prevent its subsequent disappearance, but at least he could have told Clive that he was not mad. "The ninth level," Clive muttered. "Where else could we be?"

Chang Guafe lifted his shoulders in a hideous parody of a shrug. When Clive had first encountered the alien cyborg, it had been able to change its shape almost at will, extruding new mechanical parts and reconfiguring its organic components to suit the needs of the moment. The Dungeonmasters, those enigmatic manipulators of the destinies of uncounted victims, had crippled Chang Guafe's ability. But perhaps Chang Guafe had overcome the handicap. A being of the immense will and intelligence of Chang Guafe might overcome almost anything. Almost anything. Almost, almost . . .

"A good question, Being Clive." Chang Guafe nodded his head, artificial sensors reflecting the whiteness. Although the sun was not clearly visible through the cloud cover, it could be seen as a glowing patch of brightness not far above the horizon. "We learned that the Dungeon is of nine levels, and we traveled together through eight of them. It would seem to follow, then, that we have reached the ninth and final level. Is it, then, a featureless wilderness of whiteness? That seems an unsuitable anticlimax to our long adventure."

"But if this is not the ninth level . . ." Clive swung one hand in a circle, taking in their white surroundings with the gesture. "If this is not the ninth level of the Dungeon," he resumed, "then what is it? Where can we be? Why were we brought here, and what can we do about it?"

A violent shiver ran through him, making him realize for the first time how very cold he was. He blew on his hands to warm them, then drew another breath and released it. The exhalation plumed away like a streamer of smoke. He wore only the clothes he had worn on the eighth level of the Dungeon—hardly an adequate costume for his present icy environment.

What ignominy, if he should die here, alone, of exposure to the cold. If he should die here of exposure after all the perils of the Dungeon, the battles with men and with monsters and at one point with the very demons of Hell . . .

But an idea struck him. "Chang, you are the possessor of senses varied and keen beyond the human. Do you think—"

"—that somewhere," Chang Guafe continued Clive's thought, "maybe even somewhere nearby, there is more to this world than featureless whiteness?"

"Exactly! Something, perhaps, hidden by the glare."

"Stand by, Being Clive. I will see what I can see!"

"Have you regained any of your ability to change yourself?"

Chang Guafe uttered a hideous grating sound. The portion of the alien that Clive thought was a mouth curved into what Clive thought was a smile. "You have seen Hell itself, Being Clive, and you know something of the torments of the damned. Compared to the pain of my recovery, my friend, the torments of the damned are the pleasures of a sprat's outing. But yes, Being Clive, I have overcome the affliction placed upon me. And I shall avenge every twinge of pain that my recovery cost! But for now—behold, my friend!"

Before Clive's eyes, Chang Guafe underwent an amazing transformation. He spread his mechanical limbs like a giant spider—like the alien Shriek, Clive realized with a pang of loss—and steadied himself on the ice. Like a telescope extending, Chang Guafe extended his neck up and up until it towered twice the height of a man and then some.

Strange devices were extruded from Chang Guafe's head, feathery filaments like the antennae of African moths, and glittering, multifaceted viewers like the astonishing eyes of a fly or a honeybee. Slowly Chang Guafe rotated his head, turning it in a manner that would have been impossible to any ordinary living creature but that seemed effortless and natural to this being who was as much machine as he was organism.

At last the head completed its rotation and came to a halt. The telescoping neck retracted until the strange configuration of organs and devices that passed for Chang Guafe's face was approximately level with Clive Folliot's eyes.

"You were right, Being Clive." Chang Guafe nodded solemnly. "Beneath our feet the ice extends far downward until it comes to water little warmer than itself. But yonder"—and he raised a limb, using a clawlike extrusion as if it were a pointing finger—"the ice rises as tall as a bungalow. It is as if an iceberg had been captured and held in place within this great ice floe. And within that iceberg—"

"Is what?" Clive could not contain his eagerness.

"I could not tell in detail, but my sensors indicate an irregularity of density."

Clive was crestfallen. "An irregularity of density, Chang Guafe. And what does that mean?" Clive clutched his fists in his armpits, trying to avoid frostbitten fingers. He stamped his feet to keep them from freezing. He could last a while longer here on the ice, but only a while. And then . . .

"I will put it another way," the cyborg grated mechanically. "If the iceberg were a solid block, there would be very little variation in its density. Instead, I detected great variation. It is my inference, then, that since this variation includes zones of greater density than ordinary frozen water, the iceberg contains objects, artifacts, or even creatures frozen within itself."

Chang Guafe drew his legs up beneath his body, raising his torso and head above the ice so that he glared down into Clive Folliot's haggard face.

"The iceberg also contains pockets of far lesser density than ordinary frozen water. Pockets of so little density, I infer that they actually contain air. They may be either caves or rooms."

Caves or rooms! The iceberg might contain a means of contact with humanity, with civilization. Perhaps with the Q'oornans or with the greater masters of the Dungeon, the Chaffri, the Ren, even the most powerful and mysterious of all, those beings known as the Gennine—said by some to be the actual creators of the Dungeon.

If not—well, at least it might provide temporary respite from the chill and the wind that swept the ice floe. It might provide a few more hours of survival for Clive Folliot, hours that he and Chang Guafe could apply to trying to figure out a means of escape from this terrible place. If Clive and Chang Guafe could survive their present chilling dilemma, they might make contact with Annabelle Leigh—Clive's great-great-granddaughter—and with Horace Hamilton Smythe, with Sidi Bombay, with whoever of their beleaguered party still survived.

But Annabelle Leigh had already made contact with them! The sun-glittering aeroplane that she had obtained from the Imperial Marines at New Kwajalein—what had happened to it? Where, now, were the Nakajima and Annie?

"Come along then, Chang Guafe! You point the way, and let's get us to that wonderful iceberg of yours!"

Chang Guafe settled down between twin rows of long, metallic limbs and clattered in a direction that coincided with that of the glowing blob of the sun.

Clive fell in beside the alien cyborg. The pace that the cyborg set was a rapid one, but Clive was able to keep up and was grateful for the exercise that warmed his limbs. He knew that the cold was sapping his reservoirs of strength, and that the same exercise that provided warmth simultaneously served to drive his reserves of energy toward exhaustion. But there was nothing to be gained by remaining behind and passively awaiting the end.

Rage at destiny! Fight to the end! Then, if death must come, he would at least have lived his life to the full, to the last breath of his lungs and the last beat of his heart.

Clive staggered and reached one hand to clutch at Chang Guafe. The cyborg had detected Clive's growing weakness and had offered once to carry him, but Clive had recognized in Chang Guafe's manner the fact that the alien, too, was growing weak. His power was immense, but so also were his needs for energy. And with neither food nor fuel, struggling across the face of this ice floe, both of them were approaching exhaustion.

"Being Clive," Chang Guafe said.

Clive clutched one of Chang Guafe's metal-sheathed limbs near the point where it met his body. He knew that the metal would be devastatingly cold, but his own hands were by now so numb that he was unable to feel it.

"Being Clive," Chang Guafe repeated. "Battle onward! Our goal is within reach!"

Clive raised a hand to shade his eyes. They were walking straight into the blobby sun. The bright, fuzzy circle had hardly moved in all the time they had walked toward it. It seemed neither to be rising nor setting, but merely to be waiting for them, a quarter of the way up the sky, perpetually at late afternoon or early morning, nor had Clive Folliot any way of telling which.

Could he use mental telegraphy to reach his friend George du Maurier or any of his other acquaintances in London, from his sweetheart Annabella Leighton to his editor, Maurice Carstairs of the *London Illustrated Recorder and Dispatch*? He lacked the mental energy and power of concentration needed even to make the attempt.

He could only struggle onward, placing one foot in front of the other, holding his hand against Chang Guafe's metal carapace for guidance, hoping to reach the iceberg. He blinked, and could not be certain whether he saw the sun and the sky and the ice that surrounded him and his alien companion. There was so much whiteness, so much cold and whiteness. Was he seeing it all, or had be become blinded by the glare, a victim of snow-blindness?

He held his free hand before his eyes and was able to distinguish his spread fingers as black silhouettes against the gray-white glare of the ice. At least he was not blind! At least, not yet!

"Courage, Being Clive!"

"You can say that, Chang Guafe! You're as much machine as—"

"This is not mere bravado," the cyborg interrupted. "Look ahead, Being Clive!"

Clive Folliot halted for a moment and raised his eyes from the ice beneath his feet. Towering above him, silhouetted a darker gray-white against the glaring gray-white of the sky, loomed the iceberg.

Together, Clive Folliot and Chang Guafe managed to cover the final few rods of their trek. Clive stood, staring up at the iceberg. From this distance, he could see that it was as tall as a small tenement. If only he could enter its confines and climb the stair to Annabella Leighton's cozy flat!

But that was out of the question.

With a new burst of energy he began edging sideways, circling the iceberg. Within it he could make out vague and shadowy forms.

"Here!" he heard himself shouting hoarsely. "Here, Chang Guafe! A doorway! A doorway! We are saved, Chang Guafe! It is a doorway!"

Without waiting for the alien to catch up to him, Clive staggered through the man-high opening in the iceberg. He found himself standing in a room-shaped vacuity within the ice. It appeared to be featureless, filled with a weirdly shifting gloom, the feeble light filtering in part through the opening through which Clive had entered and in part through the living ice itself.

As far as Clive Folliot could tell, there was nothing in the room save himself. No furnishing, no chair or table or couch, no stove—oh, what he would have given for the warmth of a merrily flaming oven or hearth!—nor closet nor bed nor any other furnishing or sign of habitation.

He circled the walls, peering as best he could into the shadowy world of the living ice until he came to . . . a figure that suggested the human form! He strode forward and pounded his fists on the ice, forgetting all his cold and fatigue, his mind filled suddenly with the excitement of his discovery.

"A man! A man! Come out! Tell us your story! Tell us—" He stopped. How far was it into the ice, to reach this man? And was he indeed alive?

He did not speak, he did not move. Had he been frozen into the ice when a ship was blown off course and its passengers and crew died on the polar cap? Worse yet, had he survived the shipwreck and then been trapped by some horrid happenstance, in the ice, and frozen there alive?

Clive shuddered, half from his own coldness, half from terror at the thought of what might have happened to this mute, anonymous, unmoving stranger who seemed to gaze unblinkingly at Clive from his place deep within the ice, even as Clive gawked at him.

From behind Clive came the clicking and scrabbling sounds that meant Chang Guafe had followed him into the opening.

"Chang Guafe," Clive grunted, "come and see this." He spoke the words without so much as turning away from the terrible sight that held him mesmerized. The longer he stood before the frozen figure, the more details could he make out.

The man—for he seemed clearly to be a man—loomed well above Clive's own height, and Clive was himself a person of goodly size. The frozen one's shoulders were broad, his head tall and hatless, but surmounted by a generous mane of black, unkempt hair. His face was of an unmatched pallor; whether due to a natural lack of pigment or to the cold, Clive could not tell.

The figure wore an outfit of matching jacket and trousers, tattered and threadbare and of a dull black material. His collarless and uncravated shirt was of the same color. So huge was the man that neither the sleeves of his coat nor the cuffs of his trousers reached their normal place, but rode high above wrist and ankle. His shoes were thick-soled and heavy.

"You have made a discovery, Being Folliot," Chang Guafe's voice grated.

"Indeed I have," Clive replied. "Indeed I have!"

"Have you a plan to propose?" the cyborg asked.

"Chang Guafe!" At last Clive turned so as to face the alien. "In all your repertoire of tools and organs, do you think you could find something that will permit us to free this fellow from the ice?"

"Free him?" Chang Guafe asked. He scuttered forward to stand close to the wall of ice, peering into it with an extruded sensor that looked for all the world like a sea-captain's telescope. "Free him?" Chang Guafe asked again. "How do you know he lives, Being Folliot? And if he does live, how do you know that he will do us good rather than ill?"

"I don't know that he lives. I merely suspect it. And as for doing us harm, how can our plight be made worse than it is? As things stand now, we shall both perish. If we free this prisoner, who knows what favors he may perform for us, out of sheer gratitude? I think, Chang Guafe, that this strange pale fellow is our last, best hope. But the way to find out whether he lives, and whether he is benevolent or malign, is to liberate him from his icy prison. The question, Chang Guafe, is, can you do it?"

Chang Guafe emitted the shuddering, grating sound that reminded Clive Folliot of a piece of chalk vibrating shrilly against a polished slate, that he knew passed with Chang Guafe for laughter. "Can I do it, Being Folliot? Of course I can do it!"

"Then in the name of all that is holy, Chang Guafe, do not stand there dithering!"

Clive stepped aside to give the alien better access to the wall of ice that contained the towering human figure. He watched in awe as the alien shifted and strained. He seemed not merely to be rearranging the metal parts that made up the mechanical portions of his body, but in some miniature machine shop contained within a cavity of his body to be fabricating the very parts and mechanisms that he would shortly call into play.

At last, Chang Guafe extended toward the wall an instrument that resembled a rotary saw blade.

The blade spun.

Chang Guafe pressed it against the ice.

An ear-splitting scream rent the air, a scream that came from no throat of human or beast or alien but from the living ice itself as the saw blade marked its path against the wall. Chang Guafe guided the blade first in a vertical path, cutting a line so straight and true that Clive Folliot was unable to distinguish it from the perfection of a plumb bob.

Extending one of his telescoping organs, Chang Guafe drew the line he had scored as high as the top of the frozen man's head, and then a bit higher, as if allowing for good measure. Then he rotated the blade so that it spun in a horizontal plane and continued to cut the ice until it was time to turn the blade once again and draw it downward toward the icy floor of the cave.

In due course Chang Guafe had carved from the living wall a gigantic ice cube in which the frozen form of the giant was embedded like a fly in amber. Chang Guafe hefted the cube out of its niche in the wall and laid it on the floor so that the giant's frozen eyes glared ceaselessly at the roof of the ice cave.

While Clive Folliot gazed in awe, Chang Guafe fabricated from his internal machine-shop a weblike metallic filament that he strung about the gigantic ice cube. There was a humming sound. The filament glowed first rose, then red, then white-orange.

With perceptible speed, the ice block began to melt.

Water dripped from the block of ice, puddling and then refreezing on the icy floor of the cave. Soon a cloud of steam formed around the block, obscuring the figure that lay within. But at the last moment before the immobile giant disappeared, Clive felt a bolt of psychic energy pass through his body.

He had caught the eye of the frozen man—or the frozen man's glance had caught Clive—and the glare of pure malice that passed from the giant to Folliot was the source of that psychic jolt.

· CHAPTER 2 ·
The Frozen Giant

"Stop, Chang Guafe! Stop!"

The cyborg revolved a telescoping eyestalk toward Clive. "Why should I stop, Being Clive? You yourself indicated that this being is our best hope of survival and escape from this place."

"I did, I know. But there's something about it—about him—that is chillingly familiar to me. I feel almost as though I have met this giant before."

"You would leave him, then, frozen here?"

"Yes!"

"But if that seals our own doom, Being Clive? If it means our own death?"

"There are worse things than death, Chang Guafe!"

"And you would abandon all our companions, Annabelle Leigh, Sidi Bombay, Shriek, Horace Hamilton Smythe? Your musical companion, Finnbogg? Your own brother, Neville?"

"They can fend for themselves. They have as great a chance at survival as we, Chang Guafe—or as poor a one! For all we know, they have made good their escape and are happily pursuing their lives at home. Or, for all we know, by now they are dead. In any case, Chang Guafe, I beseech you, stop what you are doing!"

The cyborg raised metal-covered shoulders in a shrug. "As you wish, Being Clive."

The glowing filament dulled to a cool metallic gray. Like an alien Izaak Walton reeling in his trout line, Chang Guafe drew the thread-thin filament back into his metal machinery.

The last of the steam swirling about the block of ice rose like a puff of fairy-smoke. There lay now revealed the form of the frozen giant, covered by a coating of ice little thicker than the glaze of ice left on the trees of a Staffordshire forest after a freezing February rain.

The ice disintegrated into a million glittering crystals and fell from the form it had so long imprisoned as the giant raised first one mighty arm, then the other, then pushed himself upright. For a moment the giant sat like a child on the floor of its playroom, his feet stetched before him, his palms pressed to the icy cave bottom.

Then with a mighty effort he heaved himself to his feet and stood with his head almost brushing the roof of the cave. He cast his glance down at Clive and at Chang Guafe.

"Too late," Chang Guafe grated in an undertone, "too late, Being Clive. Shall I attempt to recapture him?"

Clive shook his head. "We're in it now, Chang Guafe. It's sink or swim. Let's do our best to swim!"

Chang Guafe swiveled a compound eye at Clive Folliot. "Your expressions sometimes puzzle me, Being Clive, but this one I believe I comprehend. Yes, let us see if we can swim."

"Vile insects!" The giant's voice boomed out, sounding to Clive like the bass notes of the pipe organ in St. Paul's Cathedral. "What peace I had ever found, I found here in the quiet and solitude of this ice. And you have stolen from me even that pale solace. Vengeance shall I wreak upon you for the sins committed by your kind from the day of Creation! O, despicable insects! Miserable creatures that you are, not satisfied with the degradation you have visited upon yourselves and the victimization of Heaven's innocents, yet you have chosen to bring into being a new race of blameless things only that they may suffer and weep."

Clive Folliot stared into the giant's face, appalled as much by the chilling familiarity of the monster's speech as by the terrible content of his words.

"I recognize you, Monster! I know who you are!"

"You have the advantage of me in that regard, insect! But I need not know your identity. It suffices that I recognize you as a Man, the spawn of Adam. It was one of your kind who created me, who then spurned me as a god would look upon his own creation and reject it! It was you who created for me a mate and then destroyed her before my own horrified eyes! You, or one such as you, for to me, now, all Mankind is as one. One evil and poisonous to all that is innocent and good, all that ever prayed and hoped for a single moment of innocence and joy and companionship!"

The monster drew a shuddering breath, but before Clive could respond, it resumed its tirade.

"I will crush you beneath my foot as you would crush an ant beneath your own! I will—"

"Wait, Monster!"

The words were spoken in the grating, metallic voice of Chang Guafe. "What of me? I am not a human; my kind never built you. Do you plan to crush me, also? Do you think you can?"

Slowly the giant turned, casting his glare for the first time fully upon Chang Guafe. "You are the one who freed me from the ice, are you not?"

"I am, yes."

The monster stood, to Clive Folliot's eyes lost in contemplation. What heart pulsed in that gigantic breast, what brain worked within the monster's skull to comprehend this strangest of confrontations?

"You are not a Man, you strange thing."

"I am not."

Still the monster peered at Chang Guafe. "I have never before beheld such as you." He reached forward with a pale hand, the arm protruding far beyond the end of his ragged garment. "May I touch you, strange thing?"

How odd, Clive thought, that the monster asked permission of the cyborg before laying its clammy hand upon him!

"Touch me indeed," Chang Guafe grated.

The monster extended a death-white finger and touched Chang Guafe, first upon his metallic carapace, then upon a section of the living flesh that remained exposed.

"You are indeed peculiar. Are you even of this Creation?"

"Your meaning is not clear to me."

"I sense a strangeness in you," the monster replied. "A strangeness more total and profound than the strangeness of the octopus of the deep, the wolf of the northern wood, the flashing parrot of the tropical jungle, the python that falls upon its victim in the basin of the Amazon. I sense in you an alienness, strange thing, that leads me to the inference that you are not of this Earth."

"You are right, Monster. I am not of this Earth."

"There are other worlds, then, inhabited as this one?"

"More than you can count, Monster. More than you can imagine!"

"Then what do you here? And in the company of this Man, this most despicable of all God's creatures?"

"Clive Folliot is not so bad, Monster."

"He is a Man, and that is enough for me! I curse the day that God created Adam, and I curse each and every one of that first sinner's descendants!"

"They are not all so bad."

"You dare to make league with these foulers of the Earth?"

"I am not in partnership with all humankind. But I am in alliance with Clive Folliot and a few—just a few—of his fellows."

The monster swept his glare from Chang Guafe to Clive Folliot.

"I know you," Folliot asserted once more. "I have seen you upon the London stage—you, or an actor, at least, garbed and painted to resemble you."

The monster's face crinkled into a horrifying parody of a smile, and his booming voice gave out with a similarly dreadful version of laughter.

"I—upon the London stage? Am I a vaudevillean, a music-hall clown? Better should I declaim the lines of your Shakespeare. He, at least, was able to peer into the depths of the human heart and portray in his dramas the vices and the tragedies of your despicable breed."

"No, you were not an actor! It was the actors who portrayed you. Portrayed you in the dramatizations of the Widow Shelley's great novel."

The look upon the monster's face was not more sympathetic, but its expression shifted, at least, from one of cold malice to one of contemptuous bemusement. The monster looked at Clive as one would look at a bothersome mosquito in the moment before he crushed it out of existence.

"A novel? A literary romance devoted to me? A new *Robinson Crusoe*?"

"Yes."

"And the name of this fancy?"

"*Frankenstein, or The Modern Prometheus!*"

The monster's expression grew more pensive; its posture less threatening. "Frankenstein." Its voice fell in volume. Its tone was almost musing. "Henry Frankenstein was my creator."

"And your own name?"

"None gave me he. But I suppose he was my father, and as you, Folliot— You say that is your name?"

Clive assented.

"As you received your name from your father, so I am entitled to receive my father's name from him. The modern Prometheus? No, Man, the name is one that I reject. Instead I shall take the name of my maker, my father, and my enemy. I shall be known to the generations of your kind by this name. My name will be one spoken with shuddering and fear. His name and mine, one and the same, shall echo down the corridors of time until it becomes a synonym for terror and destruction."

He drew himself up to his full height, his black-haired head nearly brushing the ice cave's frozen roof.

"I name myself—*Frankenstein!*"

As if the words had been a command issued by and to himself, the monster strode forward. For a moment Clive thought that he was about to be crushed beneath the massive boots of the mighty being, but instead the monster strode past him, past the cyborg Chang Guafe, and, ducking his head to avoid striking it against the ice, clumped from the cave.

Clive and Chang Guafe looked at each other.

"What think you, Being Clive?"

"I don't know, Chang Guafe. He hates me so. Perhaps you should accompany him. But this much I do know. At the end of the Widow Shelley's novel, the monster was left drifting upon a polar ice floe. This is the creature we have freed. We thus know where we are: upon the Earth! Don't you see, Chang Guafe? I entered the Dungeon from the surface of the Earth, and to the surface of the Earth I have returned! How close am I, now, to finding my brother Neville? Such was my original goal, and in the Dungeon I found him, yes, only to lose him again. What mad universe is this, with its clones and simulacra and illusions, its replicants and its imposters? How can one be assured of any truth?" He shook his head despairingly. "And yet, if this be Earth indeed, perhaps I may find Neville again, once and for all time. After all my travail, I feel at last that I may yet achieve the goal upon which I first set my purpose."

He thought for a moment. "But you, Chang Guafe—you are not of this Earth, nor was your mission the same as mine. Perhaps you will choose another path."

"I will not abandon you, Being Clive."

"Thank you, my friend. Thank you." Clive Folliot felt tears stinging his eyes. He wiped them away before they could freeze. "But will the monster accept me?"

"He recognizes in me an essence as alien to humankind as is his own. He seemed to accept me. I think I can persuade him to accept you as well."

"I don't know."

"What is the alternative? Would you remain here until you perish of starvation or of sheer cold? If death is what you wish, Being Clive—that, either the monster or I could provide to you more quickly than the ice. You can be spared the suffering and despair of a slow death." Chang Guafe paused, then asked, "Is that your wish?"

With only the briefest of hesitations, Clive shook his head. "No, Chang Guafe. I have not come through all that I have—we have not endured all that we have together—to give up at this point. A voluntary death—whether at your hands or those of the monster, or in the slow, frigid embrace of the ice—would be abhorrent and cowardly. I must do my best, whether it brings me to triumph or defeat, life or death. I am an English gentleman and an officer of Her Majesty's Imperial Horse Guards. As long as I live and can struggle on, I will do so!"

Chang Guafe's head dipped and rose in his cyborg's

equivalent of an assenting nod. "Come, then, Being Clive. We will do our best together!"

Chang Guafe scuttered through the opening, onto the ice floe outside the cave. As the opening of the cave was too narrow to accommodate both of them at once, Clive permitted the cyborg to precede him.

He halted, then, for a final glimpse around the cave. How long had the monster stood frozen in ice? His mind raced, trying to recapture all it had ever known of Frankenstein's monster. Mrs. Shelley had written her famous romance and published it many years before Clive's birth. By the time he was a growing boy on his father's, Baron Tewkesbury's, rural estates, *Frankenstein, or The Modern Prometheus* was a world-famed tale, printed in countless editions in England and abroad and performed in mime, drama, and even musical form on stages round about the globe.

Both Clive and his elder twin, Neville, had read the book as children, had seen it in several performances on visits to London, and had even been introduced once to the great Mrs. Shelley. The twins were mere stripling lads of fifteen at the time, and she a dignified widow within two years of her death. But even in that single encounter, the young Clive had been struck by the haunted expression in Mrs. Shelley's eyes and the distracted manner of her conversation.

It was as if there were more to *Frankenstein* than fantasy, than the supposed ghost story concocted by the young Mary Wollstonecraft. She was not yet Mrs. Shelley when she wrote the tale, and in truth was little older than the Folliot lads at the time of their meeting in 1849. Could this girl of nineteen truly create the wild tale, or had she received her data from some other source?

Clive shook himself back to the present. He would discuss this with his friend du Maurier if he ever had the opportunity to do so. But for now, he must deal with the mortal potentialities of the real world as it now confronted him. He strode from the cave and stood facing the alien cyborg and the monster.

"We must get off this ice floe," he volunteered.

"How, Being Clive?"

"I think I have a plan. We can walk to the end of the ice—at least, we can attempt that."

"And then?"

"Build a boat, and sail to land."

The monster glared at Clive. "An excellent plan, insect. And of what materials shall we build that boat? Know you of a forest where we can fell trees for timber?"

"I'm afraid not. But I remember a lesson in natural philosophy that I learned at Cambridge. We can build a boat of ice."

"Ice!" Chang Guafe's metallic grate and the monster's booming bass echoed in unison.

"Yes, ice! You can produce a heating filament similar to the one you used to thaw the monster from his frozen tomb, Chang Guafe?"

"Yes, I can do that."

"We can use it to scoop out a concave shell, and launch it from the edge of this ice floe."

"And as we sail to warmer climes and our ice shell melts, Man?" the monster questioned. "What then? Do we swim the rest of the way?"

"I'll admit that there's an element of risk," Clive conceded. "But there's a good chance that we'll drift to some northern island, or even to the mainland or Europe or Asia or the New World. Or we may encounter a sailing ship on the high seas. It's true that we'll be gambling our lives. But not to gamble them means to remain here and die."

"I was frozen here before. I can survive again," the monster boomed.

"Then that is your choice."

There was a pregnant pause. Then the monster said, "No, Folliot. I shall accompany you."

Clive nodded.

"I perceive upon your countenance an expression of skepticism," the monster resumed. "You wonder why I should accompany you, puny human bug, and your peculiar companion. But I tell you this: Even in extremis, when I sought oblivion in the eternal cold and silence of this distant realm, I was not left unmolested by Man. Man—the scourge of Creation! Man it was who created me, and lived to regret that deed—and Man it was who disturbed my rest. Thus do I vow by the very God in whose name your foul species has committed enormities uncounted from the dawn of your so-called civilization to this very cursed day, that Man shall regret once more the deed of awakening me from my frigid slumber."

The sky was no longer its featureless gray-white, nor the sea its unvarying green-black.

They had reached the edge of the ice floe after a march the length of which Clive Folliot could hardly estimate. Weak as he was, wracked by hunger and exposure to the elements, he felt that he could have lasted only a matter of hours, traveled at most a mile or two. But beneath the arctic sky, it seemed to him that he had trekked over an infinity of ice, counted an eternity of hours. He had no way of measuring the miles that they covered, and even his estimate of elapsed time was based on periods of activity and rest, waking and sleep. He was not sure what body of water they had reached, assuming that it was the Arctic Ocean. They might reach the northernmost edge of the great Eurasian land mass, or that of North America, or they might drift into the Atlantic, out of sight of land, and to their doom.

The sun seemed to describe a wobbling course around the horizon, neither rising to the zenith nor falling below the rim of distant ice fields, but instead maintaining a perpetual twilight, now marginally brighter, now almost imperceptibly dimmer, but never giving them the brightness of full daylight nor the full darkness of nightfall.

When they approached the edge, Clive could hear the gentle lapping of water against the ice. His stomach had shrunk by now from lack of food. Clean water was readily available—Chang Guafe was able to melt the ice to provide drinking water for any of the three of them. But there was no food.

Clive did not know the nourishment requirements of the metal-clad cyborg that scuttered and clicked over the face of the ice, nor those of the black-clad monster that plodded tirelessly beside the human and the cyborg. He did know that he was himself growing weaker by the day. How long he could survive on clear water was problematic.

But when they reached the edge of the ice floe and saw the green-black sea spreading unbroken to the horizon, Clive was filled with a mixture of joy and dread unmatched in his long days in the Dungeon. Was he merely exchanging one death for another? Was it going to be a contest between starvation and drowning instead of death from exposure on the ice floe?

He could not permit himself to dwell upon this. Action, movement, that was what he needed. For well or for ill, he would meet his fate struggling to the last. Surrender was not an acceptable option.

They managed to construct their boat of ice as Clive had suggested. The monster stood morosely watching and listening as Clive and Chang Guafe discussed their plans. Chang Guafe was an ideal mechanician, having not only the skills requisite to the task but a complete set of tools either built into his body or subject to his own fabrication.

Clive had not formally studied marine architecture, but he had sailed small craft as a boy and traveled on both sailing ships and the new steamers as a man, and together the two of them were able to plan an ice shell capable of bearing the three companions and surviving on the northern sea.

With Clive's plans scratched onto the smooth surface of the ice, Chang Guafe carved out the rough body of their boat, then melted and cut at the ice until the boat was completed. Chang Guafe was even able to create a sail of a thin sheet of ice, and to manufacture oars for them to use should the sail melt away. He attached a rudder at the rear of the boat and pronounced it ready.

Clive christened the boat *Victoria* in honor of the monarch he hoped still to serve. They climbed in and shoved their cockleshell away from the ice.

Even now, Chang Guafe's amazing toolshop came into play. At Clive's urging, the cyborg found that he could manufacture a crude compass. "I can sense the planet's lines of magnetic force," Chang Guafe protested, "there is no need for this toy."

But Clive had pleaded. "It isn't that I mistrust you,

Chang Guafe. But I will feel more confident if I can look at a compass and tell for myself the direction of our movement."

"As you wish, Being Clive." They set a curving course, sailing in an ever-expanding spiral southeast from their point of departure.

A course due south might have brought them to land sooner than this spiral, but it might also have sailed them to their doom. By sailing in their spiral course they inferred that they would sooner or later reach the northerly coast of a continent.

Sooner or later, Clive thought to himself. *Well, it had better be sooner than later, or our dead bodies will wash ashore rather than our boat making land!*

He knew they were making good progress, for now the sun did dip beneath the horizon, giving them periods of true night, and it did rise well into the sky to give them periods of true daylight. They took watches, turn and turn-about, keeping *Victoria* on her compass course.

Chang Guafe spun a lengthy filament and crafted a fishing lure, sending the line overboard to troll behind *Victoria*. If they could catch fish they could all obtain nourishment from it, consuming its cold raw flesh in the fashion of the exotic Japanese.

The thought of the Japanese sent Clive's mind spanning the time to their arrival in the Dungeon, and his encounter, along with his early companions, with a Japanese Imperial Marine detachment. He and Horace had already been joined by the doglike Finnbogg and by young Annabelle Leigh, and Annabelle had been captured briefly by the Japanese.

She had made good her escape in a flying machine brought to Q'oorna by the same aliens who had abducted the marines, snatching them from an island redoubt in the Pacific Ocean in the midst of a war nearly a century in Clive Folliot's future.

And Clive had seen her, had seen Annabelle, flashing her wings above the polar ice cap.

Or had he? He had seen the Nakajima 97, and had assumed that Annabelle was piloting the aeroplane. But was the pilot Annie? Or had she been taken prisoner again, either by the Imperial Marines or by someone other, who in turn had commandeered the aeroplane? And what had happened to the flying machine when it disappeared above the ice cap?

Clive and Annie, Chang Guafe and Finnbogg, Horace Hamilton Smythe and Sidi Bombay . . . the adventures they had shared, the perils and the triumphs! *And now,* he wondered, *now what was to be their fate? Dear God!* He stole a covert glance at Chang Guafe, and at the stolid, pallid form of the Frankenstein monster.

What was to be their fate?

▪ CHAPTER 3 ▪
"Your Eyes Will Remain Open!"

Clive was awakened by the weight of a massive, corpse-gray hand shaking him by the shoulder.

He blinked into the red, hating eyes of Frankenstein's monster. Although the hideous creation had claimed his maker's name as his own, Clive refused to think of him as Frankenstein. That was the name of a natural philosopher or scientist, a man of noble instincts and lofty aspirations.

According to the Widow Shelley's narrative, Frankenstein had achieved more through his experiments than he had bargained for. Unable to cope with his own creation, he had fallen prey to fear and craven impulse, to the weakness that besets any man, however well intentioned. Frankenstein had been a weak man, perhaps, but not an evil one. His name ought not to be a synonym for horror and destruction.

To Clive, the creature was now and would always be simply the monster.

"Folliot, you are dying," the monster's bass tones rumbled.

"I am not," Clive managed. "I am merely hungry and cold."

They had caught a single fish on the end of Chang Guafe's line. That was, what—two days ago? Three? It had been a small fish, and its flesh had furnished precious little nourishment for Folliot and Chang Guafe and Frankenstein's monster. Chang Guafe had divided the fish, scrupulously doling out the precious food to the others. They had wolfed down the cold flesh, and Clive decided after the fact that though the meager meal had given him a little more strength with which to survive, it had done still more to whip up his flagging appetite and increase the pangs of his hunger.

Their need for water was more easily tended to. Chang Guafe had indicated that he thought he could distill the choppy brine into potable water, but rather than risk that, the companions had loaded blocks of ice into their boat before leaving the floe. Now, when thirst demanded, Chang Guafe could carve off small slivers for the three of them. The slivers of ice, melting slowly in their mouths, slaked the thirst of all three.

"You are dying," the monster intoned over Clive Folliot. "I care but little should you perish, insect. But Chang Guafe values your continued existence. This, for some reason inexplicable to me. And so for his sake I will try to keep you alive."

"I am not dying," Clive repeated angrily. He pushed himself upright and realized, with horror, that the monster had been right. It would be all too easy to permit himself to lapse into a cold- and hunger-induced trance, and to slip thence gently from life into death, hardly taking notice of the transition himself.

The monster seized him by both shoulders and shook him. "Do not die, Folliot!" it roared. It drew back a massive, death-pale hand and slammed it, open-palmed, across Clive's cheek. The blow set his head to ringing. The humiliation of being so treated by this subhuman creation brought the blood flaming into his cheeks.

"Put me down!" he commanded.

"You may sit, but your eyes will remain open and you will move frequently, insect. Or I will give you a thrashing to make that slap seem like a lover's caress." A sneer spread over the monster's face and he released Clive.

Clive collapsed onto the bottom of the boat. He drew himself up to one of the seats that spanned its narrow width and rubbed his cheeks with both hands. A brisk breeze was shoving the boat along, pressing on its sail of ice sheeting. Chang Guafe sat in the stern, one eye fixed on the crude compass he had fabricated, guiding *Victoria* by her rudder of ice.

It had seemed like a good idea. For a time, Clive had

halfway expected them to make land within a few hours of setting sail . . . or if not within a matter of hours, then surely within the first day or two.

But they sailed on, and on, and only dark water stretched in every direction.

Clive fixed his eyes on a point at the distant horizon, a point that seemed to bob up and down before the stationary boat, even though he realized that it was the boat's own bobbing that created the illusion of the moving horizon.

He used that point at the horizon as a focus for his own consciousness, and attempted to place himself in a mental state to communicate with his friend George du Maurier, safely working away as cartoonist and critic for *Punch* magazine in London. He had tried innumerable times since entering the Dungeon to establish mental communication with du Maurier. It was amusing in an ironic fashion that back in London, du Maurier had expressed his belief in the possibility of life on other worlds, direct communication and the establishment of invisible mental bonds by sheer force of will, and other such mystical stuff.

Clive Folliot, by contrast, had scoffed at du Maurier's theories. Sensible materialist that Folliot had been, his experiences of recent times had convinced him that there were worlds within worlds, realities beyond realities, and that the skeptic spoke at his own peril when he scoffed at even the most exotic of beliefs.

Several times he had felt that he was indeed in mental communication with du Maurier—or at least that he was on the verge of establishing such contact. If only he could reach the cartoonist, he could ask du Maurier to pass word to Clive's editor, Maurice Carstairs of the *Illustrated Recorder and Dispatch:* his sweetheart, Miss Annabella Leighton of Plantagenet Court, London; his father, Baron Tewkesbury; his commanding officer, Brigadier Leicester of Her Majesty's Imperial Horse Guards.

At the very least, he might offer them some solace, the knowledge that as yet, at least, he had survived, and might someday, by some means, manage to return to England. And perhaps, just perhaps, they might mount an expedition into the Dungeon to rescue him and his descendant Miss Annabelle Leigh from their predicament.

"Oh, du Maurier," he whispered half-aloud, "my friend, can you hear me? Is there any hope, any connection, any link between us other than in my recollection of you?"

He felt hot tears welling in his eyes, and wiped at them with a hand now white with cold and near frostbite, cracked and peeling with exposure.

Is that you, Folliot?

He started and looked in all directions. Chang Guafe attended impassively to the management of their boat while the black-clad monster glared from his red-rimmed eyes. There was no sign of a speaker.

Du Maurier?

Yes! Clive Folliot, it is I! Where are you? How have you reached me?

I am adrift in the Polar Sea, accompanied by two such as you would never believe!

And you have reached me without physical or mechanical assistance?

By application of my mind alone, du Maurier.

In Clive's mind there was a ghostly suggestion of a laugh.

You were right all along, du Maurier. But, to reach you at last after so many years, so many attempts—

This is not the first time you have reached me, Folliot. Are you unaware of your former successes?

I thought we were close, Folliot. Many times, it seemed that we were close. I could sense your presence, sense the energy of your mind striving to reach my own. I tried each time to respond. Did I succeed? Did you feel the touch of my mind in your own?

More than that, my friend, du Maurier continued. *You have sketched the many sights and the strange beings you have encountered on your adventures, and those pictures have reached me here in London.*

But—I never sent you sketch-paper, du Maurier. How could my pictures reach you?

As mental images, Folliot. Perhaps because I have myself worked as a sketch artist, I was attuned to your drawings. I have received no words from you. And for all that I tried to send messages back, I had no indication of success.

No. No, my dear friend, I never knew whether I had reached you or not. At times I had vague feelings, undefined inklings of companionship. But I never knew. I could only hope. Only faith in you sustained me, du Maurier.

Faith. How amazing to hear you speak so, my friend. Faith can move mountains, Folliot, can it not?

Clive paused to collect his thoughts, yet striving to maintain the link that had been established between himself and du Maurier.

Du Maurier's silent voice resumed. *What a comfort to me, after all these years, Folliot, to know this. What a comfort it is to a dying man.*

Dying? The word hit Clive like a thunderbolt.

Dying peacefully, Folliot. I am an old man, and I lie now on my deathbed. I wonder if that helped to establish our bond. As my mind prepares to separate itself forever from my flesh, it is able to rove the dimensions and connect itself to yours. Or perhaps it is the work of Dr. Mesmer that had succeeded. I must summon her to my side while still I breathe.

I don't understand, du Maurier. You are not an old man. When I left London—do you remember that last night at your club, du Maurier, after the premiere performance of Cox and Box—how you entertained Miss Leighton and myself, our encounter with Carstairs of the Recorder and Dispatch?

Very well, Folliot. Indeed do I remember that night very, very well.

But you were a man of but middle years, du Maurier.

I was fifty.

And that was some months ago. Why do you call yourself old?

Months ago? Months! Again the laughter rang in out perfect silence. *That was 1868, Folliot.*

Yes.

This is 1896. You have been gone for twenty-eight years.

The monster's clammy hand held Clive by the throat; his other hand held him by one leg. Clive felt himself lifted in the air. Before his eyes there was a swirl of darkness, a blur of the creature's death-white face and dead-black garments, of points of starlight glimmering on the polished metal that covered much of Chang Guafe.

"Stop! What are you doing?"

Clive was suspended over black water. Chill air swept his body, his inadequate costume providing little protection from the cold. A thin spray of frigid brine splashed his skin.

"You live, insect?"

The monster threw him into the air as a playful parent would toss a merrily squealing babe. To Clive the sensation was terrifying, and when the monster caught him again he clutched at the thick black cloth of his sleeve.

"I live, I live! Put me in the boat again!"

"I warned you, despicable creature." The monster's eyes glared with hatred, the little light that reflected from them coming from the stars that dotted the black sky above.

"You warned me to live, and I am alive!"

The monster threw him contemptuously back onto his seat. "What say you, Chang Guafe?" He turned his mighty frame to face the impassive cyborg. "Did this bug give any sign of life?"

The cyborg's mechanical voice grated, "No, Frankenstein. He looked as dead as anything I've ever seen. Deader than you," Chang Guafe added sardonically.

The monster laughed, a horrible, nerve-twitching sound.

"You are fools, both of you," Clive accused. "I was in communication with George du Maurier. He is my friend, and he is in England, and I had managed to establish a mental link with him."

"Looked dead to me," the monster grumbled.

"He might have sent an expedition to help us."

Chang Guafe raised his metal-capped countenance in interest. "Sent an expedition from where?"

"England!"

"To where?"

"To find us here upon the ocean."

"You are certain we are no longer in the Dungeon?" Chang Guafe prompted. "Does he know how to reach the Dungeon?"

"I don't know. Perhaps via the Sudd."

"And this expedition, do you expect it to trace your path through the nine levels of the Dungeon and come to your rescue?"

"I told you before that I am convinced we have returned to the Earth. I am thoroughly convinced of this," Clive asserted. "I thought you had accepted my reasoning."

"Tell me once again, Being Clive. You claim that you have spoken with your mind, to the mind of your friend?"

"Yes."

"If this is true, I suppose anything may be true. Still, Being Folliot, upon what evidence do you base the belief that we are upon the Earth?"

"Upon this evidence!" He rose from his place and pointed his finger at the monster. In the faint light of distant stars, he could see his own pale flesh and the paler flesh of the monster. "I realize now that Mrs. Shelley's tale was no mere romance, no fantasy. It was absolute truth, done up in trappings of fiction to make it acceptable to a skeptical world that would otherwise have recoiled in horror from the facts laid before its collective eyes."

"And so?"

"At the end of Mrs. Shelley's tale, the monster—*this* monster!—is seen pursuing his creator across the ice floes of the arctic region. What became of that tortured soul, that fantastic experimenter, we do not know. Perhaps we will find out, perhaps the answer will remain a mystery forever. That is to be seen."

He whirled and pointed once again. "But the monster remained in that polar realm, trapped and frozen in the very ice that caps our globe. There it was that we found him. Ergo, we are not in the ninth level of the Dungeon, but have been returned in some manner to the Earth."

He paused for the beat of a heart. "Or else, we may be led to conclude that the Earth itself is the ninth level of the Dungeon!"

Chang Guafe extended one telescoping, metallic eye-stalk toward the monster, another toward Clive. "Well, Frankenstein—what do you think? What became of your maker? And what do you know of the Dungeon and its contending would-be masters?"

The monster did not answer. Perhaps it would have,

Clive thought, but a whirring, sizzling sound interrupted the conversation and drew the attention of the three upward.

There Clive saw once again a sight that he had first seen on Earth, in the sky above the coast of eastern Africa. On that occasion he had been en route from the island of Zanzibar to the mainland of the mysterious continent, in search of his missing elder twin, ignorant of the very existence of the Dungeon, the black world known as Q'oorna, the levels and layers of reality that lay hidden behind the veil of the Sudd.

Many times he had seen the sign: in the skies above Earth and Q'oorna, on the midnight-blue grip of Horace Hamilton Smythe's silver revolver, in the architecture of vaulting, ancient cities on worlds whose very existence he would never have imagined. And every time he saw that sign, it had foretold terrible events.

Now he saw it above Earth's black arctic sea.

The swirling, hypnotic spiral of stars.

And, as if coming from that spiral of stars, this peculiar, buzzing sound, remindful of a child's Guy Fawkes Day firework. Or, more sinisterly, like the sizzling, sputtering combustion of a fuse, or a powder trail that might lead to a barrel of black powder ready to explode and blow everything within range of its blast to kingdom come!

Clive stood transfixed, vaguely aware of his two inhuman companions doing the same, staring upward, attempting to locate the source of the sizzling sound.

The spiraling stars surrounded a patch of blackness far more profound than that of the ordinary polar sky that surrounded the spiral. And from the center of that blackness there now appeared the tiniest and faintest of embers, an ember that brightened and grew until it became apparent that it was itself a nearly circular figure of light.

The light grew and brightened until Clive realized that the change in its size and brightness was an illusion. It was not growing—it merely *appeared* to be growing.

It was approaching!

It was descending toward their boat!

It was speeding in a downward spiral, like a long railroad train making its way down the long course of a track that wound from the peak of a conical mountain to its base.

Downward the train moved, sizzling and flaring as it advanced.

"I've seen that before! I've seen it in the Dungeon! Chang Guafe, I cannot recall—had you yet joined our party when we encountered that train?"

"I have never seen its like," the cyborg grated.

"It is a railroad unlike any other, Chang Guafe—a railroad that travels between worlds, that picks up passengers from every locus of time and space, that moves between ordinary worlds and the Dungeon!"

"I have seen railroads," the monster boomed.

"But not such as this one!" Clive rejoined. His excitement was unbounded. If they could board this train, there was no telling where they might travel—to other levels of the Dungeon, to ancient Rome or Greece or Egypt, to far Cathay where Horace Hamilton Smythe had once traveled—perhaps to the world of the Finnboggi or even the planet where Chang Guafe had first come into being.

"Here!" Clive shouted. He seized an ice oar and waved it around his head, wishing that he had a flag of bright cloth, or better yet a flaming brand with which to attract the attention of the train and its crew.

But there was no need for that. The train continued to spiral downward, downward, circling all the time over the heads of the three oddly assorted companions.

When the bellies of the cars were a few yards above the surface of the black ocean, the very waters of the Arctic bubbled and steamed, sending clouds of vapor up into the night air to greet the circling cars.

Finally the train settled onto the face of the sea. The heat of its passage through Earth's atmosphere was transferred to the water itself, boiling away unmeasured thousands of gallons and heating the region within the circle of cars so that the ice boat Chang Guafe had carved from the arctic floe, already perilously thin and porous from its days and nights afloat, disintegrated into a hopeless scattering of icy particles that quickly melted away and disappeared.

Clive Folliot began swimming toward the nearest car of the train. Behind him he could hear the monster's clumsy but powerful strokes as it emulated his action.

But the grating voice of Chang Guafe emitted a single, despairing cry followed by a hopeless gurgle.

Clive Folliot turned to see what had become of the alien cyborg, but there was only a final flash of metal as Chang Guafe slipped beneath the surface, followed by a concatenation of bubbles. The black waters closed calmly over the cyborg.

He couldn't swim, Clive thought. *He was built mainly of metal. He was so heavy that he couldn't swim!*

The sides of the train were lined with windows, and the windows were ablaze with lights from within the train. As Clive stroked his way through the once more cooling waters, he peered at the cars of the train. One, he saw, was filled with couches and chairs where comfortable travelers inhaled fumes from long-stemmed pipes. He had encountered users of fumes in the Dungeon, intelligent men and women—and nonhuman creatures—who had found peace and happiness in the smoke-induced realm of the dreamers.

Theirs was a pleasant enough existence, but it was not for Clive. He could not give himself to an existence of idleness, however comfortable. In England and in remote military posts, he had known men who had given themselves to drink, spending their days and nights in the companionship of fellow idlers, accomplishing little. The smoke-eaters of the dungeon were no better than these!

Clive had started his long odyssey in search of his brother. He had encountered others and his sense of responsibility had grown. He could not abandon Annabelle or Horace, Sidi Bombay or Finnbogg or Chang Guafe—for he could not believe that the cyborg was dead, either. Somewhere beneath him, buried by fathoms of icy water, Clive felt that Chang Guafe still lived. He would be heard from again!

And there were other characters here in the Dungeon about whom he was less certain. There was Tomàs, the Portuguese seaman. Annie herself claimed to have found evidence that Tomàs was a distant relative of the Folliots. There was the American Philo B. Goode, and there were Goode's two confederates, Amos Ransome and Lorena

Ransome, who claimed at various times to be brother and sister or husband and wife. There was Baron Samedi.

And there were Clive's brother, Neville, and their father, Baron Tewkesbury . . . or the simulacra of Clive's brother and father. Until he had resolved their true identities, he would never know whether he could leave the Dungeon once and for all, for if they were imposters they could remain in the Dungeon and rot forever, for all Clive cared. But if they were real . . . if they were real, he could not abandon them. No, no matter how cold and unloving Baron Tewkesbury had been to Clive, blaming him for the death of his beloved baroness, and no matter how arrogant and churlish the bullying Neville might have been in their childhood and might be even now, Clive could not abandon them to the endless Gehenna of the Dungeon!

He swam to the next car. The water that the train's energetic arrival had heated to near boiling temperatures was cooling as rapidly as it had warmed, and a killing cold was seeping into his bones. Clive knew that he could not remain in the water for much longer. A matter of minutes, at most, and he would sink to the sea-bed. And, unlike Chang Guafe, he knew that he could not survive there.

He could hear the monster yet, floundering in the water behind him. The creature was a far from skillful swimmer, but Clive was confident that he would safely reach the train and haul himself from the brine.

And as for Chang Guafe, there was nothing he could do now for the alien. If he knew Chang Guafe, he would find a way to survive at the bottom of the sea, make his way back eventually to land, and then go on about his business.

But as for now—

• CHAPTER 4 •
No Roman Orgy

Clive hauled himself up, using the railing that descended along with a short metallic staircase from each car of the train. He peered behind him, over his shoulder, and saw that Frankenstein's monster had somehow turned in the water. He seemed to understand little of what he was doing. He paddled clumsily away.

Even as Clive watched, the monster reached a distant coach. The train had drawn itself into a circle, like the legendary serpent of the Scandinavians that swallowed its own tail. Whatever direction the swimming monster took, he would still return to the train. The monster raised a corpse-gray hand flounderingly from the water and managed to grasp the nearest railing. Using the overwhelming strength of his huge muscles, the monster hauled himself bodily from the sea and clung to the side of the coach.

He fumbled at the car, eventually found the handle that unlocked the door, and disappeared within.

Clive Folliot was prepared to do the same, but even as he set himself to the task he was nearly thrown from his feet, for the train had started to move.

It gained speed with breathtaking rapidity, plowing its circular course upon the face of the arctic sea. Then, with a sudden shift of direction, the engine-car of the train straightened its movement. The following cars were tugged into perfect alignment and the train accelerated wildly, throwing up spectacular walls of foaming, boiling spray that stood taller than an obelisk on either side of the train.

Then the front of the train lifted from the water, and the remainder of the coaches followed suit, tugged from the grip of the sea. The train tilted ever more precipitously upward, until Clive realized that he could not hold on to the railing longer than a few seconds more. He tugged at the coach door to open it, hauled himself into the car, and slammed the door behind him.

He turned to see what kind of world he had entered, and staggered with shock.

This was no Roman orgy nor Red Indian pow-wow, no Himalayan mountain peak nor Mississippi riverboat nor Turkish seraglio. Nor was it a world of exotic landscapes and alien habitants, for Clive knew now that the Earth was only one of a huge, perhaps infinite, number of habitable and inhabited planets.

The room was lined with dark panels, perhaps of dark-stained beechwood or even darker mahogany. The ceiling was a high one, almost lost in shadow, although he could tell that curlicues and pediments served as decoration. Tall windows reached from near the floor to very near the ceiling, but so little light penetrated them, thanks to the heavy drapes with which they were covered, that Clive could not tell whether it was daytime or night beyond the tightly sealed glass.

The room was lined with crammed bookcases. Near the shrouded window stood a massive desk of wood so dark it appeared black. The drawers were mounted with well-polished brasswork. The top of the desk was covered with sheets of paper, most of them written upon in a neat, careful hand, others bearing skillfully executed sketches. Several pens lay scattered on the documents.

The room's only illumination was provided by an oil-lamp, its wick turned low so that the golden flame cast tall, flickering shadows where it was not turned back, as by the metalwork on the heavy desk, in the form of fiery reflections.

Clive turned from the desk. Against the opposite wall, beneath a large dark canvas mounted in an ornate gilt frame, stood a huge four-poster bed. What a difference from the sleeping accommodations Clive had utilized since reaching the Dungeon: a skimpy cot, a pile of fetid rags, a leafy crotch high in a tree—wherever Fate placed him, and whenever opportunity presented itself for rest, there he rested. There had been a few comfortable beds, as well. Most he had occupied alone. Others . . . A memory of pale skin, emerald eyes, and exotic, green-tinted hair arose. Clive blinked the recollection away, his eyes stinging with sudden tears. He drew his awareness back to the present.

An elderly figure lay propped in the bed. Thin wisps of gray-white hair surmounted his nearly bald head. Muttonchop whiskers of the same pale color marked his cheeks, which were themselves of a papery dryness and pallor. This apparation of death lifted a white-gowned arm and pointed a trembling finger at Clive.

"It is he!" The voice was weak and quavered, but the words were clear enough. The thin face turned to one side, and again the old man said, "It is he!"

Clive followed the direction of the oldster's glance. For the first time he became aware of the second figure in the room, a tall, slender woman shrouded in a gown of midnight blackness from neck to shoe. As Clive studied her he realized that her hair, although drawn severely into a bun behind her neck, was lengthy and rich and of a glossy black that shone in the dim lamplight like the brasswork on the desk. Her figure, although slim, was graceful and in other circumstances might even prove voluptuous.

Her dress, he realized, was not all of black, but was trimmed with panels of a purple that approached magenta in shade.

And her face— Seldom had he looked into so compelling, so exotic, and yet so human a face! Perhaps—and he cast his mind back over the innumerable females he had encountered on Earth and in the Dungeon—perhaps only the breathtakingly beautiful, exotic woman Nrrc'kth could be compared to this woman.

"Calm yourself, Mr. du Maurier. I see him. But—*who* is he?" Her voice was cool, smooth, with a contralto deepness that set something to vibrating at the very core of Clive's being.

"It is Clive Folliot—or his son, for he appears twenty years younger than Folliot ought to be!"

"I am Clive Folliot, yes sir. But you have the advantage of me, sir."

"I am your friend du Maurier. George du Maurier. You must know me, Folliot."

Clive took a few hesitant steps across the room. He half-expected freezing brine to drip from his soaked clothing, but he looked down at himself and realized that he was dry. And instead of the tattered rags he had last worn in Chang Guafe's jerry-built iceboat, he was outfitted in a proper uniform of Her Majesty's Fifth Imperial Horse Guards—crimson tunic, glittering brass accoutrements, dark blue trousers trimmed with cloth-of-gold, polished leather boots.

He peered into the old man's face. Yes, it was George du Maurier. But this was a George du Maurier ravaged by the passage of time, and possibly by other factors of which Clive Folliot knew little if anything. The George du Maurier whom Clive had last seen in London was a vigorous man of fifty, a cartoonist of accomplishment, a musician of at least semi-professional attainments, a student of the occult and the esoteric, and an aspiring novelist.

This creature, this sorry specimen that lay propped against pillows, swaddled and warmed like an infant—this could hardly be his friend du Maurier.

"What year did you say it was, du Maurier?"

"It is of our gracious monarch's happy reign the fifty-seventh year, and of Our Lord, the one thousand eight hundred ninety-sixth."

"1896!"

"Did I not tell you that?"

"When?"

"When last we spoke. You seemed to be sailing in a very strange boat, in the company of two even stranger companions."

"Yes," Clive acknowledged almost inaudibly. His head felt light. "Yes, I remember. But I thought it was a hallucination, a fantasy, a delirium."

"It was none of those, Folliot. It was real."

"And is this real?" His gesture encompassed the room and its occupants. "Is this woman real?"

"On my deathbed, my manners desert me, Folliot. Doctor, may I present Major Clive Folliot, of Her Majesty's Fifth Imperial Horse Guards, and one of my oldest and dearest friends. Folliot, may I present Madame Clarissa Mesmer, great-granddaughter of the famed Doctor Anton Mesmer. And a doctor in her own right, I may add."

"Major." She extended her ungloved hand.

"Madame Mesmer." Clive took the hand in his own and bowed over it. Her skin was soft and smooth, cool at the first instant of contact but revealing a warmth within moments that caused Clive to raise his eyes to her own. "Is it Madame, then? You are a married woman?"

She withdrew her hand. "I have taken the title to discourage gossips—and the unwelcome advances of aggressive males." Clive pulled a breath deep into his lungs. There was a detectable—and exciting—scent in the air around Madame Mesmer.

The woman resumed. "Mr. du Maurier has spoken of you often, Major. In fact, it might be said that I stand beside Mr. du Maurier's deathbed at Mr. du Maurier's own behest, but on your account."

She spoke with an indefinable accent. Clive tried to place it—German? Hungarian? He had heard of Anton Mesmer, and held him in low regard. Mesmer had been a German, studying and working for much of his life in Austria. But there were mysteries in his life, periods unknown to history. Where had he spent those years?

"Always the ladies' man, Folliot." The feeble du Maurier managed a papery laugh. "Cat got your tongue?"

"You both speak of deathbeds," Clive blurted. "Is there no hope for your recovery, du Maurier, nothing at all that can be done?"

The old man pushed himself higher against his pillows. Madame Mesmer reached for his age-raddled arm and assisted him. Du Maurier said, "The leeches have had at me, Folliot. I've enriched half of Harley Street by now, and the other half would come panting to my door if I permitted them, each to poke and prescribe and carry away my treasure, but I've had enough of their kind. Enough and more. I am dying, but I have no fear of death. No! Death is the last of life's great mysteries. Greater than finding the sources of the Nile, greater than exploring the center of the atom, greater even than traveling to Mars or Jupiter or the planets of another star. And I am eager to unravel this final mystery."

He lay back against his pillows, catching his breath, gathering his strength.

"I'd have been gone by now, Folliot, but I wanted to see you once more before I go. And Madame Mesmer has helped me to pass the final barrier to perfect psychic communication. Communication—and more—for are you not here, drawn across the leagues of space and the pages of time and the unfathomable twists of dimension? This is my triumph, Folliot!"

The old may lay back against his pillows, his eyes drooping shut, his nearly toothless jaw sagging.

"Is he—has he?" Clive leaned forward to peer beneath the bed-curtains.

"No. He lives yet." Madame Mesmer had laid her fingers on the old man's wrist, then nodded affirmatively as his pulse made itself clear to her. "He has yet some strength. The end is drawing upon him, but it is not yet imminent."

Clive looked around himself, found a chair, and drew it close to du Maurier's bed. To Madame Mesmer he said, "Will you . . . ?"

She shook her head and walked a short distance away. Clive seated himself. Madame Mesmer had remained sufficiently nearby to continue the conversation.

She looked at Clive, raising her eyebrows inquisitively. "You have really been drawn to this place from far away?"

"From the polar sea, Madame. And I seem to have got an attentive grooming and a complete change of costume into the bargain."

"An interesting epiphenomenon. But of significance—you say that you were drawn here from another year as well."

"I left London in 1868. I have been traveling—to Zanzibar, then to the African mainland at Equatoria, and from there to other places whose locale I cannot even describe."

"And you were gone for how long, Major Folliot?"

"Du Maurier claims, twenty-eight years."

"But you look very young to have been away so long."

"To me it seems a matter of . . . I cannot be certain,

but, I would think, some months. At the most, a very few years. Two or three years. Four at the most."

"Surely not twenty-eight."

"Surely not."

Madame Mesmer clasped her hands in the small of her back and paced the room like a man. After a while she returned to du Maurier's bedside. She bent solicitously to study the man, then rose again. "He is asleep. His strength has a limit. But the end, although it is rushing upon him, is not here yet."

She turned to face Clive.

"I suppose you wonder at my role in this little drama, Major."

"Indeed!"

"You have heard of my illustrious ancestor, perhaps. The great Franz Anton Mesmer."

"I have heard of the great charlatan, Anton Mesmer. Forgive me, madame, for speaking bluntly. But I believe it more honorable to speak truthfully, even at the price of giving offense to one whom I would not wish to offend, than it would be to dissemble."

Color flared in her graceful cheeks, and the flame of the oil lamp seemed to flare briefly in its reflection. Her eyes were very dark. Perhaps, in the dim illumination of the sickroom, the irises had opened, creating a darker appearance than would normally have been the case.

"My ancestor, Major, was pilloried by the envious and the ignorant. But his theories of animal magnetism and his experiments in its control—in what has come to be known as *Mesmerism*—have never been disputed. Not once. On the contrary, experimenters on every continent have duplicated Anton Mesmer's work, and without exception their results have sustained his beliefs. The time will come when he is recognized as one of the truly great figures of human history!"

"I do not wish to quarrel, Madame. Perhaps you will kindly come to your point."

"My point, Major, is that the discrepancy in time as experienced by Mr. du Maurier and by yourself is subject to several explanations. One is that you did, indeed, live only a few years while Mr. du Maurier lived for twenty-eight. This other reality which you experienced, this . . . *Dungeon*, may exist in lockstep with the Earth. In that case—"

She had resumed her restless pacing again, her hands clasped, as before, in the small of her back. As she passed between him and the oil lamp, Clive could not but notice the flicker of lamplight upon her graceful bosom. He suppressed a sharp intake of breath and concentrated on her words.

"In that case," she repeated, "your 1870, let us say—the *Dungeon*'s 1870—exists side by side with the Earth's 1870. You lived but, let us say, two years. You reached the year 1870, at which point you were snatched up by George du Maurier's psychic force and carried twenty-six years into your future. Your future. Our present. The year 1896."

"A pretty fancy," Clive rejoined. He rose from his chair and stood facing her. "Travel through time. Thus might one journey to observe the building of the pyramids, the parting of the Red Sea, the landing upon Mount Ararat, even the Crucifixion of the Savior—"

"—or one might fly in the opposite direction and observe the slow evolution of our descendants, at least according to the theories of Messrs. Darwin and Wallace. The slowing of the Earth's rotation, the dimming of the sun to a dull red globe." She had picked up Clive's narrative in midstride and continued it without missing a beat.

"But you said there were more explanations than one," Clive said, taking up the thread. He had advanced toward the woman and stood now, facing her, noting that her unusual height, in contrast to his own middling dimensions, brought their faces to a level. The warmth which the lamplight imparted to her olive skin and great black eyes made his pulse roar in his ears.

"Suppose," she said, smiling, "that the rate of time is not absolute and universal. Suppose that the stream of time flows more rapidly in one sector of Creation than in another."

"Absurd." Clive frowned.

"But a stream of water may flow very rapidly in one region, where it rolls down a steep declivity or pours from a cliff. Did you never see the great falls in East Africa?"

"I did, Madame."

"So! And yet that same stream might slow its course where it moves slowly across a plain. It might pause to form a lake. It might even, in case of a tidal estuary, hesitate at the edge of the sea, advancing timidly when the tide flows outward, returning to visit when the tide returns."

"A very pretty set of images, Madame. I congratulate you upon your poetic attainments. But what has this to do with the Dungeon, and with du Maurier and with me?"

"I was but drawing a simile, Major Folliot." She smiled at him.

"Time is not water, nor is its flow the flow of a stream. There are no time-rapids, time-falls, time-lakes, or time-tides. Your images are affecting, but ultimately they are false. Totally, absolutely false."

He started to raise his hands toward her shoulders, but a glance from her great eyes and a curl to the corner of her mouth dissuaded him. He turned away and stood with his back to her, clasping his elbows in his palms, gazing contemplatively at the wan figure propped against its pillows.

"Leave aside your theories of time. What matters is this. For as long as I traveled through the Dungeon—and its levels and regions, its denizens and its perils are far beyond the power of word to convey or imagination to picture—I attempted to communicate with George du Maurier."

He took the frail, wrinkled hand that lay on the coverlet and held the fingers sadly in his own.

"Many times I thought—I just thought—that I reached him. There was a feeling, a prickling beneath my scalp, a whispering in my mind, that led me to think that he heard my mental message and was sending one of his own in response."

He whirled to face her again.

"But I was never certain of that. What I received in return for my messages was never more than the vaguest of suggestions of contact. Then, mere hours ago—or at least, so it seemed to me—du Maurier spoke quite clearly. Hah!"

He crossed the room to a stone-faced hearth where the makings of a fire had been arranged but never ignited. He looked around for flint and steel, found instead a tall box of long-stemmed sulfur matches, and without obtaining permission of either du Maurier or Madame Mesmer, set the kindling straws alight. Even as he watched, the flame spread from straws to twigs, from twigs to heavier slivers, and thence to the substantial logs that lay upon a heavy iron grate.

"There is in the Dungeon a wondrous thing, a kind of train that moves not on tracks as does a railroad train, but on whatever course it chooses. It runs upon land, upon water, even in the sky. And its cars are not mere coaches filled with seats and travelers. Each coach represents a different period or locale in time or space. Once before I visited this train, and had a surprising experience in a Roman bath. That was long ago and far away from here."

He looked at Clarissa Mesmer, and saw that she was following his words with fascination and eagerness.

"Today I entered that train again, entered a car wondering where I would find myself, in what era and what nation. The last that I would have guessed would have been George du Maurier's private bedchamber!"

He stood with head bowed, studying the polished tips of his boots. "I could leave here, I suppose."

He crossed the room and drew aside the heavy curtain with one hand, peering through the tall window into the London street. It was indeed night—full dark had fallen upon the city, and the street outside, deserted except by a dank-appearing fog, was illuminated only by the points of gaslamps and a few shade-covered windows in other houses, windows that glowed orange behind their translucent shades.

"I could leave here and find my family's country seat, or return to my Guards unit. I could search for my sweetheart, Miss Leighton—although by now, damn it, she would be old enough to be my mother! *Damn!* Pardon me, Madame Mesmer. I could raise an expedition and return to the Sudd, seek out the point of transition to the Dungeon, and attempt to rescue my fellows."

"Or?" Clarissa Mesmer prompted.

"Or?" Clive Folliot echoed.

"Or what? It is clear that you do not intend to leave here. Not through the doorway like an ordinary visitor. No, Major Folliot. Grant me that much, as a judge of human nature. I do not know your intentions, but they are not to walk from this house into the London night. What, then, are they?"

"As yet, Madame," Clive replied, "I do not know."

· CHAPTER 5 ·
"Death Is the Least Fearsome Thing"

After a while there came a rustling from the bed.

Clive Folliot and Clarissa Mesmer raced to the edge of the four-poster.

"I slept," du Maurier's papery whisper announced. "Each time I close my eyes, I wonder if it will be the last. Do I cross the line that separates life from death? Do I face, at last, the final and greatest of all mysteries? Or do I merely lapse for a time into the realm of dreams, to return after a while and live a bit longer in this material world of ours?"

"You merely slept," Clive Folliot told him. "We are here, old friend. There is nothing you need to fear."

"Fear?" The old man's eyes brightened as he spoke the word. He turned his face and looked at the fire now burning on the hearth. He smiled approvingly. "Of course there is nothing to fear. Death may be many things, but fearsome it is not. Life is fearsome. Life hold threats and anguishes without number, but death is the least fearsome thing there is."

The old man took Clive's hand in his two. "There is nothing to fear beyond the veil—that much I know."

"How did you reach me?" Clive asked. "Did you bring me here, or did I come by some other agency?"

"Give credit to Madame Mesmer," the old man said. "By her methods I was able to concentrate my psychic forces upon reaching you. And, behold, first clear communication, then you are translated from that other time and place—wherever they may be—and here! A marvel, Folliot, a marvel!"

"How much do you know of my adventures in the Dungeon, old friend?"

"Enough. At first, of course, your dispatches reached home. Carstairs was delighted. His rag scored one beat after another. Even your sketches, Folliot, became quite a rage. You'll pardon me if I mention that they're somewhat faulty in technique. But then, you are an amateur, are you not? It would be unfair to demand professional skill of an amateur."

"But those were all sent before we entered the Sudd," Clive demurred. "Once Smythe and Sidi Bombay and I were in the swamp, and once we passed through the heart of ruby to enter the Dungeon, I was able to send back no reports."

"That I realize." The old man hoisted himself higher against the piled pillows. Even though the room had not been cold when Clive arrived, there had been a dank quality to the air. The fire he had lighted on the hearth was doing much to alleviate that condition, and du Maurier seemed to draw strength from the flickering flames and the lighter air.

Du Maurier crooked a skeletal finger at Clarissa Mesmer. "Come closer, my dear. You have provided the means for this joyous reunion. You deserve to participate in it."

The tall woman knelt beside du Maurier's bed. The old man held Clive's hand in one of his, took Clarissa's in the other, then drew them together so the three were linked. Clive felt the energy of the three of them flow together. Clearly, Madame Mesmer felt the same exchange. She shot a glance at Clive and their eyes locked and held. Even George du Maurier, sinking slowly toward his death, was temporarily buoyed by the strength he drew from the others.

Clive turned his face toward du Maurier. "Once we had entered the Dungeon, when I was no longer able to send dispatches . . . how much of my mental emanation were you able to receive?"

"In a way, Folliot, I was able to receive everything. The mind is a subtle and complex organ. Madame Mesmer's ancestor gave his life to its study, and only began to scratch the surface. When you tried to send me messages, they penetrated the barriers that separate our world from the Dungeon. But you must realize, Folliot—the events that you experienced, compressed into, let us say, two years—these events were spread for me over a span of twenty-eight years."

He released Clive's and Clarissa's hands and dropped his own to the coverlet. "May I have a cup of tea and brandy, please? Will you ring for a servant, Madame Mesmer?"

Clarissa rose to her feet. As she stood over him, Clive detected the scent of her, a subtle essence. It penetrated to his core.

"Let us avoid the presence of servants, Mr. du Maurier. I know my way about your establishment. I shall fetch tea and brandy myself."

She swept from the room.

Du Maurier gestured to Clive, who bent close to the old man's face.

"Be careful of her, Folliot."

Clive drew back, astonished. "She is your personal aide, is she not? You attribute to her wondrous powers."

"Those she has."

"But then—?"

"It is neither her powers nor her works that I suspect. It is her motives. Her intentions."

"What do you know of her?"

"I summoned her from the Continent."

"And she came."

"Ah—but not directly. After arriving from the Continent, Madame Mesmer first paid a visit in the countryside."

The old man dropped his voice to a whisper. Already he had been speaking so softly that Clive had to lean over the bed, but now du Maurier looked fearfully about, assuring himself that no one overheard their conversation. "Before coming to see me," he explained, "she visited Tewkesbury."

"Tewkesbury!"

"Yes."

"But . . . that is my ancestral home. It was the home of my childhood. It is the Barony of Tewkesbury that my brother, Neville, will inherit if he lives and returns from the Dungeon—and that I will inherit if Neville dies."

"All of that I know, Folliot."

"And in Tewkesbury . . . what did Madame Mesmer do?"

"I know only that she visited Tewkesbury Manor. That, when there, she saw your father the baron, and—"

"Are you certain?" Clive interrupted. "I thought I saw the baron in the Dungeon, but then it appeared that it was not truly he, but an amazing simulacrum of him."

"Arthur Folliot, Baron Tewkesbury, has not been out of England in all the years you were away. If you saw a man who purported to be him, you were surely dealing with an imposter of some kind."

"Then I must go to Tewkesbury! My father, for all his shortcomings, is yet the holder of the title of baron and is head of our family. He is entitled to a report on the search for his heir." Clive hesitated, struck by another thought.

"But if it is really 1896, du Maurier, the baron is twenty-eight years older than when last I saw him. He will be . . ." He permitted himself to lapse into silence.

"Yes." Du Maurier smiled. "He will be an old man, like me. "Growing old has indeed been somewhat of a burden to me, Folliot. Don't be afraid to say it. Don't be afraid to acknowledge it. I assure you, I vastly prefer growing old to the only alternative I know of."

He waited patiently, smiling his indulgence while Clive unraveled the circuitous logic of his statement.

"Not only is Baron Tewkesbury in residence at Tewkesbury Manor, I have reason to believe that he is being attended by your brother, who arrived recently in company of a missionary priest, a Father O'Hara."

"Father O'Hara!"

The words had barely escaped Clive's lips when the door to du Maurier's chamber swung open and Clarissa Mesmer stepped through.

"Silence," du Maurier whispered to Clive. He pushed himself upright once again and reached toward the woman. "You are too kind, Madame," the old man said.

"I would be of what service as I am able, Mr. du Maurier." She carried an ornate silver tray to the massive desk across the room. On the tray were cups and saucers, a steaming silver pot of tea, and a crystal decanter. As she prepared du Maurier's cup, she said, "Mr. Folliot, may I offer you refreshment?"

Clive declined the offer.

Clarissa Mesmer carried a cup of gold-trimmed china to du Maurier's bed. Whatever else had befallen him in twenty-eight years, Clive thought, George du Maurier had surely prospered in things material.

But his friend and mentor's words had put new worries into Clive's mind. New worries, and a new sense of urgency.

He must return to the Dungeon and see about Annie, Horace, Sidi Bombay, and the rest. But what was it that du Maurier had said about Neville Folliot's being back in England? And Father O'Hara!

Obviously, the transition from the mundane world to the Dungeon was one that could be made in either direction. Clive had known that—or at least suspected it—since his early days on Q'oorna. There he had visited a town that bore an astonishing resemblance to a bucolic English village. And there, in the home of the elderly mayor and his wife, he had seen a wedding portrait that showed not only the happy couple but the officiating clergyman as well.

And that clergyman, also younger by many years but unmistakable nevertheless, was Timothy F. X. O'Hara. The same Father O'Hara whom Clive had encountered in the East African village of Bagomoyo!

To this point, O'Hara was the only individual whom Clive had been certain—or almost certain—to be capable of traveling between the Dungeon and the surface of the Earth. Clive didn't even know where the Dungeon was. For a time he had thought of it as a series of spheres similar to the pre-Copernican notion of spheres surrounding the Earth and carrying upon their transparent surfaces the moon, planets, and distant stars.

Only the Dungeon was a series of spheres that lay *beneath* the surface of the Earth. As one penetrated each, one approached closer and closer to the ultimate center of the Dungeon—which might or might not coexist with the geological center of the Earth.

That was a theory that Clive had entertained. But later experience had caused him to doubt its validity. It was comfortingly graspable to the mundane mind. But, alas, the more Clive experienced of the Dungeon, the less was he able to maintain his belief in that notion.

Q'oorna itself had proven, in due course, to be a planet comparable to the Earth. But it was one that existed on the very edge of being, a rogue world whose rotation brought it to face the vast sea of astral objects known to nineteenth century man for half Q'oorna's diurnal cycle. And for the other half, Q'oorna faced an unplumbable blackness wherein only the enigmatic spiral of stars offered any relief at all.

And if Q'oorna was truly a planet at the edge of all being, then what of the other levels of the Dungeon, worlds of jungle and desert, of rolling sea and granite peak? And what of the ultimate level of the Dungeon, the ninth level? Was it truly the Earth itself? Was the whole terrifying geometry of the Dungeon but a loop that returned after its wild coursings to its own point of origin?

Father O'Hara seemed to hold a clue to that riddle!

And now Clive had learned that his brother Neville, in search of whom he had set out upon his adventure, had also returned from the Dungeon. If Neville was back, then what of that other baffling trio, Philo B. Goode and Amos and Lorena Ransome?

Clive leaped from his chair and bolted for the door.

"Mr. Folliot!" Clarissa Mesmer called after him. "Mr. Folliot, where are you going? Mr. Folliot!"

Clive paused in the doorway but a moment. "To Tewkesbury! I must go to Tewkesbury! Farewell, du Maurier! I hope you are not disappointed with the answer you find to death's mystery! And you, Madame Mesmer—it has been a pleasure making your acquaintance!"

The blackness outside was as nothing compared to the blackness Clive Folliot had encountered in the Dungeon, and the loneliness of this deserted London street was as nothing to the loneliness Clive had encountered in the Dungeon.

No, the fog that billowed around him as he stood on the

stone steps of du Maurier's house—and only now did he realize what a large and splendid establishment that house was—seemed like an old friend welcoming him home to England. The ghostly gaslights that lined the kerb and the windows that were illuminated were like welcoming eyes. The cobblestones of the thoroughfare felt comfortable and familiar beneath his boots.

He jammed his military cap onto his head and strode toward the nearest intersection. For the first time he examined his accoutrement, finding it completely in order and trim. He even carried a ceremonial saber in a scabbard depending from his belt, and a purse full of currency at his waist. Did Her Majesty's officers wear the same uniform in 1896 that they had in 1868? Clive smiled at the thought of a man from 1836 appearing for formation in 1868. Were he to reappear like a figure from the past, he would face curiosity, ridicule . . . but that was a small problem compared to the others he faced.

The intersection led to a street vaguely familiar to Clive. He was certain that he had been there before, but the buildings seemed to have changed.

Of course! he realized with a start. In twenty-eight years, stately Georgian buildings would have fallen into disrepair and ruin, greed-driven land speculators would have bought them up to be demolished and replaced by the atrocities considered smart by newer, cleverer generations.

Clive strode along, his heart filled with pangs of recollection. For a moment he thought of making his way to Plantagenet Court, in hopes of catching a glimpse of Annabella Leighton. But he knew that she was no longer there. His descendant Annie had given him the history of her family, and he was aware that Annabella, despairing of his return to give a name to the child he had got upon her, had long since departed for the New World. Why, he might be a grandfather by now!

He picked up his stride. He came to the entry to an underground railroad station and contemplated briefly taking passage on a train to carry him to a major railroad terminus. But he feared to bring himself to do so. It was too much like reentering the Dungeon.

He shuddered and passed by.

He had become disoriented midst the unfamiliar architecture of this modern London, and when he saw a window gleaming across the way and heard the sounds of commerce and social intercourse from within, he headed toward the establishment.

What was the hour? It had already been full dark when he arrived at du Maurier's home, but depending on the time of year—he didn't even know the time of year! —nightfall might come anywhere from five o'clock in the afternoon to eight in the evening. And making allowance for the time he had spent with du Maurier and Madame Mesmer, it still might be anywhere from an early and respectable hour to shortly before dawn.

Surely the quiet and almost wholly deserted streets he had traversed suggested that the hour was indeed very late.

He stood before a lighted window and peered through. The neighborhood, he realized, had altered in nature as he walked, and he was now in a working-class section not very far from the West India Docks.

Another irony, he realized. For it had been from the West India Docks that he had sailed aboard the *Empress Philippa* that early morning in 1868. Where now were the captain and crew of that ship? Where the other passengers, including the mysterious mandarin who had proven to be his onetime batman, Quartermaster Sergeant Horace Hamilton Smythe, and the trio of Philo B. Goode and Amos and Lorena Ransome?

He swung open the door of the lighted establishment and was staggered by the volume and intensity of the light, the noise, and the odors that assailed him. Clearly he had found his way into a lower class dive, and he hesitated, thinking that it might be wisest to beat a hasty retreat and seek elsewhere for passage to the railroad terminus.

But he had no chance to retreat.

Almost before his eyes had had a chance to adjust to the increased illumination, he found himself taken by both elbows and half-invited, half-dragged into the room. Not that the two individuals who had seized him did so by virtue of brute force. No, they were two of the most astonishingly attractive—and forward—women he had ever encountered.

He had seen slave women for sale in Zanzibar; he had encountered African maidens who thought no more of showing themselves as naked as Eve than did an English lady of showing her flashing eyes. But he had never seen women as done up to arouse the animal side of a man as were these two.

One of them had blond hair, a heart-shaped face, long, curving eyelashes, rouged cheeks, and painted lips. Her gown, of a brilliant shade of blue, was cut so low at the bodice that her more than ample breasts were clearly visible to the taller Clive Folliot. Her arms were naked from shoulder to elbow, her long gloves covering them from that point to her fingertips. Her skirt was generous, but the gown was cut so closely to her torso that every curve was clearly visible.

Her counterpart, grasping Clive by the other arm, had hair of a shade of red that clearly Nature had never given her. Her eyebrows were darkened and her eyes ringed with paint so that her viewer's attention was drawn to them and the startling green shade that contrasted with her hair but was matched almost perfectly by her gown. The bosom of this garment was cut low, although not as low as that of her partner. But as she twisted in place, Clive became aware that the back of her garment was cut in a declivity that extended far below her waist.

He gasped and started to back away, but the women drew him forward. The blonde said, "Look 'oo we 'ave 'ere, dearie!"

The redhead said, "This is the prettiest fing I've seen tonight, ain't it?"

They laughed, and before Clive knew what had happened to him he was halfway across the room. A long bar of mahogany wood stood against one wall of the establishment, and a crew of bartenders handed out beverages and took payment for them. In a distant corner of the establishment a small stage bore a trio of females harmonizing wistfully to the accompaniment of a three-piece orchestra. The refrain of the song, and (Clive presumed) its title, was

"Her Hair Was Hanging Down Her Back." Both the lyrics and the singers' delivery were startling to Clive, accustomed as he was to the more sedate practices of a quarter-century earlier.

The two women maneuvered Clive to an empty table, apparently the only such in the establishment.

"Have a drink, sweetie," the blonde urged Clive.

"Get a bottle," the redhead amended. "A bottle and three glasses and we'll have ourselves a party, we will!" She leaned toward him and he smelled the gin on her breath and the perfume in her hair.

"I have to go," Clive pleaded.

"In a bit, dearie."

"Soon's we've 'ad our party, cutes."

The tables surrounding Clive's were packed with burly men and flashy women. A broad-shouldered tough in a striped shirt and seafarer's cap turned and fixed Clive with a curious stare.

"Will ya have a look at the fancy Dan, mates?" he addressed his companions.

"Ain't you in the wrong part of town?" another seaman growled.

"You think you're goin' ter amuse yourself, taking in the lowlife, then beating it back to your swell friends, brigadier?"

Clive shook his head, frowning. "Now, look here, you men, I just wandered in here looking for a railroad station, and I'll be very happy to leave if someone can simply show me the way."

"Just wandered in!" the first seafarer roared.

"Show me the way!" the second one mimicked, following the words with derisive laughter. "We'll show yer the way, fancy Dan, if that's what yer wants!"

The seamen were on their feet and heading, none too steadily, toward Clive. His two female companions, no longer plastering themselves to his scarlet-clad arms, were squealing and scrambling to get away from the imminent battle.

Clive was glad that he hadn't had time to consume any liquor. He leaped to his feet and balanced to meet a potential attack. He thought for a moment of the saber that was part of his accoutrement, but left it in his scabbard. If he could limit the confrontation to a verbal level, he would be relieved. If not, then let it at least remain a battle of bare fists, not the lethal hardware of war.

• CHAPTER 6 •
"I Am Not at All Surprised!"

The two bruisers came at Clive, fists raised, looks of menace and determination on their faces. Carousers at nearby tables drew back. Clive's two erstwhile friends seemed to fade into the crowd. Even the singers on the stage and the musicians clustered before it grew quiet.

It appeared that fights were not uncommon in this den. If anything, they were looked upon as a frequent source of amusement.

The first tough who had spoken to Clive leaned across the table toward him. Clive, standing to face the man, realized that the bruiser was a full head taller than himself and proportionately more wide. His breath carried a dizzying mixture of tobacco fumes, alcohol, and another essence that Clive could only guess was dope of some sort. The man was of dubious race. His skin was swarthy, his eyes carried an exotic look, his hair was worn long, plaited into a greasy queue that hung down his grimy striped shirt.

The second tough hovered behind his companion, darting menacing looks and gestures around his massive shoulders.

The first tough said, "We don't like your kind aroun' here, mister! Fancies and swells what thinks they's better 'an us. Comes aroun' here lookin' for fast women and cheap thrills!"

Clive was on his own feet, facing the man. "I told you, my good fellow, that I was merely looking for the railroad terminus. These two ladies chose to make my acquaintance, not I theirs."

He looked around but the redhead and the blonde had disappeared.

"I'm gonna teach you a lesson, Mister Redcoat!" The ruffian lifted the table that separated himself from Clive and hurled it sideways. It crashed to the floor, sending spectators scrambling for their safety.

The man raised a beefy fist and launched a crude blow at Clive's face. Clive ducked the blow easily, feinting with his own fist to keep the fellow at bay. Behind the big man he could see his smaller companion and hear him calling advice. Still farther away, Clive caught a glimpse of the huge mirror that backed the serving bar, and the bartender standing before it, observing the confrontation.

The big man launched another blow, this time with more care than he had the first, but with equal lack of effect. The blow was a straight jab with his fist, and Clive evaded it with a simple shift of his head.

Enraged, the man attempted a brutal kick. His muscular legs were encased in thick-soled boots, and Clive suspected that if he should ever be knocked down by the man, his ribs would fall rapid prey to that heavy footgear.

But the lessons that Clive had received in personal combat were coming into play. He had fought countless boxing matches with his brother Neville, and while Neville was the more accomplished fighter—and also possessed far stronger instincts to compete and punish, while Clive's predilection was to cooperate and assist—still, the younger twin had picked up many a useful move. He had learned both fencing and further lessons in fisticuffs at the behest of Horace Hamilton Smythe while serving with the Imperial Horse Guards, and his fighting prowess had been perfected, willy-nilly, in his journey through some eight levels of the Dungeon.

As the giant bruiser hurled his massive boot at Clive, Clive stepped aside and slipped behind his assailant and added his own strength to the man's momentum by the simple device of shoving him with both hands, as hard as he could.

The bruiser staggered forward, lost his balance, and tumbled into the crowd.

Jeers rose. "Not so tough tonight, Bruno!" "What's the

matter, man, losin' yer touch?" "Bruno's takin' a lickin' for once!"

And even a few encouraging calls directed at himself. "Nice work, Redcoat!" "The toff's a slick one, i'n 'e?" "Where'd yer learn that, fancy Dan?"

Clive turned to face the giant Bruno, who was struggling to regain his feet. He heard a scuffling behind him, and a voice—a woman's voice, perhaps that of one of his erstwhile companions—called a warning.

He whirled in time to see Bruno's smaller companion charge at him, a heavy-handled dagger in his hand.

Clive was able to sidestep in the nick of time, accelerating his second attacker into his still wobbly first. There was a resounding thump as the two of them crashed to the floor, but Clive realized now that his attackers had further allies. Moans of protest rose from the crowd, but hands remained unraised in Clive's defense as a half-dozen ruffians arrayed themselves in alliance with Bruno and his first confederate.

Clive backed away, trying to avoid being surrounded and sapped or stabbed from behind, as he was sure would be his fate if his enemies managed to circle him. He scrambled through sweating men and perfumed women until he stood with his back to the bar. No fewer than eight men, a phalanx four wide and two deep, confronted him. The giant Bruno had also drawn a dirk, and he and his first confederate stood front and center, crouched and ready to attack.

For the first time Clive considered defending himself with a weapon other than his wits and his bare hands. His ornate saber still hung from his waist, a weapon whose significance to Her Majesty's servants was increasingly ceremonial rather than practical. Even in earlier times, the saber with its curving blade and razor edge was intended for use by the cavalry, by fast-moving horsemen who would slash at an enemy in a fleeting instant of combat. A sharp-pointed rapier, such as Clive had used so long ago in the castle of N'wrbb Crrd'f, would have been more suitable.

Still, the saber was the best weapon available to Clive, and use it he would. He gripped the scabbard in his left hand, ran the fingers of his right through the basket hilt, and drew the blade.

A sound rose from the crowd. It was a collective response to Clive's gesture, a combination of sigh and moan and gasp and a half-articulated exhalation of encouragement.

Then, for a tingling moment, the room lapsed into a silence so nearly perfect that the rhythmic breathing of its many occupants united to form a weird, organic harmony.

"I did not come here to fight," Clive said. "I will still leave peacefully if you will but open a way for me."

He raised the basket-hilt of his saber before his chin, almost as if in salute, then swept its point downward to the horizontal, pointing it toward the exit that gave back onto the street.

As Clive's blade stood quivering at the horizontal, the companion of giant Bruno stuck sideways at it, a twisting, lunging blow designed to sweep the saber from Clive's hand and bring the man's dagger slicing dangerously toward Clive's torso.

With a practiced twist of his own wrist, Clive sent the man's dagger whirling across the room to fall with a clatter near the now-deserted stage. Again a collective response rose from the crowd. Clive could sense that he, who had arrived a stranger and been greeted as an unwelcome interloper in the establishment, was winning their support with his sportsmanship and his skill in the face of bullies.

Someone in the second row of Clive's attackers handed a bottle to an unarmed man in the front row. The man held the bottle by its neck and smashed it across a table. Clive had heard of such a tactic, wondering if it could succeed. More likely the bottle would simply spin across the room, knocked from its wielder's hand by the force of its impact.

But the ruffian showed every sign of the experienced killer. Under his control, the bottle was converted in a moment to a deadly weapon. The thug lunged at Clive, the glittering shard of glass thrusting to impale its victim. Now the sharpened edge of Clive's saber came into play. He slashed at his newest attacker with it, slicing into the man's forearm above the wrist. With a curse and a howl the fellow dropped the bottle and plunged backward into the crowd, blood spraying from his wounded arm.

Now two more attackers came at Clive, one from either side, with Bruno following, crouched low and slashing at Clive's legs with his dagger. Clive landed a boot on the point of Bruno's jaw and the man flew backward, his dagger, too, flying above the massed onlookers to clatter against the far wall of the room.

But even his superior combative skills—in a calm corner of his mind Clive blessed both Horace Hamilton Smythe and his bullying brother Neville for the lessons they had taught him—even Clive's superior skills could not hold out indefinitely against the odds that he faced.

He leaped backward and up, hoisting himself with one hand onto the service bar as he did so. For a moment he stood on the polished wooden surface, spied the naked shoulders and colorful dresses of his two erstwhile female companions milling in the midst of others, then dropped behind the bar.

The tender there hustled Clive toward one end of the narrow space. "This way, sah! This way!" They scurried toward a door of dark-stained wood and polished brass fittings. "We'll get yer out of 'ere in a mo' now, yes we will, sah!"

Clive had a bare instant as the barkeep twisted the doorknob for him, opening the door and shoving Clive through it. Even as he stood in darkness, cavalry saber in hand, Clive blinked, stunned by the face he had beheld.

Was that malleable countenance the one he thought it was? One who had appeared first as a Chinese mandarin on the West India docks, and then again aboard the *Empress Philippa*, as an Arab guard in the heated atmosphere of Zanzibar, as a onetime duelist in the American city of New Orleans?

Was this none other than Quartermaster Sergeant Horace Hamilton Smythe?

Before Clive could clear his mind, before his eyes could adjust to the new darkness that surrounded him, there came the sound of a safety match being scratched into flame, then a tiny pop as a gas fixture was lighted.

The man who had ignited the illuminating gas turned to

face Clive. He wore a frock coat, a frilled white shirt, and a cravat of purple silk. His hair was curled, and rich muttonchop whiskers met to form a luxuriant mustache.

"A drawn saber, Major Folliot? Such melodrama, really." The man extended an elegantly manicured hand, not to be shaken but merely to indicate a brass-studded, leather-covered chair that stood between himself and Clive. "Please, Major. Put up your wog-sticker, you will not need it here. Or, if you did, it would be to meet a challenge for which it would be a wholly inadequate response. Of that, I can assure you."

He paused for a beat, two. Then, "Please, Major. I appeal to you."

Cautiously, looking in all directions to assure himself that no third party was present in the room, Clive returned his saber to its scabbard. Slowly he lowered himself into the indicated seat.

The frock-coated man nodded approvingly. "You do look splendid in your uniform, Major. Red is not a color all men can wear, but against your patrician features it is most flattering."

Clive gazed, astonished, at his host. He had been startled just moments before to recognize the bartender as Horace Hamilton Smythe. But if his encounter with Smythe had been a startlement to him, it was nothing compared to the shock of recognition he now experienced.

"Philo B. Goode!"

"Yes"—the other man bowed graciously—"at your service, sir." A table stood nearby, and Goode drew a chair for himself and sat at the table. "Will you join me, Major Folliot? I think we have a great deal to discuss."

Clive's head swam. Philo Goode! Philo Goode! The mountebank gambler from whose cardsharpery Horace Smythe had saved Clive in the passenger saloon of the *Empress Philippa*. Clive had exposed Goode and his two confederates to the ship's captain, and they had been put ashore in West Africa to fend for themselves.

Later Clive learned from Horace Smythe that Goode and his confederates, Amos and Lorena Ransome, had caught him, Smythe, in a complicated scheme aboard a Mississippi River steamer. The scheme had led to a duel in New Orleans and the snaring of Horace into an even wider conspiracy involving the three others. It was a scheme that involved them in the Dungeon, Clive knew, although in what capacity he had only the fuzziest of ideas.

Now that Clive had been drawn back to London in the year 1896, he had found Horace Hamilton Smythe tending bar in this disreputable establishment, while Philo Goode stood ready to greet him as a long-lost associate in the back office.

It was too much to assimilate in such a brief moment. Clive lowered his face to his hands, rubbed his eyes, then raised his face once again and sat in anticipatory silence.

In the sparsely furnished, officelike room, the only sound for a few moments was the soft hissing of the gas fixture. Sounds from the outer establishment, apparently a combination saloon and small-time music hall, with a possible additional function as a place of assignation, penetrated to the rear chamber.

Clive's precipitous departure from his confrontation with Bruno and his associates had prompted a major uproar in the place. But after a brief period the voice of the bartender could be heard, restoring order with a series of commands given in crisp, authoritarian tones.

The music started up again. Clive heard a piano, cornet, and drumbeat. Then came female voices uncertainly harmonizing upon a tune unfamiliar to Clive, its semi-audible lyrics apparently dealing with a request from a young lady and addressed to her gentleman. "Do, do, my huckleberry, do," Clive heard, without noting a clear specification as to what it was the huckleberry was supposed to do. His imagination supplied a variety of answers.

"You *are* Mr. Philo Goode, of America, are you not, sir?" Clive addressed the frock-coated man.

"That I am, sir."

"And that"—Clive gestured with a jerk of his head—"that was Sergeant Smythe? Sergeant Horace Hamilton Smythe?"

"It is indeed Horace Hamilton Smythe, Major Folliot. As for the title you give him—*sergeant*—I suppose it is one to which he is entitled. But to me he is known in a far more exalted role. One which you yourself might envy."

"And what rank is that?"

"I fear that I am not at liberty to reveal that information to you, Major. There are organizations and entities of immense power and importance whose very existence would startle a man of your modest attainments. Forgive my candor, please."

Clive flushed. "The rank of major is a not inconsiderable one, Mr. Goode, the attaining of which is no inconsiderable feat. Nor is it altogether beyond imagining that I may yet accede to the title of baron, although my elder twin Neville is at present the heir presumptive to the rank and its accompanying lands and perquisites."

"I quite understand that, Major Folliot." Goode leaned part of the way across the ornate table and opened a humidor of polished walnut and brass. He extended the humidor toward Clive. "May I offer you a cheroot, Major? I have them imported from Cuba, made to my personal specifications, rum-soaked and carefully seasoned."

Clive shook his head.

"I am sure you will not mind, then." Goode extracted a brown cigar, lighted it, and exhaled a cloud of heavy blue smoke toward the ceiling. "Now, sir," he addressed Clive after removing the cheroot from his mouth, "I should not be surprised at all to learn that you have some questions for me."

"I already asked you the first, Mr. Goode. What is Sergeant Smythe doing in this establishment, tending bar for a saloon's worth of ruffians and harlots?"

"For one thing, Major Folliot, he was saving your neck. As I understand he has a habit of doing."

Again Clive flushed. He had to admit, at least to himself, that he had been saved more than once by Horace Hamilton Smythe. To Philo Goode, however, he said nothing at this point.

"You do understand that you faced a severe battering at the very least, at the hands of my . . . guests." Goode tipped his own head toward the outer room. "A severe battering at the very least," he repeated, "if not a maiming—or even your death."

"I was holding my own quite nicely, thank you very much."

"Indeed you were. I was most impressed by your performance, Major Folliot." Goode rose and strode to a drapery that stretched from ceiling to floor. With a single sweep of his arm, he drew it aside to reveal the inside of the saloon. The long mirror behind the bar was transparent from its rear; any occupant of the office could thus observe activities in the business establishment without himself being noticed.

"You are no longer the soft weakling who set out from London in 1868 to find your brother, Major."

"What do you know of my adventures, Mr. Goode? And what has been your role in them? A cardsharper? A mountebank operating on a Mississippi steamer?"

"Those things, yes," Goode acknowledged. He returned to the table, drew and released another long plume of blue smoke from his cheroot, and tapped ashes from it into a heavy ashtray. "Those things and more, I suppose I ought to say."

"You ought to say, indeed, sir! You are connected with the Dungeon. I saw you on the level which I can only describe as"— he flushed to speak the word—"Hell."

"Well, one has one's duties, Major Folliot. One has one's duties."

"Are you the master of the Dungeon?"

Goode collapsed into his chair, doubled over with laughter. When he had recovered himself, he said, still chuckling, "I—the master of the Dungeon? Well, I suppose a cat can look at a king. A street-urchin can envy a senator. Oh, I am far, far from being master of the Dungeon."

"Are you connected with the Ren? With the Chaffri? With the Gennine?"

"Ah, now you address me with a more realistic question. Yes, I am connected with . . . a group."

"With which? And for what purpose?"

"You will learn everything that you need to know, Major Folliot—when you need to know it."

"I can see that I am going to receive no satisfaction from you, Mr. Goode. It would be tempting to take action against you directly—I know enough of you to know that you are up to no decent end—but for the moment, I will simply take my leave of you. Good day, sir—or should I say, good night!"

Clive rose from his seat and strode back toward the door.

Philo Goode moved more rapidly even than Clive, but rather than blocking his path to the exit, he moved to the mirrored panel that revealed the outer room. "Look before you leap, Major Folliot. Look well!"

Clive stood staring at the glass panel. He saw not a saloon filled with carousers and harlots, but a pit of roaring, dancing flames.

"It is Hell!" Clive exclaimed.

"You would not survive five minutes out there, Major Folliot. In fact, not one minute. But there is another means of egress." He bent and pulled up the corner of an oriental carpet. Beneath it, a trapdoor fitted with a heavy iron ring was revealed.

With a grunt, Philo Goode tugged the trapdoor open. A flight of stone steps led downward into the gloom.

"You want me to go down there? To face I know not what? To face, perhaps, my death?"

"Major Folliot, had I desired your death, I assure you, you would have been thoroughly and irrevocably dead long before now. Take my word for that. Please, go down these steps. They are the only way out of this place—for you."

Clive hesitated. He considered trying to leave the same way he had arrived in this room. Perhaps the vision of the flaming, hellish inferno was an illusion, a trick designed to mislead him. But he did not believe that was so. Still, he carried his saber yet. He could draw it, possibly take Philo Goode prisoner, force him to reveal what he knew, force him to reveal a safe means of egress from this trap.

But Goode *had* revealed a safe means of egress. Or such was his claim. The longer Clive pondered, the more convinced he became that Goode's suggestion was the only reasonable course of action for him to follow.

He rose from his chair, adjusting his tunic, saber, and cap, and stood over the open trapdoor. "If this is a trick, Goode, I warn you, sir—I have survived perils that you would not believe."

"I must differ with you, sir. I know more than you could possibly realize. I would believe everything you could tell me. That is the only reason you are here this night, sir, and the only reason that I offer you the opportunity that now stands at your feet."

"Nonetheless, if this staircase represents still another act of treachery on your part, Goode, I will extract from you a dear price indeed!"

"And I shall pay it gladly, Major Folliot. Now, if you see no further need to delay . . ."

Clive set his polished brown boot upon the first step of dank gray stone.

· CHAPTER 7 ·
But the Smallest Hint

The steps led downward into darkness, curving in a spiral that swiftly carried Clive into the unknown. He paused for a moment to glance upward. The open trap had shrunk to a tiny square, had done so far more rapidly than Clive would have expected.

Even as he stood gazing up, the square of light disappeared. Apparently Philo Goode had slammed shut the trapdoor. If he turned back, Clive suspected, and climbed the steps once again, he would find the door unmovable from below.

Not that he had any intention of turning back. He had committed himself to a course of action, and if there was one thing he had learned through his adventures in the Dungeon, it was to press ahead. Always, to press ahead. Peril might lie in his path, doom might await him. But no matter what the odds, there was always a chance of success. There was nothing to be gained by turning back. Surely not now.

Although the steep staircase led through darkness, there was a sufficient emanation of luminosity from the steps themselves to guide his feet. Clive set a steady pace for himself, neither counting steps nor attempting to calculate the passage of time. Eventually he would come to the end of his descent, and then he would find out what lay beneath Philo Goode's establishment.

Something brushed against his face and was gone. He wondered what it could be—a bat, perhaps. Some dark-adjusted creature flying through the blackness here, as much at home in the subterranean gloom as Clive would have been on his father's estate in Tewkesbury.

At length he emerged onto a level patch of flagstones. Here panels of illumination in one wall revealed that the stone flooring ended abruptly. There was a low drop, then a roadbed of sorts.

As if in response to Clive's presence, although he wondered if the timing were coordinated or merely happenstantial, he felt a rush of cold wind and heard a sound that grew from a soft *whooshing* to the scream of fast-driven wind.

He turned to see a lighted car barreling up the roadbed. It appeared to be made of glass or some similar transparent substance, molded over a framework of metal. He could see within the car a passenger compartment bearing a solitary traveler. The car resembled those of the train he had encountered first on the plain of Q'oorna and then again in the arctic waters of Earth.

The car slid to a halt. Clive could hear its engine pulsating like a living heart.

He looked toward the passenger compartment, started violently, then ran at top speed to the car. The passenger swung the door open and called to him. "Clive!"

"Annie!"

Without hesitation he jumped into the car. The young woman stood and Clive swept her into his arms, whirling her in a joyous circle. "Annie, my darling girl! My dear great-great-granddaughter Annie!"

"Put me down, Clive. Grandpa!" She used the term rarely, preferring to remain on a given-name basis. Her time was one of informality, and besides, in real age Clive was but a dozen years older than she, although through the twisted chronology of the Dungeon she was in truth his descendant, born some 144 years later than he.

"The joy I feel!" Clive exclaimed. "At first I feared that you were lost forever on the eighth level of the Dungeon. Lost forever—or worse! And then, when I stood upon the polar ice floe and saw the sun glinting off the wings of the aeroplane in which you escaped from the Japanese . . . There is so much I yearn to ask you, my darling Annie!

But for now, all that matters is that you are unharmed. You have not been . . . ?"

"No, I am well—as you can see, Clive." She curtsied before him. "And don't you look splendid in your scarlet tunic and clean-shaved cheeks!"

Although her attitude was still that of a woman prepared to make her way in the twenty-first century, she had been done up as a proper young lady of the nineteenth. Her hair was arranged in a crown of braids that coiled around her white forehead. Her face was modestly made up. Her gown was of a light color and material, cut modestly across the bosom and tightly at the waist. She was a contrast of one sort against the two harlots who had cozened up to Clive in the drinking den, of another against the severe Madame Mesmer in her high-necked, long-skirted outfit.

"Annie! You must tell me everything, everything that has happened."

"That will take a long time, Clive."

"But first—what is this car? What is this all about? How did you get back to England, to 1896? This is 1896, is it not? I saw du Maurier. I last saw him as a vigorous man of fifty. Now he is old. He says he is dying. He says I have been away for twenty-eight years."

"It is indeed 1896, Clive. Sit now, or you'll be knocked over!" The pulsation of the car's engine had increased in force and frequency, and Clive and Annie indeed had barely time to seat themselves, cozily side by side, before the car slid forward, pressing them against the padded back of their couchlike seat.

The car accelerated until Clive calculated that it was proceeding at a high rate of speed. It moved through a nearly featureless tunnel. Now and then a lighted panel cast a dim glow through the gloom. Now and then Clive caught sight of a branch or side passage curving away from their own. Where these branches led, he had no idea save for the wild conjecture that they were connected to different levels or sectors of the Dungeon.

For that matter, he had no idea where the car was bearing them. They were alone in it, and neither he nor

Annie did anything to control its progress or its course. There were no visible controls to be seen.

"My dear child, Annie—" Clive began.

Before he could continue, Annie said, "Clive, tell me—do you still have Neville's journal?"

Clive patted his tunic, investigating its pockets for the precious volume. "I fear not," he said. "When I was translated to London, I—" He paused to gather his thoughts, then began again. "On the eighth level—you remember that some of us were reduced in size to Lilliputian proportions, others enlarged to Brobdingnagian."

"How could I forget!"

"Fortunately, well before I was transported to the ninth level—or back here to Earth—perhaps they are the same—I had regained my normal stature."

She nodded, encouraging him to continue.

"I found myself on the arctic ice cap, along with Chang Guafe. It was just before I found him that you flew over in the Nakajima."

She made no comment on the aeroplane. Instead she inquired only about Chang Guafe. "And he, Clive?"

"He is there on the sea-bottom, as best I can surmise. What will become of him, I know not."

"And you?"

"The, well, I shall call it the space-train, arrived, and I climbed aboard, and found myself here in London. In 1896. Surrounded not by phantoms but, as far as I can tell, by reality. Including yourself." He paused to catch his breath and to gather his thoughts. He peered through the transparent wall of the car.

To appearances, the car had emerged from its long tunnel and was making its way along a wholly ordinary railway line. The long night was ending; Clive could detect the rosy blush of dawn to the east, behind the car, which sped along the tracks in a westerly direction.

As the car passed an early-rising farmer driving his hay-laden wagon along a dirt track beside the railroad bed, Annie took Clive's wrist. "He cannot see us, Clive. We can see all the world from this car, but we are protected from being seen."

"What is this car?" Clive demanded. "Have you made

league with . . . whoever is behind this? With Philo Goode and his confederates?"

She smiled up at him. "All in good time, Clive. You were telling me what happened to Neville's journal."

"The messages we received were seldom reliable anyway. I question both Neville's motivation in writing them and the authenticity of at least a number of them."

"You met Neville in the Dungeon."

"Yes. Neville—or a simulacrum."

"Did he acknowledge that he truly wrote all the messages in his journal?"

"He denied them all!"

She looked stunned, struck speechless.

Clive continued. "But now—was it truly Neville who denied writing the journal entries? And even if it was, can we believe him?"

Annie frowned. "Maybe we'll be able to find that out, somehow. But for now, where *is* the journal, Clive?"

"As I was explaining to you—when I entered the space-train, I was ragged, unshaven, half-starved, half-drowned, and half-frozen. When I found myself in London—in the bedchamber of my old friend du Maurier—I was nourished, shaven, magnificently togged, and bone dry. I do not understand what happened. I can only attribute it, like so many other mysteries, to the Dungeon."

"And Neville's journal?"

"I have no idea."

"Did you have it on the ice cap, Clive?"

"I don't know. I don't remember having it there, but I had other things to occupy my attention than thinking about my brother's notebook."

"Then it might still be on the ice cap. Or on the train. Or in George du Maurier's home, I suppose."

"Or back on the eighth level, in fact."

"Never mind. Never mind. We must cope with our situation as we find it."

The light from the east had increased, and Clive's observation of the green fields and budding trees that lined the railroad bed told him that it was a spring morning in the English countryside. One of nature's most beautiful creations—an English country spring.

"Where are we headed?" Clive asked.

Annie smiled. "Don't you recognize the landscape?"

Clive studied the vegetation and the lay of the land. "It looks like Gloucestershire."

"Right on the first response!"

"We're going to Tewkesbury!"

"Correct."

"Who is there, and what is your connection with them, Annie "

"Why, your family seat is there, Clive. At Tewkesbury Manor!"

"I know that. I did not ask *what* is there. I asked *who* is there."

"We'll access that data when our cursor reaches the designated address."

Oh, Lord, Clive thought, *she's lapsing into that strange futuristic jargon of hers.* "Annie, please—can't you speak in everyday language? Is the Queen's English inadequate to meet your needs?"

"Sorry, User. Uh, Clive. I forget myself. We'll find out when we get there, okay?"

"Very well. But Annie—so much has happened! Where are the others? Finnbogg and Shriek, Tomàs and Sidi Bombay . . ."

"You didn't mention Horace, Clive."

"I have seen Horace."

"At the North Pole?"

"No. In London. I was with him, although briefly, not more than an hour ago."

Annie's manner grew far more serious than it had been since their reunion in the transparent car. "You must tell me exactly where you saw him. How he looked. What he was doing."

"Well—" Clive hardly knew where to start. While he strove to set his thoughts in order, he peered through the glass wall of the car. Morning was well along by now, the English sky a brilliant shade of blue, dotted with tiny puffs of cloud. The railroad passed through farming country, and happy countrymen followed horse-drawn plows putting in their summer crops.

Before Clive had answered Annie's question, their little

car slowed precipitously. Annie peered ahead of them. "It's a roadblock, Clive! Quick, we'll have to defend ourselves."

She leaped from the seat and shoved the startled Clive Folliot from it. Despite her wide skirt she quickly knelt before the seat and raised its padded cushion to reveal an arsenal of astonishing weapons stowed beneath.

"Here, Clive—you can use one of these!" She handed him a machine that bore a certain resemblance to a carbine. He held it to his shoulder and lowered his face to peer through its sights. To his astonishment, he seemed to be looking through a telescope of some incredible, unfamiliar sort.

Annie took another of the weapons from its place, slammed shut the seat, and turned to take Clive's elbow.

"Annie—I should have thought to ask you—do you still have your Baalbec?"

"It's here, Grandpa!" She tapped a thumb against her bodice, indicating the place beneath her sternum where the versatile device was installed. She ran her other fingers over the skin of her forearm where the controls of the machine had been installed in the strange world of the future whence she came.

"Are we being attacked, Annie? Who is the enemy? Can you use the Baalbec to protect us?"

"Quick, out of here!" She swung open the door through which Clive had previously entered the car and gave him a vigorous shove. He tumbled from the car and onto soft English grass and felt her collide briefly with him as she landed.

There was a flash of brilliant green from a point ahead of their car, and the machine went up in a flash that blinded Clive for a moment. As he recovered his sight he saw bits of bent metal, fragments of shattered glass, odd pieces of wrecked machinery scattered over and around the railroad tracks.

"The next train to pass will be derailed!" he exclaimed.

"No it won't, and that's not our worry anyhow, Clive. Here comes our worry!"

Advancing toward them on the opposite side of the tracks came a squad of beings that bore a distant resemblance to humans. They were helmeted, and garbed in black uniforms with green insignia and piping on them.

Their metal fittings—Clive assumed they were metal— were all of the same glowing green that was almost impossible to look at. Clive's eyes stung and watered and he had to look away to avoid unbearable pain.

Even so, the soldiers seemed to fade and waver as Clive looked at them. Now and again one of them disappeared altogether, only to reappear as a vague, ghostly image of himself, yards away from the point of his disappearance.

"What—what are they?"

"Chaffri," Annie whispered. "This is as close to them as a true human normally gets. And if you bring yourself to their attention, you're not likely to survive the meeting! Stay down, Clive! Be wary!"

"I cannot see them clearly. Something here is not right."

"They can't see us either. Not any better than we can see them. Probably not that well, even."

The Chaffri had reached the wreckage of the car in which Clive and Annie had been riding. The apparent leader of the squad bent and picked up a piece of twisted metal tubing. He held it close to his face, then opened a pouch in his uniform and dropped it in.

Even as the Chaffri advanced and Clive and Annie watched, the wrecked car seemed to waver and run like a melting ice cube. In minutes it had soaked into the ground—or so it appeared to Clive.

The Chaffri were speaking in a language that bore no resemblance to anything Clive had ever heard before— emphatically including the patois that was common in most regions of the Dungeon. The Chaffri squad had divided in two, and half its members advanced along either side of the track.

Annie was right. The Chaffri gave no evidence of even being able to see the erstwhile passengers. Annie rolled away from the tracks as the Chaffri soldiers advanced, signaling for silence and tugging Clive to get him to move with her, out of the path of the advancing troopers.

But it was too late. The last of the Chaffri stepped squarely on Clive's chest.

To Clive's astonishment, the Chaffri's foot sank into his

body, like a boot sinking into thin mud. The sensation was one of the most vivid and unpleasant that Clive had felt in his lifetime. It wasn't exactly pain—it was more a sense of wrongness, a revulsion and disgust, as if he had been touched by, violated by, something not only ineffably alien but utterly perverted and disgusting.

The Chaffri leaped back, as if his response to contact with Clive was similar to Clive's reaction to him. He began gesticulating and shouting to his fellows. He already held a weapon at the ready and he swept it over the ground at his feet, obviously intending to blast Clive out of existence.

But he was fated for disappointment. Clive had already rolled away, and he and Annie were sprinting toward a nearby field.

Seedlings and earth spurted around Clive's feet. His military instincts asserting themselves, he threw himself to the ground, rolled twice, and sighted back at the Chaffri. The Chaffri's weapon fired again. More accurately, it sizzled, emitting something that looked like a bolt of lightning. Even though no tangible projectile was involved, Clive was convinced that a hit from that bolt of electricity —or whatever it was—would prove no less damaging to its victim than would a lead bullet.

He could see Annie nearby, crouched on the earth. She was moving, but there seemed to be something wrong with her. Perhaps she had taken a hit from one of the Chaffri weapons.

Clive called to her to get lower to the ground, but she gave no indication that she heard his words.

He sighted his weapon at the nearest Chaffri. Its sights almost had a life of their own, drawing his aim onto the target with uncanny sureness. He squeezed the weapon's not-unfamiliar trigger and it made a sound that seemed almost to be a sigh. Its sight dropped away from the Chaffri and Clive lowered the weapon and looked at his target.

The Chaffri wavered and faded in the fashion Clive had previously observed, but this time he did not reappear.

Clive aimed at a second Chaffri trooper. Again his weapon assisted him as if it had a life and a will. He squeezed the trigger, the weapon sighed and dipped like an athlete relaxing at the termination of a contest. The second trooper wavered and threw his arms into the air, his own weapon clattering to earth. As the Chaffri faded into nothingness, his abandoned weapon did the same.

Clive scuttled sideways across the grassy earth. He reached Annie's side, dividing his attention between her and the remaining Chaffri. He was still severely outnumbered, especially as Annie, although showing no visible wound, had been clearly rendered *hors de combat*.

A Chaffri trooper pointed his weapon at Clive and Annie. Clive raised his own weapon and they fired simultaneously. Clive felt the bolt of energy that flew past him, making the very air quiver and drawing Clive like an iron filing suddenly exposed to a magnet. But close as it was, the Chaffri's shot failed to harm Clive or Annie.

Not so the answering shot from Clive's weapon. The third Chaffri followed his two predecessors, wavering in air, fading, and disappearing. At this the apparent commander of the Chaffri detachment shouted an incomprehensible order to his troopers.

The commander ran along the railroad bed. He brought down a booted foot that did not quite reach the level of the earth. His next step terminated a short distance higher in the air. With each successive stride he rose higher and higher, his troopers following him not only along the railbed but into the air, until the Chaffri had all disappeared.

Clive shook his head. He turned to Annie. She had curled into a ball and was quivering visibly. He tried desperately to determine the cause of her distress. "Annie! Can you answer me? What is the matter? How can I help you?"

She turned panic-stricken eyes upon him. "Baalbec. Baalbec. Circuits scrambled. Software—catastrophic error—master reset. Here! Here! Here!"

She jerked away from him spasmodically. Her hands were balled into fists, pounding futilely at the earth. She managed to bring one to her bodice. "Here! Clive! Master system reset! Here! Only hope!"

His face flaming the very scarlet of his tunic, Clive followed Annie's frantic commands, tearing at her cos-

tume, reaching toward her sternum. He felt a blow from
her fist but it was not designed to drive him off, but to
encourage his assistance. He pressed frantic fingertips to
her sternum, at first feeling only soft flesh, but then a
switch.

"Left! Left!" Annie cried. "Master reset to left!"

His own left? he wondered. His mind raced. Clearly
this was no time for calm dialogue. He had to think fast.
No—Annie would think of this operation in terms of her
own perspective. His own left, as he faced her, was equivalent to her right, and vice versa. They were like mirror
images of each other.

His left—her right.

Her left—his right.

"Yes! Quick, Clive! Reset! Master reset! Switch left!"
Her heels were kicking at the earth and her fists beating at
her sides. Her face was turning a horrid shade and her
breathing was coming in desperate, irregular gasps. Clive
thought he could hear her very heart pounding, desperately pounding, as if about to burst. Perhaps it was. The
Baalbec was a device of unknown capabilities as far as
Clive was concerned. He had seen it used as a weapon, as
an aid to navigation, as a device for storing and manipulating information, and on one occasion as a power source for
a flying machine brought to the Dungeon from a South
Seas island in the course of a future war between European and Japanese forces. Where was the Nakajima 97?
There was no time to worry about that now!

What was the Baalbec doing to Annie now?

Clive studied Annie's body for a moment, desperate
that he not make an erroneous—and potentially disastrous—
move. But he must act quickly, for it was obvious that if
he did not do so, Annie would die. His own great-great-
granddaughter, this child-woman who in some odd way
had become the most precious person in the world to him
. . . if he did not act quickly, and correctly, Annie would
surely die.

The lives of others had been in Clive Folliot's hands
before now. Some he had saved, some he had spared,
some he had failed to save, and some he had taken by
means of his own, conscious, deliberate act. Some would

call such conduct a usurpation of a function belonging rightly to God alone. But this was not a power that Clive had sought, and it was not one that he wished. It was one that had been forced upon him—more times than he cared to remember.

Now it was forced upon him again. And this time the person whose destiny he would decide was neither enemy nor stranger nor friend, but his own flesh and blood, his own descendant, his own darling girl Annie. Not a religious man in normal times—in fact a doubter at times of the very existence of the Divine—now Clive closed his eyes and, under his breath, yielded up a brief, silent prayer.

Feeling Annie's flesh soft and warm and yielding beneath his hand, he managed a momentary grip on the switch and swung it to . . . the right!

· CHAPTER 8 ·
Into the Very Den of Peril

Annie quivered and toppled onto the greensward.

Clive drew her bodice back into place, covering her tender bosom. He held her hand, peered into her precious face. Her hand was relaxed, no longer balled into a fist. Her legs lay still on the earth, no longer pounding out their desperate tarantella.

The scarlet coloration was fading from her features. Would it be replaced by a normal rosy shade, or by the pallor of death? Her frantic, ragged gasps had ceased. Would they be replaced by calm, normal breathing, or by stillness?

Clive pressed his ear against her bosom. He heard her heart's beating, her lungs' breathing. Both were steady, unlabored.

Annie would recover!

He had moved the switch on the Baalbec in the proper direction!

Hard on the heels of his prayer of supplication, he sent up a second prayer: this one, of thanks. He slid a hand beneath Annie's shoulders and assisted her to a sitting position.

"Clive—grandfather—what happened to me?"

"You were struck by a bolt from the Chaffri's weapon. I feared for your survival, Annie."

She clung to him. "You must have— It's coming back to me now. You—you saved my life, Clive. The energy from the Chaffri's weapon scrambled my Baalbec. You reset the Baalbec for me, didn't you?"

Blushing, Clive admitted that he had done so.

"Thank you, Clive. Thank you."

"Annie, you told me to switch the device to the left for the master reset."

"Yes."

"What would have happened if I had switched it the right?"

She frowned. "Under normal conditions, nothing. The Baalbec's SD unit is interlocked so it can't be activated by misadventure—say, by an accidental elbow in a crowded elevator or a mistake by some overamorous groper."

"And under abnormal conditions?"

"If the interlock is disabled, you mean?"

"I don't know what an interlock is, but I suppose so. You said that the Chaffri weapon scrambled your device. Would that, ah, disable the interlock?"

"Absolutely!"

"Well, then—what would have happened if I'd set the switch the wrong way?"

"Why, the SD unit would have been activated." She smiled. "I thought I'd made that clear."

"But what is the SD unit, Annie?"

"Self-destruct. It would be too dangerous to let a Baalbec A-9 get into unauthorized hands. So anyone who tries to tamper with it, say, by removing it surgically from my body, or by scrambling the circuits and not hitting the master reset correctly— It just destroys itself."

"And what happens to you, Annie? Are you harmed by this?"

"Oh, I wouldn't be there anymore. If the Baalbec SD's, I'm gone. So is everybody and everything for about a mile in any direction. There's just a big hole in the ground."

She got to her feet, drawing Clive with her. She still had the weapon she had removed from the seat of the now-destroyed car, as Clive had his, also.

"Let's get out of here, Clive."

"Perhaps there will be a train along soon," he suggested.

"We'd do better on the road, I think." She took him by the hand and led him away from the railbed, toward the rural dirt road that paralleled the metal rails.

Before they had walked for an hour the sound of a creaking wagon, its iron-rimmed wheels jouncing when it struck a rut, could be heard. They turned and waited while the wagon hove into sight. It carried a load of vegetables. The driver sat alone on the box, reins in his hands, as two horses plodded docilely along.

Clive and Annie planted themselves in the center of the track and flagged down the slow-moving vehicle. The driver peered at them from beneath the broad brim of his hat. His hands and face showed the calloused roughness of an outdoorsman; his clothing, the dust of the dry dirt road.

The man sat peering down at Clive and at Annie. His face strained with deep thought. At length he spoke. "Young Master Folliot, is't?"

"I am Clive Folliot." Clive peered up into the other's face. "Farmer Cawder? Old Mr. Cawder, are you? Old Jim Cawder?"

"Nay, old Jim be dead these full score years, sir. I be young Jamie."

"Jamie! I remember you! Your dad was one of my father's finest men."

"Aye! A good and loyal fellow was me dad! And I'm as loyal to the Folliots as any Cawder has been for a thousand year! Can I give you and the missus a lift anywhere, Master Folliot?"

"She isn't the missus, Jamie. But we'd be most obliged for transportation to Tewkesbury Manor."

"Well, I hope that the young lady don't mind ridin' on a farm wagon, then, sir. But it's all I've got."

"I don't mind, Jamie," Annie said.

They climbed aboard. Jamie whistled up the patient horses and they resumed their slow pace.

All the way to Tewkesbury Manor, Jamie maintained a slow, droning delivery of Gloucestershire activities in recent years. Most of the news concerned marriages, births, and deaths. There was the occasional scandal, the occasional oddity. Farmer Mayhew's wife had given birth to triplets, the first set on record hereabouts. Yes, all were well and the children were now toddling about and speaking a few baby words. Farmer Morgan's cow had given birth to a two-headed calf, which had not fared as well as Missus Mayhew's triplets. Farmer Horder's son Pauly had run off with Farmer Johnson's daughter Alice, setting all the shire abuzz not once but twice, both when they ran off and then again when they came back and Alice returned home looking angry as a hornet and not willing to talk about the matter at all while Pauly looked chagrined but equally unwilling to talk.

Somehow, in the midst of all the gossip, he never commented on Clive's reappearance after so many years, or his surprising youthfulness after so long an absence.

Jamie pulled up his team at the cast-iron gates of Tewkesbury Manor. "If you and the young lady don't mind, Master Folliot. My team are aged and the track from here is steep. If we might drop yourself and the young lady here, sir, I would be ever so grateful, sir."

"Of course." Clive and Annie climbed down from the wagon. "Thank you, Jamie. And good luck to you!"

The wagon creaked away.

"What did you make of that?" Clive asked.

"He saved us a long walk."

"Yes, he did that. But I knew that man as a child. I was a few years older than he. His father—ah, what a man! He used to come up to the manor now and then, and Neville and I would run out to see him. He could pick us up, one in each hand. And he always had a piece of fruit for each of us. Gone now, gone and his son a man of middle years, too beaten down by his life and too cowed by the Folliots to notice that I haven't aged in a quarter-century."

"Never mind that, Clive. Let's get a move on. We're practically there."

The gates swung open at the pressure of his hands, and they strode up the long approach to Tewkesbury Manor. The manor was a huge building, dating back almost to the time of the Norman conquest. Clive had played there as a child, running up and down its long corridors, ducking into concealed passageways hidden by tapestries and high-backed wooden chairs.

"Have you been here before, Annie?"

She hesitated before answering, then gave a soft, affirmative response.

"I should like to know the details of that," Clive said.

"Please—there's so much you don't know, Clive. I wouldn't know where to start. Let's just get there."

"I can remember as if it were yesterday," Clive said. "The great hall, the armory, the kitchens where Neville and I were never supposed to go."

"But of course you did." Annie laughed. She seemed relieved to let Clive reminisce. As long as he did so, she did not have to answer his difficult questions.

"We did. There were other places we were forbidden to go, also. Sealed rooms. The subcellar. The inner library."

"You were forbidden to enter the library?"

"The manor has a great library, Annie. Father encouraged us to use it. But that was only the outer library. There was an inner library, as well. The door that opened to it was never left unlocked. Father alone possessed the key. Every Baron Tewkesbury for—well, for so long that the origin of the custom has been lost—every baron has had custody of the key to the sealed library, and the key has been handed down along with the succession to the title."

"Then you never saw the inner library."

"Never."

They had reached the grand entryway of the manor. A liveried footman bowed and reached for the huge iron knocker before Clive could reach for it. The footman pounded the cast-iron implement against its sounding plate, and its boom echoed from the house.

The front door swung open, and Clive ushered Annie in ahead of himself.

"Miss Annabelle." The butler bowed her into the hall. "And Major Clive. A pleasure to see you again, young sir."

Clive looked into the butler's face. The man was ancient, his sparse hair a mere white wisp surrounding his nearly naked scalp, his pink face a sea of wrinkles. "Jenkins?"

"Yes, sir."

"I'm happy to see you again, Jenkins. And Mrs. Jenkins, and the little ones?"

"The missus is still in the kitchen, sir. Most kind of you to ask. With your permission, sir, I shall convey your greetings."

"By all means. And I'll stop by to see her."

"She'll be very happy, sir. And you asked of the youngsters. They're grown now. Young Madeleine is married to a barrister in London. We're very proud of her, sir. I hope you won't think ill of her for rising above her station, sir. And the boy Tom has gone out to Australia to start a sheep station."

"That's wonderful, Jenkins. Wonderful."

"The baron wishes to see you in the library, Mr. Clive. If you feel up to it, sir. If I may venture, you do look a trifle ruffled."

Annie said, "I've other things to do, Clive. I'll see you later." She disappeared through a drape-hung archway. Clive had wondered about her having previously visited the manor; that question was now answered by Jenkins' promptly recognizing her and by her own obvious familiarity with the layout of the house.

Jenkins preceded Clive to the library. His formality was surprising, but Clive didn't question it. More to the point was Jenkins' instant recognition of him—and the fact that the man did not comment on Clive's youth.

The butler had aged normally in the past twenty-eight years, while Clive had aged by a matter of months. Surely Jenkins had noticed the change—rather, Clive thought, the *lack* of change—in the younger man. Why had he not commented? Jamie Cawder, the farmer who'd given Clive and Annie a ride on his wagon, was a dull soul who might simply have failed to take any note. But Jenkins was a bright man with a good mind. That, Clive remembered from his own childhood.

It was inconceivable that Jenkins, having bid farewell to Clive in 1868, would welcome him back to the manor in 1896, a Clive who looked hardly older than he had twenty-eight years earlier, and fail to notice something very strange about the series of events. Perhaps it was professional reserve on Jenkins' part. Or perhaps it was . . . something else.

Jenkins knocked on the door of the library. A voice called from within, and the butler opened the door for Clive, standing aside and closing it behind him as Clive entered the room.

Clive stared thunderstruck at the two men who awaited him.

His father, Arthur Folliot, Baron Tewkesbury, stood beside his high-backed, ornate chair behind his familiar desk. In childhood. Clive had thought the chair a throne, and had fantasized endlessly of his father as a king, himself as a prince who stole moments of sitting on that throne when no one else was in the room.

Baron Tewkesbury had aged indeed in the past twenty-eight years. When Clive last saw him in England, the baron had been a vigorous man of late middle years. In the Dungeon, Clive had encountered his father again—or a simulacrum of the man—and he had been little changed, if any, from his former state of being.

But now the baron had aged shockingly. He was wizened and bent. He had lost all of his hair and most of his teeth, and he stood—rather, swayed—peering at Clive through pale, milky eyes. Holding on to his chair with one hand, he raised the other, pointing a trembling, bony finger at Clive.

"So," he managed in a voice that conveyed bitter hatred despite its quavering weakness, "the traitor returns!"

"I? Father—*traitor?*—how can you call me that? I have never been a traitor to you or to the Folliots. It was you who always scorned me, who blamed me for my mother's death. And after our reconciliation in the Dungeon, I thought that all was peace between us!"

The baron stared at Clive, saying nothing.

"No." Clive held a hand to his brow. "No, it was not you, was it, Father? I remember now. I learned, even before I left the Palace of the Morning Star, that I had expressed my love and fealty to a simulacrum. Not to you."

"Correct," the old man whispered. "You made up like a sniveling bastard with a simulacrum of your father. No, Clive," he repeated, "I was never in the Dungeon."

"But *I* was." The words were spoken by another voice, a voice that broke in shockingly upon Clive's confrontation with his father. Clive turned at the sound of the second voice. So flabbergasted had he been at the sight of his father, and so distressed at the old man's accusations, that he had ignored this other.

The second man looked like an older version of Clive.

His hair was longer, steel-gray throughout, and his heavy mustache was of the same metallic hue. His face was tanned with decades of sunlight and seamed with long years of exertions. His blouse showed a slight paunch, but overall he gave the appearance of a man in excellent physical condition for his years. The uniform he wore somewhat resembled Clive's, but the design was that of a different unit and the insignia of rank indicated that the wearer held the rank of lieutenant general.

"Neville?"

"Indeed."

"But you—you have aged so—"

"I have aged but normally. Like you, I was born in the Year of Our Lord 1834. It is now 1896. Do I not look like a man of two and sixty years?"

"You do. You look remarkably fit for a man of sixty-two. But . . ." Words failed him. Instead, he indicated himself with a gesture of his hands, implying silently the comparison of his relative youth with his brother's apparent age.

"Of course, brother. You were brought here from the year 1871. You are but thirty-seven years old. And your charming descendant, I might mention—"

"You know Annabelle?"

"Were you not present at our first meeting, brother? Or have your encounters with simulacra so confused you that you doubt it was truly I—or truly she! We were both ourselves, authentically and in the flesh." He smiled suggestively. "Oh, I know her very well indeed, brother!"

Clive balled his fists and started to lunge at his brother before drawing himself back. "Only the difference in our ages keeps me from giving you a lesson, Neville! Be careful how you speak of my granddaughter! If not by reason of common decency, then because she is also your own grandniece."

"Why, brother—what did I say to offend you? Miss Leigh is a charming young person. Some of the customs and standards of her generation are different from those of our own, to be sure. Some of them may even be shocking. But I assure you, I hold her in only the most affectionate avuncular regard."

The old man had slumped into his seat, and now he

managed to call the others' attention. "To business, to business, Neville and Clive."

Neville drew a chair for himself; Clive did likewise.

"I am a very old man," Baron Tewkesbury quavered. "I have not long to live, and when I die the title of baron and all its perquisites and obligations shall pass to one of you. To you, Neville, if you survive me."

"I intend to do that, sir."

The baron turned Neville's response aside with a twitch of his head. "To you, Clive, if Neville does not survive me. And if you can purge yourself of your treasonous acts and affiliations."

"But, Father—you continue to accuse me of treason, and I am innocent of the charge!"

"Did you not make league with the Ren in the eighth level of the Dungeon? Is that not treason enough?"

"Father—I entered the Dungeon involuntarily, and only because Neville had disappeared and I was attempting to follow his trail. Everything I did in the Dungeon, on whatever level, has been done out of loyalty to the Folliots—and out of the needs of survival."

Lord Tewkesbury peered at Clive. The room was silent, its atmosphere charged as Lieutenant General Sir Neville Folliot and Sir Arthur Folliot, Baron Tewkesbury, waited for Clive to continue.

"I seem to have blundered into—or been lured into! —the greatest conspiracy in the history of the world. Philo Goode, Amos Ransome, Lorena Ransome . . . my long-faithful batman Horace Hamilton Smythe! He has saved my life repeatedly, Father, in the course of my adventures—only to disappear, then reappear in one exotic guise after another. Is the man a turncoat, or is he himself a victim of some alien force?"

He shook his head. Where to take this bizarre conversation? He would attempt a different tack.

"You, Neville." He rounded on his older brother. "You are sixty-two years of age?"

"I am that."

"And I am not yet forty. Yet we were mere minutes apart in time of birth. The year is 1896. I was snatched here from 1871. I have traveled across landscapes as terrifyingly unearthly as the mind can grasp, I have fought monsters the likes of which . . ."

He studied the faces of his two closest living relatives, his father and his elder twin. The baron seemed to be drifting, in the manner of a man approaching his ninetieth year. But Neville Folliot, immaculately groomed and punctiliously outfitted as a lieutenant general of Her Majesty's Royal Somerset Grenadier Guards, was listening intently. His expression was inscrutable as to his reaction to Clive's words and as to his own intention, but at the very least he was listening closely to Clive.

"Neville, my brother, let me tell you of one of my first encounters upon entering the Dungeon. In the company of my former batman Smythe and his East Indian associate Sidi Bombay—"

"I know Sidi Bombay," Neville interrupted. "I had the pleasure of making his acquaintance in the city of Zanzibar."

"Yes. And quite some reputation you left behind with our consul in Zanzibar, and with the Sultan Seyyid Majid bin Said!"

"Ah, some of the colorful residents of Zanzibar! And of the mainland of East Africa! I fear that I shall not see their likes again. The responsibilities of rank, the weariness of age—they conspire to keep an old veteran like me close to the flagpole. You younger chaps get to play at heroics."

"I refer not to heroics, Neville! Wherever I went, your reputation preceded me! I was branded a blackguard and a scoundrel—by utter strangers, Neville!—thanks to the mischief you had wrought."

"A pity. But it was all so long ago, Clive. Back in the sixties, ah, we were such wild youths, were we not? Colorful and rebellious, ready for any experiment, eager for every new experience. There will never again be an era like the sixties—at least not for us. But we live in a later decade now. The nineties may be better than the sixties, or they may be worse. Opinions must needs differ. But in either case, let us contend with the realities of the present."

"You will have to explain to me what you mean by the realities of the present, Neville. Precisely what realities are those? I know only that George du Maurier claims that he brought me here by the power of his mind and with the aid of Madame Clarissa Mesmer."

"Du Maurier? You have been in communication with du Maurier?"

"I came here from his home."

"What were you doing there?" The look in Neville's eyes was intense, the pupils glowed like coals. The expression on his face was severe.

"He is one of my oldest friends, Neville. The man is on his deathbed. In no way could I withhold from him whatever small comfort my presence can provide."

"But he is allied with our enemies! You fool, Clive! How much did you tell him? How much does he know?"

"What does it matter, Neville? I told you, the man is dying. As for our enemies—your phrase, brother, *our enemies*—you act is if the Folliots were engaged in a feud, like some wild American mountaineers. You—"

"This is far worse than a feud, Clive! *War* would be a more appropriate word for it. But a war that would make the contests of Greeks against Persians, Hebrews against Philistines, Romans against Carthaginians—even our own parents' struggle against the conquerer Napoleon—all pale by comparison. We are engaged in a war of worlds, of realities, of dimensions of being so vast in scope that precedent and comparison are pointless."

"That I doubt not, brother. Not after what I have seen in the Dungeon. But your adjectives convey little meaning to me. Pray, give me some facts."

Neville lowered his brow into his hands. Looking at the top of his brother's steely gray head, Clive was struck by an unexpected pang of compassion and, yes, even of brotherly love. Neville had chivied and bullied him for decades, but his brother he was, and more than a brother, a twin. Even in the Dungeon, Neville's presence had dominated Clive's actions at times—and his absence, at others.

Now, for all that he was a vigorous man and healthy for his years, still Neville was well into his middle life, beginning to approach the long and irreversible decline of old age—while Clive was a far younger man with many more years ahead of him.

Clive reached his fingers hesitantly and touched his brother on the back of his hand.

Neville jerked away from the contact as he would have from the touch of a hand of red-hot iron. He jumped to his feet. "All right, brother. It's facts you wish, and it's facts you shall receive."

Neville crossed to his father, who had slumped in his great thronelike chair and was snoring softly. "Summon Jenkins to help Father to his bed. A nap is a good restorative for him."

Clive called the butler. Neville helped Baron Tewkesbury to his feet, embraced him briefly, and then turned him over to Jenkins. Gently leading the frail baron by the hand, the elderly servant guided his even more aged master from the library.

Neville Folliot turned to face Clive. "Follow me, brother." He raised his hand and displayed the huge, ornate key that Clive knew unlocked the door to the sealed sanctum sanctorum, the mysterious secret library of Tewkesbury Manor.

• CHAPTER 9 •
The First of the Folliots

Clive stood gaping after his brother. "The—the key! You have the key to the sealed library, Neville?"

"Is that not self-evident?"

"But that key is supposed to be the exclusive domain of Lord Tewkesbury."

"Is it really?"

The sardonic note in Neville's voice grated on Clive, but Clive chose to ignore that and pursue his questioning. "Is that a duplicate? Or did you take the key from Father?"

"Oh, Clive, Clive, little brother . . . what difference does it make? I have the key. The sealed room is open. You've been so full of questions—I'll concede that you are justified in your curiosity—but come along and you shall have some answers."

He disappeared through the doorway. Clive followed.

The sealed library was utterly dark. Clive heard the scrape of a match, saw it flare into sulfurous life. Then the match flame was replaced by the warmer, gentler illumination of a lighted candle. Clive could see the face of his brother Neville sinisterly illuminated from below by the golden light of the candle.

"Please close the door behind you, and make sure that it is bolted, Clive. I do not wish others to enter this room. Ah, thank you, little brother. And beside you there, you will see a comfortable seat. If you please—"

Clive complied, sliding into the comfort of an over-stuffed, leather-covered easy chair. He watched Neville take similar action, having first placed the candlestick on a convenient table. Beyond Neville the room remained in darkness. There was a flow of fresh air, and now and then, when an errant air current set the candle-flame in motion, huge shadows danced against an uncertain background.

"You seem quite familiar with this room, Neville. I take it you have been here often."

"Perhaps not so often, Clive. But I come here from time to time. As my duties require."

"What duties? I see by your shoulders and collar that you have risen in Her Majesty's service. You are no longer restricted to the Grenadier Guards, but have attained the status of a general officer."

"My privilege to serve crown and country, Clive."

"Then you must spend most of your time inspecting units."

"Good staff work, brother, associates carefully selected and properly trained, and a commander may come and go at will. Fortunately, for I fear that I am gone from my command a great deal of the time."

"I doubt it not."

"Still, I am a man of patriotic impulse. I have had several audiences with Her Majesty, Clive. I take great pride in that."

"Your loyalty is not to this sceptered isle, Neville."

"Put it this way, brother. A man may love both his mother and his wife. May love each, truly and loyally. Yet these are different loves and different loyalties."

"Very well, Neville. If Britain is your mother, who is your wife?"

"A greater power than any empire of this little Earth, Clive."

Clive shook his head sadly. "The Ren, Neville, or the Chaffri? Does it even matter? Who are the true masters of the Dungeon? Beings alien, heartless, and cruel. Your loyalties are to them, then? To these abductors, tyrants, murderers? Your loyalty to them shames you, brother. It shames me and all of our blood."

Illuminated only by candlelight, Neville's face was hard to read. Yet Clive thought he saw the flash of anger in his brother's eyes.

"You know not whereof you speak, little brother! You think you have seen the Dungeon, and having seen the

Dungeon you think you have seen all that is terrible and strange in this universe. But listen to me, brother. I tell you that you have seen only the smallest sampling of the Dungeon. You are like a man who spends an hour on the beach at Dar es Salaam and thinks he knows all of Africa. Believe me in this—I know whereof I speak! You have barely sampled the perils and the horrors that the Dungeon contains. And the Dungeon is but a tiny microcosm, the tiniest sample of the perils and the horrors of this universe!"

His eyes reflected the candlelight, brighter and hotter than the flame they gave back. "I know whereof I speak, Clive. In this thing if in nothing else, you must believe me."

"My question, then, that you so adroitly avoided when I started to ask you it."

"What question is that?"

"In the Dungeon—on Q'oorna—I encountered a monstrosity almost beyond description in its horror. It was crossing a bridge of midnight obsidian across the abyss near the City of the Tower."

Neville nodded. "Ah, yes—I remember it well."

"The monster was equipped with tentacles, feelers, claws, mouths, fangs—every appurtenance imaginable, with which to horrify and then dismember its prey."

Behind Neville, in the darkness of this sealed library in the safety of Tewkesbury Manor, still Clive could see the monster, looming and dripping its horrendous exudations. He could almost see Sidi Bombay scrambling up the monster's flank, disappearing into its clusters of waving tentacles like a South Sea islander scrambling up the trunk of a wind-angled coconut palm, disappearing into its waving fronds.

"We fought that monstrosity, fought it to the very limit and end of our resources. Fought it—well, not to victory, but at least to a stalemate, so that at last it tumbled from the bridge and disappeared into the blackness beneath that span, the blackness of the abyss."

"Yes, Clive, yes. But you said you had a question."

"When that monster went tumbling, I was able to catch a glimpse, first of its underside, and then of its crown."

Clive's brow was coated with perspiration and his hands twitched in subconscious reenactment of the titanic battle. "Its underside was a horror all its own. A transparent membrane held sealed a compartment in which miniature replicas of the monster floated. I took these to be its young."

Neville nodded, the movement of his head making his shadow dance menacingly. "You are correct."

"Among those young," Clive continued, "I saw other creatures, victims I assume of the monster, engulfed by the parent and held as food for the horrid spawn."

"Correct again, brother."

"But most horrifying of all, as the monster tumbled from the bridge, I saw revealed upon its peak a giant replica of a human face. Of your face, Neville! And as it fell from view, that face spoke to me. It cursed me. It cursed me, Neville—with your face, and in your voice."

Neville Folliot hid his face in his well-groomed hands. "Your memory serves you truly, Clive. The creature did have my face and it did curse you there on Q'oorna. I can say only that the creature was not I, for all that it looked like me and sounded like me. It had my face, or an image thereof at any rate. It even had my recollections, my mind or part of my mind, for a time. But it was not I, nor I it. I will not apologize, for it was by no will of mine that that event took place. No. I did not and would not do such a thing. As brothers we have had our differences, Clive— any pair of siblings will have their differences—but I would not treat my brother in the manner you describe."

Clive Folliot considered, then said, "I cannot accept an apology not tendered. Therefore let it suffice that I understand your explanation, and will consider the matter closed."

"Good!" A faint smile creased Neville's face. "Now— what else do you wish to ask?"

"Who are the Ren, Neville? How did you become involved with them? Is Father aware of your affiliation?"

"Clive, I will endeavor to satisfy you. But to understand this, you must have prior knowledge. Prior knowledge of the universe around you. When we were younger, I attended Sandhurst and received an education in military science and engineering. That education—plus my service in Her Majesty's campaigns—served to make me a hard-headed, practical man. I can look at a revolver, at a fortification—or at a distant star—and see it and attempt to comprehend it in practical, realistic terms."

He shook his head, then continued. "You attended Cambridge, Clive. Your studies were in the realm of art, literature, music, and philosophy. Remember our debates, when we were home from university for the holidays, Clive? Remember how Father would ask us to report on our learning, and I would discuss campaigns and fortifications and lines of supply—and you would speak of Homer and of Virgil, of Spenser and Marlowe and Michelangelo and Mozart?"

"I remember all too well, Neville."

"I remind you not for purposes of disparagement, but because you may simply not comprehend what I am about to tell you, brother. But try to accept what I say."

"Pray, proceed."

"You know that the Greeks believed that the fixed stars in the sky were suns like our own, only incredibly distant from the Earth. And that they believed that the moving planets were worlds not unlike our own. Hence even the strange fable—"

"That I know better than you, Neville. Lucian's *True History* with its populated Sun and Moon and Venus, its intelligent cabbages and its ship that sailed through the void between worlds."

"Indeed, Clive! Well, I tell you that the *True History* contained more truth than its author may have realized. Not that the sun and moon are populated. But that there are other populated worlds, more than we puny humans can imagine, more than we can count, more than we can even comprehend. The number of stars is so huge as to defy calculation, and among those uncountable stars are scattered uncountable worlds, and on those uncountable worlds there swell uncountable races of men. Of men, and of manlike but unhuman species. And of species so utterly unlike us that the monster you saw with my face would be as familiar as a tabby cat by comparison."

"A tale I am more prepared to accept after my journeys and my travail in the Dungeon than I was before, Neville.

I will posit the truth of all you have said. Where do the Ren and the Chaffri fit in? And, still, what is your connection with them? And what is the Dungeon? What is the *purpose* of the Dungeon, Neville?"

"You would have guessed that the Ren and the Chaffri are but two of the uncounted races scattered through our universe who—at least in a poetic sense, to adopt your mode of discourse, Clive—inhabit the stars. These races are endlessly varied. Some of them are more primitive than the naked bushmen of our Earth's remotest regions. Others are so advanced as to make a Faraday or a Herschel look like children splashing in puddles and wondering at the worms they dislodge from the mud."

"The Ren, then, are such a star-race?"

Neville nodded.

"I am not as surprised to hear that as you might think, brother. In the Dungeon I encountered beings from many worlds. The faithful doglike Finnbogg, the spidery Shriek, and Chang Guafe, strangest of all."

"There are those who are not so strange, too."

"Indeed. The Lady 'Nrrc'kth and her false consort N'wrbb Crrd'f. I might have loved the Lady 'Nrrc'kth. Her beauty was exotic—her skin a white as pale as freshly fallen snow, her long hair and deep eyes the green of a forest rising through that snow. In all my travels I never encountered one to compare with the Lady 'Nrrc'kth."

"And where is she now, brother?"

"Dead," Clive whispered. "Fallen in the course of a peril-ridden descent from one level of the Dungeon to another. For that alone, Neville, I despise the Ren. If they are the masters of the Dungeon, then they are responsible for the Lady 'Nrrc'kth's demise. I will never forgive them for that, Neville!"

"But you approve of the Chaffri?"

"I know little of them, but what little I know indicates that they are no better than the Ren. No better."

Neville held up one hand. "The Ren are not the masters of the Dungeon, Clive! Do not be deceived into thinking that." He emitted a sardonic laugh, the greatest show of emotion on his part since his reunion with his younger twin. "The Ren are but one of the competing powers in the Dungeon. And the Chaffri are another."

Clive made no further comment. There was little new to him in his brother's words. Much of this he had long known—but to hear it from his own brother's mouth brought it home to him more chillingly than even the reality of his own all-too-vivid recollections.

After a while, Neville spoke again. "As for your paramour, what was her name—'Nrrc'kth—do not lose hope. You tell me that she died in the Dungeon, but what if we were to intervene at a moment *prior* to her death? What if a force should enter the event-line between levels of the Dungeon and move her to a point of safety elsewhere in the Dungeon—or out of it?"

"Can that be done? Neville, can it?"

"But, brother, I thought you were pledged to a Miss Leighton."

"Miss Leighton, I have been led to believe, left London in 1868, shortly after my departure for Zanzibar and Africa in search of you. By now she is well established in the city of Boston in the United States. From the things Miss Leigh—Annie—has told me, Annabella has no desire to have anything to do with me."

"But think, little brother—if you could return to a moment before she left London—?"

"I have thought of that, Neville. It is a tempting prospect, an intriguing prospect, but I am finally reluctant to tamper with Annabella's life. To save 'Nrrc'kth—well, to save an innocent woman from her undeserved death, that is a prospect I would wish to pursue. But the case with Miss Annabella Leighton is a different one. Not only would such interference amount to tampering with her own life, it would also interdict the establishment of a whole line of descent, leading from her to Annie Leigh. No." He shook his head. "No, Neville. It tempts me, but I will resist."

Neville rose and carried the now-guttering candle to the far side of the room. He reached to a gas jet affixed high upon the wall, turned the cock to permit the flow of illuminating gas, and raised the candle to set the gas alight.

"Are you ready, then, to proceed, Clive?"

The room was now lighted by the gas jet, and as he

waited for Clive's response, he moved about the room lighting additional fixtures.

"Proceed to what, Neville?"

"To meet the Ren."

"You mean, to return to the Dungeon? Will Annie accompany me? Is she, too, part of this strange conspiracy of yours?"

Neville's face darkened and the corners of his mouth twitched downward, pulling the tips of his mustache so as to add to the power of his angry frown. "I need not tell you that I find your language and your implications offensive, little brother!"

Clive found himself growing equally angry in response to Neville's conduct. He rose to his feet and leaned toward his brother. "I have conducted myself with propriety throughout this affair, Neville! I set out in hopes of rescuing you—"

"Or of finding me dead," the older man interrupted, "so as to assure yourself of succession to the family title and estates upon our father's death!"

Reddening at the aptness of the accusation, Clive resumed. "I suffered shipwreck and suffered a near-fatal dose of spider's venom. I struggled through jungle and swamp, endured tropic heat, and risked attack by lion, crocodile, or snake. All of this occurred before I even entered the Dungeon! While you, Neville, have been in this—this collusive plot—from the outset! To apply the term *conspirator* to you is not merely accurate, brother, it is positively charitable!"

Neville turned his back. The only sound in the room was the soft *shush*ing of the gas jets. When Neville turned back to face Clive, it was as if he had aged another five years in the minute or less that his back had been turned.

"There is some truth in what you say, Clive. I have been involved with the Ren . . . all my adult life, and even since childhood. This was to have been a secret shared only by Father and me. Such has been the case, generation after generation, for as long as there have been Folliots in Tewkesbury. Truth be known, Clive, the record of our affiliation with the Ren extends into the distant past, to the creation of the first Baron Tewkesbury by Richard the Third in 1483."

Neville was pacing now, and Clive found himself following his brother's progress back and forth, back and forth, as an Egyptian cobra follows the piping music of a snake-charmer. "The leaf on our crest, the very word *Folliot* itself, proclaims our alliance and our allegiance to the Plantagenets. Since Richard's death in 1485 the throne of England has been occupied by usurpers. When the Ren triumph in the Dungeon they shall install a Plantagenet on the throne of England! The throne shall be restored to its rightful heir! Clive, that heir shall be a Folliot!"

"Treason!" Clive could contain himself no longer. "You speak high treason, sir! You, who aspire to the title of baron, who have taken Her Majesty's shilling and served in her Grenadier Guards, who have commanded her troops in battle and seen them die in defense of crown and country—you have been a traitor to Queen Victoria all along!"

"Not a traitor, sir! A patriot!"

Clive spun on his heel and headed for the door.

"It's locked, little brother."

"Then I shall break it down or else wrest the key from your possession. I will not remain a minute longer in the presence of such foul perfidy."

"There will be no need for that, Clive. It is true that you have been put through your paces in this affair, all against your will and largely without your knowledge of what you were in."

"Yes—and so you propose what, Neville? I tell you, I desire no part of your treasonous scheme, and if justice have its way, I shall live to see you strangled with a silken cord."

"I have no such expectation, Clive. But you may be right. You may be right. The more we learn of things, even of the past and of the future, the less we are able to call the turn of Fate. But I shall unlock the door and permit you to exit if you will agree to travel with me to the home of the Ren, and confer with them there. Once you have done so, you will be free to choose your course. I will not attempt to force your choice, Clive."

Clive stood silently, studying the strange installation behind his brother, waiting for Neville to continue.

"Will you give me your pledge, Clive? Will you return to Tewkesbury Manor and travel with me to the home of the Ren?"

"There is business I must first transact in London. I but arrived there last night and was leaving du Maurier's home when I was shanghaied by your agents, Neville. There is more I must do in the metropolis."

"You have not given your pledge to return to Tewkesbury Manor, Clive, but I will accept your statement as a tacit pledge. Go, then." He reached past his brother and unlocked the door. "Transact your business, Clive Folliot, and Godspeed to you, and I pray I shall see you again."

Clive stood in the doorway one moment longer, fixing his brother with a glare. "Well may you pray, brother. But first consider well what you pray for."

He found Annabelle in the kitchen, visiting Mrs. Jenkins. Annie had admitted to Clive her former visits to Tewkesbury Manor, and it was clear that on such earlier occasions she had made the acquaintance of the faithful cook and housekeeper, and they had become instant, fast friends. Thus, the egalitarian customs of Annie's home, the American city of San Francisco in the year 1999.

Seeing Mrs. Jenkins stirred profound feelings in Clive. His mother had died at the time of his own birth. He and Neville had been raised by their father with the assistance of a series of nursemaids, governesses, and tutors, one more stern and unyielding than the next. Baron Tewkesbury had reserved his own affection for his firstborn, Neville. Even though the brothers were separated by mere minutes in time of birth, their father had lavished his affection upon the elder of the two, blaming the secondborn for the death of his mother and treating him with cold hostility from the day of his birth.

Mrs. Jenkins had been the closest thing that Clive had ever known to a mother, his dearest companion and strongest ally. Her kitchen was always his place of refuge in times of trouble. She always had a hug available for him, and a sweetmeat. Her apron had absorbed uncounted tears and her hands had soothed away uncounted hurts.

Today she held Clive at arm's length. "How wonderful, Mr. Clive. My little Clive, my little friend. You do look so young, compared to Mr. Neville. Of course, I know that he's the elder." She chuckled at her own witticism. "Miss Annie is a wonderful young lady, Mr. Clive. Do you plan to . . . ?" she winked and tipped her head suggestively.

"I fear not, Mrs. Jenkins. I am as fond of Annie as it is possible to be, but there are reasons—reasons I cannot explain." He turned to face Annie. "I must return to London. There is much that you must explain to me, Annie."

"I know. I'll do my best."

"Are you involved with—"

"Please," she said, cutting him off. "These are things that are best discussed tête-à-tête. You understand that, surely." She rolled her eyes almost imperceptibly toward Mrs. Jenkins.

"Of course, I quite understand," Clive said. "Do you wish to accompany me on my journey to London?"

"Will you return to Tewkesbury?"

"Very soon."

"Then I shall await you here, Clive."

• CHAPTER 10 •
He Is Long Dead

Jenkins arranged a trap to take Clive to the station at Tewkesbury Village, and from there he rode unimpeded to London. It was a journey that contrasted with his wild progress from London to Tewkesbury with Annabelle Leigh. This time there was no Chaffri attack, and Clive's fellow passengers were a typical assortment of country folk headed for London to transact business of their own.

When Clive reached the great metropolis he headed at once for the offices of the *Illustrated Recorder and Dispatch*. When last Clive Folliot had visited those offices, they were located in a dingy series of cubbyholes. Overaged scriveners, failed would-have-been literary lions, slicksters, and hacks had held court in a dilapidated building that smelled of ancient meals of uncertain origin and of musty clothing and men, the two equally in need of a proper scrubbing and refurbishment.

Now a tall, modern building stood in place of the old *Recorder and Dispatch,* while a modern sign prominently affixed to the front of the establishment proclaimed it still to be the home of that formerly disreputable daily.

Clive had changed from his somewhat tattered uniform to an outfit of civilian garb that he found still awaiting him in his room at Tewkesbury Manor. He smiled to find his card case still handy, and he left the manor with a full purse and a supply of calling cards. The clothing, so long unworn, was a good fit still. But it was a quarter-century out of date, and he found himself encountering stares of curiosity both aboard the railroad coach that carried him from Gloustershire and in the streets of London.

He entered the offices of the *Recorder and Dispatch* and was greeted by an efficient-mannered young lady seated at a walnut table near the building's portal.

She inquired as to whether she might be of assistance to him. Clive took note that her hair appeared to be long and glossy, of a most appealing chestnut shade, although she wore it done up atop her head where it would not interfere with the efficient performance of her work. Her figure, too, appealed to Clive's eye, perhaps the more so because of the demure outfit with which she attempted unsuccessfully to conceal it.

"I am seeking the editor of this paper, Mr. Carstairs, young lady. Is he in?"

"Have you an appointment, sir?"

"No."

"May I inquire your business, then, with Mr. Carstairs? He is very busy, and if you are a tradesman there are other persons here with whom you might transact your business."

"I am a correspondent of this paper, young lady, and Mr. Carstairs is my editor." He took a calling card from his pocket and handed it the young woman.

After peering at the card, she raised her eyes once more to Clive, then dropped them once again. "Major Folliot, Fifth Imperial Horse Guards," she read.

"Perhaps you are familiar with my work—with my dispatches and illustrative sketches."

"No, sir, I fear such is not the case."

"But they have but recently run in this very— But no, I beg pardon." Clive chided himself silently. Of course the young person had not seen his pieces in the *Recorder and Dispatch*. They had appeared before her very birth! "Never mind. If I may see Mr. Carstairs."

"Very well, sir." She signaled a young boy to show Clive to Carstairs' office, first turning over Clive's card to him. Clive followed the lad down a corridor, up a stairway, and into a palatial suite of offices that would have contained the entire staff and much of the production facility of the *Recorder and Dispatch* of an earlier era.

Clive's guide rapped clean-scrubbed knuckles against well-polished mahogany, received an answering summons, and disappeared though the portal. Clive heard a brief, muffled conversation through the door, then it opened and the youngster reappeared. The lad nodded to Clive and held the door for him as he entered the editor's inner sanctum.

A very young man—he could hardly have been five and twenty years of age—looked up from a desk cluttered with sheets of paper. He was well, even wealthily, dressed. His hair was thick, and curled about his head. He squinted at Clive as if weak of vision, fumbled amid his papers for a pair of steel-rimmed spectacles, then frowned and rose tentatively to his feet.

"*Mister*"—he lifted Clive's card in one hand and held it close to his eyes to study it—"or is it *Major* Folliot?"

"Either will do, sir. But may I ask who you are?"

"Carstairs. I am the editor of the *Recorder and Dispatch*. May I inquire, sir, your business with me?"

"Perhaps I have the wrong Carstairs. I am seeking Mr. Maurice Carstairs."

"I am he, sir."

"Impossible. Maurice Carstairs engaged me to furnish the *Recorder and Dispatch* a series of reports on my expedition to Equatoria in search of my lost brother."

"I am very sorry, sir. I have no recollection of any such arrangement, nor do I have any recollection of you. When do you claim this, ah, arrangement was made?"

"It was the month of May, sir. The end of the month of May."

"Of this year, Mister Folliot?"

"It was May of the year 1868, sir."

The bespectacled young man slid precipitously into his seat. "You are aware of the present year, are you not, Mister Folliot? If you ever received such a commission, it would hardly have been from my hand. It was the year 1871 in which I first saw the light of day."

"And the Maurice Carstairs who was the editor of this paper in 1868—where is he, sir?"

"Alas," the young man said, "that Maurice Carstairs was my father. I regret that he is long dead. Long dead and buried, Mister Folliot. I'm afraid that in the years since his death—"

"In what year did Maurice Carstairs die?" Clive interrupted.

"It was 1886. I was fifteen at the time, and had to fight tooth and claw to claim my position as proprietor and editor of this newspaper. But as you can see, sir, I succeeded."

"Oh." That was all Clive could gasp, for the moment. He took a chair, all unbidden, and stared in silence at young Carstairs. Then he said, "Maurice was your father."

"He was, sir."

"The *Recorder and Dispatch* was a far less splendid enterprise in 1868 than it appears today. I fear that the paper and its editor at that time both suffered somewhat in repute."

"I have no illusions regarding my late father's character." The young man smiled whimsically. "But he was a man of real talent and possessed a certain eccentric integrity all his own, Mister Folliot. He taught me a great deal about the newspaper business—pardon my use of the cliché, but I might even say that he taught me everything that I know. It was by the application of his lessons, and upon the foundation that he laid with the *Recorder and Dispatch,* that I was able to bring the paper to its present position of prosperity and respect."

The young man looked down and opened a drawer of his desk. He bent very close to the drawer, squinting into it. At length he looked up at Clive. "If you are indeed the same Major Folliot whom my father employed in 1868, perhaps you will be able to answer a question or two, to verify your identity."

"Are neither my card nor my word sufficient, sir?"

"Ah, there you have the great paradox, sir. If you are truly Major Folliot, your word alone would surely suffice. Your card is a mere fillip of superfluous substantiation. But if you are an imposter, you would easily lie as to your identity, and you could surely furnish yourself with a false calling card. So we are caught between Scylla and Charibdys, Major Folliot. If you are he."

"Very well. What are your questions?"

Carstairs peered into his desk drawer once again. It looked almost as if he were going to climb into it, but at length he sat upright. "First, sir, what is the name of the missionary-priest whom you encountered in the village of Bagomoyo? And, second, who was the East Indian gentleman who joined the party comprising yourself and the traitorous Sergeant Horace Hamilton Smythe shortly before you entered the Sudd?"

Clive leaped to his feet, anger boiling within him. "Your questions are easily enough answered, sir. Those two I shall never forget—although for very different reasons, sir. The priest was the Reverend Father Timothy F. X. O'Hara. And the East Indian was a most remarkable personage who called himself Sidi Bombay."

Carstairs nodded noncommittally.

"But your application of the adjective *traitorous* to Sergeant Smythe is most offensive!" Clive resumed. "If it were possible for me to strike a person wearing spectacles, I might just seek immediate satisfaction for that insult to my companion. Horace Smythe is—was—as noble and gritty a man as ever it was my privilege to serve with in Her Majesty's Guards. And in our adventures in the Dungeon he performed uncounted deeds of heroism. His behavior was inconsistent and at times may have *appeared* disloyal. But he had been victimized by nefarious operatives and was acting under an irresistible compulsion at those times!"

He drew a deep breath, then added, "Sergeant Smythe is an upstanding man, and I will not permit him to be slandered by any ink-fingered panderer of Fleet Street. In fact—"

Clive halted in amazement as young Carstairs, without a change in his expression, disappeared still again beneath the level of his desk. There was a lengthy delay punctuated by soft thumps and ill-suppressed exclamations.

Then the chair was shoved back from behind the desk and Quartermaster Sergeant Horace Hamilton Smythe, smiling brilliantly, rose with his hand extended to Clive.

There was a moment of stunned immobility. Then Clive sprang to his feet, circled the desk, and embraced the other man. "Smythe! Smythe! I knew you could not have gone over to Philo Goode!"

"Of course not, sah. And I trust that you'll forgive my

little charade of a moment past. You see, what I said—what Mr. Carstairs said—was quite true, sah. There are forces at play, sah, to whom the secrets of disguise are as an open book, and to whom the creation of an apparently living, perfect simulacrum is little more than child's play."

"I know that, Smythe, all too well. I have encountered simulacra of both my father and my brother, as well as at least one female member of my family, all to my regret. But tell me, please—were you the publican who rescued me from a mob of ruffians the other night, only to turn me over to the untender mercies of Philo Goode? It was this incident to which I just referred."

"No, sah—that was not I. And what you tell me raises an alarm within me!"

"Then where have you been? If you have not been employed as a publican, have you been engaged in the publishing trade? Is this identity of a younger Maurice Carstairs a fictitious persona which you have assumed?"

"No, sah. Young Mr. Carstairs is a real enough person, and is indeed the editor of this paper. He is a good man, sah! One of our own, sah! I assume his identity from time to time, as necessity dictates. You might say that on occasion I act as Mr. Carstairs' very shadow."

"His shadow, eh? Well, shadow, tell me—what do you mean by the expression, *one of our own?*"

"I'll willingly tell you all that I know, sah. As ever, I am your ally. You will recall my occasional lapses." An expression of discouragement appeared on the man's face. "Such conduct was the product of devices implanted in my brain. In my very brain, sah! But I have managed to overcome their influence. I am myself now, my true self. I hope the Major will believe me!"

"I believe you, Horace."

"The Major has my gratitude. And I will tell you what I meant by *one of our own,* sah. But first, sah, there is another man here at the *Recorder and Dispatch* whom you must meet. A gentleman of color. The first such, I believe, employed by a London daily in a position of authority and respect."

Clive accompanied Smythe to an adjoining office, where

a man of dark skin, with black hair and mustache, labored behind a desk. He looked up as the others entered.

"Major Folliot," Carstairs-Smythe said, "may I introduce our chief editor for overseas reportage, Mr. Pandit Singh."

The Indian rose to his feet. He was costumed in morning coat, wing collar, and cravat. As he stepped from behind his desk he revealed striped trousers, spats, and properly polished boots.

Clive gaped and his jaw fell open. "Sidi Bombay!" Once more he embraced another. Then he said, "I have already seen Miss Annabelle Leigh, my brother Neville, my father, and Philo Goode since my return to London. I suppose the only one left to make a miraculous reappearance is Father O'Hara."

It was as if a pall had fallen on the room. Horace Smythe and Sidi Bombay looked at each other in silence. Clive felt that he had said something dreadfully wrong.

Horace Hamilton Smythe broke the long silence. "P'raps I'd better explain, sah. I promised that I'd elucidate upon the phrase, *one of our own.* I might begin by saying, sah, that Philo Goode is *not* one of our own. He is the very opposite of being one of our own, sah. The very antithesis, sah."

"You mean he is of the Chaffri?"

"I wish that were all I meant, sah. It's far worse than that—although I wasn't aware of how much you know of the Chaffri, sah."

"I know of the Chaffri. And of the Ren. And somewhat, I know of the Gennine, although almost nothing save that they exist and that their home world is a place mentioned only in whispers and dread."

"If the Major will pardon my playing schoolmaster, just what is it that the Major *does* know of the Chaffri and the Ren and the Gennine? Specifically, sah, if the Major doesn't mind."

"Why, that the Q'oornans and others that we encountered in the Dungeon are the pawns, some of them—and the agents, others—of two great warring empires. These are the Chaffri and the Ren. Their homes are on planets far beyond the scope of our astronomical knowledge. And they are engaged in a longtime, deadly struggle. So great is their power, there are some who suspect that they are the basis for the Zoroastrian tradition of the struggle between Ahriman and Ahura Mazda."

Pandit Singh—or Sidi Bombay—nodded. "You know of the beliefs of the Zoroastrians, then?"

"Travelers returning from journeys to Persia and Irak have described that fascinating religion. At Cambridge, it might have been compared to some of the heresies that wracked the early Christian church."

Throughout Clive's peroration, Horace Smythe and Sidi Bombay had exchanged significant glances and nods. Now Smythe said, "That's very apt, sah. And of course, the Dungeon is their chief field of struggle, with uncounted persons and uncounted other creatures snatched up from this world or that, from this era or that, and transported to the Dungeon to serve as pawns in their grand chess game."

"But what of the Gennine, Smythe?"

"The Gennine are most troublesome, sah. They seem to regard the Chaffri and the Ren equally as foes—or as rebellious inferiors. Consequently, sah, the Chaffri and the Ren have been known to make alliance, from time to time, in opposition to the Gennine. Sort of, the enemy of my enemy is my friend."

"There is a maxim in the Arab world," put in the man who was Sidi Bombay, " 'I fight my brother until our cousin appears, then we fight him together until a neighbor appears, then we fight *him* together until a stranger appears, and we *all* fight against the stranger.' "

"What is the point of all this?" Clive asked.

"The point, sah, is that there is a great organization whose purpose is to fight the Chaffri and the Ren—*and* the Gennine. There are agents in place in every era and every region. In the Dungeon and on the Earth and on other planets as well. They are among the Finnboggi, among Shriek's people, among Chang Guafe's, among the people of the world of Lord N'wrbb and Lady 'Nrrc'kth."

"And the name and purpose of this organization?"

"It is known—somewhat ironically, if I might add my comment—as the Universal Neighborhood Improvement Association. Its purpose is simply to resist the hegemonistic schemes of the others—equally of the Chaffri, the Ren, and the Gennine. Our enemies have agents as well. We have all encountered them, Major. Philo Goode, the Ransome couple, Father O'Hara—"

"But—a priest? A man of God? Whether one subscribes to Father O'Hara's faith or not, the fact that he has given his life to the service of the Divine—"

"Priest or not, Timothy F. X. O'Hara is still a man. Whether he joined the enemy voluntarily or was somehow hoodwinked or blackmailed or mesmerized into his role, still it is one he plays." Sergeant Smythe paused contemplatively. Then he said, "They can fuddle a man's mind, Major Folliot. Cast clouds upon the brain. I know whereof I speak, sah."

"Yes, Smythe. I recall your distress when you recalled the incidents of your trip to the burgeoning American metropolis of New Orleans. I am sorry."

" 'Nothing of it, sah. Perhaps Father O'Hara is more to be pitied than despised, but he is nevertheless an enemy. If we can win him back—that is, clear the pall from his mind and restore his loyalty to the human species and the respect of all intelligent beings—so much the better. If we cannot, we must fight him as we fight the Ren and the Chaffri and the Gennine."

"What, then, are we to do?"

"We'll get out of here, sah, for starters. If the Major will kindly wait a few ticks while I resume a safer identity . . ."

Smythe returned through the interconnecting door that led to Maurice Carstairs' office. He returned promptly in the guise of the nattily dressed, nearsighted Carstairs, squinting and blinking his weak eyes and blundering into furniture and doorways. He carried a gold-headed walking stick, using it almost as a blind man uses his cane.

"Mr. Singh, please—will you accompany Major Folliot and myself?"

"Of course, Mr. Carstairs," replied Sidi Bombay.

They left the offices of the *Illustrated Recorder and Dispatch* and climbed into a hansom that waited at the door. The driver peered down through the roof-trap and "Carstairs" gave him instructions.

"Can you trust a cabbie?" Clive inquired.

"He is one of us," Smythe answered.

"But if the enemy is capable of mesmerizing men—of planting devices for control in their very brains, or of abducting them and replacing them with simulacra—how can you know even that?"

"A good question, Major," Sidi Bombay interjected. "There are ways of knowing a natural being from a simulacrum, although they are less than certain and there is always an element of danger. Similarly, sir, when a man has been mesmerized, his behavior is often distinguishable from that of his true nature. But one always faces risks, and one must always take precautions. As you shall see, Major."

Clive bowed his head as the hansom pulled away from the kerb. He closed his eyes and pressed his forefinger and thumb against their lids. How to tell reality from illusion? Whom to trust? Were these two, Horace Smythe and Sidi Bombay, truly his companions of old, or were they illusions placed here to mislead him? If Smythe could pose as a mandarin, an Arab boy, a nearsighted publisher—could not an enemy pose as Smythe?

The hansom's wheels rumbled over cobbled streets.

Another question perplexed Clive. If it was George du Maurier's mental power, as augmented by Madame Mesmer's influence, that had drawn Clive across time and space to this London of 1896 . . . then how had Smythe and Sidi Bombay arrived here? They said nothing of having traveled across the years, but if they had lived continuously for these twenty-eight years, they should have aged, as had Clive's brother. And yet, neither seemed older than he had when last Clive had seen them in the Dungeon.

A shudder passed through Clive's body. There seemed no ready solution to his dilemma. He drew himself upright, dropped his hand, and looked around. The partly familiar, partly altered vista of London still surrounded him.

The hansom pulled to a halt in front of a building Clive had not seen since 1868—the gentleman's club where George du Maurier had brought him and Miss Leighton for a celebration following the premiere of *Cox and Box*, and where Clive had also last seen the senior Maurice Carstairs.

The front door of the club bore a black wreath.

"Carstairs" sent the cab on its way and the three men stood for a moment before the wreath. A small card, edged also in black, was affixed at its center. It read, GEORGE DU MAURIER, 1834–1896.

"Carstairs" rapped at the polished wood beside the wreath with his gold-headed walking stick. A liveried footman opened the door and bowed them inside, giving a series of startled glances, first at Horace Smythe, then at Sidi Bombay, and finally at Clive.

Sergeant Smythe peered nearsightedly at the footman. "Is that you, Browning?"

"Yes, sir."

"Is anything the matter, man?"

"No, sir. I just—I . . ."

"Out with it, man!"

"I could have sworn that you entered the club just a few minutes ago, sir. But that's impossible, for here you are." The footman managed a feeble smile.

"My associates and I will be using my private room for a short while. We are not to be disturbed."

Smythe stepped resolutely past the baffled footman, blundered off an overstuffed chair, grumbled at the staff for moving the furniture, collided with an elderly gentleman who tried frantically—but unsuccessfully—to avoid his pebble-visioned progress, and succeeded at last in leading the others to an inconspicuous corridor. This brought them to an even more inconspicuous room.

Bringing a key from his weskit, Smythe unlocked the door and ushered the others in. He locked the door behind them.

"No one is allowed in here," he explained. "No one, ever." As Clive looked around, Smythe said, "Dreadfully sorry about that encounter with the door-dragon. The real Carstairs must be in the building. This has never happened before—my fault, Major. Careless. No excuse for that."

"Spilled milk, Smythe. What now?"

"Now we change our identities, Major. I told you that we take precautions, and this is one such."

"Won't it appear odd, three persons entering this room and three others leaving?"

"We've a different way out, sah."

Minutes later three figures emerged from a florist's shop in a street not far from Carstairs' club. One was an officer of the Tsarist diplomatic service. The second appeared to be a laboring member of one of the darker races. The third was a jauntily costumed gentleman whose mustaches were waxed and twirled with self-indulgent care and whose right eye was magnified grotesquely by the thick lens of a monocle.

"Thus, in the fashion described so skillfully by the American author Mr. Poe, we hide ourselves from our enemies by making ourselves conspicuous." Horace Smythe nodded approvingly at the appearances of the others. "Come then, my friends. There's a marvelous game afoot!"

· CHAPTER 11 ·
Neither Fang nor Claw nor Venomous Barb

The three ill-assorted figures—the Tsarist diplomat who was really a quartermaster sergeant, the unimposing workman who was really a master of intrigue and of esoteric studies, and the Continental dandy who was really the younger son of a Gloucestershire nobleman—cast eerie shadows in the lights of the strange instruments that covered a full wall of the room.

They had entered one of London's most splendid hostelries, made their way to a room kept in the name of Count Splitofsky, and descended by private elevator car to a chamber buried deep beneath the streets of the metropolis.

"This is a strangely timeless place," Sidi Bombay commented. "I find it peaceful to visit, it renews my soul. Here there is neither night nor day, neither summer nor winter. The illumination, the temperature, the degree of moisture here never vary. One can attune oneself to the infinite and the eternal."

"Good for the equippage, also," Smythe put in pragmatically. "This comes from a later time—p'raps Miss Annie would find herself at home here. Might even recognize some of the devices. The experts who installed this said that unchanging temperature and humidity would be best for all the gear."

"What about Annie?" Clive asked. "She is my own descendant, Smythe, as you learned when we encountered her in the Dungeon. Has she been hoodwinked by the enemy? Is she under a mesmeric spell?"

"When did you see Miss Annie last, Major?"

"Why, mere hours ago. She was at Tewkesbury Manor. She remained there when I came to London to see Mr. Carstairs. The real Mr. Carstairs, that is—Maurice Carstairs, senior."

"Quite understood, sah. I'm very sorry, sah. That could not have been Miss Annie. You were dealing with a simulacrum. Where did you first encounter her, sah, if I might inquire?"

"She appeared in a very peculiar sort of railway car, in a tunnel beneath a saloon where I had previously encountered Mr. Philo Goode. The publican in that saloon was . . . yourself, Sergeant Smythe."

"Yes, sah. As I mentioned, sah, there are simulacra to be dealt with. I assure the Major, I have no recollection of the incident he describes. Nor have I been under the controlling influence of the Ransomes and their mesmeric talents. My mind has been cleared. I worked long and hard with Sidi Bombay, and there is no longer the cobweb of mesmeric influence left in my cranium. I assure you of that, sah!"

Horace Smythe swept the hair from his brow to show a surgical scar, stark and white against the darker skin. "It took the skills of the ancient Egyptians to remove those devices from my brain, sah. It was a painful procedure and a risky one. But I am rid of them, and it was all worth the trouble to me, sah."

Sidi Bombay nodded his endorsement of Smythe's statement.

Clive put his head in his hands. "Oh, my God! And my brother and father—at Tewkesbury?"

Smythe exchanged a glance with Sidi Bombay. "One cannot be certain," the Indian replied, "but there is reason to believe that neither of those men was real. The Folliots are at the center of the struggle of Chaffri and Ren, Gennine and Neighbors."

"Neighbors?"

"A little joke, sah," Smythe said. "A taste for irony. The grand alliance that is forged to oppose the Chaffri, Ren, and Gennine, is known as the Universal Neighborhood Improvement Association. As I mentioned to the Major earlier, sah. Wherever you travel, sah, if you can locate an office of the association—its members are known simply as the Neighbors—you are in communication with our alliance."

"But Annabelle, Neville, the old Baron—if those are merely simulacra in Tewkesbury, where are the real persons? How can I find them?"

"That's a difficult problem, sah. You're sure you saw Miss Annie only in that underground railway, and then at Tewkesbury, afterward?"

"When I first emerged—Sergeant, Sidi Bombay—is this the ninth level of the Dungeon? Is Earth the ninth level?"

The Tsarist official and the Indian workingman exchanged glances. Sidi Bombay said, "You must try to understand, Clive Folliot, that the levels of the Dungeon are not simple things. Your progress through them—the progress of all of our party—was not accomplished as simply as one would descend from story to story in a tall building here in London. How did you reach London? Where were you last, in the Dungeon?"

"I—it's all so confusing." Clive clutched his head. "On the eighth level, everything seemed to be building to a climax. The Ren and Chaffri had shown their hands at last. On the other levels, they operated through agents and surrogates. But on the eighth level they were present in *propriae personae.* Then, almost miraculously I found myself stranded on the polar ice cap."

He paced the room, looking up at the great instrument panel that covered a wall. What was the purpose of the meters with their swinging pointers, the tiny lamps that flashed on and off in various colors, the panels upon which enigmatic messages flashed into and out of being, some of them in the English language, some in other languages which Clive at least recognized, still others in symbols so alien to his eye that he was able only to infer that they were language at all?

"There on the ice I saw Annie. You remember the Japanese marines we encountered in the Dungeon?"

"Indeed, sah!" Smythe responded.

"And surely you remember the flying machine—the aeroplane—in which Annie escaped from them, and with which she joined us at the castle of N'wrrb. Smythe, Sidi

Bombay—I saw Annie flying overhead at the pole, flying in that Japanese aeroplane. I waved to her and I'm sure she saw me. She waggled the wings of the aeroplane. I believe she intended to land and rescue me, only to disappear in the wink of an eye!"

The recollection brought a lump to his throat. He was convinced that the woman in the aeroplane was the *real* Annabelle Leigh. The woman in the subterranean car, the woman he had left at Tewkesbury Manor with a promise to return after visiting Carstairs in London—that woman was almost certainly a fraud. He tried to recall: Had he mentioned their polar encounter to her? Had she remembered it? Or had she feigned the recollection, permitting him to mislead himself in his eagerness to believe in her?

Where was the real Annabelle Leigh? Trapped in the Dungeon? Here on Earth, but stranded in the year 1868 while Clive and Horace Smythe and Sidi Bombay were in 1896, hardly a day older than they had been twenty-eight years before?

"Let's take this carefully, sah." Horace Hamilton Smythe had seated himself before a small panel of buttons and keys not unlike those used by the typewritists employed by newspapers and publishing firms. Clive had seen the like during his visit to the *Illustrated Recorder and Dispatch.*

"What do you intend to do, Smythe? This machine brings to mind those that Chang Guafe and I saw on the eighth level. Wondrous machines capable of storing amazing amounts of information, sorting through it and arranging it in many ways, then returning it to us upon request. Whole libraries and staffs of researchers concentrated like the Lord's Prayer engraved on the head of a pin!"

"Yes," Smythe said. "I know whereof the Major speaks. I know of such machines. And this here's the greatest of 'em all. Or, at least, it connects us to the greatest of 'em. Where the grand master machine is, I don't rightly know, sah. But what we've here is good enough for most jobs, and connects to the *real* big 'un if it's given a task it can't handle."

"And you're going to, ah, tell this machine my story? And ask it the meaning of my experiences?"

"Something like that, sah."

Even as he spoke, Horace Hamilton Smythe's dexterous hands had been flying over the face of the panel, tapping at keys, setting and resetting switches. The lights on the wall above him flared and flickered in bewildering patterns. The message board upon which Clive had seen so bewildering an array of languages carried on a dialogue of its own with Smythe's little panel.

"Perhaps the Major would be so good as to tell us what happened after the aeroplane disappeared." These words came from Sidi Bombay. Clive found himself wondering at the Indian's unfailing equanimity. When first Clive had met him, Sidi Bombay had been an ancient, wizened husk of a man. He had emerged from the horrors of the Dungeon a third his former age—young, virile, energetic. He had been dressed, in the time Clive had known him, as a humble trader, a morning-coated gentleman, a ragged workman. And yet he never lost his calm.

Clive recounted his experiences with Chang Guafe, describing the alien cyborg's disappearance beneath the Arctic waters. He described his encounter with the horrendous monster built by Dr. Frankenstein, the arrival of the space-train, the way that the two of them, Clive Folliot and the lumbering monster, had entered widely separated cars on the train. Horace Smythe's fingers flew over the keys and buttons. The message panel flashed a response, cryptic and unreadable to Clive but apparently meaningful to Smythe. The pseudo–Count Splitofsky said, "Chang Guafe survived that experience, Major, and is busy and well. What then, sah?"

"What then, Smythe? Is that all you have to say? 'Chang Guafe is busy and well.' Where is he, man? What is he doing? How did he escape from beneath the ice cap?"

"Easy, sah, easy," Horace Smythe said, attempting to calm Clive.

But Clive would not be soothed. "And how do you know where he is? I demand that you tell me, Sergeant Smythe, before we do anything else." When Smythe was slow to respond, Clive seized him by the lapels. "Tell me, man!"

Before Smythe responded, Clive felt the hand of Sidi

Bombay on his shoulder. "Calm yourself, Clive Folliot. There is nothing to be gained by treating one's friend as one's enemy."

Clive relaxed his grip. He was shaking. "You're right, Sidi Bombay. Sergeant Smythe, I apologize. I shouldn't have—have acted in such a manner. But if you know what became of Chang Guafe, you must tell me. At once."

"That's all right, Major Folliot." Horace Smythe, still garbed as the Tsarist Count Splitofsky, brushed his coat and adjusted his lapels. I can show the Major what became of Chang Guafe more clearly than I could ever explain it, sah. With the Major's permission, then . . ."

Unable to control his voice, Clive nodded.

"If the Major will take a seat, then." Smythe flicked a series of switches, adjusted a series of levers on the machine. The light in the room grew dim. Before Clive's amazed eyes a cloud of fog or smoky material arose and floated at eye level. Within it a scene slowly took form.

"Why—why it is myself! Myself and Chang Guafe and the Widow Shelley's monstrous creation. See us there, struggling across the ice floe. And see us, now, sailing before the Arctic zephyr. Sergeant Smythe, how can this be? What do I see?"

He plunged his hand into the fog—or tried to do so. It was no use, for the fog resisted, gradually, gently. He could shove his fingertips into it easily, but after the first few inches they felt a counterpressure, and the harder Clive pressed, the deeper into the fog he penetrated, the stronger the resistance became. After the first four or five inches, he found himself pressing with all his strength, perspiration breaking out on his brow, unable to reach any of the figures that he beheld.

He ended his efforts, withdrew his hand, slumped back in his chair.

"If you would merely observe, Clive Folliot," Sidi Bombay urged, "you would accomplish more than you would by attempting to intervene. It is the karma, after all, of those you behold. It is the will of heaven. One must not interfere."

"But—but it is I myself!"

"Indeed it is."

"Is this an image merely?"

"I think not, Clive Folliot," the Indian said.

"Nor do I, sah." Horace Smythe adjusted a knob, and the figures in the fog grew until they seemed the size of a child's dolls. "I believe we are actually seeing the Major, along with Chang Guafe and that other chap, the tall, pale one."

"You *believe*, Smythe?" Clive saw the space-train come to a rest on the arctic water. He saw himself and the Frankenstein monster clamber onto cars. He saw Chang Guafe slip beneath the surface of the frigid polar sea. "Can we do nothing to help him?" he exclaimed.

"We must not interfere, Clive Folliot." Sidi Bombay's voice was as calm as ever. "Nor could we. You saw what happened when you attempted to penetrate the fog."

"They don't know we're watching them. Are we actually seeing the past as it takes place, or is this an image merely?"

"Don't know as it matters, sah."

"The Major speculates upon matters of metaphysics." Sidi Bombay smiled.

"Can we see anything we want? Any scene in time or space?" Clive demanded.

" 'Tisn't easily done, sah. The controls of this thingama-bob are devilish hard to master. I can only tune in now and then. But I think I reached Chang Guafe because you was with him, sah. And now you're here. It all connects up somehow, sah."

"But you saw him before, you say?"

"Yes, sah. But you, sah, you're here now, ain't you?"

Clive nodded dumbly. Metaphysics indeed. It was all beyond him. "What's happening to Chang Guafe? Can you show me him?"

Without speaking, Horace Smythe operated the machine's controls. Water rushed upward, filling the volume of fog in the center of the room. Murk filled the space. A feeling of chill and moisture pervaded the room. Dark green forms wavered and silvery ones darted by like bullets. Clive realized that he was observing the bottom of the polar sea. A large shape, in part covered with a smooth, metallic carapace, crawled forward.

"It's Chang Guafe!" Clive exclaimed. "He's all right!"

Neither Horace Smythe nor Sidi Bombay spoke.

The phantom Chang Guafe crawled, crablike, along the bottom of the sea. Briefly the waters swirled and boiled, and by dropping down and peering up into the foggy area Clive could see the surface of the sea in an uproar, and the space-train above it, rising into the cold sky. Clive returned his attention to Chang Guafe.

The alien cyborg extruded a shovel-like scoop and lifted a gob of material from the sea-bed. With tiny tools that he extruded from his body, Chang Guage shaped the material into a tube and sent it rising to the surface of the sea. He sucked in air, inflating elastic sacs that appeared through openings in his carapace.

Gracefully, Chang Guafe rose to the surface. Again he changed his configuration, filling newly created fuel tanks with water. The water fed into Chang Guafe's body, reappeared as glittering particles through tubes that emerged beneath the cyborg's body.

Chang Guafe rose into the air, sped away from the Earth, and was lost to sight.

The fog grew as dim as if night were falling.

"That's all, sah."

"But where did he go, Smythe?"

"I don't know, sah. It 'pears as if the Major got too far away from Chang Guafe. Or Chang Guafe, from the Major, sah. Leastways, I can't hold the image past that point, sah."

"It is my guess," Sidi Bombay put in, "that Chang Guafe has gone in search of his people. Or perhaps he is headed elsewhere."

"And this is happening . . . now?" Clive inquired.

"This happened long ago."

"And where is Chang Guafe *now*—in 1896?"

The Indian shrugged. "Sergeant Smythe told you that Chang Guafe was well and busy, Clive Folliot. But that was in part surmise. I believe, also, that we will see him again, although I do not know when or where that will be."

Horace Smythe was manipulating the controls of the machinery, but the image in the fog faded, and he was not able to call it back. "What happened after that, sah?" he asked. "I mean, sah, after the Major climbed aboard the train, and the train rose into the sky. What then, sah?"

"And then, I found myself in London. In the home of my dying friend, George du Maurier. I had spoken with him, from the Dungeon. It was never clear to me whether we had truly communicated or whether it had been an illusion, a dream or mirage or hallucination. But it was no illusion—it was real."

"Mr. du Maurier is dead," Sidi Bombay said.

"He is now."

"Was he alone when you saw him? Was he conscious? Was he in command of his faculties?" Horace Smythe asked.

"He was not alone. He was attended by Madame Clarissa Mesmer, the granddaughter of the famous Anton Mesmer. He was conscious and fully coherent when I left him."

Horace Smythe and Sidi Bombay exchanged another glance. Smythe's fingers flew. Enigmatic words and symbols flashed across the message panel.

"Madame Mesmer is a very powerful woman, Major Folliot," Sidi Bombay said.

"Powerful?" Clive responded. "Do you refer to psychic power, or to human influence, Sidi Bombay?"

"Both, Major Folliot. And more."

"More, Sidi Bombay? Please elucidate."

"Her influence extends not merely to human agencies, Major Folliot. That is what I meant."

"Sidi Bombay, Sergeant Smythe . . . I fear that I have gotten into a situation that is far beyond my depth. At times I feel like a solitary adventurer, a Hercules or a Parsifal, facing monsters on the one hand and traitors on the other. Yet even that I can cope with. There was a time in my life when I should have cringed helplessly before these odds. Such is no longer the case. The Dungeon has changed me, strengthened me, altered me for the better."

He looked from Horace Hamilton Smythe to Sidi Bombay. "But at other times I feel like a piece on a chessboard," he continued, "moved about at the whims of others, a helpless pawn being played in a game I neither comprehend nor control."

"Chess is an ancient game," Sidi Bombay replied. "It was known in the Middle East and in my own country long before it reached Europe. We are, perhaps, all chessmen in the game of the gods. But we are not pawns. Sergeant Smythe I should take as a rook—powerful, straightforward, stalwart. As for myself—well, perhaps a bishop, cutting across the paths of others, striking at distant and unsuspecting targets, Major Folliot."

"And I? What chess-piece am I, do you think, Sidi Bombay?"

"You, sir? In my mind there is no question, sir. You are a knight. Your power is not so obvious, but then, sir, neither are your intentions. You seem to be moving straight ahead, only to strike to the side. Yet again, you move to the left or the right, then veer and plunge where your attack is unexpected. Or you retreat and at the last moment turn and slay your pursuer. You may never survive to become a baron, Major Folliot, but in the game of chess you are already a knight!"

Clive could not suppress a smile. He looked from Sidi Bombay to Horace Hamilton Smythe. "It was we three who entered the Dungeon together. You, Horace . . . and you, Sidi Bombay . . . and I. The rook, the bishop, and the knight—perhaps. But who is the king? Baron Tewkesbury? My brother, Neville? Baron Samedi? Father O'Hara? George du Maurier?"

"The king is dead, long live the king," Sidi Bombay intoned in a low, solemn voice.

Clive flashed him a look.

Sidi Bombay returned it but said no more.

"And who is the queen?" Clive resumed. "The Lady 'Nrrc'kth? My great-great-granddaughter Annabelle Leigh? Madame Mesmer? Lorena Ransome?"

Sidi Bombay spread his hands in silence.

"Time and again I have encountered chess sets in the Dungeon," Clive said. "In Green's house, for one. And in the strange room that was like a scene from the fantasies of Dr. Dodgson, for another. Chess sets, with real personages replacing the pieces. I appeal to you. You appear to know far more than I of our mutual situation. Share with me your information."

Sergeant Smythe said, "That we shall, sah. That we shall do." He took Clive's elbow and guided him to the seat that, in his guise as young Maurice Carstairs, he had just vacated. "If you'll sit yourself down right 'ere, sah, you shall have plenty of information. More, p'raps, than you'll enjoy!"

Clive fixed his companions with his gaze. "After this, my friends, I shall propose a further course of action."

"Yes, sah. As you say, sah."

"Sergeant, I shall thank you not to patronize me. We three entered the Dungeon together, there at the ruby heart within the Sudd. All that followed, all that befell us within the Dungeon, is the sequel of that event. I propose, therefore, that we three join—or rejoin—forces, and see this thing through to its end. *Now*, Sergeant Smythe and Sidi Bombay. *Now*, and without further delay or distraction. We have been through much, together and apart. We have suffered fang and claw and venomous barb. We have been imprisoned, have known privation and pain."

He pounded a fist into the palm of his other hand. "I propose that the three of us form a pact, that we swear a great vow, as blood brothers—yes, as blood brothers, despite the disparity in our station and the differences of our races—and see this through to its end!"

Without another word, the three men, a patrician Englishman, a hardy yeoman and professional soldier, and a dark-skinned Indian mystic, clasped one another's hands.

There was a moment of silence. Then Horace Hamilton Smythe winked his eye. "I was hopin' yer'd say somethin' like that, sah. Something exactly like that! Thank yer, sah! Thank yer! All very good, and it's time to get to work, then, sah!"

"Very well. Our first task shall be to reassemble the party of adventurers who have shared most of our experiences in the Dungeon."

"I thought it was just the three of us, sah. The Major and Sidi Bombay and meself, sah." Smythe's voice and the expression on his face betrayed a measure of disappointment.

"I understand your feelings, Sergeant Smythe," Clive said. "We three are more than associates, more than members of a business enterprise or a sporting team or a military unit. Yes, we are brothers! But we three cannot undertake this task without help."

"There's the Universal Neighborhood Improvement Association, sah."

"Indeed there is. And we shall act under their ensign, if you and Sidi Bombay so deem, Horace. But you must pardon me for feeling that we will do better if we but locate our own comrades. Those, at least, who still survive, and who are willing to join us in what must surely be the final confrontation between the champions of all that is just and decent and moral—and their sworn foes."

"Just who is it that the Major has in mind, sah?" Horace was looking more and more morose. "Surely we won't have to break up this team, I hope."

"Never." Clive shook his head. He saw the look of relief on Horace Smythe's face. Even the normally stolid and undemonstrative Sidi Bombay smiled and nodded.

"But look here, Horace, Sidi Bombay," Clive resumed. He pressed his thumb to one side of his nose, his forefinger to the other. Before his mind's eye there appeared images of uncounted adventures, unmeasured perils and privations in the Dungeon. And yet, all the suffering that he had undergone seemed, in retrospect, strangely sweet to him.

"But look," he repeated, "let me call to mind just a few. Horace, Sidi Bombay—is that marvelous mechanism not capable of tracking down a handful of individuals?"

"I do not know, Clive Folliot." The Indian looked doubtful. "You must tell me as much as you can, and I shall attempt to do as much as I can."

Clearly, Clive thought, it was Sidi Bombay who was the master of the machine.

"Chang Guafe you have already shown me."

Sidi Bombay nodded.

"And Annie, my darling Annabelle Leigh. If that was truly she, flying the aeroplane above the polar ice—but *not* truly she whom I left in Gloucestershire—then where is Annie now? And where is the aeroplane?"

The Indian held his palms outward in a strangely Western gesture. It was not necessary for him to say that he did not know the answers to Clive's queries.

"You do not know, but you can find out?"

The Indian frowned.

"Before you even try," Clive said, "let me complete the list. There is Shriek—"

"That bloody gigantic spider?" Horace Smythe's face reddened.

"Yes, Horace. A strange and alien being, but one who stood beside us through peril and privation. When last I saw her, the poor thing had been reduced to the size of an ordinary domestic arachnid. But where is she now? Can we bring her to us? And can we restore her to her proper stature?"

"That is as it may be," Sidi Bombay said. "We shall have to consider. But have you completed your list, Clive Folliot?"

Clive shook his head. "By no means, Sidi Bombay. There is Finnbogg—a dear, faithful creature and a staunch ally. He managed to return to his own world, did he not? There he would have been reunited with his own kind, but did he locate the littermates whom he so desperately sought? Has he made for himself a happy life, or does he yet bear the wounds of his suffering in the Dungeon? Ah, Sidi, I do miss Finnbogg. He was not the cleverest of fellows, to be sure, but there burned within his breast a flame of purity that we more sophisticated folk have long since lost." He paused before resuming. "And there is Tomàs—"

"Tomàs!" Horace Smythe practically exploded. "He showed no concern for us, Major, not even for you. And you told me that he was your blood relative, a Folliot!"

"Yes, Horace, that he is. Yet even the noblest house may, from time to time, spawn a rogue. Tomàs would be by no means the first such. And yet, Tomàs is not a thoroughgoing scoundrel. Good and evil war perpetually in the soul of every man. Why should a Folliot be an exception? And for well or for ill, it remains true that Tomàs is a Folliot."

"Even so, Major—even so! Why should we care for him, when he didn't care for us? Why, for all we know, he's just as likely to betray us again as he was when we first met him!"

"Everything you say is true, Horace. I cannot deny it. But still and all, he is of my blood—and he was our companion. I cannot see my way clear to simply abandoning Tomàs to whatever fate has befallen him. At least, not if there is anything we can do."

Sidi Bombay put in, "Is that the completion of your list, Clive Folliot?"

Clive stood with head bowed, as if he were studying the toes of his boots. He rubbed his chin between forefinger and thumb. "There is one other, my friends."

"Not the Lady 'Nrrc'kth, sah! I know how the Major felt, but the lady is dead, sah. We can't change that, sah."

"Not the Lady 'Nrrc'kth." Clive raised his eyes to his companions and lowered his hand to his side. "No, not she. I shall carry her image forever in my heart, my friends, but I know that I shall never see that beloved face, feel that precious touch again. Not in this world. Perhaps in another."

"Then who, sah?"

"Baron Samedi."

"That being of Hades?"

"We do not know that he is a being of Hades."

"But we saw him there!"

"As did he, us! Did you never hear of him during your sojourn to the city of New Orleans, Horace?"

"I—I'm not sure, sah. Should I have?"

"There is a cult there—at least we were lectured upon it, at Cambridge—called Hoodoo, or Voodoo, or Vodun. Imported to the Louisiana Territory with slaves from the island of Hayti. The cult is a combination of Christianity and animistic beliefs from the African region of Senegal. African gods and nature spirits, Christian figures, sacrifices and enchantments . . . it is a strange and wonderful religion."

"Yes, sah, I'm sure it is, sah. I'm sure that the Major's professors at Cambridge made it fascinating, sah. But what's it to do with me?"

"Baron Samedi is an important figure in the cult of Hoodoo. With his top hat and tails and his cigar—with his arrogant strutting and his cocky manner—he mocks death and all the powers of evil. He aided us in our escape from the nether regions—or from the level of the Dungeon that we took for them. I would be proud to have him at my side in the final confrontation with our enemies."

"And that's all, sah? There's no one else the Major wants?"

"Sergeant Smythe, do I detect a note of sarcasm in your tone?"

"Sarcasm, sah? In *my* tone? Sah, I'm just a straightforward farm lad wot's found a home in the army. Such things as sarcasm is beyond a simple soldier like me, Major."

"Very well, then. Let it go." Clive whirled toward the Indian. "Sidi Bombay, what do you think? You seem more than competent to operate these instruments. Is it possible to locate our former companions?"

"Perhaps, Clive Folliot."

"And to reach them? To communicate with them, to bring them here?"

"Perhaps, Clive Folliot. I will see what I can do. Perhaps you and Horace Smythe would care to leave me in solitude while I make the attempt."

Clive felt Horace's hand on his elbow. "Sidi can do it if anyone can, Major."

"But the space-train—"

"This would be another method altogether, Clive Folliot," Sidi Bombay said softly. He turned his back on the others and busied himself with the machinery.

"If Sidi wants ter be left alone, sah, I think we'd better leave him alone."

"What have you in mind, Horace?"

"I don't know, sah. P'raps a glass of ale. I know a pleasant pub not far from here."

• CHAPTER 12 •
The Dandy and the Count

The Continental dandy and the bogus Tsarist count left the building via a cobbled alley. A pack of cats pawing through an accumulation of trash snarled in defiance, then gave way before the waved walking sticks of the two men.

"Will we need a hansom, Sergeant?" Clive asked as they reached the sidewalk.

"Count Splitofsky, if you please, sir."

Clive grinned. "Beg your pardon, your excellency! And you may call me—" he thought for a moment, "Monsieur Terremonde."

"Is a short walk only, M'sieur. Come, let us go."

Horace Hamilton Smythe—Count Splitofsky—slipped his arm through his companion's elbow and urged him from the mouth of the alley, into the bustle of a late London afternoon. As they stepped into the passing throng, a well-dressed couple drew back, casting hostile glances at them and commenting behind raised hands to each other.

Splitofsky guided Terremonde through the gray streets. A fog had already risen from the Thames, and the air was dark and chill. The feeble sun was a mere disk of milky pallor against the gray-brown sky. Drays, diligences, broughams, and hansoms filled the thoroughfare, their wooden fittings creaking and their iron tires clattering on the cobblestones.

At a busy intersection a harried bobby wearing the smart new tunic and copper helmet of the Metropolitan Police waved gloved hands frantically, trying to sort the onrushing traffic into some semblance of order. As Splitofsky and Terremonde strode past him, the bobby saluted smartly. Splitofsky and Terremonde, with almost military precision, returned the gesture by raising their walking sticks to the brims of their silk hats.

With startling suddenness the neighborhood changed its character. What had been a bustling district of neat offices and smart shops gave way to a grimy quarter filled with dosshouses, storage sheds, sewing lofts, and low dives. It was into one of these last that the Count Splitofsky guided Monsieur Terremonde.

"Are you sure?" Terremonde inquired. But before Splitofsky could reply, the other exclaimed, "I know this place! Why, this is the saloon where I was approached by the two women—where the publican was—"

"Don't say it!" Splitofsky hissed.

Clive—Terremonde—held his tongue.

The heavy door swung closed behind the two men. Terremonde stood gazing about himself while Splitofsky moved past him, toward the long wooden counter behind which an aproned publican slouched, elbows on the mahogany surface, engaged in conversation with a woman. She was one whom Terremonde had never seen before, but she was of a type with which he had of late become painfully familiar.

Splitofsky rapped his walking stick against the wooden railing. "Service, if you please, sir!" He spoke with a marked accent.

Folliot/Terremonde peered through an atmosphere composed of tobacco fumes, exudations of distilled alcohol, attar of roses, musk, stale perspiration, and London fog. The publican had looked up and was engaged in dialogue with Smythe/Splitofsky.

Could Terremonde believe his eyes? He rubbed them with gray-gloved knuckles. Using his walking stick as a pry and a prod, he managed to make his way through the tightly packed patrons of the saloon.

"Horace!"

The exclamation had no sooner passed Terremonde's lips when he realized that he had committed a potentially dangerous faux pas. The identities and loyalties of the denizens of the den were unknown to him, but after his previous encounter with the two loose women, their ruffian associates, and the startling barkeep and "owner" of the establishment, he feared that the very mention of Count Splitofsky's true name might imperil the man.

But in the noise and bustle of the saloon, Terremonde's word went unheeded.

Splitofsky's hand darted between two heavy types and clutched Terremonde by the elbow, drawing him toward the bar. Terremonde darted a look into Splitofsky's face, then into the uncannily familiar face of the barkeep. "Who are you, man?" Terremonde hissed.

"Smith, sir."

"That's Smith with an *eye* and no *ee*," Count Splitofsky put in.

"That's right, milord." The barkeep tugged at his forelock. "Matthew McAteer Smith."

"And who is the proprietor of this establishment?"

"That would be Mr. Smithson, milord. Mr. Oliver Oscar Smithson."

"And the woman with whom you were just speaking?"

Smith peered past Terremonde. "The lady with the feather in her hair? That would be Miss Smithers, milord. Miss Dorothy Daphne Smithers. And she is a lovely lass, wouldn't you agree, milord, if I might venture an opinion."

Terremonde pressed his hand to his brow. His skin felt clammy and there was a ringing in his ears. As if from a distance he heard the bartender Smith speaking to Count Splitofsky. "His lordship looks a bit peaked. Maybe we should help him into the back room."

Splitofsky grunted assent.

Terremonde felt himself sliding, then a pair of strong hands catching him under the arms. He didn't quite pass out, but felt himself carried through the pressing crowd of the saloon's patrons. Gaslight roared and wove, smoke drifted through the miasmic atmosphere. He felt himself laid on a couch, smelled the leather upholstery, tried to focus his eyes on the wooden paneling overhead.

He found himself wondering what had become of his silk hat and his polished walking stick. Faces peered down at him. Voices buzzed and cloth rustled.

"You all right, sah?"

Clive pushed against the couch, struggling upright. Strong hands supported him. His head still spun, but he felt himself regaining strength. A glass was pressed to his lips. He swallowed a burning liquid, felt strength radiating from his belly even as the drink hit home. Brandy.

"I—I'm all right. I just—It was all too much for me." Clive raised a hand to his brow, and found that he was still wearing the gray gloves proper for an afternoon in the city. It must be evening now, and he still in daytime clothes!

"Horace?" He peered into the face nearest him. Was it that of the Count Splitofsky, or was it that of Horace Hamilton Smythe?

"Try to breath deeply, sah. You're looking better already, Major Folliot."

"I—I feel ashamed, Horace. To faint like a weak woman."

"It could happen to anyone, sah. As the Major says, sometimes it's all just too much. You'll be all right now, sah. Would the Major like another sip of restorative?"

Clive nodded, drank deeper, swallowed. "Thank you, Horace." His head was clear enough now to notice that his hat and stick had been brought along and placed on a nearby table. He looked from Horace Hamilton Smythe— yes, even in his identity of Count Splitofsky, there was no doubt in Clive's mind that the man was Horace Smythe— around at the others. The barkeep, the man who had been introduced as Matthew McAteer Smith. The woman, Dorothy Daphne Smithers. And the dignified individual looking on, surely that must be Oliver Oscar Smithson.

"You—you're all the same!" Clive heard his own voice exclaim.

"After a manner of speaking, sir, we are indeed." It was Smithson who spoke.

"But we have our differences, as well," said the woman Dorothy Daphne Smithers.

Clive looked at her more closely now. Her hair was long and lush, as black as jet and swept in graceful waves that set off her face to advantage. Her eyebrows were of the same shade, startling against a pale complexion made paler by the application of white powder. Her eyes were a deep and gorgeous blue, her features fine and graceful. Her figure, showcased as it was by the low-cut bodice and wasp-waist of her dark red gown, was lush.

Blinking with admiration, Clive smiled at her. "You do indeed, my dear. But still, Horace," this latter spoken to the Count Splitofsky, "who are these persons? What is this place? It was strange enough when I encountered Philo Goode in this very room—I think it was this very room. But I see only modified forms of your visage in every face I encounter. What is happening?"

"If I may answer, M'sieu Terremonde." The speaker was the impressive Oliver Oscar Smithson. He drew upon a black Cuban cheroot. His face was florid, set off by side whiskers that joined his graying mustache. His hair was thin, his belly not at all so. His brocaded weskit and finely tailored suiting marked him as a man of substance.

"Please," Clive replied.

"Welcome, Clive Folliot, to the Bathgate Chapter of the Universal Neighborhood Improvement Association. You have heard of us, I trust, sir."

"Heard of you?" Clive managed to climb to his feet. His knees were still wobbly but his dizziness was now past. He reached toward Dorothy Daphne Smithers. She handed him the brandy snifter. That was not what he wished to receive, but he took another sip of the liquor and set the snifter upon a low table. "Yes, I've heard of you, Mr. Smithson. Horace—Count Splitofsky—told me about the association. Horace and Sidi Bombay. That is not what I meant, sir. I mean, are you all relatives? Or are you simulacra, or those strange creatures that I am told are called *clones*?"

"Something like that," Smithson said.

"But not quite." That was Miss Smithers. Clive realized that her voice was as charming as her appearance. Cool, low, soft—yet with a suggestion of warmth, as if glowing embers had been banked against the time when they might be fanned back to passionate flame.

"Not quite? If you please, then . . ."

Miss Smithers exchanged glances with Smythe, Smith, and Smithson. "There are more worlds than you dream of, M'sieur Terremonde."

"I have learned much in the Dungeon, Miss Smithers."

"Of that I have no doubt, Monsieur. I have read your dispatches with enjoyment and admiration."

Clive felt himself coloring, yet feeling considerable pleasure at the recognition of his efforts. "Then you are aware of my adventures."

"Your adventures, Monsieur, have made you famous on more worlds than you can imagine. Those who know of them—of you—and of your companions . . . are widespread. You might walk down a street in Buenos Aires, in St. Petersburg, in Istanboul, or in Tokio, and barely one person in ten thousand would know of you. But yet there would be that one in ten thousand. And such is true not only in every great city of this planet, but also of Mars, of the worlds circling the great stars Procyon and Deneb, of planets circling suns so far from here that the very galaxies of which they are members are invisible to the unaided eye. Oh, yes, M'sieu Terremonde. Oh, yes. Wherever human foot treads—and indeed on worlds where no human being has ever set foot, but where the spark of awareness has blazed in forms more strange than any you have ever encountered—you are known."

"But about the Smiths," Count Splitofsky put in. "Would a word of explanation not be apt?"

"Indeed it would." Oliver Oscar Smithson, florid of face and fulsome of manner, took center stage.

"Each station of the U.N.I.A. is set up to serve a sector of some world. Except for those in more sparsely populated regions of the universe. There, a station may serve an entire planet—or many planets. And each such station, whenever possible, is staffed by persons of sanguinary connection. The association has long since learned that bonds of blood serve to reinforce bonds of political or other loyalties. Thus, this station is staffed by Smiths, and Smythes, and Smithsons, and Smithers. . . ."

"Our station in the American city of New York," Dorothy Daphne Smithers took over, "is staffed by Joneses. Joneses, Johns, Johnsons, Johansons, Jacksons."

"And our station at Marsport Central . . ." Matthew McAteer Smith added. The others turned to face him. "Well, the Martians' names are not easy for human tongues to pronounce."

"Are the Martians not themselves human?" Terremonde inquired.

Smith smiled. "Not—ah, not quite, M'sieur Terremonde."

"Ah, well—but then, I have made alliance in the past with creatures not of human form, nor of earthly origin. What form do these habitants of the red planet manifest?"

Smith shot an inquiring look at Smithson. The latter nodded an affirmative and the erstwhile publican struck a concealed stud worked into the woodwork of the wall. A section of solid walnut seemed to become transparent, as transparent as clear window glass. Terremonde found himself staring at a creature shaped something like a tropical jellyfish, floating high in the thin atmosphere of another world.

"As nearly as I can pronounce the station manager's name," Matthew McAteer Smith resumed, "it sounds something like this—" and he made a sound unlike any Terremonde had heard in his life, a cross between a rasp and a hiss and a dry, tortured rattling. "Every member of that station is related to the manager, and their names so indicate—although you will pardon me if I do not attempt to reproduce them for you."

Terremonde made a sound of acquiescence.

"And thus you see, sir, the importance of the Folliot family to the Universal Neighborhood Improvement Association." It was Count Splitofsky who spoke. "And perhaps," he added, "we would do well to make our way back to the place where our associate waits."

Terremonde blinked. "Yes. Yes, ah, let us do that."

"Are you well enough?" Splitofsky asked solicitously.

Terremonde indicated that he was. With the Russian at his side, he started for the door. Oliver Oscar Smithson and Matthew McAteer Smith offered their hands to each of the visitors. Dorothy Daphne Smithers did the same— to Splitofsky. Terremonde she treated differently, holding him in her arms and offering lush lips, breathlessly parted. Terremonde hesitated but a fraction of a second, then lowered his face to hers. The warmth of her reaction stirred him. He drew back. Some unspoken message passed between them.

He exhaled, released her. He wondered if he would

ever see her again—and if he did, what would be the result.

Oliver Oscar Smithson placed his hand on the elaborately worked brass door handle. "Before you go, my friends . . ."

Terremonde and Splitofsky halted.

". . . I must warn you. This building is located on an instability."

"Yes. That I know," Splitofsky said.

"When last I was here—" Terremonde began, but a look from Smith told him that there was no need to continue.

"I shall serve as M'sieur Terremonde's guide," Splitofsky said.

"Very well. Just . . . be careful, my friends. And Godspeed!" Smithson turned the metal handle and Clive Folliot and Horace Hamilton Smythe stepped through the portal of hell.

I've been here before, Clive thought. Flames leaped about him. Puffs of smoke erupted from miniature volcanoes that spread across a landscape unlike any on the Earth. The stench of sulfur stung his nostrils and the acrid atmosphere brought hot tears to his eyes. There was no visible sky. Instead, overhead, where leaping flames and roiling clouds of black vapor broke upon jagged points, a hellish inversion of the monstrous landscape that surrounded him loomed angrily, terrifyingly, threatening to fall and crush all that lay below it.

Somewhere in the distance a shriek rang out. Truly and literally, it was the despairing cry of the damned.

Clive Folliot felt a hand grasping his sleeve. He turned and looked into the face of Horace Hamilton Smythe.

"Say it ain't so, Major! Sure as me ma'am warned me, it's Satan's own realm and we're doomed. We'll cook for the devil's own dinner!"

The cosmopolitan manner of Count Splitofsky had fallen away, and though the man still wore the formal garb of the Tsarist diplomat, his manner was once again that of his true identity.

In like manner, M. Terremonde had become once again Clive Folliot, younger son of a country nobleman, major in the service of Her Majesty the Queen.

"It's hell, surely enough, Sergeant. But we are hardly damned! Get hold of yourself, man! You passed through the Dungeon; you know that Hell—*this* Hell, at any rate—is merely another level of the Dungeon."

"I remember, sah." Smythe was visibly calmer now. He released Clive's sleeve. "I'm sorry, sah."

"It's all right, Horace. I quite understand."

"I knew that this was a variable location, Major Folliot, but I never expected to find myself stepping from an Association office directly into Hades itself."

"Quite all right, Smythe. But now we've got to find our way out of here. You don't suppose Sidi Bombay has an eye on us, by any chance?"

"Don't think so, sah. He was going to try and locate our missing companions. Still, if we don't return . . ."

"All right. But we won't count on assistance from that quarter."

Their conversation was interrupted by a shriek as a devilish figure hurled a flaming trident at them. Clive dived to the right, Horace to the left. The trident whizzed between them, sizzling and crackling, leaving behind it a trail of noxious vapor.

Clive had landed on his hands and knees. Even as he scrambled to regain his feet, he spotted Horace in dire peril. The two had found themselves on a walkway of stone, hardly wider than a man is tall. When they had dived to avoid the flaming trident, Clive had landed at the edge of the walkway, but Horace, opposite him, had slipped from the edge of the path and was hanging by his fingertips, scrabbling to retain his weakening grasp on the stone.

If he lost his grasp he would tumble into a pit of roaring flames.

Clive literally threw himself across the pathway, flying through the roiling, sulfur-laden air. He crashed to the edge of the walkway just as the fingers of Horace's left hand lost their purchase. Clive grabbed Horace's right hand.

"Hold on there, Horace! I've got you!"

Clive held on to Horace's right hand with both of his own.

Horace reached with his left and grasped Clive's wrist. "Help me! Major, help me!"

Clive tugged at Horace's arm, shoving backward with his elbows, dragging Horace back onto the walkway. "Don't worry, my friend. Don't panic."

He was already half the length of a forearm from the edge of the walkway. He could see the look of panic beginning to fade from Horace Smythe's face. Behind and beneath Smythe he could see the leaping flames and, amazingly, the fiendish forms that pranced and capered among them, howling their frustration at the loss of prey that they had thought their own.

"Shift your hand now! Grasp my shoulder, Horace!"

Smythe obeyed.

Clive now had one hand free. He braced it against the pathway, heaved himself to his knees, and simultaneously managed to pull Horace Smythe fully back over the edge. The two men clambered to their feet. Horace's face bore an expression of relief; Clive's, one of satisfaction.

In the pit behind Horace, a furious demon screeched his rage and hurled a trident at his departing prey. Clive shoved Horace aside—there was no time for a warning shout and the latter's reaction—and with reflexes speeded by long and arduous exposure to peril, snatched the trident from the air, even as it whizzed past them.

"Let us see what we have here." Clive studied the weapon. The shaft was as long as a man is tall; the tines as long as a sapper's carbine bayonet and as wickedly barbed as an Equatorian hunting spear. The weapon was made all of metal, and its heat pulsed through Clive's hands—but he did not yield it.

"Sergeant Smythe—can we return to the U.N.I.A. office?"

Horace turned in a circle. "I don't see how, sah. I don't see any doorway to take us back."

Clive nodded. "Nothing so surprising to that. We've encountered doorways before that seem to lead only one way and that disappear once you've stepped through them. Well then, there's only one thing to do—push on! We'll find our way out of this place and get on with our mission."

They set off down the pathway. There was nothing to either side but scenes of horror and torment. Flames shot upward, jets of noxious fumes assaulted their nostrils, the screams of the damned and the gleeful screeches of their tormentors tore at their eardrums.

The brightness of the flames and the blackness of the clouds of filthy smoke that arose from the pits obscured their vision, but now and then a vagrant current of foul air would part the flames and the rising fumes, and Clive and Horace could peer into the pits. The faces of the tormented tore at their heartstrings, their pleas for succor eloquent even in pantomime.

Clive stopped and leaned over the edge, the trident resting on its hilt, tines upraised.

"Can't stop, sah! Can't help them! We'd best move on!"

"But—I recognized a face! Those eyes, that hair! I cannot leave her to—"

"We can't help them, sah! And for all we know, those are either simulacra or illusions. We've encountered plenty of those, have we not, sah?"

A beautiful face peered up at Clive, appeal written in its eyes.

"She's on her knees, Horace! Look at her torment! We cannot—"

"We must, sah!" Horace was tugging at Clive's elbow, dragging him by main force from the tormented woman. Before they had taken half a dozen steps the flames roared up with renewed intensity. The woman disappeared.

"That was—"

"Never mind who it was, sah! Don't torment yourself, Major Folliot."

A huge batwinged form detached itself from the roof far overhead and swooped at Clive and Horace. Only the beating of its wings, the thump of their opening and folding, the hot rush of stinging sulfur fumes as it plummeted, warned the two men.

Clive turned his face upward, facing the apparition with new shock. "Tomàs!"

The thing pulled up half the height of a man above Clive and Horace. It had a hair-covered body that was an obscene parody of a human's trunk, but its legs were truncated and ended in feet like those of a great, ugly bird, in razor-sharp claws. Instead of arms it had wings like those of a bat, the rudimentary fingertips armed also with scythelike claws.

And its face—oh, its face was that of man.

"Tomàs!" Clive moaned a second time.

The thing swooped away and rose back toward the foul flame pits and hideous rookeries of the roof of Hades. It was as small as a calf, then as small as a duck, then it turned again and dived straight at the two men.

"Fight it, sah!" Horace Hamilton Smythe had broken his stunned paralysis and regained his voice. "It's going to kill us, sah—and I have no weapon!"

The monstrosity was diving toward them, driving itself to ever greater speed with its bat wings. Its form filled Clive with a mixture of horror and revulsion, its face was filled with demonic rage and an insane hatred, its eyes glared like living yellow-white coals.

And its voice—its voice screamed in a tone as loud and as piercing as the screeching brakes of a great steam locomotive: *"Die, Clive Folliot! Die and be damned here among the damned!"*

Clive ducked as the monster passed over him, and from the corner of his eye he could see Horace Hamilton Smythe do the same.

The monster pulled up and swooped away again, but not before raking the backs of both men with its talons. The claws ripped Clive's garments and tore at the skin of his back. He felt as though he had been scourged with two sets of white-hot barbs. He emitted an involuntary scream of pain, and heard Horace Hamilton Smythe echo that scream.

"It will come again, sah! It will come again! Fight it!"

"But it is Tomàs! He is my own kin! Horace, how can I—"

There was no time for the rest of Clive's question. The hideous being had flapped and stroked its way upward again, and now it dipped once more and plunged toward the walkway, its claws extended to rake and rip, its mouth open in a scream of rage half-human and half-demonic.

Clive sank to one knee, grasped the trident in both hands, and faced squarely upward into the eyes of the onrushing monstrosity. "Get down, Horace!" he shouted.

At the very moment that the creature's claws swept through the sulfurous air where Smythe's body had been, Smythe landed with a thud on the surface of the walkway. Tomàs—or the being with Tomàs' face and with the parody of his voice—swooped through steaming air, drove forward with another thrust of its powerful, leathery wings, then reared in midair and plunged razor-sharp claws straight at Clive Folliot's horrified face.

Clive launched himself forward and upward, the hot trident extended before him. With a jolt that ran up Clive's arms and rocked him onto his heels, batwinged monster and sharpened prongs met—and the monster was impaled on the trident.

Fuming, green-black ichor spurted from the monster's torso.

Clive dropped the trident.

The monster tumbled to the walkway and thudded onto its back, the shaft of the trident protruding from its fleshy torso.

Horrified, baffled, yet moved by the pathos of the wounded creature, Clive knelt at its side. "Tomàs? Tomàs? Is it truly you? Why did you—how—your own kind, Tomàs—"

He was halted by the pure hatred that blazed from the monster's eyes. "Better to die in my true form," the voice that was half Tomàs and half that of a screeching beast tore at Clive's ears. "Better to die in my true form than to live any longer as a putrid human, a corrupt Folliot!"

"But you were—" Clive got no further. The face that was that of Tomàs Folliot, the Portuguese sailor, writhed in its final rictus. The mouth pursed; Clive wondered if Tomàs was trying to whistle, but unstead Tomàs launched a gob of spittle. Only it was not spittle, it was the same ichor that still oozed from around the tines of the trident embedded in his torso. The fetid, slimy substance burned where it struck Clive's face, and he wiped it away with the cloth of his sleeve.

Tomàs' eyes glazed, his labored breathing ceased.

Clive felt Horace tugging him gently by the shoulders. "Come away, sah. Come away. He's gone." Clive allowed himself to be drawn to his feet. He watched as Horace placed a foot against Tomàs' corpse and pulled the trident from his body in the manner that Her Majesty's soldiers were trained to use when they retrieved bayonets from the bodies of enemy troops.

"Is there nothing I can do for him?" Clive murmured softly. "He was still of my blood."

"All we can do so, sah. Either leave him here, or . . ." Smythe gestured.

Clive hesitated for a moment, then nodded, breathing a silent prayer to whatever deity there might be, for the repose of whatever soul Tomàs might have had.

Horace Hamilton Smythe tipped the body over the edge of the walkway, using the toe of his boot to do so. The body tumbled into the flaming pit below and disappeared.

Clive Folliot tried not to hear the shrieks of glee that rose from the pit, nor to think too much about what they meant.

They proceeded along the walkway, Horace Smythe now carrying the trident that he had retrieved from Tomàs's body. How long they trudged, how many miles they covered, Clive and Horace could not gauge. The path that they walked changed in composition, now with a surface like marble, now like basalt. At one point it seemed to turn to metal, a gridwork of girders not unlike the structure of a railroad trestle. Beneath their feet stretched an abyss, and its bottom, lakes of molten sulfur.

Flames and clouds of foul gases rose from beneath the trestle. Clive turned his eyes upward. The hellish pit beneath his feet was duplicated above him, and he saw flocks of the hideous batwinged creatures clustered around pits and glowing mounds of sulfurous lava that rose like volcanoes from the hot rocks beneath their feet.

The creatures had human faces, and Clive saw the hate-filled visages of men and women he had fought on level after level of the Dungeon.

One of the batwinged creatures in particular caught Clive's attention. It was smaller than the others; for a moment Clive wondered if they bred as do humans, and if so, whether this was the child of such a process.

The creature locked eyes with Clive. Its face could have been that of an angel in some medieval painting, yet one filled with such pure malice as to send a shiver down Clive's spine despite the suffocating heat of his surroundings. Suddenly Clive recognized that scene before him. It was not the work of a medieval master, but of the fantasist Hieronymous Bosch.

The demon smiled and launched itself into the air. Its flock of companions followed—dozens of them, then scores, then hundreds. They did not head for Clive and Horace directly, but circled around them, cawing and shrieking in their horrid half-human voices.

"Let's hurry on, sah!" Horace urged. He increased his pace to a steady trot, heading for the far end of the trestle, but one of the demons landed squarely in the center of their path. Another followed, and another, until fully a hundred of the monstrosities blocked the trestle.

"Back, Horace—back the other way!" Clive and his companion whirled and started to retrace their steps, only to find their path blocked by another crowd of the demons.

Hopping like birds, flapping their great leathery wings like giant bats, flexing their talons in eagerness, the twin bands of demons closed upon Clive and Horace.

"It's the end, sah! I've that trident, and I'll take as many of them with me as I can. But still, sah—this is the end!"

Clive clasped Horace's hand in his own. "We'll go down fighting, Sergeant, if go down we must. But—"

He peered into the flaming pit that flanked the trestle. Craters smoked, sheets of flame flared upward, clouds of black, sickening smoke wafted around them. Screams of anguish and shrieks of glee rose to smite their ears.

And in a particularly dark and solid-looking cloud of smoke, a formally garbed human figure danced a jig, tipped his black stovepipe hat, and bowed satirically. From a pocket in his swallowtail morning coat, the newcomer drew a crooked stogie. He bit off its tip and spit it at the monster nearest to Clive and Horace. He placed the stogie between his teeth, leaned into a shaft of crackling flame, and drew it into life.

He blew a cloud of smoke from the stogie, into a crowd of batwinged monsters. Coughing and cringing, they drew away. He turned, drew on his stogie, and blew another cloud of smoke at the monsters menacing Clive and Horace from the other direction.

"Welcome, my friends," he smiled.

"Baron Samedi!"

"Major Folliot. Sergeant Smythe. A pleasure to welcome you to Hades."

"You saved our lives."

"A trifle. These demons are a nuisance. Not to be taken seriously."

"But one of them was my kinsman, the sailor Tomàs. I—I killed him."

"Regrettable."

"We have to get out of here, Baron. Can you get us back to London? Will you join us?"

"Join you? Oh, no, no, no! I'm much too busy. I have my duties here. I seldom visit your world—although I've had some interesting times in the island of Hayti. And there's a nice city called New Orleans that I visit on occasion."

"I think I know a bit of that, Your Grace." That was Horace Hamilton Smythe speaking.

"Indeed, colleague."

Clive said, "Colleague?"

"I believe that Baron Samedi works with the U.N.I.A."

"Correct, colleague. In Port-au-Prince. And in New Orleans. As I recall, Horace, our paths first crossed in New Orleans. You were in a bit of trouble there."

"Yes, I was, Your Grace."

"You're sure you won't come with us, Baron Samedi?" Clive was wondering, now, whether he had crossed paths with the U.N.I.A. himself, at different levels of the Dungeon. When things had looked hopeless, when he had thought himself lost, only to win through to surprising victories, had it been sheer luck, or sheer grit—or the concealed intervention of the Universal Neighborhood Improvement Association?

"*Non, mes amis,* I cannot accompany you. But you wish to leave Hades? Despite the salubrious climate, the colorful scenery, the active social life, and the presence of famous personages? Very well. You wish to return to London?"

"To see if Sidi Bombay has located Finnbogg—"

"Finnbogg?" Baron Samedi waved his cigar in the manner of a stage illusionist waving his magic wand.

Hell disappeared.

Clive Folliot found himself surrounded by blue trees. Overhead, filtering through the leafy canopy, in the center of a red sky, three green suns blazed downward.

· CHAPTER 13 ·
As an Alien in Eden

He whirled, looking for Horace Smythe, for the Baron Samedi, for the monsters and demons who had surrounded him until a split second ago. They were nowhere to be seen.

The cries of the damned, the gleeful laughter of their tormentors . . . were gone. Clive was surrounded by silence. The air was sweet, the only sound was the soft rustle of a zephyr in the tall, friendly trees.

Somewhere a bird sang. Its call, a trilling, warbling song, was so beautiful that it brought tears to Clive Folliot's eyes. He raised his hands to brush away the tears, then looked down to discover that he was newly garbed in a soft outfit of green and brown.

He exclaimed aloud, voicing wonder at where he was.

No one answered.

There was no point in standing still. He sighted in on the three green suns that blazed above the leafy canopy, trying to determine a direction by which to orient himself. He was not a tracker by any means. If he could only have the skills of a Red Indian! But he had learned something of geography at Cambridge, and some lore in Her Majesty's service, and once satisfied he set out a steady pace.

As he strode along, he took stock of himself and his clothing and possessions. His garments were made of sturdy cloth, carefully tailored and excellently fitted. There were no pockets in the tight-fitting shirt, the looser jacket, or the trousers. He had neither weapon nor tool in his possession: obviously, then, he had been transported to this place and left with only the proverbial clothes on his back.

But his boots were sturdy, the temperature was comfortable, and he himself was unharmed in any way. A fine escape from Hades!

The Baron Samedi was nowhere to be seen. He'd said that he could not—or would not—leave Hell with Clive and Horace Smythe.

Clive halted. Horace—where was he? The man had accompanied Clive to the establishment that housed the U.N.I.A's London station. Where was he now—still trapped in the realm of sulfur and brimstone? Or returned to the quarters where they had left Sidi Bombay?

There was no way for Clive to find out.

He continued his march, passing through clearings, crossing meadows, but always returning to the woods. This place—this world—might well be a paradise of its own sort, but Clive felt himself growing fatigued, and assaulted by hunger and thirst. He still had no idea where he was, whether this was yet another level of the Dungeon, an exotic realm upon the Earth, or a land of fantasy—even of illusion—into which Baron Samedi had cast him.

He came to a section where the forest was less dense, and where a stream bubbled clear and inviting over a bed of fine sand and small rocks. He halted, lowered himself to the strange, bluish grass, and studied the stream. It *looked* like pure water, but he knew nothing of the local environment, of the life and the materials of this place. For all he knew, the stream did not consist of water at all, but of some deadly chemical that would prove fatal should he imbibe a single sip.

But the Baron Samedi had been friendly. He had helped Clive and his companions on their first encounter in the Dungeon, and he had rescued Clive and Horace from the demons on the trestle in their recent and unexpected reunion. Clive would have to trust that Samedi had not sent him to his death.

He stretched out and plunged his face into the stream. It was cold, pure, delicious! He drank, then splashed his face and hands.

He sat back on his heels, studying the sky. The three suns stretched away from him. He had no means of gauging their distance, but if he assumed they were all of the same size in actuality, he could infer that they stood in direct alignment. This world, this planet, was circling the nearest of the three—that was obvious. Then, depending on the time of year, the nature of the world's day and night would differ.

When the planet was at one end of its orbit, the three suns would appear in line across the sky by day, and would be hidden by the bulk of the planet by night. As the year progressed, the planet would pass between its own sun and that sun's two stellar companions, and true day would alternate with a ghostly false day as the two companion suns rose in what would otherwise be the planet's dark night.

A net descended over Clive's shoulders.

He tried to spring to his feet, but he was held down by the webwork of knotted cords. He twisted, seeking a look at his attacker, but he managed to obtain only a glimpse of pale hands and dark, ruddy cloth before a sack was placed over his head. He redoubled his struggles, then there was a stunning blow and everything was darkness.

He regained consciousness in a room that could have come out of a novel by Sir Walter Scott. Stone walls, vaulted ceilings, flaring torches, giant tapestries. He found himself facing a familiar visage. Raging, he hurled himself to his feet—or tried to, for he was held to a sturdy wooden chair by heavily knotted cords. And he was staring into a chillingly familiar visage.

"N'wrbb Crrd'f!"

"Indeed," the other hissed. "I thought I would never see you again, Clive Folliot. Our previous encounter was unpleasant enough for me."

The man was tall and slim. Even seated as he was, in a great stone seat more throne than chair, he towered above Clive. Now he stood and strode forward, leaning over his captive. His skin was as pale as an albino's. His hair was black with more than a suggestion of midnight green in it. His eyes burned with the brilliance of dark emeralds.

"You took the Lady 'Nrrc'kth from me, Folliot. And now she is . . ."

"Dead," Clive supplied. "Dead in the Dungeon. Lost to us both."

"Yes." N'wrbb Crrd'f nodded. He wore a silky mustache and a thin beard. In thought, he raised a long-fingered hand and slid bejeweled fingers the length of the beard. "Yes, she is dead. There is no way you can return her to me, but I will take some satisfaction from you instead."

He circled Clive's chair. Unable to rise or to use his hands, Clive could only follow his captor with his eyes. Finally N'wrbb Crrd'f stood before Clive once more. "Tell me, Folliot—how did you find me? How did you come to Djajj?"

"That's the name of this place?"

"It is. I thought you knew that."

Clive said nothing.

"I learned a wonderful expression from a fellow native of your world, Folliot. It is, *cat got your tongue?* I fear, I have no cat. But I have a wonderful kennel of dogs, Folliot. Very large, very hungry dogs. Do you like the beasts?"

Clive continued to study his captor. He would say nothing; instead of speaking, his mind raced. *Djajj,* yes, that was the world from which the beautiful 'Nrrc'kth had come to the Dungeon. She had been the captive and unwilling mistress of this N'wrbb Crrd'f. Clive had rescued her from her bondage, had fought and defeated Crrd'f. The Lady 'Nrrc'kth had joined Clive's band in their adventures, had become his own lady love—and had died in the Dungeon.

He had believed Crrd'f dead as well. Instead, here the man had returned to the world called Djajj, and Baron Samedi had sent Clive to that world! Why? Samedi had always been friendly—but he was also notoriously mischievous. And what merrier mischief than to send the unsuspecting Folliot to the world of Djajj!

Clive said, "What do you want, N'wrbb Crrd'f? You've got me at your mercy—at least for the moment! Are you going to do something about it, or are you just going to gloat?"

"Oh, I'm going to do something, my friend. You will not like what I do, but you will not suffer for long. Or from boredom!" The taller man's laughter was harsh.

Crrd'f stretched to his full height and paced once more around Folliot's seat. He paused again, hands clasped before his straggly beard. There was something about him that reminded Clive of a praying mantis. "I have something wonderful in mind for you, Folliot. But I don't want to dirty my hands. I'll have someone else help out."

He turned away and shouted, "Nvv'n! Nvv'n Yrr'll!"

There was a rustling, slithering sound, and from a doorway Clive saw a hideous parody of a man creep into the room. Was he unable to stand and walk like a normal human, or was it merely the fellow's manner that made him creep and twist forward like a snake? He was stocky, with shaggy unkempt hair that ran directly into a filthy, spade-shaped beard. Even across the stone chamber, Folliot could detect the stale odor of burnt weeds that clung to the man's ragged clothing of some pale shade that might once have been crimson.

"Master, master," the creature whined. It knelt before Crrd'f, fawning and cringing.

Unlike Folliot, Crrd'f carried a leather pouch slung by a strap over one shoulder. He opened the pouch and reached inside to draw a scrap of greasy, half-rotted flesh and throw it to the depraved wretch at his feet.

Nvv'n fell to his knees, scooped the disgusting scrap into his mouth, and swallowed noisily. A noisy eructation came from him. "Kind master! Good master!"

Crrd'f placed a heavily booted foot on Nvv'n's back and shoved him toward Folliot. "Put that in the shrinkage machine. And be quick—and I want you out of my sight, filth!"

Clive shouted questions and demands at Crrd'f but the latter had nothing to say. He merely stood, smiling cruelly, as the degenerate Nvv'n dragged Clive, chair and all, through a stone archway.

Folliot was astonished. This was another surprise on top of all the surprises he had already experienced. The chamber in which he found himself was tiled in white and fitted with tables and apparatuses such as he had seen only in the laboratories of natural philosophers at Cambridge.

What was this world of Djajj? It had seemed at first a virtual Eden wherein Clive was a lonely alien. Then he was captured by N'wrbb Crrd'f—or by the latter's unseen henchmen—and brought to a castle out of a past century.

And now . . . now he found himself in a modern laboratory. What had N'wrbb Crrd'f in mind?

The vile Nvv'n giggled and muttered to himself, half-intelligible words that told Clive nothing sensible or useful. Clive could see a strange apparatus on one laboratory table, a peculiar mechanism of glass retorts and metal parts, with a variety of oddly colored fluids and a pair of wires leading to something that he identified only distantly as a galvanic battery.

Nvv'n lifted the cover of a round, opaque container and scooped a handful of ground, greenish-brown strands from it. He packed these into a bowl connected to a thin, hollow tube. There was a flickering flame beneath one of the retorts; Nvv'n used this to draw fire into the bowl of earth-colored strands. He turned and blew a disgustingly odorous cloud at Folliot.

Clive turned his head away, clenched his lips shut, and strove mightily to avoid breathing in the disgusting smoke. But the bestial Nvv'n drew again at his makeshift pipe and sent cloud after cloud of noxious fumes at Clive.

At length, unable to hold his breath any longer, Clive inhaled a single wisp of the smoke. His head grew light. a roaring filled his ears, lights danced and spiraled before his eyes. He felt his stomach clench in an involuntary retching reflex, and all was once more black.

How long a time passed while he was unconscious, he could not tell. Strange dreams came and went, dreams in which the Lady 'Nrrc'kth was restored to him only to die again and again, dreams in which the Frankenstein monster grasped him by the throat and plunged his head time after time into ice-rimed brine, dreams in which detachments of Japanese marines equipped with buzzing aeroplanes attacked Mississippi River steamers.

He did not lapse into a normal slumber and then waken gradually. Instead, from the grips of a nightmare image in which a monstrous Philo Goode and Lorena Ransome batted him back and forth between them like a shuttlecock, he awoke into instant and crystal clarity.

"Being Clive!"

He looked and saw Shriek, the arachnoid alien who had shared so many of his adventures in the Dungeon, but whom he had not seen since his return to Earth and to the London of 1896. "Shriek!" he cried. He reached for the spidery creature and grasped one of its pincers between his hands, as he would have grasped the hand of a long-lost comrade.

Once he would not have reacted so to the alien. Once he would have recoiled in fear and revulsion. But his experiences in the Dungeon had taught Clive Folliot many lessons. Among them was the truth that the appearance of a creature had little to do with its inner nature.

Whereas the cruelly calculating N'wrbb and the disgusting degenerate Nvv'n both looked like men, they were at heart little more than vile beasts. While the spidery Shriek—as well as the half-mechanical Chang Guafe and the doglike Finnbogg—possessed the most admirable of human traits.

"Being Clive," Shriek grated again, "you live! I had abandoned hope for you, yet you live!"

"As do you, Shriek." Even in the dire situation that confronted him, Clive rejoiced. "Where are we now—and what have these beasts done to us?"

The arachnoid made that weird grating sound that passed for her as laughter. "Do I look any different to you, Being Clive, from the way I looked in the Dungeon?"

Folliot studied the arachnoid. He recalled, with a shudder that he hoped was not too visible, Shriek's expressed affection for him. He thought of the bizarre mating ritual of some spiders—perhaps of Shriek's kind—in which the female beheads and devours the male at the completion of their union. Shriek had shown her attraction to Clive, and he had managed as adeptly as he could to repel her advances. He managed to say, "You look just the same to me."

. Shriek made her grating noise again. "And you, to me, Being! But look around you. Has anything changed?"

Clive realized that he was no longer in the laboratory. He had been returned to the chamber in which he had previously confronted N'wrbb Crrd'f. Only he stood on a wooden surface instead of the stone floor of the room. N'wrbb Crrd'f stood near his thronelike seat, smiling maliciously at Clive.

And there was something strange. Clive looked up at

the ceiling, and saw wooden beams and blazing cressets. Only they appeared to be hundreds of feet in the air. He looked at the walls, and they seemed as distant as the stone pilasters and stained-glass windows of a cathedral.

And N'wrbb Crrd'f . . .

N'wrbb Crrd'f strode ponderously toward Clive. Each step seemed to send shock waves through the air, each stride brought Crrd'f closer and made him appear larger and larger until he loomed over Folliot and Shriek like a titan.

He raised a fist the size of a boulder and brought it smashing down on the wooden surface. Clive managed to leap away just in time to avoid being crushed like a mouse beneath a mallet. The wood rebounded at the impact, throwing Clive into the air.

Shriek emitted a bloodcurdling cry and began snatching clusters of barblike hairs from her back. Folliot remembered her ability to alter the chemical content of her own glands and create substances that could produce many reactions in any victim who chanced to be stuck by the barbs.

Screaming at the top of her voice, Shriek hurled cluster after cluster of barbs at the giant hands of N'wrbb Crrd'f. Clive heard Crrd'f shout with pain and rage, saw him dance away, shaking the entire wooden surface with each ponderous step. But now Clive realized that the giant Crrd'f did not stand on the same level with himself and Shriek.

There was an edge to the wooden surface, and Clive ran to reach it. Half a dozen strides from the edge he realized that it was a platform raised many times the height of a man above the stone floor of the chamber. He approached the edge gingerly, careful of losing his footing and toppling from the edge. But before he could reach the edge of the platform he felt a terrible surge of pain. He was literally knocked backward and off his feet. He stood dizzily. Shriek was at his side.

"You understand now, Being Clive?"

"Has N'wrbb Crrd'f become a giant?"

"No, Being Clive. You and I are as mites."

Clive sunk to his haunches, holding his head in despair. "Is there no hope for us, then?"

"Who knows, Being Clive? I was already shrunken when I arrived here. But I have seen N'wrbb Crrd'f and his disgusting lackey Nvv'n shrink others. He throws them to his Finnboggi for sport."

"Finnboggi? He has Finnboggi here? Is *our* Finnbogg here, then?"

Shriek made a gesture that could almost have passed for a shrug. "If he is, he has been so beaten down mentally that he is as a dog. They all are as dogs. I have seen other victims of Crrd'f's treatment . . . some who regain their size, if they live long enough. I think you would regain your size, Being Folliot. I might even regain mine—if he does not shrink us again, and if his Finnboggi do not kill us first."

"They're bloodthirsty, then?"

"I don't know. More likely, playful. But their play—on your own Earth, Being Folliot, did you ever see two puppies playing tug-of-war with a strip of rawhide?"

Clive closed his eyes. "If only there were some way to—to reawaken the intelligence in Finnbogg. I know he is as smart as many a man I have known. But like a dog he is subject to control. When I first met him he was serving as a guardian, serving masters who held him in contempt. But with my friends, he was awakened to his own nature, and he served with us long and well. Now, he is reduced again, almost as if he were a victim of mesmerism."

"You have an idea?"

"All we can do is prepare ourselves. Our opportunity will come, my friend Shriek."

And it was not long before that opportunity came.

The despicable Nvv'n came first. Clive Folliot and Shriek had been kept on the wooden platform—Clive realized that it was nothing more than a tabletop—for days. Nvv'n came each day to throw them scraps of food and to offer them sips of water. Sometimes N'wrbb Crrd'f stood and watched; sometimes he stood close over them, taunting and laughing.

Shriek tore her hair and threw it at him, but N'wrbb Crrd'f dodged aside, laughing all the more. Shriek and Clive together tried to escape from their tabletop prison, but the zone of pain that surrounded it halted them. Even when they tried to hurl themselves through it, leaping from a distance half their own height, the force threw them back.

But today Nvv'n approached them wearing heavy gauntlets. He stood over the table, reached for them from above, and caught Clive first in one gloved hand. With crude skill he held Clive, bound him hand and foot, and dropped him helpless upon the stone floor. Briefly he repeated the exercise, this time making Shriek his victim.

N'wrbb Crrd'f sat in his thronelike chair, gloatingly overseeing the operation.

Now Nvv'n disappeared from the room. There was a sound of snuffling, of claws scratching on flagstone, of baying. Nvv'n reappeared, the leads of half a dozen slavering hounds grasped in his grimy fingers.

"Let the nice doggies go, Nvv'n," N'wrbb Crrd'f purred.

"Uh, yuh, yuh," Nvv'n slobbered. He unsnapped the leads from the collars of the hounds. With a chorus of howls and yelps, the half-dozen dogs, each of them ten times Clive's present height, charged forward.

"They aren't dogs!" Clive exclaimed. "Not real dogs. They're Finnboggi. They've lost their humanity—they've reverted!"

The nearest canine was almost upon Clive and Shriek. Clive twisted from side to side, desperately searching for a weapon—and not finding one. Even bound as he was, if he had a sword or a knife he might free himself and then try to stand off his gigantic attackers. But there was nothing—nothing! It would have to be his bare hands, then. Bare hands, and bound hands at that, against a pack of hounds as big as elephants.

But no—Shriek had weapons of her own! The clumsy-fingered Nvv'n had done a poor job on Shriek, and she was able to writhe and scramble until her claws were free of her bonds. She reached for clusters of quill-like hairs growing on her back. With pincerlike claws she hurled them at the leading hound. The hairs struck with unerring accuracy, planting themselves in the creature's soft, tender nose.

The hound sent up a yowl of pain and terror, screeching to a halt barely a yard from the two small creatures who had been slated for a cruel attack.

A second hound charged into the lead. Again Shriek pulled hairs from her back. Clive knew that the arachnoid alien could control the chemical secretions of her own body. She could choose the chemicals with which the tips of her barbed hairs would be coated, and thereby choose the reaction she would provoke in her enemies.

For a fleeting instant, Clive wondered how Shriek had been captured. More to the point, how she had been held captive, when she might have used her arsenal of emotion-inducing chemicals against the cruel Crrd'f and the drooling, subservient Nvv'n. Perhaps she had been captured unawares and held in a sealed chamber that prevented her from hurling her barbs. Perhaps . . . well, now was not the time to speculate. She *had* been captured, as had Clive, and now was their moment to die—or to escape!

Nvv'n was slobbering, wild-eyed with puzzlement and distress at the backfiring of his master's plan. The nearly mindless servant capered first to one side, then to the other. He made gestures with his hands, repetitive gestures that seemed at first to be meaningless, even mad. But Clive realized that he was in fact patting his clothing, looking around, searching for the pipe and ground material to which he was obviously addicted.

Poor Nvv'n, Clive thought. Double enslaved: to his master N'wrbb Crrd'f and to the foul stuff that he smoked in his pipe!

As for Crrd'f himself, the man was hopping about nearly as wildly as was his brainless lackey. First Crrd'f would yell at Nvv'n to bring the Finnboggi back to the attack, then he would bypass the slobbering dolt and urge on the dogs himself, slapping and shouting at them to attack. He backed away, ran from the room, returned in just seconds with a shortsword, and used it to poke the dogs' rumps, screaming at them to renew their attack.

And the Finnboggi, caught between Shriek's maddening barbs and Crrd'f's poniard, were yelping, cringing, tumbling upon themselves and one another.

What would Clive do to gain advantage of the situation? The tumbling hounds were indistinguishable from one another, but one of them, he hoped, was his own friend Finnbogg. If he could only do something to stop the mad tumbling, to get the attention of the hounds—especially of his friend!—he might yet turn the tables on the wicked Crdd'f and the buffoonish Nvv'n.

Finnbogg had loved songs, Folliot remembered. He'd loved singing. But Clive's mind went blank. Of all the hundreds of hymns, art songs, popular ditties, and soldier's marching tunes he'd ever known, not one could he summon up! Then he remembered. This whole mad adventure in the Dungeon had begun with a visit with his sweetheart to a music hall, as the guest of his friend du Maurier.

The play was *Cox and Box* by Sullivan and Burnand. And there was a tune that Clive had particularly liked, a ditty with lyrics that went around and around in the hearer's head. Yes! They were coming back to him!

In a tiny, piping voice he began to sing:

> *Not long ago, it was my fate,*
> *To captivate a widow*
> *At Ramsgate . . .*

And from one of the Finnboggi, astonishing in its canine yowling and yet clear in every syllable, the counterpoint:

> *I, 'tis odd to state,*
> *The same at Margate did, oh!*

And then Clive and six Finnboggi, in triumphant chorus and glorious harmony, concluded:

> *The happy day came near at length—*
> *We hoped it would be sunny;*
> *I found I needed all my strength*
> *To face the ceremony.*

Shriek had ceased throwing her barbed hairs. The cruel N'wrbb had drawn back, nonplussed. Even the slobbering Nvv'n stood, awestruck.

"Finnbogg!" Clive Folliot cried.

"Folliot!" The canine who had sung most vigorously of all that vigorous chorus leaped to the fore. In one pawlike hand he scooped Clive up and held him before his face. "Clive Folliot, what happened to you!"

Before Clive could reply, Finnbogg looked around, an expression of canine bafflement on his face. "What happened to me? To all of my littermates—to my own mate and our pups?"

"Your littermate and pups?" Clive echoed.

"I wed, Folliot. Of course, you'd never have known. I found my mates, and I wed and sired six splendid pups on my lady-love. Three splendid males, as stout and active as their sire. Three splendid females, as fetching and affectionate as their dam. But—but after that, Folliot, more tragedy befell." He began to croon a mournful dirge, something that Clive recognized as "Addio, Mia Bella Napoli."

And even as Clive watched in amazement, the light of awareness and of recollection brightened in the eyes of all the Finnboggi. Hastily, Finnbogg placed Folliot on the floor near Shriek. Then, as if by plan, the six canines turned in their tracks. A sound unlike any ever before heard by Clive rose from six canine throats. It was an amalgam of grief and rage as six minds, six beings descended from a doglike ancestor but raised to human intelligence and sensitivity, regained the lost awareness of maltreatment meted out to them and their kind, to them and their loved ones.

And before Clive Folliot could so much as move, the Finnboggi had leaped upon N'wrbb Crrd'f. There were cries from the slender man, sobs and pleas for mercy. But there was no mercy.

What Crrd'f had done to the Finnboggi and their kin, Clive Folliot could not know. But what the Finnboggi did to N'wrbb Crrd'f was painful . . . and bloody . . . and final.

When it was over, when all that remained of N'wrbb Crrd'f lay still and steaming before the throne that Crrd'f had himself affected, Finnbogg—the original Finnbogg whom Folliot had met at the bridge on Q'oorna—came to Folliot.

"He made you little, eh?" Finnbogg sniffed at Folliot, then at Shriek. "Made you both little, eh?"

"I—I think Nvv'n was involved, too, old friend."

"Huh—Nvv'n. Nvv'n stupider as slug. Bad Nvv'n, but very stupid. Crrd'f smart. Bad, smart Crrd'f, hurt Finnboggi no more."

· CHAPTER 14 ·
"Your Dinner Had
Grown Cold"

Clive Folliot blinked, shook his head, and gazed around him. The sounds of alien voices and distant places faded from his ears. Although no blinders had been placed before his eyes, the visions he had seen were similarly exotic. He had left this room in company of Horace Hamilton Smythe. With Horace he had visited the London headquarters of the Universal Neighborhood Improvement Association.

With Horace he had visited Hell—and brought about the demise of his rogue cousin, Tomàs—and very nearly perished—and been rescued by the Baron Samedi. He wondered, for a moment, what would become of the soul of a person who had already achieved Hell, and died there. That conundrum he would gladly leave to the theologians.

And from Hell he had been transported to the exotic world of Djajj, home of the green-haired villain he had first met so long ago in the Dungeon. How, he wondered, had he and Horace been transported back to this room? Had Sidi Bombay summoned them by means of some psychic energy?

Would he even have survived his latest trials, had he not previously been tempered in the Dungeon? Had he ever been able to stand up to his elder twin, Neville? Was he ready at last to meet that test?

Clive had grown in the Dungeon. The emotionally stunted and deprived younger brother had come into his own. Yes, he realized—he was ready to face whatever lay ahead.

Rising, Clive said, "Sidi Bombay, Horace Smythe—we have made a terrible mistake."

"Mistake, sah?"

"Yes, Sergeant. I share the blame for it. We all share the blame for it. But I, most of all—for my blood and my position call upon me to furnish leadership, and I have instead awaited the breezes and the buffets of fate to direct my course."

"What do you propose to do then, sah?"

"We have allowed ourselves to be manipulated by the Chaffri and by the Ren, by Father O'Hara and Philo Goode and N'wrbb Crrd'f and by my brother Neville Folliot. N'wrbb Crrd'f is no more—he came to a painful but not undeserved end. Still, my friends, we have suffered, and our companions and allies have suffered and some of them have died."

"I understand your feelings about the Lady 'Nrrc'kth, sah."

"Yes. I shall never forget that lady, and I shall not forgive myself for leading her into the situation that brought about her death. She is avenged, now, I suppose." He closed his eyes and conjured up for a fleeting moment a face of pale grace and tenderness, then banished it with a sigh. "And our other friends, Horace, Sidi," he resumed. "Faithful Finnbogg, Shriek, Chang Guafe. The Baron Samedi—a strange being, but with a noble heart at the last. They, too, I have seen. Horace—you were with me when I saw Baron Samedi."

"Aye, sah—that I was! And a welcome sight the fellow was, for all that he's an odd one! But for the Baron and his magical cheroot, you and I would have been meat for those winged demons, I'll take my oath on that, sah!"

Clive nodded. "And my own descendant, Annabelle Leigh. Where is she now? Horace Smythe, Sidi Bombay—where is she now?"

Before either could reply, Clive resumed. "We must take the initiative, my friends. We must not wait for the enemy to attack, for our friends and allies to cry out for our assistance. What we must do is strike to the heart of the problem. We must carry the attack to our foes."

He rose to his full height and shot a piercing look into

the faces of his companions. "Whatever weapons may be turned against us, we must not flinch! Neither fang nor claw nor venomous barb shall halt us!"

Sidi Bombay said, "What do you propose, then, Major Clive Folliot? And might I ask, Major—where have you been?"

Clive smiled. "I stepped out with Sergeant Smythe for a few moments of relaxation at a neighborhood pub. Would you not agree with me, Horace?"

"Yes, sah. But I might say, sah—we had a hellish time leaving the establishment."

The two Englishmen, one of noble birth and one of penurious farm stock, shared a hearty laugh.

Sidi Bombay looked on in puzzlement.

"But after we left the hot region, courtesy of Baron Samedi and his magical cheroot," Horace Smythe said, "I found myself back here, while you, sah, did not return for some time."

"Some time indeed," Sidi Bombay interjected in an annoyed tone. "In addition to the investigation in which I engaged myself during your absence, I also prepared a repast for the three of us, to be consumed upon your return. Your dinner had grown cold before your return, Clive Folliot. Where were you in the interim?"

"Indeed, sah!" Horace Smythe added. "Where were you for all that time?"

"You never were able to locate our lost companions, were you, Sidi Bombay?"

The Indian shook his head sadly. "I was not, Clive Folliot. I do not know whether the limitation lies within the mechanism at hand, or within my own poor intellect. Perhaps with unlimited time in which to work . . ."

"Perhaps my descendant Annabelle Leigh could solve the problem with one of her—now, what was the term she used? Yes! One of her drygoods schedules." He squeezed his eyes shut in concentration. "No, not drygoods schedules—*software programs*, that was the term she used. But she is not here either."

"We did see Baron Samedi," Horace Smythe said. "And the Major's distant cousin Tomàs. I think we shall never see Cousin Tomàs again—and good riddance say I. Begging the Major's forgiveness, sah."

"Losing a kinsman is never a happy event, Horace. But in this case, I cannot truthfully claim any great sense of bereavement."

"As for Baron Samedi," Smythe continued, "why, that gentleman says that he visits the Earth now and then. If any of us ever set foot upon the island of Hayti—a tropic paradise, I believe it to be, covered with lush rain forests from primeval times—we might encounter him there. Or even in the American city of New Orleans."

"At the moment Samedi waved his cheroot, Horace," Clive said, "do you recall your final thought before leaving Hades?"

"I thought of the London station of the U.N.I.A, Major. In fact, as I recall it, sah, I had quite a vivid mental image of the front door of the establishment."

"Indeed." Clive nodded. "And that was where you found yourself, I should think."

"Yes, sah."

"Whence you returned here directly?"

"I stepped back inside the pub for a moment, sah. In fact, I stayed for a while in hopes of Your Majorship's own return."

"Yes. I would imagine that you even partook of a sip of the establishment's wares. No, there's no need for excuses." He held up a hand, precluding a rush of explanation. "I did not return there, so in due course you returned here. Is that correct, Horace?"

"It is, sah."

Clive paced in a circle, the energy of concentrated thought translating itself to physical movement. "At the moment that Baron Samedi waved his cheroot, I was thinking of Finnbogg. And I found myself transported to the world where Finnbogg was at that very moment."

"His home world, Clive Folliot?" Sidi Bombay's interest had clearly been piqued.

"No, Sidi Bombay. He was on the planet Djajj—the original home of N'wrbb Crrd'f and the Lady 'Nrrc'kth. Finnbogg was there, and so also was our old friend Shriek. Both were prisoners of N'wrbb Crrd'f. By the time I left there, both were free—and the unspeakable crimes of N'wrbb Crrd'f had been avenged upon their perpetrator!"

"But how did you return here, Clive Folliot? And where are Shriek and Finnbogg now?"

Clive shrugged. "I cannot answer either question, Sidi Bombay, with assurance. Although I would guess—and only guess—that since I was returned to Earth, then Shriek and Finnbogg are now back upon their own respective planets. I cannot tell for certain."

There was a long silence in the room. The mechanisms that filled so much of it flickered and glowed in their own arcane rhythms. Outside, in the streets of modern London, Clive Folliot could imagine the sights and sounds and smells of a million men and women, horses and dogs and cats, steam railroads and iron-wheeled drays.

Victoria was yet monarch of the island realm and its far-flung empire. England was secure, her people prosperous and happy, and quite unworried about Chaffri or Ren or Gennine, traitors menacing her from within and invaders threatening her from without. England was powerful and serene.

Only those few who knew the secrets of the Dungeon knew how fragile was that power, how deceptive that serenity.

It would be easy for Clive Folliot to part with Sidi Bombay and Horace Hamilton Smythe. He could announce himself to British society as the long-lost African explorer, returned at last to his motherland. He would have to find a way to appear older than he did now, so that the discrepancy between his physical condition and his putative age might not arouse embarrassing questions. If the problems of reemergence grew too great, he could emigrate to Canada or Australia or some other of Her Majesty's distant possessions, and make a new life for himself.

But he would know all the while that England was in peril. Not merely England, but all of the Empire—all of the Earth—and even more! At any hour, at any moment, some agent of the Dungeon might strike. No—he could not escape his responsibility. He could not escape his opportunity.

"What lies behind all of our experiences in the Dungeon?" he asked his companions. And without waiting for a reply, he answered his own question: "The spiral of stars!"

Horace Smythe nodded. "You're right on that score, sah!"

"And if we were to travel to the heart of the spiral of stars—what do you think we would find there?"

"I don't know, sah," Smythe replied.

"It has never been done, Clive Folliot," Sidi Bombay added.

"I am not surprised to hear that," Clive said. "We have spent our energies in combat with henchmen. Divide and rule, that has been the policy of the enemy. And he has succeeded. He has set us at each other's throats, fighting, killing, imprisoning, and torturing one another. Every act of cruelty has created enmity and hatred and a desire for revenge. So it has ever been. Hittites against Egyptians, Hebrews against Philistines, Romans against Christians. The Spanish against the Incas—ah, there was one of the noblest of Man's endeavors, set upon, betrayed, and destroyed by greedy despoilers acting in the name of God! How many sins have been committed in the name of God!"

Clive shook his head. "Roundheads against Royalists here in England, the Union against the Confederacy in America. Wellington against Napoléon in our parents' day, Hannibal against Scipio in our ancestors', and doubtless there will be war, war, war in our descendants' day as well."

"So it has always been, Major. Ever since Cain slew Abel!"

"But why, Sergeant, *why?*"

"It's human nature, sah. Warfare and killing—it fits in with Mr. Darwin's theories of evolution. When nations battle, the strong and the clever survive. The weak and the stupid perish. It's cruel, sah, that I will admit, but it strengthens and purifies the breed."

"I cannot agree," Sidi Bombay interrupted.

"But I've seen you fight, Sidi! At my side, and at the risk of your own life for the savin' of mine! I'm grateful as an Englishman can be, Sidi, but your actions go against your words."

"I have fought when it was needful, my friend Horace, but such has not been my choice. And as for the notion that the weak and the stupid perish while the strong and the clever survive . . ." The Indian shook his head sadly.

"Well, what d'yer mean, Sidi?"

"Who goes to war, friend Horace. Betwixt two brothers—I make no reference to yourself and Neville Folliot, friend Clive—if one is powerful, courageous, active, whilst his sibling is a weakling and a coward, I ask you, Horace, which will go to war? Which is the more likely to die?"

"Well—but—but—" Smythe sputtered.

"The courageous brother will go to war, and in all likelihood he will lose his life. While the cowardly brother, remaining at home, will survive and marry and father children. Thus, according to your famous Monk Mendel and your Mr. Darwin as well, the race will grow weak and cowardly as the strong and the courageous are weeded out. Not the other way around, Horace. Oh, no, not the other way around."

Clive nodded in agreement. "What you suggest then, Sidi Bombay, is that war does not strengthen and purify the species, but serves rather to weaken and degrade it."

"Precisely, friend Clive."

"I won't quarrel," Horace Hamilton Smythe said. "You're a devilishly clever fellow, Sidi. Sometimes I think you missed your calling—you should have been a barrister!"

"Oh, no! As Dick the butcher said in your great Shakespeare's play, 'The first thing we do, let's kill all the lawyers.' No, a barrister I would not be, Horace."

"We digress!" Clive broke in. The others acted as if they were ashamed of themselves. "Intellectual discourse. Mr. Darwin, Monk Mendel, Shakespeare—all have their place, but I fear that London life has made you both soft and passive. You intellectualize, quarreling like a pair of Hebrews over their Talmud, when you should act!"

Horace, stung, returned, "An' what has it done for you, sah?"

"I have not lived a London life, my friends. Not these past years. It is life in the Dungeon that has shaped me.

That has made me hard, that has turned me, all against my will and my innate nature, into a man of action!"

He pounded fist into palm, stalking angrily.

"It is the Gennine who stand behind the Chaffri and the Ren alike. It is the Gennine, from all that we have been able to learn, who created the Dungeon. It is the Gennine, acting through Chaffri and Ren and doubtless through other forces and agents down through the ages, on the Earth and on Djajj and on the worlds of Chang Guafe and Finnbogg and Shriek and on what other worlds we know not and about which we can hardly even guess, who have fostered suffering and conquest and war."

He stood with his back to the others, gathering his thoughts. When he was ready, he turned once more to face them both.

"It is the Gennine who are responsible for the death of the Lady 'Nrrc'kth, who have worked unspeakable changes upon my brother and father, who have done I know not what to my own dearest great-great-granddaughter Annabelle."

Horace Hamilton Smythe and Sidi Bombay looked at each other. They exchanged low, grumbling words.

"It is the Gennine whom we must confront, my friends." Clive spoke with passion. "And their home, I believe, lies at the center of the spiraling stars. Somehow we must get there. If we must walk, Horace, Sidi, we will get there!"

· CHAPTER 15 ·
By Cab to the Stars

"We can get there, Major, sah," Sergeant Smythe said. "And we won't have ter walk, neither."

"How, Sergeant?"

"The Major is familiar with the space-train, I know, sah."

"All too familiar. The monster created by Dr. Frankenstein is still aboard it, as far as I know. And we all saw it during its visit to the polar sea."

"Yes, sah, we did indeed. Well, that is as it may be, but there's more than one such train. There's a lot of 'em, connecting this and that point in the universe, sah. They don't just go everywhere, you see, sah. 'Tisn't like walkin' about in a clear field, you see. Even though the train don't use tracks like a steam railway, it's still a lot like one. It can only go on certain paths. There's obstacles and forces, like reefs and currents that stop a ship from goin' just anywhere."

"Yes, I understand, Sergeant Smythe."

"But there's also little cars that can run, well, like dinghies, y'see, Major. Small boats, as it were, that can go where a great ocean liner could never go."

"I believe I traveled in one such when I went to Tewkesbury."

"Like as not yer did, sah. They runs 'em, sometimes, on actual railway tracks. But that's just for convenience, sah. They can go pretty near anywhere. I reckon there's places the little cars can't go, either, but they can go a lot more places than the great trains can!"

"And they can travel through time as well as space?"

"Oh, yes, sah."

"There is a young man in Zurich, but recently arrived there from Pavia in order to attend the technical institute," Sidi Bombay put in. "Little more than a boy, Major, but a great mind already, whose thoughts will someday change the world. This boy believes that time and space are but aspects of the same essence. If we can travel in one, then why can we not travel in the other?"

"I've no quarrel with that—considering that I have come back to an England a quarter-century after leaving it, yet having lived but three or four years whilst away! Have we one of these little cars?"

"Sah—we have!"

They made their way from the hidden room, along a passageway and onto a platform similar to that beneath the saloon where Clive had previously seen Philo B. Goode and—seemingly—Horace Smythe.

"Is this corridor connected to others of its sort?" Clive asked.

"Yes, sah."

"The platform, the tracks where Annabelle and I boarded a car—whence we traveled to Tewkesbury?"

Again, Horace agreed.

"I don't understand, then. The Chaffri, the Ren, the organization that you men represent—"

"The Universal Neighborhood Improvement Association, Major Folliot," Sidi Bombay said.

"They all use the same tracks? The same system of transportation? And yet they are mortal foes?"

"Stranger things have happened, Major Folliot. Enemies who trade in wartime, rivals who conduct business at the same time that they strive for each other's destruction."

"If the Major will just climb aboard, sah." Smythe opened a door for Clive, in the side of a car similar to the one Clive had previously shared with Annabelle Leigh.

"Are we likely to be attacked?" Clive asked.

"Were you before, sah?"

Clive recounted the battle he and Annie had survived en route to Tewkesbury.

"They are everywhere," Sidi Bombay said.

"The Major is quite sure," Smythe queried, "quite sure

that the bodies of the soldiers faded from existence? They didn't remain behind, they weren't carried away by their comrades? They dissolved before the Major's eyes?"

"Precisely."

"And the survivors, sah—you say they climbed an invisible stairway and disappeared into the sky?"

"As nearly as their actions can be described, Sergeant Smythe, that is exactly what they did. I can assure you that the sight was an uncanny one—an uncanny one to my eye, even after all the strange events I experienced in the Dungeon!"

"Strange indeed. What do you make of it, Sidi?"

"I know of but one explanation. Ordolite ghosters. Does the Major know of ordolite ghosters?"

"A bit, Sidi Bombay. I learned of them on the eighth level of the Dungeon."

"Then you are aware, Major Folliot, that these ghosters are not precisely *ghosts* in the sense that our Earthly superstitions define ghosts. They are projections, phantom beings. They are simulacra of a sort, and yet not quite living simulacra. They are . . . material essences."

"So they are."

"Does the Major know the power needed to give ordolite ghosters their being?"

"The blood of a Folliot, willingly given."

"Yes. And which Folliot would willing give his blood to the Chaffri—or the Ren—for the creation of ordolite ghosters?"

"Willingly, Sidi Bombay, I would say that no Folliot would do that. Not even my brother Neville."

"Perhaps the word *willingly* is not precisely correct, Major. If a loved one were threatened, a Folliot or any man might yield voluntarily that which he would never give, under normal circumstances."

"Then you are suggesting that the troopers that Annabelle and I encountered were ordolite ghosters, powered by Folliot blood."

"When the blood is given, the donor dies. This is the way that ordolite machines work, Major. Not some of the blood, but *all* of it must be given. Still, once the donor has

died, he may be restored. That is up to the operators—
Chaffri or Ren."

"Still," Clive countered, "the secrets of life and death
are matters not to be tampered with lightly. Once dead, if
the Folliot is restored to life by mechanical means, is he
truly alive? Can the divine spark be resummoned once it
has departed, or is the Folliot restored merely to the
appearance of life? Is he once again a man cast in the
image of God, or is he what the inhabitants of the island of
Hayti call a *zombie*?" Clive shuddered.

Sidi Bombay lifted his shoulders in a curiously arresting
gesture. "Who can say, Clive Folliot? Unless one experiences this strange phenomenon, this death and restoration
to life, how can one know? And further, this is the great
paradox of the ordolite process. The blood, once given,
can be used to power great numbers of ordolite ghosters."

"I supppose, then," Clive said, "the same Folliot might
be impelled to yield up his blood and his life time after
time. Whole armies of ordolite ghosters could be created."

"So they might, sah," Horace Smythe said. "So they
might. And yet, if the sacrificed Folliot were restored as a
zombie rather than a true man, might his blood be ruined
for this use? Eh, Sidi Bombay?" He smiled, turning to the
Indian. "Another nice conundrum for you, ain't it?"

Clive shuddered. He had delayed them long enough
with his questioning. He climbed into the car, followed by
Sidi Bombay and Horace Hamilton Smythe. Sergeant
Smythe slid the transparent-paneled door shut. The three
men were seated on a cushioned lounge. It was, Clive
noted, almost identical to the one in the other car. He
wondered if this lounge, too, held a cache of weapons.

Guided by the steady hand of Sidi Bombay, the car slid
away from its platform and hissed softly into a black-walled
tunnel. Specks of light flashed by, as small as atoms and as
brilliant as flares. Illuminated patches moved past them in
a blur, so rapidly and so puzzlingly that it was impossible
to determine whether they were blobs of luminosity mere
inches away or nebular formations of stars millions of
miles from Earth.

The car swooped dizzyingly from side to side, and rose
and dipped without warning, setting Clive's stomach into

gyrations. Clive peered through the glasslike walls of the car, trying to discern features within the tunnel. From time to time it seemed that the track divided, and Clive could see passages leading off in incomprehensible directions.

Tunnels that led to . . . what? The mind faltered as it attempted to guess what cities of wonder or abysses of terror lay at the end of this passageway or that.

"Are we stil beneath London?" Clive inquired.

"Just a bit longer, sah," Horace Smythe called over his shoulder.

"And then, Sergeant Smythe?"

"We're doing what the Major said he wanted, sah. We're headed for the den of the Gennine."

But despite Horace Smythe's words, the car continued to plummet through tunnels as black as pitch, illuminated only periodically by luminous points and patches.

Once Clive caught a clear glimpse down a side tunnel and sprang upright with startlement. "Sergeant! Sidi Bombay! I could swear I saw a railroad tunnel, complete with London transportation cars and well-dressed travelers!"

"The Major is correct," Sidi Bombay announced laconically. "Not so very long ago, the London Underground was being constructed. I myself earned my shillings and pence by the sweat of my brow and the strength of my muscles, wielding a pickaxe in that enterprise," he added with a laugh.

"That project had barely begun when last I left the metropolis."

"And it is not finished yet, Clive Folliot."

"Did the workmen never break into this—this *other* network of tunnels—by error?"

"Several times."

"Then all of London must know of the Universal Neighborhood Improvement Association—and of the Chaffri and the Ren!"

"By no means, Major. We spoke before of bitterest enemies cooperating in what they find to be their mutual interest. So it is with this network of tunnels, and the concealment of these tunnels from the mundane world. Methods were used to . . . convince those who discovered our tunnels that they had accidentally penetrated ancient peat mines, burial barrows, or natural air pockets. They closed the passages and proceeded with their business. The few places where we can see into their tunnels, they cannot see into ours—or, if they do, they become convinced that they are seeing something altogether ordinary and workaday. They look, and they turn away uninterested, and they go about their business."

Clive shook his head. He peered through the forward panel of the car, over Sergeant Smythe's shoulder. Smythe, having abandoned the identity of Count Splitofsky, had resumed the costume of the nearsighted Maurice Carstairs the Younger. His walking stick lay on a cushioned seat at his side. His spectacles had been placed in a pocket of his frock coat, but he peered clear-eyed through the front of the car.

Looking ahead, Clive started. A shape! It looked vaguely human, suggestive of the armored warriors he and Annabelle had encountered near Tewkesbury. Clive began to sound the warning, but before he could utter more than half a syllable, the car had borne down upon the white form.

It shattered and splashed like a great oversized blob of sleet, spattering the angular sides of the car, flowing over the glass and past it.

Clive turned to peer behind the car. The form had regathered itself and was gesturing angrily after the car and its occupants. "That—what was that?"

"An ordolite ghoster, Major."

"It was unharmed by our impact upon it?"

"And we by its impact upon us."

"But Annabelle and I shot several of the armed troopers."

"You were using ordolite weapons, then, Major. You must have been. We've a stock of them in the car here!"

As if in response to a cue, Sidi Bombay lifted a cushioned seat and revealed a miniature arsenal. After passing weapons the size of carbines to Clive and Horace, he slung another such over his own shoulder.

Horace patted his weapon with one hand. "So much for universal peace and brotherhood, eh, Sidi?"

"War is an evil thing, Horace, and imperfect men commit evil deeds. I am neither proud nor eager to kill any being, but what one must do, one does. And one accepts the responsibility for one's acts."

A trio of luminous blobs appeared far ahead of the car.

"These . . . ordolite weapons . . . will work against the ghosters? The weapons will kill these creatures?" Clive asked.

"In effect they will, Major. Since the ghoster is not truly alive, of course, it is not exactly true to say that it is killed. But it is destroyed."

"And the ghosters have similar weapons, that will work against us—against solid, mortal, material beings?"

"Indeed. And since we are alive, we can truly be killed!"

"Then look ahead, Sidi Bombay!"

The three blobs—ordolite ghosters—were fleeing along the tunnel. Their speed was less than that of the car, and as a consequence the car was gradually overtaking them—but it was doing so at a snail-like pace. It seemed altogether possible that the car might strike them without shattering them as it had the previous ghoster.

Horace Hamilton Smythe pressed the car to its maximum speed.

The ghosters accelerated as well, using some principle of movement unknown to Clive. They had limbs and extremities, but they did not run along the tunnel floor so much as they floated above it. Floated and . . . *flowed*.

The car overtook them and the ghosters passed through its transparent forward panels.

Sidi Bombay had unslung his weapon and fired it at a ghoster. As had happened when Clive and Annabelle fought the troopers near Tewkesbury, no projectile sped from the ordolite weapon. Instead a beam of pure energy, pulsating and emitting light of a lurid, unnameable shade, shot from the muzzle of the weapon.

One of the ghosters faded from being.

Another of them was upon Clive. Rather than firing its weapon at him, the creation chose to envelope Clive, swarming over him and covering him like a thin layer of icy mist. It grew colder and more dense. Clive felt that he was simultaneously smothering and freezing.

Through the translucent ghoster he could see Horace Hamilton Smythe confronting the third visitant. Even as

Clive watched, both Horace and the ordolite creature struck gnarled studs on the stocks of their weapons and knifelike projections sprang bayonetlike from the tips of the weapons.

Before Clive's helpless eyes, Horace and the ghoster engaged in a deadly alternation of parry and thrust.

One lunged forward.

The other dodged inside, striking with the butt of his weapon.

The first whirled, lowering his head, butting at the other's face.

The second blocked the blow, brought his piece down stock-first to strike the other on the back of his skull.

Sidi Bombay stood watching, nearly as helpless as Clive.

Horace Smythe and the ordolite ghoster tumbled to the floor. Their impact shook the car and knocked them apart.

For a moment only, the ghoster was separated from Horace Hamilton Smythe. But in that moment Sidi Bombay brought his own ordolite carbine to bear, sending a bolt of glowing energy into the ghoster.

With a single grunt of pain and an audible sigh of despair, the ghoster faded from visibility.

Sidi Bombay reached for the disheveled Horace Hamilton Smythe, tugging him to his feet. The ghoster's carbine had faded along with its owner. Horace's lay harmless on the floor. Together, Sidi Bombay and Horace Smythe faced Clive Folliot.

Clive's field of vision was turning red. Through it he caught a last glimpse of the horror that marked the visages of his two sworn blood brothers. There was a ringing in Clive's ears, and he could feel himself beginning to lose consciousness.

He tumbled to the floor. He could see no more. But even through the rubbery clamminess of the ghoster he could feel the sharp blade of Horace Hamilton Smythe's ordolite bayonet.

At the risk of his flesh Clive seized the blade. It slid through the rubbery material of the ghoster and penetrated Clive's palm. He felt a moment of pain and then the hot pulsation of his own blood. He dropped the bayonet.

But it was as if his entire being were bathed in flame—a

flame that produced an agony unimaginable in all Clive's previous life, yet one that cleansed and purified and re-- stored him. A scream filled his ears and he was unable to tell whether it was his own voice shouting in triumph or tha of the despairing ordolite ghoster which had until this moment covered every inch of his being.

For a fraction of an instant he caught sight of himself in the glasslike wall of the car. He had staggered to his feet and now his reflection blazed at him like a human torch.

The ordolite ghoster was gone.

It was Clive's blood, he realized, that had destroyed the ghoster. Folliot blood, he remembered, was the powering principle of the ordolite ghoster machines—but it had to be blood willingly given. Blood taken without the consent of the donor was fatal to these strange, unliving creatures. It was Clive's blood that had destroyed the ghoster and saved his own life.

Clive leaned his head against the forward wall of the car. A shudder passed through his torso. With each gasped breath his body was regaining control.

"Will we encounter more of those?" he managed to ask his companions.

"We will encounter far worse than those," Sidi Bombay declaimed solemnly. "We will encounter creatures that will make the Major recall these ordolite ghosters with fondness."

Clive retrieved his carbine. He seated himself and began to study the weapon. It was a fascinating device, its stock smooth, and formed in a manner he had never before encountered. He held it to his shoulder and sighted along it. It was possessed of an aiming device such as he had never seen before. Even when he and Annie had faced the troopers near Tewkesbury, the battle had been so frantically fought and so quickly ended that he had lacked the time to examine his weapon.

And on this occasion, his scrutiny of the ordolite carbine was interrupted by the voice of Horace Hamilton Smythe.

"Better hold on, sah. We're about to leave the Earth."

Clive slung the carbine over his shoulder and clung with both hands to a nearby railing, preparing for the car to rise precipitously and plunge from the mouth of the tunnel, up into the sky.

Instead, with a stomach-sickening *whoosh*, it tipped forward. The tunnel in which they had been traveling took by far the steepest dip it had yet done. In less than a second it seemed that they were plunging straight toward the center of the Earth.

"Are we not headed for the spiral of stars?" Clive shouted at Horace.

"That we are, sah!" the sergeant hollered back over his shoulder.

"Then why are we headed downward instead of upward?"

"Things are not what they seem, Major!"

That was all Smythe had to say, and further questions from Clive brought no response from either him or Sidi Bombay.

Air screamed around the car, and the patches and points of light—nebular galaxies or luminous fungoids, blazing stars or glowing sparks—flashed past at dizzying speed.

Without warning the screaming ceased.

But the lights did not disappear.

Instead, a breathtaking panorama spread before Clive's eyes. He saw—or thought he saw—the sun itself, blazing and flaring in solitary majesty. But this was not the sun as seen at noonday, a ball of brilliant white against a field of sparkling blue. Nor was it the pallid disk of a watery English afternoon, nor the glorious orange flare of a mid-summer's dawn.

This was the naked sun, a seething globe of white-hot gases standing against the blackness of the void. At first, Clive's eyes were unable to cope with its brilliance. Clive looked away, the afterimage of the sun still roiling, it seemed, against the insides of his eyelids.

Then he saw the worlds, and their moons, and the asteroidal worldlets and soaring comets, and the distant suns and nebulae in brilliant white and yellow and cream. And somehow he imagined that he could sense still more planets and suns and nebulae, black worlds and black stars whose radiance lay far outside the normal band of human vision, but whose reality he could not deny.

Perhaps Q'oorna was such a world, and perhaps he was gazing even now upon the Dungeon.

He scanned the sky for the telltale spiral of points of glimmering white. Somewhere, he knew, they glittered and whirled. Somehow, he knew, he had to go there.

· CHAPTER 16 ·
Expedition from Earth

"Look ahead there, sah!"

It was the voice of Horace Hamilton Smythe, breaking in as it had done so many times upon Clive Folliot's reverie. The sergeant was pointing at a region of space ahead of the car and somewhat above it.

"Is it the world of the Gennine?"

"Not nearly, sah! It's the belt of asteroids, or planetoids to give 'em their proper name. Not little stars, they are, sah, but little worlds. Little worlds! Hundreds of 'em! Thousands!"

"I never knew such existed, Smythe! What distant star are we circling?"

"Our own star, sah. Our own! The asteroids circle the sun forever, fragments of a planet that may once have existed or that may never have come into being. No one knows the answer to that one, sah, but here they are nevertheless."

Sidi Bombay stepped past Clive and touched Horace Smythe on the shoulder. "Look thither, O brother. Thy lecture may impart knowledge more precious than pearl, but peril, not pearl, is our fate!"

He pointed, and both Horace and Clive gazed through the transparent roof of the car. Clive could feel his hand throbbing where the ordolite bayonet had punctured his skin. He was grateful for the semi-accident that had destroyed the enveloping ghoster and saved his own life, but he worried now that his wound would become infected. What strange effect might result from the cut he had incurred!

He peered at the wound. It was a small one, coinciding with the lifeline on the palm of his hand. It was no longer bleeding, nor had serious swelling developed. Still, he was not pleased with the color of the wound, nor with the throbbing, pulsing sensation that radiated up his arm from it.

"Sidi, Horace," he began, "does either of you know—"

But he got no further. A distant something glinted in the light of the even more distant sun. "What was that?" Clive gasped.

"Looks like a Ren ship!" Horace snapped back.

"Ren ship? You mean a space-train? Or a separate car like this one?"

"Not exactly, sah! Haven't time to explain! Sidi, man the mortar!"

To Clive's astonishment, Sidi Bombay could be seen once more opening the seat that revealed the little car's miniature arsenal. He removed a weapon with a tubular barrel and a heavy base-plate closely resembling the mortars with which Clive had become familiar while serving in Her Majestey's Horse Guards.

"Is that really a mortar?" Clive exclaimed.

Sidi Bombay said, "Of a sort, it is, Major Folliot."

"But you'll blow out the roof of our car if you fire it."

"The Major forgets that ordolite weapons fire bolts of pure energy, not material objects. The purpose of the mortar tube is to focus that energy so that it does no harm to our own car, but has its desired effect on that against which it is fired."

Clive bided his time, watching Sidi set up the mortar. It was obvious that he knew exactly what he was doing, and was an expert at his task. To offer assistance—interference! —would have been worse than useless.

Through the transparent wall of the car, Clive could see the Ren ship growing closer. It was unlike their own.

"It reminds me somehow of Chang Guafe!" Clive exclaimed, peering past Horace Hamilton Smythe.

"How's that, sah?"

"It looks like—like a combination of a machine and a living thing. Look, Horace! It has antennae and claws like a crab's! It's changing, shifting its shape even as it approaches us!"

"Yes, sah! I'm familiar with Ren ships, sah!"

"You must have learned this during the years we were separated, Horace! And yet you appear no older than you did when last we saw each other on the eighth level!"

"You're right about that, sah!" was Smythe's laconic reply.

"But how can that be, Horace? Both my brother and my father have aged normally, as had my friend du Maurier, to the very brink of the grave."

"If I may explain, please," Sidi Bombay put in. "As one who has both aged and grown young, I have some understanding, perhaps." When neither Clive nor Horace demurred, Sidi Bombay continued. "Sergeant Smythe and I have lived our lives in spurts, one might say. Like a flat stone skipped across the face of a pond, Clive Folliot—am I expressing myself clearly enough?"

"I'm not sure that you are, Sidi Bombay. I'm not sure that I take your point."

"Well, you see, Clive Folliot, the stone may cross a pond a rod or more in width, while actually touching the surface of the water a few times, skipping onward each time. Thus Sergeant Smythe and I have skipped over the years, dropping in now and then to accomplish such tasks as were needed. You were away from the Earth for twenty-eight years—we have been away only for a few years at a time, but have spanned the same twenty-eight years all told."

Behind Clive there was a *thump* and a *whoosh*. He could detect a strange odor in the car, and inferred that it was an ordolite propellant substance.

Above the car a blob of energy arced through the black sky. Clive tried to follow its course. At first it was easy enough. The blob was a brilliant magenta in color, and it pulsed and glowed even as it flew away from their car.

The magenta blob writhed and turned visibly, as if it were a thing alive. Although it made no detectable sound, Clive had the impression that it was hissing like an angry panther. It swooped toward the Ren craft.

The Ren craft dodged to avoid the blob.

The magenta blob altered its course to pursue the craft.

The blob, sizzling and throwing off specks and fragments like a Guy Fawkes Day rocket, flew past the Ren ship.

The Ren ship, meanwhile, slid toward the car containing Clive and his companions. It flexed its external claws, opening and closing their pincers, showing their razor-sharp serrated edges.

Behind Clive, Sidi Bombay fired another round of ordolite ammunition from the mortar.

This time the ordolite ray coalesced into a blob of brilliant yellowish-green. The distinctive odor smote Clive's nostrils, and the sound each time the mortar was fired left Clive with a ringing in his ears. As he regained hearing he said, "They aren't firing back. Perhaps their intentions are peaceful."

Horace Hamilton Smythe growled. "Might be, might not be, sah. Take a look at that thing, eh, sah?" He pointed toward the Ren craft. It was impossible to tell whether the mixture of organism and mechanism was truly glaring hatefully at the transparent car. Perhaps the bulging, reflective features that looked like eyes were merely observation ports.

Perhaps not.

In any case, they gave the appearance of hate-filled, intelligent eyes.

"We are far beyond the Earth's atmosphere," Clive said. "Do you know where the Ren came from, Horace? Are they from another world circling our own sun, or are they from a more distant locale?"

"We don't know their home, sah! We—" Horace paused, pointing in horror at the Ren craft.

It had voided both rounds fired from the ordolite mortar. Now it was nearly upon the transparent car. It altered its position, upending itself so that its rearmost segment was exposed, moving toward the car.

It was shaped like the hindquarter of a scorpion—a curving, segmented organ with a barbed protuberance at its tip. Were the Ren ship truly a scorpion, the barb would have been coated with deadly venom. As it was . . . who could guess?

Horace threw the control lever of the car to the side, and the little craft dipped and swooped away from the scorpion-tail of the Ren.

Clive tumbled against a glass panel.

Sidi Bombay swung the morter away, so Clive would not collide with it. "Be careful, Clive Folliot! If we lose the services of our ordolite weapon, we are in peril even more grave than that which we already face!"

Through the glass panel, Clive could see the Ren's scorpion-tail twitch convulsively. A glowing blob detached itself from the barbed stinger and flew sizzling toward the car.

Horace Smythe jockeyed the controls, swinging the car through a series of evasive gyrations.

The luminescent blob—an angry, glowing orange—sped past. So close to the glass did its course carry it that Clive could make out individual sparks and tails of flame flickering across its surface. Again, while there was no audible sound, it seemed to Clive that the ordolite energy-blob hissed its hatred in some psychic manner as it sped past the car.

"What would happen if it struck us?" Clive asked. "Would it envelop our ship as the ordolite ghoster enveloped me in the tunnel?"

"It would do something worse than that, Clive Folliot. It could penetrate our car's wall as the rounds from our own mortar penetrate that wall. Once inside the car, it would disperse its evil, destructive energy into our bodies."

"Would it kill us?"

"Only if we were fortunate beyond belief. More likely it would—perhaps it is better not to say, Major Folliot."

"Tell me, damn it! Tell me, Sidi Bombay!"

"It would kill only our minds. Our wills. It would turn us into hopeless slaves of the Ren. We would obey them because we would lack the force to place our own choices above their commands. That is what the ordolite would do to us, Clive Folliot. To Sergeant Smythe and myself, at any rate."

"But not me? It wouldn't do that to me?"

"You are of the Folliot blood, Major. You might be exempt from its malign influence. There is no knowing without testing, and it seems foolish at this moment to make that test."

"I might not react to the ordolite at all?"

"Or you might be—you just might be, Major Folliot—the Master of the Ordolite!"

Before Clive could demand an explanation of that extraordinary term, the car in which the three adventurers were traveling was filled with a new light so brilliant that it dazzled the eyes. Clive threw a hand before his face. When he sensed that the flash of light had ended, he lowered his arm and opened his eyes again.

Afterimages danced dizzyingly. He blinked and caught a glimpse of Horace Hamilton Smythe struggling frantically with the car's controls. Facing about, he saw Sidi Bombay clutching the mortar tube. The car bucked violently. Clive grasped a handhold to keep from being thrown against one of his companions.

"What happened?"

Horace Smythe concentrated on the controls of the car, unspeaking.

Sidi Bombay said, "We're being attacked from the rear!"

Horace swung the car in a loop. As it swooped past the upended Ren ship, Clive caught sight of a being through one of the transparent domes that gave the Ren ship the appearance of a great face.

Then Horace had the car successfully turned and speeding in the opposite direction. Ahead of them a squadron of slim shapes appeared. They were gracefully formed, as artistically curved as oriental dancers. Their skins shone in metallic hues: the blue of a dragonfly's wings, the green of a hummingbird's breast, the red of newly shed blood.

Behind them flared the exhaust of rockets. Clive was stunned at the notion of using fireworks to propel great ships, but even as he recognized the nature of these craft, the logic of their means of propulsion became clear. One after another, they discharged what appeared to be concentrated bursts of energy.

Clive could not tell whether these were yet another form of ordolite weapon or some different device. Whatever the case, one of the newcomers scored a glancing blow upon the Ren ship. Clive saw the crumpling of metal plates and watched as the Ren ship reconfigured itself before his very eyes.

Another of the graceful metallic craft scored a hit on the Ren ship, this time to greater effect. The scorpionlike weapon of the Ren ship snapped at its base and tumbled through the blackness, swiftly disappearing.

Now the Ren ship sped forward, ignoring Clive and his companions in their transparent car. The Ren charged directly at the metal squadron. Blow after blow was struck against it, and the Ren ship did nothing to respond. It took each strike in turn, writhing and tumbling, sliding metal plates and organic components into place but struggling toward its foes nevertheless.

When it reached the metal squadron it spurted forward once again. Clive lost sight of it for a moment, but even as he strained his still-stinging eyes to see the ship, he realized that Horace Smythe and Sidi Bombay, also, had been gazing transfixed at the ongoing combat.

Sidi Bombay raised a dark hand and pointed a long finger. "Behold! The enemies, locked in final embrace!"

Clive followed Sidi's direction. Yes, the Ren ship had penetrated the metallic squadron's formation and had cleaved to a red-shining ship. More than ever, the Ren craft resembled Clive's erstwhile companion Chang Guafe. It was a living thing, and it clung and tore at the metal ship with great metal claws and saw-edged extrusions.

The other members of the metallic squadron swung or drifted in disorder. It was obvious to Clive that the ships—or their crews—were desperate to come to the aid of their comrade. Yet the energy-weapon that had temporarily blinded Clive earlier seemed to be all that was available to them. And they dared not fire upon the Ren for fear of hitting their own ruddy-skinned companion.

A circular saw blade was whirring against the skin of the metal ship. The red ship was larger than the Ren but appeared helpless to counter the attack. There were windows or glassed portholes on the scarlet ship. Clive could see movement within it, but could not discern the nature of the ship's crew.

At last the blade bit successfully through the skin of the scarlet ship. A gaping hole appeared as the Ren ship grasped the edges of the opening and tore at the ship, peeling away its skin like a hungry child tearing at the skin of an orange.

One of the occupants of the metallic ship pulled himself through the opening. For a moment Clive caught a glimpse of him. The crewman appeared to be human enough, wearing a helmet and baggy suit not unlike those used by deep-sea divers.

The Ren ship caught the baggy-suited crewman in a pair of pincers that resembled those of a shore-crab. For a fraction of a second Clive could see the man's mouth open to give out a scream of agony and terror. Although Clive could not hear the man, he imagined the sound.

Then the man was halved, snipped through the middle by the saw-edged pincers. Blood and viscera spurted from both halves of the body even as it tumbled away, trailing crimson gobbets.

Clive felt his gorge rising. His hand covered his mouth and he looked away for a moment, but almost involuntarily he turned back, transfixed by the scene of battle.

He had seen many sights of combat and bloodshed, had in fact participated in many, both in his first career as an officer of Her Majesty's Imperial Horse Guards and in his second as an adventurer in the Dungeon. But seldom had he witnessed such carnage, such horror as this. Perhaps the monster at the bridge in Q'oorna, on the first level of the Dungeon . . . or perhaps the cavern of the hideous sacs in which Sidi Bombay had been held prisoner and then rescued, rejuvenated . . . but even those scenes . . . he could not be certain.

The Ren ship—or being—reached through the rent in the metal craft's skin. It inched forward. It looked to Clive as if the Ren ship was trying to climb inside the metallic craft.

But the metallic ship's defenders must have beaten back the invasion, for the Ren ship pulled back its pincers, retreating before a counterattack that saw a squad of bulky-suited individuals clamber through that same rent, some of them clinging to the Ren ship's great claw and others pulling themselves forward in pursuit.

They were men, or at least they had the appearance of

diving-suited men, and they were connected to their own ship by what appeared to be hawsers. That was necessary, Clive realized, as the counterattacking troopers bounded from the skin of their ship.

The rest of the slim, metallic fleet filled the sky, circling the combatants but taking no other part in their struggle.

The troopers were armed with primitive weapons. Clive pressed his face to the transparent wall of the car, straining his eyes for the best possible view of the battle. The troopers were carrying—astonishingly, appallingly—axes.

No civilized man had fought with a battle-axe for three hundred years or more! But in Africa, Clive had seen men go into war armed only with spears. Had seen them bring down great murderous beasts with nothing more.

And in the Dungeon, at the castle of N'wrbb Crrd'f and the Lady 'Nrrc'kth, men had fought with halberds and daggers and swords. Clive had done so himself. Even upon his return to London in the year 1896, he had carried a saber. Its intended use had been purely ceremonial, yet he had carried it with him, and in dire circumstances he had been willing to use it.

The troopers were swarming over the Ren ship, chopping and prying with their axes. Clearly, they meant to get between the metal plates of the ship-creature, to attack the softer and more vulnerable organic components that the metal plates protected. They pried between the plates with their axes while the Ren ship shifted its shape, snapping at them with its pincers. Whatever smith had provided these axes, making possible the astounding tactics of these warriors, must surely have been one of the primitive geniuses of all time!

The Ren ship extruded a new scorpion-tail. It emerged from between metal plates, shining and dripping fluids. It enlarged before Clive's eyes, slowly flexing, then curling, then flexing again.

The Ren ship used its new tail as a prehensile instrument and a stinger all in one, snapping at its attackers. At his side, Clive heard a horrified gasp as the new tail struck a bulky-suited trooper. The trooper was impaled on the barbed tip of the tail. Clive saw him fling his limbs out in a powerful convulsion of agony and death.

Now the Ren ship flexed its tail in a snapping motion, pulling the trooper with it, cracking the hawser that attached the trooper to the metallic ship as an animal-trainer cracks a whip. The trooper was flung away from the ship, tumbling and dwindling into the distance. For a moment Clive caught a glimpse of the trooper's belly, where the Ren ship's tail had torn away a segment of the trooper's suit, leaving a hole the size of a dinner plate.

The Ren ship's barbed tail was covered with gore, and the opening in the trooper's suit showed black and red. Clive prayed silently that the trooper had died instantly when struck by the barbed tail, and did not have to suffer the agonies of this moment.

But for all the effectiveness of the Ren ship's attack, it was a battle of one against many, and every bulky-suited trooper who was rendered *hors de combat* by the Ren ship was replaced by two more, furiously wielding their axes.

Now fluids began to appear on the Ren ship, horrid ichor flowing from between its metal plates. It was not the red of blood, but a hideous purplish color that made Clive gag once again. The Ren ship moved more slowly, its jabs and slices exerted more in self-defense than in the interests of its attack on the metallic ship.

More and more troopers swarmed onto the back of the Ren ship. The being's scorpion-tail flailed and struck, smashing another trooper with its heavy, barbed tip. A pair of pincers snipped off the head of a trooper, and blood spurted from the collar of his suit. But it was clear that the tide of battle had turned.

The Ren ship loosened its grasp on the metal ship and pushed itself away. A squad of troopers could be seen hacking with axe-heads at the hawsers that held them to the ship. They curved away from their ship, clinging to the Ren, chopping at it with their axes.

Clive saw the transparent globes that seemed to be the Ren ship's eyes swing open. From one of them gore spurted. But from the other emerged something pure white that writhed and spun as it tumbled through the blackness.

Like a squid spurting through the ocean, the white thing squirmed and slithered through the blackness.

As it moved away from the Ren ship, it headed directly

toward the car containing Clive and Horace and Sidi Bombay.

As it approached the car it grew, and Clive was able to make out its shape in every horrid detail. Although it was as white as a field of fresh-fallen snow in the English countryside, it was identical in form to the black monster Clive and his companions had fought on the bridge at Q'oorna!

· CHAPTER 17 ·
Novum Araltum

The white creature was hardly larger than an English spaniel.

It whirled past the car, swung back, grasped with writhing tentacles, and plastered itself to the outside of the car. Through the transparent walls of the car, Clive could see that no feature of the hideous monstrosity of Q'oorna was missing from this pallid miniature.

As the white monster pressed its top against the flat panel of the car, Clive could see that this included even the human face on the top of its trunk. Where the black monster of Q'oorna bore the incredibly enlarged visage of Clive's brother Neville, a visage that cursed him even as the monster plummeted from the high basalt bridge, this white miniature bore another face equally familiar to Clive—and equally shocking!

It was the face of Annabella Leighton.

Clive's eyes bugged at the moment of recognition. He lunged across the car toward the white thing with Annabella's features. He pressed his own face against the cold, flat glass.

Yes, every feature, every line that marked Annabella was here. The softly flowing hair. The gently arched eyebrows. The eyes themselves, crying out with the depths of Annabella's love for Clive and the pain of his abandonment of her in her home in Plantagenet Court in London. The graceful, delicate shape of her nose and the generous fullness of her lips . . .

"Annabella!" Clive cried out.

He did not know whether the glass wall of the car would

carry his words to her, but he pressed his ear to the glass in hope that she would respond.

"Clive! My darling!"

Yes! It was Annabella's voice, thinned and strained by the thickness of the glass, yet unmistakably hers.

"Let me in! Oh, Clive, I beg you!"

"Sidi! Horace!" He turned to his companions. "It is Annabella! Help me! We must admit her to the car!"

"No, Clive Folliot. It is not Annabella."

"It is! How this monster has gotten her, I cannot even imagine, but it is she! I know it is she!"

"It's a Ren, sah! They can do that, sah!"

"No! Horace, you must remember the monster of the bridge. It had my brother's face. Now this one has captured Annabella. We must let her into our car. We must rescue her."

"It's all a trick, sah. It's just the Ren."

"I know, I know!" Clive turned away from the glass, forcing himself not to look at the face of his sweetheart. "I know of these monsters. But how can I—?" He could not continue.

"Please, Clive," Annabella's voice came again through the glass.

Beyond the white thing with Annabella's face, Clive could see the heavily suited troopers, those who had survived the battle between the red metallic ship and the Ren craft. They had launched themselves and were floating toward the transparent car. They held their battle axes at the ready.

"Oh, Clive, do not leave me to die! Please, Clive! In the name of our common love! Please! In the name of our common humanity!"

Clive grasped the handle that would unlatch the door of the car and permit Annabella to enter. He tugged at it, struggling to turn it.

Horace Hamilton Smythe grasped Clive's wrist in both his hands. He tugged Clive away from the door.

"Smythe, what are you doing? Release me! If you will do nothing to help me to rescue Miss Leighton, at least do not interfere with my own efforts!"

Horace Smythe grasped Clive by the shoulders and

shook him. "Get ahold of yourself, Major! You know that isn't Annabella. You know that very well, sah! You just said as much! You can't let her—it—in here. It can't be done, sah! We'd lose all our air, we should all die rather than one. But that doesn't matter, sah—that isn't Miss Leighton. I swear to you, sah, that isn't Miss Leighton!"

The troopers were close behind the white thing, axes raised.

"She will die!"

Like a man of two minds, Clive both knew that the monster was not Annabella, yet could not restrain himself from trying to save her. He very nearly succeeded in wrenching away from Smythe, but at the crucial moment, Sidi Bombay grasped Clive's other wrist. Together, the two men held him.

The first of the troopers was upon Annabella. She let go her hold on the glass of the car and pushed herself a few yards from it, ready to meet the trooper's attack.

The white thing was equipped with tentacles and claws and rows of fangs and venomous stingers, but instead of fighting the troopers, it merely waited for them.

At the first blow of an axe, the white thing bounded back toward the car. For a fleeting moment it regained its grasp on the car, pressed its trunk against the flatness. Again Clive found himself looking into the face of Annabella Leighton. "Good-bye, my darling," he heard the beloved voice whisper. "Even this, my love gives me the strength to forgive you, Clive. Even this."

With a maddened effort Clive broke free of Sidi Bombay and Horace Hamilton Smythe's grasp and lunged for the handle of the door. But even as he gripped the metal, a trooper was upon Annabella, his axe swinging.

The single blow split the white thing's trunk from top to bottom. Tentacles writhed, the mouth that Clive had loved opened and closed in a final scream of agony—a scream that was wholly silent—and gouts of ichor spouted from the two halves of the white thing.

The troopers continued to chop away at the pieces until the largest one remaining was smaller than the palm of a child's hand. Clive fell to his knees, convulsed by a dry retching as his empty stomach clenched and clenched again in horrified disgust.

"It wasn't Miss Leighton," Horace Hamilton Smythe told Clive again. "I didn't understand the Ren when we met that black giant on Q'oorna, Major, sah, or I'd have known that you was seein' yer brother's face and hearin' his voice. I saw another face, Major, back there on Q'oorna. When you saw yer brother, I saw me own ma'am. It was hard not doin' what she wanted."

"And I saw my own beloved child, Major Folliot," Sidi Bombay put in. "My child who had been taken by a tiger in the forest of Bengal—for whom I have never ceased to grieve, Major Folliot. The Ren have the power to summon from our minds the images of those whom we love. They use these images against us. But they are not real. They are deceptions, Major Folliot."

Clive wiped his watering eyes. "I know. I know that, Sidi, Horace. But still, seeing the beloved face, hearing the so-sweet voice—can you blame me, my friends, for—for a moment of confusion? For a moment of madness?"

"No sah. No one could blame you, sah."

"But we must come to terms, Clive Folliot, with the challenge that we face." Sidi Bombay pointed one finger, as if at a stain that needed to be removed from a garment. "We must not allow that moment of madness to persist."

"And if I had opened the door to her—to it?"

"Chances are, sah, we'd simply have lost all our air. Likely we'd have been swept out of the car, and died. Or else remained here and suffocated. Small choice, eh?"

"What filthy beasts they are! I thought the Ren were human—in our encounters with them in the Dungeon, as suspect as their motives might have been, at least I thought they were human."

"They take many forms," Sidi Bombay said. "But the form in which we first saw the monster upon Q'oorna, and the form of this small white Ren, seem to be their natural shape. I do not understand the differences in their size and coloring, Clive Folliot. But they are the true Ren."

A full dozen troopers by now surrounded the car, some of them floating as gently as gulls caught in an updraft, others grasping at knobs and protruberant features on the outside of the car to steady themselves. Now and then, a trooper would peer curiously through the glass at Clive and Sidi and Horace, but for the most part they simply went about their business.

Their business was the attachment of tether-lines to the car.

Before long the car was hawsered to half a dozen metallic craft. The troopers had departed, returning without a word of communication to their own ships. The fleet began to move, and with it, Clive could feel the glass car moving as well.

"Where are they taking us?" he asked his companions.

"I'd guess they're taking us to their home world, sah," Horace answered.

"To . . . Aralt? I thought Aralt had been destroyed, Horace."

"Yes, sah. Din't know the Major was aware of that, sah."

"I learned it on the eighth level. There was a woman, a beautiful woman. Her name was Lena."

"I quite understand, sah."

"No you don't, Smythe. She was a Chaffri woman, and from her I learned that their home was a tiny world located in the sun's asteroid belt. You thought I was unaware of the existence of asteroids—planetoids—but Lena told me of them. She told me that the home of the Chaffri was Aralt—had been Aralt—but that Aralt no longer existed. It was destroyed."

"That is correct, sah. But the Chaffri are not a minor power. They most surely have an alternative headquarters. They will have moved their operations either to that headquarters, or to some lesser outpost. Those are surely Chaffri ships, and I'd wager all I've got that they're taking us to their base."

Clive slumped against the cushioned back of the plush, padded, dark-red seat. He covered his eyes with his hands. It might have been better, might have been better, he permitted himself to muse, if he'd succeeded in opening the panel, letting the air rush out of the car, letting himself die in the moment of his reunion with Annabella. Of course, it would have been an illusion. If Horace and

Sidi were right, if the white thing had been a Ren and if the Ren had the power to capture images out of their victims' minds and create convincing fancies of them . . . it might have been better to die.

"There it is, Sidi!"

Horace Smythe's voice interrupted Clive's reverie. Smythe stood at the now-useless controls of the car, pointing ahead. By looking around the car, Clive could see the metallic ships above and below, left and right of them. He could see the hawsers that connected the transparent car with the metallic ships, though the area behind each ship was distorted by the wavering pattern of its exhaust. The ships tugged gently, steadily.

Dead ahead of them lay a tiny disk, a perfect worldlet not significantly unlike the Earth, yet only a fraction of its size. Unsullied polar ice caps gleamed in the sunlight. Blue seas and green-forested continents could be seen through breaks in cotton-white clouds.

The metallic ships dropped toward the atmosphere of the miniature planet, guiding the little transparent car. The movement of the car from the point where the ships had attached their hawsers to its arrival at this planetoid had been a smooth and easy one.

But still Clive wondered at the nature and the intent of the Chaffri. The battle between the Chaffri ship and the Ren had been a classic confrontation suitable only in the conduct of implacable foes. The destruction of the white Ren was beyond Clive's comprehension. Representatives of a culture so advanced that it built craft to travel almost casually between the planets had then engaged in mortal combat armed only with axes. Clive had expected them at the very least to use ordolite energy weapons.

But axes?

They circled above a flat, grassy plain located on one of the islands that had to pass for continents on the planetoid. The passage of air created a screaming sound that shook the walls and vibrated the glass panels of the car, but they held.

The metallic ships dropped the hawsers, but they still surrounded the car and maneuvered it toward the plain.

"Can we escape, Smythe?" Clive asked.

"Not possible, sah. And besides, I thought the Major wanted to beard the lion in his den, so to speak, sah."

"The lion—the Gennine! But we have reached the headquarters—or at least a base—of the Chaffri, not the Gennine."

"Even so, sah. At any rate, sah, we couldn't get away even if we wished to. Those metallic ships have us outnumbered, outpowered, and outmaneuvered. This little car was never meant for serious combat. The ordolite mortar is a child's popgun compared to the armament of those metallic ships, Major Folliot, sah."

Clive pondered. "I suppose you're right, Smythe. Sidi Bombay, do you concur?"

"Without hesitation, Clive Folliot."

"Very well, then. Set her down, Smythe."

"Yes, sah. I've already commenced to obey, sah."

The transparent car spiraled downward. The grassy plain had been converted into something resembling a naval facility. Clive could see strips laid out that resembled docks, buildings that were the equivalent of pier facilities, and roads leading away from the area, disappearing into lush woods. He could only guess at their destinations.

The car touched down on rich grass and slid gently to a halt. Horace Hamilton Smythe methodically shut off its propulsive units and turned to unlatch the glass panels through which they had entered the car. He stood aside to permit Clive the privilege of being the first to step from the car.

All around them, Clive could see metallic craft coming in for their landings. Each of them was far larger than the glass car, could easily have dropped the car and a dozen more into its cargo hold, if the metal ships had cargo holds.

Red, gold, blue, green, silver, orange, bronze, one after another the sleek machines landed.

As each touched the earth and came to a halt, its ports opened and crew members poured forth.

But Clive and his companions were greeted by a party that emerged from a shed located near the woods.

The party consisted of men in splendid military garb, fancy uniforms of crimson and gold and blue and green that would have set to shame the fanciest dress uniforms of Her Majesty's military establishment.

The leader was a splendidly attired fellow whose gold-fringed shoulder boards swayed with his every step. His headgear resembled that of an admiral, and a tall plume rose from it to dip before the gentle breeze that coursed across the landing plain.

A sash that swept from shoulder to waist was covered with orders and decorations. A ceremonial shortsword clanked in its scabbard.

Clive peered at the man, trying to determine his rank, or even the branch of service of which he was an officer.

The man halted and saluted smartly. "In the name of the Chaffri, Clive Folliot, I welcome you and your companions to Novum Araltum. I am Muntor Eshverud."

Startled, Clive darted glances to Sidi Bombay and Horace Hamilton Smythe. They offered no suggestions. Muntor Eshverud—the name offered no clue as to the man's origins, nor did his speech, which was slightly accented but which Clive was baffled to place. Except—

Except that Eshverud used English, not the patois that Clive had learned was common in most regions of the Dungeon.

What could that mean?

Eshverud had lifted his spotlessly gloved hand in a military salute, and Clive returned the gesture uncomfortably.

"If the distinguished guests would be so kind as to accompany me to the field office." He gestured to the shed from which he had appeared. But—Clive blinked—was it a shed? The building was a bit larger than he'd thought at first, and its architecture was homey and attractive, rather different from the crude board construction he thought he'd seen.

He fell in beside Eshverud and noted that Horace Hamilton Smythe and Sidi Bombay similarly paired off with members of Eshverud's party. They set off at a brisk pace toward the building. Clive heard Horace Smythe anxiously questioning his companion about the care that their car would receive. The replies were reassuring. Sidi Bombay was engaged in dialogue, apparently on the subject of mess facilities and supplies.

"We observed your encounter with the Ren ship, Major

Folliot," Muntor Eshverud said. "You were fortunate that our patrol encountered you in time. Those are nasty things, those Ren craft. Nasty as the creatures that build and fly them!"

"You are at war with the Ren, sir? I did not quite catch your proper title."

"Muntor. My name is Eshverud. The other is my grade and position in Chaffri society."

"Very well, sir. And my prior question, if you please?"

"Yes. At war with the Ren. I suppose you might call it war. If a campaign of extermination is suitably termed a war."

"Extermination, sir? I have never heard of a war in which it was the acknowledged objective of one party to exterminate the other. Do you mean to annihilate the enemy to the last man, woman, and child?"

Eshverud smiled bitterly. His brow was massive, his whole face was broad. A thick mustache, perhaps blond in the Muntor's youth, now almost white with age, rose at its tips toward muttonchop whiskers.

"The last man, woman, and child, Major Folliot? A poignant phrase. Yes, I believe that the Ren would exterminate us to the last man, woman, and child. If they had the power to do so. Unless they chose to maintain a domesticated stock for food. They dine on the flesh of Chaffri, you know. Not often—there aren't enough of us to meet the demand. So we're considered a great delicacy among the Ren."

"I encountered a giant Ren when I first entered the Dungeon, Muntor Eshverud. In 1868, when I was in search of my brother."

Eshverud nodded. "They infest the Dungeon."

"The one we encountered—it had devoured humans and it displayed the countenance of my own brother. It cursed me in his voice!"

"The Ren have terrible powers of the mind. I do not doubt your story, Major—it is altogether credible. But I would suggest that the Ren plucked the image and the sound of your brother's voice from your own brain, and fed the information back to you in order to serve its own ends."

"I have come to believe that, yes, Muntor."

They were close to the shed. Now Clive realized that it was an inn, built in the Tudor style, half-timbered and covered with a roof of thick thatch. It had been full day when the glass car landed on the grassy field, but night fell swiftly on Novum Araltum, and the sky was already darkening. The sun was half hidden beneath the horizon, stars twinkled, and nearby asteroids wove a broad, glittering belt across the sky.

From a low chimney, a lazy stream of smoke rose slowly, and Clive could smell the familiar odor of burning peat.

The door of the inn was fitted with pebbled panes of amber-tinted glass. Lights from within gave the glass a warm, golden glow. Muntor Eshverud ushered Clive through the doorway into a world at once hauntingly familiar and disquietingly strange.

As an English gentleman he would not have frequented workingmen's pubs, yet he certainly knew what they were. There had been reason to visit them in the Dungeon, and he had encountered one, to his distress, upon his return to London.

Yet this establishment was not exactly a nineteenth-century pub. It had some of the feel of a country inn of an earlier and more wholesome age. He half-expected to see rural bumpkins, the hayseeds falling from their hair, raising tankards of ale and haunches of mutton. There was indeed a genial publican presiding over the proceedings, while serving wenches in daringly cut blouses and billowing skirts made their way skillfully among long common tables of broad, rough-hewn planks.

"Is this—pardon me, Muntor—" Clive addressed his companion, "is this the headquarters of an aerial base of the Chaffri? I fear that I do not understand, sir—although I will concede that it is a homey and pleasant place."

Eshverud smiled. He guided Clive by one elbow, maneuvering him through the crowded common room. He stopped at the bar and bent to speak with the publican. Even above the din of the room, filled as it was with drinking, eating, joking, singing, roistering Chaffri, Clive had no difficulty in making out the Muntor's words.

"Two everflowing tankards of your best, Jivach, for *Ma-*

jor Folliot and myself. A platter of good hot food. We'll be
in a private dining room, the major and myself. And if I
know my guest's tastes, Jivach, make it a point to send in
your prettiest serving wench. And don't expect to see her
back too quickly, Jivach."

And the man actually winked!

Clive let himself be steered into a private room where
the furniture, although crudely hewn, was more than comfortable. Light came from an oil lamp, and the air smelled
like England.

The two men sat on opposite sides of the wooden table.
There were a million questions that Clive wanted to ask
Eshverud. Questions about the Chaffri, about the Ren,
about the Dungeon—and about the Gennine. There were
so many questions, covering so immense a variety of
topics, that Clive hardly knew where to begin.

But before the dialogue had gotten very far, there was a
knock at the door and Muntor Eshverud called, "Come
ahead, then!"

The door swung open, and the serving wench turned to
shut it behind her even before she had set down her
cargo. Clive caught but a fleeting glance of her, yet even
in that instant he was utterly taken with her dark, glossy
hair, her soft skin that glowed creamy and golden in the
light of the oil lamp, the graceful figure and the generous
bosom that swelled beneath the inadequate confines of her
low and flimsy blouse.

He sat up with appreciation and waited for her to turn
back toward him. She bent over her task, placing tankards
of ale and platters of meat and rolls on the wooden table.
As she did so, the material of her blouse billowed away
from her warm bosom.

Clive blinked.

The serving wench straightened.

Their eyes met in startled recognition, and simultaneously they cried each other's names.

"Clive!"

"Annabella!"

· CHAPTER 18 ·
"Clive, My Darling Clive"

Without thinking, Clive rushed to Annabella—and she, to him. They embraced in a breathless rush of passion, their bodies pressed together like those of eager lovers, their mouths pressed to each other's as if each held for the other the ambrosia of life.

At last, for the moment sated, yet trembling, they managed to seat themselves. Still they remained, each with an arm around the other's shoulders, each holding the other's hand, each gazing into the other's eyes.

A chill ran through Clive at the thought that this Annabella was still another trick, a simulacrum or an illusion created to mislead him. But she was so warm, so real—the heightened beating of his heart, the tightening of his chest, the excited joy that he felt would not be denied. She had to be real! How had she come to Novum Araltum? How could this woman of nineteenth-century England be employed as a serving wench in an establishment on another world?

The questions would keep. She was Annabella!

"I expected never to see you again. Oh, my darling Annabella! I wanted to go to your home—to Plantagenet Court—but I knew you were no longer there. That in shame you had sailed away to America and settled there forever."

"I did that, Clive. I waited as long as I could for your return to England. I was . . . with child, Clive. Clive, with your child. With your daughter."

"Yes, yes Annabella. I know the whole story. I—"

"How do you know?"

"I was told by my great-great-granddaughter. *Our* great-great-granddaughter, my darling Annabella. Is it so strange to think that we have so remote a descendant? She is Annabelle Leigh, of the city of San Francisco in the United States of America. And she came to London in 1999, and from there was transported to the Dungeon."

"I have heard of the Dungeon, Clive."

"You were never there?"

"No, my darling. I never left Boston. Once I reached the New World, I determined that I would never turn back, never return to England. But I had no idea of the Dungeon. I lived my life, raised my daughter, taught her——" She blushed, the crimsoning of her skin visible not only on the softness of her cheeks but on the tenderness of her bosom.

"I know the law of your family. *Do as you will, take such lovers as you choose, bear a daughter, and teach her to do the same . . . and never, never marry.*"

"And my girls have kept that law—unto the year 1999, you say, Clive?"

"They have."

A smile crossed her face, a smile less soft than those Clive Folliot was accustomed to seeing on Annabella. "But how did you come here, to Novum Araltum? And . . . your age, Annabella. You appear little older than the tender maid I knew in Plantagenet Court."

"I would have waited for you in England, Clive, if I had been given any reason to expect your return."

"Did you never hear from me after I left? I wrote you letters—many of them."

"I never received them."

"I know. That was my shame. I wrote them only in my mind."

"I saw your dispatches in the *Illustrated Recorder and Dispatch*. Your reports and your sketches were excellent."

"I had hoped to collect them into a book."

"Your editors did so in your behalf, Clive. In both England and America you were an author of some fame. Alas, fame is fleeting, and after a few years you were forgotten. I fear that the readers of a later decade may never have heard of Clive Folliot. Still, scholars and collectors of volumes on exotic lands honor you."

"I was a famed author? My fame came and went, all unbeknownst to me, and I am now the pet of musty bibliophiles. Aye, so it ever was, I suppose." Clive shook his head, a wry smile upon his lips. His reports had been modest, his drawings crude and unpolished—at least in his own estimation. But apparently they were not so, in the judgment of others. Du Maurier's redactional services and Maurice Carstairs' promotional efforts must have done him better than ever he had guessed.

"And du Maurier?" he asked Annabella. "Did you ever hear from him?"

"He came to see me. He said that he had received emanations from you, from a distant and terrible realm. Clearly, that was the Dungeon, Clive."

"I visited him in London just days ago, Annabella. I saw him on his deathbed. He was attended by Clarissa Mesmer, the granddaughter of the famous—or infamous—Anton."

"George du Maurier was a good man, Clive. A visionary. A great soul who was born many years ahead of his time."

"And did any others come to see you?"

"Your father and brother."

"My *brother*! Neville came to see you?"

"He did."

"They came together to see me in Plantagenet Court. After a little while Neville sent the baron upon some errand, and then . . ." She turned away from him. As she did so, an errant tendril of dark hair fell across her bosom, drawing his attention to the tender valley of her breasts, where warm golden lamplight played.

"And then what?" Clive prompted.

She turned back but hid her face against his shoulder. "He told me that you were dead. He attempted to—to comfort me, Clive. He was so much like you, my darling, in every way. The curl of his hair, the features of his face, his hands, the very—the very smell of him, Clive."

"The monster!" Clive bounded to his feet. For the first time since Annabella's arrival, he thought of Muntor Eshverud. He looked for the Chaffri, but Eshverud had slipped from the room. Annabella had risen to her feet and now Clive placed his hands on her cheeks, peering deep into her eyes. "Did Neville . . . ?"

"Yes," she whispered. "I felt such confusion at the time, such weakness and despair. And afterward, Clive, such shame. That was the real reason I left England. I would have stayed and proudly borne your child. But after Neville . . . I could not stay."

"Are you sure that the child—?"

"It is your child, Clive. That I *know*! And the girls who descended from her, even unto Annabelle Leigh, are your descendants. All of them carry the Folliot blood. For better or for worse, Clive. I do not carry it, but all of our descendants do."

With a start, Clive realized that he was hungry. Through the entire trip in the glass car, the battle in space, and the landing on Novum Araltum, he had not eaten a bite. Now the smell of the hot food that Annabella had brought assaulted his nostrils. And with his hunger came a great thirst, and he lifted the tall tankard of ale and held it between himself and Annabella.

"We are together again, my darling girl. Together again!"

With their eyes they exchanged further thoughts. Annabella lifted the second tankard, and they toasted with elbows linked, then set to on the still-steaming haunch and rolls. Between mouthfulls of food and hearty draughts of ale they exchanged kisses and looks and caresses, and before the meal was over Clive felt himself yielding to old attractions, and found Annabella returning his attentions with the passion that had locked him to her in Plantagenet Court in long-ago London.

He slipped a hand into her bodice and she pressed against him, pressing her cheek against his and whispering in his ear daring syllables that he had not heard for months or years or a quarter-century.

The room was set up for private assignations, and thus they used it, Clive all forgetful of the Dungeon and its horrors and its perils. Forgetful of the sultry Lorena Ransome and the strangely colored Lady 'Nrrc'kth with her pale skin and green-tinted hair and eyes. Forgetful of the spider Shriek and the alien cyborg Chang Guafe and the faithful, doglike Finnbogg and the top-hatted Baron Samedi with his sardonic laughter and the lumbering Frankenstein monster. Forgetful of the Muntor Eshverud and of Clive's own companions Sidi Bombay and Horace Hamilton Smythe.

Happy and sated, with his arms around the soft shoulders of Annabella Leighton and her breath warm and soft on his own unclad chest, Clive slept. He was happy at last, happy save for something that nagged at a distant corner of his mind even as he slumbered in the soft golden lamplight.

The warm, pliant flesh was the hard carapace of an Egyptian scarab.

The deep, loving eyes were the faceted and glittering organs of an insect.

The strong yet gentle hands were chitinous claws.

The voluptuous torso that had so inflamed his passions was the segmented body of an—

Of an—

Clive wakened in terror, his being drenched in cold sweat. The lamp had burned the last of its oil. The room was plunged into darkness. Clive had no way of telling how much time had passed, but no sounds came from the tavern.

He pushed himself to his feet, clumsily pulling his clothing into a semblance of order, and staggered to the wall. There were a few errant rays of light, not so much illuminating the little room as suggesting the faint possibilities of illumination.

Clive staggered toward the source of the light. He collided with the wooden table and reached out to catch himself. His hand slid across a heavy platter now thick with congealing grease. A tall tankard, still half-full of strong ale, flew from the table and smashed upon the crude plank floor. Its contents splattered upward, spattering Clive's face and clothing like mud splashed from a London gutter.

He crashed against the wall and stared back at the place where he had lain with Annabella, straining his eyes to see her there. It had to have been a dream! He had been through too much. The rug had been pulled from beneath his reality once too often. That was it—that had to be it!

The lovely woman whose lush body he had so enjoyed could not be other than real. She could not!

The faint light did not permit him to see her clearly.

"Annabella!"

She stirred—but her stirring carried to his ears the dry scrabbling sound of an exoskeleton. Clive could not believe that this was real.

"Annabella!" he repeated.

Again she stirred. He could see the vague, shadowy outline of her form rising.

He threw out his arms and one of his grease-coated hands collided with a closed shutter. He whirled and struggled frantically with the latches, and finally was able to pull back the wooden panels.

He had no time to appreciate the sight of the night sky above Novum Araltum. He turned back to the room and saw Annabella in a state of flustered dishabille. Her skirt was still pulled up around her waist and one sweet breast was exposed above her disarranged bodice.

"Clive!" Even through the semi-darkness of the room she conveyed the impression of a blush. She pulled up her blouse and arranged her skirt decorously. "Clive, I am embarrassed."

He gawked.

"It was unladylike of me, I know, Clive darling. But it had been so long, I missed you and longed for you so, my darling. You cannot imagine the times I dreamed of you— entertaining fantasies of you as I lay on my mattress— pretending that each tread on the stair, each voice of a passerby in the street, each clatter of carriage-wheel on cobblestone, was the sign of your return. Oh, my darling!"

She moved across the room toward him.

He recoiled.

"Clive! Please, Clive! Have I lost you? Did my appetites of the night disgust you? Am I branded now a licentious harlot? Oh, please, my darling Clive!"

He backed away from her, blinking his eyes in the semi-darkness. For a moment she would be his own dear Annabella, the warm woman whose scents still filled his nostrils, whose flavor still roused his taste buds. Then he would blink and behold a creature of horror and revulsion, something like a beetle and something like a mantis and something altogether alien that made his scalp crawl and his skin shrivel at the thought of what had transpired between them.

He bolted for the door. He pushed against it and found it unyielding. Then he hurled himself against it, unmindful of the pain that shot through him with each impact. Finally he grasped the handle and found that the door opened toward him, into the room.

He did not look back as he sprinted through the still night-shrouded inn, searching for an exit. He stumbled into the common room he had seen hours earlier. The tables had been cleared, the occupants had long departed. A great stone fireplace that had held a roaring log now contained warm embers from which rose a thin stream of gray smoke.

Behind him, Clive could hear Annabella's voice, breaking with sobs. "Clive, my darling, my love!" There was a shuddering intake of breath, as would be appropriate to a heart-shattered woman. "Come back to me, Clive! What have I done? Why have you left me?"

But the sound that accompanied that voice was not the sound of unshod feet. It was the horrid, dry scraping and rasping of the carapace of a giant insect!

Clive plunged through the wooden door, pounding onto a grassy area. Who were the Chaffri? In the Dungeon he had thought them human—had thought both the Chaffri and the Ren were human. But if the Ren were really the same species as the tentacled monsters he had encountered on Q'oorna and then in the sky above Novum Araltum, and if the Chaffri were in truth horrifying giant insects . . .

He was struck by another thought.

In the battle between the Ren and the Chaffri, the Chaffri had appeared to be human. He had not actually seen any of them, but their baggy costumes had betrayed a clearly human form. What could this mean?

Chaffri and Ren alike seemed to have the ability to pull images from the mind. Both of them could then fool their victims into seeing what the alien races wished them to see. It was a power not unlike the power to create simulacra and invest them with an imitation of life. This was the power to mask themselves with illusions, and pass off their own actions as those of others. A victim might see himself, his brother, his lover—*anyone!*—when in fact he was in the presence of an alien monster.

"Clive, come back!"

He heard the voice of his beloved, coming from behind him. But he dared not turn, paralyzed equally by the fear that he would see a gigantic mantislike creature and that he would see Annabella—or the illusion of Annabella.

"Clive, please! Clive, last night was so wonderful! Oh Clive, I need you! Come to me, please, my darling!"

He shuddered so violently that he almost fell. He ran blindly from the inn. He knew that he was at the edge of the grassy field where both his own transparent car and the metallic ships of the Chaffri had landed. The sky was ablaze with distant stars and nebulae and with the reflected light of the uncounted miniature worlds that made up the asteroid belt.

He set off at a run, paralleling the edge of the woods that surrounded the landing field. He could not hear Annabella Leighton following, nor was there any indication of the presence of the Muntor Eshverud.

But ahead there loomed another low building not unlike the inn that Clive had fled. Was it another inn, or was it a structure of some wholly different sort, disguised by the mental powers of the Chaffri to seem an inn? He wished he could call upon George du Maurier to help him unravel the puzzle. This was du Maurier's kind of conundrum.

For a moment he tried sending a mental call to du Maurier. Then he remembered that du Maurier was dead. Dead and gone, forever beyond recall or communication from the living.

You are wrong, Clive Folliot.

He whirled. Where had the voice come from?

Don't look for me, Clive. You cannot see me.

"Du Maurier?"

Yes.

"Where are you?"

I am with your brother.

"With Neville?"

No. I am with your brother Esmond.

"But—Esmond was never born! Esmond spoke to me when I was in the Dungeon. Esmond was to have been the triplet brother of Neville and myself, and he died before birth."

That's right, brother.

"Esmond? Is it you?" Clive found himself swept by a rush of emotion unlike any he had felt in his life. "Are you my lost brother?"

I am.

"Where are you? Are you in Heaven? Does your soul reside with God?"

Heaven? God? What do I know of such things, brother Clive?

"But you are with du Maurier. He is dead. You must both be disembodied souls—the soul of the dead and the soul of the never-born."

Deep in Clive Folliot's mind there sounded the ghostly, psychic laughter of George du Maurier and Esmond Folliot. Then du Maurier's voice echoed once more, so that Clive could hear it but none other could. *There's no time to debate metaphysics, Folliot. You've got to get away from Novum Araltum. Rescue your friends if you can, but even if you cannot save them, you yourself must leave Novum Araltum.*

"Why, du Maurier? Leave Novum Araltum for where? Shall I return to Earth? To London? To Tewkesbury? To the Dungeon?"

None of these, Folliot. You yourself spoke of bearding the lion in his den. The lion is the Gennine, and you are the Master of the Ordolite. That must be the final battle in this monstrous war—and lecture me not on the virtues of peace. It takes two to make peace, only one to make war. When a warmaker and a peacemaker collide, the warmaker emerges covered with blood—the blood of his enemy!

Behind Clive he could hear a dry scraping, and a sweet voice crying out. "Beloved! Come back, my beloved!"

He raced through the night. The lights of distant stars and nearby asteroids cast a myriad of shadows on the grassy plain. Clive found himself studying them distractedly while he ran. He could hardly tell which was his own shadow, which that of a high clump of grass or a bush.

With a crash, he tumbled to the ground. He had tripped over something. He pushed himself to his hands and knees and stared in horror at the body of Muntor Eshverud.

The Muntor lay face-up, staring glassily at the star-ribboned sky. His eyes were wide and filled with horror. There was no apparent wound on his body, yet when Clive felt his chest there was neither heartbeat nor respiration, and when Clive felt his skin it was cold. Eshverud had been dead for hours—probably, Clive inferred, the Muntor had left the inn at the moment of Clive and Annabella's first ecstatic embrace. He must have been killed almost immediately.

And he was, to all discernible evidence, truly human.

Clive seized the body by one shoulder and a trouser leg and turned Eshverud onto his face. The cause of death was immediately apparent—his neck had been severed from the rear, so that only a flap of skin held his head in place. Something incredibly sharp and driven with overwhelming force had come within a hair's breadth of decapitating Eshverud.

There was a rustling behind Clive. He pushed himself to his knees and took a final look at Eshverud. The man's ceremonial shortsword still rested in its ornate scabbard. Clive grasped the sword, drew it from the scabbard, and ran once more. Behind him the sound of Annabella's cries grew faint and then ceased.

Clive halted, thunderstruck, when he found himself standing at the inn once again. Or was it the same inn? The architecture was similar but some subtle difference in the building's situation told Clive that it was not the same one he had left behind. He circled it, Muntor Eshverud's shortsword at the ready. He found a shuttered window and shoved carefully at the weathered wood.

The shutters had been left unbarred! Within the room Clive could see a few guttering candles, and in their orange-tinted light, a sight that sent horror coursing through him.

Horace Hamilton Smythe, erstwhile military man, mandarin, Arab boy, and Tsarist nobleman, now in his garb as a London scrivener, sat in a rough-hewn wooden chair. A beatific smile lighted his doughty face, and he was speaking with animation. Clive could make out only a portion of his words, but they were clearly a long, detailed recitation of his adventures in the Dungeon. From time to time he would speak in direct address, calling his listener "Mother," or "Ma'am."

The listener, sedulously sharpening serrated claws upon each other, was a giant insect that looked like a cross between a scarab and a gigantic wasp!

Even as Clive clambered through the window, the insect launched its attack on Horace Hamilton Smythe. The battle lasted mere seconds, but to Clive it might have been hours.

Clive crashed shoulder-first against the carapace of the insect, knocking it sideways mere fractions of an inch short of inflicting a horrendous wound on Horace Hamilton Smythe. The insect recovered its balance and came at Clive, striking out with razor-edged claws. Clive lunged at it, using the Muntor Eshverud's shortsword as if it were a dueling saber. The insect was as tall as Clive, and its claw-tipped limbs flicked at him with amazing speed.

Years of training by his father, Baron Tewkesbury, and his brother Neville, had given Clive a command of technique with the blade. On Earth he had never been a match for Neville, but years of adventuring in the Dungeon had hardened his muscles, quickened his reflexes, and given him the attitude needful to the fighting man whose every engagement can mean his life or his death.

A feint at the insect's face brought its claws up to protect glittering, faceted eyes. Like lightning, Clive dropped his point and lunged instead at the thin, muscular target that connected segments of the insect's thorax.

In the blink of an eye, Clive switched his tactics from those of a foil-wielding duelist to those of a broadsword-wielding yeoman. He flicked left with the honed edge of the sword, then right.

The insect fell to the floor, neatly severed in two.

To Clive's horror, both segments continued to twitch and to strike out at him.

Horace Hamilton Smythe stood by in a daze. Clive leaped over a razor-sharp claw as the insect continued to snap and swipe at him. He grasped Smythe's elbow and hustled him from the room.

· CHAPTER 19 ·
Prepare for the Final Onslaught!

Horace Hamilton Smythe stumbling at his side, Clive Folliot made his way back into the night. Novum Araltum's sky was still suffused with the ghostly glow of the asteroid belt, and in that light the two men staggered from the inn.

"She was—she was my—" Horace Hamilton Smythe stammered half-incoherently, permitting himself to be guided by the more determined Clive. Clive permitted himself to slow his pace and peer back at the building. There was no sign of pursuit.

Smythe was still muttering and mumbling.

Clive grasped him by the shoulders and shook him. "Sergeant Smythe! Come to order, man! You cannot permit yourself this kind of conduct!"

Slowly the light of reason grew in the Smythe's eyes. He raised a trembling hand and drew it across his face, then dropped the hand to his side and brought himself to a modified form of attention. "I'm sorry, Major, sah. I must have been— I thought I'd been freed of the Ransomes' mesmeric control, but I fear I was mistaken, sah."

Clive shook his head. "I don't think it was the Ransomes, Sergeant. They've enough evil to answer for, should we succeed in hauling them before the bar of justice . . . but I don't think they can be blamed for the evil that is taking place here on this world of Novum Araltum. I think the Chaffri are to blame for that!"

"But I could have sworn, Major, that I was back on the family farm, in the arms of my dear mother. She lived a horrid life, Major, a horrid life."

"I understand that, Horace."

"And here she was, restored to me, as pure and beloved as when I was a boy."

"Don't you see, Horace, what has happened? The Chaffri—they seem to be a race of giant, intelligent insects. A cross between a scarab and a mantis." Clive shuddered. "And they have an ability that permits them to reach into a victim's brain and draw from it whatever image most powerfully controls that victim."

"Then it wasn't my ma'am at all, Major?"

"It was a monstrous insect that would have slaughtered you as coldly and deliberately as a mantis slaughters an aphid! And as likely drained your vital fluids for its own delectation, into the bargain!"

"*Phaugh!*"

"Indeed, Sergeant Smythe. *Phaugh.* I couldn't have put it better myself."

"And you saw your own ma'am, too, Major Folliot?"

"No, Smythe. I saw . . . another. A woman who gave me her best, her tenderest, and most honest faith and service. And I gave her—well, never mind that. It was not she. It was merely another of these murdering Chaffri."

"You killed that one, too, did you, sah?"

"I escaped it, anyway."

Smythe turned, surveying the horizon. On this tiny world it lay close by, and the turnings of day and night were quick.

Clive followed Smythe's example. The first blush of morning was coming upon them. He could see the Chaffri's landing field, the warlike ships, and the complicated equipment used to fuel and service them. What should Clive's next move entail?

Horace Smythe interrupted the nobleman's musings. "Sah—Major Folliot, sah! What of Sidi Bombay?"

"Good heavens! The Chaffri must have him yet! Quick, Smythe, did you see any other building—other than the one where I found you?"

"I'm not sure, sah. I think there was another structure beyond yon stand of trees. I was in my childhood home, in our little cottage on the farm. There would have been a shed for the animals not far off, sah."

"Take me to it. At once!"

They ran there quickly. As they drew to a halt, Smythe pointed. "There it is, sah! I'd swear, it was just the shed we had in Sussex back in the twenties!"

"And to me it resembles a rustic inn, such as would stand in Devonshire in the sixties. But it's neither, Horace! It's one of the Chaffri's horrid nests, and poor Sidi Bombay is inside it, at this very moment falling victim to God knows what terrible fate."

"Do you see two doors to it, sah?"

The question went through Clive like a bolt of galvanic electricity. If he and Sergeant Smythe saw the building differently, could they coordinate their efforts to rescue Sidi Bombay? Or would they blunder about helplessly, each entrapped by his own set of illusions, neither capable of penetrating his true surroundings?

"I do see two doors, Horace! A main entrance to the inn, and another that must be the means of access to the kitchen."

"I'll take the one to our right, sah. You take the other. We'll find our way to poor Sidi—somehow."

"Stout man, Sergeant Smythe!" He clapped the other on the shoulder and set off, sword still in his hand, for the more distant of the two entrances to the building.

Even in the instant that Clive paused before plunging into the building, he was struck by the perfect imitation—or illusion—that the Chaffri had achieved. The walls were of timber and rough white plaster, the roof was thick rustic thatch, the windows fitted with diamond-paned glass. There was even the scent of the English countryside.

He shoved open the door and plunged into the common room of a typical Devonshire inn. The hearth, the rough tables and sturdy benches, the serving bar, even the wall decorations were chosen and arranged to perfection. But, Clive realized, they had not been chosen and arranged by the Chaffri themselves so much as they had been constructed by his own mind, functioning under the arcane compulsion of the Chaffri. Clive had summoned images from the half-remembered, half-idealized world of his young manhood as the cadet son of a country baron.

What reality lay behind the illusion of rustic woods and rough-hewn stone, he shuddered even to guess.

Clive had no time to stand and ponder. Sidi Bombay, for all he knew, lay in another room of the structure, in dire peril of his life. His mind might at this very moment be under the control of a mantislike Chaffri. The Hindu might be seeing a scene from the days of his youth, might imagine that he was in the village of his childhood, somewhere in the jungles of the Punjab or on the plains of Equatoria. Or he might be reliving a past experience that had involved him in the doings of the convoluted politics of the Indian subcontinent.

For an instant there flashed through Clive Folliot's own mind the horrifying thought that the mesmeric control and frightening responses of the otherwise stalwart Horace Hamilton Smythe might be the product of the same sinister powers of the Chaffri that he himself had experienced a few hours past.

Philo B. Goode . . . the self-styled Reverend Amos Ransome . . . the seductive Lorena Ransome, she of the shimmering black hair and dark liquid eyes and willowy figure so ill-concealed beneath her seemingly modest but subtly provocative costumes. Were any of them what they seemed? Were any of them even humans? Or were these three nothing more than hideous chitin-covered monstrosities masquerading in human society?

And if Philo Goode and the Ransomes were hideous monsters making for themselves the most effective of all disguises—the disguise of their own victims' minds and memories—then who else might be monsters as well? Clive's brother Neville? His father, the Baron Tewkesbury? His closest friend, the recently deceased George du Maurier? Annabella Leighton and her descendant Annabelle Leigh, the dear, eccentric "User Annie" of the year 1999?

Clive shuddered.

A voice seemed to whisper from within his mind. *Hold fast,* it urged him. *Hold fast to your grip on reality, Clive Folliot!*

Clive looked around. "Is that you, du Maurier?"

It is I.

"But you're dead."

Again you point out the obvious, Folliot. Do not let yourself be distracted by such trivialities as death. Plot your course, my friend. Do what you must. Much rests upon your shoulders, Clive Folliot. The fate of millions. Whole worlds, Clive! Do not be distracted by trivialities!

Clive heard a popping and crackling.

He peered around the common room and saw embers still glowing in the great hearth, threads of smoke rising slowly from the glowing embers of a huge backlog that must never grow fully cold and dark.

Was it truly a log, or a simulacrum of a log?

He rushed through the opening that led to the private rooms of the inn. He thrust open the first of them and found nothing of interest within. The second room proved equally unrewarding.

The sound of heavy boots captured his attention and he saw Sergeant Smythe approaching from the opposite end of the inn, checking rooms just as Clive was, snorting and slamming doors in impatience and disappointment as he found each chamber untenanted.

"Sergeant!"

They had met at the center of the hallway. Two doors remained to be tried, one on either side of the passage. Without a word, each man reached to open the door on his right.

Clive heard a grunt of surprise from Sergeant Smythe, followed by a sound of impact, as of a blunt and heavy object connecting with a human cranium. But Clive had no time to go to Smythe's assistance. He had already shoved open the door of the room to his own right, and he stood thunderstruck by the sight it contained.

A thing as alien and terrible as any Clive had ever beheld towered above him, its gargantuan trunk and massive crown bent to avoid scraping the beamed ceiling of the room. Great masses of tentacles writhed and snapped about it, rows and clusters of them dripping a noisome gelatinous slime. Clawed appendages, suction rings, and pseudopods appeared and disappeared, twisting sickeningly. Clive's stomach heaved.

The thing tilted in an arc so that its top was pointed at

Clive. It was a circular membrane surrounded by waving, reaching tentacles.

The thing was one of the monsters that Clive had first encountered at the bridge of black obsidian on Q'oorna. That one had shown him the face of his brother Neville and had spoken to him in an obscene parody of Neville's voice.

This one showed him the face of . . . *Sidi Bombay*.

Clive was thunderstruck. But even as he stood gawking at the hideous sight, the face melted and ran like soft wax, reforming itself into the pale beauty of the Lady 'Nrrc'kth. The white skin, the emerald eyes, the shining, green-tinted hair were so real that Clive involuntarily raised his hand to touch the lady's cheek.

But 'Nrrc'kth was dead!

But George du Maurier was dead also, and yet du Maurier spoke to Clive and told him not to be distracted by the triviality of death!

" 'Nrrc'kth!" Clive cried out.

The emerald eyes pierced his own. The lips opened. A hideous roar emerged, not from the lips of the lady, but from the round membrane of a monster, that vibrated like the head of a drum.

Clive recoiled—but for a mere instant. He was armed with the sword he had taken from the Muntor Eshverud; and with a determination that the old Clive Folliot could never have exhibited, he lunged at the monster.

It snapped its trunk away from him and scuttered across the room with astonishing agility, propelling itself with its rows and clusters of tentacles.

"Enough, Clive Folliot! Enough!"

The voice was that of Sidi Bombay, and the words were followed by the distinctive laughter that Clive had so many times heard from the Indian.

Even as Clive stood, pop-eyed and open-mouthed, the monster began again to melt and reform itself in a manner not unlike that of the alien shape-changer Chang Guafe. It changed its form, its size, its coloration. It became a man, dark-skinned and nearly naked, garbed only in a white turban and spotless breechclout.

"Clive Folliot," Sidi Bombay said. He bowed extravagantly, giving the gesture a touch of irony that robbed it of all obsequy.

"The monster," Clive gasped, "the Chaffri! They're hideous things, Sidi Bombay, hideous great insect-things that can reach into our minds and steal the images of those we hold dear, and fool us into thinking that they're humans themselves!"

"I know that well, Clive Folliot."

"But—are you Sidi Bombay? Or are you one of them?"

"Here is the Chaffri who tried to work that deception on me, O Major." The African turned and with a graceful gesture indicated a rough cage. Where Sidi Bombay had obtained the cage, or how he himself had constructed it from scrap, Clive had no idea—nor any time to worry.

He took the few strides that brought him close to the cage. It was no larger than the carrying case that a lady would use to transport a pampered miniature spaniel on a country outing. It appeared to be constructed of ordinary wood, but the creature that it held made no effort to break its way free.

When Clive caught his first glimpse of the creature it resembled the Chaffri scarab-mantises with which he was already unpleasantly familiar. But even before he could catch a clear image of the thing, it changed. For a moment it was a miniature figure of the Lady 'Nrrc'kth, all pale skin and shimmering forest green hair and flashing emerald green eyes. And nude, utterly nude, its milk-white flesh the very image of cold yet voluptuous grace.

And then before Clive's eyes it turned to the image of his father, Baron Tewkesbury. But the baron as Clive had known him as a fierce and terrifying tyrant of middle years, not the pitiable husk of a man Clive had last seen in the library at their Devonshire estate.

Clive recoiled.

The baron raised a fist, and in a shrill voice began to berate him for treason to the House of Folliot.

And then he wavered again, and melted, and reformed into an image of a great hair-covered spider.

"Shriek!" For an instant Clive was filled with a pang of longing and yearned-for reunion with the alien arachnid who had been his companion on so many adventures in the Dungeon. But he had left Shriek, along with Finnbogg, on the planet Djajj. Could this be the alien?

But then the spidery Shriek changed again and was the nameless monster created by the cursed experimenter Frankenstein, the monster last seen by Clive climbing aboard a compartment of the space-train near Earth's polar ice cap.

"Enough!" Clive cried out. "Stop it! Reveal your true form!"

The monster shook its fists at him, then lowered them slowly to its sides. It wavered several more times, offering suggestions of Annabelle, of the tentacled monster once more, of Clive's brother Neville—or perhaps of Clive himself—before lapsing into the scarab-mantis configuration that Clive at last knew to be its true form.

"A lovely creature, is it not, Clive Folliot?" Sidi Bombay stood near Clive, smiling at him. He lifted the wooden cage in one dark-skinned hand and held it close to his face, smiling benignly at the creature within.

Clive saw the creature gesture helplessly at Sidi Bombay —once, then again—then relapse onto the wooden bottom of its prison.

"Is this the true Chaffri?" Clive asked.

"So it is, Clive Folliot. When we are fooled by it, a terrifying enemy. When we see through its deceptions, when we realize that it draws all its power over us from the recesses of our own minds—a piteous, helpless bug."

He placed the cage on the floor.

"But Sidi Bombay . . . when I arrived in this room, I saw one of the tentacled monsters that we now know are Ren. And it turned into *you*! Are you a Ren? Were you transformed?"

"No, Clive Folliot." Sidi Bombay shook his head. "I am nothing but a man, nor have I ever been other than a man. I can only guess that the Chaffri"—he nodded his head toward the insect in the cage—"plucked *that* image from your mind. Instead of creating the illusion that it was a Ren, it fooled you into thinking that I was one."

Clive leaped. "Sergeant Smythe!"

Sidi Bombay looked inquiringly at him.

"He is across the hall. He entered another room, Sidi

Bombay. Smythe and I were looking for you. We feared that you had been taken in by the trickery of these monsters."

"Hardly." Sidi Bombay smiled.

"But we must see what happened to Sergeant Smythe!"

With Sidi Bombay in his wake, the Indian stopping only to snatch up the wooden cage that held the now seemingly helpless Chaffri, Clive plunged from the room, crossed the hall in a hurried stride, and thrust open the door opposite.

Quartermaster Sergeant Horace Hamilton Smythe lay on his back. His eyes were closed, and blood dripped from the corner of his mouth.

Clive peeled back his eyelids. The man moaned and struggled. Clive helped him to a sitting position.

"What happened, Sergeant?"

"Uh . . . uhh," Smythe tried to speak.

Sidi Bombay placed the wooden cage on the floor and took Horace Hamilton Smythe's hands in one of his own. The other he placed gently on the sergeant's forehead. The Indian muttered a few words. Clive could not make sense of them. Sidi Bombay released Smythe's hand, then removed his palm from the sergeant's forehead.

Smythe blinked and looked at Clive Folliot and Sidi Bombay. He was clearly suffering still from the effects of shock, but his eyes were clear and his manner was lucid.

"I think someone hit me, sah," he said to Clive.

Clive could barely restrain a smile. "I believe so, Sergeant. Did you catch a look at your assailant?"

Smythe blinked with effort. "I'm sorry, sah. All I can remember is setting foot inside the room and—*crash!*—if the Major knows what I mean, sah. All the usual effects that the sensation-mongers speak of, sah. Rushing darkness, sparkling stars, and so forth, sah. Next thing I knew, there you were, sah. Your Majorship and Sidi Bombay."

The Indian was leaning from behind Clive, smiling reassuringly at Sergeant Smythe.

"Sidi Bombay!" Smythe exclaimed. "You're all right, my old friend."

"But of course, Horace."

"They didn't fool you, Sidi Bombay? The Chaffri didn't cast a glamour over your mind?"

"They tried," Sidi Bombay said. "I was not fooled by their childish prank, Horace."

Smythe grunted. "Me 'n Major Folliot was fooled for a bit. I wouldn't call that a childish prank, Sidi Bombay!"

"Someday you Europeans will catch up with the rest of the world, Horace. I pray only that you do not destroy it first!"

Clive asserted his leadership. "We'll leave such debate for a night's conversation over the campfire, men. For now, we've got to get away from this place and get on with business."

The others assented.

"Come along, then."

They exited the inn, Sidi Bombay carrying the wooden cage with the apparently subdued Chaffri in it.

Clive peered between the slats of the Chaffri's cage. "Are they really that size, Sidi Bombay? Hardly bigger than a housecat!"

"They are, Major Folliot."

"But their spacecraft—they seemed to be of a size to be manned by ordinary folk. People such as we. And even after I fought off the spell of the Chaffri that tried to destroy me—"

"I congratulate you on fighting off that spell, Clive Folliot." Sidi grinned. "Would you reveal to me how you did it?"

Clive reddened. "Perhaps later, Sidi Bombay. We have not the time for details now. Please to answer my question."

Sidi Bombay held up the Chaffri. It raged ineffectually against the bars. "They vary, Clive Folliot. They vary." He lowered the cage.

A bolt of vivid verdure flashed past them. Without a word, the three men flung themselves to the ground. Clive peered ahead. Full morning—or what passed for full morning on the planetoid Novum Araltum—had overtaken them. In the dim light Clive could make out the form that he recognized as that of the Muntor Eshverud, crouched some fifty yards away.

But Clive had seen Eshverud lying dead, his head very

nearly severed from his trunk. But if Eshverud's living form had been an illusion, a glamour cast over Clive's mind to conceal the Chaffri's true monstrous appearance . . . if that had been the case to begin with, then the sight of Eshverud dead might equally have been a deception. But if . . . but if . . .

Clive squeezed his eyes shut, striving to clear his mind. He opened his eyes again.

The Muntor had raised a rifle to his shoulder. In Novum Araltum's morning light, Clive identified it as a Snider, one of the Royal Army's breech-loading conversions based on the old Enfield muzzle-loader. It was a weapon Clive knew well. But instead of its normal ball ammunition, the Muntor's Snider seemed to be firing the powerful ordolite ray!

Muntor Eshverud loosed another ray that sizzled the very air as it whipped past the three Earthmen. Then the Chaffri was on his feet again, fleeing.

A single Chaffri spacecraft stood ready on the field, and Eshverud leaped into it, slamming the metal port behind himself.

Clive gave chase, Sidi Bombay and Horace Hamilton Smythe following in his wake. But before they could reach the craft, it had lifted from the field and flashed into Novum Araltum's asteroid-sprinkled sky.

"Major, sah! I can see our own car! Let's get out of here, sah!"

For a moment, Clive stood his ground, surveying the situation. The Muntor Eshverud—presumably, one of the scarab-mantis creatures himself, despite his astonishingly persistent disguise as a human—had made good his escape.

Had not Clive seen Eshverud's nearly decapitated corpse lying near the erstwhile inn? Another illusion, he mused bitterly, another illusion on this planet of illusions. The Chaffri must have plucked another image from Clive's own brain and reflected it back to his sensorium so that he perceived the corpse of a martyr when he actually beheld a foul and definitely living monstrosity. The Chaffri must have known that it was incapable of standing up to a man such as Clive Folliot in honest combat, so had chosen to hide behind a glamour and thus avoid the fight.

But even if Eshverud had escaped, the three Earthmen had still captured one of the Chaffri, and the three comrades were largely unharmed.

How many more of the enemy might surround them, what fate lay in store should they remain on Novum Araltum, could only be guessed.

But the three had left London on a mission to the home not of the Chaffri nor of the Ren, but of their common enemy, the mysterious and mighty Gennine. Why should they become bogged down here on Novum Araltum? There was little to be gained in this place!

"Right, Horace! Sidi Bombay, bring that Chaffri along—it may come in handy later on."

He set out, cutting the distance that separated him from the glass-walled car that had brought them here from Earth.

• CHAPTER 20 •
"From Among Mine Enemies, Clive Folliot!"

The ship had apparently been left unmolested and unguarded. The entire aerodrome, in fact, seemed to be deserted, and Clive found himself wondering once again where the Chaffri had gone. Two he had killed, one Sidi Bombay had captured, and the Muntor Eshverud had made good his escape.

But there had been scores, perhaps hundreds of the Chaffri at this base. There must be thousands on Novum Araltum. Many thousands, perhaps. Where had everyone gone?

"Are we agreed, my friends? Do we resume our mission?"

Horace Hamilton Smythe and Sidi Bombay exchanged glances.

"You are our leader, Clive Folliot," the turbaned Sidi Bombay replied.

Horace Smythe merely nodded his assent.

Clive tried the door of the car in which they had traveled from Earth to Novum Araltum. It was not fastened. He opened it and climbed inside.

Horace Smythe followed Clive and busied himself with checking the car's controls, while Sidi Bombay circled the car examining its exterior, now scrambling across its top like a squirrel, now squirming beneath it like a ferret. Eventually he entered the car and sealed the door behind himself.

Sidi Bombay said, "Clive Folliot, the car seems unharmed."

"Everything's on the up-and-up," Horace Smythe put in.

Once again Clive Folliot felt the weight of leadership upon his shoulders. This was a position he had not sought, nor was it one that he wished to fill. But it had been thrust upon him. Were he a Fabian addressed by Malvolio, he could not have felt more heavily his responsibility.

Leadership was his—must he be burdened next with greatness?

"Have a seat, Major. It's a long journey we're undertaking, and there's no need to stand."

Even as Clive complied with Horace Smythe's suggestion, he closed his eyes and concentrated his mental powers, attempting to renew his contact with George du Maurier. For a fleeting moment he felt strange tendrils of thought and personality. He might be brushing du Maurier's psychic being, or perhaps that of his own unborn brother Esmond—or someone else. How many of his acquaintances were dead? Even the Lady 'Nrrc'kth resided now in that unknown realm that lay beyond the veil of death.

When he felt a brush of icelike cold yet feathery lightness, was his mind brushing against that of the lady of emerald and diamond?

Where, in the bewildering scheme of things, was God?

He felt the car shift beneath him, and opened his eyes. The car lifted from the surface of Novum Araltum, rocking and tilting like a wooden boat pulling away from a pier.

Beneath the car, the asteroid shrank with visible speed, the forests surrounding the aerodrome rapidly swallowing the tiny open patch from which the ship had risen. The few buildings that stood at the edges of the clearing were visible momentarily like the houses in a miniature Christmas display, and then they were gone.

Sidi Bombay had taken the controls of the car, and Clive sat watching the Indian. He stood barefoot and nearly naked, clad only in the white turban and breechclout he had worn when Clive and Horace found him at the inn. His dark skin, old and wizened when first Clive had encountered him in Equatoria and then stripped away and regrown as that of a young man amid the horrors of the Dungeon, glinted like fine onyx in the light of the distant sun and the still more distant stars.

Beside Sidi Bombay stood the wooden carrying case

that held the caged and helpless Chaffri. As Clive stared at the creature he let his mind summon up images of the men and women—and other beings!—he had faced in his adventures.

Amazingly, the Chaffri took on the form of each one as Clive thought of him or her. For a moment it was the oily and obsequious Tippu Tib, a slave trader whose enmity Clive had gained in Zanzibar so long ago. Then it became the ruthless and treacherous N'wrbb Crrd'f, the companion and self-proclaimed consort of the lost Lady 'Nrrc'kth—into whose clutches Clive had fallen on the planet Djajj.

Then for a moment Clive's thoughts settled upon the faithful, massive, doglike dwarf Finnbogg, also a former prisoner on Djajj. In that moment the captive Chaffri seemed to turn into Finnbogg. Finnbogg in miniature, Finnbogg reduced from the size of a good-sized pony to that of a housecat, but otherwise a perfect and living Finnbogg.

Sidi Bombay turned his head and looked, startled, at the Chaffri. He reached toward the case carefully, hesitantly.

Finnbogg sprang toward Sidi Bombay's extended fingers. The dwarf carried the half-organic, half-mechanical claw weapon that he had obtained at the battle with the Ren, that terrible battle atop the black, arching bridge on faraway Q'oorna. That claw, plus a set of murderous fangs as menacing as those of the underslung-jawed bulldog, were Finnbogg's armaments.

The Indian snatched his hand back from the Chaffri's cage in the nick of time.

Teeth and claw clashed against the wooden bars that held the Chaffri, and Finnbogg fell back against the floor of its cage, shifting from shape to shape to shape with a speed that defied the eye to follow or the mind to grasp.

"It was our friend Finnbogg," Sidi Bombay gasped.

"It never was, Sidi!" Horace Smythe demurred.

"You are right, Horace Smythe. It was I who saw through the illusions of the Chaffri on Novum Araltum—only to be taken in by this puny creature's flummery. A fool I am. The merest momentary relaxation of one's alertness, of one's mental barriers, and disaster awaits!"

"But it was I who was thinking of Finnbogg," Clive

half-apologized. "The creature must have been picking up my thoughts. But I thought that the images we saw of the Chaffri were mere illusions, and that only the one who provided the recollection upon which the illusion was based could see it."

Clive wondered how much time they had to pursue the question of the captive Chaffri—the use to which it might be put, the danger which it might present. "How long to reach our destination, Sidi Bombay?"

The Indian said, "We should reach our goal before long, Clive Folliot. The distance involved is very, very great. Far more of your English miles must be crossed than we three could count among us, but the car can cut across the distances rather than travel them. We will be there when we are only hours older than we were when we left Novum Araltum."

Clive turned from Sidi Bombay and Horace Hamilton Smythe. Outside the car's transparent walls, the darkness of the sky was pierced by the brilliance of uncounted remote stars, each blazing with its own frozen fire.

Feeling a hand on his shoulder, Clive turned to see Horace Hamilton Smythe. "It's a splendid sight, innit, sah?"

"You've been here before, Horace?"

"You were lost in the Dungeon a long time, sah. Sidi Bombay and I—and a good many others who have enlisted in the cause, sah—yes, Major, I've been here before."

Clive shook his head. "Understand, Sergeant Smythe, I was not in the Dungeon for the entire twenty-eight years. Far from it. The space-train that I boarded on Earth's polar region brought me across the years as well as the miles. It brought me and Henry Frankenstein's monster—and where is the monster now, I wish I knew. But you've been to many places, I suppose, Horace. Places unknown to me."

"Yes, sah. But I'm sure the Major has been to as many, and as strange."

"Perhaps, Horace. Perhaps."

Sidi Bombay reached to nudge Horace Smythe. The Indian pointed to an instrument mounted beneath the front window of the car. Smythe peered past Sidi Bombay and grunted his understanding. To Clive Folliot he said, "Best hold on tight, sah. This is the hard part."

Clive had no time to ask for clarification. Sidi Bombay pressed a lever, the ship lurched, and Clive Folliot found himself holding on for dear life.

It was like taking the famous coaster ride at Brighton. The car surged forward. Clive felt as if his intestines had been left behind. The distant stars, fixed though they were, seemed to move toward the car, accelerating by the moment. Their colors blurred and shifted as if every point of light in the firmament had been drenched in freshly shed blood.

The Chaffri behind its wooden bars launched itself into a paroxysm of terror and rage, racing around its cage, changing its form by the moment from beast to insect to indescribable monstrosity, screaming what might have been curses in a language resembling none that Clive Folliot had ever heard.

Then with a final surge and a jolt that produced an almost audible snap, the stars that surrounded the little glass car winked out of existence.

Clive felt as if he were floating, weightless, in the car. He held on to a brass rod, peering through the glass, trying to see what had happened. The car's mad acceleration had ceased, or at least it appeared to have done so. The star-scattered blackness that had surrounded the ship was no longer to be seen. Nothing was to be seen through the glass.

For all that Clive could perceive, the car might have been plunged into a sea of gray, featureless sludge. Above and below, ahead and behind, all were the same.

The Chaffri had collapsed on the bottom of its cage and lay there motionless—as far as Clive could perceive, lifeless. It had lost all form and had the appearance of a gray mass of undifferentiated protoplasm. As Clive watched, the blob stirred feebly. Apparently, all it could do was quiver.

"Is this all? Sidi Bombay, Horace, is this all?"

"No, Clive Folliot. Now we wait."

"For what? For how long?"

"Forever, Clive Folliot, and for no time at all."

Clive squinted into the gray nothingness. Forever and for no time at all—what did that mean? He looked at Sidi Bombay, looked at Horace Hamilton Smythe. Were they the vigorous specimens of young middle years with whom he had left Novum Araltum?

For a moment, Sidi Bombay appeared an infant.

For a breath, Horace Smythe appeared a feeble oldster.

Clive blinked.

No, it was Horace who was a child, bald and toothless, and Sidi Bombay who was an ancient, bald and toothless.

Clive raised his hand before his eyes. Was his skin smooth and chubby and unmarked, the hand of a baby? Was it papery dry and bloodless, the age-marked skin of a gaffer?

He blinked.

Outside the car the gray sludge was receding, organizing itself into a coherent form.

The grayness was flattening, hardening into a discernible surface. It extended in all directions, lying far beneath the car. Above the glass panes was blackness again, but this was not the star-sprinkled blackness that Clive Folliot had seen when the car was speeding away from Novum Araltum in vain hope of overtaking the Muntor Eshverud's Chaffri ship. This was an absolute and unbroken blackness, a blackness that might only be imagined by a collier trapped deep beneath the surface of the deepest coal pit in Wales.

Then slowly, so slowly and insidiously that Clive could not be certain of the moment it was first visible to him, there appeared high overhead the swirling, spinning, mesmeric pattern that he had seen so often before.

The spiral of stars!

Clive reached to grasp Horace Hamilton Smythe's sleeve.

"I see it, sah. No need to ask me if I do, Major."

"But what does it mean, Horace? We saw it in Equatoria, it was blazoned on the grip of that revolver you once carried, I saw it again at Earth's polar ice cap!"

From beyond Horace Smythe, Sidi Bombay said, "It is the Sign of the Ordolite, Clive Folliot. It is the home of the Gennine."

"Then it is our goal! Our goal at last!"

"It is indeed."

"Can the car carry us there?"

"It can, Clive Folliot."

"Then take us there, Sidi Bombay! Take us there, and our long struggle shall end in triumph at last!"

Clive caught Sidi Bombay and Horace Smythe exchanging glances again, but before he could demand an explanation, the world went spinning.

Clive's ears were smitten by a horrendous crash. Shards of shattered glass flew in every direction. Clive's clothing was shredded and his skin pierced or slashed in a hundred places. It was a miracle that neither he nor either of his companions was mortally wounded.

The car was spinning insanely, the gray surface and the black sky with its spiraling stars whirling vertiginously, first the plain above and the sky beneath the car, then the other way about.

Clive clutched at a metal bar but it came loose in his hand. As the car went end over end he tumbled with limbs akimbo. He felt himself collide with the bare flesh that must belong to Sidi Bombay. Metal rods and clumps of wooden furnishing and cloth upholstery torn loose by the impact tumbled and bounced crazily.

There was a shriek of triumph and Clive turned to see that the wooden cage that had held the Chaffri prisoner had been shattered, squashed flat by a piece of flying machinery. The Chaffri itself, reduced to little more than a puddle of grayish mud, formed its protoplasm into a perfect globe. It bounded once from a fragment of broken glass, assumed the form of a horrendous winged reptile, and launched itself from the car, flying through the unknown medium as fast as its flapping wings could carry it.

For a moment the car partially stabilized. Clive could see Sidi Bombay struggling frantically with what remained of the little craft's controls, and the machine responded—in part.

Sidi Bombay was unable to restore the car's level path, much less direct it upward again as he would need to do to reach the spiral of stars. But at least he managed to stop its dizzying tumble and achieve a precarious, wobbling descent toward the gray plain.

Long black lines became visible, dividing the plain into what seemed an endless pattern of parallel strips. Far beneath the car Clive could see the cause of the disastrous impact: it was the train that he had seen both in Q'oorna and at the Earth's pole—the train that traveled not along a pair of hand-laid tracks but through the labyrinthine maze of time and space.

The train had apparently descended from above the car. Perhaps deliberately, perhaps inadvertently, its engineer had rammed the glass car.

Now the train was descending ahead of the car. Folliot could see that the train was badly damaged, too. Not as badly damaged, to be sure, as was the car. But the crumpled metal and broken glass that could be seen on the train gave evidence that it had not emerged unscathed from its recent encounter.

"It's going to land beneath us," Clive cried out.

"Do you wish me to avoid it, Clive Folliot? I can bring us to rest some distance from it, and there we can make our plans."

Clive took quick assessment of the progress of the train and of their own. It would be less than a minute before they came to rest. "No, Sidi Bombay. We shall have to confront those rascals. We might as well do so at once."

Sidi Bombay cast a glance at Clive, behind his naked shoulder. "As you wish, Clive Folliot. You are our leader."

It was impossible for Clive to determine whether the Indian's speech contained a tincture of irony. He chose to remain silent.

"Best batten down, sah," the faithful Horace Hamilton Smythe reminded him. "This 'un may be a rough landing."

With Sidi Bombay still engaged at the controls, the other men cleared as much of the wreckage and debris as they could from the interior of the car. As he contemplated the remnants of the erstwhile Chaffri cage, Smythe sighed. "We almost had us one that time, di'n we, sah? We surely almost did!"

"Save the wreckage of the cage, Horace," Clive urged.

"But, why, sah?"

"I don't know. It may be useful."

The car bounced from the gray plain, bounded into the

air and struck again, slid in a skewing, curving course, and rocked to a halt. Clive peered at the already stationary space-train and calculated the distance between the craft as less than that of a cricket pitch.

Movement was visible among the cars of the train. Clive strained his eyes for a clear look at what was going on. To his horror and astonishment, black-and-green-armored troopers like those he had seen near his ancestral estate at Tewkesbury were clambering from several cars, and were setting up patrols the length of the train.

"Enemies again!"

"We can face 'em, sah!"

"But if the Ren are those tentacled monstrosities we encountered on Q'oorna and the Chaffri are these mantislike creatures . . ."

"They take many forms, Clive Folliot. That you must surely comprehend by now."

"Of course," Clive managed, "of course. But then—" He shook his head, unable to continue.

A squad of the troopers had left the train and were jogging along at a brisk, military double-time, headed for the remnants of the glass car.

"So much for the Universal Neighborhood Improvement Association," Clive managed. He climbed from the car, carefully avoiding the shards of shattered glass and broken metal. "Come along, men!"

"Ain't we goin' ter fight 'em, Major?"

"It would be hopeless, Sergeant. We'll talk to them and see what we can accomplish."

"But they'll take us prisoner, sah!" Horace's eyes registered the terror and distaste with which he viewed that prospect.

Clive did not answer, for he was standing near the crumpled and blackened prow of the ruined vehicle.

The squad of troopers trotted to within a dozen yards of Clive and halted in perfect unison. The commander of the squad, his visor pushed back to the top of his helmet to reveal a remarkably boyish and good-looking countenance, stood face-to-face with Clive.

Before Clive could speak a word, he was astonished to see the green-and-black-armored officer snap a smart salute, and say in a youthful and cultured voice, "My commander's apologies to Major Folliot and his companions for the unfortunate damage to their vehicle. Full compensation will of course be paid—and my commander invites the Major and his party to join us aboard the train."

While Clive pondered his answer, the officer reached up with green-gauntleted hands and began unscrewing the gleaming black-and-green helmet as if it were a part of a diving costume. The helmet removed and clutched beneath one elbow, the armor-clad commander shook out "his" long blond tresses.

The commander was a young woman—hardly more than a girl!

"I accept your commander's apologies and the invitation you convey as well," Clive responded. "But you have the advantage of me, Miss. You know my name and I do not know yours."

A winning smile creased the full lips that Clive no longer found boyish at all. "You do not recognize me?"

"I fear not."

"Well, I shall not tease you, Great-Uncle. I am your own flesh and blood, Clive Folliot. I am Anna Maria Folliot."

"Folliot!"

"Yes, Great-Uncle."

"But—but how—?"

"You are the younger brother of Sir Neville Folliot."

"I am that."

"Neville was my grandfather."

A frown creased Clive's brow. "How old are you, Anna Maria?"

"I am twenty."

"Then you were born in 1876."

The young woman's laughter tinkled like tiny silver bells sounding clearly through the crisp air of a winter morn in the English countryside. "You think so stolidly, Great-Uncle. Surely you must realize that time is neither so simple nor logic so straightforward as that."

Clive frowned. There was no end, no end to the surprises that the universe held. Every time he thought that he had found a simple and irrefutable truth, Nature proved him wrong. "I'm trying to calculate the year of your father's birth, Anna Maria. Your father, who would have been my nephew."

Anna Maria interrupted his thoughts. "He was born in 1858, Great-Uncle."

"But I never knew that Neville had married."

Again the beautiful girl laughed, and her laugh set Clive's blood rushing through his veins, his skin tingling in every limb. But no, this girl was his own flesh and blood! Once before he had come close to the unspeakable, before he had realized that Annabelle Leigh, his beloved User Annie, she of the incomprehensible speech and the irresistible manner, was his own direct descendant.

Anna Maria Folliot was *not* his direct descendant, but she was the granddaughter of his brother, and that knowledge forced Clive to abandon a certain line of thought that had barely opened to his contemplation.

"I don't mean to be discourteous, Great-Uncle, but we haven't the time to stand here and trace our family history. There's too much to do, too little time in which to do it. We can catch up on bloodlines and family gossip later on."

Clive looked at Sidi Bombay and at Horace Hamilton Smythe. Clearly, either of his companions was prepared to lift from his shoulders the responsibility for making such decisions as had to be made. There were earlier times in which they had taken the initiative, and there might be later ones in which they would do so again. But for now, Clive Folliot alone bore the responsibility of leadership. The responsibility of decision.

"Let's go!"

"You have no gear to remove from your car?" Anna Maria asked.

Clive shook his head.

The two Folliots, Clive in his London clothes of 1896 and Anna Maria in her gleaming armor, fell in side by side and began tramping toward the train. Clive cast a single glance over his shoulder. Behind them, Sidi Bombay and Sergeant Horace Hamilton Smythe were being marched by Anna Maria's armor-clad troopers. The relationship and manner of march could be interpreted as that of an honor guard—or that of troops policing prisoners of war.

Sidi Bombay had returned to the wreckage of the car and retrieved something. As Clive watched, he waved it once around his turbaned head, then placed it conspicuously in his breechclout. It was the cyberclaw which Sidi Bombay had obtained on Q'oorna, and which Clive had not seen since leaving that black planet. How Sidi Bombay managed still to have it, Clive thought, was merely one more of the endless mysteries of the Dungeon. But if Sidi Bombay felt that the cyberclaw might again be of use, Clive was pleased to see him carrying it.

At the train the party halted. Anna Maria took Clive's arm, separating him from his companions and herself from her command. At her encouragement, Clive climbed the steps to a seemingly undamaged car. Anna Maria followed close behind him.

She stood beside him, facing a splendidly uniformed man who sat behind an ornate desk.

"Grandfather," Anna Maria said to the older man, "Great-Uncle Clive is here at last."

Neville Folliot looked up from his desk and smiled at his younger brother. "So nice to see you again, Clive. Would you like a glass of brandy?"

▪ CHAPTER 21 ▪
"I Thought I Had Seen the Ultimate!"

Stunned, Clive stood gaping at his brother. He was unable to speak.

"Have you been deafened by some incident, Clive? Can you not hear me? I offered you a libation."

"What are you doing here, Neville? I saw you last at Tewkesbury. You and Father. And Annabelle Leigh, my great-great-granddaughter."

"But Clive, you have come to see me—not I, you. Why must I explain myself?" Neville's lip curled in a smile that was not unmixed with a sneer.

Clive's mind raced. Was this truly Neville—or a simulacrum? Or was he merely an illusion created by a Ren or a Chaffri? Clive had encountered all three. In fact, he had been told that the father and grandfather he had seen in Tewkesbury were false, as was Annabelle Leigh—the Annabelle Leigh who had accompanied him to the country manor. He stared at Neville, trying to determine whether or not he truly beheld his brother.

"What is the matter, little brother? Little Miss Minnie got your tongue?"

Little Miss Minnie! Yes, a variation on the expression, *cat got your tongue?* Little Miss Minnie had been Clive and Neville's childhood pet. Their love for the plump black and white feline was one of the few things upon which they had ever managed to agree. Both boys had adored the little cat, had doted on her, competing for her affection.

No simulacrum could know about Little Miss Minnie,

no clone would possess that information. As for an illusion, that was more difficult to determine. If Neville were really an alien, drawing the image and the very recollections from Clive's mind, then the emotionally charged memory of Little Miss Minnie would be a powerful tool for use in controlling him.

If only there were someone he could ask—someone to offer advice.

A ghostly voice whispered in Folliot's mind. *Clive, he is real.*

Du Maurier? Clive queried mentally.

No Clive. It is I, your brother Esmond.

Esmond? But how do I know . . . how can I trust . . .

There comes a time, my brother, when one must trust. One must! For you, that time has come, my brother. For you, that time is this very moment.

"It was your space-train that collided with the car in which my companions and I were traveling," Clive said to Neville.

"Oh, yes. I hope no one was badly hurt?"

"Through no agency of yours, Neville! It was sheer fortune that Sidi Bombay and Horace Smythe and I survived. I still—"

"You've made the acquaintance of your grandniece, I see."

"If you will be so kind as not to interrupt me, brother! We are working in the interest of all mankind. Of all mankind and more! The Gennine—"

"Please!" Neville held up his hand. "Please, little brother. I'm sorry I've upset you. I understand your being upset, of course. But—"

"What happened at Tewkesbury? What happened after I departed for London? Where is Annabelle? What of Father?"

Again, Neville interrupted by holding up a hand. In an odd moment of abstraction, Clive found himself concentrating on the intricate patterns worked into the cuff of Neville's sleeve. At first blush, the metallic threads were embroidered in a wholly abstract and even random pattern, but upon closer examination an orderly arrangement became visible. Buried within the swirls and streaks of the embroidery was the familiar spiral of stars.

"Please," Neville said, "seat yourself and be comfortable, little brother. We are not squabbling schoolboys any longer. At least, I hope we are not."

Fuming, Clive complied with Neville's request. The brothers locked eyes. Clive said, "I make no warrant to you, Neville. The stakes are far too high for me to bind myself to petty rules. But for the moment, at least—proceed."

Neville Folliot inclined his head. "Fair enough, brother Clive. Father is dead."

"Dead?"

"I spoke clearly, I believe."

"In what manner did he die? And when?"

"He was an old man when last we were together at Tewkesbury. The end came shortly after you took your leave. It was a peaceful end, Clive. In the midst of our ordinary rustic existence, Father slipped away quite quietly and peacefully. He was napping, and when it came time to waken him, the old man had simply ceased to live."

"Together at Tewkesbury? I do not recall such a meeting—unless you refer to an occasion in 1868 or earlier, Neville."

"I refer to our meeting less than twenty-four hours ago, little brother. Our meeting in the library at Folliot Manor."

"Was that truly you, Neville? I thought that was some surrogate of yours?"

"No, Clive. What gave you that idea?"

What had given him that idea, indeed? His conversation with Horace Smythe and Sidi Bombay. Had they, his two dearest companions, lied to him? Or had they been mistaken? Or was *Neville* the liar? Was his older brother lying *now*?

Esmond Folliot whispered in Clive's mind. *Trust him, brother. Now is the moment. You must trust him.*

"Never mind, Neville," Clive forced himself to say. "Never mind all that. It was you, then, at Tewkesbury. I trust you."

Clive dropped his head into his hands. Though he and

his father had been less than close, though the old baron had favored Neville over Clive and blamed Clive throughout his life for the death of his mother—a tragedy for which Clive was by no means culpable—still, he had been bound to the baron by the closest tie of blood, that of parent and offspring. The loss of his father affected him more powerfully than he had expected it ever would.

"I shall never see him again, then, Neville."

"Oh—you may!"

Clive raised his eyes to those of his brother. "What do you mean?" Perhaps, he conjectured, Neville, too, had been in communication with their never-born brother Esmond. Clive's own contacts with Esmond had been few and faint, more tantalizing than fulfilling. And yet . . . and yet . . . what an irony, if the disembodied soul of their never-born sibling should prove the great link that reunited the estranged brothers Folliot!

There were also Clive's contacts with George du Maurier. Those disembodied dialogues had commenced before du Maurier's death. Perhaps it was the forging of the mental bond with du Maurier while he still lived that permitted the more nearly complete exchange of thoughts to whatever realm it was that lay beyond the veil. . . .

"I mean," Neville Folliot said, "that to those who can travel through the web of time and space, all men are both dead and alive. Yes, both dead and alive. Father and Mother, you and I, your various sweethearts . . ."

Clive sputtered in protest at Neville's casual use of the term *sweethearts*.

Neville smiled. "Clive, you got a child upon Miss Leighton, then you abandoned her to go chasing off after . . . who was that strange creature with the death-white skin and the forest-green hair?"

"The Lady 'Nrrc'kth," Clive whispered. "She told me that she knew you, Neville."

A wistful smile brushed Neville's face, then departed. "That is true, brother Clive. The Lady 'Nrrc'kth and I were acquainted, and the pleasure was altogether mine."

Clive clenched his fists and his teeth, holding himself in check. When he was able once more to speak, he said, "The Lady 'Nrrc'kth was a finer woman than you are worthy to consort with, Neville. She was brought into this matter against her will, she served nobly and she died bravely in the struggle against the Chaffri and the Ren."

'Well, that is as it may be."

'And if I could return to the Dungeon, rescue her at the moment of her death, bring her to a safer place—would she truly live, Neville?"

"Alas, brother, she would not. That is the one immutable law of existence, both in the Dungeon and out of it. One lives one's life, one suffers one's death. We can visit the past and the future, to a degree we can change them. But the law of life and death is greater than our poor power to change."

"Then Father, too, is truly dead."

"Oh yes."

Clive raised his eyes once more to lock with his brother's. "And you are Baron Tewkesbury."

Neville smiled. There was a mockery of the self-effacement in his expression, and more than a hint of smugness. "I am, indeed."

"Shame to our house, Neville. That you should become Lord Folliot, you who are a traitor not merely to your sovereign but to your race, your world—a traitor to all free beings! Shame, Neville! I thought I had seen the ultimate in the venial and the traitorous, but you have exceeded anything I have seen before!"

Neville Folliot burst out laughing. "You are such a prig, Clive! And a hypocrite as well. You've confronted me over my little dalliances of long ago—".

"For which I paid the price!"

"—and I suppose you will condemn me for the union from which the lovely Anna Maria is descended."

"I do not know, Neville. Who is the girl's grandmother? Was Anna Maria's father conceived under honorable circumstances? Where is he? Who is he? Who is her mother? And where is your own spouse, brother Neville? You have much to answer for."

"Read me no sermons, Clive, and do not question me as if I were an erring schoolboy and you a master. You have begun to try my patience! I allow you your foolishness because you are my brother. And because you are fairly harmless. You border, occasionally, upon the amusing. But enough is enough. Now I shall have to decide what to do with you and your companions."

"What about my companions?"

"Oh, your country bumpkin and your dusky friend are safe enough. I've sent them off to work for their keep."

"Bumpkin! Dusky friend! Horace Smythe and Sidi Bombay are each a dozen times the man you are, Neville! If you knew the deeds of heroism they have performed— each of them, and many times, each of them!"

The heated exchange was interrupted by a series of thumps and cries from outside the train. Neville Folliot shoved himself from his seat and leaped to the side of the coach, where heavy drapes covered large windows. He shove aside the drapes, Clive Folliot at his elbow, their quarrel for the moment forgotten.

Outside the coach, the gray plain stretched endlessly in all directions. The black lines that Clive had seen from the aerial car—or that he had thought he had seen—were no longer visible. Perhaps they had been an illusion, after all.

Green-and-black-armored troopers were dashing from the coaches, forming into precisely aligned military units and trotting away.

Without a word, the two brothers headed for the exit. They clambered onto the gray plain. Clive bent for an instant to feel the surface. To the eye it appeared hard, solid, featureless. But to his hands it seemed to have no surface. He extended his fingertips, anticipating a substance like slate, but felt . . . nothing. There was no surface, no plane. Instead, Clive pressed his hand down, and at a certain point, it simply went no farther.

He straightened.

A mass of troopers had assembled, formed up in ranks and columns with a precision that would have made Her Majesty's Guards envious.

Standing before the troopers, her trim armor gleaming (and where, Clive asked himself, did the light come from?), stood Anna Maria Folliot. She held her helmet beneath her arm. Her hair swirled in a passing breeze, and Clive wondered where the wind came from.

For an instant he was immobilized by her beauty. She

had all the best characteristics of the Folliots—strong, solid bones, the complexion of the English countryside, softly shining tresses that flirted languorously with each zephyr. And she had another set of characteristics. If Neville was her grandfather, then three-fourths of her heritage were unknown to Clive.

Where had she traveled? What had transpired in her life? What had brought her to this strange locale, to the position of command and authority she clearly held?

Anna Maria faced about, looked questioningly at Neville, then nodded her acceptance of a set of instructions that he uttered so rapidly and cryptically that Clive was unable to comprehend their meaning. She turned away, toward the troopers, and issued a sharp command.

The troopers turned and moved off, trotting smartly toward the rear of the train.

Clive reached to touch his brother's arm, to demand an explanation of this newest turn of events. But Neville was himself moving away from Clive, trotting parallel to Anna Maria Folliot and the gleaming, armored troopers.

A mass of movement drew his attention and he sprinted forward, distancing the military unit. His brother was close behind.

The movement became clearer. It was a collection of bodies, all of them human, but garbed in a melange of styles ranging from the exotic and unfamiliar to that of urban civilization, from the ancient and primitive to the up-to-date, and, Clive suspected, beyond.

For a moment he was reminded of the polyglot corps he had faced when first he had sounded the huge gong in Q'oorna. Roman legionnaire, Apache warrior, Japanese Samurai, and European Zouave mixed indiscriminately. Some of the warriors, he discerned, were female—but that should have been no surprise, in view of his grand-niece's position of command under Neville.

And as the aggregation of arms and legs and torsoes writhed, a greater, darker mass rose from their center.

For an instant Clive thought it might be one of the monster Ren, replete with tentacles and suckers and claws, but this being was a monster of a very different sort.

It was clad in a black suit with tattered jacket and

ill-fitting trousers. Its skin was as pale as death—or as that of the Lady 'Nrrc'kth—but with the sickly palor of the grave rather than the exotic whiteness of that woman's icelike beauty.

Like a stag beleaguered by wolves, Henry Frankenstein's unnatural creation struggled to its feet. A spearman clad as in the days of Pharaonic Egypt clung to one arm, and a female individual wearing incandescent trousers and a blouse of what appeared to be writhing worms held to the other.

The monster spun, flinging its arms outward.

In a moment, his two attackers lost their grips on his black-clad arms and flew above the heads of their erstwhile comrades, crashing down onto persons unable to avoid the impact.

The monster roared. He lifted a foot. Another attacker, this one looking like an Aztec priest, clung to his leg. The monster uttered another cry of rage and swept his hand at the Aztec. The latter was dislodged, fell back to the gray earth, and was trampled, for his trouble, beneath the monster's massive boot.

Clive heard the crunch of human bones.

The monster turned as if seeking desperately for an avenue of escape. He locked eyes with Clive. The exchange lasted for only the briefest of moments, but in that fleeting instant Clive could read the monster's message.

Why had the soldiers attacked him to begin with? Clive wondered. But there was no time to resolve that question. The monster was an inhuman revenant, a being constructed blasphemously from the remnants of the grave. Clive's stomach twisted at the recollection of his encounter with the monster at Earth's polar cap. Clive had climbed aboard one coach of the train as it settled there amid the groaning ice. And the monster had boarded another.

Clive had found himself in London, in the last decade of the nineteenth century. Yet somehow the monster had wound up here—here in this strange, unworldly locale that was the nearest approach yet to the spiraling stars and the home of the Gennine.

The monster was struggling to extricate himself from the disorganized attack of his polyglot assailants. Beyond the clustered figures, Clive thought he could make out two more familiar forms, racing toward him. Yes, it was they! It was Sidi Bombay and Horace Hamilton Smythe!

The monster had recognized in Clive a familiar face. Though the dead-alive creation had expressed his hatred of Clive in their previous encounter, he was now struggling to make his way to Clive. He knew Clive, knew that he would remember him, and that he might be an ally, an ally of familiarity in the face of the alien and the hostile.

Flailing with his mighty arms, hurling attackers aside with every stride, the monster advanced. Clive was reminded of a mighty beast throwing aside ravening wolves. Who was the monster, who the assailant? To Clive's recollection, in Mrs. Shelley's novel and in the dramatizations that had brought her story to the playhouses of the world, the monster had been—at least initially—a creature of innocence. Called into being not by his own will but by that of the intemperate Dr. Frankenstein, the monster had been set upon by man and dog, had found in a blind hermit his single friend, only to be driven from the hermit's hovel by sighted men. Despised and rejected by all, even by his own creator, the monster had been abandoned to his fate, drifting to his inevitable death amid the polar ice floes.

But his death had not been inevitable!

Somehow the monster had found refuge in a cave of ice. Frozen there, he had remained for untold years, until released from his icy imprisonment by Clive and Chang Guafe. And now he was here!

Was he menace, or was he victim?

Had his rage at Clive been the pervasive instinct of a creature whose only desire was to rend and murder? Or was the monster simply reflecting the emotions that had been meted upon him?

Clive managed a feeble grin and the semblance of a welcoming, encouraging gesture.

The ghastly simulacrum of a smile on his cadaverous features, the monster lurched even more desperately toward Clive. He managed to break loose from his attackers, and then he covered the gray distance between himself and Clive Folliot with astonishing speed.

Even as the monster escaped his besiegers, Sidi Bombay and Horace Smythe were racing toward Clive. The three arrived simultaneously. Sidi Bombay and Horace Smythe could see that Clive and the monster were in some fashion acquainted, but they cautiously kept Clive between themselves and the giant being.

The brigade of armor-clad troopers under command of Anna Maria Folliot were tramping toward the quartet. In the opposite direction, the monster's ragtag erstwhile pursuers had formed into a disorganized band and were advancing again.

Behind them was the train. Ahead of them, an infinite and featureless gray expanse.

They could try to board the train, they could flee across the featureless plain, or they could stand and fight, caught between two parties of attackers.

And Clive could feel the eyes of his three companions upon him. They had turned to him for leadership—for decision!

Only for the barest fraction of a second, Clive Folliot squeezed his eyes shut and made a supreme mental effort. He felt as if he had left his body. He could look back and see himself and his three companions, the ragtag gang that had attacked the monster and the black-and-green-clad brigade commanded by Anna Maria, all of them frozen as if they were captured in a daguerreotype.

Nearby, Clive could see his brother Neville.

Neville alone, of the uncounted men and women before him, seemed unfrozen, aware of the situation, able to act. He raised a fist and shook it toward Clive. His mouth moved and words emerged.

But all in a strange, slow tempo, as if Neville were moving at half-time, quarter-time, one-eighth-time. Slower, slower, and still slower.

Clive found himself suffused in a blinding illumination.

George du Maurier said, *You are in command!*

Esmond Folliot said, *You are the Master of the Ordolite! Esmond!*

I tell you that you are the Master of the Ordolite!

What does that mean to you? Clive asked.

Go back!

*You were never born. You never lived, Clive retorted.
What can you care?*

You must command!

I will not go, Esmond! Not until you answer my question.

Du Maurier—our schoolboy asserts himself.

Better that he does, du Maurier said. *Should a weakling
rule?*

He has known sultans.

*He has known Philo Goode, Esmond. He has known
Timothy F. X. O'Hara!*

*And he has survived. What odds were quoted at the
outset, du Maurier?*

*He has not merely survived. He has grown. He is nearly
ready.*

Hmm. Perhaps he is ready, then.

*It is my fault, brother Clive. You were to have been
firstborn. I tried to usurp your place and failed—*

*What do you mean? We know nothing of our lives
before birth,* Clive said silently.

You remember *nothing of them, you mean!*

*What difference does it make? The succession of a rural
barony, Esmond, really!*

*You do not understand, Clive! The next Baron Tewkes-
bury should have been the Master of the Ordolite! And
that baron is rightfully* you, *Clive! But by my ambition, I
denied myself life and I caused such disarray that Neville
was born before you. Thus, he is now Baron Tewkesbury,
while you are the rightful Master of the Ordolite! The two
roles—that of the baron, and that of Master of the Ordolite,
have been sundered. Go back and claim what is yours!
Command in the name of your rightful authority! That is
all that can save—*

There was a crack as of nearby sheet lightning in an
Equatorian thunderstorm, and Clive was standing surrounded by Sidi Bombay and Horace Hamilton Smythe
and the Frankenstein monster.

He touched each of them, briefly, laying his palm upon
the crown of their heads. To reach the monster's head, he
had to stand on tippy-toe and reach as high as he could,
but he succeeded.

All three moved. Their two bands of attackers remained frozen.

Neville Folliot, hatred and fear blazing in his eyes, continued to stride toward Clive, moving with terrible, slow deliberation. He had drawn a pistol and was raising it toward his brother.

Clive covered the distance separating himself and his brother before Neville could bring the weapon fully to bear. Clive placed his hand upon his brother's wrist. He exerted no pressure, made no effort to turn the pistol aside.

Instead, he said, "Neville, I am the Master of the Ordolite. I command you to lower your pistol."

With infinite slowness, Neville moved to comply. Desperation flashed from his eyes, his muscles twitched, sweat sprang from his brow. But with unerring certainty, he returned the weapon to its holster. He opened his mouth to speak, but his movements were so slow that Clive simply ignored them.

To his followers, Clive said, "I know what is to be done. Come with me."

He did not look back to see if they followed. The question did not enter into consideration. He set off at a trot, efficient and space-consuming but unhurried. He passed the band of armored troopers, slowed for a moment to contemplate his grandniece, Anna Maria, then shook his head regretfully. There was no time to learn to know her better.

Reaching the front of the train, he grasped a metal rod and hauled himself into the engine compartment. A normal crew was present—an engineer, a pilot, a plotter, a mechanician. They appeared unharmed but were as motionless as the warriors outside on the endless gray plain.

Clive turned to Sidi Bombay and the others. "Don't hurt them. But get them out of here."

"What—?"

"Obey."

As his aides removed the crewmen, Clive said, "We shall decouple this engine from the cars behind. We are going on!"

• CHAPTER 22 •
"The Gennine—Face to Face!"

The engine that pulled the space-train bore only a slight resemblance to the locomotives with which Clive was familiar.

"It looks like one of them bloody things that Missoor Verne writes about," Horace Smythe commented. "All pointy and smoothed off, like a bloomin' gigantic bullet."

"That doesn't matter," Clive said. "Just—can we run it?"

Smythe studied the controls, rubbing his chin and humming tunelessly the while. Clive's eyes darted toward Sidi Bombay. The Indian stood impassively; he, too, was watching Horace Smythe. Clive turned to look at Dr. Frankenstein's creation. The monster, like Sidi Bombay, was gazing at Horace Smythe in rapt concentration.

Unable to restrain his impatience, Clive peered from the cab. The enigmatic spiral of stars still hung in the blackness above the train.

Was the spiral revolving—or was Clive's distress causing him to imagine that it was? Were the stars burning suns uncounted millions of miles from the Earth and its own illuminating flame—or were they merely tiny points of light, no more than candles or miniature gas flames that hung tantalizingly just beyond human reach?

Clive knew that Annie had recovered the polished metallic machine she had obtained from the Japanese force at New Kwajalein Atoll. Could she now soar in it to those stars?

Back on the endless gray plain, Clive could see the two forces from which he and his companions had escaped. One party was still arrayed in precise alignment, clad in identical suits of gleaming armor; the other was as varied as the first was uniform, as disordered as the first was disciplined. And in either force, not a muscle moved.

Only the form of Clive's brother Neville moved. With agonizing slowness, Neville Folliot struggled toward the cab. His face was suffused with concentrated effort, his muscles bulged. His appearance was that of a man running through a vat of viscous fluid.

"Come along, then, Sergeant!" Clive could contain himself no longer. "Can you run this thing?"

Smythe turned from the complicated control panel. He frowned, then seemed to make an internal decision. "Yes, sah! I can do it, Major! I apologize for the delay, sah, but these controls are very strange to me. But I believe I can do it, sah. I'm willing to give it a go!"

"Fine, Sergeant Smythe!"

Sidi Bombay and the monster set about uncoupling the engine from the leading coach of the train.

Neville Folliot was nearing the platform.

Horace Smythe was working over the controls.

The engine vibrated.

Neville reached a hand toward the railing.

The coupler holding the engine to the rest of the train opened with a metallic clang.

The engine lurched forward.

Neville's fingers closed on the railing.

Sergeant Smythe pulled back on a lever.

The engine lifted from the featureless gray plain.

Although the engine was accelerating steadily, it had not yet achieved a great rate of speed. Far outside the window, silhouetted against the featureless sky like a black period on a sheet of gray foolscap, something was flying frantically toward the engine. As Clive stared, the point of blackness grew large. It took clear shape. It was a perfect miniature of the Lady 'Nrrc'kth.

Clive cried out, reaching for the beautiful creature.

"Stop, sah! Can't you see what it is?"

"It is the Lady 'Nrrc'kth, Horace!"

"No, sah! It's the Chaffri! It's concentrating all its force on you, sah! That's why I can see its true form! Don't let it in here again, sah!"

"Horace is right," Sidi Bombay called. "Keep it out, Clive Folliot!"

"No!" Clive shouted. "Even if you're right, it may be of use to us! Horace—see if you can get that cage back in order!"

In moments, Horace Smythe had jury-rigged the Chaffri's smashed cage, rebuilding it from its own smashed fragments. It was a makeshift job, but it looked sturdy enough, albeit untidy. Smythe stood aside, invisible from outside the engine.

Clive stood with his arms outstretched. "My darling! My Lady 'Nrrc'kth! You have returned to me!"

The Chaffri flew through the engine's window. Clive lunged aside as Horace Hamilton Smythe swooped upon the Chaffri, locking it once more in its cage.

Penned helplessly in its makeshift prison, the outwitted Chaffri went wild. In rapid sequence it assumed a dozen forms. Feathers, tentacles, scales, plates, fur chased one another across its skin. A series of piercing wails rose from it. Horrible fangs and claws scraped at the inside of its prison.

Finally it collapsed into a corner of its cage. It slithered, grew molten, puddled. With a twinge of guilt at his own gallows humor, Clive noted aloud that it looked like nothing more than a spoiled blancmange. It had only one discernible feature, a set of great teeth that it gnashed in frustration.

The engine accelerated, heaving forward and upward.

Outside the engine, Neville Folliot had finally drawn abreast of a window. The contrivance had lifted from the plain, but it moved at a height little greater than a tall man's thigh.

Clive bent and looked into his brother's face. Neville had managed to raise one arm painfully and grasp a metal railing on the side of the engine. But Clive realized instantly that Neville, unassisted, could not pull himself into the engine compartment. Left to his own devices, he would lose his grip and fall back onto the plain.

The engine was rising and accelerating ever more rapidly. Neville's feet had left the ground and he was clinging desperately to the side of the engine. Higher the engine moved, and faster.

Peering into the grayness, Clive estimated the distance the engine had now risen. If Neville fell from here he would surely die.

A hundred mixed emotions surged through Clive Folliot, a thousand memories flickered across the screen of his mind like images at a magic lantern show. Neville ragging and bullying him as a child. Neville leading him on a wild goose chase through East Africa. Neville appearing to rise from his casket and offer Clive the enigmatic journal that had led him to more grief in his journey through the Dungeon. Neville betraying Clive's trust time and again. Neville selling the Folliot honor

All Clive needed to do was permit Neville to fall and he might be rid of him forever. Other considerations aside, this event might leave Clive to inherit the title of Baron Tewkesbury. Neville had married and fathered a son, and that son had married and fathered a daughter, Anna Maria Folliot. Was Anna Maria's father still alive? If so, then with Neville's death the Tewkesbury title would devolve upon him; otherwise, upon Anna Maria. Clive had slipped to third place in the line of succession. But title or no, he could not cold-bloodedly permit his brother to die.

"This is not for your sake, Neville," Clive grunted under his breath. "This is for dear Little Miss Minnie!"

He reached his hand to his brother and drew him into the cab. He had every justification in the world to abandon Neville to his fate. But he could not do this.

The two brothers stood toe-to-toe. Each waited for the other to speak. At last Neville said, "Thank you, Clive."

With equal stiffness, Clive replied, "You are welcome, brother."

Neville surveyed the situation in the engine cab. He peered back at the gray plain where the remainder of the space-train still stood. He nodded as if he had been considering a difficult problem and had finally reached his conclusion. He looked closely at Horace Hamilton Smythe, nodded curtly to the man; then, at Sidi Bombay, and repeated the gesture, this time even more quickly and perfunctorily. At Frankenstein's monster he simply gazed, struck motionless as well as dumb.

The monster, hitherto as unmoving as a statue, opened

his eyes wide and raised a hand toward Neville. "Insect, do you wonder at the sight you behold? Know you not my origin and nature? As your puny race is to the God who made you, or whom you imagine to have made you, so is my kind to yours. My kind, of which I am the single representative, thanks to the wickedness of the very Man who built me and who then both created and destroyed the helpmate whose companionship was the sole beseechment of my prayer!"

Eyes fiery, the monster turned to Clive. "You, Clive Folliot, surprise me!"

"Do I?"

"I had thought ill of you, Clive Folliot."

"Indeed you must have! You tried to drown me by casting me from the boat crafted by Chang Guafe."

"I have a penchant for drownings, Clive Folliot. Try not my patience. Nonetheless, I have learned a good deal of your brother Neville Folliot, and it is clear to the judgment of any fair-minded observer that you have been harmed and offended by him. Even so, *in extremis,* when you could have consigned him to his doom simply by withholding from him your assistance—without taking positive action to his detriment, Clive Folliot—you granted that assistance. Tell me, Clive Folliot, why that was your act. I am puzzled. I had consigned you to the grade of mortal whose evil warrants no slightest consideration save to be crushed beneath the heel of an avenger as a helpless ant is squashed beneath a bumpkin's boot. I had considered you no more worthy of moral consideration than the gibbering, chittering thing that cowers in yon cage."

The monster paused and pointed dramatically at the Chaffri crouched against its bars, quivering and squealing softly and piteously.

Clive began to answer the monster, but before he could speak, the monster resumed his tirade. "You held the most violent of grudges, were the victim of the most heinous of affronts and provocations at the hands of your brother. And yet you have displayed a selfless consideration for his welfare and survival. Why, Clive Folliot, why? You are a member of the privileged and oppressing class of the most depraved and indulgent society on the face of the Earth, and even so, you perform an act of selfless charity. Do you even comprehend the motivation within your own breast that moved you to this act? Do you possess, after all, a moral sense worthy of my note? Tell me these things, Clive Folliot. Speak!"

Before the monster could catch his breath and resume still again, Clive managed to get his answer out. "I saved him for the sake of a little cat, Monster. That is the whole of it."

The monster drew a deep breath. But before he could launch another tirade, Neville laid a carefully manicured hand on Clive's wrist. "Does he always talk like that, brother?"

"Always, brother. For a while there, when he was trying to drown me, I thought it might be worth the experience to let him go ahead purely in order to escape his rantings."

Neville stared at his toes, obviously deep in thought. "Why *did* you save me, brother? Your answer to this exotic fellow may satisfy him, but I demand more of you. I did wrong you grievously, Clive. Have you forgiven me?"

"I have, Neville."

"But I have betrayed you more times than once."

Clive gave a bitter laugh. "Many more, indeed."

"And yet you forgive me again and again. Why, Clive? How many times will I wrong you, and how many will you forgive?"

"Seven times, Neville. Or seven times seven. Are we not so taught? The monster, poor soulless creature, may be motivated by revenge and consequently incapable of forgiveness. But our friend Sidi Bombay's philosophy is not so very different from that which is taught to us. And in the end, so Sidi has led me to understand, we determine our own fates. You will be saved or damned, my brother, by your own doing. Not by mine. I shall pray for you in either case."

"Pray for your enemies, Clive? Is that it?"

"I will pray for my brother. Enemy or friend, that is up to you, Neville. But my brother you are, will you or nil you."

Neville turned toward Horace Smythe. "Where are you headed, Sergeant?"

"There's only one place to go, sah. I'm certain that the Major knows it as well as I do."

"You are headed for the homeland of the Gennine!"

"Yes, sah!"

"Don't go there, Clive!" Neville Folliot grasped his brother's sleeve. The tables had been turned, the tyrant become supplicant. "Please, Clive!"

Neville turned from his brother, attempted to shove Horace Smythe from the engine's controls. Smythe resisted, and Clive pulled Neville away.

"What's the matter, older brother? Why are you so reluctant to visit the homeland of your masters?"

Neville sneered. "After so many years, Clive, you still maintain your invincible innocence! Very well—"

But before he could say another word, the engine was shrouded in absolute blackness and filled with a chill that penetrated to the very marrow of its occupants' bones.

"What—?"

The engine shuddered, but it seemed still to be moving forward. Clive peered outside. He could see nothing. Not the gray, distant plain below. Not the swirling spiral of stars above. The very air within the compartment seemed heavy, chill, and dark. The only light in the compartment was that emitted by the instruments before Horace Hamilton Smythe. They gave off an eerie glow, a pallid yellow that tinted everything into a monochromatic picture.

The cultured voice of Sidi Bombay said, "Major Folliot! Sergeant Smythe! Behold!" He pointed at the caged Chaffri. The others stared.

The Chaffri, which had previously subsided into a formless white puddle in the corner of its cage, now adopted a new form. It had grown arms and legs, and stood upright like a foot-tall mannequin. Its face was human, or more properly, demonic. Its nose was sharply pointed, its eyebrows arched. Its glossy black hair came to a widow's peak upon its forehead. A pair of perfectly formed horns grew from its forehead.

Its feet were cloven hoofs. It seemingly wore a scant, skin-tight costume, but as Clive strove to see it clearly in the yellow-tinged murk, he realized that it was not wearing tights at all. It was completely naked. It pranced and capered in its cage, and as it turned, Clive could see that it had a long, barb-tipped tail. In one fist it held a wicked-looking trident.

"Lor' 'elp us! What *is* it?" Horace Smythe gasped.

"We've already been through Hades in the Dungeon!" Clive exclaimed. "Not once, but twice."

"Aye." Horace nodded. "But I see no Baron Samedi to pull our chestnuts from the hearth this time, Major."

The caged creature had begun screaming at its captors, moving its free hand in a series of mystical-looking gestures and pointing its trident first at one, then at another.

"It's placing a curse on us!" Neville said.

The demon pointed an accusing finger as well as its trident at Neville. Its eyes glinted in the faint yellow light. Watching, Clive suspected that the demon would not have appeared yellow in a normal light.

Its incantation drew to a crescendo. A bolt of lurid-tinted lightning crackled from the centermost tine of its trident and spanned the distance from its cage to Neville Folliot.

Neville clutched himself where the bolt had struck. There was a peculiar scent in the air, discernible even in the dank, heavy atmosphere that filled the cabin. A wisp of smoke rose from a charred spot on Neville's gold-braided military tunic.

"You little bugger! You whippersnapper!" Neville slapped a hand on the wounded spot, rubbing vigorously. "I'll break you in two, you little fiend!"

He leaped toward the Chaffri's cage but Sidi Bombay stepped between him and the cage. "Please, Baron."

Mollified by the acknowledgment of his title, Neville drew up. The smoke had ceased to rise from his tunic, but when he took his hand away from the offended spot a circle of singed and blackened cloth remained.

"Why shouldn't I crush that little monster beneath my heel?" Neville demanded of Sidi Bombay.

"Because, Baron, he has told us something. His mind is tuned to the vibrations that surround us, and he has warned us of that which is to come. I had feared to take the Chaffri back into our company, but I see now that Clive Folliot was right to do so."

As if on cue, the engine lurched forward. The blackness that surrounded it and the dank, heavy atmosphere that filled it were gone. For a moment the compartment was filled with light, but before the travelers could take heart, the light assumed a reddish hue and a terrible howling and crashing filled the air.

"Oh, my lord!" Horace exclaimed.

A great roaring, rushing sound surrounded and penetrated the engine. Clive felt the floor shift beneath his feet. The cabin began to spin like a bullet emerging from a rifled gun barrel. Clive felt his weight increase as the centrifugal force pressed him down.

In the new light, the formerly yellow-tinted demon in its cage turned a dark, menacing red. Beyond the windows and doors of the cabin, Clive could see almost-human figures swirling and revolving along with the engine. Beyond them dancing flames and puffs of smoke made an unbroken background that surrounded the engine in all directions.

At first there were dozens of the demons flying around the engine, then Clive realized there were hundreds, thousands, countless hordes.

Like the transformed Chaffri in its prison, the demons were completely naked. And in their nakedness there was no mistaking the degree of perfection with which their anatomy mimicked that of humans. They were male and female.

A female demon approached the whirling cabin. She posed before a window, smiling invitingly and gesturing. Clive's eyes popped. She was not Annabella nor Annie nor the Lady 'Nrrc'kth. She was not Anna Maria Folliot, nor was she Clarissa Mesmer. But she possessed the female essence of each and every one of those women, and of the temptresses Clive had encountered in the saloon on his first night back in London, and of the women he had encountered on many levels of the Dungeon, and of those he had met in East Africa and in Zanzibar and aboard the ship *Empress Philippa* at the beginning of this whole incredible adventure.

She was every woman he had ever loved, every woman he had ever desired, every woman after whom he had ever lusted.

He stepped toward her.

She smiled at him. Her mouth was generous, her lips soft. Her eyes were huge and dark. They looked black until he peered into them deeply and realized that an ember glowed dark and red deep within each of them.

It was the color of Hell.

But Horace Smythe had been right, Clive thought. This was not the hell they had visited twice before, nor was there any Baron Samedi in this Hades to help them.

Clive Folliot was the leader of this party. He was the survivor of uncounted perils in his journey through the nine levels of the Dungeon. He was the Master of the Ordolite! That above all should have given him the strength and resolve that he needed to survive this moment of peril.

And yet, like a schoolboy desperate to have his first woman, he had clambered through the window and was about to launch himself at the female demon when he felt a huge, heavy hand grasp him by the ankle. He was drawn back bodily into the car.

He wanted desperately to join the female outside. He had to join her. In a moment of madness all recollection of Annabella Leighton, of the Lady 'Nrrc'kth, of Annabelle Leigh, and of Anna Maria Folliot were wiped from his brain. It was as if he had never known love, never known happiness in his life; the realization was strong upon him and he struggled to escape from the mighty grasp that restrained him, struggled to get to the one being in all of Creation capable of bringing him satisfaction.

"Insect! Hold still!"

The voice was enough to interrupt his obsession, to bring the focus of his eyes back within the car. He realized that he was in the clutches of the Frankenstein monster.

"Foolish creature! Think for a moment with your pitiful excuse for a brain! Use the feeble intelligence that the God in Whom you claim to believe provided you! What do you think you see outside this machine?"

"My love! The most desirable creature in the universe! Monster, let me go! Her face is the most beautiful I have ever gazed upon! Her breasts are of a beauty to make

Venus weep with envy! Her body is flesh that will melt beneath my hands! The honey of her loins—"

"Enough, fool!" The monster shook him until Clive Folliot's very teeth rattled. Holding him a foot off the floor at arm's length, the monster balled his fist and struck Clive in the face.

Stars danced around Clive's head. His ears rang.

"Now, weakling, look!"

The monster turned him like a helpless infant, so that he was facing out the window. For a moment the creature of demonic temptation was replaced by a male demon, rage written across his face, his trident raised as if to pierce and disembowel an enemy.

Clive Folliot blinked, shook his head like a dog emerging from a stream.

The demon was female again.

Then it was male once more.

"Know you not the tale of Incubus and Succubus, weakling?" the monster's voice ground mercilessly. "Do you wish to leave here and go with the demon?"

"No!" Clive cried. Then, "Yes!" He struggled but the monster's grip was like that of a hundred. "Let me go to it!"

"O man of India," the monster intoned, "but reach into some cabinet or chest of this machine and fetch for me a line."

Sidi Bombay complied.

Without releasing his grasp on Clive, the monster tied the line to his ankle and threw him bodily from across the compartment.

In a moment of astonishing clarity, Clive saw the car around him, the looks of amazement on the faces of Sidi Bombay and Horace Hamilton Smythe, the captive Chaffri prancing and gesturing in its cage.

As he flashed past his brother Neville, Clive saw Neville reach upward to pass him a sword.

Clive grasped the weapon's hilt. Then he was outside the car, surrounded by a raging inferno that singed his costume and raised a sweat on his brow but that somehow failed to harm him even as his hands and feet passed through dancing flames of orange and crimson.

The creature that confronted him was in its female form. The beauty of the temptress seemed greater than ever. She smiled and advanced toward Clive, arms outstretched.

He held the sword low at his side.

The female demon slid her arms against Clive's neck. She pressed her cheek to his, her lips to his. Did he gasp for breath, or did he part his lips in excitement? He felt her passion as if it were a tongue of pure flame piercing his lips and probing his mouth. The agony was unlike any he had ever experienced, ever imagined, and yet it was sweet beyond description. He found himself filled with a longing compared to which the most voluptuous of experience or of fantasy faded.

He felt her slide her hand from his neck to his shoulder, his arm, his hand. He felt—

He raised his other hand and smote himself a blow as powerful as he could manage. His head rang. The demon sprang away from him, tugging with a powerful arm at the sword his brother had given him. But Clive managed to retain his grasp on the weapon.

He blinked and stared at the demon.

It was male.

It thrust at him with its trident.

He was barely able to dodge aside. One tine of the weapon snagged his jacket and tore away a fragment of cloth.

The demon swept past him.

He turned to face it.

The demon recovered, raised its trident again, and charged toward him.

Again he was able to dodge aside, but only at the expense of a painful scratch that burned with a pain worse than the bite of a giant spider.

A third time the demon thrust its trident at Clive, but this time Clive was able to gather himself sufficiently to parry the trident with the sword his brother had given him.

The demon halted and grasped its trident in both hands, advancing like an infantryman with fixed bayonet.

The demon thrust, and Clive parried, then recovered.

Again the demon struck with its trident, forward and upward from below waist height. If the three tines embedded themselves in Clive's belly he knew that the demon could twist and pull, the barbs would hold in his flesh, and his entrails would be yanked from their cavity.

He lunged with his sword. It was shorter than the demon's trident, and Clive knew he was at a disadvantage.

He recovered, not having come anywhere near the demon in his lunge.

As the demon raised its trident to prepare for another attack on him, Clive stepped boldly forward. He was past the tip of the trident, and now the added length of his opponent's weapon was an impediment rather than an aid in the struggle.

He thrust at the demon.

The demon swung his trident in a clumsy attempt to parry. There was no contact with Clive's sword, but the shaft of the trident knocked against Clive's arm and torso, hurling him sideways. He regained his footing. For an instant, for the barest fraction of a second, there flickered across his brain the question of what he was standing on at all.

Clive saw that the demon had raised its trident in both hands and was launching a downward blow that would take him in the chest, but he hurled himself beneath the trident, striking upward with his sword, feeling it jolt against the heavier shaft of the trident, feeling the trident ride down the length of his sword and rebound off its basket.

The demon was disarmed.

It was defeated.

The flames around the engine flickered, guttered, disappeared.

Clive was floating some twenty feet from the engine, the long line that the Frankenstein monster had tied to his ankle all that held him in place. Far beneath the cabin he could see a universe of points and swirls of light, infinitely huge, infinitely distant, infinitely grand.

Above him, so close that he felt he could reach up and touch them, was a spiral of swirling stars.

· CHAPTER 23 ·
Now and for All Eternity

He felt himself turning, floating and twisting gently. Something was tugging at his ankle. He looked to see what it was and recognized the engine, saw the monster in its window. He experienced a moment of insane hilarity, imagining the monster as an angler and himself as a mountain trout being reeled in to serve as a fisherman's breakfast. He would be gutted and boned and laid out in a pan of melted butter and broiled over a woodfire beside a country stream. It would all be so peaceful and pleasant—for the fisherman.

For the fish, another story.

Neville's sword was still in his—Clive Folliot's—hand, and as his boots thudded against the frame of the engine and he climbed carefully back into the car, he held the weapon toward his brother, hilt first. Neville took the sword from him and slipped it into its scabbard.

Clive knelt to undo the line attached to his ankle. The Frankenstein monster still held the other end, and methodically wound the line into a coil as Clive released it.

The engine lurched, then accelerated more smoothly, sliding effortlessly through the blackness toward the centermost of the spiraling stars. The spiral continued to revolve, but the engine had progressed so far that the outer stars in the constellation were visible more to the sides of the vehicle than above it.

Only the centermost star, its flames dazzlingly bright, lay directly overhead.

"Look, sah!"

Horace Hamilton Smythe's voice broke in on Clive's

train of thought, drawing his attention away from the tantalizing stars and back to the interior of the engine compartment. Smythe was pointing at the caged Chaffri.

Something strange had happened to the cage itself. Although its bars and slats had spaces between them, there must have been some force that held the prison inviolate, else the Chaffri could have flowed between the bars and regained its freedom when it was in its fluid state. Twice the Chaffri had been imprisoned in that same makeshift prison, and twice it had raged and scuttered, changing its form and its behavior repeatedly, unable to escape.

But now the prison itself seemed to be filled with water, and the Chaffri, responding to whatever influence had given it the form of a prancing devil, had since assumed a new shape. It had the upper half of a human and the lower half of a great, scaled fish.

Had it read Clive's musings of himself as a trout being reeled in by the Frankenstein monster, and in some exotic manner transformed itself in response to that imagery? But Clive had not been thinking of a hellish demon prior to the Chaffri's earlier transformation. . . .

With a shudder, the engine slowed again, coming very nearly to a complete halt. Again the exterior illumination of the swirling stars was extinguished, and the interior of the compartment was lighted only by the malign glare of the instrument panel.

And the Chaffri had assumed the form of the merman of legend. Fish-tailed, bearded, crowned; armed with a trident, but one of glittering gold, unlike the black weapon of Clive's former foe. The Chaffri had become the miniature of some pagan sea-deity—the Chaldean Oannes or the Philistine Dagon!

And through the murk, Clive could see a world of green currents, waving fronds, great aquatic creatures lazily swimming past the engine. He did not, however, see any mermen other than the miniature one into which the captive Chaffri had transformed itself.

But Neville Folliot must have seen something that Clive did not, for the elder brother uttered a glad cry. Raising his arms as if to embrace a long-lost beloved, he crossed the compartment in rapid strides and began to climb from it.

The monster, moving with surprising agility, seized Neville's leg and attached the line to it, just as he had to Clive's. "Don't let him go," Clive cried—but too late.

Neville Folliot plunged from the car.

Outside, in the sea-green milieu, Neville moved like a man swimming beneath the surface of the ocean. He seemed to be alone, and yet he reached and embraced an invisible lover.

Clive dashed to the window, grasped its sill, and leaned out. He plunged his face and torso into a tropical sea! Ahead of him he could see his brother, but his brother transformed into a merman himself! Neville's lower limbs had joined to form the hindmost section of a great fish, covered with scales, punctuated by graceful fins and terminating in a powerful flipper. He was wholly naked, and when his maneuvering gave Clive a fleeting glimpse of his face it seemed to have altered subtly into the face of a creature of the sea.

It was still Neville, but it was a Neville transformed.

And in Neville's arms was a creature of unsurpassed yet alien beauty. Her hair was long and waved gracefully in the currents. Her skin was white, her torso that of a perfectly formed woman of the most charming and voluptuous form. Her hips swelled gracefully into the hindsection of a great fish.

And even as Clive watched, the two forms embraced, moving sinuously, sensually, through the water.

Shocked, Clive drew back into the engine compartment. He was perfectly dry. No drop of water adhered to his face or hair, no splash had soaked his garments. He spun and gaped at his companions, then turned back to the window. The scene had reverted to its former state. Neville was there, but he was fully human, swimming by drawing himself forward with his arms and thrusting with his legs. His sword in its scabbard hung from his waist.

Clive gasped, then leaned forward again. Again he felt himself plunge into water, its salt stinging his eyes. His reflex, learned in boyhood swimming lessons, drew shut his mouth and held the water from his nostrils.

He blinked and saw Neville once more as merman.

But this time he was not embracing a female of his kind, but dueling with a male! His sword was changed again into a trident, and through the blue-green waters Clive could see light glinting off the razor-sharp barbs of both combatants' weapons.

Neville struck a blow at his opponent, and Clive saw a greenish fluid flow languidly from the wound.

The merman thrust at Neville, but Neville dodged and plunged his trident into his enemy. The merman's trident flashed past Neville, missing him entirely but severing the line that held him to the engine with a single clean cut.

"Neville!" Clive cried. His mouth filled with brine, and he jerked involuntarily. He was back in the engine with Sidi Bombay and Horace Hamilton Smythe and the Frankenstein monster. "Neville!" he called again, hurling himself toward the window. Outside the engine he could see Neville as a man, turning and struggling in the blue-green fluid.

As Neville revolved, Clive could see his face. Agony distorted his features and a stream of bubbles rose from his lips. "I must help him! He's drowning!" Clive hurled himself toward the window but in an instant the light of brilliant stars filled the cabin.

The sea was gone.

"My brother! My brother!" Clive leaned from the engine, peering in all directions. Everything was as it had been before the engine's plunge into strange waters, save that the star directly overhead was closer than ever. Its rays bathed the engine, its coruscating colors casting strangely variegated shadows.

"We must go back! Neville will die!"

"Indeed, O Major." Sidi Bombay faced Clive solemnly. "Your brother is lost to you. To us all."

"Smythe, turn back! I command you!"

"I cannot, sah." Horace Smythe turned from the engine's controls. "There's no way I can take us back to the regions we passed through, sah."

"What do you mean, Smythe!"

Sidi Bombay placed himself between Clive Folliot and Horace Smythe. "He means, O Major, that we have passed through regions of the psyche. Hades, Poseidonis . . . there are many others. There is the icy wasteland populated by giant man-eating worms. There is the desert of storms. There is the Lake of Tantalus. There are Hells of every variety."

"Then let us return to that watery hell and rescue Neville!"

"It cannot be done, O Major. They are not places, nor can this engine bring you to them."

"You mean they are not real? But I experienced them— and this engine *did* bring us to them!"

"They are very real, O Major, but it was not the engine that brought us to them. It was the souls of the Folliots."

"Would I have truly died in the fiery Hell I visited? Can Neville still live in the watery one?"

"Folliots are tested, O Major, as other men and women are not. You passed your test, and are here with us still. Your brother, I regret, failed his."

"And died?" Clive looked up at Sidi Bombay with grief-filled eyes.

"Your friend du Maurier has taught you how little death means, Clive Folliot."

Clive balled his fist and struck it against his own thigh, a feeble release for the emotion he felt.

In his grinding, inhuman voice, the Frankenstein monster intoned, "Perhaps it was Neville Folliot who passed the test, little Clive—and you who failed."

Clive seized the tattered lapels of the monster's ill-fitting jacket and pulled himself to his fullest height. He still had to peer up into the monster's face. He attempted to read the expression that he saw in that corpselike visage, in the monster's great dark eyes. In their depths he saw only the tomb.

After a moment he released his grip on the black cloth and slumped back from the monster. "Perhaps you are right," he whispered. The words were bitter in his mouth.

With barely a whisper of metal on vegetation, the engine slid to a halt on the centermost sun of the spiral. Clive blinked. What had happened? The moment before, he had been conversing with Sidi Bombay and Horace Hamilton Smythe and the Frankenstein monster. The engine had been thrusting itself through the blackness toward the brilliant star.

And now, as if time had slipped a gear, the engine simply landed.

Clive said, "Sergeant Smythe?"

But before Smythe answered, the engine itself was gone. The metal shell, the power-plant, the glowing control panel, the chests of tools and equipment . . . were gone.

The miniature prison holding the captive Chaffri seemed to fade like mist dissolving in sunlight. The Chaffri itself hopped up and down, changing its appearance by the moment. It was an arachnoid alien like Shriek . . . a shape-changing cyborg like Chang Guafe . . . a creature of cold beauty like the Lady 'Nrrc'kth . . . a Japanese Imperial Marine . . . a canine-descended dwarf like Finnbogg. . . .

At the sight of the last, Clive was overcome by emotion. Of all his companions in his incredible trek, his perilous adventure—of all his fellows in peril and wonder—there was none more faithful than the loving, humorous, courageous doglike creature. Watching the chameleonic Chaffri cavort like a miniature Finnbogg, Clive could hear the gruff voice roaring out "Jeannie with the Light Brown Hair," "I Pagliacco," "The Little Brown Church," "Massa's in de Cold, Cold Ground," "Babylon Is Falling."

With a lump in his throat and a tear in his eye, Clive looked at his companions.

The Frankenstein monster slowly faded from sight, followed by Horace Hamilton Smythe and finally by Sidi Bombay. Even as the Indian disappeared, Clive thought that he perceived a smile on Sidi Bombay's face. A smile of understanding and acceptance.

Clive called their names, ran to the places where each of them had stood. There was no sign of their presence. He tried to reach them by the same psychic means that had brought him in touch with George du Maurier so many times, and with his unborn brother Esmond so few.

There was nothing.

Not the suggestion of an echo of a whisper.

Nothing.

Clive raised his face to survey his new surroundings.

· CHAPTER 24 ·
"It Comes in the End to This!"

He had expected the surface of a star to be fiery hot. Though the stars appeared as tiny points of light, twinkling icy crystals, when seen from afar, still Clive had studied enough of natural philosophy to know that each distant star was a sun like the Earth's. A huge ball of burning, glowing gas. But this was not the case.

He found himself standing knee-deep in a mist that flowed to the random influence of unseen breezes. It was almost like being once more in the Sudd, the great Equatorian swamp through which he had traveled so long ago. There, with Horace Hamilton Smythe and Sidi Bombay, he had entered a gemlike boulder the size of a house, and found himself embarked upon his adventure in the Dungeon.

Now, although his boots remained dry and the footing they afforded seemed solid, the prospect was that of a mist-ridden bog.

Dead-gray trees lifted their boles and their skeletal, reaching limbs into the gray air. The smell was stale, like that of a centuries-desiccated tomb rather than a damp swamp. There was a remote sound suggestive of trickling water, but no apparent source.

If this was truly a star, then light should emanate from it, and in fact such was the case. A subtle glow was diffused through the drifting mist, a glow which appeared to come from the solid surface beneath the mist rather than from the vapor itself.

The sky was a darker gray, punctuated by the light of the other stars of the familiar spiral.

A low moaning startled Clive Folliot. He peered around in search of its source until he realized that it was merely the soft wind passing through the naked branches of the trees around him.

He tried calling the names of his erstwhile companions, but received in reply only faint echoes of his own voice, muffled by the mist that rose around him.

Should I walk, or should I remain here? he pondered. There was no apparent advantage to any one location as against another. The place in which he found himself might be as good—or as bad—as any to which he could walk.

But he decided that if he was to meet his fate in this strangely desolated locale, he would rather do so by traveling to meet that fate than by waiting passively for it to come to him.

There was no way of telling north from south, east from west. But he still did not wish to travel in circles, so he sighted on two trees and began walking from one to the other. Before reaching the second tree, he aligned himself with a third so as to maintain a straight line of progress. In this manner he traversed from tree to tree, moving steadily toward a goal unknown.

When he started walking, the land had seemed flat, although beneath the mist it was hard to tell unless he happened to step into a hole or inadvertently to kick a rise of earth. But now rises and dips in the landscape became more pronounced.

In some pockets, mist had accumulated to heights greater than Clive's. In other places, where the land rose, peaks erupted above the level of the mist.

The first pocket through which he walked contained an accumulation of mist far taller than Clive. As his chin dropped beneath the surface he gasped and clamped his mouth shut like a bather striding away from a sloping beach. He found that he could breathe the mist, and that he could see through it for a short distance. When he breathed it he found that it had a distinct flavor, not unpleasant, but one suggestive of untold antiquity.

Something swept past him in the mist. He couldn't tell what it was—a creature that dwelt in the eternal grayness of this place, to be sure. A bird or bat? Perhaps even some fishlike being that drew nourishment from the mist as fish did from water, and that swam through the attenuated medium as fish swam in the sea.

He continued on; something brushed against his leg. He reached to feel it, but whatever it was had fled at the first contact. He bent to see if he could determine the composition of the surface upon which he was walking, but the mist diffused his vision and the glow emanating from the ground dazzled his eyes when he leaned far over.

He walked on. There was no sense of fatigue, at least as yet, nor of hunger or thirst. He seemed to be trekking across a wasteland in which time as well as direction had lost their meaning.

He heard more sounds. Remote sounds, difficult to identify and impossible to locate. Something that might have been a whispered conversation, punctuated by titterings and hushing sounds. Something that might have been the growl of a large animal—or of an animal-like man.

The sound of running water, once more. A sound like that of a stream pouring over a cliff into a pool.

The ground rose, and before long he broke through the surface of the mist, and continued to climb and to climb until he realized that the ground itself had risen above the mist as well. It was of a distinct yellow color, with a surface more like smooth glass than of rock or soil, and it glowed from within, a glow that seemed to pulsate with a subtle, almost indistinguishable beat.

The gray tree trunks rose at irregular intervals from the yellow land. As Clive continued to climb he found that a stream flowed from higher on the hillside. After a while the land began to have a rougher, granular composition, closer to that of true earth. Rocks in the streambed bore coatings of yellowish lichen and slime; tiny bugs scuttled about, and small creatures swam in the water.

He lowered himself to his belly and tasted the stream. It was clean and he felt freshened and energized by the water.

He crossed the stream, letting it lap around the bottoms of his boots. He came to an opening in the hillside and without hesitation stepped into it. If some peril awaited, he would face that. He had grown at once more daring and more fatalistic; he had faced too many perils, gambled with his life too many times to be concerned with one more danger, one more risk.

A great machine whirred in the center of a cavernous room. A tiny man stepped from behind it, his hairless scalp shining pinkly in the diffuse light, his thick, rimless spectacles glinting. He was dressed entirely in white.

"Welcome to Gennine, Clive Folliot." He nodded in a friendly fashion.

"This is Gennine?"

"It is."

"And you are the mind behind all I have seen? The master of the Dungeon? Of the Chaffri and the Ren alike? It is you who have interfered with the lives of beings on a thousand worlds?"

The tiny man cackled. He could hardly have been taller than Clive's collarbone, and his voice and face indicated that he was very, very old.

"No, Clive Folliot. I am but a servant. A mechanician."

"Then tell me whom you serve!"

"Find out for yourself."

The old man gestured, and Clive saw that an archway beyond the great machine led on to a distant, cavernous gallery. Clive crossed the room of the machine, feeling a peculiar tug as he passed it, as if his whole being were somehow twisted in a direction he had never before imagined.

Through the archway he found himself face to face with a goliath who towered above Clive as Clive had towered above the wizened man who tended the machine.

The giant roared and swung a great club at Clive.

Clive stepped aside and the club struck the ground where he had stood a split-second before. "If you please," Clive murmured. He gestured at the giant and a bolt of blood-red energy leaped like a wavering thread of lightning from the tip of his finger to the giant.

The giant seemed bathed in electricity. His face bore a look not of pain but of startlement. He writhed, then collapsed to the ground, where he shriveled and shrank until there was only a pile of charred rags and the shattered remnants of a charred and splintered club where the giant had been.

Clive picked through the rags. There was no flesh or bone there. He rose and continued.

A centurion in Roman armor confronted him.

"Halt!" the centurion commanded.

"No," Clive responded softly. He repeated his gesture even as the Roman hefted a metal-tipped spear. The Roman glowed in the ruddy emanation for the count of a half-dozen heartbeats. Then he fell to the ground and shriveled until only armor and cloth and horsehair-crested helmet and shortsword and spear remained.

Clive confronted a Bwaka warrior from central Africa armed with an eccentrically shaped throwing knife.

A Frankish chief with a *francisca* flying axe.

A tribesman of Borneo with poisoned blowpipe.

A Naga with *dao* sword.

A German trooper with wheel-lock pistol.

A Maori with *toki* war-adz.

A fighting man with a Persian mace.

An Indian with a whirling flail.

A phalanx of Amazons.

He gestured and moved on.

A row of the writhing, tentacled beasts he had first encountered on Q'oorna. Ren.

A battalion of scarab-mantises. Chaffri.

Clive sighed, waved, moved on.

Another exit from the cavern and he stood on a cliff overlooking a desolate landscape of naked trees and drifting mist. He felt as if he had wandered into a purgatory— nay, a limbo—where he would face challenge after challenge, meet each in turn, triumph over every foe, and accomplish . . . nothing.

A mechanical voice grated in his ear. "You look disappointed, old friend."

He turned with a gasp. "Chang Guafe!"

The half-alien, half-mechanical being made the grating noise that passed for its laughter. "It pleases me to see you again, Clive Folliot."

"I was overjoyed to see you escape from beneath the

polar sea, Chang Guafe—but how did you get here? From distant Earth to this remote edge of the cosmos?"

"Easily enough when one can control one's configuration as I can, Clive Folliot. And you? And our companions?"

"Most are well," Clive said. "Some are dead."

"In time we all die," Chang Guafe replied. "Sooner or later—it's only a matter of sooner . . . or later."

"But we have reached the center of the spiral of stars," Clive said. "I thought that this would be the grand headquarters of the Gennine. I thought that after all our travail, once here we would confront our ultimate foe. We, or . . . I. For I did not expect to see you here, Chang Guafe. For all that you are a welcome sight."

"This is not the ultimate headquarters of the Gennine, Clive."

"Is it not the center of the spiral?"

"It is the nature of the spiral to change. Stars make their way from the edge to the center . . . from the center to the edge. No, my old friend. The center has yet to be reached."

"Can we get there?"

Chang Guafe gestured upward with a metallic appliance. "There is the home of the Master of the Gennine, Clive Folliot. And you are the Master of the Ordolite. You are known throughout the universe. Beings uncounted— races uncounted—are watching you."

"I did not ask for this. I did not want it."

"You did not ask to be born. The same thing, Folliot." Clive nodded.

"Watch this." Chang Guafe began to change his shape. Extrusions and devices appeared on his carapacelike exterior skin. Plates scraped and gears whirled. An eyestalk taller than a man popped from between two rollers, swung in a circle above Chang Guafe, and pointed back so he could observe his own work from the outside.

"Now, Folliot. You can travel in style."

Chang Guafe had transformed himself into a sleek vehicle surmounted by a transparent canopy and cockpit into which Clive gingerly climbed.

"Hold on."

Chang Guafe launched himself into the air.

Clive felt a surge as Chang Guafe accelerated away from

the yellowish, mist-covered landscape. He peered back over his shoulder, wondering what ancient events had transpired on the star-world, who the aged man with the glittering spectacles could be. But there was no time to ponder.

A spectral figure loomed before them. It took Clive a moment to realize that the titanic being was of human form, so huge was it. It took him still longer to realize that despite its size—Chang Guafe and Clive could have fit into its fist like a toy—the figure was that of an infant in swaddling clothes.

"Turn aside! Turn aside, Chang Guafe!"

Instruments were extruded from the panel before Clive, as Chang Guafe adapted himself further to the role of aerial vehicle. The instruments were similar to those used by the pilot of a small boat, and Clive seized the steering device and swung away from the infant.

They confronted another gigantic figure. This time he adjusted his sight more quickly to it, and realized more quickly that it was a boy dressed in the fashion of his own childhood.

He swung away from it, tugging back at one control, swinging another to the side, guiding his host-craft above the boy, only to confront another giant figure, another youth, this one apparently of seventeen. Dark of hair, lanky of build, struggling manfully—Clive could not suppress a grin—to raise a straggly mustache.

Again and again Clive swerved, each time facing another figure, each older, each gigantic. A lad of nineteen years or so, dressed as for Cambridge. A bravo in his middle twenties, wearing the uniform of a lieutenant of Her Majesty's Horse Guards. A substantial figure in his thirties garbed in tropical pongee and pith helmet.

And others. One of forty-odd, putting on a small paunch, and one in his fifties, with graying hair and deeply lined face, and one in his sixties, bald of pate and sunken of eye.

They surrounded Clive, whichever way he swung the controls of his ship.

Clive undid a latch and swung back the glass canopy that covered his place. He climbed from the cockpit and closed the canopy behind him. The medium in which

Chang Guafe drifted was strange—it seemed as if Clive were floating in it like a fly caught in a bowl of syrup; and yet he was able to move freely, like a diver beneath the sea.

As he watched, Chang Guafe reconfigured himself. "I have done all that I can for you, Clive. You are the Master of the Ordolite. It is now for you to triumph—or to fail."

A clawlike arm emerged from Chang Guafe. It made a peculiarly human gesture, shaking hands with Clive Folliot. Then it folded back into the alien cyborg. Panel after panel folded, then turned, then folded again. Chang Guafe became smaller and smaller until there was nothing left of him but a metallic cube the size of a small dispatch case. Then that folded in upon itself and, with a small popping sound, disappeared altogether.

Uncounted giant figures stood pointing at Clive Folliot. Pointing at him from above and beneath, from every side. And every one of them was himself, as infant or as youth or as wizened gaffer. Every one of them was himself.

"I am the Master of the Ordolite," he said to them softly.

"You are that," they chorused.

He began to drift toward the star-world that was the true center of the spiral.

His many other selves trailed behind him as if on single-file parade.

• CHAPTER 25 •
Master Versus Master

He stood on a glowing surface of pearl white, a surface that curved away and seemed to rise to a distant horizon. The appearance of this world was the same in whatever direction he faced. Left and right, above and below, there was nothing but glowing whiteness.

With a thought to find some feature or denizen of this world, he tried walking. A hundred yards or so in one direction. The only way he could measure distance was by counting paces, for there was neither object nor inhabitant by which to judge his location; the prospect at the end of his walk was identical to that at its inception.

"Are you here?" he called.

Surprisingly, his voice echoed. But there was no response. He searched his garment for an object with which to experiment, found a royal sovereign in his pocket, and threw it against the white surface that served here as earth. The glittering coin bounced back as high as his waist. He caught it with a sweep of his hand and returned it to his pocket.

He heard a distant buzzing sound, as of a single giant insect. Peering in all directions, hoping to locate the hornet or bee or whatever it was that had made the sound, he saw a distant speck against the featureless white sky. He squinted, shaded his eyes with one hand, strained to make out the speck.

It grew larger, accompanied by an increase in the loudness of the buzzing.

He recognized its shape—it was the Japanese machine which his descendant Annabelle Leigh had obtained at

New Kwajalein Atoll. Even though there was no discernible source of illumination in this world, light glinted from the Nakajima as it tilted and turned in its aerial course.

Clive waved eagerly, and felt his heart leap with joy as the Nakajima waggled its wings. Annie had seen him! She was headed toward him! Based on the apparent size of the Nakajima and the pace at which it was growing, he knew that it would take a fair while to arrive, but he was overjoyed nonetheless.

He heard his name called, and he whirled to find himself confronting a quartet of individuals.

There stood Amos Ransome, garbed in his dour clergyman's outfit of black frock-coat and white ecclesiastical collar. Beside him stood his sister or wife; her true identity had never been revealed. Lorena Ransome's hair was pulled back in a severe bun. Her dress was black, and covered her from neck to ground and from shoulder to wrist. But to Clive's astonishment, her face had been made up and painted like a hoyden's, with long, artificial eyelashes, unrealistic rosy spots on the cheeks, and lips the color of blood.

And the bodice of her dress had two circular cut-outs within which her tender skin was reddened with paint like that of an ancient Babylonian temple woman.

Framing Lorena Ransome on the side opposite Amos was Philo B. Goode, the bogus American mining magnate. He wore his broad-brimmed hat, stringlike cravat, brocaded waistcoat, wide-lapelled jacket, and intricately carved boots.

A cheroot protruded from the edge of Amos Ransome's mouth. A smirk marked his countenance. One side of his coat was drawn back and his hand rested on the butt of a silver-plated Colt navy revolver. Clive Folliot could not see the grip of the revolver, but in his heart he knew that it would be of black or midnight blue polished stone set with a spiral of diamonds representing the stars of the Gennine.

"Are you the Gennine?" Clive asked.

"Smile," Philo Goode replied, "when you call me that, pardner."

"Is this the end of the Dungeon?"

"It is, Clive Folliot. There is nowhere farther to go."

"This is the true center of the swirling stars? The home of the Gennine, the ultimate rulers of the Dungeon?"

"It is the home of the Gennine."

A roaring filled Clive's ears and points of light and darkness danced before his eyes. "You are merely people. I encountered you on the *Princess Philippa*. Penny ante gamblers, sharpers, petty cheats. You cannot be the rulers of the Dungeon."

"But we are." It was Lorena Ransome who had spoken. She slipped her hand from her companion's neck and advanced toward Clive. He stared, his eyes drawn, against his will, to her bodice. He had seen women naked and half-naked on a half-dozen continents and on a dozen worlds, but never had he seen one who attracted and excited him as did Lorena Ransome.

"Stay back!"

"Clive."

"I resisted the fire-succubus!"

"An illusion. A figment of your own mind."

"I knew the Lady 'Nrrc'kth, the woman T'Nembi of Bagomoyo, females human and alien of world upon world."

"Then why fear me, Clive?" She slid her black-clad arms around his neck and pressed her lips against his own. Amos Ransome and Philo Goode dropped from his consciousness. He could think only of this woman, of Lorena Ransome. She had cast a spell upon Horace Hamilton Smythe, Clive knew, during Smythe's long-ago sojourn in wild America. Was she doing the same to him now?

He grew dizzy, felt himself falling into a state of vertigo. He could no longer identify the directions of up and down in this pearl-white world, could no longer discern the nearby from the distant. He could feel Lorena Ransome's long fingers beneath his garments, could not prevent his own hands from moving over her form.

"Good, Clive. Yes, Clive. Yes!"

A shrill voice was piping and a small weight leaped upon his back. He could feel tiny feet kicking at his neck and then a point of excruciating fire behind his ear.

Blinking and slapping at his neck, he leaped to his feet. A miniature Baron Samedi was prancing in circles, pointing at Clive with his omnipresent cigar. "Fool, fool, fool!" the baron shrilled. "Slave to your gonads! Goat! Behold your strumpet!"

Lorena Ransome stood scowling at Clive and at Baron Samedi. She was something hideous and terrible, something hardly human. It was as if the evil in human nature had been distilled and concentrated and reconstituted into a being of pure malignity.

Something furry collided with Clive's leg and he glanced downward to see that the miniature Samedi—apparently the Chaffri, the being that had somehow survived the dissolution of the space-train, reacting to some desperate subconscious thought of Clive's—had found its way here and had changed still again. It was now a miniature Finnbogg, massive in form and substance despite its diminutive stature, caninesque in its fidelity.

Lorena was the ultimate in evil, Lilith, the night monster of the Hebrew Book of Isaiah. She pointed a shriveled finger at Clive and screeched, "I'll get you, Clive Folliot!" She raised a second finger, pointed it crookedly at Finnbogg. "You and your little dog, too!"

The Chaffri/Samedi/Finnbogg hurled itself at the far larger Lorena Ransome. Together they tumbled to the pearl-white ground, rolling over and over. Amos Ransome entered the fray, struggling to pull the tiny Finnbogg from Lorena. The man's curses, the woman's screeches, the canine's snarls blended to make a mad cacophony.

Clive watched, petrified.

A cold drop spattered off Clive's face. It was followed by others. He looked up and saw that somehow the featureless glowing sky had been occluded by a massive array of black, roiling clouds. Lightning flashed, thunder rolled, sheets and torrents of rain swept the pearl-white earth.

With a scream and a hiss, Lorena Ransome and her attacker dissolved before Clive's horrified eyes.

Philo B. Goode drew his nickel-plated navy Colt. "I'd planned a more elaborate end for you than this, Folliot. You are the Master of the Ordolite, don't you know?"

"I am he, Philo Goode. Consider the meaning of that, and conduct yourself accordingly."

"You survived more challenges than I thought you would.

More than I thought you *could*." He ground his teeth audibly, then gave himself a shake. "Sometimes the simplest means is the best." He raised the Colt and pointed it directly at Clive's face.

Clive thought of the Mandarin who had saved his life repeatedly. The Mandarin who seemed to possess supernormal, even supernatural, powers. The Mandarin who had proved to be none other than Clive's old friend and onetime batman Horace Hamilton Smythe.

He could see the tightness on Goode's face, the infinitesimal tightening of his finger on the Colt's trigger. Through some oddity of light and direction he caught a glimpse of the revolver's grip—polished stone of midnight blue picked with a spiral of glittering diamonds that swirled madly even as he stared, transfixed.

He could hear the soft click of the moving trigger, the slow explosion of the powder. A flare of red flame and gray smoke poured from the muzzle of the Colt, and from it emerged the solid lead ball, whirling as it flew across the space that separated Philo B. Goode from Clive Folliot.

The Master of the Ordolite slowed the passage of time until the bullet was barely moving. Clive smiled. So slowly that each muscular rearrangement was individually visible, Philo Goode reflected a grimace of bafflement and rage.

Clive parted his lips in an expression of benevolence, opened his teeth a fraction of an inch, closed them again upon the flying bullet. He permitted its velocity to spin him a full 360 degrees.

He faced Philo Goode once again and spat.

The bullet flew toward Goode, smashed his ribs, tore his heart to shreds. Blood spattered and rained on the still-wet ground. He toppled backward, the Colt flying from his hand.

Clive caught the whirling weapon and shoved it into his waistband. He faced the sole figure who remained with him: Timothy Francis Xavier O'Hara, priest.

"Ye did mightily well, lad." O'Hara nodded, his broad scalp showing pinkly against its thin fringe of white hair. "But what d'ye plan to do now? Ye don't think ye're goin' t' shoot me with that great cannon, do ye?" O'Hara pointed at the Colt.

Clive shook his head. "I didn't come here to shoot anyone, Father."

"Forget the Father business. I dumped that long ago!"

"What is this place?"

"The home of the Gennine."

"Who are the Gennine?"

"I am the last of the Gennine. We're an ancient race, Clive Folliot. Long, long ago we realized that we were dying out. We did everything we could to save ourselves—to no avail. So we created the Dungeon to amuse ourselves. To while away the time."

"It was all . . . for your *amusement*?"

"Yes."

"And now?"

"Now I'm all that's left—and I shall go, as well. You're the only one who reached this place, Clive. You should be proud. How many millions have entered the Dungeon—some who died fighting, some who settled down and made a new life for themselves there, some few who escaped and returned to their own worlds. Oh, very, very few of those. But there were some who did, yes."

He shook his gleaming head. "But now you've made it to the home of the Gennine."

"Are you human?"

"Eh?" O'Hara had raised his hand to his chin, dropped his gaze to his feet in abstracted concentration.

"I said, are you human? Or are you something else? I've seen shape-changers enough in this mad adventure."

O'Hara shook his head as if he could hardly comprehend the question. Somewhere the distant buzzing sound had grown louder, and Clive looked up to see the sun glinting on his great-great-granddaughter Annie's Nakajima 97. The aeroplane was close now, dipping toward the ground, its propeller whirling, its wheels reaching to touch the earth.

"I don't know, lad. Human, not human? What am I now?" He raised a hand to his eyes and looked at it. Clive thought the puzzlement in O'Hara's face was real. "I can't remember. I just can't remember. How was it that God made me?"

"God?" Clive exclaimed. "I thought you'd renounced your priesthood."

The Nakajima was closer, its engine's sound louder. How could O'Hara not hear it?

"I was a weak priest, Clive. Not God's fault. Mine. I wish I could hear a voice call me Father once more, and know that I was worthy of the name. That it was not a mockery or a rebuke to me. Oh, how I wish for that!"

A shudder wracked his body. "Not you, Folliot. Don't you call me Father again. You know me too well for that. The things I've done—the cruelties I've done—I and all the Gennine! Was I human at the outset? If only I could be forgiven. Not by God, but by one whom I've wronged. By one being who suffered at my hands." He studied his hands, holding them both before his eyes. Clive Folliot saw tears in those eyes.

"I forgive you," Clive said.

Timothy F. X. O'Hara smiled. "Thank you, Folliot. Thank you." He crumpled to the pearl-white ground and lay still.

Clive Folliot stood alone, staring into the sky. The spiral of stars, which had lured him and guided his destiny for so long, now revolved about him. He had become its center.

A chill ran down his spine and left him trembling. It was a chill provoked not by cold air, but by the reaction to his position. From the role of cadet son to a minor country house, he had risen above all others. The title of Baron Tewkesbury would pass through Neville's line rather than his own, but that was the most trivial of concerns.

He was more than a baron, more than an emperor. He was the Master of the Ordolite.

A soft wind caressed his cheek, whispered in his ear. Or perhaps it was a voice. Or a chorus of voices. Did he hear the disembodied tones of George du Maurier? Of his two brothers, one unborn and the second now gone across the shadowy line that separates the living from the dead? Did he hear the voice of the Lady 'Nrrc'kth, and that of her brother N'wrbb Crrd'f? Did he hear the voices of the women he had loved in his life, and of his other companions, allies and foes alike, in his quest through the Dungeon?

He thought he heard other voices, too—Father O'Hara and Madame Mesmer and spidery Shriek and Chang Guafe and gruff hearty Finnbogg. Tomàs Folliot and Baron Samedi and the Imperial Japanese Marines he had encountered at New Kwajalein: Lieutenant Takamura and Lieutenant Yamura, Sergeant Fushida and Private Onishi. The passengers and officers he had known aboard *Empress Philippa*, the partners in the sinister Ransome/Goode/O'Hara scheme and the officials of the Universal Neighborhood Improvement Association. The Sultan of Zanzibar and the men and women he had encountered during his time in Equatoria.

The gentle breeze became a raging cyclone, the whispering voice a roaring chorus of men and women, alien creatures and artificial monsters.

The Ren.

The Chaffri.

And the Gennine.

He was the Master of the Ordolite.

A single voice emerged from the cacophonous roar. "Clive, what will you do now?" It was the voice of George du Maurier. "You are the most powerful of men. Perhaps the most powerful being in the universe."

"I am not God," Clive said.

"Still . . ."

"I don't know, du Maurier. I have striven so long. Now that my strife is completed, may I not rest for a while? The Buddhists of India, upon reaching a certain age, renounce their belongings, their occupations, even their families. They shave their heads, don saffron robes, and wander the land, their only other possession a begging bowl from which to eat brown rice."

"Does that appeal to you, Folliot?"

"I knew a farmer once, du Maurier. A fine fellow. Perhaps, if I live many years, I might become like him."

"Then there are no more worlds to conquer, no more challenges to meet?"

"Glory has lost its charm, du Maurier."

"Are there then no more wrongs to right?"

Clive nodded. "Someday, perhaps. But for now, I am weary, my friend. Weary."

Du Maurier made no comment in parting. The chorus faded, the voices stilled.

But there was another sound, a faint buzzing that had grown louder and louder even as Clive Folliot turned to follow the course of the machine that was its source.

The Nakajima 97 touched its wheels to the glowing ground. The sound of its engine ceased as Annabelle Leigh cut the ignition. The aeroplane rolled to a stop.

Annie climbed from the cockpit and ran to Clive Folliot's side. She took his two hands in her own.

"I've come to take you home, Grandfather."

Clive looked into Annie's face and wept.

Selections
From the Sketchbook
of Major Clive Folliot

The following drawings are from Major Clive Folliot's private sketchbook, which was mysteriously left on the doorstep of *The London Illustrated Recorder and Dispatch*, the newspaper that provided financing for his expedition. There was no explanation accompanying the parcel, save for an enigmatic inscription in the hand of Major Folliot himself.

"Our revels," as the bard said, "now are ended." My friend Du Maurier's hand is no longer available to improve my poor efforts, but I have his model and his advice to guide me. Let these last portraits be my farewell to a great and dramatic phase of my life.

The fires of vengeance have burned themselves out. Was my adventure a success? I have achieved a glory beyond my dreams, but at the cost of dear Annabella, and of my own brother's life. More than anything else, I am weary now, and shall rest until I am needed again.

HAIL AND FAREWELL, OLD FRIEND.
GEORGE DU MAURIER AS I LAST SAW HIM.

PHILO GODDE, WHO NEVER
LIVED UP TO HIS NAME,
AND HIS HELLISH
STAIRWAY INTO THE
BOWELS OF
LONDON.

TWO OF THE CHAFFRI SOLDIERS WHO ATTACKED ALONG THE RAILWAY TO TEWKESBURY.

MY FATHER—NO, ANOTHER SIMULACRUM, BUT THIS TIME, AT LEAST THE MANOR WAS AUTHENTIC.

CHANG GUAFE, AS HE TRANSFORMED HIMSELF IN THE SEA; BARON SAMEDI. AIDES, COMPANIONS, FRIENDS WHOSE COMPANY I WILL MISS.

ABOVE,

THE FIERY DOOR FROM PHILO GODDE'S OFFICE AT THE PUBLIC HOUSE.

VEHICLES OF PASSAGE
THROUGH SPACE
AND TIME:
THE CAR
THAT
CARRIED SGT.
SMYTHE, SIDI BOMBAY,
AND MYSELF...

...AND THE INSECTILE SHIPS OF THE REN.

AT THE CHAFFRI MILITARY
ENCAMPMENT, A BUILDING APPEARED
THUS TO ME. SNARES AND DELUSIONS!

MY BELOVED
ANNABELLA, A
DISGUISE FOR ONE
OF THE CHAFFRI.

FOR ONCE IN THIS ADVENTURE,
A TRUE FACE — A CHAFFRI IN ITS CAGE

MY GRAND·NIECE —
A WOMAN SOLDIER!
ANNA MARIA
FOLLIOT.

PERHAPS I SHALL NEVER TRULY UNDERSTAND WHAT MOVED MY BROTHER NEVILLE, BUT I CAN NOW, TOO LATE, FORGIVE HIM.

THESE DEMONS TESTED ME EN ROUTE TO THE HOME OF THE GENNINE.

NEVILLE, TOO, WAS TESTED
BY HIS OWN DEMONS.
HE COULD NOT HELP HIS
WEAKNESSES, BUT HE
PAID A FULL PRICE
FOR THEM.

WHEN I NEEDED HIS AID ONE LAST
TIME, CHANG GUAFE BECAME MY
TRANSPORTATION.

AT LAST THE STORY ENDS. ALL MY
TORMENTORS, ALL MY COMPANIONS ARE
GONE, SAVE ONLY MY BELOVED DESCENDANT,
ANNABELLE. GOOD RIDDANCE TO MY FOES,
GOODBYE TO MY FRIENDS.
LET US FIND
SOME
PEACE
WHILE WE
CAN.

Robert Gore 12/89

ALSO AVAILABLE

PHILIP JOSE FARMER'S
THE DUNGEON
Book 1

by Richard A. Lupoff & Bruce Coville
ISBN: 0-7434-5829-X

The quest starts here . . .

Plunging into a vast prison that spans a planet, Clive
Foliott faces a fantastic world of dwarves, cyborgs,
and aliens unlike anything he has ever imagined. It
is a multi-leveled collection of beings from the hidden folds of time and space.

Trapped somewhere inside is Neville Foliott,
Clive's twin brother, and no creature in the Dungeon
will stop Clive from finding him!

PHILIP JOSE FARMER'S
THE DUNGEON
Book 2

by Charles de Lint & Robin Wayne Bailey
ISBN: 0-7434-5842-7

The quest continues . . .

In *The Valley of Thunder*, Clive Folliot and his fellow captives face a new death daily. Against dinosaurs and cave creatures, giant worms and shark people, the group battles for their lives. Torn between continuing his search for his twin, the elusive Neville, or helping his comrades return home, Clive splits the party, doubling their chances of success—and their danger. Is it worth the gamble?

In *The Lake of Fire*, Clive is at last reunited with Neville, and the brothers and their troops escape to the next level of the Dungeon—a place straight out of Dante's Inferno! They must cross boiling rivers and bottomless chasms, passing the terrors of the Lake of Fire to reach their goal: the forbidding Palace of the Morning Star. What horrors await them there . . . ?

NIGHTWINGS

by Robert Silverberg
ISBN: 0-7434-7446-5

A FABULOUS TALE OF PILGRIMAGE AND HOPE,
BETRAYAL AND TRANSFORMATION, BY ONE OF
SCIENCE FICTION'S GREATEST WRITERS

Only at night, on the winds of darkness, can she soar.
And it was Avluela the Flier's ebony and scarlet wings
that led the Watcher to the seven hills of the ancient city
from which, in a moment of weakness, the watcher
failed his vigil, leaving the skies and deep space
unguarded.

The invaders came and conquered.

With Avluela lost in the turmoil of the conquest, the
watcher set out alone for the Holy City—home of the
Rememberers, keepers of the past, and where the secret
of Earth's salvation lay hidden in antiquity. On his journey, the Watcher hoped to recapture his youth and find
the soaring, beautiful woman he loved.

But Avluela held more for the Watcher—and Earth—
than love. Her wonder stretched beyond flight, for she
knew the riddle to free all men. . . .

WITH AN INTRODUCTION BY THE AUTHOR